PETER GARGETT

ON THE SEVENTH DAY

THE LORD TOOK HIS BAT HOME

Typeset in Minion Pro

Editing, design, typesetting and publishing by UK Book Publishing

www.ukbookpublishing.com

ISBN: 978-1-912183-64-7

To Sue, for always being there

Wednesday October 4th – Late morning

(He has bartered the engraved watch that was a birthday gift from his late mother).

The diminutive Inquisitor General, five foot nothing in her stockinged feet Dora Spenlow, owns a harvest moon face, which in repose bears an uncanny resemblance to a Seventeenth Century New England village idiot and yet disconcertingly, when she fashions a rare demi-smile, etches the woman in the moon face framed by Picasso frizzy blonde curls, a disquieting moonlit echo of a scaled down Rokeby Venus; Rubenesque thighs; tits to die for.

The Prisoner no longer at the bar sucks rasping breaths deep into his lungs, which is just what the lady prison psychiatrist had advised before the unfortunate incident; the prison consensus being that she had been asking for it. He really must get a grip and his life must revert to a pithier opening sentence. He really must grow up from being the clever clogs Scholarship boy. An opening sentence such as – Prison Officer Dora Spenlow led the acquitted prisoner to an empty cell for sex – would say it all. More unbalanced than usual by a totally unexpected euphoria, Jack to his cell mate friend is also being more fanciful than usual, and that is saying something. He is not used to euphoria of any kind. Dora Spenlow being the exception to any rule.

The day before yesterday his hideously tattooed and unexpectedly former Armley cell mate, Dog breath Billy Sikes, had leered tits to die for to an answering basilisk stare from 'a we are not amused' and very much naked Prison Officer Dora Spenlow. Against her better judgement she had allowed the big man to watch proceedings taking place on Jack's lower bunk. Dog breath, a failed hit man by his own admission, confided afterwards that his ultimate tit-related fantasy actually involved the no doubt silky smooth right hand of the international movie star Amelia Sedley, tits wobbling as they had spectacularly wobbled in that movie also starring her third – or was it her fourth – husband? Lucky sod being the prison consensus.

On the first morning of sharing a cell, Dog breath and Jack to his friend, had traded windmill blows over spilled coke, and Jack to his friend had landed a lucky punch smack in the middle of the death's head tattoo adorning, if that is the word, Dog breath's lantern jaw. The big man out for the count.

Another raspingly deep breath. And another. That's better. It really is a pity about the lady prison psychiatrist. She didn't really deserve that, although she was asking for it.

On that first morning on remand Dog breath and Jack to his friend had become inseparable buddies known to each other as Sikesy and Jack. No one gave them any grief. No one but no one messed with Billy Sikes because a failed hit man is still a hit man in the prison pecking order. No one but no one called him Dog breath to his face. To be honest no one got anywhere near his face and Jack to his friend worries that his own sense of smell is permanently impaired.

"What did it feel like to kill the cunt in cold blood?" In the underground holding cell just minutes after the unexpected not guilty verdict, and after their hurried half dressed coming together, the Rokeby one is archly contemplating buttoning up the eye wateringly tight fitting Prison Officer's uniform shirt, fraying at the cuffs and the collar. This could well be the half decent off the wall beginning of the state of the nation novel, which in the belching, farting darkness of the prison night Jack had promised himself he would write if he was ever released, which had seemed highly unlikely at the time. There is no excuse now and for reasons that will become apparent there will be no mention of any of the Brontës. A Room at the Top for its time – A kind of Loving probably without love. Or being more ambitious, which is relatively easy in belching, farting prison darkness – not Tolstoy by any means and not Proust naturally – perhaps more appropriately – A Man without Qualities.

Except no-one would believe a word, which is why it will have to be called a novel.

"What did it feel like to kill the cunt in cold blood?" Dora Venus is even more archly as archly does contemplating buttoning up the frayed shirt. There are ancient Egyptian sweat stains grave-marking at the tight armpits. There he goes again. He really must get a grip.

The Rokeby one has progressed to fiddling with a loose button and goggly wide apart eyes are staring him down. There really is no need.

The clever clogs show off Scholarship boy, who has always defined himself by his depth of useless knowledge in the manner of his literary hero Saul Bellow, decides a literary response is inappropriate. In any case Dora Spenlow does not do books unless there are full page pictures to colour, never mind doing enigmatic.

"What did it really feel like?" She doesn't do pregnant pauses either, the slithering Bradford accent even more pronounced than usual as she leans top heavily forward. He sincerely hopes that Dora Spenlow doesn't do pregnant. Euphoria might well have a lot to answer for.

It is sweatily airless in the Leeds Central Criminal Court underground holding cell and redolent of numerous undefined odours and several quite acutely defined.

"Tell me, Johnny boy." She expertly shifts the gob of well chewed gum from one cheek to the other. He hates being called Johnny and he was never a boy, only his poor dear mother's precious little Johnny. His bloody sister called him John because it became her mission in life, from an early age, to be at odds with their mother whenever possible. She inevitably succeeded.

"It feels…" A six months' pregnant pause just for the hell of it. Defying gravity Dora Spenlow leans as close as close, flying saucer dusky nipples coyly peeping through the ragged lacy fringes of the uncoordinated black bra. Sikesy would foam at the mouth. Sikesy had foamed at the mouth.

"It feels …you know…really really…you know…good."

Although mollified is not a word that she would recognise, she appears mollified….it is a hard habit to break. "The bastard deserved it." That demi-smile released into the wild. "You did the world a fucking favour, Johnny boy." He really wishes she wouldn't call him that. "You're a fucking hero." Dora Venus doesn't do irony either. It is true that amongst the ordinary people that make up a Jury, Jack's slaying of the paedophile child killer Franklyn Blake is seen as a heroic action.

There is a phlegmy exaggerated coughing in the corridor outside the holding cell. Dora hurriedly buttons up the frayed shirt, adjusts the hells angel style buckled belt, brushes down the creased uniform trousers and tut tuts at a tell-tale stain and rub rubs energetically. The tits to die for taking on a mesmerising Chinese lantern life all their own.

Despite the Judge's no nonsense directions to the Jury as she had glared over ridiculous half-moon spectacles and declaimed, in a cut glass accent, that John, Johnny or Jack's guilt was proven beyond any reasonable doubt; that this had been a trial by his Peers and not by Twitter trolls and had directed the Jury to a guilty verdict: he was found not guilty on all charges.

The Jury had only retired for twenty seven minutes and seven of those minutes had been taken up with a toilet break at the insistence of the Jury Spokesperson, who cannot catch sight of any kind of toilet sign without needing – as she had delicately put it – to go. There had been that time when she had – as she had delicately put it – been caught short when the public conveniences in Roundhay Park had been vandalised. Even to this day she does not like to dwell on the unfortunate consequences; she has never been so embarrassed in her life and that is saying something.

At the not guilty verdict Prisoner escort Dora Spenlow had sort of playfully squeezed his bad knee. The defective traffic light luminous flame haired Jury

Spokesperson of indeterminate age, possibly under forty, had winked at the Accused. The Accused's widowed sister had burst into loud sobs and the Accused had by no means been certain that they were loud sobs of joy. Chief Inspector Stephen Guest had stared soulfully at Jack's sister and then had stared at the smirking Jury Spokesperson in utter disbelief.

John, Johnny or Jack had stared likewise, and the meaty hand pressure that had reached his upper thigh had proved unexpectedly arousing. It being some considerable time since he had been unexpectedly aroused – at his mother's funeral to be precise. He is not including the only-to-be-expected dark of the moon arousals on the bottom bunk with a naked Dora Spenlow and Sikesy watching on. Those arousals are in a category all of their own and for the purposes of this narrative best ignored.

The bewigged toffee nosed Judge had glared balefully at the collective Jury persons and had then glared even more so at the Prisoner in the dock and the grinning pocket Venus Prisoner escort…escort being very much the word. In truth the Judge had been totally wasting all her expensively educated bale on Dora secret middle name Spenlow, who had effortlessly tongue flicked a gob of well chewed gum from one cheek to the other and moon calf stared back with knobs on.

There had been wild cheering in the packed public gallery and the Judge had looked up to see that Sir Godwyn Lydate was no longer present. With more than a touch of hysteria she had threatened to clear the Court. Dora Spenlow had openly sniggered and squeezed the tell-tale bulge in Jack's trousers. You Tube footage of the not guilty announcement has gone viral and the bulgee is an instant Social media sensation. The Prime Minister's wife is a like.

Chief Inspector Stephen Guest had closed his eyes and had shaken his grizzled grey head, enmeshed in the horror of his very own O J Simpson moment. It might be thought that on such fine margins is humanity and all its consequences shaped…there he goes again.

Barely half an hour after the verdict, stolen marker pen in hand, a flush faced Dora Spenlow now leans so close that the sweated Poundland perfume brings him to the edge of an out of season sneezing fit. Pinkie tip of tongue poking out between buttery lips, she executes a disabling vice grip of his strong right arm and then surprisingly gently turns the arm over.

It could well be an attempt at a loving gesture.

Scarce breathing in dim concentration, she painstakingly inscribes her mobile phone number on the stretched parchment skin that is beginning to reveal its separate age and he glances down. One of the far too many kinks in his brain is that he always remembers number sequences, sometimes for years afterwards. The last one moves over and no one falls out of the bed.

"Ring me." The demiest of demi-smiles. Living out the fantasy of her pagan allure she knows that they always ring. "And watch that temper, Johnny boy."

Eerily echoing the words of his late unlamented mother. Life as repetition repeating the finite stock of words. Only twenty six letters in the alphabet. Echoes within echoes.

"Now kiss me, Johnny boy." Spooky. Really, really spooky.

Wednesday October 11th 11.38am

Who was it who said a week is a long time in politics?

Certainly not the possibly late thirties, always and forever immaculately turned out and expensively coiffured, shapely in all the right places, Public Relations boss lady, who executes the merest of painted on lip synced grimaces in the manner of a we-are-not-amused Victorian schoolmarm. She appears too ethereally beautiful to quite pull it off. Jack to his friend really, really must get a grip and he takes several deep breaths through the nose. He really, really hopes that the lady prison psychiatrist is on the road to as full a recovery as possible. She used to have such a beguiling if somewhat wavery painted on smile, of someone becoming only too well aware that they are quite probably in the wrong place at the wrong time.

J'accuse, the lady of the here and now, points a Prussian blue painted fingernail at his right wrist where some faded numbers are still faintly visible. He just couldn't be bothered.

"You look like a fucking survivor from Auschwitz." Dismissive posh Home Counties... possibly Bucks or Herts. The swearing adding a rich two coat magnolia lustre to the debutante poshness. His attempt at an answering lip synced grimace contortion leaves a lot to be desired. It is in the breeding. "You have spoken to Chapman and Hall."

It is not a question but he answers anyway. "Yes." He squeaks, coughs. "Yes." That's a bit better.

The lady elegantly crosses elegant legs – it has to be said legs well worth elegantly crossing. Legs that have been admired in the most exclusive places, including Juan les Pins; never in her worst nightmares have they been ogled inside a prison cell. The red soled shoe on the crossed leg swinging, it has to be said, poshly suggestively. The Prussian blue leather armchair the same colour as her tights creaks, it has to be said, poshly suggestively – there is co-ordination and then there is Shirley Keeldar. Dora Spenlow could learn a lot from this 'all in the right places' lady who tap tap taps with the Prussian blue index fingernail of her right hand on the chunky leather chair arm. A prominent nose, but not unduly so, the unedifying family kink long since removed. "Mmm..." Tap tap. Tap tap tap. Tap tap. He never learned the Morse code having lasted only two weeks and three days in the Boy Scouts. It was not all his fault; in retrospect it was a mistake for the Boy Scouts to share a weekend camp with Girl Guides. This most formidable lady most certainly does do pregnant pauses; eleven pound baby popping out head first any minute now pregnant pauses.

They are formally seated opposite each other in matching leather armchairs each side of the ornate marble fireplace in a highly polished Mayfair office, at least twenty times the size of the prison cell he had shared with Sikesy, and the imaginary silky right hand of his movie star bitch. Shirley Keeldar purses the ever so matching Prussian blue lips and the ditto fingernail is poised in mid tap. He is not at all sure that Prussian blue is her colour.

"We..." The royal We – he likes that. "...at Smith Elder want you, John." No lip synced grimace. "I am sure that the two of us can come up with a deal breaker."

If he is not mistaken the word here is most definitely suggestive. Only seven different letters but to be fair there are only twenty six letters to work with. "The trouble is ..."

She stops him right there. She possesses incredibly piercing, not quite matching, powder blue eyes, with a hint of Sloane bloodshot. She does not at all like 'the trouble is'. She will soon find out that he is made of sterner stuff.

"The trouble is ..." He ploughs on. "... Chapman and Hall have verbally agreed serial rights with The Sun newspaper." His voice sounds oddly far away to his own sticky out ears. The room is fashionably high ceilinged.

"You have not signed a contract." It is not a question. "We will more than match their terms." The paler blue of the piercing powder blue eyes is the colour of a 1970s Manchester City shirt laundered at the wrong temperature. It is a hard habit to break.

"I can promise you..." That word again. "...we will more than match their terms." This is a lady that likes to give the impression that she gets what she wants. He is well aware that she is the best in the business and that is why he is here. It is no accident.

To be absolutely fair he is not at all used to being wanted in any capacity whatsoever by a woman such as Shirley Keeldar. He is not at all used to being in the same room and breathing the same air as a woman such as Shirley Keeldar. He screws up his mouth in that habitual gesture that so provoked his poor dear mother, and stares long and hard at a natural blemish the shape of a wingless butterfly etched in the marble fireplace; he knows how it feels. However, there is a rare species of Mongolian butterfly that can sprout new wings; hope springs eternal in the butterfly world.

"Why don't we adjourn to lunch ..." A just discovered being pregnant and frantically shaking the Boots tester because there must be some mistake pregnant pause. "...and work out the details." A much smilier smile and he is not meant to notice the slightest of tremors.

John, Johnny or Jack has invariably sheltered behind words. Words. Words. Words and more words. There is no choice if you lecture on Nineteenth Century literature to a largely indifferent ninety percent female Student Body. At least one of whom at any one time would be sniggering behind a cupped hand and several others checking their mobile phones and others taking toilet breaks without permission.

Unreal and surreal are the scratchy words scribbled on the mental white board, as he limps a few steps behind the most shapely, not the least bit Victorian, rear of Shirley Keeldar. Relatively poor, approaching middle aged, perennial bachelor university lecturers do not get taken out to lunch at the River room Restaurant at the Savoy hotel by arses like this.

"Your usual window table, my Lady?"

Imperious last days of the Raj, she waves away the proffered gold leaf embossed menus and orders drinks. An unpronounceable imported vodka for my Lady and Johnnie Walker Double Black for the gentleman – as if – all he said was whisky please. She badly needs a drink... my God does she badly need a drink... inside she is quivering.

Now she is texting at breakneck speed on the state of the art platinum mobile phone that appears welded to her left palm. There is an apologetic wafer thin wedding ring that for some reason he thinks that, just like Dora Eames, the Vicar's wife, she will not wear at certain times.

He glances at his wrist and the girly watch 'borrowed' from his bloody sister. Then he stares out of the pale autumn sun reflecting picture window overlooking the Embankment and the inevitable River Thames, and the square rigged Festival Hall on the far South Bank.

His poor dear mother had taken him there as a treat for their twelfth birthdays and his twin sister had tagged along, it being her birthday as well. She had burst into tears over nothing very much –it was not even a hard pinch – and the resultant smack had echoed and re-echoed around the stalls. The tears had ossified on her shocked face and it was at that moment that their mother's fate was sealed. Until that day in Court his sister never sobbed again.

The drinks deferentially arrive and the lady stops texting. Breeding will out.

"Cheers."

"Bottoms up."

The tantalisingly smooth whisky burns the wafer thin lining of his stomach – he has forgotten the tablets again. He slurps more tantalisingly smooth whisky. Alcohol has always leant him a false patina of inner normality. Now that is a word to include in the novel. Patina is most definitely a word to lend artistic credibility. He is not at all sure that Tolstoy ever used the word patina.

"So tell me, John Bellingham…" She rolls the name round the tongue like a 1961 Margaux. He hopes she isn't taking the piss. "…are you getting used to being a somebody?" As opposed to being a nobody he imagines the sub text. Fair enough.

"Such lovely rough justice." She gulps vodka and then, as an afterthought, holds up the cut glass tumbler in a toast. "To the People's fucking hero."

He drinks to that. The most fragrant Rosalie Murray MP, speaking in the House of Commons, had actually called him the People's hero. … no fucking involved…although he wouldn't kick the fragrant Rosalie Murray out of bed… chance would be a fine thing.

The expensive perfume scents that waft across the usual window table my Lady are most assuredly sneeze proof. She probably never sweats. Shapely whatever the rich and famous call them – certainly not tits – succinctly shaped in the fitted designer dress politely hinting at cleavage.

"An unlikely fucking hero, my dear." The instant they have escaped into the ether she wishes she could call back the words, without looking stupid of course. It is the nerves speaking. He is not at all what she expected. She is not sure what she expected but it was not this most unexplained of men, so frighteningly contained in his own brittle self. The oddly colourless eyes not at all windows on the soul…which is probably a good thing.

She needs him to sign on the dotted line. My God does she need him to sign on the dotted line. She has stopped returning the Bank's calls and she probably has forty-eight hours maximum. After the terrible indignities of last time she will not ask her husband to bail her out again.

The People's fucking hero hisses the words for her ears only. "Don't you dare judge me, you fucking snooty bitch." The words have long festered. "Don't you fucking dare." Any fucking snooty bitch in a storm will do. The misty Filey bay spittle fogs her composed in all weathers features into momentary discomposure. She knocks over the cut-glass tumbler to deluge the table with ice cube fragments. The tumbler doesn't break.

He cannot stop himself setting the tumbler upright. You can take the man out of the tumbler but you cannot take the tumbler out of the man. Where did that come from?

In the blink of an eye most apologetic waiters whisk the cloth away and realign the intricate cutlery settings. No one says thank you. … no one says sorry.

Jack to his friend indulges in several deep breaths through the nose, as demonstrated by the lady prison psychiatrist with that noticeable lisp and the short skirts – just asking for it. She had confidently advised that the anger attacks would diminith in time and the red mitth would become leth red. She had probably read Wilfred Owen for A-level English. She parroted that evil did not exist but was to find out otherwise; although the Parole board continue to follow her half-baked theories that she no longer believes.

"Sorry." He mumbles. Not thorry. Screws up his mouth in that habitual mew that used to drive his dear poor mother to even more distraction than usual. She hated stubbornness except in herself.

Shirley Keeldar appears for all the world to be quite magnificently also in the wrong place at the wrong time as she pushes back the chair. She knows only too well that evil exists. "I need to powder my nose." She just cannot afford to slap his face and storm off in a rage. She just dare not.

Jack to his friend drains his glass and a watchful waiter rushes to snatch the empty glass away to be replenished at a nod. Whisked is again the word and he could get used to this. He will get used to this. The purloined Holiday Inn pen is poised…another eminently usable word…poised. This book writing thing cannot be all that hard…surely?

It is such a new minted sensation to be anticipating the return of any kind of beautiful woman. A new minted sensation to be any kind of hero. He really must watch that red mitht.

More drinks arrive even more deferentially. A gulp of tantalisingly smooth whisky. At this time of day the window framed Thames is crowded with all manner of river traffic. In the bad times and the even worse times, he has always found the thought of water stuff soothing and therapeutic. The thought of fishing is what he missed second most of all whilst he was in prison. Slyly shyly striving not to give himself away, because he hates to do that, he peers from beneath the Heathcliffian eyebrows that badly need trimming, and looks round the busy, noisy restaurant. A blur of faces and a buzz of off key voices. He is careful not to catch anyone's eye.

As far as he is aware no female is sniggering behind a cupped hand, although several are checking mobile phones and one appears to be heading to the toilets in the wake of Shirley Keeldar. A gulp of tantalisingly smooth whisky. Stomach not unpleasantly burning. A damped down Guy Fawkes bonfire approaching midnight with storm clouds scudding from the North East. There he goes again. Perhaps a pencil rather than a pen – easier to rub out.

"Shall we start again, John?"

"My friends call me Jack." The plural a slight exaggeration although Sikesy did take up enough room for a handful of normal people. The beautiful woman of any kind has very much returned and determinedly retakes her seat. An even smilier smile with exactly the correct number of perfect white teeth. He hopes that one day he will be able to discern genuine from fake… smiles, that is.

"Bottoms up."

"Cheers."

This visually ethereal heroine of an unfinished Keats sonnet knocks back half the replenished vodka, then pinches the prominent but not unduly so nose, and inhales a deep sea breath. Probably more Larkin than Keats. The lady prison psychiatrist would have lisped thplendid and then unfortunately crossed lots and lots of legs. Lots and lots of legs are an unfortunate mistake in prison. Apropos of nothing in particular.

"You know, Shirley." The sound of her name from his lips bounces back in that same ether. "You know, Shirley, I have never visited Westminster Abbey."

Only twice in her life has the strikingly lovely Shirley Keeldar been thrown by something a man has said. She is thrown now. Only this time she cannot respond by either slapping the man's face, like the first time, or doing as she was told and taking off her knickers and bending over, like the second time. "Oh." Is marginally better than nothing.

He knows what he means. "I love cathedrals."

"Oh." There is being unsure of the terrain and then there is being lost in a deep dark forest as midnight approaches and what it is fervently hoped are owls hooting.

"The sense of eternal peace is incredibly soothing."

"Yes." She is a gutsy lady. "It must be." She finishes the vodka and signals for another one.

"The pretty leggy girl you sent to kidnap me from the Holiday Inn?" He is not good with names. Shirley Keeldar is not sure whether this is deliberate and whether to laugh out loud, or simply smile or do neither, and does neither. "The Honourable Lady Rebecca Sharp." She sniff sniffs and pinches the not unduly so nose. He finishes the whisky and signals for another one to the three bedroom semi-detached born.

"She talked to me as if she was, you know, interested." He screws up his mouth. "You know, genuinely interested." And an Honourable at that. The pampered half tamed eaglet piercing powder blue eyed, very much bushy tailed, Shirley Keeldar smiles the similiest smile yet. If it is false it could well fool an expert. "You see that table over to your right, Jack?" Fuck off Johnny boy.

There is a table where a plumpish, not unattractive, page boy cut brunette is suckling a bald headed baby at a partially exposed largish breast. The shaven headed male companion, whose face is vaguely familiar, is ignoring proceedings and avidly texting, which for the purpose of this book could well be in reply to a rude text from his young mistress. Being cheated-on brunette wife intercepts Jack's acutely embarrassed gaze and, it has to be said, smirks meaningfully, shifting the baby's head to expose just about all of the largish breast as the greedy sparrow mouth pops off the milk tipped walnut nipple. Of course the baby is probably her husband's, but there is a good chance it might be Godwyn's baby after that particularly memorable stolen weekend at his Cotswold retreat, when rather a lot of bodily fluids were exchanged. Not to mention the following even more so weekend at Lydate Hall.

"Not that table." Shirley chuckles throatily, recognising the couple and waves. Harriet Wititterly grins and Henry looks up from the mobile phone and blows a kiss. "The next table." There are two, from this distance, thirty something made up to the eyeballs women extravagantly locked in forehead to forehead chitter chit chat over bowls of what appears to be salady stuff. They are most conspicuously not looking anywhere at all. "Those two have been clocking our table since the moment we arrived. They know who you are." She just stops herself saying darling and instead sniffingly sniffs sniffs. "Notoriety possesses attraction for certain women, Jack." She believes they are on a more even keel now and is beginning to relax. The edge of desperation has smoothed more than somewhat.

"Certain women?" He knows he is blushing.

"Those with two arms and two legs." A throaty chuckle and she wisely decides to leave it at that as she pitter pat pats his strong right arm. "Welcome to fame and misfortune."

Jack gulps tantalisingly smooth whisky and his stomach hardly burns at all. He wonders what the two thirty something made up to the eyeballs women and the page boy cut brunette suckler are thinking. For that matter he wonders what Shirley Keeldar is thinking. He has never been good at knowing what women are thinking; he has never been good at women full stop. He blames his poor dear mother – he knew only too well what she was thinking.

If he did but know it Shirley Keeldar is wondering if she will get away with a deal breaking blow job... possibly not. She has never been one to spoil the ship for a haporth of tar and he does possess a certain rustic charm. She has deal broken much worse and they need him. My God do they need him.

The thoughts of the two thirty something made up to the eyeballs women and the being cheated-on cuckolding brunette suckler can only be guessed at.

"Smith Elder will look after you, Jack." A pitter pat pat of the strong right arm. "I will look after you, Jack."

"What about Chapman and Hall?"

"Leave those fuckers to me." It feels a little bit like the Third Reich to his plucky little Belgium, but not as much as he had anticipated. She is upping the ante and is very good at upping the ante, even when more than slightly pissed. If there is a sliver of desperation it is being drowned at birth by the unpronounceable vodka.

His poor dear mother will be turning in her grave, although it will be somewhat crowded down there. She hated swearing and hated rude words, particularly the word fuck. Even though it was a set book, she refused to allow Lady Chatterley's Lover into the house, which even to his schoolboy self, appeared more than a tad hypocritical.

"Now let's eat and agree…" It might well be a suggestive before getting pregnant pause. "…a deal breaker." Pitter pat pat. "The steak Diane is to die for."

What goes around comes around. Is that what he means?

Wednesday October 11th 2.06pm

John Caldigate MP stares short sightedly out of the arched mock gothic window on the top floor of the scaffolded Ministry building. He glares defiantly at the blurry River Thames far below, as he displays a show of pantomime villainy normally reserved for the Opposition Spokesperson, a woman he has been determined to ridicule at every opportunity – although it has to be said she is rather good at ridiculing back, and could well be ahead on points.

"This is not good, Godwyn." Nervously clicking the fingers and thumbs in the hands clasped behind his exceedingly broad back; an almost Churchillian pose. "Not good at all." It is not recorded if Churchill clicked his fingers and thumbs when under pressure… probably not. Nor did he bite his fingernails… nasty habit.

"Yes, Minister." Sir Godwyn Lydate, the most permanent Permanent Secretary, allows himself the driest of dry lip twitches, wasted on John Caldigate's exceedingly broad back. Churchill was never this broad. Decentish Savile Row suit although not Sir Godwyn's choice of tailor. The charcoal grey material alarmingly stretched across the Incredible Hulk shoulders. The current Minister of State executes an impressive for his bulk forty-five degree ballet pirouette. Not handmade shoes and no doubt holes in the socks. It is Sir Godwyn's considered opinion that socks maketh the man.

"So, Godwyn."

"Minister?"

"The John Bellingham situation?"

Let the Minister play Ministers, as Sir Godwyn clutches the buff manila folder to his chest and stands tall to his full five feet nine and three-quarter inches; possibly nine and seven eighths inches. In the age of the all-pervasive computer and all its nefarious invasive manifestations, in this dusty corner of Whitehall the buff manila folder is King across the water.

In Sir Godwyn's considered opinion computer inventor Alan Turing has a lot to answer for. Sir Godwyn's great Uncle Bertram Lydate worked with Turing at Bletchley Park on breaking the German Enigma code. Actually shagged Turing's camouflage girlfriend on a regular basis, which was more than Turing was prepared to do. Evidently, she was a lusty girl.

The current Minister heavyweight contender pumps a huge right fist into the huge palm of his left hand. An annoying habit that he displays when under pressure, which is more often than not. A habit mercilessly aped by his underlings to accompanying hoots and giggles, but only when he is safely holed up in his office with Agnes Grey…which is often.

"That half pint bitch." He never uses the Opposition Spokesperson's name. Never even refers to her as the Right Honourable Member; the long suffering Speaker of the House of Commons has long since given up. "That short arsed bitch is going to have a field day at my expense." He boxer pumps so violently that even the unflinchable Sir Godwyn contemplates a flinch. He likes to pretend that his preference is violence meted out from twenty thousand feet.

"Most unfortunate, Minister."

John Caldigate MP knows in his water that, even as they speak, this urbanely calculating most permanent of the Permanents is running through the possible candidates as John Caldigate's replacement. The untouchable little shit will act out his backstairs role to perfection. There have been rumours – no more than that. No one but no one has dared lay a finger on Sir Godwyn Lydate who has buried most of the bodies.

"Where are our people now?" John Caldigate does so relish having people although in reality they are Sir Godwyn's people. The current Minister prefers to converse standing with his feet well apart like a poor man's Henry the Eighth dominating with his bulk. A strategy wasted on Sir Godwyn.

"Jane Fennel is close to his suite at the Savoy." He lip twitches at the unsought fleeting image of a week ago, a pouting Jane Fennel crawling naked on his bed and emitting lioness noises as a prelude to a most memorable night and most of the next morning; he was almost late for an important luncheon appointment.

The big man rocks aggressively on his heels. It is not hard to believe that he was once suspended from the House of Commons for drunkenly punching the drunken Foreign Secretary after a late night sitting. It only seemed to enhance his career prospects in certain quarters that, for the moment, hold sway in Government.

"You know the husband, Godwyn?" He decides on the circuitous Kefalonian mountain route because, whatever else he is, John Caldigate is not a complete fool. No one tangles with the nastily vindictive Sir Bernard Keeldar out of choice.

"Occasionally we share…" A totally wasted dry lip twitch. "…a drink at the Club." The most exclusive of Pall Mall Gentleman's Clubs from which John Caldigate has been black balled three times.

"Can you speak to him? Get the good dame to throw the murdering little shit to the wolves." Anyone less like a good dame than Shirley Keeldar it would be hard to find.

"Chapman and Hall are hardly the wolves, Minister." The big man does so like being called Minister. Vanity thy name is John Caldigate MP. Sir Godwyn knows it is a weakness to file away for the future.

"They are not Shirley fucking Keeldar."

"Indeed, Minister." Sir Godwyn cannot resist the beginnings of a knowing smirk. Nanny used to slap his leg if he knowingly smirked, and then more often than not kiss it better. "We have intercepted certain communications." With the cavalier flourish that he has made all his own Sir Godwyn opens the untitled buff manila folder. He knows it irks the current Minister. "The redoubtable Lady Keeldar has agreed serial rights on the projected book with the Daily Mail for an exorbitant sum." He is reading in a deliberately flat voice because he knows it irks the current Minister. "The murdering little shit is to appear on the Phineas Finn Show on Friday evening, in tow with the international movie star Amelia Sedley." Even the Prime Minister cannot ingratiate himself onto the Phineas Finn Show, let alone in tow with Amelia Sedley, the ultimate sex goddess. He snaps the folder shut. "The United States of America beckons." A Lydate ancestor had made a fortune in Virginia tobacco and of course in slaves. It was rumoured that the ancestor sired more than a hundred children with female slaves and was a living legend in the State of Carolina…his wife remained childless. He was killed at the battle of first Bull Run, leading a gallant charge of Confederate Cavalry that won the day.

John Caldigate drags his thoughts away from an image of the unattainable Amelia Sedley. "Jesus fuck."

"Indeed."

"Has he signed a contract with the stuck up bitch?" John Caldigate has forgotten himself and not for the first time it has to be said. Sir Godwyn does not forget or forgive…unless it suits his purpose, and of course, the likes of John Caldigate can be such useful tools.

"He will." No dry lip twitch. "He most assuredly will." If John Caldigate was more astute he might be surprised at the change of tone, but he is not and is not. Instead he points accusingly at the untitled buff manila folder.

"There must be something we can use."

Sir Godwyn Lydate recites from memory. "He lives with his separated twin sister. The sister's husband has disappeared. His mother died almost a year ago. He has never married. He lectures at Leeds University on Nineteenth Century literature with a specialisation in the Brontës. He has published a slim volume on Charlotte Brontë's married year. It sold seventy-two copies and he bought ten copies. His interest is Cathedral stained glass windows particularly of the Thirteenth Century. He does not socialise with colleagues. He has no driving convictions. As far as we know he isn't gay."

"Jesus."

"Indeed." There is no point in sharing the joke. "Of course he is a cold blooded murderer but a Jury of his Peers found him not guilty."

"Stupid cunts."

Sir Godwyn Lydate does not reply. John Caldigate is never sure when this highly polished Old Etonian relic is taking the piss; it is something you were not taught at Rochdale High.

"And this is the People's fucking hero? This is the modern day fucking Robin Hood? This is Clark fucking Kent?" He bellows. Dear…dear…dear.

"Press hyperbole is sometimes a trifle far-fetched, Minister."

"There must be something."

"There is always something." Sir Godwyn Lydate is as ordainly thoughtful as ever as he thankfully closes the sound proofed door of the current Minister's lair. A twitch of the dry lips. Lairs are such tricky places. Without deigning to knock, because he never knocks, he opens an unmarked door at the far end of the doomy panelled corridor. This room, which houses the current Minister's gatekeeper, naturally appointed by Sir Godwyn, is on a much smaller scale; almost claustrophobic with the cluttered desk and two 'seen better days' dining chairs borrowed from elsewhere. A single locked two-tone grey filing cabinet. Nothing personal on display.

The keeper of the gate had found the black and white photograph of her recently deceased mother on her wedding day far too distressing. After all, she had worshipped her late father, and he would have been devastated at the manner of her mother's death. It was thanks to Sir Godwyn that the scandal was hushed up.

Luckily the keeper of the gate is on the small side herself. Not quite petite. Petite is not a word that would be used to describe Agnes Grey. She looks up from the computer screen and snatches off the unflattering black framed spectacles, which appear to be designed for a larger face. She rubs red rimmed eyes that lack sleep and gazes expectantly at Sir Godwyn Lydate, Master of the Revels born five hundred years out of time.

Agnes Grey could be anything in her forties; even at a pinch and given a fair wind, late thirties. Close cropped mousey hair greying naturally at the temples, where a visible vein throbs disconcertingly at the right temple. No discernible makeup. A pleasant enough woman other women think. Not unattractive in a pleasant, unthreatening way. Good bone structure like her late mother and very pleasantly put together like her late mother.

This makes the truth all the more remarkable. Sir Godwyn does so revel in other people's truths and the lies at the heart of those truths.

"Good afternoon, Miss Grey." She always waits for him to speak first.

"Good afternoon, Sir Godwyn." A pleasant voice and a pleasant smile. A woman who merges into backgrounds and is more often than not overlooked. Not taken account of, which is a big mistake. A mistake Sir Godwyn so rarely makes.

Fastidiously moulding his body to the nearest borrowed dining chair, he crosses immaculately trousered legs, and displaying hand stitched socks, adjusts the Old Etonian tie that never needs adjusting. Sitting as straight as the straight backed chair he rests the buff manila folder on his knee. And tap taps it with an index finger.

Agnes Grey nods to the flickering screen.

"Bellingham has become a worldwide sensation since the verdict." She pleasantly smiles displaying slightly crooked teeth that might spoil a less pleasant smile. The two of them are surprisingly easy with each other, which is not a given under the circumstances. There is so much below the surface to appreciate about Agnes Grey. "We are being made to look foolish, Sir Godwyn."

He admonishingly raises an index finger and tut tuts.

"Some of us, Miss Grey. Some of us." The tinder-dry lips closed tight as if they have never given birth to a twitch. He has never called her Agnes in all the time and in all the ways they have known each other. Nonetheless she is most definitely one of his girls. There is still a delicious frisson when she recalls the initiatory poker strip.

He always thinks she bears an uncanny facial resemblance to Queen Victoria in early middle age. Most definitely at the chins and around the ever so slightly bulbous eyes of her late mother. All in all a not unpleasant resemblance to his favourite Queen.

"Miss Grey, I do not wish yours to be one of the bodies that I alone know where it is buried. I do not think you are a particularly strong swimmer." No beating about the bush. A predatory penetrating gaze that she can well believe sees everything. She sometimes forgets there is never anywhere to hide. "Do I make myself crystal clear?"

"Yes, Sir Godwyn." She squeezes together the clammy hands clasped in her pleasant lap. Prayers are never of any use. She knows that.

Not unkindly now, human weakness being his stock in trade. "I know that needs must, my dear, but sometimes needs must not. It does not suit my purposes for Mary Caldigate to find out. Walls have ears and she is not a forgiving woman."

She stares po-faced at the hands clasped ever so tightly in that pleasant lap. If it was not for Sir Godwyn Lydate her needs must would more than once have led to unfortunate consequences. She has to be forever grateful. What goes around comes around he has said more than once.

Only when she hears the door close does she glance up and is, as always, acutely aware of his absence from the room. Not being here he is more here than ever until the fragrance of the expensive cologne fades. She smiles pleasantly at the scatter of memories and only wishes there were more.

The private line from the Minister's office buzzes and she heaves a deep sigh. Needs must are such awkward things. She answers the phone and listens. "Very well." She replaces the receiver and as instructed slips off her tights and knickers before answering the Minister's summons…he is always so impatient and she only wishes she wasn't so eager because it will have to stop and she doesn't want it to stop. She swallows in anticipation of the next few minutes and is just glad that Sir Godwyn will have left the building. It must stop though… it really must stop.

Wednesday October 11th 5.09pm

The taste of acidic change is on Jack's lips and things will never be the same again. There will be no turning back; not that he wants to turn back. The pencil has been put aside because it is cheating to rub out. This pen is green ink but no matter.

He is blissfully unaware of the monster he has created.

The view from the grimy picture window of the Grande suite with an e of one of the grandest hotels in the world is a grand view of the River Thames. There are lots of insignificant people dolls arranged on the pleasure steamers, which from this height appear to be much knocked about Dinky toys. Not that he ever played with Dinky toys. His dear poor mother hated clutter of any kind, and that included his sister.

On the nearer embankment, illuminated in the thinnest of October sunshine, there are yet more insignificant discarded Christmas gift Barbie and Ken dolls, worked by unseen children's hands. Never being allowed any of her own, at every opportunity, his sister used to pull the arms and legs off other children's Barbie and Ken dolls. The sunshine is thinning by the minute and he theatrically shivers. The post-coital cigarette tastes cindery in his mouth. Not an unpleasant taste. Staring out of the window he knows this is the way he has always desired people to be. At a distance…faceless…in boxes… preferably with the lids nailed down. Work colleagues kept at arm's length…Students ignored in the street… never answering the door. A spun cocoon to keep out a largely alien world.

He glances over his bare right shoulder at an unashamedly naked Shirley Keeldar seated on a deep sofa with legs crossed; not even thinking about covering size-perfect, pink-nippled breasts, she is conversing in hushed clipped business like tones into the state of the art phone thingy, and unthinkingly caressing the livid bite mark on her left shoulder. She is not in the least bit concerned that he is appraising her nakedness. Prussian blue toenails, but the Prussian blue lipstick has been kissed away on a perfumed taste that he had never ever imagined in his sick daydreams.

She elegantly uncrosses and crosses bare legs and gives him a posh finger wave. His poor dear mother was never seen naked by any of the men in her life, Jack's father, whoever he was, least of all. Jack shakes the cheap pen, which appears to be running out of ink. He turns reluctantly away from the lovely naked woman because he is drawn to the God-like bird's eye view.

A matchstick boy and a matchstick girl are necking up against the embankment wall in broadish daylight with people passing by. His mother would not have approved as she only ever necked in the dark.

It was at his mother's sparsely attended funeral that his dry eyed sister had introduced him to the recently widowed Lily Dale, who had clasped his chill hands in abject out of place sympathy. She wore, in the Vicar's wife's opinion, an inappropriate above the knee black dress that put the other women in the shade... decent legs. The Vicar had looked on admiringly; the Vicar's wife had looked at the Vicar not at all admiringly.

The matchstick boy and the matchstick girl have broken their attic clinch and appear to be arguing. She is angrily stubbing a finger in his face and there was Jack wishing he could be that boy. He really must break the habit of wishing that he was someone else. Someone else holding a girl's hand in the street... someone else walking arm round a girl's waist in the park... someone else necking a girl at the movies. Someone else. Always someone else and somewhere else.

He really is not at all sure about this green ink.

Shirley Keeldar moves like a cat and not just any old cat, but a pampered, half-tamed Siamese cat. Lily Dale didn't move at all like a pampered, half-tamed Siamese cat, more of an alley cat as it turned out. She had small almost pre-pubescent breasts. These breasts now pressed against his naked flesh are very much pubescent. Intrusive nipples are Dorset pebbles that could be seven times skimmed on the waves of the choppy English Channel.

There he goes again.

"You really should not stand at the window so very naked, darling." Siamese cat woman is rubbing strategic bits of body against his muscle tensed buttocks and meowing enticingly. Lily Dale consigned to history... Lily Dale should never have been born. If ever a name should have been written in pencil and then rubbed out it was Lily Dale. The matchstick boy knocks the out of proportion, slender paint-stained finger of the matchstick girl away from pointing between his eyes. He hates arguments in public.

"You bastard." Hisses the Artist Emily Rowley.

"Look up there." This is one of his days for sounding more annoyingly false cockney than even more annoyingly false mid-Atlantic drawly. "Look at that window."

Argument temporarily suspended, the wide eyed girl gazes in wide eyed, pleasurable disbelief. A naked man at an upper window. A man in a window. Window man. Staring at Emily Rowley staring back. A late period canvas by the school of Egon Schiele, if there had ever been such a school, come to life. And now a naked woman all over the naked man like a cat on a hot tin roof. She could well be meowing in his ear.

The naked couple disappear stage left. The window is empty.

"Great arse." Murmurs the matchstick boy.

"Rich cunts." Replies the matchstick girl. She has nothing against rich cunts, except that she is not one herself. Already her mind is shifting to another plane. Conjuring so many startling visions that she forgets to breathe.

Psychedelic colours are flashing through her mind's eye. Early period Emily Rowley. It has to be. It just has to be. There is no time to lose. The need to put paint on canvas is a tormenting pain in her gut.

"Fuck off." She slaps the placatory hand away and walks hurriedly in the direction of the nearest Underground station.

Thursday October 12th 1.57 am

Aso stunningly pensive it is a pity there is no one awake to appreciate Shirley Keeldar daintily sips the not quite chilled enough Pol Roger champagne…a good vintage but not the best. With her free arm she hugs herself in the fluffy Savoy hotel bathrobe.

She needs to feel safe and it always comes to this. The need to feel safe and so rarely feeling safe. She had not felt safe in Jack's arms. She had felt many things but safe was not one of them. She has tried to feel safe in Tom Sawyer's arms but she knows she is only fooling herself. Her husband's arms are the last place on Earth to feel safe: there is always Goddy of course but then Goddy is… well… Goddy.

She is seated on curled under bare legs and stares unseeing at the darkened picture window at the far end of the Grande suite. She thinks about ringing for a minion to come and close the curtains. The artful scattering of Tiffany lamps sheds a soothing rainbow glow, whilst leaving the corners of the barn like room in mysterious shadow. She had loved mysterious shadows in rooms as an unwanted child. Imagining all kinds of tiny exotic predatory creatures just biding their time before pouncing and savaging her idiotic mother. They never did. That was left to her idiotic mother's own self destructive cupidity.

The children's rhyme of the colours of the rainbow pops into her head – Richard of York gave battle in vain. As a child she had always felt sorry for that poor misunderstood King, who had lost his crown and everything else on a brave impulse…history does not belong to brave impulses. She even more daintily sips the not quite chilled enough champagne and is acutely aware of swollen lips and adjusts the position of her bare legs. The clever as clever is country bumpkin superhero has jumped her from somewhere left field. She hadn't seen that coming and seeing things coming is one of her more honed talents. She had thought that he might be a two minute let's get it over with slam bang thank you ma'am. How wrong can one be?

She perhaps hasn't taken into account that he is writing the story.

She lip syncs a cat got the cream smile. Godwyn Lydate has said to her more than once, in his own inimitable way, that in the final analysis human life is all about cocks in holes. In the final analysis it is probably true. It was certainly true when Goddy first whispered that ancient Chinese philosophy into her ear in the early hours of an abstract summer morning, which she still fondly recalls with tingles in all the accepted places.

There is a coded rap rap rap at the door.

"Come." She glances over her left shoulder. "You're late, puss."

"Lawyers eh?!"

A willowy twenty something raven haired catwalk beauty stalks into the room as if she owns the place. She shrugs off an up to the minute style leather edged black jacket that she dumps unceremoniously on the floor. She is wearing a loose fitting purple blouse because she is not happy with her small breasts, and a tight fitting above the knee black leather skirt because she is very happy with her lots and lots of ultra slim legs. Black tights with stocking seams. No visible jewellery. No make-up. Patek Phillipe man's watch that she refused to return to a particularly disappointing ex-fuck buddy.

"You get everything, puss?"

"Everything." A cut glass County set accent, as she steps off incredibly high heeled Louboutin shoes and dumps a Ducal monogrammed crocodile skin attaché case on the glass topped coffee table. Unlike the accent the coffee table doesn't splinter.

She flick flicks the raven winged shoulder length hair in an habitual gesture that had so much annoyed her last but three, or was it last but four, fuck buddy. With that disappointing size of cock he had no right to be uptight about anything…creep.

"So we have a deal?" An adorable gap toothed smile.

"Of course." Shirley gulps a mouthful of warm champagne. "Help yourself." The Honourable Lady Rebecca Sharp helps herself. "And top mine up, puss."

Champagne poured, she kneels facing Shirley Keeldar.

"How was it?"

"Good." For some reason that Shirley has not yet fathomed she doesn't want to talk about the left field stuff – occasionally she is that kind of girl. "Surprisingly good."

Lady Rebecca, who can take a hint, sip sips warm champagne. "Just like this." Sip sip sip. "Daddy bought twenty cases." So like the impecunious Duke to order not the best vintage so that several months later he can dispute the bill with Berry Brothers.

Clutching the champagne flute as to the Castle born, Lady Rebecca snuggles as close as close and Shirley tenderly kisses the impeccably parted crown of the sweet blossomed head. She has always been grateful to Goddy for introducing Becky at a Ministry cocktail party. At that time Becky had just been initiated as one of Godwyn's People, and of course Shirley had known it was a double edged sword.

"In the morning he will sign the contracts." Spoiled rotten kittenish Rebecca is cosily tucked into the generous curves of the summer's-day body heat of the woman who, despite all her frailties, she absolutely adores. Possibly because of all her frailties that can in sum total appear to be strengths.

"No need for a threesome then?"

"No need for a threesome."

"So the Bank can go fuck themselves."

"The Bank can indeed go fuck themselves."

They sip sip warm champagne in companionable silence.

"Tomorrow is another day."

"Gone with the wind."

"You watch too many movies, puss puss."

"Amelia Sedley was bloody marvellous as Scarlett O'Hara in the remake and should have got an Oscar nomination at the very least."

Shirley Keeldar does not argue and it gives her a brilliant idea, and unfortunately she always acts on her brilliant ideas.

Thursday October 12th 2.33 am

Sir Godwyn Lydate will not be side-lined, which will become more and more of a pity as time goes on.

Comfortably ensconced in the trusty old Retainer leather armchair in the study of his everything in its place Albany apartment, he sniffs appreciatively over the rim of the engraved tumbler... To Godwyn with love... to be on the safe side she only had her initials engraved in a heart.

He sniffs up the glorious grouse moor aromas of his current favourite single malt whisky – a gift from the Distillery of course. He does so enjoy the quasi-official trips to Edinburgh and the married lady who is so deliciously Scottish.

There is something about the burring Scottish accent on a woman that gives him such tweaky, all-over goosebumps. One married Scottish lady in particular. There is an extra dimension in going to bed with another man's Scottish wife; a lesson learned early at Eton.

"Ah." The whisky so pleasantly warming the cockles of the organ called a heart.

Such a rewarding dinner at the Club with the Chinese ambassador. For once the claret was perfectly acceptable. Now he can turn his undivided attention to his latest acquisition. He does so love acquisitions... Scrooge like examining rare Penny Black stamps gives him almost the same frisson as the thought of a roomful of naked Scottish married women, all chattering at the same time.

He recites the neatly, hand written of course, attached label out loud. The baritone burble of his voice honeyed on the twenty five year old rare malt whisky. This is a particular Cover that he has coveted for many years. Rare stamps and women... women and rare stamps, he would like to possess every single one, but then patience is supposedly a virtue.

"Plate 1b. 8d rate. Ex Mayflower grand prix exhibit. BPA Certificate. Twenty-eight thousand pounds." Guineas would have been more appropriate. Guineas being the lingua franca of generations of Lydates. An Eighteenth Century Lydate had lost a thousand guineas on the turn of a card, but turning the next card he had won the winner's wife. Always bragged he got the better of the bargain. She bore him six children... he gave her the pox.

Sir Godwyn gazes covetously – there is no other word for it – at the row of eight superb four margin Penny Blacks on the cover addressed to Bridlington, with an exceedingly light touching of the distinctive cancelling Leeds Maltese cross.

An early May date and he so adores early May dates. Equivalent to a small Scottish town the size of Dumbarton, the streets jam packed with naked married Scottish women all talking at the same time. Twelfth of May 1840... he must look up Parliamentary Proceedings for that day. This beauty is now part of the world renowned Lydate Collection of Imperforates. The Keeper of the Royal Collection is envious. Even that ubiquitous stamp collector King George the fifth is probably turning in his grave.

Sir Godwyn might well visit Bridlington. One never knows. Life can be full of unexpected surprises where postage stamps and married women are concerned. Setting aside the magnifying glass he takes up the buff manila folder that he had deposited on the floor next to his chair. He opens the folder and peruses the top photograph of the two dozen or so glossy coloured prints. John Caldigate MP is naked except for a pair of pale blue Marks and Spencer socks with holes in both heels. The Ministerial red box is upturned on the floor of the master bedroom of the grace and favour Admiralty Arch apartment. The tiny camera well hidden in the decorative cornice.

Sir Godwyn dry lip twitches and peruses the second glossy coloured photograph. A scarlet lipped Agnes Grey wearing only a suspender belt and attached black stockings, so reminiscent of her late mother as she lays aside the whip, and over a sequence of several photographs, takes ownership of John Caldigate's impressive erection that might frighten a more timid woman. The framed studio portrait of dear Mary his wife and their three children is laid face down on the bedside table. As it was when Sir Godwyn spent such an enjoyable night with an at first pretending to be reluctant Mary Caldigate. Her husband had been away on a foreign jaunt with Agnes Grey in tow. In the end Mary was not the least bit reluctant...nor the next night, nor the night after that.

Several more glossy coloured photographs that leave nothing to the imagination. Miss Grey really can be a very naughty pleasant looking lady. She has been somewhat neglected of late by the Neglecter in Chief; he really ought to put that right. Another glossy coloured photograph… the same room… John Caldigate who certainly puts it about, this time with a certain well known High Court Judge's long suffering, very much naked, apart from the black stockings, middle-aged wife, which gives Sir Godwyn food for thought. The mobile phone on the polished Georgian occasional table chirps Parsifal. He moves aside the empty engraved whisky tumbler. "Yes, Prime Minister."

Thursday October 12th 9.03 am

Jack Bellingham, the People's hero, is ravenously demolishing a room service breakfast with all the trimmings, including a double serving of black puddings. A post-coital morning to be as ravenous as… well as ravenous as on a post-coital morning. A vast improvement on slopping out after a wakeful night of Sikesy's adenoidal snoring and muttered death threats. Sikesy always slept like…well like Sikesy, after being serviced by the imaginary smooth right hand of the international movie star Amelia Sedley.

At Shirley Keeldar's post-coital suggestion – he loves the sound of that – post-coital. Every novel should have several; suggestive on so many levels without going into overmuch messy detail. Anyway, at her post-coital suggestion they had shared a luxury bubble bath which turned a tad coital. They are now exceedingly well scrubbed but running late. Jack had pointed out that he had been running late all his life and she had absentmindedly sympathised. Despite the running late thing, and wearing only yesterday's lacy pink knickers, Shirley had wasted an interminable amount of time applying various ointments with the perfectly sized pink-nippled breasts bouncy balling, as she massaged nameless unguents into apparently flawless skin. John Keats only ever saw the end result… hence the lyric Poetry.

Whilst skimming the morning newspapers Jack had played the voyeur, at which he has had a great deal of practice over the years. It is surreal to read so much about himself and some of it true. The double page spread in The Sun giving food for thought.

Mouth crammed full of bacon and sausage in true prison fashion, he had scribble signed the various contracts where indicated. Being only too well aware that the signing ceremony actually took place when Shirley came back to bed in the early hours of the morning. He had woken to find it wasn't a dream after all and that the entangled legs were very much for real. The close up smiley mouth the most wakeful thing he has ever experienced in his poor deluded life.

A few minutes after the signings, a fully dressed Shirley Keeldar gathered all the signed documents together, as that willowy Honourable gazelle of a girl breezed into the Grande suite with an enchanting gap toothed smile as she pinched a slice of toast. She had done the same yesterday in the crowded breakfast room at the Holiday Inn Marble Arch. It is the sense of entitlement that keeps you in your place. Or should that be keeps one in one's place. Time will tell.

Yesterday he had spent two hours dawdling over breakfast and had almost given up. Then had appeared this most beautiful Sorcerer's apprentice – sense of entitlement and all. So many admiring heads turned as one it could have been choreographed. Now the two women exchange imperceptible nods. No need for any words. Shirley Keeldar in particular is careful not to make him believe he has signed his life away. She is mistaken if she believes he would ever think that, because after all, despite the endemic cheating, he was the undisputed Chess champion of his cell block.

Now Shirley kisses him on the forehead in a throwaway possessive way that comes as natural as breathing.

"Rebecca will look after you today, darling. New clothes. New haircut."

Jack holds up the cup of coffee in a toast. There is no champagne and they both laugh or in her case larf. The Honourable Lady Rebecca Sharp does not larf.

Boss lady exits the room in a supremely efficient way in a swirl of expensive perfume. One would never know she was wearing yesterday's lacy pink knickers and, one would never know, that only yesterday the Bank had threatened to foreclose. The Bank becoming more ruthless after the takeover by the Germans. Shirley Keeldar hates Germans. More to the point so does Sir Godwyn Lydate.

Thursday October 12th 9.48 am

Unless genuinely amused at someone's unexpected downfall, speak of the devil Sir Godwyn Lydate does not do laughter. Smiling is an effort of will that most of the time he is not prepared to make.

"How is the Collection going, Godwyn?"

"Which one, Prime Minister?"

The Prime Minister smiles indulgently. It is always wise to let Sir Godwyn have his unscripted little jokes. It is unfortunate that the titular First Lord of the Treasury's smile more often than not comes across as creepily obtuse. So he doesn't smile very often. He does do sternly patriotic gazing into the far distance superbly well. Like now.

"You are absolutely certain he has to go?"

"Yes, Prime Minister."

They are seated opposite each other in Sir Godwyn's study in the hushed Albany apartment. They are meeting here because Sir Godwyn can be certain they are not being overheard. There is no such word as paranoid.

Their deliberations are momentarily interrupted by the entry of a big boned, bosomy, fiftyish woman, carrying a silver tray with two Ming china cups of coffee that rattle with her nerves to which she pretends to be a martyr. She is proud to do for Sir Godwyn Lydate and a person has to put up with minor inconveniences. Lydia Robinson never loses sight of the bigger picture. An accident of birth is just that.

"Thank you, my dear Lydia." Anyone less like a Lydia it would be hard to find.

"Indeed." The Prime Minister executes his off centre keep your distance acknowledging a faceless peasant smile. Luckily she is too overawed to look up…she is a proud woman and just stops herself curtsying as she backs out of the room. Just wait until she tells her Wilfred, although he votes for the other lot when he can be bothered. The poor love is something rotten with his chest these days. They would be in a right pickle if it wasn't for Sir Godwyn who is most generous. He has his funny little ways but they are a small price to pay. It is only occasionally, very occasionally, that she suffers any misgivings and then she gives herself a stern talking to and thinks about going to Church the next convenient Sunday. It works every time.

"Your lady what does doesn't live in?" The Prime Minister gingerly takes up the irreplaceable cup and saucer. He knows the bastard does it on purpose.

"Only when she is needed." Sir Godwyn appreciatively sips the Honduran coffee with little finger correctly pointing east. "Sometimes needs must, Prime Minister, although sometimes needs really should not."

The Prime Minister thinks it wise to sagely nod; he is also quite proficient at sagely nodding. Sir Godwyn bloody Lydate can be annoyingly obtuse. The First Lady, as Jayne likes to be known, insists that Sir Godwyn is indispensable. In fact the neurotic bitch does talk about Sir Godwyn rather a lot, although Robert Peel does switch off to most of what she says these days, and is rather relieved she has gone off sex since the latest miscarriage, and of course finding him in bed with Florence Dugdale. Only last weekend at Chequers she had spent an hour tête-à-tête with Sir Godwyn alone in the Orangery. Afterwards she denied that she had been crying and he had not bothered to press the point.

"I am not sure I want him to go, you know, Godwyn." He fashions a nervous cough and exaggeratingly carefully sets down the Ming china cup and saucer – a Lydate family heirloom he has been led to believe. Of course it goes without saying that the Lydates go back to the Norman Conquest. "He is immensely popular with the Trident wing of the Party."

Sir Godwyn sets down his own Ming china cup and saucer less carefully and retrieves the buff manila folder that has been lurking on the Turkish carpet like the proverbial elephant in the room. Opening the file with due deliberation he extracts several glossy photographs that are much more incriminating somehow than mere computer images. The most permanent of Permanents hands the glossy photographs over to a Prime Minister, who is only too well aware that with the Government's paper thin majority he is by no means permanent. Sir Godwyn hands the photographs over as if dispensing degrees at his old Oxford College. An annual task which he executes rather well, if he does say so himself. He does so enjoy the après dispensing – even in the current gender correct climate some female undergraduates are nakedly ambitious.

The husband of the First Lady shuffles through all the glossy photographs. Then does a second and third take at two images in particular of John Caldigate and Agnes Grey that leave absolutely nothing to the imagination. The ever lurking fear momentarily flaring behind most photogenic eyes that women of a certain age apparently find irresistible. There really is no accounting for taste.

"Jesus fuck." Agnes Grey's wicked come and get me grin so reminiscent of her late mother.

"Indeed, Prime Minister."

The indeeded Prime Minister hands back the incriminating evidence as if it is untreated nuclear waste, and runs an unthinking hand through the swept back gelled hair of the style of a much younger man. "When were these taken?" He croaks... coughs. Wishes he dared spit on the priceless Turkish carpet; indeed wishes he had the courage to spit in Sir Godwyn bloody Lydate's impassive Sixteenth Century Venetian Doge's face. A Renaissance creature to the life. There no doubt was a Renaissance Lydate making life hell for Thomas Cromwell... not to mention Henry the Eighth's various Queens.

"Three nights ago, Prime Minister." The Prime Minister resolves never again, which is a resolve he knows he has not the resolve to keep. Ruefully he rubs a remarkably smooth chin and tries for a matching rueful smile, which comes out creepily obtuse. "Great arse." Just one of the boys. Nudge. Nudge. Wink. Wink.

"Indeed, Prime Minister." And he doesn't need to add you should know, Prime Minister.

"You are absolutely right, Godwyn." Not one of the boys anymore. No. No. No. "If this gets out on top of the Bellingham backlash we are toast. Total fucking buttered wholemeal toast."

"Indeed you are, Prime Minister."

Sir Godwyn allows a decent interval of time to elapse for this most photogenic, weak bellied, self-serving, back stabbing, fornicating moral degenerate to properly absorb all the implications; every single one. Whatever else he is not stupid.

Sir Godwyn waits and waits... patience being a virtue best served in small doses.

"I need a drink."

Mine host pours a largish Scotch… a common or garden blend he reserves for occasional visitors, and watches the visibly failing project knock it back in one swallow and the hand steadies. He could add toper to the list… piss artist most certainly.

"I am going straight to Northolt from here, Godwyn. The Helsinki Summit." A failed attempt to take back the high ground. The moron thrives on Summit meetings and the resultant photo opportunities with equally venal world leaders. The President of the United State will be at this one – enough said. To the less cowed of his colleagues the Prime Minister is known as Summit Man. He would probably see it as a compliment.

"A replacement, Godwyn?"

"I thought Rosalie Murray, Prime Minister." The First Man looks startled as well he might. "If you recall, Prime Minister, she spoke out in support of the Bellingham verdict in the House and called him the People's hero. It played well in the country."

Of course he fucking recalls. He never forgets anyone who does not toe his increasingly isolated version of the Party line. The Chief Whip was his only close friend at their minor Public School.

"She is popular with the media, particularly the Daily Mail." A newspaper that is the Prime Minister's most implacable critic. Sir Godwyn has pretended that the Editor cannot be bought off. "And she interviews well on television." Unlike the Prime Minister who comes across as creepily patronising, except to women of a certain age.

"And she is a woman."

"Indeed, Prime Minister."

"An attractive woman."

"Indeed."

"See to it, Godwyn."

Sir Godwyn of course does not reply. When the Prime Minister has wafted on his way trailing a scent of the same expensive cologne, Sir Godwyn studies some other glossy photographs in the file. The Grace and Favour bedroom taken several weeks ago. The putting it about John Caldigate and the rather attractive middle aged, richly fleshed, wife of that well known High Court Judge. She is also wearing only a suspender belt and black stockings but no whip and no upturned red box. Sir Godwyn must whisper sweet nothings when he next meets the lady on the cocktail circuit. He tut tuts as he flicks through the photographs…these are activities that should not be indulged in by such a respectable seeming lady, and she a Magistrate.

There is a tentative knock at the study door. This lovely big woman knows her place.

"Come in, Lydia, my dear."

She balances the hallmarked silver tray and, with concentrated pinky tongue peeping out, reverently retrieves the Ming dynasty cups and saucers. There is something about the shy sensitive assertiveness of this large boned, bosomy working class woman, that he finds strangely soothing to his savage breast. She was born in Dumfries and has never quite lost the hint of a Scottish burr.

"Will there be anything else, Sir Godwyn?" She is standing round shouldered with feet planted firmly, as though the tray is a tremendous weight and an earth tremor expected at any moment.

"You know, Lydia, my dear, I rather think there will be something else."

"Very well, Sir Godwyn." She rather thought there would be something else when she realised he had been looking at those dirty pictures. She had sneaked a peek at them when he was in the bath. Being very much a red blooded woman, she is not unhappy that there will be something else. "Shall I retire to the bedroom, Sir Godwyn?" Quite matter of fact as if she is asking should she polish the family silver. She is really glad that at the last minute she decided to tidy things up down there. Her mother always called it down there. Her husband used to call it her hairy Mary... the poor love.

"Yes, Lydia. Run along and prepare yourself."

"Very well, Sir Godwyn."

He Penny Black watches Lydia Robinson leave the room with a sashaying sway of child bearing hips that is quite natural; the cups and saucers merestly rattling. He studies another photograph. John Caldigate's wife spread eagled naked on the same bed. A really wicked grin, and not for the benefit of John Caldigate, as Mary Caldigate brazenly plays with herself as the naked man approaches. So unexpected of the cocktail party circuit's prim and proper wifely wife, usually hanging onto her husband's arm for dear life. Quite a collector's item for Sir Godwyn's collection only. Not quite the real thing though...Sir Godwyn, the naked man, had forgotten about the hidden camera in the urgency of the moment. He must remember next time...although he has nothing to be ashamed of.

He mustn't keep dear Lydia waiting, who is very much the real thing in spades.

Thursday October 12th 10.32 am

"What does it feel like to kill a man in cold blood?"

The Honourable Lady Rebecca Sharp is alone in a glamorous hotel suite with a confessed murderer. The hands resting in his lap are killer's hands. Hands that could close round a woman's slender neck and choke out her precious life.

She is sitting on lots of legs à la Shirley Keeldar and is rather glad she does not possess Shirley's indelible strength of frailties. There are enough complications in her life thank you very much. "It is the first question Phineas Finn will ask you on tomorrow's show."

"My friends call me Jack."

"I know." She doesn't tell him that as far as she is concerned he is merely Project Jack and certainly does not tell him that he missed out on a threesome. "Boss lady has insisted you are the final guest on the couch. You will come on arm in arm with Amelia Sedley." An Amelia Sedley who is being treated for sex addiction she doesn't say. Scarlett O'Hara to the life.

Boss lady, who hates being called Boss Lady, is several moves ahead. She is more her old self now that the German owned Bank has had to fuck off without Dresden needing to be bombed. Sir Godwyn rarely takes prisoners and so there is that to look forward to as well.

"The movie star Amelia Sedley?" Movie legend… movie star… duh. Becky wonders who the clever one is here.

Jack could not be more taken aback if this real life vision of Sunday supplement glossiness had farted in his face like the cuckolding wife in the Canterbury tales. Of course Chaucer used a quill pen.

"She is tipped for best actress Oscar." He tries to keep the awe out of his voice. The celebrity mags were popular in jail and Sikesy purloined any with photos of Amelia Sedley. No one complained…well just the once and the complainant was fed through a straw for several weeks.

"The very one." The very one who is being snared into the tentacles of Project Jack. "And now we need to go shopping." She springs to her feet. "But first I need a pee."

He is beginning to realise the subtle poshness of certain words.

She checks the bin in the black and white tiled bathroom but there are no used condoms, only several screwed up tissues. The Boss lady should really know better after that harrowingly tearful visit to that awful clinic, ruining her makeup with Becky gripping her hands for dear life. She doesn't want to go through all that again any time soon.

There is a frowzily pretty, in a common sort of way, waitress person cleaning up the breakfast debris without undue haste.

"Is there anything else, Mr Bellingham?" Trying for posh and consciously not dropping any aitches. Common little trollop, but strangely familiar and bloody nice boobs. Becky really must get up the courage for a boob job. She is just thankful that Project Jack doesn't ask the pushy little trollop to call him Jack.

"That will be all, thank you, dear." Genuine top drawer posh so there. Becky stands magnificently gangly in the Louboutin high heeled shoes, with hands on slim hips and staring the busty slapper with the awful scuffed shoes out of the door. If looks could kill.

Becky would be indeed surprised if she was able to see through walls and see the common little trollop drop the pose and talk into a tiny microphone at her wrist. A very posh voice indeed.

Thursday October 12th 11.51 am

The forty minutes or so of invigorating naked recreation spent with a hesitantly enthusiastic as always Lydia Robinson, had set Sir Godwyn up nicely for the brief interview with the Ex-Minister, which went rather well. He tap taps the gold embossed Mont Blanc fountain pen, which was a gift from a grateful Royal Personage, against his ever so slightly protruding front teeth.

The Georgian antique desk in his Whitehall office is clear of any clutter except for the two buff manila folders. In the folder on the left is John Caldigate's signed resignation statement. After demanding to see the Prime Minister he only had to be shown two of the photographs with Agnes Grey. The incriminated one had agreed that he needed to spend more time with his family. He had bellowed hardly at all. Sir Godwyn knows that on leaving the room the ex-Minister had contacted Agnes Grey before contacting his wife; needs are so delightfully axiomatic. Sir Godwyn had contacted Mary Caldigate before the meeting and assured her that her husband's career, with all the wifely trappings, was by no means over. They had talked intimately and suggestively for several minutes and agreed to meet tomorrow evening at his Albany apartment – I cannot wait had been her breathless parting comment. Strictly for his own delectation, Sir Godwyn appraises more glossy photographs of John Caldigate's long suffering wife very much cavorting with Sir Godwyn. These pictures were kept in reserve but were not needed. The errant wife's secret is safe for the time being. The naughty lady had posed lasciviously for Sir Godwyn's eyes only and he had made dear Lydia enact a similar pose. She really is a treasure. With a self-satisfied sigh he secretes the glossy photographs in the left hand folder, and glances at the ornate George II ormolu clock that graces the marble mantelpiece, above the actual real coal fire. He checks on his mobile phone the message from the pretend lioness Jane Fennell, his operative at the Savoy Hotel. He now knows what the Bellingham creature had for breakfast. Always useful to know what a potential enemy had for breakfast. Jane has sent a selfie and looks suitably waitressey in the begged and borrowed uniform. She is sticking out her tongue and raising her skirt to prove she is wearing sensible waitress knickers. It might be an idea to show it to the Archbishop, but Sir Godwyn is not at all sure that he wants to put dear Jane through that particular ordeal. He glances again at the priceless ormolu clock, which had been especially designed for Queen Charlotte against the wishes of her husband George the Second, who had been in one of his Hanoverian small minded cost cutting moods. Another feisty lady.

He has kept this particular feisty lady waiting for twenty-two minutes. He does so enjoy a good old fashioned arm wrestle with a feisty lady and never lets them win.

"Do come in, my dear."

Rosalie Murray, Member of Parliament for Leeds North West, is the sort of late Eighteenth Century, painted by the School of Reynolds, handsome, fine boned woman, content in her own times, that he does so wish he could admire. It is a risk. He knows it is a risk.

The feisty lady unfussily seats the late Eighteenth Century posterior on the surprisingly comfortable low down Victorian armchair, facing the Georgian antique desk.

From under startling false eyelashes she slyly, but not slyly enough, appraises this Whitehall lair to which few Ministers ever gain access, never mind the hoi polloi, of which she is indubitably one. She just could not believe the call when it came this morning. Right until the last moment she half believed that someone was playing a practical joke – there are a number of potential culprits that she could name. She had half expected to be turned away from the porticoed building by the uniformed Major-domo, who had made no secret of admiring her legs.

The huge Fifteenth Century painting of Aphrodite at her toilet dominates the room… it is an original. Aphrodite bears an uncanny facial resemblance to the formidable Mary Ellen Meredith, wife of the Foreign Secretary.

Sir Godwyn has perched himself on a corner of the desk looking down on everything and within touching distance. She will not be intimidated.

"Well, my dear."

"Well, Sir Godwyn."

This fiercely intelligent, flawed woman has a very good idea why she is here. The rumour mill has been working overtime. It is hard to believe… but there it is. At the tenderish age of forty-three she will be very much the baby of the Cabinet. She has not held any bag carrying preparatory Junior Ministerial Posts, being far too outspoken for that. But she is nakedly ambitious … and, if need be, ambitiously naked… no doubt he knows that. He will know she is a risk. Jesus – she knows she is a risk. Sir Godwyn is rocking one leg to a no doubt Wagnerian tune. Rosalie knows she must be on her mettle. There will be a price to pay because there is always a price to pay. She has heard the rumours. Still, prices are there for the paying. Who was it said Paris was worth a Mass?

"The Prime Minister has asked me to sound you out, my dear."

"I wish you would call me Rosalie. I am not really a dear."

She crosses the quite magnificent legs that had been so expertly appraised by the Major-domo and rocks one of them to her own tune. She could be forgiven a lot for these legs but not everything… by no means everything. So the lady is proficient at somewhat predictable opening gambits. To tell the truth, he has never much appreciated showy opening gambits that inevitably fail miserably against a player of his skill.

"Very well." An indented pause. "Rosalie." His ever so slight exposure of teeth reminds her of one of her least favourite characters in Alice in Wonderland. As a precocious spoiled child she had always wanted to be Alice through the looking glass. She would have done things very differently if she had been Alice.

"You may call me Sir Godwyn."

Call me Rosalie has a pleasant tinkling laugh that is easy on the ear. To be honest there are many things to appreciate about this woman apart from the legs. Whether he would bid for her at auction without an expert opinion is another matter.

Recently divorced for the second time. No children. Supposedly a committed Christian, although he finds that hard to believe. A recent one night stand with the Foreign Secretary after a drunken Commons Reception; another man that puts it about. An occasional weekend married lover in her Constituency, when the married lover's wife is visiting her sick mother more frequently than strictly necessary. A brief lesbian relationship. An abortion at Cambridge where even so she achieved a double first. A more recent abortion that has remained surprisingly secret when one considers the name of the father.

It is all in the right hand buff manila folder. Naturally there are several revealing glossy photographs. "Well, Rosalie, we are in a bit of a pickle over the Bellingham situation."

"You certainly are." She will not be outstared. Most unusual striking grey eyes. Definitely a school of Reynolds portrait, but by no means a Masterpiece. Painted by one of his studio assistants, with just one or two touches from the Master. Certainly the eyes. The legs were never on display in a Reynolds portrait…more's the pity.

"We, Rosalie. We."

He is only too well aware that she also finds the game viscerally exciting. Better than sex one might think; or one might not think. He can see it shining from the foxy grey eyes. He can smell it. She gets it. So few people that play the game get it. It is it. He just hopes that in her late Eighteenth Century boldness she does not underestimate consequences. That would be most unfortunate for all concerned. "We have had our eye on you for some time, Rosalie."

She has been only too well aware of the ubiquitous Sir Godwyn Lydate studying her recent performances in the Chamber. And in the Strangers bar, when that second hand Lothario of a Foreign Secretary got her legless after that Reception for the Israelis. From what she could remember the very much unprotected sex had been surprisingly better than average. Thank God for the morning after pill.

She is trying to work out the next moves. He is making no secret of appraising her body and the low cut blouse shows off the boob job to perfection.

The shortish, pleated, almost school girlish, skirt allowing the window display of more than enough slender thighs. A Jimmy Choo high heeled shoe is dangling tantalisingly from the size four foot of the crossed leg. The shoe ready to drop when the cymbal crashes.

With the boldness that often gets her into trouble she boldly looks him over. Her parents had said, and had said often, that she should have been a boy. Rosalie is her middle name being a sop to their disappointment. Robyn is her first name. It was a difficult birth and she is an only child.

Rosalie is very much aware that he exudes raw power from every pore of his sun bronzed skin. Power that she craves and that is so close she can touch it. She must not make a false move. She must not be too bold. No risks. Please God. No risks. She knows what she is like.

He touches the knot of the old Etonian tie that he wears because the colours suit his complexion. He cannot be accused of being a snob. "I think I might be able to persuade the PM that you are the person for the job." They both know which job.

She cannot stop herself licking her lips and the taste is one she knows well. "I upset the PM and the Chief Whip with my speech calling Bellingham the People's hero." Me and my big mouth. Nevertheless an extremely apposite speech he doesn't say... a speech to sweep a knight and a bishop and several pawns from the board. Not to mention endangering the black king. He sees Rosalie Murray as playing white, but of course he might be wrong.

"What do you want me to do?"

With a suddenness that takes her breath away, he crosses to the marble fireplace and snatches up a polished brass poker and vigorously pokes amongst the blazing coals. Lighting this real coal fire and keeping it stoked is a rite of passage of the newest female member of his People. Of course it isn't as simple as that because Sir Godwyn Lydate does not do simple. There is his own unique take on strip poker. Only yesterday dear sweet lots and lots of Clarissa was a wee bit fumbley and no doubt on purpose dropped a lump of coal on the Persian carpet, for which she had to enact due penance.

Rosalie Murray has never been frightened of spiders and their webs. She has never been frightened of anything or anyone. Except perhaps her second husband on that one occasion, and that is not a mistake she will ever repeat.

After the abortion, the Vicar in her Constituency had been very understanding and consoling. Late one evening they had fervently prayed together, facing the altar thigh to thigh like it thunders in the Old Testament. The resultant David and Bathsheba coming together on the altar steps might be seen by the narrow minded as verging on the sacrilegious. She has always believed that God moves in mysterious ways and has always believed that God is a woman.

To the left of the imposing marble fireplace there is an early Regency just about, at a crush, two seater contraption thing taking up lots of space underneath an artistically lace draped window that will overlook Downing Street. On the elegant occasional table next to the two seater contraption thing stands a glorious bronze statuette of Aphrodite crouching at her toilet. There seems to be a theme here and Rosalie's eyes are drawn to the generous curves.

The mobile phone on the desk rings to something no doubt Wagnerian. He answers with a curt yes. He does not appear to be affected by the heat from the fire, but she is beginning to sweat under her arms and is glad she has dabbed, and then more for luck, that ludicrously expensive perfume in several strategic places.

"Indeed, Prime Minister." He appears to be only half listening as he sucks on the Mont Blanc pen. "Quite so, Prime Minister." He ends the call and jauntily pockets the ultra slim phone and resumes his Imperial perch on the corner of the desk. "That was the Prime Minister."

That delicious tinkling laugh.

"How is Helsinki?"

"Full of hot air." There seems to be an awful lot of legs for one woman. "We have much to discuss, my dear Rosalie."

"Indeed we do, Sir Godwyn."

"My friends call me God."

That delicious tinkling laugh might well get on one's nerves after a while. This close he inhales the perfume that is a deciduous late summer flowering in the endangered heat of the room. His favourite perfume... clever girl... he likes that. As with Jane Fennell's sensible waitress knickers, the devil is in the detail. Not too much perfume though, the senses should be piqued not overwhelmed. He appears lost in thought as he gazes into her eyes that she has been assured, on more than one occasion, are beguiling. She stares back and thinks there might well be a terrible sadness well disguised at his core. A Martian who has crash landed on Venus. Perhaps she is being unduly fanciful.

Abruptly he recalls himself to the moment and glances at the George II ormolu clock. "I have a luncheon date, my dear Rosalie." With a bruising proprietorial hold on her bare upper arm he leads her to the door. "You want the job, Rosalie." It is not a question.

"Yes." She answers anyway.

"It is best we are not seen together until after the announcement. You will appear on the Spencer Perceval Politics Show on Sunday morning." He can smell the mingled peppermint on her close breath. Dutch courage then.

"You will debate with the Shadow Minister."

"Old iron knickers."

He does not reply. Instead he pecks a powdered cheek and she is acutely aware of the tip of his tongue. "I will be there in the studios. Afterwards I insist on brunch at my Albany apartment. I do a mean scrambled eggs with smoked salmon on the side."

"Sounds delicious." She will have to cancel her Sunday plans but that will not be a hardship. When she has gone the deciduous late summer flowering lingers – echoes within echoes. What goes around comes around. The lingering is becoming a wee bit cloying. Thank goodness the hay fever season has passed.

Thursday October 12th 1.23pm

Hindered by designer bags banging against running legs and with awkwardly clasped hands, they seek sanctuary in the exclusive Italian bistro at the west end of Jermyn Street close to Burlington Arcade. So exclusive it doesn't display a name. So exclusive it waives the need for a reservation for the youngest daughter of a Duke. And it goes without saying the People's hero.

The odd couple are efficiently guided to a table at the rear of the restaurant, out of view of the street and the screaming Japanese schoolgirls peering, guppy fashion, through the plate glass window. In the art gallery next door to the restaurant a striking square faced Russian looking woman peers out to see what all the fuss is about.

The designer bags are gathered up by a simpering waiter and a gap toothed smile his ample reward. The people who booked the table weeks ago will be told there has been an unavoidable mistake. Not of course told that they do not matter in the scheme of things. A Duke's youngest daughter would only be trumped by Royalty. The People's hero is probably untrumpable.

"This is madness." It doesn't seem right to say fucking madness in the presence of this sweet, innocent looking girl, who doesn't look old enough to be out of school uniform. She flicks shoulder length hair in that utterly adorable way. If she had ever appeared at one of his sparsely attended lectures he would have bumbled more than usual, hiding behind that out of time Pickwickian persona. Later he would have painstakingly Meccano constructed a luridly intricate fantasy where the girl, after many a struggle, ended up naked in his bed where, in a paroxysm of passion, he would not quite strangle her to death. Although of course it is not an exact science.

He should not really be writing this down…he will cross it out.

"You have gone viral." She is checking the state of the art mobile thingy whatsit.

"They were pawing me." Not in his most intricately constructed Meccano sick fantasies has he been jumped by a scream of Japanese schoolgirls, any of whom would have been gladly and expectantly naked in his bed, without any struggle or any construction whatsoever.

The miasma of shocked surprise tinting the recently acquired bemusement glazing the oddly colourless eyes makes her want to slap his face.

Lady Rebecca Sharp is always prepared for the worst and the black dog is often snapping at her heels as it was for her mother and grandmother. The drugs don't always help… prescribed or otherwise. So she has enough problems of her own without caring where call me Jack is coming from. She knows he is trying to give off the impression of being an uncomplicated man, a lump of wet clay to be shaped, pretending the potter's wheel isn't broken beyond repair. There is something desperately out of kilter that makes her more than usually uneasy. She knows she should be grateful but there we are. They need the money and thank you Lord for the money. Call me Jack comes with the money and so there we are. Shirley Keeldar will do anything and almost anyone for money, which goes back to her childhood. Becky Sharp will do anything and anyone for money, which goes back to her childhood. The threesome would have been a small price to pay and Becky would have given value for money…she always gives value for money where threesomes are concerned.

Now she is tap tapping the state of the art tablet thingy whatsit. The nubile Japanese schoolgirls clocked the People's hero despite the new trendy haircut, and had surrounded their 'misunderstood' hero with Beatlemania 1960s style. Becky had reluctantly grabbed his hand and run for it. There is something about his touch that gives her the creeps.

"We must ensure a Japanese translation of the book."

"Are you serious?"

She doesn't mean that book.

"I am always serious where money is concerned." She doesn't look up so that she doesn't have to resist the temptation to slap the – are you serious – face. The all singing all dancing mobile trills an iconic pop tune that he cannot quite place; he can rarely place pop music iconic or otherwise.

"Hi." Becky answers and ostentatiously listens and he secretly admires the shapely earlobes. "That ridiculously expensive Italian near Burlington Arcade." There is no need to watch the pennies anymore… fuck off, Bank… Germany is no longer calling.

Jack appears entranced by the clipped, perfectly shaped Roedean vowels and the bewildering sense of entitlement that she exudes from every single pore.

"A swarm, if that is the correct adjective, of coming in their knickers Japanese schoolgirls spotted the actual People's hero." She doesn't look up. "It might have been the mask and tights that gave it away." She does not gap tooth smile.

She is listening intently and Jack thinks she does listening intently quite adorably.

"That's brilliant." She appears to have forgotten Jack's existence which does not surprise him in the least. But she needs to be careful because he is writing the story. He really is not sure about this green ink.

"No publicity is bad publicity." She glances at Jack, who is staring at his hands on the pristine tablecloth. The nails have been manicured and the fashionable haircut and trimmed eyebrows have transformed the gold plated bumpkin into a much younger looking Heathcliff's older brother – the almost handsome one who made a fortune out of coal. The one with the mid Nineteenth Century equivalent of Issues.

"The People's hero wants to go to the Egon Schiele Painting Exhibition at the Royal Academy." She is aware in her peripheral vision that Jack is nervously breaking bread between agile fingers.

"Daddy will get us shooed in." A deep sigh. "Right ho. Love to Uncle Goddy." She ends the call and is aware of the Project breaking more bread. The Egon Schiele Exhibition is probably the right place for Shogun Jack.

Thursday October 12th 1.43 pm

A visibly edgy Shirley Keeldar ends the call. She has taken possession of the window table at the fiendishly exclusive La Vendee Restaurant. A table from which there is an uninterrupted view of Albemarle Street and the entrance of the Ritz Hotel.

An October grey limousine with blacked out rear windows pulls up to the kerb and parks on double yellow lines. An October grey matching muscle bound uniformed chauffeur moves discreetly to the nearside rear door. Momentarily he glances in the restaurant window and makes eye contact, reminding Shirley that large parts of her experiences with men have been one car crash after another. Several passers-by pause, but no one recognises the immaculately dressed man who emerges from the limousine. That is as it should be. No reason to frighten the natives.

The recently appointed Italian Head Waiter rushes to open the restaurant door and ushers the most honoured guest to the table, where the most beautiful English lady is waiting. The Head Waiter possesses more than a passing resemblance to the late Benito Mussolini.

"My dear." The most honoured guest kisses Shirley on both lightly powdered cheeks. No air kissing here. The Italian Head Waiter pushes in the chair, only slightly missing his timing, and then scuttles away to snatch up an ice bucket and a magnum of Sir Godwyn's favourite champagne; he rushes back to the table only slightly tripping. There are no other diners. Sir Godwyn tastes. "Excellent, Giovanni." Not Benito then. Giovanni's smile is slightly disconcerting, as there appear to be too many teeth in his mouth. He has been earnestly practising the name Zur Godween… Not Zur Goodween. He pours generous amounts into the two crystal goblets. It has to be goblets, which Sir Godwyn prefers to prissy girly flutes. "A toast, my dear." She is thinking he is always the Ringmaster and all that he needs is a scarlet coat and whip. On second thoughts just a scarlet coat. "To the pendulum of life." They clink crystal goblets and sip sip appreciatively. She smacks her lips. There is nothing second best vintage about this champagne.

Such a voracious minx. Every time they meet he recalls the vision of the naked twelve year old girl staring electric blue eyed, like a Midwich cuckoo, at the naked electric blue eyed fourteen year old boy.

"So tell me, my dear, how is lover killer?"

"In the recovery position."

He doesn't properly lip twitch. Perhaps he is just a wee bit jealous… always just a wee bit jealous. A fine balance. If only he were a different kind of man.

"And you, my dear?" With the more striking electric blue eyes, she matches him blue eyed stare for blue eyed stare, as she did as a twelve year old girl who had just discovered the difference was even more different than she had ever imagined.

She sips champagne. "Also recovering."

"What can one expect when one takes a cold blooded murderer to one's bed?" Definitely a wee bit jealous. He does not at all appreciate that along with the champagne she relishes the wee bit of jealousy. Their relationship has always been one of intricate checks and balances.

"He was found not guilty Milord." Her words call up a fleeting image of the well known High Court Judge's exceedingly naughty wife, indulging in behaviour with John Caldigate of an exceedingly non-judgemental nature. It is to be hoped dear Mary does not find out. Or the High Court Judge for that matter. Of course, one never knows.

"I was there, my dear." He signals for the crystal goblets to be topped up. "The Jury system is second on my list. Judge Helen Graham is scheduled on my list for tomorrow." A touch of legalise rarely goes amiss.

"She is not taking the rap then?"

Frighteningly astute as ever. He is secretly glad that she has been saved by the bell so to speak; the Bank was being particularly intransigent and the German owners will need to be taught a lesson. It is on his list. He gazes out of the window at the cloudy grey limousine parked on the double yellow lines. The muscle bound chauffeur is slouched at the wheel reading a filched copy of yesterday's Sun newspaper. He does so hope a Traffic Warden will appear… preferably female.

"No, my dear, she is not, as you so succinctly put it, taking the rap." He has ordered the Arbroath smoked salmon and Norfolk farm scrambled eggs that are such a delightful complement, in his opinion, to the greatest vintage champagne of the previous century. One sometimes needs a change from one's favourite lunchtime Burgundy. "There are deeper waters here than twelve idiots coming to the wrong verdict, my dear."

"I know."

"I know you know."

They have always been easy together since he taught her how enjoyable the difference can be; a brother and sister with benefits. These days incest is such an over emotive word.

Giovanni maintains a surreptitious watch on the table, as his olive skinned sister-in-law is serving food to the man of a thousand secrets. There are stories about this man. A man who makes and breaks Prime Ministers. A man who shapes the seasons.

Sir Godwyn takes note of the sister-in-law's olive skinned Mediterranean colouring and the merest intriguing suggestion of a hare lip. He is always delighted at imperfections. She is probably mid-thirties and busty in a Roman peasant rolling in the hay kind of way. It was rolling in the hay as a fourteen year old that brought on his hay fever; the gardener's wife had taught him much that he has not forgotten. Tit for tat one might say, as he had taught the gardener's wife a few things that, despite the age difference, quite took her breath away, so that she was not able to ask where he had learned those things. She had to be careful ever after when making love with her randy git of a husband.

"Thank you, my dear." The busty waitress lip crookedly smiles and, after a momentary pause, he pronounces her name like a fine aged in the barrel Barolo, which is by no means easy with such a short name. "Thank you, Anna." She touches the mole on her cheek in a timeless gesture of the Camargue.

Giovanni is watching intently, which only highlights his squint... it is not certain if Benito Mussolini squinted. The whore never crookedly smiles for Giovanni; boasts that God will punish them both. Giovanni of course doesn't believe in that God. Giovanni's God is not particularly intelligent and tends to believe in the same things as Giovanni.

Sir Godwyn refuses to converse whilst eating and so they eat in that companionable non-speaking that is a cornerstone of their, he likes to think unique, filial relationship. Out of the corner of his eye he is aware of the olive skinned sister-in-law pretending not to be watching and waiting because she knows that it infuriates Giovanni. It is Sir Godwyn's business to know that Giovanni is taking full advantage of his sister-in-law and that she prefers it from behind. No doubt so that she can close her eyes and pretend it is someone else... probably anyone else.

"So, my dear." He sip sips champagne. "He has signed." Shirley has never possessed much of an appetite but he resists the temptation to steal from her plate. Manners maketh the man. He signals for the dishes to be taken away. The dusky woman gives off a musky scenty odour when she leans a little too close for comfort. An undertone of scrubbed sweat that is by no means unpleasant.

She fills out the waitress uniform in a quite distinctive way. He must bring the Archbishop to lunch because this dusky woman possesses the potential of a long overdue Nemesis. Sir Godwyn never forgets or forgives.

"You should be careful, my dear." The sister-in-law flares swampy brown eyes in shocked surprise, but realises he is talking to the beautiful blonde lady. A lady that is all the things that Anna would wish to be. "He is a dangerous man."

"He's a pussy cat." For some reason that she cannot explain, even to herself, she wants Goddy to pretend to believe this patent lie.

"My dear, he most definitely is not a pussy cat." The hovering waitress is not sure whether to take the plates away or wait for further orders. Indecisive is not a word she would understand. She is not a proper waitress anyway. It is just that the insanely possessive Giovanni rightly does not trust her out of his sight.

He treats her like a slave but she dare not go against him after what she did. Sometimes she wishes that Giovanni was dead as well, and she has lit scores of candles in Church on that very wish. Sir Godwyn signals with a Cardinal's beckoning finger and she leans as close as close. She has one earlobe markedly longer than the other and he whispers for that ear only. "I know everything." The Irrawaddy muddy eyes see what they see. "God has spoken." The improper waitress takes the dishes away watched by a narrow eyed Giovanni. One of these days he will swing for that whore.

"Now. Where were we, my dear?"

Thursday October 12th 5.05pm

The Honourable Lady Rebecca Sharp is seated, with practised ease, in a wide armchair in the Grande suite with legs tucked under her body. She glances up from the screen of the tablet to eye blinkingly study the not guilty one who, seated alone on the settee, is devouring the hardback version of the Egon Schiele Exhibition catalogue and reading without moving his lips. She wonders if he will spot himself. Untitled.

He is sucking on an Exhibition biro. He had insisted on buying a dozen Exhibition biros and had not replied to Becky saying… "Are you writing War and fucking Peace? And why not buy two dozen fucking fridge magnets while you're at it?"

The squally eyed woman of a certain age behind the Sales counter had gazed in wrapt wonder at the infamous Call me Jack. When he smiled his thanks, she had practically stripped off there and then, and begged to have his love child; Becky had looked away in disgust.

Annoyingly licking a finger he turns the pages and holds one up sideways to study two grotesquely nude women entwined, contemplating something unspeakably profane. Becky prefers proper paintings like the Singer Sargent or the Whistler owned by her father. Well, the copies owned by her father. He sold the originals before Becky was born. She has to reluctantly admit that there is something weirdly appealing about an unsureness and a vulnerability that does not sit well with something vitally bereft at Jack's core; not able to decipher the signals that people, particularly women, put out; an Enigma code that he has been unable to break and all his shipping sunk without trace, apart from a few slicks of oil. Until now, that is. Now the clever sod is learning by rote. The brutal executioner of the paedophile child killer Franklin Blake holds three of the four aces. The ace of Spades is fame. There appears to be nothing sexier than being a murderer who got away with it.

Becky can well understand why a Jury of Monday morning men and women found him not guilty – the little everyman against the venality and corruption of the Establishment. She can also fully appreciate why Sir Godwyn Lydate is on the Atlantic patrol. In his cups, which is most of the time, her father the Duke declares that all Politicians are shits, only some are shittier than others. One of his more profound observations.

The designer haircut has taken ten years off the not guilty one's age. Just a pity about the ears. He does wear the trendy designer gear surprisingly well considering… the Honourable Lady Rebecca Sharp seeks to be nothing if not fair.

"The Exhibition was amazing." He gives off a schoolboy enthusiasm that is reaching towards charming. He is working on it. There is somewhere smokily depthless in his Being that even an adorable gap toothed grin cannot reach, and so she is spared the effort. "Egon Schiele's sister Gertrude looks a lot like you."

Becky is saved from dredging up a comment, or indeed ostentatiously not making any comment, by Shirley Keeldar exploding through the door of the Grande suite.

"The media are fucking camped out downstairs." She stylishly tosses a Burberry raincoat over a chair and misses. She doesn't sound displeased at all and it is obvious she is a bit pissed from lunch.

"How was lunch?"

"Uncle Goddy sends his felicitations." She takes three attempts at felicitations. Best for all concerned to change the subject because simmering jealousy is a two-way street.

"Is Gabriel lined up?"

"Monday morning." Shirley joins Jack on the settee and pitter pat pats his good knee, which spurs on an exchange of stagily complicit smiles that Becky pointedly ignores. "We will get the Weekend TV appearances out of the way." There is money in them there appearances. Jack thinks that none of Egon Schiele's models looks the least bit like the most shapely in all the right places pre-Raphaelite Shirley Keeldar.

"Who is Gabriel?"

"The ghost writer for your forthcoming best-selling book in several languages including Japanese." She glances at Becky who glances back. No words necessary.

"I thought I would be writing the book."

"Gabriel Betteridge will of course discuss it with you, darling."

Becky shoots Shirley a hard stare that is not acknowledged. "Then he will fashion the worldwide best seller in double quick time."

He has heard the name. He ghost wrote a biography of the last but one England Football Manager. "I can write, you know." He even sounds childishly petulant to his own sticky out ears. With this stylish haircut the ears are a bit too sticky out if the truth be told. He has always been acutely conscious of his ears. At school he was nicknamed Jugs amongst other things, including Nobby.

"I have published a book you know." Childish petulance is a hard habit to break, particularly when it used to work so well.

Shirley playfully ruffles the stylish haircut. She really likes it. Becky cannot stop herself glaring.

"What was the title of your book, darling?" Shirley playfully tweaks an ear and it has to be said that there is a lot of ear to tweak. Becky is tapping down hard on her tablet. Fuck it. Anyway they can now afford tablets by the bucket load.

"Charlotte Brontë's married year."

"Gabriel Betteridge would have called it Charlotte Brontë sex slave."

Jack old fashionedly ponders this comment, as he has old fashionedly pondered on so many atrophied aspects of Nineteenth Century literature, at sparsely attended Conferences over the years, in so many out of the way places. Shirley Keeldar caresses an earlobe and he loses his train of thought. That never used to happen in the out of the way places where his earlobes remained inviolate.

"Amelia Sedley is definitely with you on the Phineas Finn show tomorrow evening." It is hard to believe. There is little else to say. "Her People are enthusiastic."

"They are shit scared the new movie will bomb." Becky does not take her eyes off the tablet that is bouncing on her knees. There is no point in making any sense of it. Amelia Sedley is the most photographed and talked about woman on this or any other known Galaxy. The ultimate unattainable sex object… just stand well back and ask Sikesy.

Jack had seen the movie, for which Amelia Sedley was last nominated for that elusive Oscar, four times in one week. On the fourth viewing he was accompanied by his bloody sister. A bald as a coot middle aged bloke was surreptitiously, but not surreptitiously enough, wanking on the row behind. Jack's sister had turned round and told him to fucking hurry up about it. Jack had been surprised she hadn't offered to finish off the bald coot. To be fair, she had thought about it.

With a heartfelt sigh he puts the Exhibition catalogue to one side. His place saved by the Egon Schiele Exhibition bookmark. Jack collects bookmarks. He has more bookmarks than he will ever use, which is information surprisingly missed by Sir Godwyn Lydate.

Shirley's mobile contraption thingy burr burrs an actual old fashioned telephone tone. She checks the caller and answers with a grunt. "Surely." She ends the call and stares at Jack, who guiltily wonders what she has found out. "Got to shoot off."

It is a pity. If Becky had not been here somebody's law would have ensured that Shirley and Jack would have ended up in bed. She is always randy when a bit pissed after lunch. She would not have answered the distress call. The call would have been taken on Becky's watch.

Shirley exchanges knowing glances with Becky. There is telepathy and then there is Shirley Keeldar and Becky Sharp.

Shirley kneels at his feet and delves in a capacious Serapian shoulder bag, and hands over a brand new state-of-the-art mobile just about everything, that wouldn't last five minutes in prison. "My number is keyed in." Then both women are heading for the door. "One of us will pick you up later, darling." Shirley waves and blows a kiss; Becky does not wave and blow a kiss. Then they are gone – just like that. Although he doesn't really mind being on his own. He has had a lot of practice over the years. In prison he was never alone and sorely missed his own company. Being a loner isn't all that bad. With practice the tasteless daydreams are real enough.

He pours a neat Double Black Scotch and wonders if he should ring his bloody sister. If the truth be known, he is glad to be away from her cloying presence and insistent demands. She will be on the second or third tall glass of Asda own brand vodka by now. No doubt lolling Josephine Bonaparte fashion on the battered family sofa and watching reruns of Homeland. The sofa where they had huddled together last week, pissed as rats, and watched the Phineas Finn Show. Jack will ring tomorrow… perchance to dream.

He swallows two potent stomach tablets washed down with the whisky that is most definitely not Asda own brand – the burning in the stomach always a reminder. Not that he needs reminding. He holds up the cut glass tumbler in a perfected perambulatory toast. "To us." And settles down patiently to wait on events. He is good at that. And of course there is the Egon Schiele Exhibition catalogue and of course Gertrude. Now there was a sister worth having.

Thursday, October 12th 9:59 pm

The Exhibition pen writes much smoother and black ink is so much more literary somehow. He had been going to write about his bloody sister but she will have to wait until he is good and ready. She will not like that… he would like to write her out of the story.

Sir Godwyn Lydate knows something about filial affection. An unaborted child cosseted almost to destruction by his Nanny, whom he still adores after his fashion. An unwanted alien from outer space to his viciously arguing parents, who divorced before he was out of nappies. They got together again when he was three years old and then separated for good when his sister was less than a year old; his father claimed, with some justification, that his sister was the gardener's child…after all, on several occasions, he had spied on his wife and the gardener very much in bed together. His parents could not live with each other and they could not live without each other. They were mistakenly led to believe that the without each other option would be less deadly. Godwyn had been claimed by his mother to spite his father and his father's relatives, the ancient tribe of Lydate. The family had half-heartedly brought up his sister after a fashion. Girls did not count, except to be passed around and then used as marriage fodder.

It was Nanny Tressel who had comforted, in her own ruminative way, the abandoned little Copperfield. Until he was shipped off to Eton, like his father and his father before him and his father before him, to the umpteenth generation of Lydates of Lydate Hall, Nether Lydate in the time honoured County of Hertfordshire. Nanny was always there for the holidays. At Christmas there was never any Christmas tree or decorations allowed in the vast draughty Elizabethan mansion; but Nanny always ensured he had postage stamps on Christmas morning for the stamp collection, which was the second love of his young life, to be secreted in the embossed dog eared stamp album he had discovered in the attic one rainy afternoon. His mother was always away somewhere sunny and abroad at Christmas.

It was an unashamedly loving Nanny Tressel, guarding at his bedroom door, who had taken him to her truckle bed when he had woken screaming from another nightmare one Christmas morning. It was Nanny who had wetly kissed and kissed and hushed the shivering little boy between substantial bosoms as she called them. She let him suckle the moon crater nipples as she had suckled him as a baby… her own baby boy being stillborn, which was probably for the best. Nanny always looked on the bright side and still does except, occasionally, where Goddy's welfare is concerned.

Then all at once it was summer, and it seems only yesterday that he had thoughtlessly charged into the dining room on an imaginary steed chasing Parliamentarians and had surprised his Royalist mother, the fashionable flowery dress ruckled round her waspish waist and lacy pink French knickers surrendered at half-mast and she being lustily – there is no other word for it – being lustily taken from behind against a rocking dining room table, by the man who had come to discuss the catering arrangements for the annual Church fete to be held in the grounds of Lydate Hall. The lady of the Manor traditionally opened the fete and judged the vegetable marrows. Their self-same eyes met but she couldn't focus properly as the rapidly approaching orgasm spiked her bent over body. The man, whose name Godwyn never knew, had momentarily grinned at the unexpected audience and pushed harder... and harder, so that Godwyn's demented mother shouted out something that was not for childish ears. The unknown man closed his eyes and pushed harder and harder. The little boy had not wanted to watch as the dining table rocked precariously on a mid-Atlantic squall, and the man emitted a bellowing bull calf groaning that mingled spectacularly with his mother's abject keening and the little boy scampered away for dear life. The Royalist soldier making good his escape to fight another day.

It was much later that same day, because there had been even noisier seconds on top of the table, when his more furious than usual mother, still wearing the crumpled flowery dress and smelling of something not very nice, had unearthed her only son hiding in a cluttered musty cupboard under the stairs. She had dragged the terrified little boy out of the false refuge, various sizes of Wellington boots and all, and beaten him with knotted fists. The marks of her rings were traceable by Nanny for many days afterwards. "Like father like son, you fucking pervert." She had spat out within an inch of his blubbering face. He was aware of Nanny Tressel close by and his out-of-control mother turned on the cheap to hire buxom village girl, whom she had more than once accused of being ten pence to the shilling. Although of course not to her face.

"Stop it." Nanny Tressel at her most intimidating. "Stop it now."

His mother had stopped it now and stared stiletto daggers at the ignorant peasant bitch. She had never called her an ignorant peasant bitch to her face. Only to others after making sure Nanny was out of earshot.

The ignorant peasant bitch had glared back sharpened kitchen knives. In fact she was holding a sharpened kitchen knife and they both knew she would use it without a second thought.

"Keep that little shit out of my sight." And his mother had stormed off, muttering incoherent curses against the male line of the Lydates back beyond Darwin's slimes of time.

Nanny had taken possession of her own little Goddy in strong arms and rocked him just like she had when he was a suckled baby. Stroking the matted hair and kissing away the tears just like she had when he was a suckled baby. Such a greedy suckled baby.

Just like it was yesterday. The musky meadow sweet scents and the crooning voice set on its very own demi octave. The gorgeous fleshy softness enfolding his terrible primeval hurt and the hard penis straining against the cobwebbed dusty trousers.

In the now, today, he adjusts the sumptuous silky Chinesey dragon robe that was a gift from a certain Chinese lady of high standing on the Prime Ministerial trade mission to Beijing, where Sir Godwyn's fluency in Mandarin Chinese had come in extremely useful. Not least when arranging the rather unusual late-night entertainment in the Prime Minister's Quarters. On the return flight Robert Peel had kept Sir Godwyn at his side. Keep your enemies close and keep Sir Godwyn Lydate closer still.

Another later summer. Just like it was yesterday. An aimless rainy afternoon and he was home from Eton for the holidays. His mother in the south of France with some disposable paramour... Nanny's word. She had read it in a true Romance magazine and she repeated the word several times that summer.

It was Nanny Tressel's idea to explore the attic.

There was no dog-eared stamp album of long forgotten Penny Blacks to unearth but there was a rusting metal trunk of his mother's discarded dresses. She hated to give anything away. Perhaps forgetting that he was not such a little boy any more Nanny Tressel had impetuously shrugged off the unevenly hemmed home-made cotton dress. Despite many maternal slaps she had never properly mastered needlework.

She had rummaged voraciously through the moth soiled seasons of dresses and she was not wearing any knickers. Like her mother and her mother before her – a village habit of long standing. Village sluts according to his mother and she should know. The not so little boy had watched intent eyed as Nanny bent forward and chose the same flowery dress, had tugged the crumpled garment over her head and split the seams on her wibbly wobbly titties; titties being a smutty Eton word the boys had sniggered about the Headmaster's much younger Scottish wife, who favoured inappropriate low-cut dresses to excite pubescent boys. Godwyn had been her own particular favourite pubescent boy and she used to ruffle his hair at every opportunity. One memorable day he had grabbed hold of the ruffling hand. It was the first time he understood that feverish eyes can shine unconditionally and bosoms actually heave.

In the present moment of the here and now, a summoned Shirley Keeldar kneels at his bare feet and discerns the familiar far away lost Continents look sheening the hooded eyes, and the right hand absentmindedly caressing nothing visible. The syringe is ready.

"Naughty little Goddy." Cast adrift in the spidery cobwebbed attic with rain dripping through unrepaired tiles, Nanny had sighed the age old sighs of needful village girls the world over, as he had rubbed the outline of the hard penis up and down the expanse of bare bottom with that dress marooned round her titties. The bare bottom more expansive than the Headmaster's much younger Scottish wife's bare bottom. "Naughty little Goddy." Nanny had made no attempt to stop naughty not so little Goddy being naughty. He had been emboldened to unbutton the cream cricket trousers and slither the released rock-hard penis up and down the secret fleshy valley. And then the delightful shock of Nanny's backward seeking hand taking charge of the rock-hardness and guiding the remarkable length surely inside. Believing it would be his first time, Nanny had especially moaned to make him feel like a man and then she had moaned for real, as he had pushed and pushed like that nameless man rocking the dining table. Nanny had groaned and groaned but he knew it was in a good way, because the Headmaster's much younger Scottish wife had groaned and groaned in the same good way, as he had pushed harder and harder that day, just as he pushed harder and harder inside Nanny. It was at that point that the Headmaster's much younger Scottish wife had briefly contemplated second thoughts, but it had been much too late for that; they had always wanted children. His eyes flare open in the here and now and they are the limitless blue of that late summer sky, after the summer storm had cleared, later on that fateful attic day and he was naked in bed in Nanny's arms.

His mother had arrived home unexpectedly. She was always such an unexpected woman. She had screamed vile obscenities and she had tried to drag Nanny Tressel out of the bed by a bare leg. That was a fatal mistake.

"My darling." In the here and now there are tears streaming down his face. "Oh! My darling." Shirley the only one who knows everything. Not even Becky Sharp knows everything. Nanny of course is taken as read.

"I need oblivion." He replies and it reads more stagily dramatic than it sounds.

Shirley Keeldar, who is wearing a silken dragon robe that once belonged to the granddaughter of an Empress, plunges the needle into his thigh. He shudders and she whispers, "You are not to blame, my darling. It was not your fault."

No soothing words can ever prevent a part of him always being that terrified little boy, watching his mother being strangled by an enraged naked Nanny. His mother horribly gasping out her life, with shoeless heels banging a death rattle on the bare dusty floorboards. Shirley leads him to the master bedroom of the Albany apartment and lies down with him and takes him in her arms and soon he is breathing deeply and evenly. She dare not leave him alone. He really was not to blame. The mad bitch deserved it.

Thursday October 12th 11.08pm

The Honourable Lady Rebecca Sharp is mind blowingly stunning in a tiny black dress and lots and lots of slim legs. She has whisked Jack away by the Savoy Hotel goods entrance and has commandeered Sir Godwyn's limousine and Chauffeur for the evening. The great man will not be needing either and the last thing she wants is to be alone with project Jack. She sits up front with the Chauffeur and strokes his thigh as they are whisked to Glencoras nightclub, situated in the most fashionable part of fashionable Knightsbridge. She and the People's hero are of course waved through to the VIP area, where the music is throbbing but not deafening. This early only a handful of leggy is as leggy does young women are perfecting catch all nubility on the dance floor; everywhere there is the hum of posh voices like honeybees queueing for their turn at the Queen Bee. A for once genuinely bemused Jack is introduced to a seventh Earl's younger son, whom Jack recognises as that smirking Usher at a Royal Wedding who had been caught on camera pinching a Bridesmaid's bum. The pincher partly owns Glencoras, which is his mother's name. They are shown to a table of scantily dressed girls all patented from the gazelle formula; Jack thinks he recognises the Bridesmaid with the pinched bum.

Lots and lots and lots of air kisses and demi-waves and toothsome grins and a smattering of oohs and aahs as convict Jack is introduced or, rather, his name tossed to the table to make of it what it will. Some naughty schoolgirl nudgy giggles and it appears that blood red piranha mouths are the next fashion. A cacophony of scents and perfumes to invade if not quite conquer the senses.

He recognises one of the leggiest of the gazelles as a minor Royal, and another as a Bridesmaid whose bum had not been pinched. Another is a well-known television Personality, whom he remembers from the time he was suspended from his job, and for several weeks watched wall to wall daytime television. He had been reinstated through lack of evidence and because the key witness had disappeared.

One flashing eyed gypsy girl, who is also vaguely familiar, blows him an exaggerated blood red kiss and beckons with a loaded index finger.

Bulbous magnums of criminally expensive champagne litter the table, together with rare labelled whisky and even rarer Russian vodka shipped from St Petersburg. And what he later learns to be absinthe flown in from Paris this morning. Becky, who is glad to see the back of her charge, pushes him towards the flashing eyed gypsy girl who grabs his arm and drags him down to share her seat. Lots and lots of thighs… legs so yesterday. Gypsy girl is preternaturally stunning, as they all are preternaturally stunning in a manufactured do not stay beyond midnight kind of way. There is something hazardous about it all that he cannot help but find appealing. Gypsy girl is wearing a silvered glittery halter top shaped to utterly rounded breasts and wearing matching incredibly short shorts. A neatly moulded belly button and delicately pale olive skin like the insides of a peeled black grape. She squeezes his bad knee and leans as close as close, but this is not the place to be reminded of an uncoordinated Dora Spenlow. "Just loved the trial, Ripper man." Cut glass Roedean accent that goes without saying. Whitby jet black close cropped hair the shade of his mother's favourite brooch, which was actually bought in Whitby one rainy August bank holiday Monday. His bloody sister had been left at home locked in her bedroom.

The gypsy girl's flashing greenish eyes are unnaturally bright like a southern hemisphere embedded in a northern sky. She is acutely jittery and constantly jiggling the lots and lots of right leg and thigh. The lots and lots of left leg and thigh stays still. Releasing the bad knee she retrieves a matching glittery clutch bag from amongst the cigarette stubs littering the floor at her surprisingly large bare feet.

She delves in the glittery clutch bag and, children's party magic trick fashion, produces an opaque plastic bottle. Taking a proprietary grip of his right hand she shakes out a green tablet and a pink tablet and then two yellow tablets by mistake, into his sweaty palm. With a toothy grinning. "Oops. What the fuck." She hands him her glass of what turns out to be absinthe in a what's mine is yours crafted gesture that is impossible to resist.

Obediently Jack swallows all the tablets. In her turn she swallows one green tablet and one pink tablet and only one yellow tablet. Jack thinks these must be real diamonds studded in her earlobes. He is later to discover that there is a real diamond studded somewhere else and realises that his sick imaginings did not go far enough, particularly when he discovered the second studded somewhere else diamond. Over a peeled black grape shoulder she is telling someone to piss off. "One lousy fuck and they think they own you." She confides in her new best friend Jack. "Perhaps you could dispose of the tosser, Ripper man." She kisses the last word. "Permanently." Red lips are not so red as the stained stones kissed by the English dead. He thinks he might have said aloud. Who gives a fuck?

He is not sure how much later they are seamlessly grinding as one body on the by now crowded dance floor. His limbs appear to have developed a St Vitus will of their own. The music is deafening and the manic flashing lights are crying havoc…. a horse… a horse…. my kingdom for a horse. The dance floor is heaving and his consciousness implodes to the sensation of existing outside the gyrating mislabelled baggage of his body, forever consigned to be unclaimed on an everlasting airport carousel.

A bluebottle that has wantonly strayed is looking down uncomprehendingly from the sweaty ceiling onto the crush of alien bodies not far enough below. Call me Jack and gypsy girl are frantically necking and he surely cannot taste something rotten in the State of Denmark. There is a hand a hand my kingdom for a hand groping inside his designer jeans. The bluebottle wisely decides to make a run for it but the wings are heavy and deciduous. It should not be here. There is a wrong place and a wrong time and this is surely both of them.

Jack has never been inside a ladies' toilet of any kind. Where he was brought up it was forbidden territory to the male of the species. Even waiting outside for a lady within was frowned upon. Unless, of course, you were a cute little boy with sticky out ears and it was your mother, as usual taking her time, and you were trying not to cry; other ladies patting your head and lipstick kissing your brow and making appropriate noises. Often holding you against squashy chests to stir up funny feelings.

Everything is a fuzzy hazy pink. There are naughty girly Nursery rhyme characters on each cubicle door. The door sporting a naked bending over Cinderella, leering over her shoulder at the naked Prince, swings open and a fuzzy hazy Lady Rebecca Sharp staggers out supported by a sleek haired youth, who Jack thinks he recognises, sporting a pair of lacy black knickers as a crown. They stagger away giggle giggling like the privileged idiots they must pretend to be.

Then she who is she drags an only too willing Jack and his beanstalk into Cinderella's lair. He knows there is something dangerous about lairs but he cannot quite put his what's it on it.

The utterly stilled bluebottle on the low ceiling is looking down through ninety degree eyes. It must remain completely still and only swivel its eyes to watch the creatures below tearing at each other's clothes. Hoping against hope they will be too preoccupied to notice an insignificant bluebottle minding its own business. It thinks it should probably look away as the lithe olive skinned female of the Species peels off the glittery tiny covering things.

The bluebottle is not to know that, as a spoiled little rich girl, the lithe olive skinned female pulled the wings off flies, squashing the wingless cripples with a slender thumb and finger, revelling in the crackling squishy sounds and vividly imagining the soundless shrieks of agony.

The by now naked male of the species slumps heavily, with a bump and a grind, onto the broken toilet seat and laughing uproariously almost tumbles off; the lithe olive skinned female does not laugh uproariously.

The male abruptly stops laughing uproariously as the naked olive skinned female lowers itself down and down to absorb the engorged reproductive organ. As the olive skinned female throws its head back in a showing off ecstasy, it spies the uninvited bluebottle on the ceiling. The bluebottle receives an unbidden mystical revelation and flexes its waxy wings to fly away no matter what.

An olive skinned thumb squashes it flat. Nothing. End of story.

Friday October 13th 7.35am

Not quite… C'est la Vie… bluebottles come and bluebottles go. Life goes on for the squashed bluebottle's numerous offspring…it was ever thus.

An unsquashed Sir Godwyn Lydate relishes the first few stolen moments of another ticked off dawn. A lovely woman asleep in his arms, which he wishes were just a wee bit longer. As that unaborted child, one summer morning he had hung from a tree branch by his arms for as long as he could bear it. There was no lasting effect.

This particular lovely lady stirs and mumbles – it sounds like a name but he cannot be sure. She is always there for him without question. They are two peas from the same pod, although of course no two peas are identical. He kisses the blonde crown and she settles back into a troubled sleep. She will have had a wakeful time until she was certain that his breathing had shallowed out. The attacks have lessened over the years and afterwards he is more and more spiritually becalmed… almost at peace… but almost at peace with what he is never certain. Certainly not the ghost of his strangled mother. Sometimes he wakes to the awful gurgling sounds of her hard dying, the shoeless heels bang banging on the bare unswept floorboards.

He strokes the arc of the shapely bottom that is within reach. Nanny Tressel, who became Nanny Linda, after that first and last summer that shaped the boy into the man, called it her bottom, as did the Headmaster's much younger Scottish wife. His mother called it her arse; stick it up my arse had been a favourite insult, until the day she was taken very much at her word. The mad bitch doesn't call it anything now that she is interred in the family vault at Lydate Hall, designed by Vanbrugh in one of his more exotic drunken moods. Surely angels never looked like that in any sane, sober person's imagination. By now her essence will be well and truly mixed with the bones of the ancestral Lydates – God help them all. His lucky father was assumed lost at sea.

He will steal a few more delicious moments before running his ritual morning tepid bath. Baths preferred since the tepid baths he shared, and occasionally still shares, with Nanny Linda. After his mother's timely demise they had both rightly believed themselves safe, and he would ease his boyish spine up against the lovely squashy titties. She would enclose him in her meaty arms and meaty thighs, and soap up her lovely boy as she crooned made up nonsense lullabies. The best of times... the worst of times.

With his mother permanently out of the picture, the doddery arthritic husband and absurdly shrewish wife that caretakered the rundown Elizabethan mansion, kept well out of Nanny Linda's orbit. They had crossed Nanny just the once and the absurdly shrewish wife bore the bruises for many weeks afterwards. The weird orangey hair never properly grew back.

They never dared breathe a word and just stopped knowing. An early lesson the young Godwyn took on board. Now he hums a snatch of the chorus from Wagner's Flying Dutchman as he runs the tepid bath. The door opens and a naked Shirley Keeldar, face angled by troubled sleep, pat patters across the imported Genoese Italian marble floor tiles. She pat patters quite superbly – Venus crossing marble floor tiles by the school of Botticelli. It is in the blood.

"You all right, Goddy darling?" She anxiously studies his face and is relieved to discern that the demons have passed over for now.

"Thanks to you, my dearest." They will share the tepid bath and he doesn't share a tepid bath with just anyone. If the truth be known he currently shares tepid baths with the gloriously bosomy Lydia Robinson probably more than most. In his view it is the third most intimate thing that a man can share with a woman.

Friday October 13th 8.19am

Known more and more to his friends as Jack jerks snorily awake from a primary coloured kaleidoscope of weird and wonderful dream sequences. He is not wearing pyjamas. Lily Dale had teased him mercilessly about his stripy pyjamas with an old-fashioned drawstring. The stupid woman said he looked like a survivor from Auschwitz... she was not to know but even so. In the here and now he is alone but there has been a woman here. There are kaleidoscopic fragments of memory and tastes that linger. A diamond? Most definitely a diamond...two diamonds... not to mention the lingering soreness that never existed in the Meccano constructed sick daydreams. This is a strange bed in a strange bedroom that is not the back bedroom of his mother's house with a black-and-white photograph, signed by Brian Close, of the Yorkshire County cricket team of 1959 framed on the wall; a cut-out magazine photograph of Venus triumphant by Lucas Cranach the elder sellotaped above the bed. The only photograph on this wall is a bloody great big Castle.

In the next room the Honourable Lady Rebecca Sharp is seated at the dinky kitchen table in the Knightsbridge apartment that her father begrudgingly allows her to use begrudgingly. She calls it his knocking shop but not to his face of course. His vile temper is legendary.

Politely sipping coffee from a huge Parisienne coffee bowl, the Duke's youngest and least favourite daughter is wearing an off the shoulder pink lacy dressing gown garment. The muscle bound man seated opposite is sporting a manly string vest and boxer shorts covered in motifs of Big Ben. There are Regimental tattoos on his forearms.

"Seems quite a stud your Jack." The muscle bound man sips coffee from an I love Beijing mug – a gift from uncle Goddy; a pair of matching mugs and a small jar containing a rare Chinese aphrodisiac making up the gift.

"Not my Jack." The gap toothed grin to raise and then see his lopsided grin. "And you should talk, studdo."

The secondhand somewhat erratic toaster pops and it could be a prop in a 1950s kitchen sink drama at the Old Vic. The toast is only marginally browned and, as she is buttering the marginal toast as thinly as possible, she is aware that project Jack has appeared uninvited in the doorway; not exactly the genie out of the bottle but pretty damned close. He is wearing pale blue boxer shorts of the latest fashion and is doing that recently acquired bemusement thing. "Coffee?" A well brought up girl.

"Please." She pours a brown liquid resembling coffee into the other I love Beijing mug that is visibly chipped. The rare Chinese aphrodisiac was used up some time ago.

"There is no bread for toast." No butter either for that matter. He looks around bemusedly. "If you are looking for Julia she has vamoosed." Lady Rebecca doesn't look at Jack.

"Julia?"

"Julia Verinder, who you were shagging half the night." Becky nibbles some toast. "Sole heir, or should that be heiress, to Julius Verinder who owns half the High Street."

"I don't remember much about last night." Fastidiously avoiding the visible chip he noisily slurps lukewarm funny tasting coffee.

Becky exchanges glances with Gilbert, known as Gil to his friends, whose hand under the table is caressing an ultra smooth thigh. She wishes he wouldn't – sufficient unto the day is not a saying she has the willpower to follow. She waits for the dust of Jack's words to settle. "You were out of your tiny mind." Daintily she munches thinly buttered toast. "Big strong Gil here had to manhandle you back here after you threatened to flatten a Prince of the blood Royal and several Door chappies." Nibble. Nibble. "You have a vile temper."

"I never used to do drugs." He does that pathetic mew thing with his stupid mouth.

"You certainly did drugs last night, matey." Gilbert Markham, who is Sir Godwyn Lydate's muscle bound most trusted chauffeur, chomps on thinly buttered toast.

Jack wisely pretends not to hear and instead peeps over the rim of the chipped mug at Lady Rebecca's pinky nipple on view, as the pink lacy garment yawns intricately open at one side. She is unconcerned; breeding will out. It is Gilbert, known as Gil to his intimates, who leans over and covers up the exposed pinky nipple.

Jack's stomach rumbles. This clever clogs grammar school boy needs to find his depth – the scholarship to Cambridge – unfashionable Sydney Sussex College but Cambridge nonetheless. The double first. The proud mother. The jealous sister. Articles and lectures. The slim book. That is just about the sum of it.

The muscle bound Charles Atlas and the stunningly gorgeous girl are conversing in undertones, heads close together. He is excluded and so nothing new there. She is the sort of unattainable girl that he used to spy on by the banks of the Cam at a spot where dense undergrowth tempted indiscreet lovers. There was one unseasonably hot May afternoon when a girl had removed her bra and revealed pinky nipples. Staring wide eyed at those particular pinky nipples had made him careless and he had been spotted. He ran off and the boyfriend in his underpants had given chase but Jack got clean away. Athletics was the only sport at which he excelled at school…he was always running away.

Friday October 13th 10.05am

Shirley Keeldar, who has had to skimp on her make up this morning and just about gets away with it, is sipping black coffee with a dainty little finger pointing towards Mecca; the coffee is foul. Standards at the Ritz are slipping. She sets the cup to one side never to darken her lips again, and checks the time on the diamond encrusted Rolex, which was a birthday gift from her husband before they were married…on her most recent birthday he gave her a fat lip.

She cannot stop herself admiring the turn of a shapely wrist. The wrist does not show the exhaustion that the rest of her body has absorbed. It is always the same after one of Goddy's "Do's". Thank the Lord they are more and more infrequent these days.

She tap taps a kidney coloured fingernail against brilliant white teeth. No exhaustion there either and so thank goodness for wrists and teeth. She crosses and then re-crosses the shapely black seamed legs and swings a loosed Jimmy Choo high heeled shoe, partly revealing a most shapely foot. The five toes remain hidden from public view because she believes that toes are very personal. Only Tom Sawyer has recently sucked those hidden toes and the thought of it produces a twist in her tummy, that is not as flat as she would wish. They really must meet up soonest…which is Tom's word.

The ever so smartly uniformed Porter at his station is ogling – there is no other word for it – with somewhat bleary eyes. Shirley never tires of being lusted after if only by a humble Porter, and he does possess an admirable military bearing. A reminder of a recent unforgivably enjoyable threesome with Becky and Gil. The only excuse being that they were being pursued by the Germans and needed distraction. They certainly got that in spades.

An Arab Prince no less, and his entourage, sweep through the desert sands of the hotel lobby. The humble porter bows as they pass through in a sandstorm swirl of robes and incense. The Arab Prince goggle eyed stares appreciatively at the achingly beautiful woman with honey blonde hair and such lovely lovely legs. He is a Princely connoisseur of lovely lovely legs and all that they entail. Smiling toothily before the unstoppable Royal sweep sweeps him past the vision of desert rose loveliness; he is also a connoisseur of minor Romantic poetry. In the street the engines of the fleet of limousines are ticking over. It would not do to keep the Foreign Secretary waiting too long.

The vision of loveliness checks her watch… five minutes late. Ultimate sex symbol Amelia Sedley hates being kept waiting. It is she who notoriously keeps other people waiting, sometimes for hours on end. Shirley Keeldar tap taps the kidney coloured fingernail against the brilliant white teeth. There is something extremely satisfying in putting that common little trollop in her place.

The humble Porter deferentially tips his cap, as another vision of untouchable loveliness bursts through the swing doors, which had been opened for the Prince and then closed again. The Porter of course recognises the Honourable Lady Rebecca Sharp. The Duke is a frequent visitor who appreciates the utmost discretion and tips accordingly… when he remembers, that is. She is accompanied by a Punch and Judy slouching individual, sporting a New York Yankees baseball cap several sizes too big and ridiculous ornamental ladies' sunglasses. The humble Porter looks down his nose, which takes some doing.

"You look ridiculous, darling." Is the mild greeting from the seated vision of loveliness as the unalike couple approach the Louis Quinzish chaise longue.

Jack somewhat peevishly snatches off the tastelessly ornamental ladies' sunglasses that Becky had shoplifted in a Puerto Banus gift shop. He tries not to catch anyone's eye, least of all the Porter, who is staring him down like a long lost cousin of Dora Spenlow.

"And you're fucking late." The ladies exchange knowing looks and Becky knows that boss lady is pleased that they are late. She doesn't forgive social slights at Movie Premieres. Shirley fussily rearranges the hem of the above-the-knee skirt and admires the knees that appear not the least bit exhausted. "It is very naughty to keep the global fucking superstar bitchette waiting." Another exchange of knowing looks.

At a gifted glance from Shirley the humble Porter scuttles across the lobby and escorts the ill-assorted threesome to the particular lift that is out of bounds to ordinary mortals when the fabled one is in residence. One of the two beefy black Bodyguards mutters into his ostentatiously attached mike and they all have to wait. The two Bodyguards stand po-faced staring into the distance with arms crossed to emphasise noticeable shoulder holster bulges.

This close the heady mix of exotic female perfumes is going to the humble Porter's head. This attendant close he wishes on a star that it had been this most shapely honey blonde bombshell, with the amazing legs and see-through eyes, that he had fucked last night and twice this morning, and not the plump teenage Bulgarian chambermaid, whose English vocabulary is limited to please and thank you. Chance would be a fine thing.

The vision of honey blonde loveliness speaks to one or both of the show off black Bodyguards. That particular movie has a lot to answer for and no blame attached to Amelia Sedley for once. "Kindly inform whoever is at the end of that ridiculous contraption attached to your cauliflower ear that if this lift is not here in one minute we are turning round..." She eyeballs the one who had muttered into the mike. "...and we are fucking off and not coming back." Magnificent. Quite magnificent. The beefiest one by a fine margin mutters into the mike and the lift arrives in forty seven seconds. They are met on the second floor by a very attractive female Personal assistant and a very attractive female Publicist. Amelia Sedley does not do jealousy of other women and she does not do ugly. Nor does she do other people's late.

"You're late." One of the very much females hisses. The other one just stares.

"Just what I said." Shirley Keeldar selects from her portfolio of putdown smiles; the wide-eyed innocent – what me taking the piss one. Not easy to pull off.

They are led at a Monty Python sketch speed walking pace along the deep pile carpeted corridor. Over one of the very much feminine shoulders they are informed that Ms Sedley has taken the whole floor. At least Jack appears impressed as he limps in the rear. He doesn't know which of the coloured tablets is responsible but he is manfully struggling with a hard on that has a will of its own. When the muscle bound chauffeur had left the apartment Jack had thought about jumping Lady Rebecca, and then wisely thought better of it. It is not helping matters following these four arses.

With all due ceremony they are ushered into the Presence. The legendary Amelia Sedley is not in a good mood. The legendary Amelia Sedley is rarely in a good mood these days. The legendary Amelia Sedley sacks staff given the least opportunity, which marginally improves any given mood. She is currently sacking her fourth husband, the conniving bastard. The Prenup had better be watertight or she will be sacking her latest exorbitantly expensive Attorney.

She has come across the snooty, so far up her own shapely arse, Lady Shirley Keeldar on several occasions and the feelings are mutual. Unfortunately the snooty arse upper cannot be sacked. The mincing Bambi girl is a Duke's daughter. So fucking what…she has bedded several Dukes. "A Yankees fan." She betokens graciousness as she betokened graciousness in that early movie where she played a youthful Duchess of Marlborough. A movie even she admits best forgotten. At least the receiver of the graciousness and of the throwaway smile, which is insured for many millions of dollars, has snatched off the fucking stupid baseball cap. Amelia Sedley hates baseball and one star baseball Pitcher in particular, the lying bastard.

At least this Jerk is not exactly ugly and she has taken worse medicine. He, as he should be, is appraising the perfect tits shaped through the diaphanous material of the kimono that also shapes the perfected nipples… a great deal of money well spent. In beribboned pet doggy style she pat pats the identical Louis Quinzish chaise longue. "We had better get acquainted, honey." An echo of early Bette Davis. "The rest of you can go." She waves them away. More late Bette Davis, when she was past her best and drinking to excess, the waving out of sync. Shirley Keeldar and Becky Sharp exchange meaningful glances as they are ushered out.

The door is closed ever so gently. She hates doors being slammed. She has sacked people for less.

"So how does it feel to be this close to Amelia Sedley?" Worryingly she more and more refers to herself in the third person.

"Unreal." She is pleased to be pleased with this response. "It feels like I ought to ask you for your autograph."

"I don't do autographs." He wonders if she is joking – hard to tell. She wishes that she was holding that mislaid fake antique Chinese fan, to fold up with a snap and tap him playfully on his strong right arm. That was the movie where she played the last Empress. A glittering triumph according to Movie Today magazine. No fucking Oscar though.

"Silly boy." She makes do with the index finger of her right hand. Not quite the same thing but being prodded by Amelia Sedley is not to be sniffed at. Her first husband, the elderly Producer now dead, God rot his guts, said how well she handled props. Mind you she was handling his cock at the time. Talking of which, she is only too well aware that there is a suspicious bulge in the Jerk's rather tight fitting designer jeans. Under strict medical advice she has taken an extra dose of the prescribed medication this morning and is feeling, shall we say, controlled.

There is a silence that could well be awkward in given circumstances; silences pregnant or otherwise are such difficult things to master in second rate movies.

"When I was in prison." He is only too well aware that she is only too well aware of the unsettling nearness of the actual Amelia Sedley, as she adjusts the silky kimono a bit too adjustingly. "My cell mate used to wank off imagining that it was your fair right hand doing the honours so to speak."

He wonders if the Egon Schiele Exhibition pen was such a good idea after all. There are far too many crossings out.

They stare in eye blinking unison at the actual fair right hand in question, which is resting on an exceedingly bare knee. Kimonos can be fucking tricky as she remembers from the movie where she played a dying Geisha to almost universal acclaim. No fucking Oscar there either.

Apparently unfazed, she properly studies this particular Jerk for the first time. Her People have convinced her that the two of them must become a media item. She just cannot afford another box office flop, and they must somehow substantiate the bare faced lie that Amelia Sedley is in line for an Oscar nomination, never mind an Oscar.

Her People insist the Jerk is supposed to be the bee's knees. An Internet sensation; a cold-blooded murderer who has got away with it. Most certainly a raw intelligence burns haphazardly behind the oddly colourless eyes. There is a contradiction of apparent vulnerability and brittle inner strength, which is a fatal combination in her not inconsiderable experience of men. A fetching out of place haircut and cute sticky out ears. She has always had a weakness for cute sticky out ears since that randy stunt man whose name she has forgotten.

She has had to bed a lot worse than this particular Jerk on her spectacular rise to where she is today, which in her darkest moments she realises is probably on the way down; unfortunately she upset an awful lot of people on the way up. "I suppose I should be flattered." The fair right hand in question is caressing her own exceedingly bare knee... she is definitely right-handed. "Didn't you imagine the same thing?" She executes Eighteenth Century coquettish trapping an unsuspecting rich husband, as she had executed in that movie where she played Mrs Siddons. There had been lots of gratuitous nudity but, needless to say, no fucking Oscar.

She doesn't exactly flutter meticulously made up eyelashes; it is much more complicated than that. This close the face that launched a thousand ships as Helen of Troy in the last but one movie that sank without trace, shows its slight imperfections. Something does not sit quite right, dig beneath the gritty Hollywood veneer and you could well unearth the supposedly vulnerable teenage girl that fled Huddersfield more years ago than she cares to admit. He is not sure that would be a good thing.

"I thought I would wait for the real thing."

She is really glad she took the stronger medicine even if it plays havoc with her periods, which have been a bitch anyway since the most recent secret abortion. The star baseball Pitcher had promised on his mother's life that he had had the snip, the lying bastard. She emits a rare million-dollar throaty laugh that men would kill for she has been told on more than one occasion. "If we are going to be an item." Such a lovely unspecific word. "You will have to learn what turns me on." She has no intention of revealing it is merely possessing a cock of any size shape or colour.

There is a most definite bulge. She has forgotten his fucking name. She doesn't always bother with names. Randy that's it… the randy stunt man was called Randy.

"Jack. My name is Jack." She is startled but recovers in the blink of a meticulously curled eyelash.

"I like Jack." She makes it sound like a piece of confectionery – would you like a nice cup of tea with your Jack?

"I know what turns you on, Amelia."

She appears genuinely taken aback. There really should be some fucking actual awe around here. The algae green irises of her only two eyes are river running and depthless and tinged with lurking crocodiles. This is the description he writes down later and, for once, he is not exaggerating. Green ink would have been appropriate for once.

"So tell me, Jack." The pertest of pert smiles to give a whole new meaning to the four lettered word pert. This could turn out to be a not unpleasant hour wasted before beauticians and hair designers descend like the locusts they are. She is aware of subdued voices in the adjoining room. And one not so subdued. She will swing for that fucking shrink…let them eat cake. Was that Marie Antoinette or Catherine the Great? She played them both the same way. Not even a fucking Oscar nomination.

"So tell me, Jack, what turns Amelia Sedley on?" If he replies cocks of any size or shape or colour she might well have to faint, but not too faintedly, what with wearing this fucking Kimono. Now he genie like rubs the eastern slopes of his aquiline nose with a manicured fingernail and winks… actually fucking winks. And then mimics in an exaggerated stage Yorkshire accent that is J.B.Priestley to the life she would think, if she had ever heard of J.B.Priestley.

"Ye can take the lass outer Uddersfield but ye cannot take Uddersfield outer the lass."

What the fuck is he trying to say? It is almost as if he is making all this up as he goes along. Like she has opened that fucking wardrobe over there and entered some parallel fucking Narnia Universe… that is if she could fight her way through all the fucking clothes. She wonders whether just to slap his face, but thinks better of it, because in real life he has killed a man in real cold blood. She does not do real blood, cold or otherwise. She needs some fucking direction here.

There follows a definite belly rounded pregnant pause, during which she abjectly fails to properly adjust the stupid fucking kimono. Stupid fucking name… stupid fucking Japs. "I am sure you're only too well aware…" She exaggerates the unplaceable transatlantic accent. "…that we are to pretend a relationship for the media." And emphasises pree-tend and mee-ja. Thank God for the fucking medication, only it fucking wears off...stupid fucking medication.

"Your movie is premiered next week." His bloody sister calls them films. His dear poor mother used to call them flicks. "And they..." He nods to the muffled voices behind the door. "...believe it will be a flop." He mews up his mouth. "Apparently I am sure-fire box office."

Yeah. Yeah. Yeah. Whatever. She wonders what will be appropriate if he dares to put a hand on the exceedingly exposed knee. More thigh than knee to be accurate. Stupid fucking kimono. Stupid fucking knee. Stupid fucking medication. She knows exactly what she will do.

She glances sideways. A glance she had perfected as Scarlett O'Hara in the remake of Gone with the Wind. Movie Gossip magazine had said she was a shoo-in for an Oscar. As fucking if – bastards.

The Jerk, she means Jack, that's it, Jack, is wasting the peepshow of the century by gazing into the fucking distance. In profile he reminds her of one of her leading men. A most passionate affair and he had sworn undying love. That was until she got pregnant and he ran for the hills, the bastard. Stupid fucking leading men... stupid fucking hills.

Shit. He is speaking. "All my life I have been used to people laughing behind my back." The gazing into the distance thing is definitely what's his name – the hill runner. She is really not in the mood for someone else's fucked up fucking life story. "They wouldn't laugh if they could see me now." This might well be a quite decent script. She touches his lips with silencing fingers in a gesture he once observed from the back row of the Vue Cinema at Kirkstall. Perhaps his favourite Amelia Sedley movie of all time.

He doesn't appear to be the least bit overawed to be actually touched by the actual legend that is Amelia Sedley.

There is a knocking at the door and rattling of the door handle.

"Fuck off." She shouts in a voice that most certainly carries and there is an immediate impending silence. Jack places a surprisingly dry palm on the knee-thigh that could not be any more exposed. Fuck the medication. And without warning the legend that is Amelia Sedley is devouring Jack, that's it Jack, with mouth-to-mouth resuscitation. The tongue that is insured for a small fortune is discovering that his tonsils are still in place.

Friday October 13th 11.12am

Jack's bloody sister kneels somewhat uncomfortably on the 2' x 2' rubber mat that their mother used for weeding the garden when she was upset and wanted to be conspicuously alone. Marion Fay is kneeling at one of the more recent graves in the more exposed north-east corner of Adel churchyard. Listlessly she thinks about doing something about the drooping anaemic roses, which are poking drunkenly out of the black fake marble chipped vase. There are weeds to be dug out. No chance. She hates to sweat unless sex is involved.

Red and white roses that were their mother's favourites. The red of Lancaster and the white of York… Richard of York gave battle in vain… the childhood rhyme for the colours of the rainbow. Their mother had wilfully deceived herself that she was a Peacemaker.

Marion Fay occasionally, normally when she is drunk on her own, wishes that she misses their mother every second of every day like her acquaintance Alice Vavasor misses her mother every second of every day, or so she claims. Occasionally, when she is more drunk than usual, she wishes that they had been more like sisters than mother and daughter like her acquaintance Mary Thorne had been more like a sister than a daughter to her mother, or so she claims.

When she is dead drunk and just before she passes out Marion really does wish that she had liked their mother just a little bit.

Marion will forever feel cheated that their mother did not live long enough to endure the ordeal of John's imprisonment and trial. Unfortunately the cancer got her first. She was never strong, as she never tired of telling anyone who would listen, and was mortified to be proved right. The Vicar would always listen and he provided great comfort to their mother towards the end.

Marion indulges in a secret knowing smile. As a child she became adept at secret knowing smiles because they used to so annoy their mother. The slaps were well worth it. The Vicar is an insidiously weak, kindly man with an insidiously wandering eye. Just ask Alice Vavasor and Mary Thorne to name but two. There are rumours about that tarty MP woman as well.

The brittle bones safely interred in this hallowed ground worshipped her Johnny as her God. The teacher's round red juicy apple of their mother's beady eye. The younger twin by seven minutes, he could do no wrong. The boy. The young Prince. Taking his absent father's place.

Marion shields the same oddly colourless eyes from the glinting autumn sunlight, and looks towards the squat humpbacked Saxon Church, which just misses being picturesque, as Saxon Churches so often do. The Church where they were both christened and where the Vicar of that day named her Miriam by mistake. She was the one who had screamed at the touch of Holy water. The Church where she was married and the Church where one day soon she will be buried.

Another secret knowing smile. The Vicar's long-suffering wife is away visiting her sick mother. The Vicar will be 'visiting' a sick parishioner no doubt and giving comfort and scattering some Holy water of his own.

Despite the Indian summer sunshine there is a distinct autumn chill in the air and she mews up her mouth and shivers theatrically, as if someone has walked over their mother's grave. There is no one. There is never anyone.

From here, if she cared to look, she could see where Lily Dale is buried. No one leaves flowers there. A secret knowing smile. Marion wishes with all the accumulated peevishness of her peevish heart that she had not introduced that duplicitous bitch to her brother John at their mother's sparsely attended funeral. He possesses enough duplicity of his own thank you very much. The duplicitous bitch would no doubt have introduced herself anyway and got what was coming to her in the end.

With a familial exaggerated sigh, Marion struggles up from her knees and briskly brushes down the skin-tight cut-off stone-washed jeans. The unbidden gust of north-easterly wind attractively ruffles the fashionably styled dyed chestnut hair.

She doesn't look her age, this perennially attractive woman with a perpetual careworn expression; the inherent meanness not always effectively masked by her bits of beauty.

A limping elderly man leading a ridiculously yapping pint sized ratty doggie thing, straining on an equally ridiculous never-ending lead thing, hobbles down the uneven paved path towards the rear gate of the churchyard. She hates dogs. She has nothing against limping elderly men, even ones wearing L.S.Lowry flat caps.

She is only too well aware that limpalong Leslie is appraising her busty figure, and she cannot stop herself brushing the scarcely windswept hair away from her oddly colourless eyes, with a most feminine gesture, that emphasises the fullness of her breasts. She of course catches his rheumy eyes and demi-smirks. Apparently panic stricken he averts his eyes and limps along with his head down; the yapping dog has stopped yapping as it is dragged along.

Smiling that habitual secret knowing smile she looks beyond the Church building to the bleak Victorian Vicarage and hears the rear gate of the churchyard slam shut. No doubt on reaching home limpalong will be getting out the porn mags for a wank. Her brother has quite a speciality collection.

She hopes her brother doesn't think he can get away with not ringing. He promised to ring and had better bloody ring or else. Purposefully tucking the rubber mat under her left arm, she marches even more purposefully towards the War Memorial lych-gate, that displays the name of her maternal grandfather amongst the many fallen of the Second World War.

The secret knowing smile has disappeared. She needs a drink.

Friday 13th October 10.35pm

These Egon Shiele Exhibition pens do not last long. He is glad he bought a dozen.

Jack is naturally perfectly at ease naturally. If the truth be told, as indeed it must, he is more than somewhat semi-detached from his body which is goodly good. The purple pills shared with the legend that is Amelia Sedley have been most conducive.

He really emotes with that word. Or should the word be embrace. Not that word. The other word. He will write it in capitals. CONDUCIVE. That word.

Deep down in the convoluted labyrinths of his morbid, some might say sick, daydream escapes from reality he had been irresistible to all women. The good the bad and of course the ugly. Beautiful unattainable women the most attainable of all. Glossy Sunday magazine girls with their come and get me eyes; lactating women pushing prams in the park; bright-eyed young things at his lectures. All attainable. He never, even in his most convoluted daydreams, believed that the legend that is Amelia Sedley was even remotely attainable.

No stretch of the imagination prepared him for the reality. The taste and the smells and the touch of the actual attainability. All different yet essentially the same... even Amelia Sedley. He is not sure whether to be disappointed or not.

Nothing has prepared him for the reality of lounging at his ease in the Green Room behind the set of the Phineas Finn Show, thighbone to thighbone with Amelia Sedley, an out of this world stunning Amelia Sedley, lusciously shaped in an above the knee purple sequined dress. The dress cleaved to the plunging neckline and leading hungry eyes bodily to purple sequined tights. It is decreed that purple sequins are very much in. There will be copies of the dress in the High Street within the week under the Amelia Sedley Gold label.

The actual one is busily deleting messages on a wafer thin gold-plated cell phone and sipping from a glass of red Burgundy. At her insistence they are sharing the wine with arms naffily interlocked. The vineyard, and the vintage, specified by her People and the bottle had to be uncorked exactly two hours before pouring.

There had not been much time for rehearsal. There was such a lot of getting in the way theatrics when she sacked the shrink, and sacked one of her People for exchanging raised eyebrows with the shrink. So in the limited time available they have just run through a few off the cuff remarks, and a few takes of Amelia to be caught on camera whispering secret nothings into a sticky out ear. She has insisted on sitting to the right on camera and so it will be his left sticky out ear, which is marginally the sticky outest.

The pumped up studio audience is an intrusive background noise. The ubiquitous – I repeat – the ubiquitous Phineas Finn is vapidly interviewing a stand-up comedian whom Jack thinks he sort of recognises. He is not very good with the names of stand-up comedians or their faces either for that matter, and a reasonably well known television Chef ditto. Amelia Sedley had not acknowledged their existence. Earlier in the green room they had gaped in awe, and the well known television Chef appeared to be chewing his own tongue.

Amelia and Jack share the red Burgundy, which caresses the pallet most caressingly, and are intently watched by a, probably mid-twenties, of course leggy pony tailed brunette, who is standing half in and half out of the doorway to the studio. One foot on the third step... one foot on the second step; tightish skirt and black tights; flat shoes; no sequins anywhere to be seen. She is sporting dinky headphones and occasionally mutters into a dinky attached microphone. There is a sense of déjà vu that he cannot quite put his finger on.

The of course leggy brunette holds up five fingers – no rings. Five minutes to go. Jack nods and inanely smiles. The fingers are ignored by Amelia Sedley who doesn't do other people's time.

Earlier, the manufactured Monkees couple had emerged from the Ritz Hotel arm in arm, to a blinding fusillade of camera flashes and shouts from the paparazzi. There had unavoidably been a leak of the time they would be leaving the hotel. Amelia had whispered sweet nothings into a sticky out ear looking as if she had just been ravished, all for tomorrow's newspapers. The Movie Premiere looms and Jack thinks the movie should really be titled... 'Last chance saloon'.

The stretch limousine on its circuitous route to Television Centre, as specified by her People, had been tailed by several motorbikes swerving and weaving in and out of the horn hooting traffic, pillion passengers riskily taking pictures. "Perhaps we should fuck." She had whispered. Snap. Snap. Snap. "That would make the front pages." He was not at all sure she was joking.

At Television Centre another fusillade of camera flashes, as steroid guzzling Security people surrounded the Uber couple. Screams and yells from adoring crowds herded at a safe distance behind crush barriers. Shouts of 'we love you Amelia'. She had waved and blown kisses like the ghost of Marilyn Monroe, which is a part she has, surprisingly, never played. "Stupid cunts." She had muttered for his sticky out ears only.

The of course leggy pony tailed brunette holds up four fingers – still no rings. No doubt his bloodied... he means bloody sister will be ensconced on the scene... he means seen better days sofa at their mother's house... always and forever their mother's house. The bloody sister will watch the Phineas Finn Show clutching a large vodka and small tonic – he cannot think infinitesimal. He is not sure it is even a word. Unless she has passed out already of course and he would not be at all surprised. Although he hates to be surprised by his bloodied sister. Yes... well.

Watched intently by the leggy brunette, the even leggier Amelia Sedley secretes the wafer thin gold-plated cell phone in the matching purple sequined clutch bag. Acting all conspiratorial she shows Jack the hidden contents of the clutch bag. "What every girl should carry at all times." She horse, he means hoarse whispers loud enough for the fucking nosy bitch with the flappy ears to overhear. She will probably ask for Amelia's fucking autograph. These people should get fucking lives.

The leggy brunette holds up three fingers. Amelia Sedley snaps shut the clutch bag and, in the instant, closes her eyes as tight as tight and composes herself yoga style with deep breathing. The lady prison psychiatrist is coming less and less to mind. Jack is beginning to realise that it is the way of such things where famous people are concerned; things that are best buried in the past without a headstone stay buried. There are of course exceptions.

The leggy brunette decides not to hold up two fingers. These A-Listers are from another Planet and the rages of Amelia Sedley are legendary. "Two minutes." She squeaks and coughs. "Two minutes."

Thirty seconds later Amelia Sedley opens her eyes and decides there is not enough time to be properly enraged by the fucking nosy flappy eared bitch. She rises to her feet more like a Botticelli Venus rising from the waves than any Venus Botticelli ever dreamed up. She rearranges the masquerading as a revealing dress to her absolute satisfaction. The cheap copies under the label Amelia Gold will be in the High Street by the end of next week…he thinks he might have written that already.

She executes an elegant twirl. "How do I look?"

"A million dollars." Jack knows that he will never see anything more achingly otherworldly enticing if he lives to be as old as the Prophet Abraham.

"Only a million?" She full lip pouts and catwalk Super model poses just for Jack, with one hand on a sticky out hip and the other hand draped perfectly. The leggy brunette can only look on and contemplate the unfairness of life. Get over it, Celia.

"A billion dollars."

"That's more like it." She takes ownership of Jack's strong right arm. Amelia Sedley knows the score because this is her designated time. After a due pause they will enter stage left very much in step and very much an item. Whatever else she is the ultimate professional.

She offers Jack a votive smile that could indeed launch a thousand ships. If the real Helen of Troy had been half as beautiful the Trojan War would make more sense.

"One minute." The leggy brunette recognises the unaffordable perfume.

The audience noise is building to a deafening crescendo as Phineas Finn racks up the introduction of his beyond mega star guests. Expertly he ratchets up the tension to fever pitch. "He cannot believe it. He just cannot believe it." A forty something female member of the audience faints on camera. "Yes. Yes. Yes. Ladies and gentlemen." More than a touch of old time Music Hall without the gavel. "We only have the actual People's hero and the utterly fabulous Amelia Sedley. That's all." He screams. "That's all!"

"Go." The leggy brunette nudges Jack in the small of the back. Last week at this point an A-lister had felt up her arse. "Go." Amelia Sedley holds him back until she has finished counting to twenty. Then and only then do they go.

Friday October 13th 10.41pm

Marion Fay is well on the way to being well pissed which, so far, is as good as it gets, apart, that is, from just before she passes out. She is occupying a sisterly place on the threadbare sofa of childhood illnesses, with slim bare legs drawn up under a body that feels heavy and lumpy. When she is properly well pissed, just before passing out, it will not feel heavy and lumpy at all. In the instant before she passes out it will feel ethereal and weightless. If only those few fleeting moments could be bottled.

She is naked underneath the well-worn dressing gown that was a Christmas gift from her late husband. She had tried it on that particular Christmas morning and they had fucked under the threadbare Christmas tree and knocked it over, scattering the meagre tree ornaments and fusing the tree lights. He had taken her over his knee and spanked her bare bottom and then they had fucked some more, forgetting the turkey that had overcooked.

The television images are somewhat blurred. She must get it serviced or whatever it is you are supposed to do with blurry television sets. The studio audience is going wild on cue and some stupid woman has fainted on camera. Marion takes a gulp of vodka from the bottle. And another gulp. She forgot to buy any tonic water. Her memory is not what it was. Anyway tonic water gives her heartburn.

And there he is… mother's precious little Johnny arm in arm with the fairy tale Princess herself… Amelia bloody Frozen Cinderella. Gorgeous beyond gorgeous and stunning beyond stunning. Mother's precious little Johnny is grinning from sticky out ear to stickier out ear, as well he might, the murdering little shit. He needs to be very careful, that is all she can say. He needs to be very careful indeed. Marion knows where the bodies are buried. Oh yes! There are time bombs and then there are…well… time bombs. Yes indeedy. She burps noisily and swallows back some sick.

Phineas Finn bestows a theatrical loving hug of hugs on them both and bows them reverentially to the left side of the studio couch; the star side. If Phineas Finn bestows reverential then boy have you arrived.

Marion glugs more vodka. The toothsome twosome glide down together seemingly attached at the hip. Marion thinks Siamese twins and giggles; two heads are sometimes better than one. Amelia Sedley is caught on camera whispering into a very visible ear. The smug stand-up comedian, who Marion doesn't think the least bit funny, and the stubbly television chef bloke who seemingly can't afford a razor, are brilliantly sidelined by the broad acres of Amelia Sedley's purple sequined legs. Never were legs so purple and or so sequinned. Marion Fay burps even louder. "Pardon you."

The shortness of Amelia Sedley's purple sequined dress can be judged by the tantalising thought that she might or might not be wearing knickers. If Marion were not so pissed and had control of her facial muscles she would bestow a secret knowing smile. Blurry John is talking words and the echoes of his blurry voice are different somehow... posher... ever the Chameleon. The camera pulls away and Amelia Sedley is stroking his good knee and is drinking in his words like her take on a love-struck teenager. Marion is absolutely certain Amelia Sedley has never ever played a love-struck teenager. Marion glugs more vodka from the bottle. Amelia Sedley is now talking words in that hypnotic transatlantic drawl. The camera pulls away and John is drinking in her words like...well like a love-struck teenager. This is way beyond secret knowing smile territory and Marion spills some precious vodka on the battered family sofa. John would be furious but then John was often furious. At the second attempt Marion hits the mute button. The trouble is when she has progressed to the stage of being beyond being well on the way to being beyond well pissed, she bursts into tears for no apparent reason – like now. It is because things kick in – memory sorts of things. Not very nice memory sorts of things that cannot be muted.

The threadbare dressing gown is gaping open and through the pathetic stupid tears she looks down at her own tits which are sensitive of being appraised. The belly is more rounded than she would like and the belly button a veritable Clan of the cave bear. She picks out some fluff but doesn't look down beyond the belly button. She absolutely refuses to be a voyeur of her own reproductive organs. Yes indeedy.

Through the pathetic stupid tears she can just about make out that a blurry Phineas Finn is making a fist of half-heartedly chortling at some interjection by the unfunny stand-up comedian. The camera, though, is in love with Amelia Sedley, who isn't laughing and is staring at Jack, who is staring back with knobs on. Marion wonders if he is on something. She would burst into tears except that she has already burst into tears.

Swallowing back some more sick she blinks her eyes but it doesn't help. A blurrier Amelia Sedley is gazing at a blurrier John in apparent Mary Magdalen rapture. She cannot recall Amelia Sedley ever having played Mary Magdalen.

She scrambles for the mobile phone and at the third attempt presses a number. John had had his mobile stolen in prison. "It's me." She doesn't sound as pissed to her own ears as she had expected and is not sure that is a good thing. "Get your sorry ass over here right now." She ends the call.

On screen the like totally famous pop star, called Cabousomething or other, wearing tight black leather trousers that give a whole new meaning to lots of legs, has appeared from nowhere like a Jill in a box. She is hugging John like a mother bear finding a long lost cub and then scoots off camera to prepare to belt out her latest platinum bending number one.

If looks could obliterate.

Marion closes her eyes or rather her eyes close of their own volition. She must have dozed off. Now John is sandwiched on the studio sofa between Amelia Sedley and the world famous female pop star Cabousomething or other. There is only so much a girl can take and so Marion scrambles for the remote control and retrieves it at the fourth attempt. The vodka bottle is empty. There is a tentative knock at the kitchen door. If Marion was able to control her facial muscles she would bestow a secret knowing smile.

Friday October 13th 11.02pm

Jack is on fire. The adulation of the screaming audience has swept over him like an out of place thunderstorm sweeping across the limitless Sahara wastes – his own copyright phrase. He is the meat in the wholemeal crustless sandwich of the two most desirable women in the fantasies of countless men, not to mention women. It doesn't get any better than this one might think.

Shirley Keeldar and Rebecca Sharp are conspicuous on the front row. He just knows… he just absolutely knows that they will be delighted with their almost human performing seal. They have their heads together. He cannot lip read.

"Perfick. Perfick." Whispers Shirley.

"Money. Money. Money." Whispers Rebecca.

They are both thinking that all it needs is a spectacular no holds barred hair pulling, insult screaming, catfight to make it the best of all possible worlds.

An almost, but not quite, wetting himself Phineas Finn is reluctantly winding up the Show in his own inimitable fashion. He just knows in his retained water that viewing figures will have gone through the roof. He has ignored as long as he dare the ever more frantic Production voices in his ear. Out of the corner of his eye he is aware of that stupid leggy what's er name making cutthroat gestures. Who the fuck does she think she is?

Swirling whirling inside Jack's paper thin mappa mundi skull is the substance of the tolling of a bell… send not to ask for whom the bell tolls. The vision unbidden of his naked mother at the side of the unmade bed, praying and praying and praying on her knees. Begging forgiveness in his infinite mercy; fearing in her heart of hearts that there will be none. Her God being a jealous God; her God being all too human.

Jack blink blinks his eyes and stares into the camera lens. His bloody sister was there too and knows everything. Jack blink blinks and stares at the audience, which is hooting and applauding. They are laughing. Laughing. Laughing.

Laughing. The stand-up comedian is not laughing. The television Chef is staring at Amelia Sedley's legs. He is not sure either.

The once upon a time spotty bullied teenager Mary Taylor, now known to the world as the pop star known as Casaubon, squeezes Jack's strong right arm to break the spell. "I'm going to write you a song, man." For his sticky out ears only and he has a fleeting vision of the glaring Amelia Sedley grabbing fistfuls of Casaubon's purple-greened hair. The pop idol is a well-made lass and would probably give as good as she gets. She would probably not fight as dirty as Amelia Sedley.

Jack doesn't know what was in the multicoloured lozenges that Amelia slipped into his salty mouth to mix with the purple tablets, just before they arrived at Television Centre. They certainly were not placebos.

He is somehow back in the green room and a flute of warm champagne has magic bean appeared in his right hand. Amelia Sedley has been sidelined into animated conversation by some of her entouragey People. Casaubon pounces and steers him into a corner.

"You really give me the horn, man." He hadn't realised that manufactured pop stars talked like a parody of a manufactured pop star. She is made up like the wild woman of the jungle, sporting some random visible psychedelic catch the eye tattoos that catch the eye. He quite likes the overall effect in a wild woman of the jungle kind of way – she is no Jane. "I will sing you that song naked in bed, man." If there is an answer to this then Jack is not the man to give it. "Bell me, man." She whispers her mobile number... he will not forget it. She is hustled away by her own entouragey People to a late night gig for the eighteenth birthday party of a minor Royal.

Amelia Sedley is still corralled in animated discussion with a gaggle, or is it a swarm, of her People. All of them except one are intent on ignoring Jack as much as they dare. He is a potential threat. Everyone and everything is a potential threat in the world according to Amelia Sedley. The People get used to striving to read the unreadable but it doesn't get any easier. There is the one exception of a person who is very much staring unblinkingly at Jack, known as Jack, as he slips out of the overheated Green Room through a convenient partly open fire door. Outside he sucks up rusty breaths of damp night air deep into his lungs. The almost consigned to history lady prison psychiatrist had advised that deep breaths are always beneficial and she should know. Hunkered down on flat heels against the far wall and smoking a cigarette is the, of course, leggy brunette no longer wearing a dinky microphone. An organically pretty girl who appears shocked, as well she might, by the magical appearance out of nowhere of the actual People's hero. She is on a final warning and needs to be careful.

He breathes in the spiralling cigarette smoke and she is even more shocked when he hunkers down shoulder to shoulder and almost thigh to thigh.

Although he gets the impression that she sees legs as things to walk on rather than fashion accessories. "I don't know your name."

"Celia." She squeaks and coughs. Then in a stronger voice with a hint of poetic Cockney. "Celia Brook."

"Hi Celia."

"Hi."

"My friends call me Jack."

She hesitates. Then. "Hi Jack." There is probably a joke in there but now is not the time or the place. He is behaving just like a normal person. At this moment he is the most famous person on the Planet. Celia has followed his Twitter profile along with several million others, including the First Lady of the United States and the Chinese President's wife.

"Gie us a drag, Celia."

Shakily she hands over the partly smoked cigarette that is kissed with Boots' on offer two-for-one pale pink lipstick. He sucks in a lungful of smoke and then politely hands the cigarette back to the pretty girl next door just about any street anywhere. Expressive brown eyes though; at this moment expressing shock and disbelief. He likes that. A too generous but it works somehow mouth and natural glossy auburn hair tied in that common or garden ponytail. Almost the Belle of the High School Prom but not quite. She takes a ladylike drag and blows smoke through a cute turned up nose...he had missed that.

"Do you read much, Celia?"

It is so weird that he is actually saying her name. "Yes. Loads." She so wants it to feel like they are fifteen year olds sneaking a forbidden smoke behind the bike sheds, and then perhaps a stolen kiss if one of them can get up the courage. Stop it, Celia.

"I teach." A tight smile. "I mean I taught Nineteenth Century literature."

"I know." She blows more smoke through the cute turned up nose.

"I suppose the whole fucking world knows." He hopes so anyway.

"I don't like swearing." She replies without thinking. And then thinks... me and my big mouth. They are not two fifteen year olds, and there will be no getting up courage and no stolen kiss. This is not one of her pathetic daydreams.

After that incident last week she was warned about speaking out of turn to A-list Celebrities. Phineas Finn had shouted and stamped his feet. In her turn she had been so cross and determined not to cry. When he turned his back she had stuck out her tongue. So there.

"Sorry, Celia."

Thank goodness for that. Not knowing what else to do she hands him the cigarette and he sucks in another lungful. Fifteen year olds again; a girl can dream. She will relive all this later alone in her forever and always childhood bedroom at her mum and dad's house, with a poster of Casaubon on the wall. Celia hadn't dared to ask for an autograph.

She is acutely aware that he is staring off into the far distance. Or at least as far as the opposite shadowy wall and the rudely defaced Health and Safety notice, that she always avoids looking at.

"There is a book by Mark Twain." Cigarette smoke spirals and mingles in the damp 1950s atmosphere of an early lost sketch by L.S. Lowry. It must have rained earlier but rain is no longer a consideration in the world according to Amelia Sedley. "He wrote a book called a Connecticut Yankee at King Arthur's Court." She makes a mental note as he hands back the cigarette and is soothed by seeing the smoke twirling from her too generous etc. lips. "At this moment I am that Yankee." He just stops himself saying fucking Yankee. It is the company you keep. Or is it the company one keeps?

"The question is who is Morgan le Fay?"

Wisely she offers no comment and instead flicks the tab away. You never flicked the tab away in prison.

There is a silence of smoky breath after smoky breath, shoulder to shoulder, thigh to thigh and not the least bit pregnant silence. She is not the kind of girl who pushes herself forward to fill the gaps of silences. She is not the kind of girl who would not insist on sensible precautions.

"You like your work, Celia?"

She screws up her mouth. "It's all right."

"You meet a lot of famous people." He grins. "Like me."

"You're nice." She smiles wistfully. "Most of them are awful."

"Tell me more." He stifles a yawn.

No hesitation at all. She is glad to confide in someone she just knows will be sympathetic.

"Last week a certain so-called..." She shapes a quotation mark with index fingers. "... 'Celebrity' cornered me after the Show." She shudders at the recollection. "Grabbed both my you knows."

He nods and tries not to stare at said you knows.

"And said he wanted to take me to the toilets, would you believe, for a quick..." She stares at her clasped hands. "... for a quick you know."

"Unbelievable."

"I told him if he wasn't so rich and famous I would slap his face. I nearly said his stupid face."

"Good for you, Celia."

She just knew he would understand and is going to post a comment on his Facebook page as soon as she arrives home tonight. Mum and dad will have watched the Show and will want to hear everything, because they know it takes her mind off the break up. She is emboldened. "Phineas said I should have..." She stares harder at the clasped hands. "... at least have given him a you know." It is hard to tell in this gloom but he thinks she might be blushing. The said you knows are certainly well worth grabbing.

"A blow job?"

She nods and bites her lower lip. There is nothing at all pregnant about this pause either. She prays that she isn't going to burst into tears. Since finishing with her cheating boyfriend she bursts into tears at the least provocation.

"You know, Jack?"

"Yeah."

"You could do a lot of good."

"Good?" As if the word is an alien concept.

"Make the world a better place." Why on earth would he want to do that?

Tongue-tied in the moment he cannot put together a suitable reply that doesn't contain a swear word. She possesses a natural winsome smile that is simply that and not a disguise for something sinister. There is something infinitely peaceful and soul soothing about this nothing out of the ordinary girl, who is not the sort of girl to snigger in her hand during one of his lectures.

The fire door bursts open and a long legged Gazelle escapes from the caged hubbub of noise into this sheltered corner of the African Veldt.

"Thank the fuck." Jack doesn't look at Celia. "Amelia fucking Sedley is going fucking ape shit in there." The Duke's least favourite daughter glances dismissively at the ordinary, she supposes quite pretty, in a common sort of way, girl. Just a pity about the hair. A nobody she instantly decides. Just for a second she had worried it might be the psychedelic pop man eater.

"The mad bitch thinks Casaubon has spirited you away to the deep dark jungle from which no Explorer returns." Although project Jack would probably return, she thinks, and Casaubon would disappear without trace.

"I needed some air."

Lady Rebecca computes that this is reasonable and so moves on. The spotty common girl is dismissed from all calculations. She has no premonition that this might be a mistake. Only one spot to be fair, and hardly noticeable at that.

"Duty calls." The snooty posh girl assumes Jack will follow her back into the Green Room and he does so. At least he gives a backward glance and a rueful smile. Celia is not a fifteen year old anymore sharing a cigarette behind the bike sheds and never been properly kissed. There is no call for courage of any kind. A girl can dream. She will hug herself in her narrow childhood bed tonight and pretend they are someone else's arms. She will kiss the smooth skinned arms and pretend they are someone else's lips.

Stop it, Celia. Just stop it.

Saturday 14th
October 9.02am

C an it be made quite clear before we go any further that Sir Godwyn Lydate has no intention of being sidelined in this excuse for a novel. He is extremely annoyed that his, shall we say, doings of an intimate nature of yesterday evening involving a naked Mary Caldigate, have not been written down. Very annoyed indeed and it will not be tolerated. Those, shall we say, doings were well worth recording …she is such a delightfully inventive creature, totally wasted on that useful idiot John Caldigate. It might be thought that there is already too much sex recorded in this excuse for a novel, but that is not the point.

Watched intently by a wing clipped, but nevertheless hawk eyed, Judge Helen Graham, the most permanent of Permanents steeples his, he likes to think, classical pianist's fingers in that intimidatory manner that he has made all his own.

Someone will pay for this insult.

Anyway, enough of that. Neither is there any record of an intimidating phone conversation with a certain famous lady, who has not shared a bed with her famous husband for several months. So unfortunately the child is probably of Sir Godwyn's making; the abortion has been arranged for next week. He is surprised she didn't abort after the quite recent Olympian lovemaking. Anyway enough of that as well. That was also not written down.

A determined not to be chastened if she can possibly help it Judge Helen Graham is well aware that, although the stalactite blue eyes are staring unblinkingly at her legs, they are focused somewhere else entirely. She resists the temptation to cross the quite decent, if she does say so herself, legs because she is a Judge first and a woman second. Legs have nothing to do with any of this charade. She must think of it as a charade. She must – she really must. She is not exactly afraid, because she knew this was coming. But certainly uneasy. Yes. Uneasy. She politely coughs.

Now for a few moments longer then she deems strictly necessary, the great man does focus on the legs which she is glad she didn't cross. The skirt is shorter than she remembers and she is beginning to think that legs are getting a bit too intrusive here. Now he is staring into her eyes and that is much better. She has always been accomplished at eyeball to eyeball stuff. After all she has eyeballed some of the most notorious criminals in recent history, and that includes certain well known politicians.

"I must apologise at calling this meeting on a Saturday morning, my dear." He does not sound the least bit sorry, as he twitches the dry lips to intimate the thought of a predatory smile. She is probably being too fanciful. No, she is not being too fanciful at all. The intimation of a smile is one that an alligator might contemplate, if an alligator was able to intimate a smile. A hungry alligator at that.

Perhaps she is just a little bit afraid.

"I do hope I have not…" He pauses, searching for the exact bon mot and appears to get inspiration from the bloody intrusive legs. If she pulls down the skirt it will only draw attention to the bloody things. "… interfered…" A slightly puzzled pause as if he has just recollected why they are here. "… with your weekend plans, my dear."

Judge Helen Graham, for Christ's sake, crosses the quite decent legs that seem to have acquired a life of their own. She must not lie to herself, the skirt was intended, but to compensate she offers up for his delectation her own unique take on a world-weary heard it all before so don't fuck with me grimace, that has been used to good effect to overawe verbose Counsel up and down the land, ridiculous wigs and all. She is clever enough to know it is wasted on Sir Godwyn finger in every bloody pie known to man Lydate. She can only pray that always being the cleverest girl in whatever class is going to be enough. A somewhat forlorn hope, she is clever enough to realise.

She has been only too well aware that this meeting has been looming since that bloody little shit was pronounced not guilty by that ridiculously flame haired jury Spokesperson with the pendulous bosoms. Shitty bloody juries – shitty bloody pendulous bosoms.

She thinks she will keep bosoms out of this because she has got enough on her plate with pushy bloody legs. A Judge first… who is she kidding? She has been advised to wear a hastily purchased low-cut blouse and have at least three buttons undone. There are more than hints of a hastily purchased lacy pink bra a size too small – again taking advice. She is determined to go down with all guns blazing. She owes womankind that much at least. Who is she kidding?

She has almost a bruiser's face, he thinks. Without being unkind, an almost but not quite handsome Stan Laurel at the beginning of his career. A severe haircut only enhances the somewhat disquieting impression of a shadow etched face, like cloudy sunlight reflected on a Welsh mountainside in the late autumn afternoon. He frowns. He does not mean that at all and it must be deleted.

The frighteningly intelligent eyes of a minor bird of prey with acutely defined eyebrows; the eyes of a hawk in the face of a vulture. Strong manly veined hands resting on a bare upper knee that is not the least bit knobbly. Unpainted fingernails. Lots and lots of visible freckles on bare arms and bare legs and no doubt lots and lots of freckles not visible. A neat and tidy figure with no apparent wastage of flesh.

"So." The overall impression against all the odds being not unattractive. Not a beauty but then there are so many of those; the stalking lioness impersonation of Jane Fennell comes unbidden to mind. Helen Graham being rather the sort of woman whom a man might confide to his chum over a beer that he would not kick out of bed. "May I call you Helen?"

"Of course." There is no nervousness apparent in the firm deepish voice and he can only surmise that her insides are invisibly jelly wobbling by the way she is overly conscious of her rather decent legs. He can surmise that she has endured a sleepless night and that she could not eat breakfast. He doesn't think she is the type to imbibe Dutch courage.

"You may call me God."

The deep almost manly laugh is only a touch strident to a practised ear. More the laugh of the chum in the pub rather than the woman who wouldn't be kicked out of bed.

"So, Helen, what are we to do with you?" The steepled pyramid of his fingers collapses without warning. "I hasten to add, my dear, that I do not personally agree that you are in any way personally responsible for the…" A meditative pause. This time he appears to draw inspiration from her bloody sodding cleavage. "… for the unfortunate verdict."

She has sworn on her sick mother's life that whatever it takes she will not be a sacrificial lamb. Sacrificial lamb genes are not among the Graham genes and she is determined not to uncross her legs. She has been advised to wear skimpy black lacy panties to feel good about herself, for Christ's sake. A thoughtful Christmas gift of several years ago that she has not worn until today. The usual sensible comfortable pants would not now be sticking uncomfortably between neat and tidy bum cheeks. It is so bloody hot in this room and he is now doing his very own impersonation of a sleek bird of prey riding the currents to glide in for the kill. There is no rush as he intends to hog centre stage. Can he repeat? He has no intention of being rushed. Is that quite clear?

She is only too well aware that there is something fundamentally disquieting about this man, even to one of her formidable character and undeniable talents. Despite the temptations, and despite the inevitable rumours to the contrary, she has not slept her way to the top of the Judiciary. Well… only to get on the first rung. She has given up so much over the years and she will not let it all slip away. She is damned if she will. After all Henry of Navarre said Paris was worth a Mass. It really is bloody hot in this room with the real coal fire roaring in the grate like some medieval portent of unspeakable instruments of torture.

"I have talked to the PM."

She is finding it hard to swallow and her bowels are churning… perhaps missing breakfast was fortuitous after all. She licks her lips and he is reminded of a rare species of lizard peeping out from the midday camouflage of its mother stone. "He has agreed with my take on the…" A most portentous pause this time and she clenches the neat and tidy bum cheeks together for all she is worth. "… on the situation."

"Situation?" It comes out without thinking.

There is a visibly nervous twitch at her exposed throat. No visible jewellery but an intriguing constellation of freckles at the throat. He likes that beneath the clever as clever is Judge facade there beats a trepidatious heart. It would be most invigorating to see dear Helen wearing a Judge's wig and nothing else. He really is a fool to himself sometimes.

"Situation?" She repeats. This time with thinking.

He must pull himself together; he blames lack of sleep and of course Mary Caldigate – the little minx. "There have been strong suggestions that you should be the sacrificial lamb."

She knew it. She just bloody knew it. She opens her mouth to defend the no doubt indefensible, but he holds up an imperious hand and the Ninth Legion halts in its tracks. She shuts her mouth. This is new territory. She is sweating under her armpits which are prickly where, after a sleepless night, she shaved as best she could this morning. She crosses her legs.

"I have told the PM in no uncertain terms that I do not agree." Caesar has spoken proclaims the raised hand – for all the known world to bow down and worship – Hail Caesar! This Caesar would not enter the Senate without an armed guard; there would be no Ides of March. It is a truly magnificent gesture and for one of the few times in her life she feels more like a woman than a Judge – something she must keep to herself. The skimpy black lacy knickers have found their unexpected moment.

"I have told the PM that I want you onside." He slams both hands flat on the polished desktop and the buff manila folder bounces. "Very much onside."

"I see." She doesn't see a bloody thing and is as blind as a day-old kitten, but smiles, and has no idea how it turns out. She is fiddling with the fourth button of the low-cut blouse. For Christ's sake she never ever fiddles with buttons on low-cut blouses.

"I have followed your eminent career with great interest, my dear." The fiddled with pearl button has it. "Great interest."

She really thinks that she ought to resist being flattered by this most disingenuous of the species. She cannot help imagining the spider and the fly of the childhood nursery rhyme, but then the spider did not need to flatter the fly.

"I have always believed that your considerable talents could be put to more effective use than giving weight to the ramblings of third-rate barristers, droning on interminably day after day."

She cannot stop herself chortling in agreement. Oliver Hardy has twanged his braces and cracked an off-the-cuff joke. "I have thought the same thing many times." She hears herself agreeing.

"Just so." He can discern that she looks after herself... a regular at the gym. Never been married. Only a handful of discreet lovers over the years, the latest being Sir Bernard Keeldar. No abortions – perish the thought. Only attends Church when absolutely necessary. An occasional glass of wine. Just the one recent minorish indiscretion – unfortunately only a blurred photograph. It is all in the buff manila folder.

The severe haircut will have to go. "So, Helen, I have a proposition."

Here comes Paris. She cannot stop being a woman and it was being a woman that nearly ruined her career. It is probably in that bloody file. She wishes that she believed in God and could offer up a silent prayer.

"A seat in the House of Lords." He watches the dawning of shocked surprise with visceral pleasure. "And the role of Attorney General."

For only the second time in her life Helen Graham is at a loss for words. She opens and shuts her mouth, knowing she must look like a confused guppy at the wrong end of the pond at feeding time. It is trite to think it, but in her wildest dream she had not expected this. She seeks a voice. Any bloody voice will do. "The sacrificial lamb?"

"The Minister for Law and Order has tendered his resignation."

"John Caldigate?"

"Indeed."

She swallows hard and hopes she isn't blushing, as she glances at the buff manila folder and thinks that he probably knows anyway. She must compose herself. "But..."

"There are no buts, my dear Helen." She cannot help but ponder on the advisability of being his dear Helen. "On Monday the newly appointed Minister will rubber stamp your appointment." On balance there are probably worse things to be than his dear Helen. "And the PM will confirm your elevation to the House of Lords." Although that useless Cuckold doesn't know it yet.

"The new Minister?"

He leans forward across the desk and she leans slightly forward in a mirror gesture. Her thighs are beginning to ache with the strain. She was a reasonable athlete in her College days and it is the same muscle stretch ache. To cross or uncross that is the question.

"Can I rely on your discretion, my dear Helen?"

"Of course." She leans even closer. "You can trust me implicitly." She hears herself saying.

"I know that, my dear Helen." The lust for power is shining out of the…out of the… yes… out of the definitely hazel eyes. If she were a lighthouse shipping would be safe. One can just imagine this lady draping a black cloth over the Judge's wig and pronouncing the death sentence in funereal tones… To be hanged by the neck until dead. The death penalty is also on his list.

She is all agog with naked curiosity. Knowledge is power. She is a favoured one… a chosen one. She licks her lips. The lizard has ventured into the harsh sunlight and shed several skins.

"Rosalie Murray."

"An excellent choice, Sir Godwyn." To be fair she would have agreed that Lucrezia Borgia was an excellent choice.

"Please, Helen. You know we will be working very closely together." He leans close. She leans closer. "Very closely indeed, my dear. You really must call me Godwyn."

After a moment's hesitation… "Godwyn." She tastes the name like fine wine. He likes that. She fashions a cat got the cream smile that surprisingly rather suits the somewhat severe contours of her face. She has forgotten all about legs and cleavage and it shows. She is not sure when she unclenched her neat and tidy bum cheeks. The lacy black knickers are actually surprisingly comfortable and one hardly knows they are there.

"You have so much to offer, my dear Helen. So very much." She is only too well aware that her nipples have hardened and she wonders if they are visible through the somewhat clingy blouse. She had never thought of that and normally she thinks of everything.

"What you see is what you get, Godwyn." Under normal circumstances she would not have said that either.

"I like very much what I see, my dear Helen." An almost smile; an almost smile for the sharing of State and of course other secrets; an almost smile for plotting plots; an almost smile for liking what he sees and working very closely together indeed.

Half an hour ago she was preparing to go down with the good ship Helen Graham, saluting with all guns blazing, so to speak. Now this veritable Merlin has waved a magic wand to make all her self-absorbed dreams come true. The glittering prizes have been tossed into her lap. She doesn't normally do mixed metaphors and certainly not involving laps.

"You know, Helen my dear?"

"Yes, Godwyn."

"We are going to change the world you and I."

If she read this in an airport novel on her annual two weeks holiday at her brother's villa in Menorca, she would toss the book away in disgust. In the here and now she is only too well aware that the hard nipples are not at all on holiday.

"Are you hungry, my dear?"

"Yes." She realises that she is ravenous and that her stomach is distantly rumbling. The breakfast that she didn't have seems a long time ago.

"Do you have any plans for the rest of the day, my dear?"

"No." Not now anyway.

"Well then let us adjourn to my Albany apartment. We have much to discuss and I do a mean scrambled eggs with smoked salmon on the side."

"Sounds delicious." She doesn't care. It feels so so good to be reprieved from the scaffold so to speak. She does feel a wee bit sorry for poor John Caldigate. But still, an indiscretion is merely that. It is black lacy knickers all the way from now on. For the first time in her life, as pathetic as it might sound, she knows what it is to be drunk on life.

Saturday 14th October 10.03am

The famous not guilty one, now known as John only to his sister, is determined to be the hero of his own story. After all, that is why the book is being written. He is sipping real black coffee and gazing out of the draped bedroom window which overlooks a Green Park that is reflective in the autumn sunshine. The coffee tastes of success, but he needs to learn to stick out his little finger. But he is wearing a Ritz Hotel bathrobe and so one step at a time.

Amelia Sedley, who also tastes of success, has gone jogging in Green Park surrounded by a coterie of muscle bound Bodyguards and a gaggle of paparazzi being encouraged to keep up. Many heads turn as the tight group serpents its way towards Buckingham Palace Road.

Jack, not John and most certainly not Johnny, sets down the bone china coffee cup on the wobbly bone china saucer on the tray that displays the remnants of a shared breakfast. He turns on his heels to take in the enormous bedroom with its oriental Emperor size bed and the very much rumpled and soiled bedding. He pads on bare feet to the cavernous mirrored bathroom where they had shared a shower earlier; there is water splashed everywhere and soggy towels discarded for minions to take away. Jack hardly recognises the designer stubbly face that is staring back at him from the floor-to-ceiling mirrored wall. There is a puzzled expression on its face as it strokes its chin.

Then Jack pads on bare feet back into the bedroom – bare feet with oddly spread-eagled toes almost like a platypus… not quite… but almost. There is a seeking for deferential and missing by a mile knuckle rap on the bedroom door. He opens the door only slightly ajar, as famous people being disturbed doing nothing are wont to do. One of her People asking if there is anything he needs. An earnest looking girl somewhere in her twenties and merely beautiful of course. She is staring as if challenging him to a staring contest. Most odd – no, thank you very much, there is nothing Jack needs and so she scuttles away, with a challenging backward stare that he was not expecting.

He could get quite used to referring to himself in the third person. It is somehow not your fault then… he means it is not one's fault.

For something to do to waste time he checks the all singing all dancing cell phone. Amelia Sedley calls them cell phones. He bets no one in Huddersfield calls them cell phones.

He really should phone his bloody sister. She can be dangerously unpredictable if ignored. It is too early to ring, as she has no doubt got a hangover and is not good with mornings. Afternoons are a bit of a trial. No messages from Lady Rebecca, who is masterminding the Twitter stuff, which has gone viral since the Phineas Finn Show. Images of Jack and Amelia very much together are flooding social media. There is a message timed at two-thirty three this morning from Julia Verinder hoping that she isn't pregnant. He is not at all sure what to make of that storyline.

He checks the pen. He definitely wrote that down.

The sequined purple dress with a jagged tear down the seam is crumpled where it was shed last night; the ripped purple sequined tights ditto; there are no knickers. Tossing the cell phone onto the second day of the Somme bed, there is no need to pinch himself. This is real. Last night was real. The frantic clothes ripping sex on the floor and the relentless follow up coupling on the bed, the orgasms within the orgasms. All of it real. She had yelled out his name. He is not to know that she always yells out the names if she remembers and Jack is easier than most to remember, apart from Randy. Eventually they had collapsed unconscious with limbs entangled like two last night together wartime parting lovers. He is determined to get his money's worth out of the wartime lovers theme.

In the shower the beyond mega one had knelt at his feet in abject supplication and taken as much of his hard on as she could manage in her liquid mouth. He had looked down on the kneeling actual Amelia Sedley and it was all of it real. The blonde hair of a million posters plastered to the visible skull. Talk about intimations of mortality. Water of just the right temperature cascading down the Niagara waterfall of a spectacular cleavage, and drip dripping delightfully off coral pink nipples – the Hollywood sex goddess at his feet and all of it real… every square inch. She has promised to share another shower on her return from jogging. In his twisted daydreams there had never been shared showers and he had most definitely missed a trick there.

There is the sound of a disturbance in the living room and the door is barged open and in strides Shirley Keeldar and her Tonto sidekick. He gets the distinct feeling that Tonto doesn't like him. He might have to make it mutual and then she will be sorry… he hopes.

"Don't knock."

"We didn't." Shirley Keeldar has brushed aside Amelia Sedley's People, and in particular the weird staring girl, like so many houseflies. Shirley is strikingly elegant in a most fetching pale blue trouser suit that matches her eyes. The humble Porter had thought the lady sheer class, and had imagined it was the classy lady when he was taking advantage of the Bulgarian chambermaid; twice last night and twice this morning. She has learned a new word... Visa.

"Where is the transatlantic sexpot?"

"Jogging in the park."

"Jesus wept." With the toe of a Louboutin shoe Shirley gingerly pokes at the torn sequined dress and the torn sparkly tights. "I wouldn't have thought she would have had the energy for jogging." He wonders if she is a little bit jealous – probably not.

Rebecca Tonto emits a noncommittal grunting noise and is ignored.

"Get dressed, darling, there are things to do and people to see." He is about to protest when she holds up a silencing hand in the manner of Sir Godwyn Lydate. It would not do to admit that he is somewhat relieved. Another shower might have been a step too far.

"A private tête-à-tête luncheon has been arranged for you and the beloved one, and of course the world's press, at most exclusive La Vendee Restaurant." Just a knowing smile because only Shirley is aware just how exclusive. Jack has that sulky look which she thinks is rather attractive in the right kind of light. "Remember Lord Bacon's widow, darling?"

"She made her gentleman usher deaf with too much sex."

"Who's a clever boy then?" Just a smile. "Now get dressed, darling."

So he shrugs off the Ritz Hotel bathrobe and, despite her misgivings, the Honourable Lady Rebecca Sharp has to be impressed. Surely? No comment.

Saturday 14th October 10.23am

A gurgly snoring Marion Fay is dead to the world with her face turned to the wall of fading 1970s wallpaper. The Reverend John Eames gingerly turns back the winter duvet and studies the magnificent hindquarters; his other passion is horse racing. A spreading backside but shapely and roundly desirable... always that... compelling meatyish thighs that wrap around his body to replicate the indecorous throes of passion. There is nothing neat and tidy about making love with Marion Fay.

The lady mumbles in her sleep but doesn't wake. She is not a morning person and resists waking as if her dreams are a far better place to be. Delicately he traces the verging on plumpness of a buttock... an unbidden thought from out of the ether... the right buttock with the kissable birthmark the shape of an undiscovered South Sea island. She mumbles in her sleep at the hesitant touch but doesn't wake.

Marion phoned the Vicarage last night knowing that he would come because he had no choice. His wife is in Essex visiting that bitch of a sick mother. He would have had no choice anyway. He had been watching Marion's brother on the Phineas Finn show and, if he didn't know better, he would have found the bravura performance persuading. But he does know better – Bellingham is a dangerous man. That time Bellingham had come home unexpectedly and found the two of them naked in his mother's bed, and had dragged a naked and, he must admit at least to himself, terrified Reverend John Eames down the stairs one by one and thrown him naked out of the house. Thank God it was the early hours of the morning and thank God for shadowy hedges and thank God his wife was away. Thank God it had stopped raining.

If he was that famous movie star or that famous pop star he would be very afraid.

For a few blessed minutes John Eames rests comfortably with his hands behind his head. A good thinking position and there is so little time for thinking these dog days. What he also quite likes about Marion Fay is that there are no illusions and no emotional demands. In fact sometimes it can feel as if he is being used and most definitely not as God's instrument. On the other hand, things are getting far too emotional with Alice Vavasor, who more and more stridently insists that she is being used. And of course there is Rosalie who is not coming this weekend... again. He has his pride. It was good while it lasted and it never got better than that first time on the altar steps. Best not to think about Mary Thorne.

He supposes he should think about his wife. He has to admit that ritual sex has become a fortnightly chore to be got through as neatly and tidily as possible. In recent times she has insisted he use a needless condom so there is no mess. He supposes that theirs is a marriage of convenience that has never, after all these years, got past the inconvenience stage. Their fathers were the best of friends, and both sidelined in their careers in the Church of England for too openly believing in God.

Reluctantly he covers Marion's biblical nakedness with the winter duvet. He is inevitably hardening and she would not appreciate being woken up just for that. She has a fiery temper that is best avoided.

Indulging in an invigorating shower he renders snatches of his favourite hymns in a deep baritone voice. It was the love of hymns that led him into the Ministry against his father the Canon's advice. And of course a fervent belief in God, which he wisely keeps to himself.

He scrubs vigorously with the soaped up loofah. He cannot help but notice that his belly has grown somewhat bellier of late. His wife had pointed this out only yesterday, when to his relief, they didn't have sex before she set off to Essex and her sick bitch of a mother…his wife's own words incidentally.

Seated on the very edge of the battered sofa and trying not to breathe in too deeply, he nibbles white toast because there was no wholemeal bread and watches Sky News. There is repeated and repeated footage of Bellingham and the famous movie star arriving in the early hours at the Ritz Hotel, very much cleaved together in the biblical sense.

They appear to be smitten with each other – poor poor girl. There is footage of the poor poor girl jogging with bodyguards in a London park. Perhaps the poor poor girl might be able to look after herself – a really tight bottom. Mary Thorne has a really tight bottom which he must not think about in his present state, although he might have to carry out a Parish visit later. Poor Mary is finding the trial separation from her second husband rather a strain. The christening of her third child has been postponed for a second time. He really must stop thinking about Mary Thorne and her delectable hindquarters with somewhat intrusive tattoos.

The Reverend John Eames sips milky coffee with two sugars, and has no doubt whatsoever that Marion's brother will flourish in the swampy depths of London high society. That most atrophied of men possesses an incubus quality, which feeds off the life force of anyone unfortunate enough to get within range. A malign influence on his poor mother, although she must take her share of the blame. God might well forgive the poor deluded woman.

John Eames wishes that he had not crossed to the other side. The Good Samaritan never one of his favourite Bible stories. He had meant well …the road to Hell and all that.

Bellingham is a continuing malign influence on his sister who can manufacture quite enough malignity of her own. John Eames doesn't think he is being overdramatic. The ribs that were broken on that terrible night still ache in inclement weather and the north-east wind doesn't help. A Parish south of Watford would be more than acceptable.

There is no shred of forgiveness in his heart for John Bellingham, that curiously self-regarding and yet frightened of his own shadow creature. God will have to make up his own mind.

He is always glad to leave this house with all his clothes on. As soon as she hears the front door quietly close a fully awake Marion Fay opens her eyes and stares at the wall. He had better bloody ring. She turns onto her back and stares at the ceiling. She is not in the mood for a secret knowing smile. She is not in the mood full stop.

Saturday 14th October 11.09am

Lewis Carroll fairy wreathed in the smoky light beneath the propped open broken rooflight in the sloping attic space, in the four-storey apartment block, in one of the meaner streets of Peckham, the girl-woman, probably late twenties, is concentrating every scrap of a considerable wayward talent on a partly coloured canvas. The cigarette dangling from her mouth spiralling smoke to mingle with spiralled smoke. She would be recognised as the matchstick girl who had spied the naked man at the window of the Savoy Hotel.

The girl-woman is by no means conventionally pretty – strong featured though – certainly that. A distinguished, verging on Patrician, nose that often gets in the way – her father's nose. When her paintings sell for big-money she will reward herself with a pert nose. She does not want to consider that a pert nose would not sit well on such a determined face... that rare thing, a face that can only improve with age.

And such a determined face like now... the absolute and utter now. Determined to capture for all time the eclectic visions that imprison her mind in a multitudinous thrall. That idiot Louis had demanded sex this morning, but she had been at her easel since before dawn. Sex only ever gets in the way and Louis Trevelyan has never been all that dedicated to Art. Never been all that anything. Only ever painted to be seen to be painting to pull women. She had screamed at him to fuck off and so he had fucked off.

Emily Rowley sucks the handle of the paintbrush and is exhilarated by the woody taste... a taste that Michelangelo would have known. She means business... boy does she mean business. In her mind's eye she arranges and rearranges Cerne Abbas man aka Window man, glimpsed at the hotel window and staring straight at Emily Rowley. And then the naked blonde, all tits and thighs, imposing herself at his shoulder. A hand from nowhere sneaking round his muscular thighs to cup his balls. The titillating vision then disappearing stage left for sex in the afternoon. Privileged purposeless sex. The best sex thinks Emily Rowley who has never experienced privileged purposeless sex. She will though. She bloody will.

The naked imposing herself blonde woman is too ethereal and Emily cannot get a proper fix...there is not enough substance. But Window man is a different proposition. She is adeptly capturing her own unique take on Window man. Her own creation from life is turning her on more than the flesh and blood Louis Trevelyan ever did. Quick hard sex his forte that was purposeless but not privileged. She has fashioned two decent canvases out of the lachrymose Louis – a ludicrously Pinocchio nosed female with three breasts, and a one eyed Cyclops man rutting like stray mongrel dogs on heat. There is even an old fashioned gas street lamp with a broken light and a headless dog pissing at its base. The second canvas – a tongue lolling Cyclops man with a miniscule cock... Cyclops man being devoured by Pinocchio female's what can only loosely be called a cunt; the artistically arranged spiky hairs leading one to think it might be so. Emily heard yesterday from Nina Balatka that both have been sold.

She is working rapidly now. A gravity defying ash lengthening cigarette dangling from the corner of her slackened mouth, in the manner of her dead painter father, who hanged himself exactly ten years ago yesterday. Perhaps his unquiet ghost is watching over his errant daughter better than he ever did in life. She likes to think so when she thinks about it at all… which is not often. She has been her own father and her own mother for so long now.

She is mentally consumed by the medieval beggar stumps for legs man, with the huge out of proportion circumcised phallus – no Cyclops man he. Disturbingly empty eye sockets, because Window man was too far away to be sure of the colour. The eight fingered claw hand of the one legged blonde with six breasts and an overripe tomato drooling mouth – no eyes – no nose – straw hair like Worzel Gummidge's sister the morning after a named tornado… Storm Emily perhaps. This Artist named Emily Rowley feverishly paints on the stretched canvas the image of a nightmarish black crow with a killer beak dripping blood.

It is the extravagantly lifelike, if a touch on the gorged side, phallus that commands the viewing space. She wants men to feel inadequate and wants women to be afraid of what is in store at the ending of days.

Sucking on the brush handle, she pauses to consider the unfinished painting with narrow eyed contemplation. Emily's flat green eyes are like fake emeralds in a child's first jewellery box. The Jermyn Street Gallery have begged for more of her distinctive work… Nina Balatka's words. Emily Rowley is getting known in certain circles. It has taken years of self-sacrifice to get to pole position to be an overnight success.

She stops pausing – her brain is teeming with visions for Window man two and Window man three. She flexes the out of proportion fingers of the numb right hand. As usual she is wearing only baggy knickers and a faded T-shirt when she paints. She is desperately turned on but dare not break off to masturbate. She dare not risk a man from Porlock moment…she knows she is that good.

Saturday 14th October 1.07pm

The passionate greeting in the lobby of the Ritz Hotel will reverberate around the known world, although perhaps not until the last syllable of recorded time. Shirley Keeldar looks on with smug satisfaction and not a little subdued excitement. Lady Rebecca Sharp looks on with something approaching a smug trepidation that is bred in the bone. One of Amelia Sedley's People whispers to another of Amelia Sedley's People. "She's a bloody good actress." The humble Porter just looks on humbly. The Bulgarian chambermaid has learned several new words and one of them is quite shocking, even to the ears of the humble Porter, who is beginning to wonder if he has made a big mistake.

Amelia Sedley whispers into the more prominent of Jack's prominent ears so close that no one can lip read. There is paranoid and then there is Amelia Sedley.

A woman on Twitter has shared that her fantasy is to rub Jack's ears between her balloon tits; a selfie of the balloon tits has gone viral. Amongst other proposals, the woman has received several proposals of marriage, which makes one doubtful for the future of the human race. "Is this the real thing, Amelia?" Shouts one of the paparazzi.

One of her People whispers to another of her People. "Isn't it always?" They both giggle but not too loudly. The inordinately earnestly beautiful one of her People, somewhere in her twenties, overhears and looks on with a quite disturbing earnestness that no one bothers to notice. She has never practised not too loud giggling and Lucy Snowe is used to being ignored. She knows that her day will come because it is in the stars that are her brothers and her sisters.

The expected, shall we say for want of a better description, lovers are late at the most exclusive restaurant. Not that it matters. There is no lateness in the world according to Amelia Sedley, except by other people.

The cat on hot bricks head waiter of the most exclusive La Vendee restaurant, which is a mere thirty three paces from the Ritz Hotel, greets the two most honoured guests at the door. He is not sure whether to bow from the rounded waist and so, just to be on the safe side, bows from the rounded waist. He is ignored by Amelia Sedley and the stubbly man just looks through him as if he is a ghost. These people are from a different Planet. The media scrum stays outside shepherded by some of her People.

Lucy Snowe is nowhere to be seen.

The Mediterranean olive skinned sister-in-law, with the merest suggestion of a hare lip, thinks about curtsying. The muddy Tennessee swampy eyes take in everything, as the world famous movie star and the accompanying man, whose arm is being treated as a life raft, are shown to a table at the rear of the restaurant which is not visible from the street. Keep them guessing is the paranoid way. There are of course no other diners.

The world famous movie star, who waves the twitching Giovanni away as he is about to pull out a chair, is clothed in a figure defining white dress well above the knee. Bare arms and a fashion trending high priest collar with two slashed gaps, edged with gold leaf, and a hung line of real pearls below the outline of breasts. A second slash, edged with gold leaf, and a hung line of real pearls is caught at the waspish waist. A show of pink paleness of stomach is tantalisingly shouting – if that is the right word – look but do not touch.

The effect is out of this world.

Amelia Sedley angles the chair to her absolute satisfaction. She hates minions touching a chair which she is going to grace with her perfect posterior. Posterior being the word she prefers. The touch of minions is a pollution she refuses to countenance except…well…except.

"You look like a zillion dollars." The clever clogs Scholarship boy learns by rote.

The pearly smile perfectly complements the gorgeous dress and its myriad pearls, which delicately shiver with the least movement. He has been told in no uncertain terms that they are genuine – the pearls that is. Not to mention the gold dangly earrings like tiny Chinese lanterns set with real diamonds, that fairy tinkle when she inclines her head, which is often.

Perhaps not quite a zillion dollars but then exaggeration is the order of the day.

The ignored Giovanni is hovering with gold embossed menus and just knows that his stupid peasant sister-in-law despises his innate servility. He despises his innate servility almost as much as he despises his graphic need for the stupid peasant sister-in-law.

"Champagne. The Pol Roger '87." Demands the only too recognisable voice of the world famous movie star.

"At once, my lady." She is no lady.

The stilled as a poised praying mantis sister-in-law watches mesmerised as the famous movie star fondly caresses the stubbly man's stubbly chin. Such delicate agile fingers and such an enormous diamond ring.

"I am glad that we are…" Amelia Sedley exaggeratingly shapes quotation marks with the delicate agile fingers. "… 'supposed' to be an item." As he is not a minion the tone of voice has softened and mellowed. He realises she is perfecting the part and it is fascinating to watch. There is no need to reply as the agile fingers become even more agile. "The fucking was pretty damn fucking good." This is not a line that he remembers from any of her movies.

"You say the nicest things, Amelia." Unbidden there is a fleeting memory of a partially undressed Lily Dale saying more or less the same thing, the black dress from the same day's funeral crumpled on the floor. "You say the nicest things, Lily." He had said. Not an occasion he really wants to be even a fleeting memory. He at least has moved on, unlike Lily Dale.

A visibly sweating Giovanni hustles across the empty restaurant clutching the champagne bottle and the clinking ice bucket as if they are newborn babes in arms.

"Flutes." He snaps at Anna in passing. It is practically impossible to curl her upper lip but she makes a valiant attempt and then does as she is told. She is only too well used to doing as she is told. It is safer that way. She stores it all up though – every last doing as she is told – line by line.

"To us." Amelia proposes the toast.

"To us." They clink crystal flutes. She really is good with props. They sip champagne. They sip more champagne.

Amelia Sedley does suggestive coy quite magnificently. "I didn't need my medication this morning." Sip. Sip.

This close the champagne wetted lips are only a smidgen too full and this close the unlined forehead is only a tad too smooth and this close the black eyebrows, that are a stunning contrast to the platinum blonde hair, do not quite hide the tiny scar. This close the brilliant emerald green eyes are fabulous clashing shades of mystic green shining ever so bright with the drops of atropine. "My People." She also does dismissive quite magnificently. "My People are delighted at the publicity."

"So are mine." All two of them.

Giovanni is doing that cat on hot bricks thing as he clutches the menus and is avoiding eye contact with his sister-in-law. He will sort her out later. The most famous of famous movie stars signals with a raised finger. "Waiter." He rushes over, just about avoiding tripping over his several feet.

"Madam?"

She ignores the proffered gold embossed menus. "Recommend something light." She is gazing at the stubbly man as if he is most definitely the sweet course.

Giovanni's mind goes blank. Zur Goodween. No. No. Zur Godween. No. No. No. Zur Godwyn. A kind of prayer. "We ave a seegnature deesh of scrambled eggs and smoked salmon. Veery leet."

She switches the searchlight gaze. "Hand reared chickens?" This minion really is a very ugly man, who vaguely reminds her of somebody she would rather forget. She hates being reminded of men she would rather forget, but there are rather a lot of them if the truth be told.

"Yees, madum." It doesn't matter how famous she is she will not be able to tell the difference. "And Arbroath smoked salmon, madum." Or so he has been told.

"Sounds perfect." He is dismissed without even being dismissed. The dark eyed sister-in-law refills the crystal champagne flutes, the scents of expensive perfumes making her only too well aware of her own inherent muskiness. The stubbly man is intently watching the pouring with oddly colourless eyes that do not appear to blink. A shiver runs down her spine as if someone has walked over her mother's untended mountain grave. She dare not cross herself in full view.

"Thank you." She is politely dismissed by the stubbly man and once out of sight, extravagantly genuflects across her expansive bosom and breathlessly whispers half a Hail Mary. She avoids making eye contact with that goat Giovanni. Perhaps one of these days he will have a heart attack when they are fornicating... he makes enough strangled noises. She has given up on prayers as the Virgin Mary appears to have gone deaf. She still has hopes of the lighted candles.

"I wonder what your jailbird buddy would say if he could see you here lunching tête-à-tête with Amelia Sedley."

"Probably something that is unrepeatable in front of a lady."

"I am not always a lady."

"I know." Something tells him that she is storing this little scene away for future use. It is to be hoped that the eventual Oscar is not going to be for lifetime achievement when she is an old wizened lady; although it is impossible to believe Amelia Sedley will ever grow old and wizened.

The goat is nowhere to be seen and so Anna serves the, in her opinion, meagre food. She is only too well aware that the stubbly man is appraising her expansive bosoms of which she is always proudly conscious. The not unpleasant musky odour with undertones of scrubbed sweat she can do nothing about. It has never put off men. Even as a twelve year old village girl, every male in the village wanted a feel, and then some, of the expanding bosoms. She thinks the other half of the Hail Mary.

"This is delicious." Amelia Sedley eats affectedly in tiny mouthfuls, because her latest ridiculously expensive nutritionist has advised that she must thoroughly masticate food before swallowing.

At Amelia's insistence they masticate away without conversing. When she was a pre-pubescent girl she was often smacked on her bottie by her stepfather if she ever talked with her mouth full, and was made to go upstairs in the dark. She was quite often smacked on her bottie by her stepfather...sometimes in the dark. She has not seen him or her fucking useless mother since Amelia ran away from home as a fourteen year-old. She looked older.

That disquieting musky odour again, as the dark raven woman clears away the dishes a bit too clatteringly. Amelia Sedley hates minions to impose themselves in any way and glares quite magnificently. Jack inhales the hints of garlic on the raven woman's breath, as he idly wonders if a man could lose himself in these beyond midnight black eyes. Probably not, although it could possibly be ennobling to die in the attempt. Or possibly not.

"Will there be anything else, madam?"

"No." She is dismissed.

"Thank you." The stubbly man murmurs and stares into the dismissed one's eyes, who stares back in the moment. She of course wonders what he can possibly see in this pale anaemic girl with the appetite of a sparrow and the manners of a pig. She takes away the plates. There is no hovering Giovanni to avoid catching his eyes that never discern anything that matters.

Jack takes ownership of the distinctive shaped bottle and pours more champagne as water drips on the table. Amelia Sedley covers her flute with the nay say palm of her right hand. Yes... that right hand. "I have that photo shoot in the park this afternoon." Whatever else they say about Amelia Sedley, and my God they do say a lot, they have to admit that she is professional to the core. In between the casting couch sessions there has been hard work and dedication in bucket loads, to augment the sparse talent that accompanies the stunning beauty. "We must go." A radiant green eyed Goddess smile confirming that he is part of the chosen We. He cannot make up his mind whether that is a good thing or not. Probably not. And there is probably no nobility in dying in the attempt. Whatever else, Jack is a quick learner.

When they have gone Giovanni appears from wherever he has been sulking, takes Anna by the hand and leads the black eyed sister-in-law to the vacated table. To their table. The carelessly abandoned crystal flutes half filled with the fabulous champagne. There is plenty more in the bottle angled in the ice bucket where the ice has melted. The expensive perfumes linger.

With a southern Mediterranean plastic flourish he snatches at the dining chair still warm with the movie star's perfect posterior. Anna eases down rather more posterior that she would never claim to be perfect…lots of it yes…perfect no. There is nothing luminously magical about this black eyed rolling in the hay peasant woman, who so rarely smiles because there rarely is anything to smile about. But neither is she unattainable. She was never that and as a thirteen year old she had her first scare of a late period…it was by no means her last such scare.

Giovanni occupies the stubbly man's seat and holds up the stubbly man's fingerprinted crystal flute. On cue the sister-in-law holds up the crystal flute that is haloed with the famous movie star's blood red lipstick.

"To us." He mimic toasts as they clink crystal flutes and wrongly believes that his bravado will make her put aside his servility. They mimic sip champagne… they mimic sip more champagne and it almost comes off. From the famously shaped bottle he tops up the flutes with an unsteady hand. "They are just the same as us."

Anna merestly shakes her head and gulps champagne from the lipstick smeared crystal flute. She will not say anything because Giovanni hates to be contradicted by a woman. It is hard being a poor widow she thinks… so very hard. She wishes to God that she could say no but she has never been able to say no. She could not say no to leaving Italy although it would have been dangerous to stay. She is not that stupid.

"Go to the toilets."

They can hear the idiot Chef banging around in the kitchen. He will be leaving soon. Not soon enough for the old goat.

"Go. Now." She pushes back the chair and does as she is told. She always does as she is told.

Even after all these years Giovanni never tires of watching her richly fleshed body in motion. This big woman has had a stranglehold over his animal lusts since they were children in the same mountain village. As a girl she used to hang upside down knickerless from a tree branch pretending to be Mussolini's hanged mistress, with mouth gaping and tongue lolling out. He had refused to be Mussolini and instead had played a Partisan raping the dead body of the hanged and knickerless Claretta Petacci.

At sixteen Anna chose his older widowed brother to be her village husband. She told Giovanni that she would not make a good wife and she was right. So Giovanni married her younger by six minutes sister – the sensible stringy one. Giovanni and Anna had still animal rutted at every opportunity. He always knew he was not the only one but will never admit to himself that there will never be an only one.

His throat is too constricted to mimic sip any more champagne. She will be in place. He pushes open the door with the sign of an Edwardian lady with an open parasol. Anna is naked with the hanging Garden of Babylon bosoms and the burning bush glistening between the meaty thighs. All of it. All of it. God in heaven. Always and forever all of it until the day he dies.

If he was ever to have a recurring nightmare it would be that he would die before his time and some other man possess this woman perhaps body and oh God! Perhaps soul as well. No it will never be. They have not gone through all they have gone through for that to happen. His God will not allow that to happen.

Sporting the tall chef's hat at a jaunty angle, the beanpole Chef, who fancies himself as a bit of a ladies' man, pokes his head out of the kitchen. The restaurant is empty but then the restaurant is usually empty. There is something funny going on here and that Sir thingy whatsit bloke is up to something. Still. He who pays the piper calls the tune and his is not to reason why and all that crap. Ralph can no longer be choosy about the jobs he takes. There has been one dismissal too many along the way. At the previous job he was not to know the husband would come back unexpectedly. Ralph grins, which is not a pretty sight. At least he and the horny cow had well and truly finished. He will give that horny cow a bell when all the fuss has died down.

Whistling tunelessly he shuffles over to the table with the champagne flutes. There are mouthfuls of champagne in each flute and he tosses them both off, licking the remains of lipstick off the second one. It is as close as he will ever get to the fabled sex goddess Amelia Sedley. Apart of course from the Amelia Sedley range of racy underwear as worn by his missus.

He swigs from the bottle. Earlier he had poked his head out of the kitchen to sneak a glimpse of the fabled one in the flesh. He and the missus have seen most of her movies and the missus is a massive fan. It would have put him quids in to have got an autograph.

Being partially deaf in one ear it takes a couple of minutes before he becomes aware of the muffled noises coming from the bogs. He edges closer. The unmistakable sound of a man and a woman very much at it. Going like the clappers by the sound of it. It has to be the dago and the dago slag and he supposes he ought to be a bit jealous after yesterday, but being practical he doesn't want to get on the wrong side of the dago, who seems well in with Sir thingy whatsit. Also being practical there is plenty of the dago slag to go around.

He swigs from the champagne bottle. Sounds as though the dago is beginning to lose it big time. Ralph wonders if he ought to wait around for some tasty leavings like yesterday, or go home and give the missus a good seeing to. It is her afternoon off… difficult decision. Digging in his pocket he takes out a ten pence coin. Heads wait for the dago slag – he knows Sir thingy whatsit is sending the dago on another errand; tails the missus… he tosses the coin.

Saturday 14th October 2.58pm

Sir Godwyn Lydate will not be ignored. His doings are of more portent than the doings of anyone else in this book, of that he is certain. So write that down if you will.

It has to be recorded that he is inordinately proud of his exquisitely fluffy scrambled eggs and tasty Arbroath smoked salmon on the side. The eggs from hand reared chickens on his Norfolk farm which is handily close to Sandringham. The particular smoked salmon he had discovered on one of his quasi-official trips to Edinburgh. They had spent such a pleasant morning on the seafront at Arbroath where she would perhaps not be recognised. Then a most invigorating afternoon in a rear bedroom overlooking some dustbins of the seafront hotel…in the circumstances the honeymoon suite had not seemed appropriate.

There is of course lots and lots of wholemeal crust-less buttered toast on the side, and a bottle of his favourite lunchtime Cote de Beune uncorked on the kitchen table polished by the enthusiastic Lydia Robinson only this morning.

The house beautiful kitchen in his Albany apartment has everything in its place and a place for everything. Dear Lydia sees to that. Only the ornate pepper pot is somewhat out of place.

It is by now a tad on the late side for lunch and someone's stomach is audibly rumbling; they are both well aware that something came up unexpectedly to delay lunch.

The soon-to-be ennobled Judge Helen Graham sips appreciatively. "A very good year."

"Indeed so, my dear Helen."

She is displaying lots of quite decent, if she does say so herself, bare legs. Lots and lots of freckles. It feels so decadent at this time of day to be naked beneath the borrowed dragon-motifed dressing gown, which is so deliciously floaty around taught breasts. She aches pleasantly between quite decent bare legs. She had believed that mutual no holds barred sex was a thing of the past and in the dim and distant past at that.

Sir Bernard Keeldar is a considerate lover one might be led to believe, except sometimes in the dark when he is not the least bit considerate. She has ignored the texts pinging to her mobile phone. He will probably have guessed, and was no doubt hoping she would be dismissed from the Judiciary and accept her punishment. She hopes he will not be too upset but then he is rarely too upset, because there really is no point if one is married to Shirley Keeldar. But then he might make Helen pay a penance of his own devising and she is not at all sure she wants to go through that again.

Sipping appreciatively, she narrow eyed studies Sir Godwyn as he busies himself with the food, the silk dressing gown a twin to her own. Godwyn, as she must now think of him after mutual no holds barred just about everything. She had not realised there were so many nerve ends in a body to come to fruition in such shattering climaxes…a most generous lover in contrast to Sir Bernard. Just thinking about it is making her exceedingly edgy.

"You had weekend plans, my dear?" He glances covetously over his shoulder.

She could get to quite like being coveted and shakes her head. "No." She lies. She can half believe she is that brilliant law student reincarnated, the sex taken as and when; in her case more as than when. Always a serious girl and so rarely taking life as she found it. There were always consequences to be considered and she was not the sort of girl to be caught out unprepared.

With a Pantomime villain flourish, he brings the plates of food to the table. There is a sense of fun that she has not previously been aware of in this most powerful of men; that few people are ever aware of in this most powerful of men. Sir Bernard has no sense of fun at all and wears his power quite differently. Now Godwyn is fussing that she has everything she needs. "I adore lots of pepper on my scrambled eggs." He shakes the ornate pepper pot and then hands it over. It is in the shape of something she most definitely recognises – the naughty man – and she giggles. She never ever giggles.

"To us." And they clink engraved wine glasses in a toast that makes her shiver. She has never ever toasted to 'an us'.

"You are chilly, my dear?" He is solicitous and takes ownership of a cool freckled hand. At one point in the, shall we say, proceedings he had looked up from between her legs and rashly promised that he would kiss every single one of the freckles on her belly. She had been too close to the thousand foot cliff edge to say anything remotely coherent in reply. He had made a gallant attempt.

"No." She squeezes fingers and takes a gulp of wine. "Not at all."

They eat in a pleasantly charged silence and the only other sound is the tick tick tocking of the venerable grandfather clock imposing through the open door. Such a comforting old fashioned sound ignored by several generations of Lydates.

"This is delicious." She mumbles with her mouth full, which is a solecism she never usually commits, being such a fiercely well brought up girl of whom so much was expected.

"So are you, my dear Helen."

She is glowing… literally glowing. He had always thought her the most contained woman he had ever met, despite the evidence of the blurry glossy photographs, and had been prepared for a longish siege. He doesn't feel exactly cheated. The Trojan horse can be stored away for a future siege.

"More pepper, my dear?"

"Thank you, Godwyn." She giggles. She didn't even giggle as a child.

They eat some more in pleasantly charged silence, the only sound being the tick tick tocking of the venerable grandfather clock, which bears the sword thrust of an Eighteenth Century Lydate who took exception to the passing of time. He was killed before his time fighting for King George at the Battle of Culloden. His body was returned with all due ceremony and he is buried in the family vault at Lydate Hall.

Sir Godwyn leans across the table and cradles the right side of Helen's rose blushed face in a fond gesture that takes them both by surprise, and she takes possession of the cradling hand, kissing the criss-cross life-lined palm in an even fonder gesture.

"You know, my dear, I was there on the last day of the trial."

"I spotted you in the balcony." Another more lingering palm kiss. She doesn't say how wretched she felt when she saw that he was gone. "I thought the verdict had ended my career." And more importantly so did Sir Godwyn Lydate.

"We must ensure it never happens again, my dear." A moreish buttery kiss with wine soaked tongues. "We must ensure that trial by jury has had its day." He has spoken and so be it.

"You know, Godwyn?"

"Yes, Helen, my dear."

"I'm feeling a bit naughty." She fashions a surprisingly effective come and get me wicked grin as she presses the captured hand against a remarkably firm breast. On the small side but very much on the firm side.

All it needs is the Judge's wig and the half-moon spectacles to make it perfect as he squeezes the remarkably firm breast.

"We will leave the peaches and cream until later, my dear." After scrambled eggs with smoked salmon on the side, he is rather partial to peaches and cream washed down with the last mouthfuls of Cote de Beune. But there must be priorities in life.

"Much later." She purrs.

Much later indeed he will eat the peaches and cream off her naked body, thus proving that there is a second time for everything.

Saturday 14th October 3.44pm

If he is not careful Jack believes that, given a quarter of a chance, Sir Godwyn Lydate will take over this bloody book and that will never do. Jack has not gone through all that he has gone through to become a bit player in his own story. He has had quite enough of that sort of thing, thank you very much.

In the here and now he has sneaked away from the media madness that always and forever embraces Amelia Sedley, and which has inevitably taken over the photo shoot in Green Park. He will not be missed whilst ever she is emoting to an adoring world. He is quite certain that Amelia Sedley does not possess the brains to take over this bloody book; possesses just about everything else but thankfully not the brains…the gods are not that stupid.

It is such a pleasant sunny autumnal afternoon for a solitary stroll; solitary has never been a problem for Jack. He is wearing the Yankees baseball cap and wraparound Serengeti sunglasses courtesy of Shirley Keeldar. He has promised faithfully to leave his mobile phone turned on. He really must phone his bloody sister. The longer he leaves it the harder it gets. The bitter sibling quarrel of Tuesday afternoon is simmering on a low heat and it is not in the nature of either of them to turn off the gas. His poor dear mother would not have allowed the quarrel to linger and would have taken her Johnny's side, mistakenly believing that she had brought peace in our time.

He looks around. He is passing the Italian restaurant in Jermyn Street too posh to display a name. This brings to mind that Rebecca Sharp does not like him and that the harder he tries to ingratiate himself the worse it gets. He should not let it get to him but it does. It is his bloody book after all.

Next door to the restaurant he glances into the window of, he looks up, the Jermyn Street Gallery and stops in his tracks. He is stunned by the two canvases displayed in the picture window. The compositions – the colours – the artist screeching for you to stop – just you – yes you – stop, you fucking worm.

He has never seen anything like it and the style is only derivative of itself. A grossly oversexed Pinocchio nosed female with three breasts who is rutting with a one eyed Cyclops. The other canvas – Christ almighty – a crinkly arsed Cyclops being devoured between the elephantine thighs of the Pinocchio nosed female whose eyes are gouged-out yet all seeing – mocking the viewer. The Cyclops looking agonisingly over his shoulder as he is about to disappear from view to where the Sun don't shine; the Cyclops knowing it is too late and that it was always going to be too late. Woman for good or ill thy name is woman.

Jack pushes open the door of the gallery and a fragrant bell tinkles. There is a most pleasant perfumey atmosphere and, despite the mainly empty walls, the gallery exudes class. There is no hint of fire and brimstone.

A woman approaches who fits in rather well. Only medium height, but somehow physically intimidating, wearing sprayed on tight pink jeans and a matching pink blouse with the top three buttons undone. Thirtyish at a guess and seen something of the world that's for sure. An arresting squarish face with take it or leave it Slavic eyes, framed by reddish blonde hair cut stylishly. A pink lipsticked mouth that should be too wide and is surely created for spontaneous laughter. In all an eminently Cyclops beware package.

She is not spontaneously laughing now; not even smiling. The wide mouth is historically set, as though she will never smile until every last German soldier is driven from Mother Russia's sacred soil and a million German women raped in turn…history repeating itself as history…our bastards for yours.

"Can I help you?" The Slavic eyes are narrowed to absolute Slavic and the tone of the voice very much doubts that she can help. He is not to know that Nina Balatka has just taken a telephone call that has made her very angry… very angry indeed.

Jack snatches off the wraparound thingymejigy sun glasses and doffs the stupid Yankees baseball cap. He doesn't understand the first thing about baseball.

"Sorry. I didn't mean to alarm you."

"You didn't alarm me…" The narrowed miss nothing Slavic eyes are pale almost milky blue. "…Mr Bellingham." This worldwide fame thing does have its advantages that's also for sure.

"My friends call me Jack."

"We have only just met." He is taller than in her rude dream of last night.

"You can still call me Jack." The winning smile would gain him fourth place, possibly third place in a field of eight.

She ponders for a few moments. He is not to know. "Very well, Jack." Taking him by surprise she steps closer and holds out a squarish hand and a circle of bracelets tinkles. "Nina Balatka."

Taken by surprise Jack transfers the stupid baseball cap to the hand holding the sunglasses which he drops with a clatter. They awkwardly shake hands and then she bends to retrieve the dropped sunglasses. The tantalising glimpse of bra is also pink. Prison Officer Dora Spenlow could learn a thing or two about colour co-ordination from this four square lady.

"These are very expensive, Jack." She handles the unbroken sunglasses exaggeratedly carefully and places them on a table displaying gallery leaflets, which have just arrived from the Printers a week late. "You should be more careful."

Indeed he should. "An unusual name."

"My mother was Polish and my father was Russian." She does not say that her father raped her mother and could have been any one of half a dozen perpetrators. She has never told anyone that. "Now how can I help you?"

"The paintings in the window?"

"They are sold." And that is that. There is something inherently uncompromising about this physically intimidating woman. A hint of collars turned up and spies being exchanged on a fog shrouded bridge at midnight; starving guard dogs howling somewhere in the darkness of the Steppes. In the movie Amelia Sedley had played a prostitute who was a spy and had been executed quite artistically, although barely clothed. He idly wonders if Nina Balatka has been influenced by that movie, although she is of course fully clothed.

His bloody sister had gone around for weeks with her collar turned up and out staring the firing squad. It became quite intimidating.

"The artist?"

"Yes." Over to you Jack.

"Will there be any more paintings?"

"I sincerely hope so."

He would really like to make her smile. "Does the artist have a name?"

"Yes."

Then she takes him by surprise and laughs out loud. Spontaneous yes, but also disturbing in a hard to fathom way that makes him wonder if it would have been better to have kept on walking. The exchanging of spies is fraught with treachery.

"She is a very private person."

Deliberately avoiding eye contact, Jack glances round the mainly empty walls and notices a smaller, more traditional painting and does a second take. It is a lifelike pinky nude woman, draped full-length on an ultramodern IKEA couch and facing the viewer, head resting menacingly on a raised arm. It is Nina Balatka and very much naked, except for a pair of white panties caught on one crossed ankle.

She follows his riveted gaze.

"Yes that is me. I paint as well."

He walks over to take a very much closer look. The body even more physically intimidating without clothes. Blush pink nipples and a striking reddish blonde bush wedged between the muscled thighs.

Now she is standing next to him quite unabashed. "I am just an old-fashioned girl." He listens for the spontaneous laughter that doesn't come.

"How much is it?"

"The body is not for sale."

He doesn't make eye contact. "The painting?"

"Four thousand pounds." She has just quadrupled the price. She is not at all sure she is comfortable so close to the man with whom she shared such exceedingly intimate exchanges in her rude dream. He must never know. What goes on in rude dreams stays in rude dreams.

"I'll take it."

She always seeks to get the measure of a man... usually in a matter of seconds... this one will take a few minutes. She unhooks the painting from the wall, whose beige colour she has carefully chosen. Everything must be just so because this could well be her last chance.

"Where shall I send the painting?"

"My suite at the Savoy." Is something he never thought he would ever get to say.

"Not the Ritz?"

He shakes his head. The woman's pale almost milky blue eyes appear guileless. He has not the remotest idea what she might be thinking.

"I will take it in the back." He indeed cannot fail to appreciate the shapely pink fabric-covered backside, as she walks to the rear of the gallery, the painting securely tucked under an arm. She would expect nothing less as she glances over her shoulder. "Would you like a cup of tea?" It is the very least she can do. She had woken up from the rude dream with such pleasurable sensations invading her body, that she had held herself tight in her own arms for several minutes before more thoroughly masturbating than usual.

"Yes please."

She pushes through the gypsy bead curtain at the back of the shop. His mother always insisted that he say please and thank you. She rarely did so.

He walks to the picture window and looks out between the rears of the two canvases onto a quiet Jermyn Street. There is a name drunkenly scrawled on the backs of the canvases – Emily Rowley. A suitable name for an artist.

"Jack." She shouts his name. He is used to it now and much prefers it to John or Johnny. His mother so often whispered Johnny in that wheedling tone that made his flesh creep.

He pushes through the bead curtain and Nina indicates a stool. "Milk? Sugar?"

"Just black please." As a child he had always hated the thought of milk spurting out of cow's udders. Perching now on the three legged stool he sees that the nude painting of Nina Balatka is propped against the wall facing the room. It would demand the eyes in any room. "Have you painted anything else?"

"Several like that." She blows on the Egon Schiele Exhibition mug of milky tea and three sugars. She never apologises for her sweet tooth – in her Polish childhood it was not possible to have a sweet tooth. "They are hanging on a wall in the Chelsea Harbour apartment."

"I would like to see them." He is getting better at his follow ups. "You are very talented."

She studies Jack over the rim of the Exhibition mug, as if aligning him in her rifle sights. The Slavic features remind Jack of those wartime black and white photos of Soviet women fighter pilots.

"Do they all display a pair of white knickers?"

She looks as though she is ready to pull the trigger. The voice though is surprisingly gentle. "Yes… but not always round the ankles." She blows on the sweet milky tea and takes a tentative sip… then another one. "Since I was a little girl Mamma insisted I wear only white knickers." Another less tentative sip. "For purity." It is a brilliant throwaway line that Amelia Sedley has never mangled in a third-rate movie. He realises he is being unfair.

He decides the only sensible retort is to sip his own unsweetened black tea and pretend not to be caught at too much of a disadvantage. Set against another wall are half a dozen overlapping run of the mill London scenes.

"Are the Londonscapes yours?"

"They have been my bread and butter." She sets down the Exhibition mug and dabs the corners of her wide mouth with unpainted fingernailed fingers. She would look amazing in a Russian fighter pilot's leather helmet, with the reddish blonde hair poking out and blowing in the slipstream, as tracer bullets scream past the cockpit.

"I made a crust hawking them round City offices." Jack's oddly colourless eyes appear to be watching the words shaping out of her mouth, which she finds a trifle disconcerting, but not unexciting. She is not easily disconcerted…excited is another matter. "That is how I met my current boyfriend."

Not a proper boyfriend, but the word will do as well as any other. "He owns this building." There is a definite edge to her voice. "He also owns the Chelsea Harbour apartment building." She doesn't have to say that she cannot be owned. "Your tea is going cold." She watches and waits for him to drink all the tea. She hates waste.

"Emily Rowley walked in here ten days ago on the day we opened." She is intensely thoughtful. "Those canvases in the window were covered in newspaper." A smile that sits oddly on her face, as if she doesn't quite mean it. "I had to pay the taxi."

"Why here?"

"She had tried everywhere else." Quite simple really. Nina Balatka crosses one square hand over the other square hand on the scratched Formica table top, in a gesture that demands restraint. Supple fingers would be expert on a fighter plane machine gun, the plane diving out of the sun. The eyes would not blink. "I loved the paintings. They were a revelation." She smiles as if smiling into a mirror. "She is a genius and I persuaded my current boyfriend…" For want of a better word. "… to buy them both." He wouldn't know a masterpiece if it bit him on his fat arse.

"Revelation is the word." Jack wholeheartedly agrees.

"I tried to contact Emily earlier today but she is on a different Planet when she is working. Eventually I got through. She is working on something big. I am going over tomorrow afternoon."

"Can I come?"

The last thing Nina Balatka is is a fool. She knows that if this man sitting so cosily opposite endorses Emily Rowley then they will both make the deserved breakthrough. Fame and fortune not quite on the turn of a card, with chance and circumstance always and forever seasoning the human condition. She knows that truth better than most. Nina Balatka has always trusted to her star even though, in the worst of times, it appeared to be a falling star that would burn itself out.

"She doesn't want me to go earlier than two o'clock in the afternoon." Nina has no intention of going on living hand to mouth begging crumbs from the rich man's table; wealth is everything. Sometimes the Fates must be given a helping hand. "You can come."

Jack intently studies the inscrutable face and thinks she might be in the wrong story and even the wrong century. A fugitive from the brothers Karamazov…perhaps a younger sister on whom it would be unwise to turn one's back if there is a hatchet within reach.

"Tomorrow lunchtime I am on the Spencer Perceval Show." He thinks better of touching the crossed square hands on the table and continues to fiddle with the Exhibition mug. If he was aware of what had taken place in her rude dream last night he might not be so reticent. "I will meet you at Television Centre at eleven thirty and get you into the Show. Then we can go together to see Emily Rowley." He thinks for one awful moment that she is going to change her mind and demonstrate that newly acquired masterful has its limits.

"Very well."

The mobile ping pings is in his pocket. It is Amelia Sedley. "I must go."

When he has gone Nina Balatka remains in the same position for several minutes staring at the nude painting of Nina Balatka. Only when she becomes aware of the tinkling of the fragrant doorbell does she reluctantly move.

Saturday 14th October – Evening the first part.

The long suffering wife of the Reverend John Eames has returned unexpectedly to the paint peeling Vicarage. No phone call. Nothing. His first thought is that the mean-spirited woman is trying to catch him out. Too late – too late was the cry. Then he remembers the two vodka glasses waiting to be washed up in the kitchen; one bearing tell-tale lipstick smears.

"I wasn't expecting you." A going through the motions perfunctory peck on the proffered powder dusted cheek, and she glides through to the kitchen and retrieves an uncorked bottle of Sauvignon Blanc from the fridge. She has always moved like a 1950s fashion model. She doesn't take any notice of the fridge magnets anymore, but she does take notice of the two glasses next to the sink.

"So I see." She doesn't sniff the air as usual and appears somewhat distracted.

"Is your mother all right?" Apart from dying that is – the evil cow.

"Lingering." She three-quarter fills a tumbler with white wine and takes an unladylike swig, not at all 1950s fashion model style. He really hopes she is not going to make a scene. There is always a lingering headache after working on his Sunday sermon. Alice Vavasor has a nerve to say she is the one being used; Mary Thorne never claims she is being used.

"We need to talk, John." This is not good. "Get yourself a drink." Even worse.

She tops up the wine and clutching the bottle and the tumbler she glides through to the cluttered lounge. Nothing incriminating. Thank God he came across Alice Vavasor's ridiculously flimsy knickers when he plumped up the cushions. They are now scrunched up in his trouser pocket and he must remember not to blow his nose. Alice had only been gone ten minutes before his wife arrived home... talk about Providence at work.

"John?" Her voice is drier than the wine, as she perches on the very edge of the sofa, on the side where the springs haven't sprung, with her knees primly together. Alice Vavasor doesn't know the meaning of the word prim and she also has difficulty with the keeping knees together bit. He thinks he might have strained his back.

"John?" Still here. He inclines his head in true Nineteenth Century Clerical fashion; she believes he does his impression of a minor character from a Trollope novel just to be more annoying than usual. She takes a deep breath. "I don't know quite where to start." She stares pensively at her husband of fourteen arduous years. As usual he looks guilty as charged. Childless, he has often been more like a recalcitrant child than a grown-up husband.

The career that she once supported had started with so much promise, but even so she should have listened to her mother; but then she never did listen to her mother.

"I want a divorce, John."

"A divorce?" He twitches his head from side to side in apparent shocked disbelief. He would be even more shocked if he knew the half of it.

"I thought things were better." He is that recalcitrant child and she is done with all that.

Jesus wept... there is so much accumulated bile that she could spew out if she even loved him a little bit. She had never loved him more than a little bit.

He opens and closes his mouth – one of the lost boys – most definitely not Peter Pan.

"I have met someone else." Which is sort of true. She realises that the tumbler is empty and so she pours more wine. He appears incredulous... this cannot be happening... he will be the laughing stock of the Parish.

"Who is it?"

"You don't know him." Which is half true. His wife is sitting there with knees together all prim and proper and glugging more wine. As if. Well. Just as if. Words fail him. Words should not fail a Vicar with his failings. He remembers to drink some vodka from the lipstick smeared glass and, when he realises, nearly chokes. She doesn't slap his back.

"Let's be honest for once, John, all I have ever been to you is an occasional blow-up doll." She gulps more wine. The image she has conjured up gives them both pause for thought, and she resists the temptation to nervously giggle.

"Who is it?"

"It is the doctor attending mother." Well it could well be his baby. He is married, but even so they had fucked on several occasions in her bed-bound mother's lounge at about the right time of the month. She thinks her mother probably heard because they did make rather a lot of noise and her mother is not as deaf as she pretends. Thank God she has lost her voice.

"A doctor?"

Some of the bile seeps out. "Yes, John. Nearly as bad as committing adultery with a Vicar." She takes a deep breath because there really is no point in losing her temper at this late stage. She intends to be dignified, which is not easy when she can smell there has been a woman in this abject room.

"And you see, John…" She cannot look at him. "…I am pregnant."

If she could bear to look at him she would discern that the expression on his face is priceless. "And I intend to keep the baby."

He opens and closes his mouth. Some slight hints that Alice Vavasor dared insinuate now make sense. Of course he holds his head in his hands – she would expect nothing less.

"It definitely isn't yours." They both know that. It is some considerable time since the blow up doll has been inflated. Even then she made him use a condom. She would not risk perpetuating the Eames dynasty. She had never risked that.

Saturday 14th October – Evening the second part.

The Painter Emily Rowley is crouching like the caricature of creature at bay, possibly early Goya before he found his sure touch, in the farthest corner of the attic space. She has pissed herself but that is what creatures at bay do. She has not defecated because there are limits. In the gloom she is wide eyed and half starved, staring at the partially completed shadowy Window man canvases, which are propped higgledy-piggledy against the nastily damp patched wall. She is not able to reclaim that fleeting illusion of the intruding Cat woman. She desperately needs to pixilate that cupper of the balls.

Despite the anguished frustration, which is a physical pain in her belly, she has to grimly smile. The cupper of the balls sounds like some time-honoured sinecure at a Medieval Court. Perhaps not such a sinecure at the Court of Henry VIII.

The man she has… the man is there. It is the woman. The woman, always the woman. Emily is keening in a low monotone, as she always keens when struggling with the birth pangs of a new creation – only never ever like this. The keening grows louder and louder and is a distressed animal scarce human sound, that echoes through some eternal burning star beyond time and Space. Louis Trevelyan listens at the door and then retreats. He does not need this crap. There are plenty more fish at the easel.

Saturday 14th October – Evening the third part.

Sir Godwyn Lydate has changed his weekend plans. It is a most unusual occurrence and has caused comment in certain high places. There is some whispering that he is a law unto himself…not very loud whispering it has to be said…but whispering nonetheless.

"Are you ready, Helen my dear?"

Helen Graham is staring at her reflection in the ornate William and Mary oval mirror hanging in the hallway of Sir Godwyn's Albany apartment. The mirror had once upon a time adorned Queen Caroline's apartments at Richmond Palace.

Helen and Godwyn have very much shared a lingering bath and she is feeling exceedingly cleansed. She is wearing the shortish skirt and the low-cut blouse of this morning, and he thinks that from behind she is remarkably trim in the tight fitting skirt. She is contemplating whether to dye out the grey showings in her hair and hardly dares contemplate the transition, from sensible pants to lacy black knickers to no knickers at all. For many reasons October has always been one of her favourite months; unlike April the cruellest month.

"Ready, Goddy." Another transition difficult to contemplate.

The cloudy grey day limousine takes only a few minutes to reach one of Sir Godwyn's favourite restaurants on the edge of Chinatown. The muscle bound Gilbert Markham checks in the mirror and sees Sir Godwyn stroking the snooty woman's very much exposed thigh. A bit too stringy for Gilbert's taste… although he wouldn't kick her out of bed.

The restaurant is booked up weeks ahead, but of course Sir Godwyn Lydate's favourite table is made available. The diminutive Chinese owner bows and scrapes and greets his most honoured guest in Mandarin. The most honoured guest replies in kind. They exchange pleasantries and the weather is apparently warmer in Beijing.

Helen Graham is impressed. There appears to be no end to this man's accomplishments and she blushes at that thought as they are shown to the table. He of course orders in Mandarin without seeing a menu. A bottle of rare Chinese pale lemon coloured aperitif wine is also produced like a rabbit out of a hat. The diminutive Chinese owner and several waiters hover as the most honoured guest tastes and approves. The rare wine is on the house; they will not lose face.

"To us."

"To us." They clink wine glasses etched delicately with intricate Ming dynasty Chinese boating scenes. The wine is delicious and she licks her lips.

"There is much work to do, my dear. As well as the backstairs Jury stuff, we must kill off the Schools bill on several legal technicalities. Don't want the oiks getting above their station."

"I am looking forward to getting my teeth into it, Goddy." She joins in the most un-Sir Godwyn like infectious almost, but not quite, snorting giggling.

Thank goodness some dishes of food arrive superintended by the diminutive owner, and another bottle of even rarer white wine. A few words of Mandarin are exchanged. This most honoured guest has dined here with the Chinese President's wife no less. No other diners were allowed.

"Let us eat, my dear, and then I will share some initial thoughts."

He is brilliantly dexterous with the chopsticks and she is all fingers and thumbs. With a minimum of fuss he adjusts her hold. The adjusted hold is much more efficient.

"Thank you, Goddy."

He wonders if that might have been a mistake. If he has a fault it is to sometimes get carried away in the moment…perhaps not exactly a fault as getting carried away in the moment is not to be gainsaid. There have been so many unforgettable moments.

"Don't mention it, my dear."

"This is delicious." She speaks with her mouth full.

"You know the answer to that, my dear." She blushes like a love struck undergraduate and he thinks the effect quite touching, and quite sad, and not a little enticing.

This is all really fun she thinks. There has not been a lot of fun in her life. There has not been a lot of anything in her life except work. Work. Work. And more work. And look how that nearly ended up. She has never ever gone out in public without knickers; the only trouble is that she now needs to go to the toilet.

Saturday 14th October – Evening the fourth part.

There is a surly brazenness about Marion Fay's self-absorbed nakedness that is disquietingly unbiblical. There is something about being brazenly naked on their mother's bed in what will always be their mother's house, which is a slap in the face of their mother's shade. She has no doubt their mother's ghost will haunt this house if it possibly can. Marion Fay is well on the way to being well pissed.

"Rot in hell, mother dear." She waves the bottle and spills some vodka on her tits and there is no one to lick it off – John Eames does have his uses. She knows she is attractive to weak bellied men and that she is attracted to weak bellied men like John Eames. Of course her late husband was the weakest bellied of them all. Women… well women are a different matter.

"I am coming to get you, brother dear." The vibrations of her own deep voice reverberate in the musty shrouded room that has reverberated to the grunts and groans of their mother's unnatural lusts. Shades of their mother's ever more desperate prayers begging forgiveness, believing that John Eames could be some sort of emissary to the afterlife. Stupid deluded woman. Soon there will be no one to go through the motions of tending her grave.

Marion glug glugs from the fingerprinted bottle and then throws the empty bottle to smash against the wall. What a waste of being brazenly naked. She had caught sight of her own nakedness in the mirror and wished she was a man to ravish that so so curvy body.

She giggles and burps and farts. Then caught out by the suddenness, she leans over and pukes on their mother's carpet where the mad woman used to kneel to pray. Marion Fay very much doubts if anyone out there in eternity could ever be bothered to listen to their mother's rantings. Not after the havoc she had wreaked. She pukes some more and feels slightly more composed.

Saturday 14th October – Evening the fifth part.

Shirley Keeldar is embracing a thumb sucking Becky Sharp who is draped on her lap. The Grande suite of the Savoy Hotel is eerily translucent with the gentle dissimilar rhythms of their breathing. The rise and fall and the rise and fall of their chests the only disturbance in the Tiffany lamp lit spaces.

They are both glad to step off the world for a few precious moments and have done this before and will do it again. Theirs is a give and take relationship unique to themselves. Deeper perhaps than sisters and deeper perhaps than certain mothers and certain children. They think so anyway, not having children. Unfortunately they did have mothers.

"This is nice." The bland words fit in like the last pieces of a child's twelve piece jigsaw. Shirley strokes Becky's shoulder length hair and Becky's response is to ease herself deeper into Shirley's curvaceous lap. "It is so nice just to be here." Becky has fine silky hair made electric by the stroking.

The thumb is withdrawn. "There is a dangerous streak in that man." They are both well aware of whom she is speaking. "I want you to be careful."

"Silly puss." Shirley gently kisses the flyaway silky hair and only a small destructive part of her wishes that Jack was here; there is no point the larger destructive part wishing that Tom Sawyer was here. The visibly thinner thumb is reinserted and Becky sucks for all she is worth and closes her eyes tight, enacting the trick that rarely worked as a child, to make nasty things go away. In the vacant chair opposite, Shirley has propped the realistic nude painting of the sturdy woman with distinctive reddish blonde hair. Becky opens her eyes and releases the thumb. She really must put away childish things. They both stare at the nude painting; there is a challenging uncompromising brazen honesty in the keen eyed staring back gaze which they both find disquieting.

Saturday 14th October – Evening the sixth part.

Amelia Sedley is just about managing to disguise the abject terror lurking behind the greeny lustrous eyes. Not easy to pull off. The hands tied behind her back highlighting the bravely defiant breasts shaped in all their glory by the diaphanous material that is most definitely out of place.

She spits in the face of her tormentor and the answering cowardly slap slap in response resonates in the Ritz Hotel bedroom. The effort not to break down and beg for mercy is truly, truly heart rending.

It is a cleverly staged anti-climax when Amelia is led out of the grey damp walled Prison cell to inevitable execution. Instinctively she dominates the screen, as she walks proudly and unafraid, if a trifle under dressed, as the credits roll over the dimly lit and now empty cell. The abandoned shawl, the open Bible on the bare table and the painting of Christ the Redeemer fixed crookedly by a rusty nail to the artistically damp stained wall. A long minute later there is a distant pop pop pop of the rifles of the German firing squad, as the never ending credits keep on rolling to the Adagietto of Mahler's fifth Symphony. There will not be a dry eye in the Prison Cinema and Sikesy will be in seventh heaven.

"What do you think, Jack?" For some reason she appears apprehensive of his reaction. As if he is any man and every man and the vulnerability is brutally exposed for his eyes only. Surely to God such beauty is not skin deep?

"Fucking brilliant." Not a quote that can be used in any publicity.

They are sprawled partly clothed on the Emperor sized bed in the Ritz Hotel bedroom, corralled by the detritus of two dozen cold pizzas and two distinctive shaped empty bottles of champagne.

Her People are never sure of the preferred pizza of the moment and People have been sacked for getting it wrong. At scary eyed Lucy Snowe's suggestion they had ordered every possible combination.

Some of the People think scary eyed Lucy Snowe is getting a bit too big for her boots, although they hesitate to say so to her atrophied face.

Jack's mother would have tut-tutted at the waste – waste not want not being one of her many facile mantras that she rarely if ever followed. Too many cooks spoil the broth another one. Not that she ever did much cooking.

"She was a remarkable woman." Jack does a double take – Amelia's subdued, endearingly quavery voice is the subdued, endearingly quavery voice of nurse Edith Cavell, as portrayed by Amelia Sedley. Possibly her last chance for that elusive Oscar, although Jack is not at all sure that the actual nurse Edith Cavell was as hauntingly beautiful, or as gobsmackingly desirable as the image that has faded from the screen.

"You are a remarkable actress, Amelia." The image on the screen somehow having more substance than the real person.

"I want you to take me to the Premiere of 'Sacrifice." Speaks one of the many voices of Amelia Sedley.

"It will be a pleasure." He takes the fantasy woman of a million wet dreams in his arms and stifles a yawn.

Sunday 15th October 8.19am

The Reverend John Eames just cannot believe that his wife till death us do part spent the night in the spare room and propped a chair behind the door. She should be so lucky. Now she is annoyingly meticulously packing the larger of the battered suitcases with what she calls essentials. Including skimpy underwear for God's sake. He didn't see that coming.

Not to mention being pregnant by another man for God's sake. He so didn't see that coming that he might as well have been an inhabitant of Mars. He has always had an affinity in his own mind with the red planet, particularly the three breasted Venusian women of the early Dan Dare stories featured in the Eagle comics, that he had discovered in his late father's attic.

"I wish you would stop staring at me like that." Snaps the very much two breasted Earth woman, as she continues folding and neatly tucking under.

"I will be a laughing stock." This voice would scarcely reach the front pews where the deaf old lady sits, never mind the back of the church and the sniggering teenagers taking shelter from the rain. "A laughing stock."

She pauses momentarily to glance at her husband in name only. She must stop thinking of him as her husband of any kind. He never did look his best in this threadbare dressing gown and has never taken much care of his appearance. "Tell your precious congregation that you threw me out because I was playing around." Which is truer than he realises. She continues to fold and neatly tuck under. She always was a tidy packer. "Tell them anything you want, John. Anything at all."

"We have been married for fifteen years."

That bloody recalcitrant child. She will be glad to see the back of it.

"Does that count for nothing?"

"Fourteen years ten months and eleven days to be precise." She pauses in the folding and tucking under. "It counts for less than nothing." She squintingly glares and he hates it when she squintingly glares. "Have you the remotest idea how soul destroying it is to know your husband has only ever made love to you as a penance." Even now she is too polite to say fucked; it was never ever making love. "That he would rather make love to a fat slag like Alice Vavasor, for Christ's sake."

"She's not that fat."

"Sod off, John." She never properly swears. The spittle sprays from her mouth. "Just sod off and let me finish my packing in peace."

Safe in the kitchen he indulges in a swig from the fingerprinted vodka bottle. The table is littered with his notes for the unfinished Sermon… most of his Sermons are unfinished these days. He takes another swig. He will have to extemporise as usual. Perhaps the subject could be the woman taken in adultery… he bares his teeth… that Sermon would make a few taken women shift uneasily in their pews. There was something to be said for stoning adulterous women.

Abruptly he sits down. If the truth be told the particular adulteress upstairs has always blighted his career. There was that time when she called the Bishop, no less, a pot-bellied pervert. All because he had imbibed a drop too much of that god-awful British sherry, a gift from her god-awful mother, and slid a hand up John's wife's dress. The dress was far too short anyway. Just asking for it and the poor Bishop wasn't to know that she had run out of clean knickers. Despite the La di da airs and graces she has always been a bit of a slut. A blow up doll indeed. Blow up dolls do not offputtingly fart during let's get it over with sex, or stare at the ceiling composing the weekly shopping list.

The front door slams and the car engine throatily starts up. So that's that – not even a goodbye. Fourteen and some years well and truly up the spout. He bares his teeth… up the spout indeed. "Good riddance." He mutters. All he has to do now is concoct a believable story and, with any luck, there will be oodles of tea and sympathy. He will just have to tread carefully with Alice Vavasor, because he has made certain rash promises on the assumption that he would remain safely married. He has also made certain rashish promises to Mary Thorne, based on the same quite reasonable assumption.

Sunday 15th October 11.21am

Nina Balatka is seated in the Reception area of Broadcasting House endeavouring not to be too physically intimidating and avoiding eye contact with anyone and everyone. The pale almost milky blue eyes staring intently at the mobile phone that is held in her square hands resting in the square lap – although there are no messages; there are rarely any messages. She never paints her fingernails because her mother had never properly recovered from the gang rape and never painted her fingernails ever afterwards. As if the painted fingernails were what inflamed the Russian soldiers.

Nina is not at all sure that she truly belongs here, but then she has never truly belonged anywhere. She knows that men are eyeing her up; she is a striking woman and has never been afraid to use those striking looks. Oft-times not too wisely or too well.

After much out of character deliberation she has dressed in figure hugging pale blue jeans, a loose pale cream blouse and a gold fringed matching cardigan. The reddish blonde hair is well and truly conditioned and painstakingly styled. The only visible jewellery is a wafer thin gold watch that she wears on her right wrist; a gift from Julius in the first heady throws of what could loosely be called passion, which didn't last long beyond three fucks barely worth the name. Nevertheless a gift she intends to keep. She thinks she was probably not the first "girlfriend" to receive the watch… she will be the last.

The mobile phone pings and she checks the message. Then deletes it… thought so.

"Hello Nina."

She looks up with prepared eyes and there is famous Jack standing tall and staring down with those oddly colourless eyes. She does a manufactured smile just for his benefit, the generous mouth veering to its most uncomplicated when generously smiling. At one time she would not have given him a second glance in the street. In his turn he would have spied from afar and built-up Meccano structured daydreams that inevitably ended badly.

"We just have time for coffee."

She knows that he appreciates the rising to her feet which she does execute rather well. An appraising glance at her arse which is only to be expected. She has to admit that it feels really special to be guided towards the canteen with his hand cradling her elbow. She has never thought of an elbow as a sexual object.

People are staring and whispering and she enjoys that.

Nina doesn't tell him that she prefers tea and he doesn't ask and so they sip frothy cappuccinos at a table for two. She is very much aware that their knees are almost touching. In her experience knees are definitely sexual objects.

"So tell me about yourself, Nina." He seems much more rashly confident than yesterday and there are dark shadows fracturing the oddly colourless eyes.

"What do you want to know?"

"Are you wearing white knickers?"

"Of course." She is not surprised that he thinks he can throw her off her stride. It is what men try on with certain women.

She really is a most striking woman, displaying a touch more make-up than yesterday, which highlights the Slavic features in a dramatic way. A Patriotic war female Russian fighter pilot on leave in Moscow and looking for a good time. Life is cheap. Life is easy. He doesn't recognise the perfume. No hint of engine oil.

He sucks the Exhibition pen and knows that this war time theme is just about exhausted.

The pale almost milky blue eyes are staring him down. He is not to know that her nipples are tingling. They never tingled in the presence of Julius Verinder – in fact they almost disappeared without trace.

"So, Nina."

"So, Jack."

"How is your rich boyfriend?"

"I haven't seen him for a couple of weeks." More like three weeks – she might well get used to frothy coffee.

"All passion spent?"

"Something like that." She licks foam off her upper lip. "How is your famous girlfriend?"

He uses the teaspoon to dig out the coffee froth at the bottom of the cup. His mother would have tut-tutted. She stopped slapping his arm after that time he slapped back and she fell and broke an arm.

"So so glad you're on the Show. So so glad." Thankfully they are rudely interrupted and Nina Balatka recognises the sleekly well fed figure of Spencer Perceval, who is bending over the table, totally oblivious of interrupting anything or anyone.

"Looking forward to it." The two unalike men awkwardly shake hands. The reasonably famous Political Interviewer is accompanied by a very much leggy sort of redheaded girl clutching a clipboard to her chest – green painted fingernails and Sherwood Forest green tights that draw attention. Maid Marian of Sherwood Forest avoids meeting Nina's gaze.

"Can I introduce Nina Balatka." Insists Jack and Spencer Perceval demi-waves noncommittally. Decent looking piece – not Amelia Sedley though. The very much leggy sort of redheaded green themed girl is not introduced. "I would like Nina in the Studio."

"Of course." Behind the smoothie exterior and slicked back hair style of a much younger man, Spencer Perceval is making calculations. Although his calculations are not usually accurate. "I will lead the way."

The very much leggy sort of redheaded girl takes up the rear.

An uncomfortable wonky swivel chair is found for Nina Balatka by the very much leggy sort of redhead, who is still avoiding eye contact. Nina is positioned behind the cameras where she has an excellent view of the two facing sofas. Half recognises the two women on one sofa as opposing Politicians, who are studiously ignoring each other. They are both introduced to Jack by a slightly too obsequious Spencer Perceval, who misses the right note by several fractions. The attractive blonde introduced one smiles expansively, as if all her life has been a preparation for this moment. The pixie brunette introduced one does not smile.

Nina Balatka is not aware of the Watcher secreted in the shadows at the rear of the Studio. She has a sixth sense for being appraised but this time it has failed miserably. She has not the remotest idea that she is being favourably compared to an early May date two penny blue Imperforate, with a neat Maltese cross barely touching. Or that the appraiser is racking his brains, which have been compared to the size of Canada, as to where he has seen this striking woman in the recent past. Ah! Of course! He had caught them out in that quiet supposedly out of the way Italian Restaurant, but then they had caught him out as well… hmm…he doesn't think that Julius Verinder saw it that way.

Meanwhile Jack is ensconced on the other sofa with Spencer Perceval, facing the newly appointed Minister, an attractively made up blonde with a decent expanse of legs, and the pixie Shadow Minister, an earnest elfin brunette with an awful chopped hairstyle and wearing unflattering trousers baggy at the knees. Nina Balatka does not know a lot about Politics, but she does not think there are many votes of either sex to be had with unflattering shapeless trousers baggy at the knees. Nina Balatka stifles a yawn.

The, too earnest for her own good, elfin Shadow Minister is stabbing an aggressive finger and arguing the case with made up blonde legs. Then she has a real go at Jack for some apparently sexist remark. Jack sticks out his tongue live on camera and blows a resounding raspberry. Spencer Perceval makes no attempt to hide the matey down the pub chortle. Made up blonde legs emits a delicious, very much at the races, tinkling laugh that would get under Nina's skin after a while.

The too earnest elfin creature rips off her microphone at the second attempt and, as much as her height allows, stalks disdainfully off the set. On the way out she glares at Nina Balatka who glares back, charitably wondering if it is that time of the month, in which case Nina can have some sympathy. Her periods recently have been a bitch. Then the too earnest elfin creature momentarily pauses and stares beyond Nina, and the petite features swell in – there is no other word for it – fear. Then she is gone with more of a scurry than a stalk and Nina Balatka is left wondering.

"I thought that went well." Spencer Perceval, the consummate performer after his own lights, makes everyone chortle including the Crew… he's a card is Spencer… amongst other things. The man skulking in the shadows does not laugh. It is not recorded whether or not Nina Balatka or sort of red headed Carrie Brattle laughed. Apparently they only have walk on parts…or so it might be thought.

Spencer Perceval is orchestrating every atom of his just beyond mediocre talents to prevent the People's hero taking over the Show, which is turning into a Premier league lovefest between famous Jack and the so far up for it, it hurts, made up blonde Minister. There are certainly votes to be had here. She is the one who referred to the acquitted Jack as the People's hero in the House of Commons; the Daily Mail trumpeted that she spoke for the Nation.

Nina Balatka smooths the fabric of the sprayed on pale blue jeans along a honed thigh, as the leggy sort of redheaded Carrie Brattle, still clutching the ubiquitous, if that is the word, clipboard, is making windmill over the top winding up signs. A relieved looking Spencer Perceval is gushingly thanking his only two guests, but it seems more than two, and the elfin Shadow Minister is not even a Spectre at the feast.

"Good to see you again, my dear." A stage whisper that makes Nina almost jump out of her skin as she stares at the man who has materialised out of the shadows. She never forgets a face. She had badgered and badgered Julius to take her out for a romantic dinner, and this very same man had waved a greeting as she and Julius were being shown to a discreet table in an alcove in the supposedly out of the way Italian Restaurant. "Shit. Fuck." Julius had spat and tightened his hold on Nina's arm and there was a bruise for days afterwards. There was no turning back and the man – this man – was openly appraising the tight fitting above the knee black evening dress bought, much to his chagrin, on Julius's borrowed credit card.

"Good to see you, Julius."…"And you, Godwyn." And that was it. The stunningly beautiful raven haired unsmiling woman at this man's table was a dead lookalike for the Prime Minister's wife, except that the Prime Minister's wife is always smiling.

"I am surprised you remembered." This striking looking woman of the here and now has recovered quickly. He likes that. She remembers that the high and mighty Julius Verinder was more than a little scared at the unexpected meeting. When Nina had said the woman was a lookalike for the Prime Minister's wife Julius had hissed, "It is the fucking Prime Minister's wife, you stupid bitch."

There was no call for that. They had hardly exchanged a word for the rest of the one course meal and he had not ordered wine. Romantic it was not. Never has the shop window display of her body been so wasted, or so she had thought. She has not seen Julius since that evening. The texts are becoming more and more strident and in response she is getting angrier by the day. She can just about imagine this man of the shadows in a Russian soldier's uniform, only Nina has no intention of being forced to the ground like her mother, her clothes ripped off and her knickers stuffed in her mouth.

"I never forget a beautiful woman who fits everything so magnificently in a little black dress." He glances down the front of her blouse but that is only to be expected.

"And how is my good friend Julius?"

"I don't know." She thought about saying scared shitless but is not sure of her ground.

"I see." And she is sure that he does see.

The others are inevitably gravitating towards this man Godwyn – yes Godwyn – that's it, as he stands tall to his full 5 feet 9 3/4 inches; he seems marginally taller. He is not a man to be crossed and it might have been better if she had been content to warm Julius's bed and dream up new tricks to titillate his jaded sex drive. That is probably her level, she cannot help thinking at moments like this, when she has jumped off the high board and is not at all sure that there is water in the pool.

"So good to see you, Sir Godwyn." An even more obsequious Spencer Perceval pumps Sir Godwyn's free hand enthusiastically. "You know Rosalie Murray of course."

"Indeed."

"And Jack Bellingham?"

"I have not had that pleasure." The merest twitch of tinder dry lips. Sir Godwyn's hand is resting on Nina's shoulder as if it is the most natural gesture in the world. She doesn't move a muscle.

"Jack Bellingham... Sir Godwyn Lydate." They incline heads but there is no question of shaking hands. This is a meeting that was inevitable. The brief silence is awkward. Nina thinks it is like two boxers meeting at the weigh-in before the big fight. She is only too well aware of the suggestive pressure of the resting hand.

"Are you going to introduce me to this beautiful lady?" It is Sir Godwyn Lydate who decides to make the first move in what will be a marathon game of many moves. Chess it is not.

"Nina Balatka," Jack replies as noncommittally as he can manage. He would like to slap the intrusive hand away but knows that would not be a good move.

"So pleased to meet you properly, Nina, my dear."

Spencer Perceval makes a throat clearing noise. The leggy redheaded Carrie Brattle is very much in the background and is not being introduced to anybody. She is used to that... Sir Godwyn Lydate knows all about Carrie Brattle, although Carrie Brattle doesn't know that. Jack catches Nina Balatka's eye which is only too willing to be caught.

"We need to be going."

So even the People's hero is intimidated by the man from the shadows. Perhaps more of a threatening character from a Dashiell Hammett novel, thinks Carrie Brattle, whose favourite holiday reading is 'The Maltese Falcon' – although of course no one cares what she thinks, never mind what she reads on holiday.

"That is a pity." The hand squeezes the shoulder and is withdrawn. "I am sure we shall meet again, my dear." Jack is ignored. There goes a pawn only of course it isn't Chess.

Spencer Perceval in his turn is trying to catch Carrie Brattle's eye who is staring fascinated at Sir Godwyn Lydate and, apart from Spencer Perceval, they are all staring at Sir Godwyn with varying degrees of fascination. Spencer Perceval, who does possess a bit of an intrusive personality of his own, is wondering if there is time for a quickie in the dressing room before heading home for a late Sunday lunch in the bosom of his family – roast beef and some of the trimmings.

Sir Godwyn takes possession of Rosalie Murray's elbow which, as elbows go, is probably sexier than most. "We must also be going, my dear."

"Such a pity that poor Camilla stormed off like that," Rosalie cannot resist remarking.

"The poor dear girl is under a lot of strain," Sir Godwyn snaps back. Rosalie thinks she might have been rebuked but sincerely hopes not. It does not do for a Minister of the Crown to be rebuked in public… Sir Godwyn Lydate or no Sir Godwyn Lydate.

Thank Christ they have all pissed off. Spencer is always mentally and physically, not to say emotionally, drained after being in the presence of Sir Godwyn Lydate and whatever woman of the moment he has in tow. Spencer would not have thought that the always and forever up for it Rosalie Murray was Sir Godwyn's cup of tea. Meeting her again has reminded Spencer of the minor indiscretion during the BBC midsummer party for MPs. He has had worse shags, although the ladies' toilets is not the most comfortable seat of Eros. Talking of shags, he is only too well aware of Carrie Brattle who, with a suggestive arse wiggle, green legged and green eyed, has disappeared through the door of Spencer's dressing room.

He really is a stupid sod just to get in her knickers allowing silly Carrie to believe he would leave his wife and kids. He has tried to stop it… but… well but. She is starting to get possessive, for Christ's sake, and doesn't seem to understand that there is no possession involved. He really should go straight home because he sees little enough of the wife and lovely daughters – so he must count to ten and then leave – at eight he opens the dressing room door and slips inside. There are a few nods and winks amongst the Crew… he's a one is our Spencer… one of these days… mark my words… one of these days.

A naked Carrie Brattle is perched on his desk with smooth legs crossed and smooth arms crossed underneath sticky out tits. She beckons with a slim index finger and Spencer moans. Carrie Brattle uncrosses her bare legs and Spencer moans some more. It's just not fair. She opens wide her bare legs as Spencer frantically struggles out of his clothes in double quick time and falls flat on his face.

Sunday 15th October 2.07pm

Emily Rowley has at least changed her baggy knickers and had a shower and the smell of urine is now only an accompaniment in a minor key. She is still at an impasse with ball cupping Cat woman, who has become a cloaked shade behind the dominance of Window man and she was never that. Emily desperately needs to conjure the flesh and blood woman in her own unique image to anchor the more than flesh and blood Window man…she has never been so focused in her life.

This is the Garden of Eden at the moment of the Fall. This is Adam and Eve with knobs on. This is going to be the beginning of all things – fuck off, Charles Darwin – fuck off the Big Bang. This is where it all started. And on the seventh day the Lord was cheesed off and rested from his labours.

She has not prayed since she was a little girl but she prays now, closes her eyes and puts the palms of her hands tight together. She doesn't think to kneel because she never kneeled as a little girl. "Please God. Please God or whatever is out there. If you are out there please please help me. Please God. Please God. Please."

The following surge of eerie silence is disturbed by a knocking at the door. She ignores it. Then more insistent knocking and a rattling of the loose door handle. Fucking typical. Just when she's attempting to commune with the Almighty that loser Louis Trevelyan reappears. Fucking typical.

"Fuck off." Her voice most certainly carries.

"Emily?" A muffled woman's voice. So not Louis the loser then. It might be an Angel. You can but hope. The muffled woman's voice again. "It's Nina." An Angel called Nina? "Nina from the Gallery."

The varnish peeling door is squeakily opened just far enough to reveal the flat green eyes like fake emeralds of a child's necklace, set in the pinched paint blotted face of the artist Emily Rowley. She recognises Nina who is most definitely not an Angel and there is a man. The links in her brain have become frazzled. "What do you want?" The voice hardly carries at all.

"Can we come in, Emily?" The slight Polish accent more pronounced with nerves. There is so much at stake. "This is Jack Bellingham who loves your paintings." For Nina everything depends on this axis moment.

Emily Rowley stares hard at the Jack man. The name is vaguely familiar and the way the man is standing and staring is more than vaguely familiar – the distinctive shape of the face. She opens the door wider on a rasping squeal, which is worse since Louis the loser kicked it shut yesterday. He really has temper issues, that particular loser.

Emily Rowley is standing there magnificently uncaring in the change of baggy knickers and a see-through halter top – the outdated revolutionary logo on the top has long since worn away. She stares into the oddly colourless eyes that stare back. "Fuck. It's you." She is finding it hard to unfrazzle the links in her brain. "It is you?"

He nods his head and Emily Rowley literally launches herself into his arms and wraps her bare legs round his body. The Exhibition pen is dashed from his hand as he holds on tight to the girl who in fairness doesn't weigh a lot.

Nina Balatka is rarely at a loss for words. In this moment, as a spectator of this tableaux of the hackneyed theme of wartime lovers reunited, she is most definitely at a loss for words. He had been listed amongst the missing.

"Matchstick girl." Jack holds on tight. "You need fattening up, matchstick girl."

Emily Rowley laughs in his face and the cigaretty breath is hot to the touch. "Cheeky sod." And she kisses hungrily on his themed mouth – it is not exactly a lover's kiss but then this is Emily Rowley. Then he lets go and she leads him by the hand into the attic space like a medieval Queen with the Royal favourite of the moment; which is ridiculous but there it is.

Nina Balatka closes the warped door with difficulty and follows. She needs to catch up here.

Matchstick girl and Window man are facing each other and holding both hands and Emily's smile is beatific. She is too thin and the long legs on the cusp of spindly and no thighs to speak of, the face with the prominent nose verging on gaunt. The auburn hair lanky and unkempt and the visible tits on the small side but not the nipples. She is as tall as Jack which makes everything more apparent.

Jack is momentarily riven with a terrible shattering connection both spiritual and physical that he will do his best to put on one side. The muggy cigarette smokey hint of urine attic space makes his sensitive nose twitch. The space is dominated by the colourful canvases. She squeezes his hands. "You know who you are, don't you?" She whispers. "You are Adam." And so there can be no misunderstanding: "The first man." Then she lets go his hands and pitter pats on grubby bare feet across the attic space to take up a battered sketch pad, which earlier had been tossed on the floor in disgust.

Nina Balatka looks around in bafflement. The colourful images are definitely a version of Jack. The circumcised weapon cannot be that out of proportion in real life. Surely? Anyway. How could Emily know? They have never met.

Emily has rooted out a stumpy pencil stub and with shining green eyes, seeming as real as they ever will, she studies the one and only Window man made flesh and blood. She also studies Art gallery woman, who is now standing by his side as if she has some sort of claim. She is not Cat woman but she will most certainly do at a pinch – after all she is only Eve. Emily points the stub of the pencil. "You are Eve." And so there can be no misunderstanding: "The first woman." Emily is now no longer remotely considering taking yet another unsuccessful overdose. She points the pencil stub at Jack. "Take your clothes off."

"I beg your pardon?" His mother was a stickler for politeness. She will probably be saying please and thank you to the other inhabitants of the circle of Dante's Inferno reserved for female Gorgons. Matchstick girl is glaring fiercer than the fierce hug and is pointing the pencil stub at Jack like a primed weapon. It doesn't look ridiculous and Nina is impressed… not at all discomfited… just impressed.

"Take your fucking clothes off." Jack screws up his mouth in that habitual mew that his sister copied as a child, to further annoy their mother, and now does so from long habit. Nina Balatka glances from famous Jack to paint blotched girl, who has the looks of an underfed Amazon warrior smelling a blood sacrifice from a thousand paces. Life is cheap… life is hard in the Amazonian jungle. If Nina was Jack she would take her, or rather his, fucking clothes off. The tall thin girl in the change of baggy knickers, who is shaking with emotion, walks up to the man and stands eyeball to eyeball. It is a sight well worth writing down. Nina Balatka believes wrongly that she is intruding.

"I need you to take your clothes off." A most reasonable everyday request in a quiet determined voice, which is quite shocking in its common or garden tone. "Please." That's better. "Let's put it this way." She emphasises with the pencil stub close enough to poke out an eye. Nina Balatka winces. "I intend to immortalise your rotting body and your even more rotting soul for all eternity." A most meaningful pause." Not to mention your rotting organ of reproduction."

"There is no answer to that."

"No there is not." Emily edges away and watches like the eternal watcher on the shore, as Jack takes off and neatly folds the designer clothes – his mother always insisted on clothes being neatly folded. Then Emily studies the naked man with intense concentration that has nothing erotic about it – well – almost nothing. Nina Balatka hardly dares breathe as Emily Rowley forms an unbroken soldiery square with her paint splattered hands and studies the eternal rotting man. Nina Balatka cannot stop herself glancing sideways at the eternal rotting organ of reproduction.

"What do you see, Window man?" Emily could be talking to a child through the painterly soldiers holding the square at Waterloo.

"A matchstick girl and a matchstick boy."

"What are they doing?"

"Necking."

"Is that giving you a hard on?"

"No."

"What is giving you a hard on?"

Nina Balatka holds the sideways glance and could not look away if her life depended on it.

"The naked woman coming up behind me."

"You know what she wants?"

"Yes."

"You can smell her sex?"

"Yes."

Nina Balatka does look away and appears startled. In these few seconds she realises that Emily Rowley, doing her unique take on artistic insanity, is now very much staring at Nina with those flat green eyes.

"Take off your clothes."

"What!" Nina shakes her head in bewilderment. She actually says vat. She never says vat any more. Her mother had slapped her face every time she said vat. The tall gangly artist is now so in her face she has no face.

"Take off your fucking clothes."

Nina Balatka opens and closes her mouth.

"You are the cupper of the balls." Emily emphasises each word. The tone every day reasonable once more. Scary. Really scary. "You have been daytime fucking, you rich cunt, and are about to fuck some more."

Nina takes a pace back to be able to breathe properly but Emily takes a step forward. Now the stub of the pencil could put out one or both of Nina Balatka's eyes.

"You are a rich cunt." If only. Nina Balatka wisely keeps quiet. The flat green eyes are boring, there is no other word for it, boring into her skull. "Rich cunts fuck in the afternoon." Charles Darwin himself could not have put it more succinctly.

Nina Balatka wishes that she didn't find this off the wall Pantomime more than somewhat arousing. There is part of her that always wants to be able to please. It is a weakness. There is the beginning of wisdom then there is the end of wisdom. She begins to undress, and an obeyed Emily Rowley seats herself on the rarely if ever made bed, pencil stub poised over the curling at the edges sketch pad. This time no one has lost an eye.

"Hurry up for fuck's sake it's not a fucking striptease," Emily blurts out.

Nina Balatka hurries up and, naked, kicks the white knickers away in a tiny act of defiance that she knows is pathetic, like all her tiny acts of defiance. Jack is glancing sideways and she is glancing sideways at Jack. She is pleased to see that he is also more than somewhat aroused and that Emily's painterly rendition is pretty damned accurate.

"Now come up to him from the left side." It could be pretended that these are rehearsals for an Edinburgh Festival fringe offbeat play. Nina wishes it wasn't so draughty in the rehearsal room because goosebumps are not the least bit erotic.

"Now rub against his thigh and lick his shoulder." The pencil stub is madly criss-crossing the page of the curled at the edges sketch pad. Nina is acutely aware of his buttocks tensing against her cushioning belly. Jack in his turn is acutely aware of the pubic hair itching over his bare skin. Much hairier than the real thing, although he supposes that Emily Rowley has decreed that this is now the real thing.

Despite the obvious distractions they are both fascinated by the quicksilver movements of Emily Rowley's manic sketching. She is on the Embankment arguing with matchstick man; the People's hero is at the Savoy Hotel window looking down, the naked rich cunt at his shoulder. Emily is not to know, nor does she care, that he is a past master in the world of skewed imaginations.

"Cup his balls." Nina Balatka hesitates. She is aware of Emily Rowley opening her mouth and inhaling a deep breath, and so Nina cups his balls. The cupping is tentative and almost apologetic. She can hardly be blamed.

"Take fucking ownership," Emily Rowley barks and so Nina Balatka squeezes and caresses. The resultant moan that bubbles his lips is only to be expected.

"Bite his shoulder." Nina bites his shoulder.

"For fuck's sake!" His eyes flare open in shocked surprise and he is very much back in the here and now. Emily Rowley is frantically sketching in a nether world of her own creation. All she needs is a crown of lighted candles in the manner of Goya. She jumps to her bare feet and comes odourly close to observe Nina Balatka squeezing and caressing for all she is worth. She has most definitely taken ownership.

Emily comes closer and hesitantly touches bits and pieces of the living twosome as if almost afraid the mirage might disappear in a puff of smoke from the Genie's lamp. She fingertip follows the generous curve of a breast and touches a hard nipple and fleetingly strokes the standing cock. Then she stands back to admire the composition. "Stop now, cupper woman." She is not a bit like a cat.

I have a proper name, thinks Nina Balatka, who nevertheless stands obediently naked next to the naked man. They are both trapped under the narrow tunnel vision gaze of Emily Rowley. Nina Balatka has never felt so vulnerable in her life and that is saying something. She takes hold of Jack's near hand and she is so glad that he squeezes. He is acutely aware of the hot hand and of the hard on falling away. Nina Balatka is staring at her own painted toes; toenails are usually hidden but fingernails are not. She does not look at Jack's feet.

As if listening to an inner voice Emily Rowley sagely nods her head and pushes a wedge of unkempt hair away from the contemplative flat green eyes. "Right." She turns away. "You can both get dressed and fuck off." A dramatic pause as she poses with arm outstretched. "I have Immortal longings on me." Cleopatra she is not.

Jack turns his head and looks down at a naked Nina Balatka who appears smaller and less physically intimidating without clothes, and uncharacteristically vulnerable, as she stands obediently staring at Emily Rowley, who is muttering to herself and, discarding a well-used paintbrush, selects another one.

Nina turns a head coned by slightly dishevelled reddish-blonde hair and boldly meets his gaze. They are not quite touching thighs but still holding hands, like naughty children who have been caught out playing naughty children's touching games in the garden shed out of sight of the grown-ups. One of the naughty children has knocked over a spade and they are holding their breaths, wondering how quickly they can get dressed.

Emily Rowley is now splashing colour on the partly finished canvas and is apparently oblivious to everything else. Especially to the man and the woman awkwardly retrieving clothes and trying not to get in each other's way. The artist is only dimly aware of the door closing with rasping difficulty and is humming a tuneless tune as she rapidly paints; a cigarette droops from her mouth.

Sunday 15th October 2.59pm

Spencer Perceval has parked a last year's top of the range maroon Range Rover, sporting a just about personalised number plate, round the corner from his imposing Islington residence that was a wedding gift from his redoubtable father-in-law.

He is gripping the leather steering wheel and staring bog eyed out of the streaky windscreen at nothing in particular; he is not a man for overmuch introspection. He opens the driver's door and spews and spits into the neat and tidy gutter and then he bangs his forehead against the steering wheel. His life is unravelling even more than usual and at a speed of knots.

He had meant to go home and had wanted to go home. Instead they had frantically copulated on the floor of the dressing room. Later he had bent a naked Carrie Brattle over the desk and taken her roughly from behind, slapping the lovely arse and the tasteful devil tattoo, as she begged for it harder and harder. The splattering orgasm tipping him over the edge of semi-gratuitous semi violence. She had fought back with nothing semi about it and he is acutely aware of the bruises.

"Jesus Christ." He moans aloud. "Jesus fucking Christ." He wishes to God he could turn the clock back two months six days and eleven or so hours and not practise his infallible seduction technique on the lovely, demure, newly appointed Production assistant with the sticky out tits. She, it later turned out, was only too willing to be infallibly seduced and turned out to be not the least bit demure. Only the sticky out tits proving genuine.

He bangs his forehead against the steering wheel and it fucking hurts. It has always been a perk of being a reasonably famous Political Interviewer to poke the newly appointed female Production assistant. A straightforward poke or three... that's all. A rite of passage. Tell that to Carrie fucking Brattle.

The salty real tears are meandering down his boozy cheeks and he can taste every last one. He has to think. He has to think and stay calm. He will shout a greeting and sneak upstairs for a shower and wash the stink of guilt away. Then, later than usual, Sunday lunch in the bosom of his family. As it should be. As it must be. He is never certain if he is more scared of Sir Godwyn Lydate or of his redoubtable father-in-law. It is a close-run thing.

"Jesus fucking Christ." He is gut sobbing sort of for real and he must compose himself before making the gut wrenching phone call. He has no choice. With a crisply laundered initialled handkerchief, which was a birthday gift from his eldest daughter, he scrubs his red rimmed eyes and lustily blows his nose. "Get a fucking grip." He shouts out loud and then remembers to close the car door. He can just about admit to himself at times like this that he is a vain and venal creature. He is sorry… so very sorry. It will never happen again….never….never.

He taps in the number at the second attempt. "Please answer. Please fucking answer. Please. Please." The call is answered on the sixth ring.

"Is that you?" He listens. "Yes it is important." A slight hint of pique. He doesn't have to pretend to be a tragic fool; Shakespeare would have penned him an occasional short speech to raise a few hoots and jeers from the groundlings. He stifles a sob. "I need your help." He listens for a few more precious seconds. "I know. Sorry." He listens some more and swallows some snot and clears his throat. "You remember that very attractive Production assistant on the Show?" Of course he will remember… probably knows her shoe size and the brand of razor she uses to shave her fanny every other day; probably knows she likes to be watched shaving her fanny. He moans at the memory and listens, staring bleary eyed out of the windscreen. He is grateful the street is posh enough to be deserted at this hour on a Sunday. "Yes the one with the sticky out tits." Bastard. "She told me today that she is pregnant." He listens some more and stares some more. "Of course it's mine." The voice doesn't quite rise to indignant – he hadn't thought of that. After all she is a horny little bitch.

"She wants me to leave Sarah." A moth eaten bird of some kind lands on the bonnet and squawks annoyingly and shits. Spencer bangs on the windscreen and it flies away with much beady eyed squawking. Thankfully he doesn't believe in omens, and has more than enough on his plate as it is. "Of course I don't but she threatened to tell."

Less than an hour ago the horny, possibly two timing, little bitch, after the taking from behind and the exchange of slaps, had perched naked on his naked lap and very much threatened that, if he didn't do the right thing, she would tell his wife and then the Press. She used to be almost engaged to someone who is a journalist on the Daily Express. Then, God help him, they had done it again with her on his lap and he has a fucking semi hard on just thinking about it. He listens a lot more and swallows a lot more snot and nods his head although there is no one to see. Except there is someone to see, a pinched, pale young girl's pretty face looking out of the window of a third floor apartment of the three-storey Victorian residence on the other side of the street. Then a man's face and the pale faced young pretty girl turns reluctantly away.

"Oh! Jesus thank you. Thank you. I owe you big time."

He ends the call and the mobile immediately buzzes. He checks the caller and doesn't answer. She really is the pits.

Sir Godwyn Lydate ends the call and twitches tinder dry lips.

"Anyone I know?" Asks the too nosy for her own good Rosalie Murray, who is fragrantly sipping ruby red Burgundy at Sir Godwyn's kitchen table. She will have to be taught her place and he will look forward to that. He doesn't reply. "Trouble?"

"A little local difficulty, my dear."

Rosalie Murray smiles archly. It is a smile she has almost perfected in front of the bathroom mirror and, certain of her allure, she is impatient to move things along and so puts down the glass and unbuttons her blouse.

Sunday 15th October 3.23pm

"You have to be fucking joking."

It has to be said that Amelia Sedley is not in a good mood. Jack is not answering his cell phone. After this morning's marathon shagathon she had flushed the medication down the fucking toilet in a superb gesture of the moment. The cameras should have been rolling. The cameras were not rolling.

Now she is edgy. Very very edgy.

The extremely pretty Personal assistant Person, who Amelia supposes has drawn the short straw, shakes her head but not too much and stands to attention as if about to salute. She doesn't look as if she ever cracks a smile and has a too earnest looking stare that could well be as disquieting, as she is disquietingly pretty, nay beautiful. Amelia Sedley doesn't notice.

"Where is she?"

"In Reception."

"You are sure it's not some fucking confidence trick?" Amelia Sedley knows only too well that the world is full of nutters and weirdos. She has come across more than her fair share. It had better not be one of those is the subtext in very big letters. The too earnest staring disquietingly pretty, nay beautiful, girl does not seem to be at all fazed. Amelia Sedley doesn't notice.

"She has his eyes." Lucy Snowe has daydreamed about those same eyes drinking in her own wanton nakedness. She has rehearsed wanton nakedness for when the time is right, and is quite good at it now. She will know when the time is right because it will be in the stars that are her brothers and her sisters.

Amelia Sedley closes her own eyes and attempts some joined up unmedicated thinking. Since running away from home at the tender age of fourteen she has inevitably used sex as a potent weapon. Always the nuclear option with no survivors. It has almost come to define, in her own eyes, the stunning beauty that can hold a man or a woman in thrall, if she so chooses, in thrall in the moment at least. The idiots call it sex addiction but it is probably more self-addiction. As long as men or women want to clamber all over her body she will never grow old as others grow old.

Lucy Snowe wishes with all her heart that she could be this woman at the absolute cusp of her beauty. Perhaps she can. Perhaps she will.

Amelia Sedley all at once opens her eyes. They could well be mistaken for exquisite stained glass windows on her soul. Everyone and everybody are replaceable.

"Send her up."

Lucy Snowe does not at all mind being Royally dismissed in the manner of Marie Antoinette in her pomp because one day all of this will be hers. She doesn't know that she has been aping Amelia Sedley by flushing her own medication down the toilet.

Amelia Sedley, who, if her life depended on it, would not be able to recall Lucy Snowe's face in a crowd, studies her own image in the Louis Quinzish wall mirror which is slightly askew. She will get one of her People to straighten the damn thing.

The primrose blue above the knee dress is perfectly sculpted to the perfected figure and sculpted to the perfected tits which, despite rumours to the contrary, are almost all her own…the nipples of course are another matter…nipples that are utterly compelling. She smiles and the image smiles and they are one and the same – the woman and the image. She sticks out her tongue and the image sticks out its tongue. They can all fuck off they both agree and she winks at the image and the image winks back.

There is a knock at the door and for once there are no shades of diffidence. Amelia Sedley smooths the shaped dress over perfected thighs and then raises the hem and jealously admires the slim legs in the mirror as if they belong to someone else.

"Come." She drops the hem of the dress.

Through the slightly askew mirror she watches the door open and the woman enter the room and the door closes as if by magic. Lucy Snowe is listening at the closed door.

As a disturbed small child Amelia Sedley had wished she could be sucked into the World behind mirrors because it had to be a better world. She is not to know or care that Lucy Snowe had wished the same thing so that she could scratch goody-goody Alice in Wonderland's eyes out.

"You are his sister?"

The sister gazes at this most beautiful of apparitions of the actual Amelia Sedley. It is hard to believe it has all been so easy. The apparition walks towards Marion Fay and takes hold of her two hands as if – well – as if. The heady perfume kidnaps the senses and there is not enough money in the world behind mirrors, or in any other world, to pay the ransom.

"You have his eyes." There is an inflection in her tone as if they are speaking about their loss. Possibly it is wartime and Atlanta is burning. "The shape of his face." Marion Fay remembers the scene from 'Gone with the wind'. He really will have to find an alternative to the war time theme.

"Luckily not his ears."

The spell, such as it was, is broken and their pin headed laughter mingles quite minglingly. There are depths in this sister person and Amelia Sedley borrows depths, as some people borrow library books and don't give them back.

"Can I get you a drink?" She squeezes hands. The womenfolk of the Southern States must carry on for the sake of the fatherless children. "Coffee? Tea? Or something stronger?"

"Something stronger."

"A girl after my own heart."

This time the laughter is more corrosive, but mingles nonetheless, and they can already ape being bosom friends. Lucy Snowe hears the laughter and wishes she could laugh like that, knowing that his oddly colourless eyes have seen her wantonly naked. She will practise that corrosive laughter. The wantonly naked is coming along nicely.

"What are you doing, Snowe?" Asks one of the People.

"Listening at the door." And she corrosively laughs. It definitely needs working on.

Sunday 15th October 3.38pm

Within a short stroll of the claustrophobic smoky attic space, Jack and Nina take refuge in a seen better days cafe in a side street that could easily be missed, and often is missed. They share an overwhelming need to get out of the open air which has become oppressively expansive. There is just too much sky to be imagined behind the clouds.

By tacit agreement they order hot sweet tea and, for some unaccountable reason, sticky buns. There are no other customers at this time on a Sunday afternoon and Jack pays what seems an exorbitant amount without demur. They take the table farthest from the steamed up window.

"So our rotting flesh is to be immortalised."

"Apparently so."

"You are Cupper woman."

"And you are Window man."

"I was always Window man." There is no answer to that.

They sip hot sweet tea and both appear enmeshed in a gossamer spidery veil of their own musings. That is Jack's take anyway. He is finding it impossible to read the woman who appears genuinely stunned by what has occurred. He is not aware that she does not feel able to ask about the original ball cupper aka Cat woman.

The middle aged, pot bellied, disgracefully balding man behind the counter is, with his good eye, eyeing up the lovely bit of stuff. She reminds him of someone. Although these days most bits of stuff, lovely or otherwise, remind him of someone. The Nancy Geezer sipping his tea like a puff doesn't remind him of anyone.

Nina decides to advance from another angle.

"Amelia Sedley is very beautiful."

Jack sips hot sweet tea and contorts a considered face, whilst gazing at the high cheek boned features from out of his sister's eyes. "You are very beautiful."

"Not in the same way."

"No. Not in the same way."

There is something that neither of them can get hold of in all this, an after with no before which is strangely disconcerting. Nina Balatka sips hot sweet tea and contorts a considered face in her turn; considered moulds her square features rather better. "I will not see my boyfriend again." Not that she has a choice.

"What about the Gallery? The Chelsea Harbour apartment?"

"He has to be careful." With unpainted fingernails she traces ingrained Berlin Olympics circled coffee stains on the scratched Formica table top. "There are things I know." She taps the fingernails... a hollow sound. "Bad things."

The perpetually middle aged man with the disgraceful comb over is trying to overhear but their voices are several octaves too low. His hearing is not what it was. Nothing wrong with his eyesight though – well, at least the eyesight of his good eye. She is hot stuff all right in a foreign sort of way. Nothing wrong with that... a Russky his guess. She has taken hold of the Nancy geezer's hand – lucky bastard. He has heard that these gold digging Russky tarts are real goers. A good job he is behind the counter, hiding the bulge in his trousers.

"What shall we do now?" She whispers.

"I don't really know." He realises this sounds weak. "You know, Nina, the last few days have been unbelievable." She quite naturally strokes his free hand and leans closer. "And frightening." He adds. She has an urge to take him in her arms and make soothing noises. The last time she followed up these feelings it did not end well.

The man behind the counter is polishing the gritty surface and trying to cop a look at the Russky tart's cleavage. Pretty damned spectacular.

"Do you want to come back to my apartment?"

A wan smile. The Exhibition pen is running true to form.

"Do you, Jack?"

"Yes."

"Let's go then."

The man behind the counter watches them leave hand in hand. "Great arse." He murmurs aloud. They have not touched the sticky buns and he rubs his hands at the extra profit.

With the sticky buns safely back under the plastic cover and the dead fly flicked away, he hangs up the sun faded closed sign and bolts the door and limps rapidly to the rear of the premises. The illegal Polak tart is washing-up. Not a looker like Sarah Newton and a bit weighty but willing enough, and knows on which side her bread is buttered. She looks over her shoulder to see he is unzipping his trousers over the bulge. It is the false eye that holds her squinting gaze. He is always so impatient. Her husband was always impatient and he had two good eyes. "Upstairs now."

She rapidly dries her hands on the grubby tea towel and follows up the stairs, unbuttoning her dress as she climbs.

Sunday 15th October 3.58pm

A for the time being much chastened Spencer Perceval has turned off his mobile phone. He doesn't know what possessed him to give that, probably two timing, Carrie Brattle the number in the first place. He was bewitched… that's it. They used to burn witches, didn't they?

"You seem preoccupied." Although his wife is still only just this side of drop-dead gorgeous and he isn't embarrassed to take her places, she is noticeably putting on weight. She comes to sit heavily on his lap. He wonders if she does it on purpose. After the more subdued than usual Sunday lunch the girls have gone to their rooms. A pinched, pale-faced Frances, their fifteen year old eldest daughter, had rushed home a few minutes after Spencer. She claimed she had been at a friend's house and had lost track of the time. She was just grateful she wasn't interrogated.

Spencer's lunch had been made up mostly of red wine and now he is drinking neat whisky. Sarah prises the tumbler out of his drowning man's grasp and steals a generous slurp and then another one, as she always likes to share. He takes back the whisky. There is no reason he should feel so guilty. Good Lord, he has been told in strictest confidence that his neighbour, Felix Spearman, is knocking off a fifteen year old schoolgirl, for Christ's sake.

"I was thinking about today's Show." He replies and not that Show either. He finishes the whisky in a hurry.

"You were brilliant as usual." She doesn't call him darling anymore and ruffles the slicked back hair because she knows he hates that.

"What do you think about the daft cow walking off set?" He asks, smoothing down his hair, thinking that she likes to believe that he values her opinion. He could not be more wrong.

"The killer chap was making her look stupid." Another annoying hair ruffle for luck. "And that man eater Rosalie Murray was for once winning on points." Spencer shuffles uneasily. There is no way Sarah can know, they were only gone ten minutes and Sarah was deep in conversation with that tosser of a Foreign Secretary, George Meredith.

Sarah Perceval smiles to herself. Her darling husband doesn't know that she opened the unlocked toilet cubicle door and caught more than a glimpse of a naked female backside, a bit too shapely for Sarah's liking, bouncing up and down just like that. She couldn't see the man's face but she recognised the bruises mapped on his visible bare shins where she had kicked him earlier. And of course the unmistakeable selfish tenor of the deep seated groans as he approached the point of anti-climax. She almost felt sorry for the bouncing slag.

Neither does the once upon a time darling have any idea that, two minutes later, his just this side of drop dead gorgeous wife had entered the next but one cubicle, hand in hand with an out of breath George Meredith. He had been pestering her whenever they met to go to bed with him. She had coyly resisted but found it flattering. Spotting the no longer darling following Rosalie Murray, that Concise Oxford Dictionary definition of a man eater, in the direction of the toilets had made up her mind on the spot.

Poor George could not believe his luck and, learning from the mistakes of others, they locked the cubicle door. The sex had been surprisingly good considering that the toilet seat was absurdly wonky. So good that it had got a bit too noisy considering. So good in fact that within the week they had made it to an actual bed and several times since, including yesterday. In fact she is getting incredibly horny just thinking about yesterday.

Spencer is not expecting the intrusive tonguey kiss. "The children are occupied." She whisperingly nibbles an ear and in response he pushes her backwards across the sofa. Closing her eyes she tugs up the loose skirt and expertly slips out of flowery knickers that George Meredith would recognise from yesterday. It is a long time since Spencer's wife has been this willing, at least with Spencer.

They are far too preoccupied to realise that their eldest daughter, fifteen year old Frances, is peeping round the door. She had sneaked to the kitchen for a glass of water when she became aware of the unmistakable noises emanating from the lounge. She watches wide eyed as daddy's pale thrusting backside is on full view entrapped by mummy's bare thighs. Frances is surprised because there had been a real atmosphere at lunch. Her mother had been furious that the roast potatoes were yet again ruined. Thank goodness that she, of course, blamed daddy and not Frances. No one dared speak at the table which suited Frances, who could give herself up to thoughts of Felix. Mummy and daddy are very much at it, as her best friend in the whole world, Katie Woodward, calls this sort of thing. Katie has seen her mummy and daddy at it more than once.

Usually when they are drunk which is most of the time. Frances has heard her parents at it before, but has never seen them at it, and it is making her feel a bit funny down there. Unlike Katie she has never allowed a boy actually inside her knickers – only touching on the outside. She has allowed tittie touching because everyone does that, even Mina Lavry who Katie insists is frigid.

Frances is on the pill because of her erratic periods and is seriously considering allowing her much older sort of boyfriend to at least do some proper touching and stuff down there, and then who knows. Today she had stroked his hard cock but not for long. He was very annoyed when she stopped and called her a cock tease, which she didn't think was very nice. But when she burst into tears he had said he was sorry and they made up with some really nice kissing, and she allowed some tittie touching, and had let him kiss her titties and that was very nice. He had sucked her nipples which she was not at all sure about but it was also very nice. She had stroked his hard cock some more, because no way did she want to be a cock tease. Katie Woodward has gone all the way with her much older sort of boyfriend and said it was brilliant. It looks and sounds like mummy is finding it brilliant as well. Frances is glad because her parents have done nothing but argue recently, and when he is home daddy has been sleeping in the spare room. At this moment he is threatening some very rude things indeed. She is not at all not sure she wants Felix threatening those sorts of rude things; it is not very romantic.

A red-faced and embarrassed Frances tiptoes up the stairs to the privacy of her bedroom, locks the door and exhales a deep sigh. If her much older sort of boyfriend was here now she would probably let him go most of the way. That would show Katie Woodward so there, and Frances sticks out her tongue. She efficiently undresses and critically studies her slim naked body in the full-length mirror.

She knows she is pretty with honey blonde hair and pale blue eyes like mummy. Uncle Goddy says that she is as beautiful as her mummy was at this age. He also says that she is a bit too grown up to sit on his knee and to stop wriggling.

She stares narrow eyed at her own slim naked body that is magically becoming more shapely and womanly with each passing day; the titties are really filling out. She ignores the bite mark; it really hurt but he said he was sorry. She turns sideways and knows that her bum looks good in tight jeans. She overheard a boy on the street say she had a great arse, although she finds boys of her own age childish and boring.

She wonders if she ought to attempt to shave down there. Katie shaves down there but then she is very dark.

On arriving home Frances sexted Felix a picture of her titties which he has promised to keep to himself; of course she trusts him implicitly. She knows it is wrong to be going out with someone whose divorce is not yet through, but they love each other so much. The age gap means nothing he has said.

Katie Woodward's much older sort of boyfriend is still married and Frances thinks he is only after one thing, which of course he has now got. But she would never say that to Katie Woodward who would stop being her best friend in the whole world. She has already threatened to make Mina Lavry her best friend in the whole world if Frances chickens out of going the whole way with Felix – although of course Katie doesn't know his name. He has said Frances mustn't tell anyone his name until they are properly together. He had made her swear on the Bible, which she thought was very romantic.

She watches the image in the mirror touching between the slim legs; there is a bruise on a thigh where she was whacked with a hockey stick scoring the winning goal. At this moment she wishes that Felix was here to take care of things down there but as per usual she will have to take care of herself. But not for much longer. Felix has promised they will soon be together... Frances Spearman has a ring to it. She rummages at the bottom of her underwear drawer and takes out the dinky vibrator which she has pinched from mummy's collection of all shapes and sizes, hidden under the underwear in mummy's bedside drawer. She will never miss it. Uncle George is always bringing new ones to make mummy giggle and Frances has heard them at it too.

When she has finished taking care of herself she is going to sext a full frontal picture to Felix. She has never dared do that before... it will be a commitment. She hears her parents banging and clattering up the stairs and their bedroom door slamming. Her father will not be sleeping in the spare room tonight. Conjuring a vision from earlier of Felix's hard cock spurting in her hands, Frances switches on the vibrator.

Sunday 15th October 4.49pm

Marion Fay is well on the way to being pissed and her new best friend in all the world is not far behind. They have both kicked off their shoes and made themselves comfortable on facing Louis Quinzish chaise longues, showing lots of legs to emphasise the girly nature of things. They have no secrets. They are both drinking from bottles of high-end vodka which amuses Amelia Sedley. She was fourteen years old when she last drank vodka from the bottle.

"He's always doing this." Marion Fay concentrates hard on not slurring. There are furrows on her brow; there are no furrows on Amelia Sedley's brow.

"Doing what?" Amelia Sedley cradles the bottle and tries to focus the lovely eyes that have launched several thousand ships. The gods have been too kind and there will be a price to pay for such ambrosial generosity, thinks Marion Fay...she is not sure where that word came from.

"Not answering his mobile."

"Bashtard."

"I'll drink to that." Marion holds up the bottle in a mock toast and they giggle like naughty schoolgirls and glug glug more high-end vodka.

The time is rapidly approaching for sharing intimate secrets, real and imagined, in the dorm after lights out.

"He really is a bashtard." Marion Fay hitches up her skirt and looks down between the quite decent legs. She badly needs new undies. "You know. A real bashtard."

Amelia Sedley is staring intently through the gathering gloom. She wonders if knickers with strategic holes might be the next big thing in the Amelia Sedley branded range of underwear. Then with difficulty she focuses on the blurry face. "A real bashtard?"

"Our mother washn't married."

This time the naughty schoolgirl giggling threatens to get out of hand and it is to be hoped that Matron is not patrolling the corridor. Amelia Sedley spills some high end vodka on the designer dress and doesn't give a fuck…she might get one of her People to lick it off. "That means you're a bashtard ash well." More giggling and a bit of choking and coughing. It is a good job Matron won't admit to going deaf. Lucy Snowe, who is listening at the door, is certainly not the least bit deaf.

After a decent interval Marion holds up her nearly empty vodka bottle. "To dark family secrets." The deepish voice reverberates in the darkening hotel room and Amelia Sedley magnificently shivers. She knows all about dark family secrets.

"Your turn." Marion points the bottle. "Fair doosh." She studies a blurry Amelia Sedley gathering her thoughts most thoughtfully. It reminds Marion of that movie where Amelia played a white lady lawyer in 1930s America fighting to save her innocent Negro husband's life. She kept taking off and putting on ugly horn rimmed spectacles most effectively. Saddo John would know the name of the movie…being well pissed she refuses to think of him as Jack.

"My shtepfather fucked me when I wash jusht fourteen."

Now Marion didn't see that one coming and her jaw literally drops as if the puppet master has momentarily let go of the string. It makes Amelia Sedley giggle and she spills some more high end vodka. Fuck the dress. She will give it to one of her useless fucking People who will probably sell it on eBay. Bashtards.

"You mean he raped you?"

"No." Amelia takes a slurp. "Fucked me."

"Jesush."

"No. My shtepfather." Another fit of giggles and a bit of phlegmy choking from Marion Fay, the giggling a bit rusty.

"The perv was always trying to catch a peep." Another slurp. "Know what I mean?"

Marion noddingly nods knowing exactly what she means. The accent is hard to define.

"Shometimes I let him catch one." Slurp. Slurp. "Then one day I bunked off shchool. The perv worked nightsh so I knew he would be at home." The word home doesn't sit right somehow. Marion Fay looks on from the back row fascinated. "The previoush morning I lishened to him and my mother at it in bed. There had been a lot of moaning and groaning and begging." She pauses and grins mischievously. "I got really turned on." Marion noddingly nods. "I'm getting a bit turned on jusht talking about it."

"Me too."

There is a darkening silence for a few moments that Jack would recognise as verging on pregnant.

"He was watching fucking horsh rashing on the telly." Slurp. She takes a deep breath. "He was a real looshing gambler. Anyway I shtood in front of the telly and shtripped off my school uniform like a proper shtripper. You know bit by bit and humming the tune." A salacious grin that she has perfected in so many movies. "He washn't watching the fucking horsh racing any more when, naked as the day I wash born, I crawled on all foursh towardsh him like the oddsh-on favourite."

Marion Fay would not be able to look away from this other worldly beautiful creature commanding the stage if the Ritz Hotel was burning to the ground. There is a limitless perversion here that probably destroyed the stepfather in the end; the bald coot on the back row of the Vue Cinema at Kirkstall had a narrow escape.

"I washn't a virgin. There been a couple of creepsh at shchool." She slurps and realises the bottle is empty. This realisation makes the words even slurrier. "But the perv wash sho…you know…big." She drops the empty bottle and holds her hands well apart. "I mean really really big."

Marion noddingly nods as Amelia presses her head back against a chaise longue cushion and sighingly sighs. "I still think about it." Another sigh. "My firsht ever proper orgashm."

The silence that follows is almost dreamlike in a contrived way and it is Marion who reluctantly breaks the spell.

"You think he thinksh about it?"

"Every fucking time he shees my image." Yes. Of course he would. "You remember the firsht time you orgashmed on a cock, Marion?"

Even though she is getting being well beyond being well pissed Marion needs to tread carefully. Dark family secrets are dark and secret for a very good reason. They are supposed to be taken to the grave. Or, in fact, several graves. She does not reply.

"Come over here, Marion."

Marion Fay awkwardly swings her quite decent legs to a floor that is remarkably unstable. They appear to be crossing the Tasman Sea in a force ten gale. By now the ship – sorry – room is almost totally dark and appears to be turning on some malevolent axis.

They fumble tumble into each other's arms, in the manner of well pissed naughty schoolgirls, knowing they will have to face Matron in the morning and so might as well be hung for a sheep as a lamb – Lady Rebecca Sharp would be able to advise. Amelia Sedley smells wonderful and Marion Fay smells like an itchy Marion Fay, which is not a problem because Amelia Sedley has no sense of smell; another secret kept from her adoring public.

Sunday 15th October 7.19pm

A second generously filled tumbler of the unaware Julius Verinder's whisky in hand, John to his sister, but Jack to just about everybody else by now, is admiring the group of paintings on the beige emulsioned wall opposite the panoramic picture window. Half a dozen paintings of the naked Nina Balatka with white panties in various strategic positions. He smiles at one in particular where she is wearing the white panties jauntily, as a crown, and smiling somewhat enigmatically, with one hand resting on wide hips and one hand moving to cover the bush between her legs, but not quite reaching in time. Enigmatic is certainly the lead word here. It is the painted on smile that compels. Not quite a come and get me smile… more a come and get me if you think you're up for it and rich enough big boy, and you'd better not be a five minutes wonder, smile.

"You like that one." She slips her arms round his waist and rests a square chin on his shoulder. Even fully clothed it feels good, particularly when Emily Rowley and her primed pencil stub are not in the vicinity.

"You have real talent."

"But not genius, thank the Lord."

"Genius should be kept in a bottle with the lid screwed on tight."

For a few blessed seconds they both quietly contemplate thoughts of the mad girl in the attic who, even as they speak, will be geniusing away for all she is worth. He had never given much thought apropos the mad woman in the attic in Jane Eyre; that was a learned article and a follow up lecture missed. They would have loved the mad girl in the attic theme at the Vladivostok Conference.

"The spaghetti bolognese will be ready soon." She eases the tumbler from between his fingers and swallows a generous gulp of whisky and hands the tumbler back.

"I am ravenous." He doesn't feel it appropriate to say that he could eat a horse, which was a delicacy in post-war Poland.

"We never ate the sticky buns."

She retreats to the kitchen area and he crosses to the spectacular panoramic picture window overlooking the Thames at Chelsea Reach. The myriad lights in the darkness have a distinct fairytale quality and for once he feels relaxed and unthreatened. There have not been many times in his life when there has not been one threat or another… some imaginary… some all too real. "Come and get it." He is meant to smile and so he smiles.

The outrageously out of proportion black marble dining table dominates the open plan kitchen area. She has uncorked a bottle of Julius Verinder's favourite Claret, and the fiendishly subdued lighting really suits the intricately jigsawed Slavic features. She is not a woman to be afraid for no reason.

"To us." Jack holds up his glass.

"From where I come from that is a dangerous toast."

"To danger." They clink glasses and he sips appreciatively. "This is excellent."

"Nothing but the best for Julius Verinder."

"So I see." He really is a quick learner. They eat in relatively companionable silence and both realise that needful silences are something that could well define their relationship, whatever it turns out to be. There is never a right time for counting chickens; a Polish saying that she thinks rather than speaks.

"This is delicious." Not being as adept at needful silences he mumbles with his mouth full. His poor dear mother would have slapped his hand and then stroked it better until that time he retaliated…there were no more slaps after that. They continue eating in a flat bellied silence that is not in the least bit pregnant. Only when the plate is conspicuously empty does Jack lean back in the manner of a Nineteenth Century Bradford Mill owner and take ownership of the glass of Claret. "Where there's muck there's brass. There's been an Arkwright at Arkwright's Mill for a hundred years." A joke phrase that used to amuse his dear poor Mother ad nauseum.

Nineteenth Century Mill Owner proprietorially eyeing up a shapely Mill girl fashion, he watches Nina deftly fork the spaghetti and put just enough in her mouth at any one time. He refills both the wine glasses. … "Yer needn't cum ere wi yer College ways." A pause is as a pause does. "We might need another bottle."

She waits until she has swallowed the food. "There are plenty more where that came from." Which is not a saying from her Polish childhood.

"How long will he let you stay here?" He glances round at the luxurious surroundings and then turns the wine glass in his hand to appreciate the ruby reflections glinting in the subdued lighting. "Particularly when there are no benefits."

Nina pauses with the last forkful of spaghetti held over the Harrods seconds willow patterned china plate. "Believe me there were precious few of those." She executes an assertively self-deprecating gesture with the forkful of spaghetti. Not easy to carry off.

"Like many rich and powerful men it was not the sex with Julius." She swoops down the last mouthful and patiently chews and then sips some wine. "Most of the time he got his excuse for rocks off watching me undress and parade around in just stockings." She licks the sauce off generous lips. "No white panties." She sips more wine and studies Jack over the rim of the wine glass. "For some reason his spoiled rotten daughter hates me with a vengeance." Nina is only too well aware of the reason. The daughter walked in on them on one of the few occasions that parading in stockings led to minimal sex hardly worth the name.

Jack looks profoundly thoughtful. He is still receiving texts from Julia Verinder which he now deletes without reading. Nina thinks that profoundly thoughtful is a look that suits the bleak moorland lay of his features. There is an attractive broodiness that asserts itself when he is not trying to be someone he is not which, unfortunately, is most of the time.

"You do not seem to be a happy man."

"I am happy. Here. Now. With you." He had said the exact same thing to Shirley Keeldar.

"Good." A really square attempt at a giving smile. "To answer your question. Julius is putting pressure on me." She sips more wine. "He will have his next for his eyes only stripper lined up." A derogatory smile. "There are only the paintings and the photograph on the bedside table that are mine." She glances around the bad taste decor. "He can keep all this. It is the Gallery I want." There is tensile steel here. "There are two rooms above where I can live." She can see it all in the swirling wine and he watches fascinated. They are both aware that she is more than the equal of any man that she chooses. She just needs a lucky break. "The last time I saw Julius he took me to an out of the way restaurant and was shocked to see and be seen by two people at another table." She sets down the wine glass. "He warned me never to tell a living soul."

Jack doesn't say anything; he always feels awkward if there is any talk of souls.

"It was that Sir Godwyn Lydate." The steely gaze is utterly compelling. "Who owns that lady Minister."

"Owns?"

"Yes." No hint of a smile, steely or otherwise. "That man owns people body and soul." She purses her lips. "Julius Verinder was mortally afraid of that man."

She takes a generous gulp of wine. "I think I should also be afraid of that man."

After uncorking a second bottle of the excellent Claret they are indelibly settled at one end of a wide expanse of tasteless chocolate coloured sofa, close together but scarcely touching thighs, sipping wine and staring into the simulated flames of the hideous wall mounted gas fire. The coal effect is remarkably real though, reminding Nina of all too meagre childhood hearths in Poland. She wonders if she will ever be able to leave her childhood behind.

"Who was the woman?"

"The Prime Minister's wife."

"Jesus Christ." If he was able to whistle he would whistle.

She turns her head so that she can take in the craggy Victorian broodiness flickering in the dancing flames. She thinks he is probably a man born out of his time...more probably born out of any time. "He makes and breaks people, that man."

"I was annoyed that he was touching your shoulder."

It takes a minute or two to respond as she stares into the coal effect flames. "He wanted me to feel the power."

"And did you?"

"Yes I felt the power." She will not tell Jack that she also felt the sexual voraciousness, so that her nerve ends tingled and her body threatened to let her down. Some things you do not tell. There must be no more talking about such things. She puts down the empty wine glass and takes Jack's glass to make a pair, and gently strokes the craggy face that visibly relaxes under her touch. They are both surprised by the resultant gentle kissing, like two rare butterflies coming together late in the life cycle, in the sun dappled budding of an Indian summer garden. He sucks the end of the Exhibition pen... too fanciful?

"You look bone weary, Jack." Not waiting for an answer, she takes him by the hand and leads him to the sumptuous bedroom – Julius Verinder spends well if oftimes not too wisely.

On the bedside table there is an out of place black and white photograph in a battered metal frame, of a teenage Nina Balatka and an older woman, obviously her mother, and neither of them is smiling. Nina turns the black and white photograph face downwards.

Sunday 15th October – Late evening – the first part.

Sir Godwyn Lydate is very much at ease propped up against several pillows and staring thoughtfully at the shadowy ceiling, with Rosalie Murray drowsily naked in his arms. Lots and lots of entangled bare legs that are a wee bit intrusive if the truth be told. But there it is. Needs as always and forever must, except of course on the rare occasions when they must not. Tomorrow morning he will take care of that stupid boy's little difficulty, and then a visit to the soon to be ennobled Judge Helen Graham is on the list.

He surprises himself by almost wishing it was the plainer Helen Graham drowsily naked in his arms. There is something tantalisingly surprising about that particular lady. There is nothing tantalisingly surprising about Rosalie Murray. Still… she is here and now and in his plans and so he shakes her awake.

"Again?" She mumbles. She might show a little more enthusiasm. Most definitely not a Penny Black. In fact he fears she might turn out to be a common or garden perforated Penny Red, and not a rare plate.

"No, my dear." No merest twitch of dry lips as he knocks the intrusive hand away. "Now pay attention." She pays attention. "We have to discuss the most important thing of all." She keeps paying attention. "You do realise that the Prime Minister is a dead man walking?" It is a phrase he used about the previous Prime Minister and the one before that. He was proved right on both occasions.

The newly minted Cabinet Minister eases away from his clutches and raises herself on her left elbow, staring with the striking grey eyes of a sleek urban fox caught in the headlights too close to the dustbins. Quite decentish firm breasts but there will have to be much less public cleavage from now on. A pity for those in the House of Commons Public Gallery.

"You are in the right place at the right time."

"You are joking?"

"I never joke about such matters."

He studies the startled emotions dancing out of step over the decently put together features. This close there is some visible facial work… not too much… nothing too obtrusive. A clever girl who might be lucky that all her nasty little secrets will remain in his safe keeping. That is if she stays a clever girl, which is not a given… time will tell. He cannot help thinking, not for the first time, that she should have been a Courtesan at the Court of Charles II. She would have been clever enough to get away with such a lot. Not treason though – that might have been her undoing.

She licks her lips that are never ever tinder dry. "Are you saying what I think you are saying?"

He caresses under her chin and works the cutish dimple with a brailed thumb. "That is exactly what I am saying, my dear."

"But…but… but…"

"There are no buts for people like us, my dear."

People like us… she rather likes the sound of that. The out of step startlement has been replaced by something much more tenuous, inevitably spiced with a spark of fear of the unknown. A fear he has never known because the unknown is where he operates.

"The game is afoot, my dear."

Almost of its own volition, her body slithers into his arms and is shaking with the knowledge that everything is within her grasp. All that she has ever dreamed on – her very own bit of Shakespeare. "How will I ever repay you?" There is a tipping point where reality and unreality meet and this is it.

He caresses, he has to admit, a shapely buttock – no boy playing a woman's part here. "I will surely think of something, my dear."

The unknown can be such a gloriously dangerous place and this time he doesn't knock the intrusive hand away.

Sunday 15th October – Late evening – the second part.

The Reverend John Eames is hunched over in the chilled and darkened room, clutching to his chest the battered family Bible that belonged to his late father. Through the window of the eerily silent Vicarage a three-quarter moon is precariously dangling through the bare limbs of the beech trees, clustered like ghostly watchers in the north-east corner of the churchyard, where the newest graves are dug.

There is a funeral tomorrow.

The off key Sunday Evensong had been even more sparsely attended than usual, and is sparser and sparser with each passing week. A Vocation that started with such glittering promise is fizzling out before his once upon a time eyes. A dud rocket if ever there was one.

Rumours are all at once snapping at his heels and they have sharp teeth these rumours. Alice Vavasor's supposedly estranged husband had been in the congregation. He had stared malevolently at the Vicar stumbling through the pathetic Sermon, that most certainly dared not allude to women taken in adultery.

No Alice Vavasor in the congregation and no Mary Thorne. There had been whispers… lots of whispers. The giggling teenagers at the back of the church were not giggling for once and, as omens go, that was pretty damning. The deaf old lady in the front pew had avoided eye contact. She never avoids eye contact.

It is as though his wife leaving has pulled the stopper out of the bottle and something rotten is set loose. Ye gods… his wife pregnant by another man. A blow up doll would not have got pregnant by another man.

The silence in the house is beyond oppressive. The fall of the house of Eames – such as it was – the silence crushing his spirit – such as it is. If he were a braver man he would contemplate suicide. There are plenty of his wife's sleeping pills upstairs and he even wonders if she left them behind on purpose.

The Chief Sidesman had cornered him as he sneaked away from the Service and had demanded there must be an urgent meeting of the Church Wardens… Monday morning at the Vicarage. The Verger had looked on po-faced. Alice Vavasor's supposedly estranged husband had spat on the ground and then, for some inexplicable reason, looked searchingly towards the Vicarage.

Alice Vavasor was a mistake, he can see that now. John Eames clutches the dog eared Bible to his chest and for the first time in many years prays out loud. No…unfortunately that is not correct. He had prayed out loud with Bellingham's mother on that awful night. She had taken great comfort as they had knelt together and later, naked in bed, she had whispered into his naked ear that it was like making love with Jesus. A mistake. A big big mistake. He should have passed by on the other side.

"Please God. Help me. I need help. Father. Father. Eternal Father."

He closes his eyes to blot out the strung up three-quarter moon mocking at his nothingness made less than nothing. If only he could remember an appropriate psalm.

"Please God. Please Almighty God." The tears are meandering down his puffy cheeks and he is mortally afraid. "Please. God of Ages. Help me, a poor sinner." He falls to his knees and is unaware of the tentative knocking at the locked and bolted kitchen door. The handle is rattled and then a faded, pretty young woman's anxiously pale, tear-stained face peers through the grimy window. The house is in total darkness and Mary Thorne slinks reluctantly away.

Monday 16th October 7.17am

A determinedly square faced Nina Balatka is sitting alone at the gross black marble dining table and noisily slurping black coffee. The noisy slurping a residue from an embittered childhood…at least the coffee is real. But she is angry… very angry and there is no nerve strained mother to shout in Nina's face. No mother's lover of the moment to slap her into submission. The reddish blonde hair is tied at her neck in severe business-like fashion. She has efficiently showered and dressed in a loose non-descript grey woollen sweater and skin-tight peppermint green jeans. She is wide awake and clothed in molten rage, still very much aware of the memory of Jack's insistence straining against her cushioning belly, that woke her from the inculpate dream cycle, to a surprisingly pleasurable waking. Taking a deep breath, she knows that she has never been able to string such pleasurable moments together into a work in progress.

The man himself had drifted back into a troubled sleep as she had ever so quietly closed the bedroom door. His mobile phone is placed neatly on the black marble surface and no one would know it had been tampered with. She has read the messages both deleted and undeleted, a skill she mastered to keep one step ahead of the various men friends of one hue or another. The term boyfriend does not adequately cover it.

Nina thinks it might be a weakness, but she has always needed to put a face to her enemies. She stares narrow eyed at a scattering of Constable-like Suffolk clouds visible through the spectacular picture window, but the scattered ill-natured clouds are by no means her enemies as they are the enemies of Lucy Snowe. Life is to choose or be chosen and from now on Nina is determined to choose whether or not to be chosen…in fact whether or not to choose. The Gallery project needs Jack for the moment and so she needs Jack for the moment.

Nina slams down the purloined cheapskate Starbucks coffee mug and some coffee spills. The sharp edged sound echoes like one of her mother's lover of the moment's vicious slaps. She strides to the double entrance doors styled, would you believe, on the entrance doors of a late Fourteenth Century Florentine Basilica.

Speedily she ascends in the private lift to the Penthouse floor. Previously she had ascended only when Julius Verinder rang to order her upstairs like a Chinese takeaway for one…often followed by a Chinese takeaway for one.

Now it is her choice. The lift combination has not been changed because the arrogant fools have, of course, underestimated Nina Balatka's capacity for being her mother's daughter. If her mother had had her choice, she would have slaughtered every single Russian soldier on the Planet, then their wives, then their children, then their mothers after making them watch. Nina Balatka's revenge is on a more manageable scale, but no less pitiless, as one of her mother's lovers of the wrong moment found to his cost.

Within twenty seven seconds she is facing an identical set of mock late Fourteenth Century Florentine Basilica double doors. The bad taste is on an epic scale. One day she will visit Florence and spit on the original doors, but for now she makes do with spitting on these replica doors.

Ignoring the intrusive bell, not yet invented in late Fourteenth Century Florence, Nina Balatka hammers on the Basilica doors like a crippled Penitent at the end of her tether demanding sanctuary… the end of the world is nigh. She hammers… she hammers and there is blood on her knuckles. The plague ravaged eyes forging bloodshot with the terrible nearness of Divine retribution. There are lessons here for Amelia Sedley, the ultimate method actress. Nina Balatka's mother died insane. Nina Balatka's subtler insanity will live and breathe and propagate. One day she will be rich beyond the dreams of avarice.

The left-hand door is wrenched open. This is taking a fucking liberty. The fucking Polak tart will pay for this. The drug pinched, slumber dragged down after a wakeful night features of Julia Verinder do not have time to switch, from preparing a fusillade of foul mouthed invective, to registering shock horror. The crazed harpie grabs a handful of Julia Verinder's loose mined black hair, dragging the only daughter of Julius Verinder, like that out of favour rag doll recovered from the dustbin, across the Genoese marble floor slabs.

This particular rag doll unstitches its mouth to scream in mockery of that other discarded Christmas toy, when it is silenced by two resonating slaps. The hastily thrown on black silk Chinesey robe sags open, to reveal a vulnerable work in progress body, which Nina Balatka now uses as a throne. She lowers and lowers her enraged face to within a few spitting inches of the agonised features. "You listen, Jew bitch." The spittle sprays and the Warsaw Ghetto never happened. "You do not contact Jack Bellingham ever again." Slap. Slap. "Do you understand?" Slap. Slap. "Do you understand?" Slap. Slap.

"Yeeeeeeeees…" She wails.

"Are you pregnant?"

"Nooooooooo…" She wails.

"If you ever contact him again I will…" Nina takes ownership of an exposed breast and squeezes hard. "I promise you." The spittle mid Ocean sprays. "I will cut off your tits." And Julia Verinder Oh so believes the mad Polak bitch, as the mad Polak bitch squeezes and squeezes until the enhanced nipple threatens to explode.

Julia Verinder whimper wails, "It hurts." Then she just wails until the hardest of slaps silences the wail. The rag doll is heading back to the dustbin along with the bead picture making kit and the jigsaw with pieces missing.

Abandoning the wretched specimen of washed-up humanity cowering on the floor, Nina Balatka marches to the partly opened door of the Master bedroom that she knows only too well. She turns and points the barrel of a finger at Julia Verinder. "Don't you dare move, Jew bitch." And then she kicks the bedroom door open. It is a role that perhaps not even Amelia Sedley, directed to within an inch of her life, could play so effectively.

A diminutive Julius Verinder is garden gnome perched on the edge of the vast acreage of bed clutching random bedding to his naked body. Nina Balatka boldly strides across the room and knocks the mobile phone out of the two hands and their frantically shaking fingers and thumbs. There has been far too much shaking to summon Security.

"Get away from me." His voice several octaves too high as, hands on hips, the mad bitch is bending over his clutched body. Her mere physical presence dominating the world that has shrunk to this room and to this bed. "You mad… mad…" He dare not say bitch.

"I would not soil my hands." She spits in his face and he clutches the random bedding tighter and blink blink blinks which only makes it worse. "Now you listen, you greasy Jew pig." The ratcheting accent is more Polish than she would wish, but then she has not felt this murderous since her mother's suicide pact with the last waste of space lover. "I will be out of the apartment by the end of the week." He is goggle eyed watching the working of the lips as if this is an alien creature just landed from an unknown Galaxy. "You will transfer the Gallery into my name."

"No…no…"

"TO-DAY. And you will transfer £50,000 into this account TO-DAY."

She tosses a slip of paper onto the bed. He flinches; it doesn't explode. There are the disturbing intrusive sounds of hysterical sobbing from the next room, where the daughter of half the High street is curled up in the foetal position not daring to move. The Genoese marble is an Icelandic chill to her mottled flesh and, unsurprisingly, no one gives a damn that her teeth are chattering. She is not used to not being given a damn about.

"I have no doubt whatsoever that Sir Godwyn Lydate is only too well aware that you are screwing your own daughter." The mad Polak bitch appears blurred and indistinct as he blinks and blinks on the gobs of spittle blinding his better eye. He dare not let go of the armour plated bedding. "I am sure you do not want the rest of the world to know." She moves closer and he edges away but not nearly far enough. "Do it.TO-DAY!"

He mumbles something remotely incoherent and he can smell the sardonic coffee on her breath. He hates the smell of coffee on someone's breath and he knows that she knows that.

"What did you say, Jew boy?"

"You won't get away with this." He struggles to articulate the words on a strangled indrawn sob.

"TO-DAY! Small dick." The grin is more of a Venetian Carnival mask gone horribly wrong, and is really really scary. She is brandishing a knife. Holy Moses, she is brandishing a knife. Where did that come from? "TO-DAY! Or else it will be no dick."

She marches out of the bedroom at the head of her troops and it is only then that Julius Verinder, who owns half the High Street, is aware that he has pissed himself.

The outer double doors slam and he counts to fifty and only then, and not before, with fingers for thumbs difficulty does he untangle himself from the soiled bedding. He just dare not think about it. Not now and perhaps not ever. He pad pads on bare feet into the living room, sinking to his knees to gather the feverishly shaking body of his only daughter into his arms, which have been drained of whatever muscle power they once possessed.

"There. There. She will pay for this. She will. She must." There is always someone else to pay.

"No! No!" His only daughter – his only child – shrieks and breaks away from the pathetic cushion of his pot belly. She stares appalled into his face and knows him for what she has always striven to believe he is not. "You give the mad Polak bitch what she wants." She pushes him away and the silken robe has fallen away and despite everything he avidly licks his lips. "Now!" She struggles to her knees as if rising from a quicksand, appearing unexpectedly magnificent in a naked Cassandra pose that is anything but a pose. "Do it NOW!" She has the exact same goggle eyes. "Whatever she wants." She grabs a useless arm and shakes him like a hunting dog with its easy prey. "NOW. DO IT!" Shake. Shake. "Just fucking DO IT, you useless wanker."

The useless wanker pad pads on the same bare feet towards the state of the art computer.

Monday 16th October 7.58am

Much against his better judgement Sir Godwyn Lydate has shared a tepid bath with a well scrubbed and rosy cheeked Rosalie Murray and now the striking grey eyes are intently watching across the kitchen table. They share wholemeal toast and percolated coffee of just the right consistency. The pepper pot stands aloof.

"You really think so?" She responds somewhat timidly. He is not fooled.

"Under the circumstances it would be sensible."

She is only too well aware that she does timid responding rather fetchingly, and that it is a look which suits her slightly misaligned features. It is a pose she has struck several times to good effect on camera in the House of Commons.

"Needs must I suppose." She is not at all enthusiastic. "Very well." Not that she has any choice. "You say his wife has walked out?" She adds.

"Apparently she is pregnant by another man."

He pours the dregs of the coffee into his own cup. He does so love the dregs.

"I am lunching with the Archbishop at the Club." Her striking grey eyes never cease their intense watching. "I am sure there will be a suitable Bishopric." The bitterest dregs of the coffee the best of all. "From now on you must be circumspect, my dear." The striking grey eyes appear a trifle disconcerting when they are drinking in words like the proverbial Arab maiden at the Oasis well. "No more drunken fumblings with members of the third estate in broom cupboards."

"It wasn't a broom cupboard."

He lets it pass. "Get Vicar man down to London." All briskness now. Time must be shown to be of the essence. "Today."

"He will have Parish duties." She catches the look that flashes in the hypnotic pale blue eyes. "Of course. Today."

"That's a good girl."

She is not at all sure that it is appropriate to be called a good girl. Not at all sure that it sits well with the dignity of a Minister of State and Privy Counsellor.

Monday 16th October 8.23am

It is a rain damaged misty autumnal morning in the north east corner of Adel churchyard. The Reverend John Eames theatrically shivers as he stares down at the reasonably well kept grave of the awful Bellingham mother. With his weak chest he should have worn a thermal vest.

It had not been all his fault. Probably most of it was not his fault if the truth be known. She led him on. He sees that now. The awful Mother had begged him to let her confess her sins and to be absolved. Not forgiven... but absolved. He had refused. This is the Church of England he had declaimed. There will be no Rome here. No Popery; mimicking the uncompromising liturgical voices of his late father and his late father-in-law.

She had begged on bended knees and hugged his legs. There had been wailing and gnashing of teeth. The Book of Ruth come to life and he had given way and they had knelt and prayed together, gripping hands as he heard the awful confession from beginning to end. It was hard to believe the number of sins weighing down the soul of that most ordinary seeming, Church going, flower arranging woman.

She had confessed in throaty whispers so close to his ear. The all-pervading perfume and the compelling touch of delicate hands. It was all too much to bear and they had embraced to share comfort in the Lord's forgiveness – that was all. To give succour to the torment of souls – that was all. Absolution. It was hard. Too hard. Oh God! Too hard to bear.

Looking back it is almost as if it was deliberate, every word of it, as if she could discern the molten core of his eternal weakness. Almost evil in fact. It all started to go horribly wrong in those moments of that understandable weakness. He can see that now. The compelling touch of the delicate flower arranging hands and the all pervading perfume of perished roses. The mother and, days later, the daughter as the price of her complicit silence. Ye gods. There is nowhere for him to confess. No one to absolve the burden on his soul. Only God in his Infinite mercy.

John Eames looks up to the oppressive sky. He is chilled to the bone and it will serve them all right if he catches pneumonia. They will be sorry then.

He cannot stop himself glancing over to the unmarked grave of Lily Dale which no one visits. The terrible burden of what Marion Fay had spilled out in her drunken ravings to torment him for his weakness. The mother and then the daughter expecting him to absolve such terrible sins.

I am not God, he had pleaded. I am not God.

A shuddering sigh. Anyway it is all over now. The meeting to decide his fate is at nine o'clock this morning in the lonely, deserted, wifeless Vicarage. God knows what he will do or where he will go. Away from this place anyway. Perhaps a monkish retreat shut away from this rotten stinking world, where such unabsolved sins will never see the light of day. Never mind receive absolution, or whatever other word hapless sinners might care to choose to cloak their unforgivable sins.

"Help me, Lord God of Hosts…please help me…please…please."

Last night he had fallen asleep in the chair in his crumpled clothes and clutching the battered Bible. Sweet Jesus what am I to do? The forgotten mobile phone in his pocket trills to a well known hymn tune that used to annoy his wife. Jesus Christ, what now? God in heaven, Leave me alone. Leave me alone.

"Yes." Defensively hunching his stooped shoulders he listens… and he listens… and he listens and then falls to his knees on the soaking wet grass and looks up to the heavens.

Monday 16th October 8.37am

In a frighteningly stapled together voice, Nina Balatka has matter of factly related the recent events in the Penthouse suite.

Jack could never have dreamed up such goings on for his Twenty first Century state of the nation novel. All he has to do is record all of this and call it fiction. The twenty six letters of the alphabet arranged in a proper and suitable order. There must be truth. Surely there must be truth…truth is fiction…fiction is truth, the kind of trite repeated saying that could have been lifted from any one of his lectures on Nineteenth Century literature…take your pick.

"I wish I'd been there." He offers a most conspiratorial smile as she generously butters the ever so slightly burnt toast and passes him a slice. He takes a buttery bite. The narrowed Slavic eyes as ever take it all in and she brushes a strand of reddish blonde hair out of those eyes, which is an unusually feminine gesture for Nina Balatka…a gesture of her mother's.

He sips black coffee and to change the subject says, "What was the word you shouted out this morning in bed?"

She knows exactly which word he means, shouted at the hurried apex of their coming together.

"It is hard to translate."

"Please try." He indulges in another buttery bite.

"It is village Polish." She looks away. "It means something like… my body burns with your need."

"In that one word?"

"Yes."

She takes possession of his buttery hands and licks the buttery fingers one by one – he wonders if she is a butter freak.

"You must teach me village Polish," is his expected response.

"It is a tragic tongue." She entwines the licked fingers with her own fingers. "There has been a brutal history. So many battles lost. So many Conquerors."

"Teach me anyway."

Her only reply is to sadly smile at his misplaced cupidity…there is the chooser and there is the chosen and above all there is the choice at the rainbow's end. As meal tickets go he is more presentable than most.

Monday 16th October 8.59am

The fairytale Princess that is Amelia Sedley snuggles closer to the sleeping woman in a sharing richness of flesh. She cannot resist kissing the tip of what some might say is a prominentish nose and the colourless eyes flicker open. "Not good in the mornings," mumbles Marion Fay and the colourless eyes show puzzlement. She wonders if there has been some dreadful misalignment, which can happen in a fairytale, or it might just be a tantalising dream. She has had a lot of those and will wake up in the familiar bedroom that will never be free of the unmistakable scents of their rotten at the core mother.

She rapidly opens and closes her eyes. No. Cinderella's beautiful face is still on the page, the hot breath spicing Marion's senses with such lovely naked kisses. What a waste all the other mornings have been she might think, if she was the least bit poetic.

Monday 16th October 9.12am

A frowning Sir Godwyn Lydate – and that should be a warning to the unwary – with undisguised distaste studies the bleak frontage of the red pitted brick apartment building. Not the best area of London and not the best building in not the best area of London. Flaking paintwork has always been one of his pet hates, being a reminder of the days when his mother let Lydate Hall go to the dogs.

The smartly uniformed chauffeur is frowning in his turn.

"Wait here, Gilbert. I don't think I will need you in there."

"Very well, Sir Godwyn." A military man to his fingertips, Gilbert touches the peak of his cap. There were never the fringe benefits in the Regiment that there are working for Sir Godwyn. There are the women of course and he gets to hurt more people. What's not to like?

Sir Godwyn flicks immaculately laundered cuffs and adjusts the gold monogrammed cufflinks, as he approaches the higgledy-piggledy display of named bells of different shapes and sizes. It is not difficult to pick out the correct one. He does so worry about that boy and his lack of imagination, as in so much else.

He presses the bell with a disdainful elbow and then waits. He is not good at waiting in such circumstances. There is a distinctive unpleasant odour that he cannot quite place and he is about to lean on the bell again when a sleepy girly voice answers. "Llo…"

"Special delivery from Spencer Perceval."

The door immediately buzzes and with a wry backward glance at the on guard chauffeur, who makes a decent attempt for wry in return, he pushes open the door with a polished brogue. The place of Perceval assignations is on the first floor and so he climbs the stairs. He once got stuck in a lift and it led to certain unfortunate consequences.

He rap raps on the door that has probably never seen better days and tries not to breathe in; he is going to have to think of a suitable punishment for that stupid boy. Sir Godwyn's patience, such as it is, is wafer thin.

An attractive, more ginger in this light, tousled head peeps around the door jamb. She has only opened the door just far enough. Sensible precaution although there is no chain.

"Carrie Brattle?"

She nods and yawns quite fetchingly. She thought it would be flowers or chocolates to say sorry because it usually is flowers or chocolates to say sorry. She is about to rub sleep out of her eyes when the delivery man pushes past the startled girl and closes the door. She is opening and closing her mouth like a dishevelledly attractive female guppy, computing if this is still the bad dream. She clutches the Harrods seconds pink silky dressing gown, a gift from Spencer who had said that nothing was too good for his best girl, to her now very much wide-awake body.

"Don't be alarmed." A soothing Patrician's voice. "You know who I am?"

She stares and nods. He is the man who makes Spencer come out in a rash.

"Excellent." He leads the way down the narrow passageway as if he owns the place and looks into the first room. An unmade bed and a not unpleasant smell. The second room is an untidy kitchen. Then a bathroom… ditto.

At the far end of the gloomy corridor is a square boxy living room with cheap and tasteless furniture by no means expertly put together. Definitely no one else here. The poor girl is apparently being faithful to the faithless little shit. He has lost a wager with himself and is surprised and not a little intrigued.

Sir Godwyn, Christian Martyr fashion, seats himself on the rickety sofa on which Carrie and Spencer had made impromptu love that very first time. The girl clutches the pink silky dressing gown for all she is worth, as the man pat pats the sofa and reassuringly smiles. It is not a frightening smile and if only she wasn't naked beneath the clutched pink silky dressing gown she would not feel at such a disadvantage. She rarely feels at a disadvantage with older men. He has a really nice smile. Carrie is not so burnished at this time in a morning, hair has tumbled over one eye. She dare not let go of the dressing gown which on another morning she had catwalk modelled for Spencer, leading to mad passionate love on this very floor. He had put out his back and had to go to A&E. She had tried not to laugh.

The man pat pats the sofa for a second time… there will not be a third time.

"Sit here, my dear. We have things to discuss."

"Has something happened to Spencer?"

No smile, merely a twitch of the dry lips. "Unfortunately not."

"I need a pee."

He considers for a moment. He is not an unreasonable man. "Very well." And he waves a dismissive hand.

Whilst she is absent he studies the out of place bits and pieces room. An ugly, soul destroying, place of transit. Somewhere cheap and nasty to secrete what used to be called a mistress by his father's generation. It could be a minimalist stage setting for a dispiriting play about the pretence of love and the reality of deceit and betrayal – something Russian perhaps – or quite possibly Swedish. He almost feels sorry for this poor deluded ten a penny pretty girl. Pretty even without make-up and so perhaps five a penny.

A toilet flushes. A tap is turned on... turned off.

The less than a penny pretty girl is standing in the doorway clutching the pink silky dressing gown. There is nowhere to hide. She does wear the on the shortish side dressing gown several sizes too large, as well as it can be worn. Very nice legs and lots of red toes. She is growing on him.

"Can I get dressed?" She really should learn to say please. His mother never said please, or thank you, for that matter. She had the limited vocabulary of girls of her class of that period.

"My time is valuable, my dear. Come here and sit down."

She goes there and sits down, because when this man isn't smiling she knows why he makes Spencer come out in a rash. She cannot remember his name – Sir something or other; somebody very important she knows that. She wants to know what all this is about. Spencer should be here to hold her hand but then Spencer is so rarely here to hold her hand.

"That's better, my dear." Almost as an afterthought he pats a bare revealed knee. He has incredibly soft hands like a doctor. She has always been a sucker for doctors. Spencer's hands are not at all soft, although he had joked that his dream job would be a gynaecologist. At least she thinks he was joking.

"Has young Perceval minor promised he will leave his wife?"

Carrie Brattle nods and nervously licks dry lips. She has not had time to do anything with her face and it is always too shiny first thing in the morning. This time the patting hand lingers on her bare knee. That is the thing with afterthoughts.

"There is no easy way to say this, Carrie, my dear. Can I call you Carrie?"

Carrie Brattle nods.

"Perceval minor was one of my fags at Eton. He was a lying little shit then and he is a lying little shit now." The impunitive hand demands attention. "He will never leave his wife. She is the money, you see, my dear."

"He promised. He promised." The hand is now inevitably accepted. "He said I was the love of his life. He did. He did." She can hear his voice saying it in this very room. She makes a concerted effort to cry. "He promised. He did. He did."

Quite naturally he gathers the gulping for air girl in his arms and strokes her backbone through the silky material. She does smell rather good considering, and the backbone is most backboney; he is trying to remember who it was had a thing about backbones – Ah! Of course.

"There there, my dear."

She is just about sobbing for real now. A girl has her pride. He has experienced enough of these situations to let nature take its course. There are worse things to have in one's arms than an old-fashioned abandoned woman trying to make the best of it. Although perhaps self-deluded might be a more appropriate description.

"Listen to me, Carrie." At his most persuasive, he holds the insistently blubbering girl at arm's length. The dressing gown has fallen open to reveal sticky out breasts. She doesn't care. In a non-threatening gesture that takes the girl by surprise he covers up the sticky out breasts.

"Are you pregnant, Carrie?"

She shakes her head and sniff sniffs defensively. She is not that stupid.

In a similar gesture he brushes the lock of, it has to be said, gingerish hair away from her eye.

"I do not blame you in the least, my dear." She clutches the silky dressing gown, which does seem to have carved out a fairly intrusive role for itself in proceedings, and sweeps a snotty nose with the other hand. He notices the fake designer watch as he hands over an initialled handkerchief. "Blow, my dear."

She blows and then clutches the handkerchief in a balled fist. She had thought about getting pregnant, then decided it was too big a risk to take. She really could not face another abortion.

"That better, my dear?"

She nods her head. He really seems very nice... a real gentleman and such soft hands. She knows in her heart of hearts that he is telling the truth.

"Now listen, Carrie." She listens so listeningly it could be a parody of listening. "I am going to take care of you." The nearest thing to hazel eyes flare in what he takes for surprise. "Your degree was a two-one in Fine Arts."

How does he know that? How can he possibly know that? She doesn't nod.

"My family seat is Lydate Hall in Hertfordshire." That's it. Sir something Lydate. "I need someone to catalogue some valuable paintings." They had been placed in a family trust so that the hell cat Mother could not sell, although she disposed of just about everything else that was of any value. Other paintings have been acquired by Sir Godwyn in more recent times. He takes ownership of the unclutching hand and the balled fist and rests everything quite naturally in the scarcely covered lap. "There might well be a most prestigious book to come out of it, my dear." The fact that he has a financial interest in the Burlington Magazine will ensure that.

She looks down at everything resting naturally in her scarcely covered lap and licks not so dry lips. As a man of voracious appetites he recognises the unmistakeable shadow of voraciousness on those licked lips. She hides it but not too well. The dishevelled frizzy ginger hair is really a quite fetching colour, from the palette of a follower of a follower of Titian perhaps.

"You cannot go back to the BBC. You do see that?" She nods and the nearest things to hazel eyes fill with tears but he is not fooled. "I will arrange that your own apartment is prepared for you at Lydate Hall." The dressing gown has fallen open just about everywhere a dressing gown several sizes too large can fall open.

She thinks she might as well be sitting here naked. "Get dressed and pack your belongings. My chauffeur will drop me at Whitehall and will take you on to Lydate Hall. I will forewarn the Bertrams, the husband and wife who run things for me." Nanny would most definitely tut tut at that job description… and would most definitely tut tut tut at the plural.

Carrie will be only too willing to be persuaded to shed the dressing gown, which is gaping open to reveal both sticky out breasts, not to mention lots of scarcely covered lap. She always wakes up horny.

Spencer Perceval is already dumped in the dustbin of her own particular history where he patently belongs, with the other trash. Stupid stupid boy indeed. The heat of her lap is tempting, and he is tempted, but there must be a consideration of time and place to fully appreciate the run of things. Patience in these matters is more than a virtue and he is already regretting his impetuosity with Rosalie Murray. One must never take one's eye off the ball…Sir Leonard Hutton's advice to Sir Godwyn's Great Uncle Maurice Lydate, when he came in at number ten against the Australians in a Lord's Test match; although Sir Leonard used more industrial language, before hitting the winning runs.

"It will all be for the best, my dear." She is sure of that, and is loath to let go of his doctor's hands that transmit reassuring feelings to a woman who has been unceremoniously dumped.

"Why are you doing this?" Apart from the obvious she doesn't have to say.

"You are a damsel in distress, my dear."

The meagre tears have dried up, otherwise she would smile through them like a brave little left behind sweetheart when the bugle calls…not that Spencer Perceval would ever follow a bugle call.

"Now go and dress." She rises agilely to her feet and he pats the bum tantalisingly shaped through the clinging ersatz material. "My dear." It is a promise and she takes it as such.

The mobile phone buzzes in his jacket pocket to what she takes to be a posh tune, and she pauses in the doorway. Spencer, God rot his guts, fondly called her a nosy cow… amongst other things.

"Yes, Prime Minister."

Carrie Brattle just about manages not to gape. Sir what's it Lydate raises his eyebrows and twitches dry lips. "Quite, Prime Minister."

Once out of the room Carrie Brattle grins and punches the air. She might just turn out to be a lucky cow as well, and sticks out her tongue at the shade of Spencer Perceval, the lying little toad.

Monday 16th October 9.57am

It is all busy busy in the Grande suite at the Savoy Hotel.

"Where are you, Jack?" Shirley Keeldar holds the slim platinum mobile phone to an ear and tap taps the slimmest of gold pens against the gleaming white teeth – money well spent. The piercing electric blue eyes stare off at some far off Galaxy beyond Hubble. "What fucking Gallery?"

Refocusing from several billion miles away, she raises immaculately plucked eyebrows to eyeball Rebecca Sharp, who flick flicks shoulder length hair as she glances up from the flickering tablet on her lap. There is a naughty message from naughty Gil to naughty knickers that Rebecca has answered briefly but naughtily. She knows that as a shared joke he uses her tits as his space saver. She has reluctantly decided not to use his cock as a space saver, because she has learned only too well that one never knows. She has no illusions about Gilbert Markham…or about any man for that matter.

"Never heard of it." Not being in one of her collection of ethereal moods, Shirley strides Nazi Gauleiter fashion to the picture window and focuses on the nearer Galaxy of the River Thames and all its related irrelevancies. She decides they must cut Jack darling some slack because after all he has signed on several dotted lines. "Fine. No problems. Listen, Jack darling." She pauses knowing that Jack darling will be methodically counting the seconds of the pause. "There is a meeting here at three o'clock about the bestseller and you need to be here." Another tantalising pause.

Jack is counting out the pause and watching Nina Balatka, measuring tape in hand, measuring in the largest of the two rooms above the gallery that is to be the sitting room-cum-bedroom – come just about everything else. The £50,000 has been transferred to her account and the Verinder lawyers are feverishly working on transferring the Gallery into her name. Part of the deal is that she will never make contact with Julius or Julia Verinder ever again, to which she has verbally agreed.

"Jack?" He is still here. "The BBC wants you on Question Time on Thursday evening live from Leeds Town Hall. Spencer Perceval is the guest host." Shirley has accepted on his behalf and with his acknowledging grunt the call is ended.

"Who is Nina Balatka?"

"Not the remotest." Lady Rebecca is remembering that drunken grope with Spencer Perceval at Glencoras night club, then all the subsequent usual stuff back at daddy's knocking shop.

"Jack is bringing the creature with him this afternoon."

"Really?" That smarmy Perceval had promised to ring. Lady Rebecca Sharp is not used to being not called back after the usual stuff and, to add insult to injury, the next week at Glencoras the slime ball had been all over that yid bitch Julia Verinder.

"Are you listening, puss?"

"Sorry… what?"

"I was saying that your Uncle Goddy has gone too far this time."

"He is not my real uncle." They both know that but they enjoy her saying it. "He can never go too far because he sets the rules." One of those pauses that Jack would need to count out. "There are no actual rules."

Shirley turns her back on the picture window and tap taps the slim gold pen against those perfect white teeth; the all singing all dancing mobile phone tap tapping against a slender thigh and not quite in tune. She has never had an ear for music and always finds their box at Covent Garden such a trial, often falling asleep, much to her husband's annoyance.

"He has taken Judge Helen Graham to his bed." She knows that Becky is right and that there never have been any rules; Shirley knows that she should know that better than anyone.

"So?" Becky regretted afterwards not slapping Perceval's stupid face to embarrass the yid bitch.

"So she is not returning my husband's calls. So they were meant to spend Sunday together."

"So?" Becky had also regretted not slapping the stupid face of Julia Verinder, although that would have been the waste of a perfectly good slap.

"So he is pretending to be devastated just to annoy me." A deep sigh. "He rather played around with the idea that they were soul mates." In their circles it is the height of bad manners to exchange souls, as it inevitably leads to complications. They both know that Sir Bernard Keeldar has a serious problem totally unrelated to souls, but very much related to just about everything else.

Realising that boss lady is nonplussed Lady Rebecca pays attention. Boss lady doesn't usually do nonplussed, so this could be awkward.

"So what is the problem with no rules Goddy fucking – because that's all it is – the Judge woman?"

"Firstly. The relationship with the Judge woman has kept Bernard out of trouble." That is true. Thank God for Sir Godwyn Lydate's intervention that last time, when even the Keeldar millions might not have been enough to make the bad things go away.

"Secondly it looks like Judge lady thinks it is, you know, serious with Goddy." A tight smile. Shirley Keeldar is glad she can always confide in this willowy slip of a girl where appearances are always deceptive.

"You are telling me that the plain Jane Judge thinks she is the one?"

"Apparently so."

"Jesus wept." Becky Sharp shakes her head in disbelief. She has never been one for the sisterhood.

"Bernard was getting himself into one of those awful threatening moods as if was all my fault and so I had to phone Goddy there and then. He thought it was faintly amusing."

"Yes. He would."

"Bernard really is being a fucking pain."

"Poor you, it must have been awful." She takes Shirley Keeldar in her arms. They both know that deep down the Honourable Lady Rebecca Sharp is the strong one, and has a core of tensile steel and is not the least bit willowy. Except, perhaps,when the black dog is snapping at her heels.

"I will talk to Goddy." She fondly strokes Shirley's hair that always smells so swept clean. "I will persuade him to get the poor fools back together. After all they deserve each other." There is not an ounce of romance in Lady Rebecca's soul and Shirley appreciates that.

The two unalike women embrace and Shirley is leaking tears. She would not let anyone else in the world know that she is capable of leaking tears over something so apparently ridiculous as her husband.

"Stop it now, you daft cow." Becky nuzzles an ear. "He will listen to me." Another ear nuzzle. "He always listens to me." Shirley knows this is true. "Perhaps I am the one." Becky mimics and Shirley cannot stop herself chuckling through the leaking tears.

"That's better." They stand apart holding hands. "Now go and repair the damage and I will ring him now."

"He might not answer."

"He always answers for me." Whilst Shirley hesitates at the bathroom door, Sir Godwyn Lydate does indeed answer on the third ring.

"Are you listening, uncle dearest?"

"Are you on speakerphone?"

"Yes."

"Good morning, Shirley, my dear." There is a pause. "I always listen to my favourite niece. You know that, Rebecca my dearest."

"Please ensure that the poor deluded Judge personage is restored to the spider's web arms of Sir Bernard Keeldar forthwith. There can still be discreet fucks."

"I love those."

"I know."

"You are a bossy little madam."

"Pretty please."

"You know I can never resist your abject pleadings."

"You are just a dirty old man."

"Not so much of the old."

"Would you do it soonest?"

"For you, Rebecca my dearest, it is already done." Shirley Keeldar has gone into the bathroom and closed the door. Becky goes off speakerphone.

"You deserve a special reward, uncle dearest."

"I will think of something."

"Not if I think of something first." Lady Rebecca has the knack of making such promises sound like threats.

Sir Godwyn Lydate ends the call and stares at the back of the chauffeur's head, the grey uniform cap set at a slightly rakish angle and the ears no doubt burning.

Becky Sharp is one of the few women who can leave Sir Godwyn Lydate somewhat off-balance. It started several years ago at that shooting weekend at Lydate Hall, when Becky had accompanied her father, the Duke, because she was in disgrace having been expelled from Roedean; no one who could afford the exorbitant fees was expelled from Roedean and she had to be watched. There were rumours of most regrettable behaviour of a most definitely sexually depraved nature ; there were rumours of a teacher's suicide. Although no one would speak about it, least of all the Duke – pots and kettles came to mind. It had been hard to believe such rumours of that butter wouldn't melt in the mouth, adorably gap toothed and wide-eyed gangly teenager. He smiles to himself and forgetfully rests a hand on Carrie Brattle's green tighted knee. She doesn't flinch. Knowing she is being watched in the mirror by the chauffeur she slightly opens her legs; it is a bugger waking up randy and alone.

That first night of that weekend, Sir Godwyn, after drinking the Duke under the table, had been caressed awake at some ungodly hour. Caressed or more like harried awake by a naked gangly Becky Sharp very much everywhere in his bed. She had hoarsely whispered what she wanted him to do as she enveloped his body with lots and lots of Bambi limbs. It was not wide-eyed and it was most certainly not innocent. Butter would certainly have melted.

"Here we are, my dear." He squeezes the green tighted knee and is aware of the slightly open legs. "This is where I leave you for now." The grey limousine with blacked out rear windows glides under the impressive Georgian arch that Pevsner once extolled. "Gilbert will whisk you down to Nether Lydate in no time at all and the Bertrams will see you settled in. You will be safe there." The probably hazel eyes in which a man would struggle to drown are intently watching his lips. He wonders if she is partially deaf. "I will pop down at the weekend." A promise is a promise. He catches Gilbert's eye in the rear view mirror and imperceptibly nods.

He watches the limousine pull away and braces his shoulders and deeply breathes in the cloudy morning air. The Ministry doors are guarded by the uniformed major-domo who smartly salutes. He lives in hope that Sir Godwyn might use him on other matters. He has heard the rumours.

"Good morning, Sir Godwyn." He holds the military salute.

"Good morning, Oliver." It is so good to be alive.

In the pulling away limousine Carrie Brattle opens her legs wider and catches the hunky chauffeur's eye in the rear view mirror.

Monday 16th October 12.25pm

The Archbishop, displaying his non-committedly most pleasant he appreciates Lord God Almighty is not for everyone's face, is shown with due deference into the members' smoking room of the exclusive gentlemen's club. Non-members are not allowed in the room but smoking is allowed to certain members in defiance of the law.

"Hugh, so good to see you." The only member currently in occupation of the members' smoking room is Sir Godwyn Lydate, who half heartedly sort of rises from his favoured table by the old-fashioned partly mullioned first floor window overlooking Pall Mall. A little touch of Dickens in the night which had been Sir Godwyn's idea. "I have taken the liberty of ordering the Club whisky."

"You know my tastes, my dear fellow."

"Indeed I do." Indeed he does. Just for the form of it they sip the Club whisky and smack lips appreciatively. It was a habit they developed at the Harry Hotspur club at Oxford – a club even more weirdly exclusive than the Piers Gaveston Society and every bit as destructive as the less exclusive Bullingdon club. Only Hotspurs know what occurred and still occurs at the annual reunions. No one has ever lived to tell the tale.

"So, Godwyn."

"So, Hugh."

The Archbishop stretches his long gaitered legs and studies his one and only University friend; studies with those immensely intelligent deep-set brown eyes of a crossbred cocker spaniel, which he likes to think gives the impression of seeing into men's souls. A useful attribute for an Archbishop.

No beating about the bush. That is his way. "So tell me, my dear fellow, what it is you want? I will of course agree and then we can enjoy luncheon." Despite the gaiters, always a man of appetites. "The Club claret is most acceptable." He smiles benignly. "Particularly as it is not French." They both amicably set their faces at the in-joke.

"The new Minister needs a husband."

"Makes a change from the farmer needs a wife." He appears thoughtful. Archbishop Hugh Clavering often finds it useful to appear thoughtful and pulls off appearing thoughtful rather well, if he does say so himself. "I hear she is a somewhat racy lady."

"Indeed." Sir Godwyn recalls the somewhat intrusive use of the loofah in the tepid shared bath.

The Archbishop ponders, and also does pondering rather well. "But perhaps shall we say a trifle flaky round the edges?"

"Quite." They are both thinking the same thing. "Hence the need for a husband pdq."

The Archbishop decides not to comment on what this most dangerous of disingenuous plotters is plotting. Best not to know… best not to even hazard a guess. Instead he tops up the whiskies from the bottle on the table. No one likes to disturb Sir Godwyn when he is having one of his little tête-à-têtes. A certain ex- member once called him an unforgiving sod; which is not the half of it.

"Who is the chosen one?"

"A Vicar in Leeds. His wife, who is apparently pregnant by another man, has conveniently walked out of the marital home." A twitch of dry lips. "He has already been found acceptable in the beast with two backs department."

"Only acceptable?"

"The lady has exacting standards." The vision of the loofah will linger for some time.

Instead of saying 'you should know' the Archbishop executes something complicated with quite magnificent eyebrows and Sir Godwyn looks on with admiration. On initiation into the Harry Hotspur club the eyebrows are shaved off, together with all bodily hair. And, normally under protest, a hired for the evening prostitute is ritually shaved and then ritually penetrated in all orifices in the time honoured fashion, normally under further protest, but always well paid off. Sensible girls take the threat seriously. Only once had retribution needed to be meted out and the girl found it difficult to work in Oxford after that…found it difficult to work full stop.

"I take it then that a humble Vicar will not be acceptable as the exacting lady's Prince Consort?"

"You take it correctly."

They sip the Club whisky. Whenever they meet there are always disparate memories of those Oxford days. Sir Godwyn as President of the Union and of the Harry Hotspur club, always one step ahead of everyone else, including the Dons and, of course, their wives. Plus ça change. It was thanks to Godwyn that the unfortunate, some might call it rape, of that busty waitress was somehow hushed up. A miracle if ever there was one.

"The Bishopric of Staines has just become vacant."

"Excellent."

A well-known member peeps into the smoking room and then scurries away in alarm, hoping he hasn't been recognised.

"Is there a quid pro quo, my dear fellow?"

Sir Godwyn knows that Hugh Clavering likes to go round the houses on these occasions, and so he glances at the antique Rolex watch that belonged to his father, and then studies his manicured fingernails. He gives thought to

Carrie Brattle, who gives a whole new meaning to changing horses in midstream and suspects she is a voracious little minx. Possibly Renoir might have done her justice. He knows under which Renoir painting he will pose her naked. He thinks it quite likely that Gilbert took a detour on the way to Lydate Hall and wonders in which secluded wooded location he parked up the limousine this time.

The Archbishop coughs into his hand and Sir Godwyn pours more whisky. He already has a most suitable quid pro quo lady in mind. Once a slutty waitress always a slutty waitress in the world according to Hugh Clavering.

Monday 16th October 1.02pm

The two of them are outdoing each other giggle giggling for all the world like those archetypal empty headed schoolgirls. They are seated at the table hidden from the street in the Italian restaurant, so posh it doesn't display a name, next door to the newly opened Art Gallery on Jermyn Street. The second bottle of outrageously overpriced Chardonnay is nearly empty, the over the top monogrammed china plates gooey with tomatoey pasta sauce.

It is a well on the way to being well pissed Marion Fay who opens the plain brown carrier bag and sensually caresses the hidden from view dildo.

"It doesn't seem to be growing."

There appears to be an inexhaustible supply of giggly giggles and the ignored waiter is maintaining a discreet distance. He has been instructed in no uncertain terms that this is the actual Amelia Sedley and friend, so keep your distance and look away. The muscle bound Security people have turned disgruntled customers away… no argument… no discussion. This is the actual Amelia Sedley. Some of the disgruntled customers are hanging around to catch a glimpse of the fabled one.

The hired limousine is parked on double yellow lines and a gaggle of tipped off media are waiting to pounce. The empty headed St Trinian's duo are blissfully unaware that Jack Bellingham, munching a common or garden cheese sandwich, is staring out of the windows on the first floor of the new Art Gallery at the undignified scrum in the street below. Neither do they know that a formidable Nina Balatka is at his side.

"Don't you wish you were there with Amelia Sedley?"

He shakes his head as if at a buzzing fly and munches the tasty cheese sandwich. He ate a lot of his mother's cheese sandwiches when he was a University lecturer.

"Social media insists you are the golden couple." She attempts a sigh. "That is where you belong."

Jack glances sideways at the contained profile that gives nothing away. "I do not belong anywhere." The sandwich is rather good, much better than the ones his mother used to make. She was always stingy with the cheese, bread often verging on stale because she had a blind spot where sell by dates were concerned – including her own.

He swallows the last of the rather good cheese sandwich.

"The bed will be arriving this afternoon." She says knowing full well that the needs of the moment are just that and nothing more. That love is a fallacy that entrapped her mother in the end. The only thing that counts is money... lots of money.

"Great."

A growing crowd of onlookers is being held back by the grim faced Security people who are loving every minute. The six foot seven black guy with a distinctive earpiece had once guarded the last but one President of the United States. Jack had overheard him confide in a muscle bound colleague that he much preferred guarding Amelia Sedley, because he never got to fuck the President.

The empty headed pretend schoolgirls emerge from the restaurant very much arm in arm. It is most definitely his bloody sister clutching a brown paper bag. To a background of screams and shouts the rear door of the limousine is flung open and the onlookers are allowed to press not too close. With lots of legs on display the two women scramble into the limousine, helped by the helping hands of the six foot seven bodyguard, who is particularly helping Amelia Sedley's posterior.

The limousine purrs away chased by most of the media and some of the crowd. A hand can be spied waving through the rear window. The six foot seven black Security guard speaks to a muscle bound colleague and they both grin, displaying several gold teeth.

"So that was Amelia Sedley."

"That indeed was Amelia Sedley." And friend. He should have known. A bane is a bane is a bane.

There is something undeclared in his tone of voice that makes Nina Balatka intently study his utterly composed profile. There is nothing to be read and she thinks he whispers 'bitch' as he stares and stares, with those oddly colourless eyes, at the emptiness where the limousine has turned the corner.

Nina touches his arm in a reassuring gesture that is the last thing he needs. Anyway, she is not very good at reassuring gestures because she never means them.

Monday 16th October 2.17pm

The Attorney General and soon-to-be ennobled Judge Helen Graham has left exclusive La Vendee restaurant arm in arm with a tight lipped Sir Bernard

Keeldar. She has been surprisingly affectionate and promised faithfully that nothing happened of an intimate nature with Godwyn Lydate, or at least nothing of which Bernard would not approve, which leaves rather a wide field. He had done a second take at the disingenuous words, spoken in that voice of telling the truth the whole truth and nothing but the truth so help her God, knowing that she was lying through her four times a day brushed teeth. Annoyingly there is an almost luminous quality to her skin that he hasn't been aware of before today.

During the awkward meal she had reassuringly stroked his liver spotted hand and had intrusively fingertip touched his face and played footsie under the table. She never instigates footsie under the table.

She called him darling a lot, which was unusual, but then disappeared to the toilet for rather a long time. Now she has to rush off and he is beginning to think that his soul might be better off in someone else's keeping. Although he is running out of options and she does deserve to be punished. They are the only customers and as they leave arm in arm an anxious Giovanni bows them out and locks the door from the outside. He has an important errand to run for Zur Goodween and he must not be late.

The beanpole chef Ralph Newton has heard the door of the restaurant ceremoniously locked and so has the black eyed sister-in-law, who is bending over, loading the few dishes into the antiquated dishwasher anchored in the gloomiest corner of the kitchen. As that idiot Giovanni cannot resist bragging, she knows something of the errand, knows it will take at least an hour. Stupid is as stupid does or, as they say in the mountains, a donkey in festival finery is still a donkey.

Ralph Newton, who, for some unfathomable reason fancies himself as a bit of a ladies' man, sneaks up behind the invitingly bent over dago slut and breathes in the musky scenty odours and the undertones of scrubbed sweat. She is rattling dishes and pretending to be unaware that the idiot is about to feel up her invitingly bent over arse, and just wishes he would get on with it.

She gives out some encouraging noises at the first hesitant touch. So far so good. She allows the waitress uniform dress to be raised to her waist. The chef's trousers are unzipped at the second attempt, because the hard on makes it awkward. The stonewashed purple knickers are invitingly stretched over the bent over arse. To speed things up she eases the knickers down over meaty thighs.

Meanwhile Giovanni is striding past the Ritz Hotel and entering Green Park by the Piccadilly entrance. Zur Goodween apparently trusts Giovanni with this most important errand and so he must not fail. The trust of such a man is worth its weight in gold, frankincense and myrrh. He stops in mid stride and theatrically smacks a sweaty palm to his brow and two pretty girls take avoiding action. In his haste he has forgotten the piece of paper... Cretino... Cretino. At an almost run he retraces his steps and for once is not ogling pretty girls, who are rarely aware that they are being ogled; he is of the age that pretty girls do not register the ogling.

The partially deaf Ralph Newton does not hear the door being unceremoniously unlocked as the beanpole chef moves, perhaps more rapidly than a red bloodied lady might wish, towards a conclusion and is shouting that she is a filthy slut. He had shouted the same thing at the missus this morning, who had said nothing and was just glad it was soon over. Sarah Newton really is beginning to wonder why she puts up with it...any benefits of being married to Ralph, apart from a decidedly transient pleasure, ceased to exist a long time ago.

This particular conclusion is promising to be more spectacular than usual, as she more than matches him push for thrust. The gushing needs begin to drown the other senses and she screeches like a mountain cat on heat. That does it. That fucking does it.

"Slut. Slut...aaargh..." And he comes and he comes and he comes. Where has she been all his sorry life? The last thing Ralph Newton hears this side of Paradise is the screaming of "Cretino". Then and then and then the searing pain overwhelming all his little bits of knowing.

He will never know that it was a snatched up frying pan that smashes into an exposed temple as the poor sap topples inelegantly sideways, slopping out of the bent over woman and smashing into the sharp corner of the steelwork surface with the same temple as if on purpose. Then blackness. Then nothing.

Anna provocatively maintains the most revealing position and looks backwards over her shoulder with the black eyes that reveal less than nothing. The beanpole chef is spread eagled on his back with shocked unseeing eyes wide open. He looks ridiculous with the trousers and underpants trapped round his bony knees and the instrument of such recent transient pleasure shrivelled to a glistening slug.

Unhurriedly she pulls up and adjusts the stretched stonewashed purple pants and pats down the waitress uniform dress. Then quite deliberately turns to face the appalled features of the hyperventilating excuse of a brother-in-law. He drops the frying pan with a clatter as Anna kneels beside the body, which is posed awkwardly, like a shot cowboy in a B-movie Western. There surely should be an arrow. She matter of factly closes the eyelids. She had done the same for both her husbands and two of her brothers.

"He is dead." She states the obvious without any show of emotion. "You killed him, Giovanni." The shock of her level, accusing voice drags him back to some semblance of a gathering of scattered senses.

"Please no. Please no." He holds out his clasped hands in a mockery of supplication. "I didn't mean it." He falls to his knees and covers his face with his two trembling hands. "Please no. Please no."

As prayers go she thinks they are pretty pathetic. Without a second thought and knowing time to be of the essence she eases up the dead body's grey underpants and then the squared patterned chef's trousers and adeptly fastens the twisted belt. She even thinks to pull up the zip. Only then does she shuffle on her knees next to her weeping brother-in-law and takes possession of the cold cold hands.

"Listen, Giovanni." She is uncharacteristically gentle now. He must not go into shock. He is a weak man… a very weak man and there is no time for the indulgence of shock. He opens his eyes and sees the unmoving dead body and closes them even tighter. Perhaps he will wake up from this particular nightmare as he has woken from so many others.

"It was an accident, Giovanni." He recognises his name and opens his eyes and stares at the dark brooding face where the black eyes are made compelling. "It was an accident, Giovanni." As if she is talking to her mentally deficient little cousin whose eyes she also closed in death. "An accident, that is all." She cannot bring herself to touch the stupid living face.

"Yes. Yes. An accident." He can make believe that some of her innate peasant immobility in the face of disaster is flowing into his own body. "That's it. That's it. An accident." He hated being a peasant, but he listens intently as this peasant woman explains how the accident happened, and goes over it three times.

She even arranges her mouth to the nearest approximation of a reassuring smile that she can manage. "Ring Sir Godwyn. He needs to know." She is not stupid. He needs to know everything. It is the only way.

"Yes. Yes. He needs to know."

Without a glance at the useless thing that used to be Ralph Newton, the would-be ladies' man, Anna leaves the kitchen and heads for the ladies' toilets. She pauses and is satisfied to hear the muffled voice of that idiot Giovanni pleading with Sir Godwyn. She feels the urgency to thoroughly wash away any obvious evidence of Ralph Newton's bodily fluids, before facing that most formidable of men.

Sir Godwyn is leaving that most exclusive Pall Mall Club and takes the call with one foot in his limousine. The Archbishop is striding away whistling a hymn tune and with a spring in his step. The po-faced chauffeur is holding open the door, being careful to keep the memory of an incredibly horny, naked on the back seat Carrie Brattle, smile off his face. "I will be there in five minutes." Four minutes later a scared out of his excuse for wits Giovanni is waiting at the door of exclusive La Vendee restaurant as the limousine glides to a halt.

"Where is the body?"

"In ze keetchen, Zur Goodween."

"Show me."

Sir Godwyn prods the ridiculously inert body with the toe of a highly polished handstitched brogue. Glancing with distaste at Giovanni who is uselessly wringing his hands, Sir Godwyn sniffs the air, and looks around the kitchen, missing nothing.

"How did it happen?"

Giovanni gulps and captures a shuddering breath. "We eard a shout and we rushed een and found eem like zees." All in a rush. "Ee must ave sleeped and banged ees Ed on zee corner of zee work surface. Zere." He dramatically points so there can be no mistake. "Zere."

"We?"

"Anna and me."

"Where is she?"

"In zee laidees."

Sir Godwyn lip twitches the beginnings of an ironic smile. These Italian peasants really take the biscuit. "Washing away the evidence?"

"Zur Goodween?" This man is the devil incarnate. Giovanni has to make a supreme effort not to cross himself. He cannot remember the last time he crossed himself.

And here is the lady in question standing at the doorway in all her pride and malice. Sir Godwyn beckons with an imperious index finger and she edges as close as she deems appropriate, which is closer than Giovanni thinks wise. She has always been what in the mountains they call a woman of the nostrils.

He takes a step closer. "So tell me, my dear." She can smell the whisky and wine on his breath. "Tell me what happened."

She stands her ground, not sure what that idiot has spewed out. This man, who is most assuredly not an idiot, takes firm hold of the chins and she will not flinch. He likes that. She really is an imposing woman, to be taken roughly in a hidden corner of the olive grove with the pitiless sun burning one's backside.

"Shall I tell you what I think happened?" The reflecting blackness of her eyes is quite intriguing, although of course it is an overused word. This is turning out to be an enjoyable interlude. "I think the deceased was fucking you and almost certainly from behind." He squeezes the chins. She has probably never ever flinched in her life and is not about to flinch now.

"I think that snivelling moron caught you at it, so to speak." The snivelling moron in question knows that his face is giving him away. "I think he grabbed the frying pan which is now hanging the wrong way round on its hook." The black eyes shut down even blacker. "He then hit the deceased, whose belt is twisted, and who then fell and banged his head on the sharp corner of the work surface." He releases the chins marked with the fierce grip of his fingers. "Is that what happened, my dear?"

For several seconds she matches him stare for stare just to show she will not be beaten down. He really likes that. "Is that what happened?" Surprisingly he gently massages the suggestion of a harelip. "Tell me."

Curtly she nods her head and the snivelling moron falls to his knees and covers his face with palsied hands. Sir Godwyn lip twitches as Anna traps a manicured finger between wolfish teeth.

"Have you thoroughly washed away the evidence, my dear?"

Curtly she nods her head and releases the trapped finger which is covered in her saliva.

"Good. I have a little mission for you, my dear."

She excavates a deep voice that could echo from a mountain pass at daybreak.

"You are not calling ze Police?"

"Good God, no. It will be our little secret."

The snivelling moron risks a hopeful peak through latticed fingers.

"It was a dreadful accident. I will make a call. The body will be removed. His widow will be more than compensated." Just like that.

"What is the mission?" Ever practical. He likes that and there is so much to like.

"A little re-enactment, my dear." He touches the end of her nose in an intimate gesture all his own. "The past come to life with a busty waitress too forward for her own good, more than a hint of stocking top and of course a future Archbishop." He looks down at Giovanni. "You stay here until the body is removed."

"My errand, Zur Goodween?"

"Stay here."

"Yees, Zur Goodween." Giovanni avoids all eye contact with his sister-in-law.

"Come, my dear." Sir Godwyn takes ownership of an elbow. "Your somewhat limited but nevertheless formidable talents are wasted here."

Giovanni waits until they have been gone for several minutes before scrambling to his unsteady feet and spitting on the corpse. Only the spittle dribbles down his chin. So he thinks about kicking the dead man but lacks the courage.

Monday 16th October 4.01pm

Jack Bellingham is experiencing the all too familiar sensation of the thinness of the Earth's crust beneath his feet. He is staring out of the picture window of the Grande suite of the Savoy Hotel but there is no matchstick girl to anchor his gaze. The dragon at the molten core of the Earth has snatched the memory back to its fearsome lair.

Dear. Dear. This will never do. It will have to be crossed out.

It is the reality of a reality that has always been just out of reach, twisted daydreams not an adequate substitute, and the right and proper substance of things always just out of reach. He blames his dear poor mother whose reality was very much within reach.

"A penny for them, darling." The original Cat woman, now fully clothed, is at his shoulder and hands him a tumbler of whisky. The meeting went well and

Gabriel Betteridge has gone away to write the instant bestseller. Jack answered all the probing questions… one or two of them truthfully.

He takes a gulp of whisky and accepts the not unpleasant stomach burning. "I was thinking how my bloody sister has been the bane of my life since the day we were born."

It was not the answer Shirley Keeldar had been anticipating. There is something inherently left-field about the People's hero that catches people off balance. She sips neat vodka. Becky is probably right – Becky is usually right. Not that it makes any difference.

"Becky doesn't like me." Spooky. Really spooky.

"She is wary of you."

"I am wary of me."

Shirley Keeldar feels it is appropriate to slip a possessive arm round his waist. After all, the last time they had been together on this spot they had been naked and she had rubbed against his bare thigh and cupped his balls. "The world is at your feet, darling Jack."

He points out of the window. "That world?"

"That world." As if there is any other world, for fuck's sake.

He screws up his mouth, knowing that his poor dear mother would have slapped his leg and kissed it better. Until that return slap with the falling over and breaking arm stuff. He is only too acutely aware of Shirley's exotic perfumed closeness. "Do you like me, Shirley?"

There is no hesitation. She is very good. "Of course, darling."

"Nina Balatka likes me."

Who the Fuck is Nina Balatka she doesn't say. "I thought she was coming with you this afternoon." The gold digging little bitch she doesn't say.

"She had to go and see Emily Rowley." Who the fuck is Emily Rowley Shirley doesn't say. There is only so much fucking not saying one cannot say. She nuzzles against his neck, which is a reaction of sorts, to reclaim the high ground.

"You must be careful, darling. People will use you." She should know.

"It is probably better than not being used by people." Another heart burning slurp of whisky. In truth he is beginning to think he is being used by Nina Balatka until something better comes along. She would not have looked at him twice in the street prior to his hero status.

Shirley Keeldar is glad that Becky is not here because Shirley actually does, on some deep level, relate to this bundle of contradictions who is no doubt quite capable of using the users to his own advantage.

"Where is the worldwide superbitch Amelia Sedley?"

He shrugs his shoulders and they sip their drinks. It is getting dark outside with lowering clouds threatening a storm. "I'm hungry."

"What do you say to room service?"

"As long as it's not pizza." He hands over the empty tumbler and kisses Shirley full on the lips and she kisses back. Daydreams never had this third dimension and they lacked taste.

Monday 16th October 5.19pm

The pretend real waitress is dolled up in a cobbled together waitress uniform that would not be out of place in a 1950s Lyons Corner house tea rooms… the sort of uniform that screams do not touch from the 1950s smoke engulfed rooftops. The hint of stocking tops perhaps a trifle overdone, but that was where the trouble had started all those years ago. An unforgivably pissed up dinner at the Harry Hotspur club. That particular busty, no longer in the bloom of youth, waitress had leaned over the table to reach for some broken crockery, inadvertently displaying more than a hint of stocking top… mistake number one.

Club President Godwyn Lydate had already puked most of the six course dinner all down his new dress shirt and been unable to stand up, let alone intervene. It would never happen again. The others were equally comatose, if not more so, apart from hollow legs Hugh Clavering. The busty waitress had extravagantly tut tut-tutted at the mess on the table, which in retrospect was mistake number two. The future Archbishop, whose head for drink was already legendary, grabbed the leaning over waitress from behind and she had ear splittingly screamed… mistake number three. Afterwards Hugh Clavering had claimed it was the tut tut-tutting that made him teach the common tart a lesson and not the more than a hint of stocking top. Nor indeed the ear splitting scream. But then he was a congenital liar even before he had discovered Church of England Sermons.

Punching the poor woman to the floor she had been silenced, losing three teeth in the process, only adding to the eventual payoff. The carpet was pale blue where it wasn't spotted with blood. At the time a befuddled Godwyn had thought it was one of those side swipe coincidences that makes a mockery of just about everything. Afterwards he could never remember why he had thought that.

The rape had been brutal. Godwyn had watched because he had lost control of the muscles that closed his eyes. The poor woman gurgle screamed and was silenced with a cowardly rabbit punch. The last of the ancient line of Claverings had ripped open the bodice of the waitress uniform, exposing breasts that shook like pink blancmanges on a pre-war Pullman Express racing over points. He had almost bitten off one of the nipples but she was unable to scream. The nipple would eventually heal but would be always tantalisingly off centre. Even to this day she and Godwyn laugh about it; the off centre nipple being incredibly sensitive and hot-wired.

There had been an equally repellent Hugh de Clavering in William the Conqueror's retinue at the Battle of Hastings; a Godwyn de Lydate had been his put upon Squire. As the future Archbishop later pointed out in his mock defence, there had been much rape of Saxon women in the aftermath of that battle and they were not compensated. The common tart should be grateful and anyway she was asking for it. President Godwyn Lydate knew only too well that it would be pointless to tease out the flaws in this argument.

Thank God the rape hadn't taken long, as this particular Hugh Clavering had jerkily ejaculated with a third team rugby fifteen victory whoop, and rolled off the semi-conscious woman to crawl away bare arsed to unearth more alcohol. A shocked – he had thought unshockable – Godwyn Lydate had wanted to cover up the poor woman's very much exposed and violated private parts. Ridiculously he had worried that there should be some dignity involved. He was unable to move or stop up his ears to the graphic keening of a gin trapped animal in distress. It was a sound he would never forget and there was a small part of him that would never forgive.

In the aftermath, the poor woman had been so grateful for Godwyn's most apologetic involvement that had enabled her to keep the child. Not to mention the new teeth or the generous allowance negotiated from the Clavering sauces and condiments millions. They meet up whenever Sir Godwyn returns to Oxford which is quite often. They laugh over it now. The stupid thing is she would have readily agreed to a sexual liaison if Hugh Clavering had asked nicely.

Anna, the Mediterranean sister-in-law, is studying Sir Godwyn intently with those fathomless dark eyes, as he drags his mind back from the past and becomes aware of the staring. It might well be disconcerting to the uninitiated, like ants crawling over one's face when one wakes afterwards in the Tuscan sunshine.

He checks the time on the expensive looking antique Rolex. He is due at a Downing Street Reception.

They have rehearsed the bending over the highly polished dining table in the Albany apartment. "Not too much stocking top." He had admonished and she had looked over her shoulder, not able to read this man. At least she doesn't yet despise him as she despises other men. "That is much better." And he had patted the bare bottom; all those years ago that had been mistake number four.

"Remember." She turns to face him, standing with the peasant hands dutifully at her side as if it actually is the 1950s. This impressive big woman could probably knock the Archbishop out cold with a single blow. "If you scream he will punch your face."

"I veel not scream." She would not want it to end before it had properly started.

"You must struggle and you must resist." He fussily straightens the give away cravat at her neck. The suggestion of a harelip is more suggestive than usual and he cannot quite place where she belongs in the ordained scheme of things. There is a substance about this woman that is intriguing – that word again. He does so love being intrigued. There were worse ways for the idiot chef to spend his last moments on earth.

Memo. Must square the widow.

"I veel struggle. I veell reesist. I veel not screem."

"That's a good girl." He caresses a cheek. She has probably always been a woman of substance even as a girl. The doorbell chimes some notes from Isolde's lament for Tristan –not at all appropriate given the circumstances.

Monday 16th October 5.48pm

The Reverend John Eames has loosened the constricting dog collar, uncorked a rather good Margaux and is appreciatively sipping the velvety smooth claret. He raises a glass to the God that heard his pleas. His late father would be so proud, although of course it might not be the same God. A more than slightly harassed brand spanking new Government Minister instructed him to make himself at home, before she rushed off to a Downing Street Reception.

He has only been allowed to visit this Westminster bolt hole on one previous occasion several weeks ago, when he was attending a Church Conference. The visit had not been a great success. She had been distracted about upsetting some powerful personage and sex had been minimally undressed and more than somewhat hurried. He remembered thinking at the time it had been like being with a prostitute faking an orgasm, whilst already thinking about the next client – a bit off-putting. It made him appreciate Mary Thorne all the more.

He sips more velvety smooth claret. The Minister has told him not to call her cuddle bunny any more. He thinks she might be beginning to take herself far too seriously.

As soon as he had arrived with his hastily packed bag, she had pecked him perfunctorily on the cheek and asked him to zip up the little black dress that she had chosen after much due deliberation. She was running late. She had eased the dress up to her waist as if he wasn't in the room, revealing diaphanous black knickers and had adjusted one of the seamed black stockings. Then, with a distracted wave, had dashed out. The Ministerial car was waiting with the engine running. The only other time they have been together since that previous visit was a couple of weeks ago at the Vicarage when his wife had been away. The sex had been acceptable. He sips more velvety smooth claret. He has to be honest, she had seemed distracted at first, but then things had warmed up quite nicely and he had no reason to think the quite peremptory obscene demands were not genuine. Disappointingly she had left the next morning straight after a hurried breakfast.

He wanders into the bedroom, where her distinctive perfume forever lingers, and sniffs the air and checks the bedside drawer, being careful not to disturb anything. Several pairs of knickers... some crotch less... the pill... good... flesh pink vibrator large-size... it works... several loose condoms of assorted flavours. A neatly folded man-size handkerchief with embroidered initials TLP, and several tell-tale stains...mmmmmm.

On the unmade bed are half a dozen discarded cocktail dresses, one split almost to the waist. She was obviously determined to look sexily Ministerial, but not too much so, at the Downing Street Reception. Not an easy look to pull off. She has the sexily bit in spades; it is probably the Ministerial bit that's a bit tricky.

There is an insistent ringing of the somewhat high pitched doorbell and he starts guiltily, closes the bedside drawer, and gets his breathing under control as he walks to the front door. Taking a deep breath he opens the door as if he owns the place. His welcoming smile is genuine and is reserved for women of any age, whether attractive or not. The pony tailed mousy haired girl, late 20s at a guess, is wearing rimless spectacles and is primly pretty. Extremely red lips.

She does not smile back. Instead she continues talking into the mobile phone pressed to her left ear. "Of course, Minister." She ends the call. "That was your blushing bride-to-be."

"I haven't said yes yet." The smile is now conspiratorial and shared jokey but she does not smile back. She is not the kind of girl to share any kind of joke, however unfunny, before proper introductions.

"You will, buster. You surely will." Bulging shoulder bag and all, she rudely pushes past as if she in fact owns the place. No one has ever called John Eames buster, and he checks that the constricting Clerical dog collar is still in place. Feeling more than somewhat foolish, he follows the resoundingly tight bottom, shaped in the well-cut navy blue trousers, as it enters the everything always and forever in its place living room, that has the ambience of an airport transit lounge in the early hours of the morning; there has not been a lot of family time in this designer space. The resoundingly tight bottom collapses in a controlled way on the least uncomfortable tubular chair, and its owner unzips the bulging shoulder bag resting on her lap. "There are some documents for you to sign."

"And you are?"

"Cecilia Hunt." She rummages in the shoulder bag. "Rhymes with cunt. Pleased to meet you, John." Now they can share a joke.

He has to say something. "Likewise I'm sure." He stands masterfully with his back to the bleak picture less white wall, facing the second floor window that overlooks communal dustbins. A returned from the American wars Captain Poldark to the life... or so he fondly imagines. Cecilia Hunt dumps the bulging shoulder bag on the pale blue carpet and shuffles the papers in her lap into some semblance of order. Then makes eye contact. A verging on disconcerting appraising stare through the rather severe round spectacles. No. The stare is, in fact, disconcerting. "These are documents relating to your divorce."

"Divorce?" He needs to assert himself here. "What has my divorce got to do with you?" That's much better.

"I work in Sir Godwyn Lydate's office." There is a meaningful pause, although what it signifies he is not at all sure.

"So?"

"He is your blushing bride-to-be's boss."

"I wish you would stop saying my blushing bride-to-be." He cannot help but feel that he is being railroaded here. "And I thought her boss was the Prime Minister."

Cecilia Hunt shoots a withering look that suggests she had not realised he was simple minded. "Don't be stupid."

He opens and shuts his mouth. "Sir Godwyn has arranged with the Attorney General, no less, that your divorce will go through by the end of next week."

"End of next week?"

"Your wife." Another of those pauses. "Your soon-to-be ex-wife, has agreed to a very generous settlement." He just stops himself saying – settlement? "She has signed the papers."

This most efficiently put together young woman shuffles said semblanced papers in her no doubt resoundingly well bred lap. "There is an appointment for you to meet the Archbishop tomorrow."

"The Archbishop?" Bugger.

"The Bishopric." As they have been introduced she pauses on the verge of a joke. "The Bishopric of Staines has become unexpectedly vacant and you are to be the next Bishop of Staines." A pause of course. "My Lord to be." He opens and closes his mouth whilst indecorously sliding down the wall, not at all like the returning Captain Poldark, and coming to rest on the pale blue carpet. Luckily he doesn't spill any wine and so drains the glass.

"Are you happy now for me to refer to your bride-to-be as your bride-to-be? Admittedly blushing was perhaps a step too far."

If he had ever met Sir Godwyn Lydate he would discern the uncanny resemblance of the copied dry lips twitch. When he meets the Archbishop he will see the likeness full stop. This pertly pretty girl does not take no for an answer, as his soon-to-be ex-wife had found out in no uncertain terms. Cecilia Hunt makes things happen and even Sir Godwyn is ever so slightly wary of her many and varied accomplishments. Her mother has always had the same effect on Sir Godwyn…but then…well…but then.

"Where do I sign?"

"That's more like it, Bish." He just stops himself opening and closing his mouth, certain that his poor man's imitation of the eternal dying guppy will not impress the redoubtable Cecilia Hunt. They perch close together on rickety high stools at the kitchen breakfast bar and she indicates where he must sign. She has provided a cheap black biro.

"There." She points with a red fingernail. "And there." She gives off a rather pleasant summery scent. "And there." It reminds him of someone but his memory is not what it was.

"Should I read all of this?" He flicks the papers, seeking for dismissive I do this all the time. She thinks he is really cute in a sliding down the wall flicking through unread papers kind of way…not at all bad looking.

"Don't worry." The red lips smile most smilingly. "You are not signing your life away." She dissembles from long practice.

He pauses with the cheap biro poised and arranges his face as if about to recite a speech from the school production of Hamlet, where he was the understudy for the Prince, and there could well be a ghostly prompter in the wings. "Oh! Sweet Cecilia that is just what I am doing."

She has to admit that she finds him strangely attractive in a very much the wrong man for her blindly following the itch between her legs kind of way. Not at all what she expected. "Just fucking sign and I most certainly am not sweet."

Without another word he hurriedly signs on the indicated places and she most efficiently gathers the papers together.

"And now we can celebrate."

"Celebrate?" Double bugger.

"Your elevation so to speak." He cannot be certain if she does double entendres – she is giving nothing away and instead points at the opened wine bottle. "A glass of that rather decent plonk will be most acceptable for starters." She kicks off her shoes and he wonders if, like him, she believes in a God who moves in mysterious ways and is no doubt female…to be honest he could probably accept that…it would make a lot of sense.

Monday 16th October 6.29pm

Sir Godwyn Lydate is taking pygmy sips of the warm, flat, non-vintage champagne and boredly studying the assembled multitude. The Green Salon at ten Downing Street echoes and re-echoes to inane chatter and insincere laughter. The Prime Minister is talking as earnestly as only he can fake, to Rosalie Murray, whilst his ever watchful eyes roam the room. She is certainly ostentatiously scrumptious in a spectacular little black number. Quite superb legs. Sir Godwyn sips and makes a face and appraises some more.

The striking grey eyes of the new Minister are inviting Prime Ministerial confidences. The tinkling laughter enough to draw in any man under the age of ninety nine – make that a hundred and nine. The Prime Minister is no longer looking round the room and is checking down the front of the little black dress. It gives a whole new meaning.

Sir Godwyn takes another teenie weenie sip. He really must have a word about the foul champagne at these Receptions. Studying the little black charade, he is not displeased that he has invited those quite superb legs and cleavage back to Albany after the Reception. There are some things the lady Minister needs to fully take on board and she is more receptive after sex. The quite distinctive perfume that never fails to send shivers down his spine is mysteriously at his elbow; he turns his head and lowers his voice. "You look absolutely ravishing." He lowers his voice even more. "Darling."

Never to be outshone, the First Lady is also wearing a spectacular little number and deep crimson really suits the sweet auburn colouring. She really makes an effort at these ridiculous soirées. This close the appraising is much more personal and there is even more cleavage than Rosalie Murray is displaying. The First Lady has never been one to hold back on cleavage and, for obvious reasons, there is no love lost between the First Lady and Rosalie Murray.

"Are you sneaking a peak at my boobs?"

"Guilty as charged."

The First Lady wets her lips with as little of the warm champagne as humanly possible. She lowers the superbly modulated voice, but no one can overhear in this nervous sweaty hubbub, although lip reading is another matter.

"Is everything arranged, Godwyn?" She has eyes on that pushy tart Rosalie Murray.

"You are quite certain, my dear?" He inadvertently catches the roving eye of Helen Graham who raises a glass. Her number is not so little but equally effective in its way. She is accompanying Sir Bernard Keeldar, an inevitable guest on these occasions, as his most generous donations are acceptable to all Parties and have smoothed away many difficulties.

"Quite sure. I think." She licks the rim of the glass in that way that sets his nerves on edge.

"Is it what you want, Godwyn?"

"We agreed it is what we both want."

"There really is no choice, is there." It is not a question. The tone of her voice is out of sync with the words.

Sir Godwyn heaves a deep sigh for her benefit. There is only so much soul-searching a man can take. He wishes that he was a different kind of man. He doesn't do if onlys – one of the many curses of the Lydates.

"I want you to go with me, Godwyn."

"Of course, my darling."

Reluctantly she drifts away to do the dutiful mingling, at which she has always excelled, and really is a most stunning looking woman to which almost all eyes are drawn. Except those of Sir Godwyn who glances at the oil paintings of long forgotten Eighteenth Century politicians adorning the gilded flock walls. One of the long forgotten politicians was a Lydate ancestor, a Minister in William Pitt the Elder's first Administration. There he is… exuding the certainty of the Lydates of that Century, so sure of his place in the order of things and now long forgotten.

"You are very pensive, Sir Godwyn." The diminutive Chinese ambassador addresses him in Mandarin Chinese and Sir Godwyn replies likewise.

"There is much to be pensive about, Ambassador." They stand shoulder down to shoulder and cast their miss nothing eyes over the oh so invited crowd. They always take time out together at these stale functions. It suits both their purposes.

"The Prime Minister's good lady is quite quite lovely." There follows a thoughtful nonspeaking. "One could almost say blooming."

"Indeed."

A minute or two of, some might think, quite comradely silence. Their secrets go back a long way and the things they know never come knowingly between their joint and several purposes. They even share similar, what some might call, weaknesses and know it only too well.

"There are so many women in this room who seek you out with their eyes, Sir Godwyn."

"You are as observant as always, Ambassador." A dry lips twitch that has been captured for all time in that Eighteenth Century portrait hanging on the wall, and thus something of the needless past lives on unremarked from generation to generation.

They are being given a wide berth, as if conversing in Mandarin sets them apart from the common herd, as indeed it does. They are probably discussing matters of great State. It is the bird in a gilded cage language for it.

"By the way I am the bearer of warm felicitations from our President's good lady." Some more nonspeaking at which the Ambassador is an expert. "I mean of course his wife." More nonspeaking. "She will be visiting London very soon for some early Christmas shopping."

No reply is needed or expected; they merestly sip warm champagne and both make attempts at gurning halloween faces at each other. Then Sir Godwyn holds up the half full glass to toast a lady across the room who has caught his eye. He recognises the homely, attractive face but the name escapes him and he hates names, however insignificant, to escape him. She glances away and blushes. She is fortyish and big busted with good clothes sense; the shades of purple showing off the matronly bosoms to perfection. The verging on distinguished older man, to whom she is clinging for dear life, must be the nondescript husband – there is usually one in tow on these occasions. The lady cannot stop herself glancing over to see if he is still, she imagines, stripping her naked in his mind's eye and she glances guiltily away. The blush spreading to her neck. She will need to go to the toilet.

"Yet another conquest, Sir Godwyn."

"It would appear so." He frowns over the name. It will come to him. It takes longer these days. "Who is the rather delectable Chinese girl who is accompanying you this evening, Ambassador?"

"She wants to be introduced to you."

"How nice."

The delectable Chinese girl in question is in animated conversation with George Meredith, the Foreign Secretary. Much to the discomfort of his rather frumpy, but in a nice way, long-suffering wife, who is aggressively tap tapping a well heeled foot. She catches Sir Godwyn's eye and raises impeccably plucked eyebrows in over the top exasperation. These days she spends a lot of time at the beauticians to make it appear that she doesn't spend a lot of time at the beauticians. They exchange knowing looks. The Chinese ambassador does not make any comment.

"The delectable Chinese girl has heard all about you, Sir Godwyn."

"I do hope not, Ambassador."

The inscrutably smiling Ambassador steers Sir Godwyn by the elbow towards the two and a half some and several people move hastily out of the way. As he approaches the shades of purple bosomy lady his formidable memory click clicks – of course, stupid of him. He pauses in mid stride, as does the attached Ambassador, who looks with interest at the blushing middle-aged hausfrau. Not for the first time is he in total awe of his occasional good friend. Too good a friend being the worst kind of enemy, is the old Chinese proverb.

"How lovely to see you again, Marian." As he captures the outstretched hand. "Such an unexpected pleasure."

"I didn't think you would remember, Sir Godwyn." The warm plumpish hand remains captured without a fight.

"I never forget a beautiful woman." Which is true. He caresses just about everything with those luminously pale blue eyes; come to bed eyes they would have been called when she was a silly schoolgirl. She alone is aware that the naughty man is caressing the palm of the warm plumpish hand with a hidden finger.

The Chinese ambassador thinks that if this goes on much longer the good woman will probably have an unfortunate occurrence in the nether regions. He interrupts in perfectly accented English... the years at Eton were well spent. "So pleased to meet you." He leans forward from the waist and the even warmer plumpish hand is transferred to his loose cool papery grip.

"The Chinese ambassador." Murmurs Sir Godwyn most confidentially. He thinks the poor lady could well swoon away at any moment. Such lovely big bosoms to put even Mediterranean Anna in the shade. The Archbishop is noticeable by his absence.

"This is Marian Fairburne." The bosoms are palpably heaving. "She was recently appointed to the Patrons Trust at the National Gallery." He doesn't add that the husband's accountancy firm are generous sponsors.

The Ambassador releases the hot, plumpish hand and smiles benignly. He has already forgotten her name. Sir Godwyn takes over.

"We met most opportunely at the opening of the Egon Schiele Exhibition, where she was kind enough to congratulate me on my little welcoming speech."

She licks naturally generous lips. "This is my husband." Who nods stiffly and appears ill at ease… as well he might. "He is the senior partner with the Accountants GWD." She has been loyally in his shadow for so long it is a hard habit to break.

The Ambassador smiles benignly. "You have offices in Shanghai I believe."

"Indeed we do, Ambassador." The husband appears slightly less ill at ease. "I was over there last month."

Sir Godwyn seizes the opportunity to edge Marian Fairburne and her bosoms to one side. They should perhaps be given names like weather fronts. "You must give me your mobile phone number, my dear. I am looking for someone of your calibre to chair a prestigious new Quango on Art in the workplace."

He leans so close that she can breathe in the sourness of the champagne on his breath to mingle with the sourness on her breath. "We should meet over lunch to discuss. I am certain you would be ideal for the role."

"Oh! Sir Godwyn."

"Godwyn please. I will ring you."

She half whispers the number all in a rush. "Shall I write it down… Godwyn?" She breathlessly whispers.

"I have an excellent memory for numbers, my dear Marian."

"You will ring me?" She squeezes the nearest arm. The one he bruised earlier at a rather energetic meeting at the office of the newly appointed Attorney General, where an antique inkwell was damaged beyond repair. He doesn't flinch.

"You can count on it, my dear Marian." He lip brushes a plumpish cheek in a purely social way and only she is aware of the tip of his tongue. Unless of course it was her overwrought imagination. She does rather suffer from an overwrought imagination…no… she is sure it was the tip of his tongue.

The Ambassador leads Sir Godwyn by the elbow to resume their interrupted journey towards the ill-assorted two and a half some. The Foreign Secretary is deep in abject conversation with the delectable Chinese girl, who is very much aware of their approach.

"My dear Mary Ellen." Sir Godwyn kisses the rather frumpy but in a nice way, Foreign Secretary's wife on both ruddy cheeks; very much a Country girl riding to hounds –it is not the time or place to use her nickname.

"You were going to ring me." She whispers and her breath always smells so fresh and minty. She is rather pointedly drinking what he assumes to be orange juice.

"Soon." He whispers back. "Promise." And he squeezes a substantial, but in a nice way, bottom. The last time he squeezed this bottom it was substantially naked.

"Ah! Godwyn my dear fellow." George Meredith does hail fellow well met and almost pulls it off, but cannot quite disguise the underlying fear. The Chinese ambassador is an expert on underlying fear.

"May I introduce Li Soo Ying, temporary third secretary at my Embassy. Sir Godwyn Lydate."

"Sir Godwyn needs no introduction." The slim hand is cool and slender. The size of the nameless bosoms well and truly hidden in the modest silk garment.

The Ambassador expertly edges the Foreign Secretary and his formidably long-suffering wife a little to one side.

"You are the most beautiful woman in the room, Li Soo Ying." It sounds more convincing and less corny in Mandarin Chinese.

"I know." In Mandarin Chinese. The First Lady, not to mention Rosalie Murray, might challenge the slender Chinese girl to an arm wrestle on that score. They are both only too well aware of what is going on.

"The Ambassador tells me you wished to be introduced to me." He is holding the slender cool hand and all its slender cool fingers. Marian Fairburne has disappeared to the toilet.

"Your reputation in China is immense, Sir Godwyn." One of those nonspeaking moments the Chinese do so well. "Immense, Sir Godwyn."

"Godwyn please." The driest of dry lip twitches. "We must meet for lunch, my dear."

Rosalie Murray is looking pearl handled daggers across the room. The First Lady is nowhere to be seen. The Attorney General is gulping champagne and ignoring whatever Sir Bernard is bleating on about, as he surreptitiously touches up a waitress.

"You had better give me back my hand, Godwyn." More nonspeaking. "People will talk." He makes a show of reluctantly releasing the slender cool fingers. "I will be free on Wednesday." She murmurs for his ears only.

"Excellent." In for a penny in for a pound could well be the reserve motto of the Lydates of Lydate Hall. "Shall we say one o'clock at my Albany apartment." If she is surprised she doesn't show it. "I would love to cook for you, Li Soo Ying."

"Li please."

"Will you do me a big favour, Li?" She inclines her head in inscrutable Oriental style. She will of course say yes – or just perhaps no. She needs to be careful.

"Will you wear this lovely dress?" She smiles a porcelain statuette's painted on smile, and the dusted brown eyes literally sparkle with the Master's brush. Such perfect tiny white teeth. Such perfect heart-shaped lips.

"If you wish, Godwyn."

"Thank you, Li."

She looks as though she might break if dropped carelessly, but he knows only too well that appearances in China are invariably deceptive.

There is an intrusively discreet touch on Sir Godwyn's right shoulder. He steps politely sideways and is confronted by blonde frizzy haired Lizzie Hastings, the First Lady's personal assistant and naturally one of Sir Godwyn's appointees. One can never be too careful.

"Yes, Lizzie, what is it?" A touch of asperity. She whispers close so that his ear tickles quite deliciously. She has an organically pretty face and a full figure to draw some of the sharper eyes in the room. A sidelined Li Soo Ying appears inscrutable.

"You must come at once, Sir Godwyn." She whispers even closer. One never knows who might overhear. "She is in a terrible state." There is only one such she. He is immediately on the alert and glances round the room. The Prime Minister is deep in discussion with the French ambassador's wife, who is of a certain age, and very French of course. There is no sign of the First Lady.

"Where is she?"

"In her rooms." The First Lady has not shared accommodation with her husband for several months. It is one of the worst kept secrets in Whitehall. "I didn't want to leave her on her own but you must come."

"Please do excuse me, Li." He brushes the cool slender hand and all its fingers with his tinder dry lips and whispers for her ears only. "Until Wednesday." He nods to the others and, not too hurriedly, accompanies a red-faced Lizzie Hastings out of the Green Salon by the private side entrance. Several heads turn. Rosalie Murray cannot believe her eyes. She just cannot believe her fucking eyes.

Over the head of the French ambassador's wife, the Prime Minister exchanges conspiratorial smiles with the Li Soo Ying. She needs to be very careful indeed.

Later Monday Evening 16th October – The first part

It is probably best to draw a discreet veil over the doings in the second-floor bedroom at the Ritz Hotel occupied by Hollywood superstar Amelia Sedley, the face of Dior. She is practically paralytic with the amount of glug glugged champagne, not to mention the cocktail of drugs.

She is finding it impossible to focus on the naked Marion Fay and the glistening dildo. She is unable to resist as Marion Fay wedges a triangle of cold pizza between Amelia's wide open legs and begins to nibble aggressively. Amelia Sedley endeavours to speak but there is just a throaty gurgle as the greedy mouth devours the crust.

Later Monday Evening 16th October – The second part

Trapped in the dim lit attic studio, Emily Rowley is clinging for dear life to Nina Balatka and keening like that gin trapped animal in some wild dark place. Nina Balatka is stroking the unkempt hair and hiding the triumphant smile, although Emily Rowley is not in any fit state to notice the triumphant smile.

The Window man canvases propped round the damp stained walls are the most amazing paintings Nina has ever seen. The pale almost milky blue eyes cannot look away from one particular canvas. At the same time she is making absent-minded hushing noises, as if Emily Rowley is a child in distress and the mother's thoughts are very much elsewhere – the sounds of the far off battlefield are carrying on the wind. Yes….well. She kisses the top of the head and strokes the knobbly backbone. Emily Rowley is shivering and shaking. Jack is right – she does need fattening up.

"They are brilliant, Emily. Brilliant." The Exhibition that will make their fortunes is already taking shape in Nina's head. Opened by the People's hero, Window man himself, to universal acclaim with Window lady – aka cupper of the balls, at his side.

"They're awful." Emily wails and grips tighter. She is still wearing only the baggy knickers and the paint splattered words worn off T-shirt. "I wish I was dead." This particular gin trapped animal is annoyingly keening on a banshee wail.

Right. Enough. At her intimidating best, or worst depending where you are standing, Nina breaks the clinch and holds the snivelling snot nosed excuse for humanity at arm's length. The take it or leave it square face demands attention.

"Stop it. Now!" She shakes the shaking girl until the uneven teeth rattle. "Do you hear me, Emily? Stop it. Now!" The Slavic eyes are in sniper mode – the wide mouth set on automatic.

The artist known as Emily Rowley stares and stares with those fake emerald green eyes in offbeat wide-eyed wonder. "Cupper woman?" She whispers.

Nina has not got time for this. "Shall I tell you what we are going to do, Emily?" The artist known as Emily Rowley nodding dog nods her head – jump off a high building she might wonder – take a massive overdose, only that didn't work – slit her wrists, although she tried that once and it didn't work either, despite the river of crimson flowered blood whose colour she has never been able to reproduce in paint. She has not tried jumping off a high building.

"We are going to have a hot shower." At least Nina hopes so, glancing sceptically at the stuck on shower cubicle in the murkiest corner of the attic room. "I am going to soap you up all over until you are as clean as a new pin." An English expression she has heard more than once and has always wanted to use. "Do you understand?"

The artist known as Emily Rowley noddingly nods her head, wondering if you can drown in a shower.

"And I am going to make sure that the world hears about your genius. And you are a genius. Do you understand, Emily?"

"Yes, cupper woman." A still small voice.

"My name is Nina. Say it."

"Nina." An even stiller smaller voice.

"We are together in this…" A gentle stroke of a paint splattered cheek that somehow contains a veiled threat. "You…me, Nina… and Jack." Not that he is fully aware of it yet.

"Window man?"

"Yes. Window man." They stare at each other for several charged seconds. "Right. Shower time."

Nina Balatka begins to undress and Emily Rowley hesitates. "I don't want to be on my own tonight, cupper…I mean Nina. I don't know what I might do. Would you stay with me? Please."

Wearing only white knickers Nina pauses. Perhaps it will do Jack good to know she is not available at the drop of a hat. She does not intend to be available at the drop of a hat ever again. She will text him because after all she is safeguarding their best interests. "Of course I will stay, Emily."

The answering smile is utterly beatific.

Later Monday Evening 16th October – The third part

Sir Godwyn Lydate pauses in the open doorway and takes in the grand operatic scene. The little red dress cast aside in an untidy heap and the First Lady's make-up gothically streaked with weeping. She is sitting cross legged on the floor in revealing red underwear with one stocking visibly laddered and both stockings precariously attached to the lacy red fragile suspender belt.

She stares at his impending intrusion more like an animal at bay than an animal at bay… for goodness sake.

Lizzie Hastings holds back because Lizzie Hastings believes that she is nobody's fool.

"That will be all for now, Lizzie my dear." He merestly touches a bare arm and she endeavours not to shiver. There has been enough insane jealousy for one night. "Shut the door, my dear." The door is then conspicuously locked from the inside.

Lizzie Hastings is glad to leave. There is something about the ferociously self-obsessed First Lady that has always frightened Lizzie in her bones, and she is an eminently sensible girl not given to hyperbole. Lizzie of course worships Sir Godwyn and hopes and prays that she is wrong in thinking that even he has gone too far this time. She has to admit there is a tiny frisson that hopes he has gone too far, because Lizzie Hastings will not abandon him come what may; she will be there to pick up the pieces. In her heart of hearts she knows she is only a bit player in anyone's story. At least she is in this story and plots can thicken in surprising ways. That achingly beautiful woman behind the locked door appears fragile and breakable, like the finest Meissen, and yet there is a steeliness at odds…there would be something unbreakable amongst the shattered fragments and even his sure touch might not be sure enough. If he ever did fall to earth the repercussions would be incalculable but Lizzie would never turn on him. Never. Never in a million years.

There is nothing more she can do for the moment. He might need Lizzie later. He quite often needs Lizzie later, if the First Lady has taken the strong sleeping pills and is dead to the world. Or if…well…or if. There are things Lizzie knows that she dare not tell. Lizzie tiptoes towards her own room and cannot help wishing that he will come to her bed tonight, as he has come on other nights. Just the thought of it is making her moist. She doesn't like to dwell on the fact that he has spoiled her for other men. It was her choice after all.

Behind that conspicuously locked door Sir Godwyn gathers the Prime Minister's might as well be naked wife in his strong arms. He is preternaturally calm whilst she weeps and sobs and beats ineffectually with flailing clenched fists. There is as ever the underlying scents of her desperate needs, which have somehow sneaked through the fissures in his formidable defences. He of course does know.

When she is quiet at last, he strokes the smooth blood sealed spine and waits as always for the ragged breathing to come under control, as it always does. She is a Stradivarius of a woman and can only be tuned by a Master… even then… even then.

He carries the unresisting bride to the sofa and cradles the hauntingly lovely woman on his lap.

This most calculating of men had never calculated for any of this to happen. She had appeared so grieved and broken when she discovered the sheer magnitude of her husband's infidelities. She had striven to keep it hidden for all their sakes. The two of them had once upon a time been very much in love and she had given up so much to support her husband's surprisingly meteoric career.

Then on that fateful morning when the infidelities all became too much, Sir Godwyn had touched her bare knee on this very sofa and sympathetically asked how she was bearing up. Of course he knew what was wrong. He knows everything. He certainly knew that infidelity was a two way street.

He had spent the previous night with that most energetic puppy of a girl, Lizzie Hastings, and was more than a trifle befuddled after a sleepless few hours. He had been surprised to see the First Lady, who was supposed to be accompanying the Prime Minister on a bridge building visit to Merseyside. Sir Godwyn had squeezed the bare knee without thinking, as one does, and the Modder dam had broken and swept away all common sense with everything else. He had taken her in his arms – there was nothing else to do – they had made love there and then on the sofa and later in bed. She had desperately clung to him and he thought he had probably made the second biggest mistake of his life. And then they made love again and he knew that he had made the biggest mistake of his life.

"Darling Goddy." Back to the here and now. The past is indeed a foreign country.

"My darling." He kisses the classic furrowed brow.

"I love you, Goddy."

"I love you, Jayne." He thinks he does after his fashion, and that is the tragedy. He really thinks he does love this most fragile of women, and knows it is almost certainly not enough because love is only a four letter word…unlike infidelity.

"I don't want to go through with the abortion, Goddy." Such a tiny anguished voice, almost a child's voice afraid of the dark. Instead of saying please leave the light on she says, "I want to have our baby." The next few minutes will be crucial. Ye gods. He doesn't know if he has the will and the guile to argue and cajole any more. He only knows it would have been better if he had stayed longer in Lizzie Hastings' bed, as she had begged him to do on that fateful morning. Always a boisterously adventurous girl and he had been sorely tempted. But he did not stay in Lizzie's bed and he did find the First Lady, semi-draped in her revealing dressing gown, with salty tears streaming down the hauntingly beautiful face. Shakespearean tragedy at its most damning. The stinking groundlings for once silent and open gobbed.

In that befuddlement, after the night with Lizzie Hastings, he had not been able to make a cold blooded calculation and did not make any other calculations. That is probably why a Lydate ancestor on the Duke of Wellington's staff lost both his legs to a cannon ball and thus died gloriously at Waterloo. And why another Lydate ancestor died in the Crimea sword raised leading the charge of the Light Brigade. And why yet another Lydate ancestor had been blown to pieces leading a Company of his Regiment over the top on the first day of the Somme, instead of staying safe at the headquarters Château with the other Staff officers. The Victoria Cross is on display at the Regimental Museum. Sir Godwyn has refused to sell.

"Goddy, my darling."

"Yes, my darling."

"I must have our baby." And of course not forgetting Dunkirk. His great uncle Neville Lydate had refused to leave on one of the little boats. Had insisted on staying to fight for the honour of the Regiment. His body was never found.

That day in the overheated Orangery at Chequers she had told him she was pregnant. There had been no one else it could be, she lied, least of all the Prime Minister. She always refers to her husband as the Prime Minister, never Robert, and certainly not the Bobby of his intimates. She had insisted she wanted to keep their love child and Godwyn had insisted there must be an abortion. In the end she had reluctantly agreed. He should have known… he really should have known.

"Goddy, my darling."

"Yes, my darling."

"Take me to bed."

An expectantly naked Lizzie Hastings cuddles her most shapely body in her own arms and gives it an hour. Surely tonight that brutally lovely woman will take at least one of the strong sleeping pills. Only when the hour is up does Lizzie, with a disappointed sigh, open the bedside drawer and retrieve the rabbit vibrator, a birthday gift from a previous boyfriend who did not possess Sir Godwyn's legendary stamina.

Later Monday Evening 16th October – the fourth part

Ensconced in the Grande suite at the Savoy Hotel, the once upon a time call me Jack has received the text from Nina Balatka and is somewhat annoyed. Gulping whisky he hangdog stares at the painting of the nude Nina with the white panties round an ankle – a slightly thick ankle if he is being picky. The painting is propped up against a coffee table as if not exactly forgotten. It is most definitely striking and he is not at all sure if he wishes he had the power to make it come alive. That kind of wish is a bit too close to the twisted daydreams that were the closest thing he ever got to real women with actual ankles. His mother being the exception that proved the rule…his bloody sister, as in so much else, did not prove anything.

He is pleasantly distracted by the arrival of Shirley Keeldar, very much a real woman, sashaying her elegant way around the Grande suite and turning on the Tiffany lamps one by one. Superb legs in sheer black tights and a tight fitted black skirt and a sculpted crimson silk blouse with several buttons undone.

"A top up?" She asks and he acknowledges, remembering to practise a winning smile. She bends close and pours gurgling golden whisky into the cut glass tumbler.

They settle close, but not touching, on the comfiest of the couches and sip their drinks in the comfiest of silences. They are both staring at the painting... it really is striking. Almost too challengingly lifelike in Shirley's valued opinion. There is a definite likeness to that formidably gay games mistress at school...a memory of being smothered by huge breasts and finding it hard to breathe, best left unremembered.

"She is quite talented," Shirley Keeldar has to admit and has to admit that she quite likes being with Jack. She doesn't know why she feels so much at ease because she is not an at ease person – there is Tom Sawyer of course, but he leads such a busy life and they have to be so careful with their secret trysts – there is so much at stake.

There is the inherent vulnerability in Jack that she finds endearing – enticing even. Of course he possesses a vile temper but then one would be disappointed if a murderer did not possess a vile temper. "Nina is very alluring in an uncompromising East European kind of way." Is Shirley's considered opinion. The formidably gay games mistress was half Polish, or it might have been half Czech. She is not sure of the other half.

Jack murmurs agreement, giving the impression that he knows exactly what she means. She takes hold of his free hand with her own free hand. "We can go to bed if you like, Jack. I am a wee bit horny." She doesn't like to admit that she is a wee bit horny most of the time these days and wonders if it is an age thing.

He turns his head and fashions a Peter Pan lost boy smile that should tug at her heartstrings; the mood music would be an easily forgotten lilting Viennese waltz melody.

"Later. I just want to sit here for a bit." He sweetens the pill. "With you."

"You know, Jack, you are really rather good in bed." She crosses her legs and reveals lots of sheer black tights. She will be even hornier for the waiting... definitely an age thing.

"Better than Sir Godwyn Lydate?"

"How do you know about Goddy?"

"Becky told me." That figures. She can be a real tell-tale and very much a puss with sharp claws when it suits. Shirley retains his hand and they entwine fingers and it is rather soothing, in an ersatz kind of way.

"There is no doubt much that Becky did not tell you, darling." To be going on with she presses the clasped hands inside the blouse against a squashy breast. She launches straight in. "Goddy and I were in the attic at Lydate Hall... he was fourteen and I was twelve...we were sort of siblings and I was staying for that summer... we were very much left to our own devices... Godwyn had been....” She carefully considers the choice of words. “Irreparably damaged by his Nanny...” As an afterthought, she adds, “Who always hated me...and still does.”

He takes a gulp of whisky – irreparably damaged – words he would do well to remember.

“Nanny seduced him when he was twelve years old.” Jack doesn’t say anything. “She was a sly buxom village lass who got to him before his mother did, which one might say was the lesser of two evils. The mother was a supreme bitch of the highest order but was afraid of Nanny. Everyone except Goddy was afraid of Nanny.” She slurps vodka. “One day when it was supposed to be Nanny’s day off she cycled up from the village because she had forgotten some knitting, or so she said. She walked in on the foul mother naked, except for her stockings, with a naked and aroused Goddy on her lap sucking a nipple he was never allowed to suckle as a baby. Nanny Tressel went ape shit and beat the mother senseless. Nanny kidnapped Goddy to her own mother’s cottage in the village. That same day the evil witch mother left Lydate Hall and rarely returned. It was rumoured that her nose had been broken.”

“The mother didn’t bring charges for the beating?” He is thinking of his own mother.

“She wasn’t that stupid.” Shirley stares off into the far distance and Jack is learning when to keep quiet.

“The summer when I was twelve, but to be fair nearly thirteen, Nanny was unwell. There were rumours of course.” Shirley doesn’t elaborate. “So Godwyn and I were very much, as I said, left to our own devices. The old couple who led everyone to believe they ran the house kept very much to themselves. They were frightened of Nanny even when she wasn’t there. So it was in the attic where we first played the game of Nanny and Goddy. I had to take off my dress and panties and bend over the dressing up trunk. He took me from behind...but gently.”

She pauses for another slurp of vodka and he feels he ought to say something. There is still a lot of learning to do.

“I’m sorry.”

“Don’t be silly.” She laughs but not in an amused way. “It was very pleasurable. Much more pleasurable than pleasuring the older girls at boarding school.” A benighted smile. “Not to mention the odd school mistress or three.”

Jack slurps and spills some whisky.

“Goddy had learned a lot from Nanny Tressel.”

They both take slurps. Neither one spilling this time.

“After that I used to sneak into his bed every night. I felt so loved and grown up and strange to say, it was one of the happiest times of my life.”

Jack knows that he does not have to say anything. He really does know that happy sadness, or is it sad happiness, is beyond any form of words. For several minutes they remain comfortably ensconced in their separate pensive attitudes in the rainbow's end lighted room. They finish their drinks but neither one seeks to break the spell.

Then something makes him speak out. It was not what he intended to say when he opened his mouth.

"One afternoon just after our tenth birthdays my sister took me by the hand and led me upstairs to our mother's bedroom. My sister was giggling in an odder way than usual. Our mother's bedroom door was ajar and my sister edged it further open. My mother had gone to lie down with a headache. She went to lie down with a headache most afternoons."

The tumblers are empty and there are no drinks to ritually slurp. "She was beached on her back on top of the covers with the flowered skirt up around her waist and sensible white pants, that I recognised from the washing line, bundled on the floor. Her legs were spread wide open as if she had fallen from a great height. I remember there was a noticeable ladder at the top of one of the stockings; she always wore stockings. She said they were more hygienic than tights." She would, thinks Shirley. The clasped hand is pressed more possessively against a squashed breast.

"Her right hand was moving between her legs and she was moaning. Her eyes were tight shut and her mouth gaping." He pauses for breath and the scarcely breathing Shirley presses the hand so tight, there is no more breast to squash. She is feeling very horny indeed.

"My sister did that naughty schoolgirl manic giggle that she still does to this day." His voice rises a few octaves, as though he is that boy and the rest of his life is yet to be fucked up. Despite appearances to the contrary it is not the painting of Nina Balatka at which he is staring but the real-life body of his mother all those years ago. "Neither of us could look away as her body went rigid and her hips thrust into the air, as if she had been shot, then she fell backwards and appeared to stop breathing. I was frightened and I began to cry. My dry eyed sister shoved me forward and I stumbled to the bed. Mummy's bed."

It was the last day he ever called her mummy.

"I said are you all right mummy mummy mummy and she opened her eyes. It took some moments for her eyes to focus properly. Then she spread her lips in a weird lopsided grin. I was old enough to think she might have had a stroke. She pulled me close and whispered I was a good boy. There was a funny sort of smell that reminded me of school dinners."

He pauses and gulps some air and swallows hard. "That night mummy came for me when my sister was safe asleep and dragged me to her bed." The tears are streaming down his schoolboy face. "I said mummy I don't want to. Please mummy I don't want to..." It was the last time he ever called her mummy.

"It's all right, Jack. It's all right." Shirley is holding his shaking body in a tight embrace. "Really it's all right, darling." She is getting rather expert at this sort of thing after all the times with Goddy.

"I've never told anyone."

For what seems a very long time they rock backwards and forwards in the parody of a too fond embrace. Two lost children holding each other as only lost children can ever hold each other in a grown up world.

Later Monday Evening 16th October – The fifth part

Rosalie Murray is absolutely furious… absolutely fucking furious. The Ministerial car to which she is entitled drops her off at the door of her Westminster apartment. She slams the car door and the driver tut tuts under his breath. It is a good thing she is unaware of the tut-tutting.

How dare Sir bloody Godwyn sodding Lydate sneak out of the Downing Street Reception with that horse faced trollop Lizzie fucking something or other. Rosalie had been only too well aware of his smarming around that older woman, batting her false eyelashes and pushing out her false tits. That is par for the course. Even slobbering over the hand of that chinkie slut only to be expected.

Rosalie had had to admit it was all racking up her excitement at the thought of going back to Albany. Had even wondered if he was doing it on purpose for Rosalie's benefit – a kind of foreplay. The sexy black knickers were sticking pleasantly in all the right places.

She slams into the bedroom and flicks on the light. She has forgotten all about the arranged husband… and there he is naked… and there is Celia what'sit naked. At least he has the good grace to appear nakedly shocked at the unexpected appearance of the apparition of the Goddess of Vengeance. The brass necked little tart Cecilia what'sit does not appear in the least bit shocked.

"I thought you were otherwise engaged tonight." A pause… "Minister." The little tart adds very much as an afterthought. There is a visible livid love bite – make that two visible livid love bites.

"So I see."

"We got a bit carried away." Another of those pauses… "Minister."

"So I fucking see." The two formidable women are eyeball to eyeball and, being fully clothed, Rosalie Murray should have a marginal advantage.

"You were told to babysit him, not shag him." She stands with hands on her hips. "What bit of babysitting did you fail to understand?"

"I was never good with verbal instructions. Tourette's or something… Minister. So I equate babies with shagging." The eyeballing is probably a score draw and it is by no means certain who will edge the penalty shootout.

John Eames is wisely not eyeballing anyone. As surreptitiously as possible he is pulling up the blushed pink sheet, but not far enough to cover up most of Cecilia Hunt. At least the other bite marks are well hidden. He doesn't know where to look and so he doesn't look anywhere.

"Oh! What the fuck." Now he does very much look at his future blushing bride, as she expertly sheds the skimpy black dress. They are both very much looking, as she shrugs out of the skimpy uplift bra, and then even more expertly steps out of the sexy black knickers that have been sticking pleasantly in all the right places.

Cecilia Hunt makes a mental note and is good at mental notes – Tourette's or no Tourette's.

"Any port in a storm." Exasperates Rosalie Murray who doesn't bother shedding the stockings.

"Shouldn't that be ports?" A pause is a pause is a pause. …"Minister."

"Make some room." So they make some room.

Tuesday 17th
October 7.42am

No message from Jack and a more pensive than usual Nina Balatka is beginning to wonder if she was a bit too hasty and ought to be worried,. There is so much at stake. She tap taps the two-year-old mobile phone against her chin. Against her better judgement she has tried ringing and it has gone to voicemail. At least she has not left a message.

Emily Rowley is fiercely concentrating on dabbing the all-important finishing touches to one of the remarkable Window man canvases; the one where a three eyed Window lady, as Nina prefers to think of her other self, displays a burning bush between elephantine thighs – very Biblical but by no means flattering.

"You okay, Em?"

Emily Rowley has shyly asked Nina to call her Em. The poor girl has always wanted to be called Em by a special friend and has never had a special friend. Nina thinks that call me Em sounds like the name of a Second World War radio programme, but doesn't say so.

Emily, now known as Em to her special friend, nods but doesn't look away from the canvas. "Have you got any food, Em?" Nina possesses a healthy appetite and cannot think straight on an empty stomach. Emily nodding dog shakes her head – a bump in the road. Last night she had fallen into a deep sleep in Nina's arms, tits squashed together in the three-quarter bed, on a mattress that has definitely seen better days. Nothing untoward happened or had been contemplated. Emily just wanted to feel safe and watched over by her very own guardian angel.

She really is a sweet, almost simple-minded, girl underneath the multi-coloured cloak of vergent insanity. Genius in its many guises.

"Are you hungry, Em?" Emily nodding dog shakes her head. The recently shampooed hair ripples on her nebulous thin shoulders. Nina looks over those thin shoulders at the brilliant work in progress. She must keep in with Jack because she cannot wait to organise the Exhibition. It will be stunning.

Where are you, Jack? She tap taps the mobile against squared teeth. She closes her eyes and prays in Polish. She always prays in Polish.

The mobile buzzes. "Hi, Jack." She is not sure if she has kept the relief out of her voice. It is a very long time since she has been relieved to hear a man's voice. It is an even longer time since one of her prayers has been answered. "She's fine." Emily smiles without looking away from the canvas. Nina touches the rippled hair. "Hard at work."

Emily waves a brush in the air.

"She waves hi." Before falling asleep Emily confided that she found Jack a real turn on when she is in the mood, which to be fair is not often. Nina had not agreed or disagreed but had concentrated on being the guardian angel – not a role for which she is particularly suited.

Jack is telling Nina that he is with his agent, which is true. Nina doesn't think he has ever told her the agent's name and doesn't ask. Evidently there has been an early meeting about some dates on American TV, because they are desperate to get Jack over there. Nina hopes the pangs of hunger are not jealousy, but she has never ever been jealous and has no intention of starting this late in the day.

To lighten the mood she jokes that her stomach is rumbling. Evidently his stomach is rumbling as well. He says come over to the Savoy and share breakfast on room service. Anything you want.

"You all right if I leave you, Em?" Emily Rowley nods and adds a dab of deeper crimson red to the amazing burning bush. Nina fondly pats her head. "See you later, Em."

Emily nodding dog nods her head and spits on the canvas and works the deeper crimson red with a broken thumbnail. The effect is amazing, but still not the shade of the flowered life ebbing away blood that she seeks.

Tuesday 17th October 7.53am

Jack ends the call and eyes up – there are no other words for it – Shirley Keeldar easing up black tights over black knickers. She wickedly grins and wiggles the shapeliest of bums and Jack grins back not feeling the least bit like a voyeur. In fact he feels remarkably grounded this morning, the earth beneath his feet just the flat earth. There be no dragons lurking, although they are probably only sleeping. It will not last. At least nothing needs to be crossed out.

They had gone to bed together as something quite natural and preordained. The first bout of confessional lovemaking had been brutal and self-serving on both their parts. The second bout was brief and sentimental and in some way celebratory, although celebratory of what they are not at all sure.

Then unashamedly naked in each other's arms, they had talked lots more. She had divulged more secrets and so had Jack. He had thought she would be shocked but she had stroked his face and brushed away the few, too few, unwanted tears with a delicate thumb, as if putting the finishing touches to a clay bust.

They had fallen asleep in each other's arms as exhausted lovers surely must in a state of the nation novel. Sometime before dawn they had woken up melded in each other's arms and kissed and caressed and made love. Then they had whispered some more and he thinks she must have surely to God told him everything. They each hold the key to the other is what they ought to believe. They would probably be half right.

"This is the closest I have ever been to anyone." She had lied kissing a sticky out ear.

"Me too." He had lied.

"Nina would be jealous if she could see us now."

"Perhaps."

"We must never be jealous." She is good... very good.

"No."

It is good to watch Shirley getting dressed and not feel the least bit voyeuristic. In fact it is a word that the People's hero must strike from his vocabulary. She adjusts the above the knee skirt at the waist and tells him that she is going to the office to work on his affairs. After all, he is the golden goose, she does not say. She will just have to brave puss's hard stares. Becky always thinks that Shirley goes several steps too far where certain men are concerned and she is probably right...although she need talk.

"Nina is coming over for breakfast." Shirley Keeldar is not the least bit jealous but pretends a half decent pout.

"What are you doing this evening, darling?" She asks.

"I haven't thought that far ahead." He smiles that lost boy's smile that now appears quite natural.

"We have a lot of work stuff to discuss." She smooths down the skirt. "There is a cosy little restaurant where I would like to take you." She tells him the name and he has of course read about it in the Sunday supplements. "I will meet you there at eight."

A kiss full on the lips and she is gone in a haze of the distinctive perfume that he had watched her spray on in several places. The taste of her lipstick lingers on the palate.

After a few minutes of him being lost in thought, the room phone rings. "Send her up."

Tuesday 17th October 8.21am

Standing at her side of the bed Sir Godwyn Lydate intently studies the before waking woman, which could well be the title of a lost painting by Manet or more likely Monet. Enmeshed in sleep she is as hauntingly beautiful as ever. Perhaps more a Pre-Raphaelite image of some perverted medieval scene that only ever existed in an artist's overheated imagination. She always looks eternally at peace in the minutes before she wakes, when the Sleeping Beauty eyelashes beginning to quiver.

As always some sixth sense tells her that the man is no longer in the bed. She moves restlessly and moans and flutter flutters the eyelashes. Flinging out her arms to bare the Grecian statue breasts in a gesture that never ceases to flutter his excuse for a heart. Flutter perhaps like a late summer butterfly in the tended gardens of Lydate Hall; a most apposite metaphor.

"You are leaving, my darling?" How could he bear to leave such compelling naked beauty is the message in the bottle.

"Someone has to run the Country, my darling."

"I thought that was my husband." She kicks away the duvet to reveal every square inch of her naked body in all its prepossessing glory.

"No you did not."

"No I did not." A quite bewitching smile – beautiful naked lady on waking with a bewitching smile. He is full of painterly titles this ticked off morning. Then all at once she is that serious child who will not be thwarted. "I want our baby, Goddy." If he could only be sure but it would appear churlish to demand a paternity test.

"I know, my darling. I know." He had not been going to touch her body anywhere because he knows where it will lead. When has he ever made wise decisions where this enchanting creature is concerned?

He cannot stop himself sweet tooth kissing each Belgian chocolate nipple; this gesture of surrender almost brings tears to her eyes. "You must rest now, my darling." She gratefully clasps and gratefully holds a hand to her face." Later today Lizzie will take you to my cottage retreat in Chipping Camden." He smiles what some people might take for a sad resigned smile, but they would be wrong, because this time he has calculated the odds. At Oxford no one would play him at chess unless he was handicapped in some way. It became ridiculous. "Lizzie will stay with you." The Cotswold retreat is the one place he goes to be uncontactable, even by Nanny.

"You will come to me, my darling." She nuzzles the unborn clasped hand and he is only too acutely aware of being stared at by the kissed nipples and has to look away.

"As soon as I can get away, my darling."

She has a sudden thought. "There are my diary commitments." She has grown to loathe her diary commitments, especially if they involve the Prime Minister.

"I will take care of things." Of course he will.

"And him?" She has childishly resolved never to speak his name again; the betrayer of all the days of such early promise. Finding out about those awful things so soon after the latest miscarriage. Then finding him in bed with Florence Dugdale had been a bitter blow, although she loved the drama of it. They had so wanted children or so she had led herself to believe.

"Leave it to me, darling." Of course she will.

Avidly she kisses that unborn child of a hand. She can be so much like a child herself when not being the most seductive woman he has ever known, and that is saying something.

"I love you so much, Goddy, my own darling." She has conveniently forgotten that she once called the nameless one her own darling and told him she loved him more than life. Not to mention…

"And I love you, my darling."

"Kiss me, Goddy."

A disappointed Lizzie Hastings decides to tiptoe away. Listening at keyholes can be such a thankless task, albeit in a minor key.

Tuesday 17th October 8.34am

The Reverend John Eames surfaces somewhat reluctantly from the drug like slumber. It is his own reverberating snoring that wakes him from a most realistic Sapphic dream. He has never ever woken with such a rocklike hard on from such a rocklike dream. In the early hours the threesome swallowed some diamond shaped purple tablets and John had continued to satisfy the two women long after it had been strictly necessary.

So it is an actual drugged sleep from which he is most reluctantly emerging, weirdly having dreamt of taking Mary Thorne that first time, against her better judgement, but it had not been in the Churchyard bending over a gravestone, like in the dream.

He becomes dimly aware that there is someone else in the very much disordered bed. Just one someone else. He sniffs… no clue there, although obviously not the vanilla Mary Thorne. He reaches out to feel up the bare hindquarters and thinks he knows which one. Enveloping the someone else in a bear hug, rubbing the drug enhanced hardness between the thoroughbred flanks…that reminds him…he must seek out a Bookmaker to place some bets. There is a runner in the two thirty at Doncaster called three in a bed…it has to be worth a decent punt.

"Jesus." She murmurs. "You're insatiable, Bish."

"I am for you."

She pushes back against the hardness. "Horny bastard."

"Dirty bitch." He has never ever called a woman that, although he came close with Mary Thorne that second time. He hopes his blushing bride-to-be is not within earshot. He is not sure the threesome thing is quite his cup of tea... he is more a one woman at a time sort of chap. In the neat and tidy kitchen, Rosalie Murray is munching on some crunchy cereal muck that is supposed to be healthy. She does want to lose a pound or three. Pointedly ignoring the red stain ingrained wine glasses, and the two empty wine bottles, she is checking messages on her mobile phone. Nothing from Sir Godwyn high and mighty Lydate, but there is a most interesting message from the Foreign Secretary. Sipping strong black coffee she becomes aware of the unmistakable noises coming from the bedroom, and smirks. She has not felt this, shall we say, inundated for some considerable time, if somewhat sore in certain intimate places. The poor sap had excelled himself with a little help from his purple friends. Just thinking about it is making her realise the enhancing drugs are still in her own system. The noises in the bedroom are reaching a crescendo and she is tempted... sorely tempted. Perhaps the marriage of convenience might not be such a bad thing after all. Perhaps Cecilia what's it should go on honeymoon as first reserve. She certainly has a certain way with her, the brass necked little tart.

The mobile phone pings. The Ministerial car is waiting. A farewell slurp of strong black coffee and designer bag over shoulder she heads for the door. The noises emanating from the bedroom showing that that was not a crescendo after all. "Let's go kick ass." She punches the air and winces at the soreness. Rosalie had fallen asleep whilst the other two were still very much at it. That brass necked little tart has capacity in spades.

The Minister hesitates... no... duty calls.

The clever clogs Cecilia what's it might have bitten off more than she can nibble on this time. There are well hidden depths in John Eames and well hidden depths can hide such nasty surprises.

Despite the soreness there is a spring in Rosalie Murray's step and if she was able to whistle she would whistle. There is nothing she cannot do, apart from whistle of course. Be very afraid, Sir Godwyn Lydate – be very afraid. She slams the apartment door on an obscene plea in anyone's language.

Tuesday 17th October 8.44am

Spencer Perceval is really really annoyed. As a spoiled little brat he used to jump up and down and scream at the top of his voice when he was really really annoyed. Sometimes he would hold his breath to terrify his doting parents. He feels like doing that now. In fact he does hold his breath for several seconds but there is no one left alive to be terrified and so he breathes. The less gorgeous than she used to be, but still pretty gorgeous if she makes an effort, wife has really pissed him off. I mean really really pissed him off.

He had woken from a dream of Carrie Brattle with a bit of a stiffy and slapped the wife's lots of bum to wake her up and told her to get on top. She had point-blank refused. I mean he was doing her a fucking favour right? Her period has started. Even if true, which he very much doubts, as if that ever stopped the horny cow in the past. He had slapped her about a bit and she had kneed the stiffy for Christ's sake. It still fucking hurts.

Then she had given him the full fucking silent treatment. He hates the full fucking silent treatment. She has taken the girls to school and is, no doubt, meeting one of her posh overweight chums for coffee and a good old bitch about the other posh overweight chums.

Well fuck her, that's all he can say. Perhaps he was a bit hasty dumping Carrie Brattle. After all, abortions are quick and easy these days… just like going to the dentist. He shouldn't have panicked and boy did an equally horny Carrie Brattle know how to take care of his morning stiffies. Her mobile number is unobtainable and no answer at the sort of love nest. Sir Godwyn is nothing if not thorough. Spencer should really not have panicked. A big mistake and another page to add to the War and Peace of big mistakes.

The state-of-the-art toaster pops. The toast is burned and he burns his fingers. "Jesus fuck." The still gorgeous when she makes an effort one has set the toaster on the highest setting. His foul expletives are interrupted by a tentative knock at the front door.

Tuesday 17th October 11.24am

Sir Godwyn Lydate possesses the enviable man from Mars talent of being able to compartmentalise every aspect of his life and times, which is a talent that has served him remarkably well over the years. He doesn't brood after rare defeats, he just plots revenge. Nor does he exult over the countless victories, he just plans the next one and the one after that. The pulling of strings is second nature to this most permanent of the Permanent Punch and Judy men.

The impeccably uniformed chauffeur glances in the rear view mirror of the limousine and recognises the 'he be plotting' face of his Lord and Master so knows not to make small talk. There are no doubt great matters of state involved. Instead Gilbert Markham ponders on the liquorice allsorts naughtiness of the Honourable Lady Rebecca Sharp. That girl could have satisfied his old Regiment and not turned a hair.

Sir Godwyn is instinctively aware when and how far to retreat. It is a skill possessed by all great Generals and a skill that both Napoleon and Hitler could have benefited from. Stroking his baby's bottom smooth chin, Sir Godwyn stares out of the darkened window at the passing street scenes… the people more than the buildings.

Buildings are merely arrangements of bricks and stones, whereas people have failings and foibles and bravery and cowardice and not forgetting lust. Buildings can be repaired as he has proved at Lydate Hall; damaged people thankfully can rarely be repaired.

The Panther grey limousine pulls up outside the unprepossessing block of seedy apartments, in not the best street in not the best part of London, bringing a sense of déjà vu. This time he fears there will be no sticky out Carrie Brattle to make things interesting.

"Wait here, Gilbert."

"Yes, Sir Godwyn." He touches his cap. Nothing the great man does is a surprise.

The late Chef's habitation is on the fourth floor and Sir Godwyn takes the stairs two at a time, trying not to breathe in through his nose. That people live and propagate like rabbits in hutches never ceases to fascinate the dapper Old Etonian. There can be so many nasty surprises attached to people that live like rabbits in hutches that one has to stay on the alert.

The woman who eventually answers the peremptory knocking at the rattling door with the rusty numbers is not at all what he expected. The surprised Sir Godwyn cannot prevent the dry lips twitch, even though it might give the wrong impression. In the instant his features are rearranged to convey 'is there anything I can do to help at this difficult time' and if he was wearing a hat he would raise it politely.

"Mrs Newton?"

The woman is probably five foot five or six, bare footed with an everything in its place worn down heart-shaped face, which could be almost beautiful given the right circumstances. These are patently not the right circumstances. Mousey hair not too badly cut; a surprisingly dishevelled look and gentle brown eyes that will always seek reassurance from a man – no signs of red eyed weeping. Shapely figure in the cheap above the knee print dress and nice legs below the knees to the bare feet. Sometimes thighs can be a nasty surprise although probably not in this case. No visible trace of mourning black. All this he absorbs before she has finished nodding.

"My name is Sir Godwyn Lydate." He announces with all due emphasis.

The gentle brown eyes momentarily flare in momentary surprise that lends a certain animation to the blocked out face. Then nothing. A firework that has been lighted and then fizzled out on the ground. That is the thing with fireworks that fizzle out on the ground -- stand well back.

"Do come in, Sir Godwyn."

He notices the staged hesitation as she opens the door wider and stands her ground as he brushes past. A nicely modulated voice with just a puzzling hint of somewhere North. A quite evocative scent and lots of it. She might well have married beneath her. There will certainly be an untold story , although possibly only a short novella. He pauses and breathes in the lots of scents, as she shuts the ill-fitting door and strides purposefully down the gloomy passage, bare feet pitter pattering on the patched linoleum. The gloomy passage permeated with an odour that he can only compare to wet clothes after a rainy fox hunt. They pass two closed doors to reach the door of the living room, which is standing invitingly ajar.

"Please take a seat, Sir Godwyn." A neat and tidy square low ceilinged room with everything, such as it is, in its place it would seem. Some cheap souvenirs on a ledge catch the eye. The Pyramids a trifle out of proportion and the Sphinx definitely so.

"After you, my dear."

She takes a seat on the black leather effect settee, which sinks alarmingly under her slight weight. He decides to remain standing as he studies the new widow deftly arranging her position and tugging at the ragged hem of the cheap print dress. This manoeuvre only highlights the bare leg which is no doubt what she intends. He is fairly certain there will be no nasty surprises with thighs.

"Please accept my sincere condolences, my dear." She stares dolefully at her own working girl's hands clasped in her lap. "He will be greatly missed."

"They said it was an accident." Definitely some North there... North Yorkshire perhaps?

"Most unfortunate." He is standing to his full height as she shyly looks up from under what he wrongly takes to be false eyelashes. She knows this impeccably attired top drawer gentleman is mysteriously important because Ralph had been, in his own peculiar way, in awe; but the gentleman seems very nice considering. She had not in her wildest dreams expected him to call in person. His startlingly pale blue eyes are well used to drawing confidences from people, especially women she thinks. She knows that she reads too many romantic novels, where she daydreams of being the heroine ending up in the arms of the hero on the last page. As if.

"They say there will have to be..." She hesitates. "...a post mortem." Ralph would have hated that. He hated operations, but it does somehow lend him a significance in death he never possessed in life, however hard he tried, poor lamb. He would never even admit to a low sperm count and instead convinced himself that she was barren; such a terrible defining word and untrue, which is what hurts.

"Just routine, my dear." He perches gingerly on the settee, it sags gently and she resists the temptation to edge closer. That might appear too forward in the circumstances. She is a well brought up girl, who knows only too well that she should not have married for love, which turned out to be something else entirely.

"With it being an accident, my dear." It is with difficulty he suppresses a dry lip twitch.

She is very much aware of no doubt expensive aftershave and wonders if he shaves himself. His chin being as smooth as the chin of the hero of a romantic novel. "Is there anyone who can be with you, Mrs Newton?"

"Please call me Sarah."

"Very well. Sarah." Her name sounds more resonant when spoken by his exceedingly plummy voice. The watch he is wearing is probably worth more than Ralph earned in a year. That is when the lazy sod was working – thinking of him as a poor lamb did not last long.

"We have no family." She realises too late that there should have been a break in her voice. Still, it is not the time or the place to say there are no children. Although they had tried once upon a time… my God how they had tried. There were no problems in the trying department.

"Friends? Neighbours?" A Pause. "A work colleague perhaps?"

She shakes her head and he notices that she appears a trifle diccomfited. A lank of mousey hair falls across an unlined forehead and she resists the temptation to brush it away. He wonders if she might be about to cry, and so takes hold of one of the workaday hands clasped in her lap. Rubbing gently in a sympathetically natural way that no one could take objection to, least of all the murdered chef. There are proprieties after all.

She finds the unexpected contact comforting when there is no real need of comfort. He is not to know that of course, although she cannot help wondering if he guesses.

"Is there anything I can do, my dear?" It is probably his imagination but she appears to be slightly on edge, as if listening for something. "Are you expecting someone, my dear?"

She hastily shakes her head. "No. No one." With a gesture of suppressed annoyance, she brushes the fall of hair away from her perfectly in proportion unlined forehead. The ragged hem of the dress has ruckled up to reveal a birthmark the size of a two pound coin on the inside of a slender thigh. The knees not the least bit knobbly. This well put together woman could surely have done better for herself than the adulterous beanpole Chef, but then women are sometimes so unreadable in translation.

"There is something, Sir Godwyn." The accented voice almost a whisper that suits the timbre of the voice. He can only too well imagine this throaty whispering in far different circumstances. There are just not enough hours in the day.

"Godwyn, please." He squeezes the captured workaday hand and, with the free hand, she scrapes some loose hair behind an ear in a feminine gesture. Cheap earrings but tasteful.

"Ralph was a good man."

"Of course."

"But…" She prettily hesitates. "…He was not very good with money." She licks the rosebudish lips and prettily cannot seem to find the right words to carry on. This new minted widow is not at all what he expected as he waits several heartbeats and then several more. "I haven't any money for the funeral." She huskily whispers all in a rush.

He takes possession of both hands. "I will take care of everything, my dear."

"Oh! Thank you." She is even more prettily confused. He is enjoying himself much more than he thought he would. There are depths here. She allows another hand squeeze. It is the least she can do. "Thank you, Godwyn."

The gentle brown eyes are reassured; the eyes of a doe that has found sanctuary in the depths of the forest… just how deep the forest she has not the remotest idea. If she did know how deep, she might well try and seek sanctuary elsewhere.

"Are there any other financial requirements, my dear?"

She nods her head and then feels she must explain herself. "I work at the cafe across the street but it is hard to make ends meet. Ralph was so often out of work."

"Quite so."

"You are being so kind, Sir Godwyn and I don't like to impose." An eyelash flutter. "I mean Godwyn."

"I will arrange the funeral and then we can sort out any other issues." This time she squeezes back. "I will take care of everything, my dear."

"Thank you, Godwyn." The still small voice. "I was really worried." This time she squeezes first. "I didn't know which way to turn." Well she did, but she does not like it one little bit.

"You have been a clever girl to turn to me." It is a long time since she has been called a clever girl.

One final both way squeeze. "Now I must go." He releases the hot workaday hands into the wild and takes out his wafer thin mobile phone. "Give me your number and I will ring you when everything is arranged." He pats a brave bare knee. "And we can meet up again very soon. Would you like that, my dear?"

"Very much, Godwyn. I feel so much alone."

"Not anymore, my dear. Not anymore." He squeezes an even braver bare knee and then taps in the number that he will remember anyway…there really really are just not enough hours in the day.

"He would want to be cremated, Godwyn." She doesn't want to take any chance of being haunted by his ghost. He could be such a jealous bastard and sometimes without cause.

"Of course…" He can also do hesitation but not so prettily. "…Sarah, my dear." He pat pats a bearing up bare knee; a wandering little finger dusts the two pound mole. Sarah sees it as a gesture of a dog preparing to piss against a lamppost. A male territory thing which is fair enough.

"When will you ring, Godwyn?"

"Later today, my dear." Pitter pat pat. Wander. Wander. "And that's a promise, my dear." She covers the pitter pat patting hand gently with her right hand like a late summer butterfly landing on a flower. He is much taken with the late summer butterfly theme.

The widow precedes her distinguished visitor down the gloomy passage to the front door. There seems to be more of a sway to the hips and everything else. The odour of wet clothes not quite so noticeable.

"I can't thank you enough." She touches his arm. "Godwyn."

He thinks it is appropriate in the circumstances to kiss the unfurrowed brow in a 90% cousinly way. Then she, it appears almost instinctively, offers the almost rosebud lips. The brief kiss has elements of chasteness, because after all one has to be aware of protocol with the husband unburied or, indeed, unburned.

"I will see you very soon, my dear."

He is rewarded with a hesitant soul-searching smile. Nice teeth. There is no excuse for not looking after one's teeth.

Safe in the living room she breathes in the expensive aftershave as she crosses to the grime smeared window overlooking the vagrant street below. Staying back so as not to be spotted, she watches entranced as the grey uniformed chauffeur smartly salutes and opens the rear door of the huge grey limousine. Grey is one of her favourite colours; she was always a fey child. She is pleased that Godwyn glances up at the window, before returning to a secret world behind the blackened windows.

The well-built chauffeur gently closes the door and marches smartly to the driver's door and also glances up at the window. She can spot an ex-military man at fifty paces, having been brought up at Catterick, she knows all about military men and their unpatriotic little ways. She holds herself tight in her arms and daydreams about being in the back of that limousine with the all powerful Sir Godwyn Lydate taking liberties. He will have an Achilles heel and she will find it if she gets the chance. She always finds the Achilles heel and it is not always a low sperm count. She is not to know that it is best to stay well clear of Sir Godwyn Lydate's Achilles heel.

As the grey limousine pulls away, she glances at the cafe across the narrow street and smiles. The Polish waitress with the funny name is at the doorway anxiously looking up and down the street. She hates to be left alone in the café because her English is not very good.

A grim faced Sarah goes back to the bedroom, opens the door and hesitates on the threshold. The naked man on the bed would be recognised by Jack and Nina as the perpetually middle-aged cafe owner with the disgraceful comb over.

"Has he gone?"

"Yes."

"Thank Christ for that." He is literally slobbering. "Come back to bed, sweetheart." They had not progressed beyond some mistimed necking and a bit of a feel.

"You need to go."

"What!?"

"You heard." She stays in the doorway and crosses her arms. She is able to make herself look formidable if she puts her mind to it. Just a few minutes ago she had reluctantly agreed to let her creepy boss at the cafe have his way with her, as they say in the best romantic novels. In fact a phrase from one of the romantic novels on the bedside table, the page saved by a bus ticket. He has offered a substantial increase in wages if she is – nice to him. There seemed no realistic alternative. After all she had put up with Ralph's increasingly bizarre sexual demands for long enough.

She knows only too well that she is one of those women who need the physicality of a man in her life. Even this pathetic specimen is just about better than nothing.

"Do you want to keep your job?"

"I suppose so." She really hopes she can trust Sir Godwyn but she is not used to trusting people and a man like him is outside her experience. He had stroked her knee but that might mean anything. He should have gone a bit further and then she would have been sure, but given the circumstances she didn't feel it appropriate to offer encouragement. She might have been wrong.

"Then take care of this." He lies back proudly. "And be quick about it."

She has her lips pressed tight together and is thinking. The sight of the quite respectable hard on is most definitely distracting. Then she comes to a decision because she has no choice but to look after her best interests and has to play the cards as they are dealt. Today is today. Tomorrow is tomorrow.

"I want five hundred cash. Now." She knows he always carries a bundle of used notes.

"What!?"

In one sleek movement she shrugs off the dress and stands naked well out of reach. She couldn't find her knickers when there was the peremptory knocking at the door. If Sir Godwyn had gone a bit further he might have experienced a most pleasant surprise.

"I am well worth it." She hopes Sir Godwyn thinks so but she cannot be sure.

"Bitch!"

"You call me that again and you can piss off back to the Polak." Who thinks bitch is a term of endearment.

Sarah Newton stands magnificently nakedly angry with hands on slim hips. She really is a most alluring woman and he can hardly breathe, which is not a good thing with his dicky heart. "My wallet is in my trouser pocket." He breathlessly whispers.

"Sorry?"

"I said my wallet is in my trouser pocket."

She folds up the grubby notes and turns her back and secretes them in her knicker drawer. He groans. She has a gorgeous arse. "Please hurry up, sweetheart." He pleads with more abjection than he would wish.

"You should be ashamed." She walks towards the bed. "Taking advantage of a poor widow woman."

"I will look after you, Sarah. Honest I will."

She supposes a bird in the hand, however scraggy, is worth two in the bush. She looks down between her legs and sighs – she needs a shave. She looks at the man on the bed who has followed her gaze and who groans on the groan. She might as well enjoy it until hopefully something, fingers crossed, better comes along.

As well as the money she has taken a condom from the wallet, which she throws in the general direction of the erection. There is no question of a low sperm count because she knows the Polak has had a recent abortion.

"Put that on. The last thing I need right now is a baby." His hands are shaking so much she has to help out.

Tuesday 17th October 12.15pm

A pensive Sir Godwyn Lydate is staring out of the darkened windows of the grey limousine. Something about the widowed Sarah Newton is needling him. Something didn't quite add up. He hates things to not quite add up. The mobile phone vibrates to Parsifal and, still pondering, he doesn't check the caller.

"Yes, my dear." He listens intently as he studies the back of Gilbert's perfectly aligned military haircut. He even sits to attention when he drives. Sir Godwyn appreciates loyalty, rewards loyalty and has well rewarded Gilbert. He punishes disloyalty without mercy and knows that Gilbert will never be disloyal.

"He should not have done that, my dear." He listens some more. "He really is a stupid stupid boy." He checks his manicured fingernails. "It is not like you to be so upset, my dear. Do pull yourself together. I will come straight over."

On the detour to Spencer Perceval's mansionette, bought as a wedding gift by the lady's father at Sir Godwyn's insistence, he makes several phone calls. On one of the calls his replies are so pincer sharp that Gilbert glances in the rear view mirror and hurriedly glances away. He wouldn't like to be in that lady's high heeled shoes… Minister or no Minister. Sir Godwyn abruptly ends the call as they arrive at their destination.

"Wait here, Gilbert."

"Of course, Sir Godwyn."

There is a lady's high heeled shoe abandoned in the middle of the driveway and a neat flowerbed has been trampled. The second high heeled shoe is snagged in a rose bush. 'Bittersweet' is the name of the rose on the attached label.

A theatrically weeping Jane Perceval opens the door before he knocks and impetuously jumps into Sir Godwyn's arms and wraps bare legs around his body. Sir Godwyn closes the door with his foot, holds tight and shoos and coos because he knows from experience not to say anything. Poor Jane has always lived life on a knife edge of raw emotion and it can prove so very tiring. If he had not been distracted with disturbing thoughts of the dry eyed widow he would not have answered the call. He is not really in the mood for all this nonsense. These days he is rarely in the mood for all this nonsense.

Not without visible effort he carries the clinging on burden through to the extensive lounge and they collapse in an undignified heap on the immense sofa. She is most definitely putting on weight. He gives it a couple of minutes of shooing and cooing and stroking before taking hold of her chins and squeezing. This close they need a bit of tweezer work; she has always tended to let herself go at the least minor setback in her privileged life.

"I am getting too old for all this, my dear."

She takes a deep shuddering breath. "I used to be your darling."

He knows only too well that it is a veiled threat. "Tell me what happened, darling?"

She takes another slightly less shuddering breath. "You know I have tried to make it work, Goddy darling. You know I have tried and tried." He kisses the tip of a damp nose which always seems to have a calming effect. If she was a dog she would probably wag a tail. "I have forgiven his infidelities for the children's sakes and for all of this." She dramatically flings out a bare arm that he would hesitate to describe as fleshy.

Amateur dramatics has been her one and only talent and she is rather good in a minor key – more of a serving wench than Queen Mab. "I have even let him do disgusting things." She theatrically shudders. "Disgusting things." Spencer Perceval would be taken aback at this statement and wonder who she was talking about.

Sir Godwyn thinks it best to move on quickly. "Tell me what happened… darling?"

She thought he would never ask. "We had a god-awful row this morning." She points to a livid bruise on her cheek and pauses for the audience to gasp in horror. Sir Godwyn tut tuts. "I ran the girls to school."

Never having run girls to school he nevertheless nods encouragingly. He knows running children to school is something a lot of people do.

"I was meeting a friend for coffee but her mother was taken ill and I came home unexpectedly." The uplift bra highlights breasts that have been the winners in the weight gain stakes. "I found the fornicating little shit fucking that fat bitch from next door." Sir Godwyn tut tuts and fights off a dry lip twitch. It is not a line one will hear in most Amateur dramatic productions – most certainly not a line that J.B.Priestley would have conjured. "They were naked on the kitchen floor." At that unforgettable mental picture Sir Godwyn forgets to tut-tut.

Instead he absentmindedly brushes spittle away from her tastefully enhanced lips. The make-up has run but Jane Perceval, overweight or not, could never look like a clown. The what she takes for a caring gesture brings more tears to her eyes. Knife edges are so precarious.

"The fat bitch was bouncing on top making enough noise to wake the dead." Jack Priestley really did miss a trick there.

"Dear. Dear." Another unforgettable mental picture and a bit more brushing away of spittle.

"I have thrown the fornicating shit out." If there was an audience in the Church hall, those few remaining would break out into spontaneous applause.

"And the fat bitch?"

"I kicked her out on her fat arse." Pots and kettles come to mind. She looks so much younger when she wickedly grins, even if the wicked grin turns grimly malevolent.

"Dear. Dear." Now that would have been a sight for sore eyes. From what he recalls from a rainy summer barbecue, the fat arsed one was a rather generously proportioned lady with please please come to bed eyes; or as it turns out please please take me on the kitchen floor eyes. It is no laughing matter. He remembers the fat arsed one's rather sleazy husband paying rather a lot of attention to the eldest Perceval girl, who reminds Godwyn so much of her empty headed mother in her prime. There will be trouble ahead.

"I am not taking him back this time." She caresses Godwyn's smooth chin with fingers that are not as delicate as they used to be once upon a time. She kisses the smooth chin. "We should have married, Goddy."

"We did say at the time it would have been a terrible mistake... darling." Or rather he had said and she had reluctantly agreed.

"I WAS pregnant with YOUR child."

There is no answer to that. Enter the useful idiot stage left – who has now apparently exited stage right, accompanied by much hissing and booing.

They both glance at the polished silver framed photograph that has ostentatious pride of place on the mock Georgian occasional table. A much younger and much slimmer version of Jane Perceval, smiling archly, and cradling a baby enfolded in an ancestral Christening gown; standing to one side is a boyishly grinning Spencer Perceval striving not to look out of place. On the other side the reluctant Godfather who is not grinning. Sir Godwyn Lydate as Godfather to his own child… most definitely not a laughing matter.

The irony never escapes him every time he sees the photograph that is so deliberately displayed. The Godfathering was one of Jane's insisted on conditions and Jane's insistings have continued to this day. He sometimes wonders if it would have been easier to have married the stupid girl and have done with it. By now they would have been safely divorced. But then he would have had to see the children every other weekend, or some such nonsense.

"How is the child?"

"Frances is looking more and more like you every day."

There is no answer to that either. There is a blessed silence for a few moments and, with nothing better to do, he admires the pushed up breasts.

"I mean it about not taking him back."

"What about the children?"

"They hardly see him anyway. He is more like a favourite uncle." In her mind Sunday lunches with spoiled roast potatoes do not count. This week's afters has turned out to be a strictly one off performance. "Forget the favourite bit."

His mobile phone vibrates to Parsifal and she raises a quizzical eyebrow, as she did so effectively in the amateur production of 'When we are married'. She has always been good with eyebrows. On the night when she apparently conceived Frances they had made love to the music of Parsifal in the background. She had called it making love, but he had had his mind on other things that particular night; that is until she had done something that had riveted his attention and the subsequent, if you will, lovemaking certainly warranted an end product.

He answers his mobile phone. "Yes, Prime Minister." He strokes a bare knee without thinking and that was where all the trouble started on that memorable night and many many more nights since then. There has always been some doubt about the third child whose name escapes him. "The statement has been prepared, Prime Minister."

She has to smile at his making the words 'Prime Minister' sound like he is referring to a lesser species of dung beetle. She takes hold of the knee stroking hand and traps it between fleshy thighs, as she had done on that memorable night when she evidently conceived Frances.

"Your wife is indisposed and has been advised to rest." Everything about Goddy has always excited Jane, from the first moment they were introduced by her father. She had been acutely aware of the embarrassing dampness between her legs all the time they had outrageously flirted at that function.

She had wanted a job and he had duly given her a job, he had told himself to please her father. A week or so later she had contrived a messy breaking up with the latest unsuitable boyfriend of two whole weeks. She had rung Godwyn in hysterics and said she was taking an overdose. The girl with whom she shared the apartment was away in Mustique. There was no one and she was at the end of her tether. Against his better judgement Godwyn had rushed round. It only took nine minutes.

He had been so sympathetic and so understanding and she was only wearing a shortie nightie. She had quite reasonably explained that she had no wish to be found naked by the ambulance persons after taking an overdose. She had perched on his lap and promised to stop being a silly girl and the rest followed as night follows day. In fact it was a night and a day.

"That really is not the point, Prime Minister." She unzips his trousers and burrows with four rabbit fingers and a mole thumb and has most definitely not lost her touch. The Prime Minister wonders why Sir Godwyn breaks off in mid-sentence.

"Leave it to me, Prime Minister." He ends the call and turns off the phone. "What are we going to do with you... darling"

"Take me to bed."

"I mean after that."

The answering grin is not the least bit malevolent. It is the wantonly abandoned grin of the time they had been introduced by her father, pretending he was not pimping his youngest daughter in exchange for Political favours.

"I will not take him back, Goddy." She necks fiercely on his mouth and all the reasons for him being here come flooding back. The greedy searching of her tongue worked that first time and it works now. He knows about the others, including George Meredith, who has lasted longer than most, but Sir Godwyn is hardly in a position to take the moral high ground.

She leads him by the hand across the imposing hallway past the kicked off one hinge door of the state of the art kitchen, to the foot of the always impressive marble staircase. She pointedly ignores the fat bitch's cast off bra and knickers but the crumpled dress she kicks aside. Godwyn cannot help noticing the motto on the knickers... most appropriate.

Tuesday 17th October 12.57pm

Gilbert Markham squints at his Rolex. It is a fake but a very good fake. He knows from experience that if Sir Godwyn stays more than twenty minutes in that house it will be at least two hours before he emerges, appearing more sleek and well-honed than usual.

Gilbert has to admit that she is a tasty piece of posh Totty, if a tad weighty these days. He lives in hope that Sir Godwyn will ask Gilbert to step into the breach and help keep the lady sweet. It will not be the first time he has acted as a sweetening surrogate – just ask Carrie Brattle – but never with this particular lady. Gilbert wonders if she has something on Sir Godwyn. Gilbert has something on Sir Godwyn; but then Sir Godwyn has much more on Gilbert Markham, who is enough of an old soldier to know that if you strike first at Sir Godwyn Lydate it had better be a killer blow...he has no intention of taking that chance.

He eases back the driver's seat and tips the neb of the uniform cap over his eyes. He might as well catch up on some kip. Lady Rebecca can be very demanding and keeping that girl sweet is a full-time job. He wonders if it might be time to cool things, although she might not like that. More importantly, Sir Godwyn might not like that. He likes Lady Rebecca kept sweet, although now of course an unbelievably randy Carrie Brattle has come into play.

Gilbert is just dropping off with a smile on his face, when there is a tentative tap tapping on the driver's window. Not Sir Godwyn then. He flicks up the cap and opens his eyes and presses a button. The window noiselessly descends.

"Sorry to bother you."

"Not at all, madam." Another tasty piece of weighty posh Totty. It is the street for it. It should be renamed weighty posh Totty Avenue. This one is a mouth watering platinum blonde, fortyish at a guess, with a low-cut top and expressive low cut eyes. All in all well worth a second squint.

"Could you possibly do me a huge favour?"

"Hopefully, madam." He presses another of the plethora of buttons and noiselessly raises the seat.

"I would be very grateful." He can see over her shoulder that the bedroom blinds Chez Perceval have pinged shut. At least a two hour stint, possibly more, because Sir Godwyn seems to be in one of those funny moods today, when he needs to lose himself in the fabric of a woman and Gilbert sympathises...there was a lot of fabric involved with Carrie Brattle.

"Indeed, madam."

She leans forward. There appears to be no hinterland of a bra. Lady Rebecca talks about hinterlands rather a lot at the moment. "I had a bit of an argument with my next door neighbour and one of my shoes is on the drive, the other one is in a rose bush. I wonder if you could possibly retrieve them for me?" A hundred metres sprint winning smile that is all perfected lips and perfected teeth. "They are rather expensive." There is no way on God's earth that she is setting foot on that drive ever again. For the last hour she has had to sit down on a cushion.

Gilbert Markham knows that she knows, but what he doesn't know, is that less than an hour ago she was unceremoniously dragged naked off that, in Gilbert's opinion, tosser Spencer Perceval. Dragged off by the expensively coiffured hair just this side of what promised to be a climax of sorts. To make matters worse, if that was possible, she cannot find any of her vibrators – not a single one. She wonders if Felix has stolen anything else; the locks will have to be changed. That was the reason she had called next door, to borrow a vibrator from Jane. Not counting on the real thing answering the door.

"Certainly, madam." She takes a step backwards as he opens the door. A really curvy piece. Lady Rebecca is not a curvy piece – lots of hinterland but not a lot of curves.

Avidly, the weighty posh Totty watches him retrieve from the recent war zone the shoes that cost an arm and a leg. Since the start of divorce proceedings she has not thought it appropriate to treat herself to any new shoes, as there is no man in her life to suck her toes. She can observe that the shoe in the rose bush is not easy to extricate and she hates rose bushes. As a child she had been rushed to hospital with a rose thorn poisoning her thumb and had to wait in Casualty with a lot of smelly people. She sucks the thumb where there is a tiny scar. She still hates smelly people.

"There we are, madam." Not being the least bit smelly, her knight in shining armour holds the shoes aloft like a remnant of a piece of the true cross brought back from the second Crusade. "I'm afraid one of the heels is broken."

Genuine tears are stinging the most expressive eyes. There is only so much a girl can take and there are times when she wishes she didn't hate swearing so much. She does glare at the Perceval house, the eyes expressing come outside if you dare and I will pull your hair out by the dyed roots you what's it what's it. She takes an involuntary step towards the offending house.

"I can get them repaired, madam."

"You can?" The eyes now expressing who needs a second-hand vibrator with a big strong man like you around, which is by no means a subtle look.

"I know a man." He winks. Gilbert Markham is the sort of alpha male who can get away with winking at just about any woman, even a tasty piece of overweight posh Totty. "I know a man for most eventualities, madam."

There is a pregnant pause. It is a long time since she gave up trying to get pregnant. She extends a finely manicured hand.

"My name is Rosanna. Rosanna Spearman." She has thought about going back to her maiden name but lacks the social courage. This hunk of a man secretes one of the shoes in the crook of his arm and grips the finely manicured hand – there are some things a girl cannot give up.

"Gilbert Markham." He keeps hold of the finely manicured hand. "Gil to my friends."

"Am I a friend?" She sounds nonplussed and he hopes she isn't taking it the wrong way.

"I hope so, Rosanna." In for a penny in for a pound... he squeezes. "I really hope so." She really did not intend to squeeze back.

"Hi Gil."

"Hi Roz." She has never been called Roz and after the initial shock she quite likes it. Neither of them says it rhymes with Boz.

It makes everything so very personal. Spencer Perceval would never have called her Roz and probably couldn't even remember her name. He had called her babe...harder, babe.

The colour of her expressive eyes is not easy to describe – he takes a stab at gunmetal grey. There is a livid bruise on one cheek, so she was the loser on points. He is not aware yet of the other bruises.

"Are you hungry, Gil?"

"Famished, Roz."

"I will fix you a sandwich, Gil." Which is the extent of her culinary skills. She retrieves the squeezed hand and touches her expensively fashioned hair in a most feminine gesture. "It is the very least I can do." There is just a tad overmuch perfection. Once upon a time she must have been a natural stunner. "Follow me, Gil."

"With pleasure, Roz." She really is a curvy piece of posh Totty. One of those women where extra pounds are put on in all the right places. The unlooked for thought flits in his mind that she actually seems a very kind woman.

Tuesday 17th October 1.14pm

The somewhat lanky Archbishop is standing tall to his full six foot two and a quarter inches. At Eton he was nicknamed longshanks, but that stayed at Eton with so much else. He is always careful not to stand tall in the presence of Sir Godwyn Lydate. The beringed hands are clutched behind his back as he stares out of the mullioned window at the immaculately maintained Palace gardens that are wasted on his gaze. He sees there are far too many dead leaves for his liking. He will have a stern word. He is rather good at stern words, if he does say so himself.

This pose is one he deems appropriate. Lord Cardinal of all he surveys and Prince Palatine of the Church Militant. It could well be the Fifteenth Century and a man so blindly sure in his own skin that he doesn't need skin. Skin. Flesh. Ah! The way of all flesh.

He smiles benignly at his own reflection, as if mulling over a complex matter of Church theology, and early Church theology at that... possibly Fourth Century. He had so enjoyed the dark eyed waitress fighting back this morning. Such a lovely exchange of slaps and punches and then she had all at once surrendered… such a surrender! Those lovely big dusky breasts created to suckle a host of children… suffer the little children.

He must stop thinking about it. He really really must. The second coming. Oh! Dear God the second coming.

There is an under rehearsed deferential knock at the study door. He takes the usual few moments to compose himself. "Come."

The balder than a coot arthritic Chaplain Secretary bows himself, with some difficulty, into the Presence. He has served four Archbishops and this one is the most disingenuous by a country mile. "The one fifteen appointment, your Grace."

The Archbishop maintains the theological pose, giving off that profound impression of pondering some controversial declaration of the early Church Fathers. The Chaplain Secretary is not fooled. "The Reverend John Eames and Miss Cecilia Hunt." She had said Ms, but the Chaplain Secretary does not recognise that term.

Allowing the duly announced twosome several moments to take a few hesitant steps into the August Presence and appreciate the pose, he swivels majestically and holds out the ring hand. Cardinal Wolsey to the life. Deigning to be amused that the weary looking Vicar fellow, with bags under his eyes, is not sure whether to shake hands or kiss the blood red stone.

Ah! Wolsey. Wolsey. A Clavering ancestor had loyally served the Cardinal and had gone to the scaffold on the same day. Ah! The treachery of Princes. Indeed. Indeed.

He breaks the spell. "Enchanted to meet you." The two men awkwardly shake hands. "And you too, Miss Hunt." A brief minion's fingershake. Women knew their place in Tudor times.

"It's Ms actually."

"Quite so." A virginally untouched kitchen wench sort of prettyish girl. No doubt misleading on the virginal bit. Rimless spectacles that add to the effect and paint a rather stern appearance – more a 1930s village schoolteacher out of AJ Cronin, his favourite author. One of Godwyn's creatures, no doubt and so definitely misleading on the virginal bit. There is something vaguely familiar about her features that he cannot quite put his finger on.

"I have arranged for a selection of sandwiches and a decent Claret so that we can consume whilst we converse." Busy. Busy. Not enough hours in the day. Time is of the essence and all that. Who would be a Prince Palatine of the Church Militant?

He leads the way to a small circular William and Mary style dining table, ornately set for three people, and they seat themselves at his fussy direction. The Archbishop is pleased to see that Miss Cecilia Hunt is displaying rather a lot of leg… nevertheless perhaps more than might be deemed appropriate for the occasion. It is not given to many to consume and converse with the actual Archbishop. He smiles forgivingly and she smiles primly. She certainly has the figure for a Lyons Corner house waitress in the nascent years.

With a Papal flourish he shakes the dinky little antique bell at his right hand.

The understandably overawed Reverend John Eames is endeavouring to gather his scattered thoughts. So much has happened in such a short time. It is hard to believe he is breaking bread with the actual Archbishop who is so often in the news. The shaken bell takes him by surprise – bring out your dead he absurdly thinks – he is definitely not getting enough sleep.

Cecilia Hunt's thoughts are not in the least bit scattered. She is wondering whether some of the whispered rumours in certain high places could possibly be true. Something in the Archbishop's closeness gives her the creepy feeling that they probably are true, and that she is showing far too much leg. Thank goodness they are not alone.

Showing too much leg is a temptation she finds hard to resist because she knows her legs are a gold-plated asset in what is still largely a leg man's world. Less than an hour ago the legs were wrapped round John Eames's face and she shuffles in her seat at the unbidden thought. Johnny really is surprisingly adept at satisfying a girl who is so rarely satisfied. There could be interesting times ahead on the satisfaction front.

A startlingly busty Mediterranean-looking woman opens the study door and, Acorn antiques style, pushes in a hilariously squeaky trolley. There are several monogrammed plates of dinky crust-less sandwiches, two opened bottles of claret and three intricately engraved wine goblets. There is a most pleasant tinkle tinkling to accompany the squeaky squeakings as she pushes the trolley towards the table. Cecilia is surprised, but doesn't show it, to see that the black eyed pusher is wearing a 1940s waitress uniform, like a fugitive from a lesser known Ealing comedy.

In the recent past Cecilia has dressed up as a schoolgirl and as a nurse, for the delectation of recent boyfriends – never as a 1940s waitress. Perhaps she has been missing a trick. A momentary knowing glance passes between the Ealing fugitive and their creepy host. Cecilia Hunt decides that she is most definitely showing much too much leg.

The olive skinned glancee stagily rearranges the plates of crust-less sandwiches on the circular table. Then the opened bottles of claret are placed within reach of their host. Almost as an afterthought, the intricately engraved wine goblets are set out to some mysterious holding pattern. Cecilia thinks this is very much Sir Godwyn Lydate territory, as she becomes aware of the not unpleasant musty scenty odours and undertones of scrubbed sweat. She glances at Johnny who is – and who can blame him – captivated by the woman's Breasts with a capital B. Cecilia glances down at her own breasts with a small b, dinkily shaped under the pink silky clingy blouse. Quite sufficient thank you very much; Johnny has had no complaints thank you very much. The Busty one with a capital B dribbles some claret for the Archbishop to taste. He smacks his lips and closes his eyes. "Excellent, Anna."

"Shall I pour, your Grace?" A surprisingly deep accented voice, surrounded by rouged lips that do not quite add up. Cecilia gets the impression that she and Johnny are most definitely intruding in something namelessly pre-historic and best avoided at all costs.

Cecilia Hunt has just discovered a deep-seated aversion to husky accented deep voiced women. There is something almost of the deadly nightshade about this dark woman. Something almost sulphurous. Something almost of the praying mantis might not be taking it too far. Cecilia Hunt is rarely wrong in her reading of other women. Reading of men, yes... far too often wrong... women...no.

"Please do, Anna."

She eye wateringly deliberates over the pouring, ably assisted by the twin Breasts acting more like triplets. Anna is only too well aware that the two men are, of course, entranced by the Moscow State Circus wibble wobbling and that the snooty spectacled leggy girl is not in the least bit entranced. So she is poured less wine.

The snooty spectatacled leggy girl is thinking that if this woman had been a genuine 1940s waitress she would have been arrested for gross indecency.

"Thank you, Anna." A swift giving and receiving of knowing glances. "That will be all for the moment."

"Very good, your Grace." The Reverend John Eames thinks that the foreign accent lends the husky voice a named Ocean of undiluted promise, best left as promise for everyone's sake, probably including the Archbishop.

These Exhibition pens seem to have a life of their own.

Anna is watched out of the room by two sets of eyes, and the trolley pushing departure is followed by several moments of contemplative silence. John Eames cannot help but think it is like the first moments of entering a Church at a Wedding, or a Funeral, when people pretend to pray. He glances guiltily at Cecilia, who is demurely sipping wine and staring at nothing in particular. She looks so cutely scholarly wearing the round spectacles – an old-fashioned schoolteacher who would beat your knuckles with a ruler as soon as look at you.

"So tell me, John." The Archbishop likes to believe that he is rather good with names, if he does say so himself. "How much have you been told?" He takes up two crust-less sandwiches and one by one he pops them in his mouth.

"Hardly anything, your Grace." Well... nothing at all. He glances in the direction of Cecilia, who is daintily nibbling a crust-less sandwich and staring at nothing in particular.

"We feel things need shaking up a bit er...John." The Archbishop slurps claret to wash down the cream cheese and smoked salmon sandwiches. "Rather a good year." He murmurs to himself. He is murmuring to himself rather a lot these days. "We feel you are the man for the job." Another evaluating slurp. " Er…John."

"The Bishopric of Staines," Cecilia interjects, primly nipping crumbs from the corners of her mouth.

"Quite so." For Christ's sake he cannot be expected to remember everything … for Christ's sake. He has just been imagining Miss Cecilia Hunt in waitress garb, and she goes and spoils it by being pushy. She is just asking to be disciplined. "So tell me er… Cecilia." Jesus he almost said my dear. "How long have you been working for the ubiquitous Sir Godwyn Lydate?" They both know he would not take this superior tone if Sir Godwyn was within ubiquitous earshot.

Quite exceptional lots of legs and so he will forgive the pushiness just this once. There is that skimpy futuristic Star Wars waitress uniform with the exceedingly short skirt, more a pelmet really. Dear God… the vision.

After a measured pause for the Archbishop to gather his thoughts she replies, "Three years and eleven months and six days…" She checks the chunky girly watch on her left wrist. "Four hours and twelve minutes."

The Archbishop almost spills some claret. "I see."

Cecilia elegantly inclines her head and intercepts his startled buck in the headlights stare head on. He is not used to that. The, he thinks more greenish than anything, eyes are far too sparkly for their own good behind the rather severe spectacles.

"I do not think you do see, your Grace." A smile that does not reach the more greenish than anything eyes, but looks rather fetching shaped on the mouth of incredibly small teeth; mayhap a waitress who is sick and tired of her mundane day after day job and does not register the customers' faces anymore; a waitress that needs to be taught a lesson when all the faceless customers have gone.

The soon-to-be enthroned Bishop of Staines bemusedly looks on and struggles to stifle a yawn and then yawns. He knows that he is out of his depth but doesn't care anymore. Any fool can learn to doggy paddle.

Tuesday 17th October 1.59pm

Spencer Perceval is pathetically slouched at his cluttered desk in the shared office at the studios. With his head in his hands he can almost fool himself into believing that the lovely willing, oh so lovely and oh so willing, Carrie Brattle is poised to knock and enter. Wafting the distinctive Carrie Brattle scents of Carrie Brattle, that he is missing so much more than he ever thought possible. This has rarely happened with the others. It does not help that his neurotic shrew of a wife has thrown him out of the house. It was a pity she walked in at such an inopportune moment, which was embarrassing for all concerned.

Mind you he had to stifle a chortle when, as naked as the day she was born, what's er name from next door was dragged by the hair and then punched and kicked out of the door. She had scampered away dodging the shoes. It was very funny. But then the neurotic shrew had shouted some hurtful things at Spencer… really hurtful things and there was no need for that. Then to cap it all to be thrown out of the house in his turn. She will take him back, because she always takes him back. It is the resultant phone calls with his father-in-law he finds depressing, not to say debilitating. He has to put up with a lot.

Sweet, willing Carrie Brattle would have been so understanding. They would have been at it by now making things better and enjoying a no doubt spectacular climax, without some sclerotic madwoman bursting in at the crucial moment. Carrie. Carrie. Carrie. Thy name is Carrie.

Sir Godwyn had texted one word – sorted. One of his unfunny little jokes. Now he is not answering his phone and no doubt having his end away somewhere; that man is a legend. In any case he would not tell Spencer where Carrie is secreted away. She might as well be on the dark side of the moon.

There is an ever so polite knock at the door. So polite that one of the crew is probably taking the piss.

"Fuck off." He shouts and then breathes deeply of the fading remembered scents of a Carrie Brattle who used to knock and come straight in. Offering that come and get me smile as she lap danced round the desk unbuttoning a tight skirt, and then… and then. Carrie. Carrie. Carrie. Perhaps it was the real thing. Perhaps they can get back together after the abortion and be more careful next time. Anyway it wasn't his fault because she said she was on the fucking pill. That's what she said. He had no reason to think she was lying. Then of course there is the possible two timing thing. There is another less ever so polite knock at the door.

"What! For fuck's sake."

Taking this as an invitation, a head peers round the half open door. An utterly distinctive curly orange haired female head that he has a feeling he should recognise. He straightens up, shakes himself down and adjusts his face.

"Well?"

He looks so pathetically pathetic that Helen Huntingdon has to suppress a giggle. She is prone to fits of manic giggling at the best of times. He was so pissed he will not remember.

"It's about Question Time in Leeds on Thursday."

"And who the fuck are you?" Start as you mean to go on is Spencer's motto of the day.

"Your new assistant." There is something vaguely familiar about the scary hair.

"Says who?"

"Sir Godwyn Lydate."

Fuck. Fuck. Fuck.

"Come in. Come in." And he waves a regalish right hand in an imperious gesture that the crew often impersonate. "Sit down. Sit down." He might as well make it appear that the old fart has done him a favour. "Your name is? Your name is?" The crew often impersonate his habit of breathlessly repeating himself... of breathlessly repeating himself.

She really must not giggle, but is prone to manic giggling at the most inopportune moments. It can be endearing, but it can also be infuriating, especially if it involves coitus interruptus.

"Helen Huntington." She crosses the room in catwalk steps not dissimilar to the sadly missed Carrie Brattle. Only Helen what's er name is very much not undoing the buttons of a tight fitting skirt. Nor is she smiling come and get me big boy. She is also probably wearing knickers.

What she does do is to most efficiently remove the pile of ill assorted papers off the only chair, sit down and cross noticeable legs in orange tights that match the curly hair. Small delicate features with scarcely drawn on eyebrows, which give her eyes a washed out, consumptive look. A Pre-Raphaelite painting come to life – one of the models who died young. From what he can discern possibly a tad flat-chested but, after this morning's debacle on the kitchen floor, he has gone off intrusive triple AAAs for the time being. There is definitely something vaguely familiar.

"So." He steeples his fingers in imitation of Sir Godwyn Lydate. "So."

She suppresses a giggle as he smiles without showing his teeth – his questioning let's get on with the job but, hey, I quite like you unless you do something to make me not like you smile. Not an easy one to fake, as he has just proved. One to practise in front of the bathroom mirror if one had the patience.

"How old are you, Helen?"

"Is that relevant?" A bit too much in his face for his liking. Does she fucking know who he is?

"You look about fourteen, Helen." So there. So fucking there. He would outstare her as well only she places a delicate hand over her mouth and convulsively giggles more like a fourteen year-old schoolgirl than any fourteen year old schoolgirl known to man. The giggles are definitely ringing some bells.

He turns down the volume of the complicated smile and holds up his hands in mock surrender. There is something soothingly infectious about this girl's oddball good humour and so he grins naturally for once. "Shall we call it a score draw? A score draw?" With boyishly floppy blonde hair she thinks he looks no more than fifteen years old. Until one looks closely that is.

Enough is enough. She let's get down to business places her hands squarely in her lap. There is quite an odd smell in the office that she cannot quite place. "The Queens Hotel is booked from tonight." The voice all business like as well.

A fourteen year old determined not to mess up on work experience. "Seats are booked on the five o'clock flight this evening."

He almost as business like, if not more so – so put that in your pipe and smoke it – checks the gold Rolex that is the thing he loves most in all the world and that he never loses any opportunity to flaunt. A gift on their first wedding anniversary when they were still pretending. He doesn't bother reading the engraved message any more. He dare not have it erased.

"Not much time, Helen. Not much time"

"No indeed. We need to get going, Spencer."

"We?"

"I have been told that Carrie Brattle is indisposed."

He does a double take. That is one way of putting it.

"So I will be taking her place…" Another double take. "…as your assistant."

He nods and chews a thumbnail. A bad habit when he is unsure of the ground.

"I have a case packed, Spencer." More nail chewing. She thinks it is a really nasty habit but resists the temptation to smack his hand. That would make things far too personal in the circumstances. "I see you have a bag packed as well." She uncrosses the matching orange legs. There is a battered holdall dumped on the floor into which he crammed as much as possible, with the neurotic shrew screaming in his face and hitting out with balled up fists. He winces at the thought. She landed one or two telling punches and it was probably a technical knockout.

"Let's go."

He was just about to say that. The holdall is fucking heavy. He doesn't offer to carry Helen Huntington's dinky designer case which is outside the door, and then realises it is on wheels.

Tuesday 17th October 2.16pm

An entranced Carrie Brattle, whose ears are not in the least bit burning, gazes up at the Old Master painting with a genuine sense of awe. Mars and Venus surprised by Vulcan – a massive ornately framed canvas that is taking pride of place in this first room of the picture gallery of Lydate Hall.

She of course recognises the Sixteenth Century Spanish painter's name… of course she does. It must be worth a small fortune if genuine. She peers closely… the brushstrokes appear absolutely right. She had once told a previous boyfriend that standing this close to a genuine Old Master was better than sex… well… better than sex with him anyway.

The face of Mars bears a striking resemblance to Sir Godwyn Lydate… no doubt an ancestor. She studies the face of Venus and wonders if that might be the face of the ancestor's wife, or mistress more likely, who certainly appears to be enjoying being pleasured by Mars, that certain look on her face that Carrie recognises only too well. Decent tits with cherry nipples and in your face meaty thighs, that were all the rage then, even for a pretend Goddess being pleasured by a pretend God.

Carrie Brattle smiles a smile of having been there many times. It is a pity there is no one in the room to appreciate the lustre the smile lends to Carrie's otherwise street corner pretty face. A next-door neighbour's daughter's pretty face; the sort of pretty face that populates a working day in the streets of London and in the Tube at rush hour, where no one smiles but where pretty girls are noticed in passing.

She knows she is no great beauty – not dissimilar to Venus in the painting. Decent tits and cherry nipples and thighs slender, but this is now and that was then. There were no complaints when the student Carrie modelled for the life classes and had plenty of dates as a result. She has used what God gave her pretty damn effectively. There were most certainly no complaints from Gil on the back seat of the limousine, and after he had watched her squat and pee on the grass, they had done it again. She had fooled herself into thinking that Spencer Perceval was well and truly snared. He bloody well should have been with all the effort that she had put in, not to mention getting her timing right to fake the orgasms, which is not easy when someone is slobbering all over your tits. She had not faked the orgasms with Gilbert Markham.

Unlike Venus, she has stopped smiling. Spencer had promised they would be together and she believed him because he was so plausible. She is sure he even believed it himself when he was parroting the words. In response, she had excelled herself – in another age she could have been an in demand Courtesan. She has always believed that she has used men just as much as they have used her, and is probably right. With Spencer she let her guard down and it will not happen again. To break Venus's hypnotic gaze Carrie walks across to the floor to ceiling window that overlooks the extensive grounds undulating as far as the eye can see. An elderly gardener is most methodically sweeping up leaves. Carrie studies this subject for a painting of the Dutch school and holds herself tight in her own arms. She doesn't miss cowardy custard Spencer as much she thought she would and, in fact, despises him for hiding behind the formidable Sir Godwyn Lydate, not having the guts to do his own dirty work. If she had been pregnant his actions would have been beyond the pale.

She smiles that lustrous been there done that smile. Of course she wasn't pregnant – she is not that stupid. The intriguing Sir Godwyn divined the truth straightaway. She had overplayed her hand, so live and let learn, because you cannot pretend an ace with such a man when you only hold a four of diamonds.

She has been told by the really nice seeming, nothing is too much trouble, Bertrams that the Master, as they call him, is coming down late on Friday evening for the weekend. There is some important meeting and she must stay out of contact with anyone until he arrives.

She wonders if that includes Gilbert and hopes not. She glances round, catches Venus's eye and could almost believe that she winked…it was probably a naughty coachman in those days. Carrie has three days to think things through, and something tells her that there will be much to learn from the Master of Lydate Hall – it could be the title of a lost Brontë novel. She has not read any not lost Brontë novels, although she has of course heard of Charlotte Brontë… Amelia Sedley played her in that movie that was much criticised for the graphically no holds barred gratuitous lesbian scenes.

The elderly gardener, whom she will find out is not so elderly close-up, straightens and stretches his back, looks up and waves a gloved hand and the quite pretty girl waves back. She reminds him a little of his youngest daughter, also a quite pretty little thing who caught Sir Godwyn's roving eye. He returns to his task enervated by the vicarious contact with the quite pretty girl.

A few minutes later he looks up and the window is empty. Growing old is not such a good thing. The quite pretty girls he rolled in the hay are not the least bit pretty anymore and some are just not any more. The times when Sir Godwyn's mother used to wave from that same window to signal that the coast was clear seem several lifetimes ago. Not to mention that time when her husband returned unexpectedly, discovered them in bed together and had insisted on watching.

Tuesday 17th October 3.47pm

The tornado named Sir Godwyn Lydate bursts unannounced into the office of the recently appointed Minister of State and Privy Counsellor. There is perpetual scaffolding visible outside the arched mock Gothic window overlooking the Thames far below.

"What the fuck…?" A startled Rosalie Murray looks up from the laptop computer on her desk. There is no time to shut it down, as she half rises from the deep blue padded leather chair chosen by John Caldigate MP. "What the fuck do you think…?"

She is not able to rise the other half because, seemingly coming out of nowhere, a fisted one-two-three smashes into her preordained face and she spectacularly crashes backwards over the tumbling chair like a rehearsing circus performer. Except that a rehearsing circus performer would probably not land so awkwardly.

Grim Reaper faced Sir Godwyn checks the screen and click clicks the mouse. Within thirty seconds there is confirmation of his worst fears: he has backed the wrong horse and this could get very messy. He needs all his wits about him and they will be.

The treacherous harpy is now groaning into consciousness and instinctively attempting to tug down the hem of the concertinaed skirt. That is the very least of her worries.

He picks up the phone. "Get in here now, Miss Grey."

Within seven seconds the padded soundproofed door is opened just far enough to allow an ashen faced Agnes Grey to slip apologetically into the room. A visible vein is throbbing at her right temple; she is only too well aware of the pathetic groans coming from somewhere out of sight and she swallows hard. "Come here, Miss Grey."

She goes there and he points to the screen. Momentarily she glances at the groaning body on the carpet and at its futile attempts to cover its redundant modesty, then she looks at the screen. She knows everything there is to know about computer systems. "Yes. That's it, Sir Godwyn. I felt you ought to know."

He stares reflectively at the not unattractive, in a pleasant unthreatening way, little woman. The close-cropped mousey hair, greying naturally at the temples, only adding to the non-threatening attractiveness. The ever so slightly bulbous eyes are, as usual, avoiding eye contact unless it becomes absolutely necessary. The likeness to an approaching middle aged Queen Victoria is quite unsettling, but not in an unpleasant way. No one would ever guess and, after all, Queen Victoria had her naughty secrets.

Luckily the, intense as always, lovemaking at chez Perceval had already come to a natural climax when he took Agnes Grey's call – he always takes Agnes Grey's calls. Even though poor Jane was unhappy that he had to depart the scene without any after play. The trouble is that Jane Perceval's after play invariably turns into more play. He has promised to go back for dinner this evening, not a hardship, because she is a decent cook and the daughters always appreciate the, all too rare, visits of generous to a fault Uncle Goddy. They think it is a huge joke when he forgets their names.

When he had approached the parked limousine a flustered Gilbert had come rushing out of the next door house, dragging on his uniform jacket.

The woman with the come to bed etc eyes was looking out of an upstairs window with more been to bed etc eyes. Sir Godwyn had dry lip twitched. He might even allow Gilbert to get his grubby little paws on this pathetic groaning thing.

"You have done well, Miss Grey."

"Thank you, Sir Godwyn."

As they are speaking the pathetic, not to say intrusive, groaning is morphing into a throaty, retching sobbing. They both glance, with different shows of distaste, at the pathetic retching sobbing thing. A paint flaking puppet with a broken string, thinks Agnes Grey and is rather taken with the image. Sir Godwyn's thoughts are unprintable. They both look away.

"How long have you worked for me, Miss Grey?"

"Eleven years two months and three weeks, Sir Godwyn." And three days and eleven hours she thinks will be too sad seeming to divulge. Never mind the minutes… the seconds are ticking away.

"My goodness how time flies."

"Yes, Sir Godwyn."

"I remember the first day you worked for me, my dear."

"So do I, Sir Godwyn." She cannot stop herself blushing, as she allows exceedingly brief eye contact. She swallows hard and looks away and doesn't see the sealing of the dry lip twitch.

Now they both have no choice but to turn their attention to the bedraggled excuse for a human being struggling personfully to its knees on rubbery limbs, spitting out salivered blood. Thankfully, thinks Miss Grey, not spitting out any teeth…oh dear…there's one…and another. The flesh-coloured tights are laddered in several places and the cream blouse liberally spotted with blood and saliva. Perhaps only an Emily Rowley could do full justice to the dialectics of the unfolding pageant.

Agnes Grey should not be glad, she knows that; however, she is very glad indeed but does not show it of course, because she likes to believe she never ever makes the same mistake twice. The blood splattered apparition that would fail an audition in a Dickensian Christmas Carol, is struggling to set up the overturned chair, as if things can thus get back to normal. At the second attempt she slumps heavily on the uprighted chair, tentatively feeling at a jaw that, surprisingly, appears to be in one piece. Out of the unclosed eye she glares balefully at Sir Godwyn Lydate and then glares balefully at Agnes Grey, who surely wouldn't say boo to a goose? She had shouted at Agnes Grey earlier and called her a moron and that might have been a mistake of abstract proportions.

The moronic bitch is whispering into Godwyn's ear and the resultant dry lip twitch, almost masquerading as the beginnings of a smile, does not augur well.

They go out of focus. What the fuck? A fool to herself, Rosalie Murray tries to speak but for some reason her tongue is too big for her mouth. She tightly closes the good eye and prays she might wake up in bed sandwiched between John Eames and Cecilia What's it.

Counting to ten she opens the good eye and Sir Godwyn Lydate's face is no more than two inches away. The silent scream is constricted in her throat and she can do nothing about the slivers of snot dangling from her nose. There is so much pain she thinks the nose might be broken.

"You are a fool. Did you think for one minute that I would not find out? Did you? Did you?"

She makes a dreadful keening sound like a strayed domestic animal gin trapped in excruciating pain it was not designed to withstand.

"Cleverer people than you, much cleverer people than you, have tried and failed and are in the gutter." His spittle is spraying her face. She has no sense of smell. "Or worse." With a snort of disgust he moves away. "You disappoint me, Murray."

She begins to leak tears over which she has no control, pearly tears rolling down a battered make-up smeared face, to mingle with the blood and snot. She is a human train crash and many casualties are trapped in the wreckage.

"Thorry." She has dredged up a voice of sorts but it is not her voice. Her hands cover her face and it hurts… it really really hurts and she dare not breathe through her nose.

Sir Godwyn turns to Agnes Grey, who is watching fascinated, as if she has never seen the tears of a woman who has been punched backwards over a tumbling chair. Add to that a woman who has just pissed herself.

"Take her away and get her cleaned up, Miss Grey." He wrinkles his nose in disgust.

"Yes, Sir Godwyn."

"And then bring her back here."

"Yes, Sir Godwyn."

The smaller woman supports the limping taller woman who is weeping and choking, and is not quite as tall, because she is not wearing the high heel shoes that shot off in the spectacular nine point eight backwards flip.

When they have gone the steely eyed Sir Godwyn goes to work on the computer. Thanks to uber-loyal Agnes Grey, who must be suitably rewarded, they have nipped another insurrection in the bud – not even deserving of that name. Swift and ruthless will be the response. Pour encourager les autres.

Sir Godwyn screws up his lips and narrows his eyes and his hands fly over the keys. One of the names stands out and so he makes a phone call that he had promised to make but not quite so soon.

"Ah! My dear Bunny, I promised you I would ring." He listens politely for as long as seems appropriate. "Quite so. Now listen carefully." She has been waiting for this moment. Revenge is indeed a dish best served cold.

Tuesday 17th October 4.03pm

Jack Bellingham is beginning to believe that he is no longer the hero of his own novel and that he has not the substance for it; others are more substantial. Others can carry it off… no names no pack drill.

He has sometimes viewed his own life as a work of fiction in progress and not a particularly encouraging work of fiction at that. A badly written novel that finds its inevitable way onto a rickety remainder table outside a seedy second-hand bookshop somewhere in Wales. There to be pulped unread in the wind and the rain.

Everything changed, or so he thought, when he accidentally killed the paedophile child killer Franklin Blake – but that is another story. Enough people said he had morphed into a hero, even if an unlikely hero; an unlikely fucking hero as Shirley Keeldar had pointed out, but a hero nonetheless. A hero for the times perhaps, which says as much as you need to know about the times. In his own mind he has likened it to Charlotte Brontë's most unlikely overnight success with Jane Eyre – from obscurity to fame in the blink of her father's eye.

Now he is not at all sure. The surreal calmness experienced last night in the arms of Shirley Keeldar is a vaporous thing, misty whisped to nothingness in the telling light of day. Perhaps he should divulge every last secret and exorcise all the ghosts, because Lily Dale was the least of it. For too long he has identified himself to himself by the disdainful sniggers of the few women who deigned to notice his taking up space on the Earth.

That was his excuse of obscurity – he was the invisible man. That should have been the title of this half-baked state of the nation novel only, as usual, H.G.Wells got there first. That is the real story of Jack's life, that someone else got there first. Only his mother ever gave him definition.

It is all brought home as he sits with his back arched against the damp stained wall watching Emily Rowley adding some vivid pink blotches to one of the triple breasted Window women. Everything she is, or ever was, is being burned into these canvases and fancifully he thinks it is like watching Turner or Goya on the cusp of fame – take your pick. It is a remarkable experience to be in the presence of the outpourings of a towering genius and, like Charlotte Brontë, the name of Emily Rowley will live forever on her overnight success.

He glances furtively at the perpetually unmade bed, where Nina Balatka in tight purple jeans is lounging at her ease, making brisk arrangements on her mobile phone for the paintings to be transported to the Gallery. Jack has confirmed he has arranged a working dinner with his agent this evening to discuss publicity and Nina Balatka is apparently thrilled.

No doubt the habit of feeling sorry for himself is just too deeply ingrained. He knows there is something ridiculous in a man who has bedded the actual Amelia Sedley feeling sorry for himself, and indeed feeling inadequate, for God's sake. Not to mention bedding the posh ethereally gorgeous Shirley Keeldar, or the sturdily energetic Nina Balatka for that matter, who, in the here and now, bestows a dinky little wave and a dimply smile as she finalises arrangements.

It is as if he is taking the part of someone else in his own life. The real Jack or John or Johnny is somewhere hidden suitably dark and fetid where he belongs. Most certainly not in the here and now, enabling the genius of Emily Rowley to be unleashed on an unsuspecting world.

There are pages missing and there are pages that are indecipherable and there are pages that are blank.

Nina Balatka laughs squarely at something said by the other person on the phone – a man no doubt. Jack looks from one woman to the other, then to the canvas of Window man IV or perhaps Window man V. The splodges of vivid pink draw the eye to the several and various, what could loosely be called, nipples of Window woman – aka cupper of the balls.

Tuesday 17th October 4.17pm

A more than somewhat cleaned up version of Rosalie Murray is tamely led limping into what she once believed, for such a brief time, was her private office and an inner sanctum. The Minister's lair no less.

Thankfully she has turned off the water works and is now merely annoyingly snivelling. The good eye red and puffy, the other eye closed on a livid bruise that covers half her face. Bathing it in cold water has made no discernible difference.

Sir Godwyn Lydate is royally seated on the decorative sofa that has always been out of place in the spartan panelled room. The sofa of a previous Minister's bad taste, the sofa where John Caldigate and Agnes Grey had shagged each other's brains out, although she tries not to think about it. Sir Godwyn is thoughtfully tapping the mobile phone against ever so slightly prominent front teeth. It is a gesture that makes strong men shudder; effects on strong women are frankly mixed. Without having to be told, a po-faced Agnes Grey nudges the barefooted penitent towards the sofa of best forgotten assignations.

"Sit down, Rosalie."

A bare legged Rosalie does as she is told and winces. Agnes Grey remains standing, ever alert to carry out his bidding as he sniff sniffs.

"I have binned the tights and knickers, Sir Godwyn." If one can call those brief things knickers she thinks to herself. Agnes Grey would not be seen dead in those flimsy things that hardly covered anything at all.

"Don't tell me she is not wearing any knickers?"

Rosalie Murray is staring hard at her own very much together bare knees that are not the least bit knobbly. They could not be more together if she was a Berlin housefrau in 1945 with Russian soldiers in the next street.

"I always carry a spare pair, Sir Godwyn." Everything is now most sensibly covered.

"You think of just about everything, Miss Grey." He gazes most thoughtfully at the indomitable Agnes Grey, who is blushing and staring at her own sensible shoes. It really is hard to believe. He takes possession of one of Rosalie Murray's bare knees and she snivels within a snivel. She wants to plead but the words are all jumbled up. She doesn't know what he knows... probably everything and she stifles a moan. George Meredith led her on. He did. He did. "What are we to do with you, Rosalie Murray?"

"Thorry. Thorry." Not her voice but the voice of an admonished child. This is Daddy when he was really really cross and was going to spank her bare bottom really hard to make her cry. Only this is worse and she cannot think straight. She cannot see straight and wishes she was anywhere but here. "Thorry."

"Yes. Yes. We take that as read." She is not his dear any more. The hand is remaining on a bare knee and weirdly that offers a smidgen of comfort and the faintest of hopes, although of what she is not at all sure. "Do you know what you have done, Rosalie Murray?"

Miserably she shakes and then nods her head and groans at the resultant poker burn of pain.

"Have you any paracetamol, Miss Grey?" He is not a monster.

"In my office, Sir Godwyn."

"Go and get some, and a glass of water."

"Yes, Sir Godwyn."

When the door has quietly closed he pat pats the bare knee and she partially opens the better eye. The searchlight glare of his gaze forces her to look away.

"Shall I tell you what you have done?"

"Yeth." A tiny whisper as if she has not the remotest idea what she has done but would very much appreciate being told.

"You have possibly ruined the career of the second worst Foreign Secretary of modern times." She doesn't know whether to laugh or cry and anyway can do neither. "Do you know something else?"

"No." An even tinier whisper as she stares one eyed at the fuzzy possessing hand covering the bare knee and is appalled at the sliver of excitement... truly truly appalled. It is slivers of excitement that have got her into this mess in the first place.

"If I had been Julius Caesar I would not have been assassinated on the Ides of March." She stares one eyed at the fuzzy possessing hand. "Brutus and Cassius would not have survived the failed attempt. Believe me, Rosalie Murray, they would not have survived that March day."

She believes him. Oh! She so so believes him.

The door opens just far enough for Agnes Grey to sidle into the room. She is carrying the glass half full of cloudy tap water and her last three paracetamol. She glances apprehensively at Sir Godwyn. She was not at all sure about leaving him alone with the wreckage of the good ship Rosalie Murray. She would hate for him to go too far. One of these times he might not get away with it.

"Thank you, Miss Grey." Thank goodness he seems calmer now and the tempest has blown itself into a mere storm. They both study what used to be a supremely confident Rosalie Murray swallowing the tablets with great difficulty. Shakily she drains the lukewarm water through puffy lips. Agnes Grey takes possession of the empty glass before it slips through slippery fingers.

The Spectre at the feast. Some Spectre. Some feast.

"So, Miss Grey. What are we to do with her?"

Agnes Grey is just loving being part of this conspiracy as a most trusted confidante at the very heart of his nefariousness. "She is truly sorry, Sir Godwyn." The subject of the discussion starts in surprise. This ultimate woman of the background had cleaned Rosalie up most intimately, checked there were no bones broken and checked the remaining teeth – only three missing. Had seen her at her most vulnerable and had been very gentle and kind. Rosalie should not have called her a moron earlier. "I think she deserves a second chance."

Rosalie had not noticed before, because she had not properly listened, that Agnes Grey has the merest hint of a Scottish accent.

"You think so, Miss Grey?"

"Yes, Sir Godwyn." She unflinchingly meets the gimlet eyes. He likes that. He likes that she thinks she can read him so well. There is something about Agnes Grey that is formidable in its own unique, locked in a dark cellar way, that reminds him of her late mother. She is a Praetorian guard. It is an important role, to give one's life if called upon.

"Very well, Miss Grey. I bow to your judgement."

Rosalie Murray begins to cry. There is nothing she can do to stop the tears. If it did not hurt so much she would hold her hands to her battered face in abject relief.

Sir Godwyn abruptly removes his hand from the bare knee which is momentarily finger tattooed by the intense pressure. Not permanently like the tasteful rose tattoo at the base of her spine he had so recently admired. What a fool she has been.

"Leave us now, Miss Grey." There is only the slightest of hesitations. "I will speak to you in a few minutes." She has no choice but to be persuaded.

"Yes, Sir Godwyn."

"Arrange for the carpet to be cleaned."

"Yes, Sir Godwyn."

"And the chair."

"Yes, Sir Godwyn."

When she has gone he strides to the mock Gothic monstrosity of a window and gazes through the massive scaffolding at the busy Thames far below. Mental note. The scaffolding will have to go.

He turns abruptly and contemplates the fallen woman out of a 1790s print by Gillray – no doubt something to do with the evils of gin inevitably leading to prostitution. He has done his calculations and the next several moves are inevitable, but nevertheless to be appreciated. One should always appreciate the inevitable because, just occasionally, the inevitable doesn't happen and that must also be calculated... hence the Foreign Secretary hanging on by his fingernails...a useful idiot must not be discarded unless absolutely necessary.

"Look at me, my dear." The partially closed one eye looks out from the bruised and broken face. She had glanced in the mirror in the toilets and cried out at the grotesque face looking back. Agnes Grey had taken Rosalie in her arms and had embraced a modicum of comfort.

"You have been a very stupid girl." His voice is not ungentle.

She wipes the snotty nose on the back of a hand. It hurts. My God it hurts.

"It is lucky for you, my girl, that giving you a second chance could well suit my purpose, otherwise they would have been fishing your body out of the Thames."

Surely he is joking? He walks from the window and looks down on the fallen spear carrier, the make-up and blood and snot all smeared into a mask that is not at all funny. "The next few days you will stay with Miss Grey." He tap taps the mobile phone against ever so slightly prominent front teeth. "She inhabits a rather pleasant apartment in Kensington and has lived there alone since her mother passed away." A most unfortunate incident but at least her mother had died with a smile on her face.

He does not expect the fallen one to say anything and the fallen one does not say anything.

"I will arrange for the Ministry to somehow struggle on in your unfortunate absence." Tap. Tap. "For the time being Miss Grey will take care of you." No dry lip twitch.

Rosalie Murray cannot stop herself emitting a grateful sob. He leans forward and she cannot stop herself flinching as his thumb traces the unbruised curve of part of her chin. "It would have been such a watery waste." Surely he is joking?

He sets the camera on his mobile phone. "Look into the camera, my dear." He zooms close. There is no question of saying cheese.

Tuesday 17th October 6.48pm

The Reverend John Eames gazes across the kitchen table at an alabaster pale Cecilia Hunt, who is concentrating on the message that has just pinged on her mobile phone and is finger scrolling down most efficiently. The prudish spectacles reflecting a badly aligned kitchen spotlight.

There is a Delftware teapot of weak tea, two matching cups and saucers and a milk jug on the table. The absent Rosalie Murray hates to drink tea from mugs, which she thinks rather common.

The Reverend raises a cup to his minor Greek Deity lips and imbibes a lukewarm mouthful. Imbibe was a word his wife frequently drew out of the hat. He dislikes tea to be too hot almost as much as he now dislikes his wife – he is not the sort of man to draw hatred out of the hat. Cecilia Hunt dislikes tea but likes the idea of taking tea and has no problem with hatred.

"Anything interesting?"

"A missive from the other Lord God Almighty, Sir Godwyn Lydate." Cecilia Hunt possesses an irreverent streak that she knows she might live to regret one day. Her mother has often pointed out that Sir Godwyn is not at all good at seeing a joke at his own expense.

As a child, Cecilia was often lovingly punished by her mother for a cheeky mouth, earning the nickname 'potty mouth' and the occasional token slap. As well as being sent upstairs in the dark, which was not particularly loving punishment; even now she sleeps with the light on.

Sir Godwyn has been rumoured to dish out far worse than token slaps to those who have the temerity to get in his way – Loyaltie me lie – that was Richard the third's motto and look what happened to that particular God's anointed. "The blushing bride is entering purdah for a few days, Bish." She scrolls down some more. "She is not contactable." A puzzled Cecilia glances teasingly at Johnny Eames. She has decided to call him Johnny at more intimate moments, as it is more romantic than harder. Bish at other times because it makes him uncomfortable, and then he looks sort of cute. She thinks, possibly wrongly, that there are not a lot of depths to Johnny. Going on past experience with men, that is to be welcomed.

Intimate moments Johnny primly imbibes more lukewarm tea, which gives him the appearance of a 1950s C list matinee idol on a provincial stage in a second-rate play. A depthless look with which she is not at all familiar, but could get to quite like.

"Aren't you going to drink your tea?" He primly asks.

"Jesus fucking Christ" is the unexpected reply. She looks even paler alabaster and her shocked features are not arranged at all, as she snatches off the severe rimless spectacles.

Other times Bish sets down the Delftware cup on the Delftware saucer. "What on earth is wrong?"

"Look." She hands over the mobile as if it is radioactive. The screen displays the barely recognisable battered face of his not at all blushing bride-to-be, who appears scared out of her wits and looks a frightful mess. He glances across the table at a shocked Cecilia Hunt who is holding a hand to her mouth. She looks so young and vulnerable without the severe rimless spectacles.

"He sent this?"

Imitating a puppet with several strings broken she haphazardly nods her head.

"He did this?" The strings appear broken beyond repair. "He cannot get away with this." Sometimes he can be quite incisive, but usually at the wrong occasion.

She dry coughs and takes a gulp of cold tea that she has forgotten she so dislikes. She swallows and coughs and appears to be making a very much visible effort to pull herself together. Pull yourself together, Cecilia she tells herself, and puts the severe rimless spectacles back on, inhaling several deep breaths as instructed by that sleazy therapist. She has a suspicion it is just to see her pert breasts rising and falling. She is a bit of an expert on pervs.

"She has somehow crossed him."

"And he does this?"

"It must have been something really serious." Now she is rub rubbing the back of her neck and stretching, unthinkingly showing off the pert breasts in the clingy blouse… the sleazy perv of a therapist would be in seventh heaven.

"He cannot get away with this."

She grabs hold of his free hand and knocks over a, thank goodness, empty Delftware cup which, thankfully, doesn't break. There is only so much a girl can take. "Oh yes he can." She glances backwards over her shoulder as if a manifestation of Sir Godwyn is lurking in the shadows… she would not be at all surprised. She snatches at the mobile phone. "I am going to delete it." He holds the phone out of reach but is not sure of the next move. Incisive only takes a man like the Reverend John Eames thus far and no further.

"Give it to me, Johnny. Now."

Meekly he hands over the phone and she deletes the terrible image and the attached message, breathing a sigh of relief, as if the deletion will mean it never happened and Rosalie Murray will come bouncing through the door at any moment, with that air of annoying invulnerability and that equally annoying smile of secrets not going to be shared.

"Jesus, Cecilia." He rarely takes the Lord's name in vain. "He is a monster and must be stopped." He does not sound at all convincing even to his own ears. She is looking at him pityingly but not at all unkindly and, snatching off the spectacles, takes possession of both his hands.

"You must understand what you have got into, Johnny darling." This is the first time she has called him darling and she has his full attention. Mary Thorne calls him darling. Cecilia looks so different without the severe spectacles. Not exactly younger and not exactly more vulnerable, just different, in a nice girl shortsighted sort of way.

"Soon you will be the Venerable Bishop John of Staines because, and only because, it suits the purpose of Sir Godwyn Lydate. You will be his creature. You will have taken the Danegeld and there will be no going back. One day he will demand his pound of flesh." She has to somewhat waveringly smile at the mixed metaphors, and at her own abject weakness, which she accepts for what it is. He thinks she is smiling pityingly at his own all too real weakness.

"I will turn it down."

"No you will not." She squeezes gently and the pressure of the softly spoken hands is so very comforting. "Do not let's go there, Johnny darling."

"I like you calling me Johnny darling."

She leans across the table, deftly kisses his pursed lips and sits back down, studying his weakly handsome face with several degrees of affection, or at least the next best thing. "My mother took the Danegeld and has never regretted it. I have also taken the Danegeld." She knew that first in history at Oxford would come in useful one day. "So has Rosalie Murray taken the Danegeld." No more jokes about the blushing bride-to-be. "She will recover from the bruises."

"A bit more than bruises!"

"Johnny!" She admonishes and squeezes with intent. Walls have ears... careless talk costs lives. She would wave an admonishing index finger if she had a free hand.

"Sorry."

"As I was saying she will recover from the bruises and she will have learned her lesson the hard way. Anyone crosses Sir Godwyn Lydate at their peril. Are we agreed?"

He doesn't answer and she resists the urge to kiss him into forgetfulness. He has the look of a Victorian schoolboy who will not repeat his lesson and has to go to the back of the class and face the wall...there was no dyslexia in those days. He is staring moodily at their entwined hands. "Are we agreed?"

Sulkily he nods and she bestows another less deft kiss as a reward.

"You are only with me because he wants you here." The entwined hands have it.

"Whilst that is true, Johnny darling, I do love being here with you." By sheer force of will she makes him meet the at odds worldly wise gaze. She fondly smiles. "That has nothing to do with Sir Godwyn or anyone else."

"Really?"

"Really." This time the kiss could most definitely be described as lingering and soon the kiss goes beyond lingering and they only just make it to the bedroom.

Tuesday 17th October 7.21pm

Spencer Perceval narrows his touchingly bloodshot eyes and hard stares at the mobile phone in his left hand, as if he is auditioning for the role of Eliot Ness and the mobile phone is public enemy number one. Knowing his luck the role will probably go to someone else. If he was not ensconced in the plush cocktail bar at the Queens Hotel in Leeds he would throw the bloody thing across the room. He has broken three mobile phones that way in the past month. The accounts department is not best pleased. There has been talk of anger management. Fucking twats.

"Fucking bitch." He hisses. The fat shrew cow is not answering his calls.

"Wife trouble?" Helen Huntingdon is looking on with undisguised amusement and showing rather more orange legs than Spencer deems appropriate in his current mood. She is drawing attention to herself and he doesn't like that in his female companions, even those who have not yet experienced the joys of sharing his bed. Although there is something he is missing here. She appears to be permanently on the edge of a fit of knowing giggles which is very off putting. "Fuck off."

"Charming." She appears to be not the least bit put out as she sucks vodka and tonic noisily through a straw. He hates that. So unladylike. He gulps a mouthful of Stella, and is aware that he is being surreptitiously watched by the peroxide blonde barmaid pretending to polish glasses. He once bedded a trainee production assistant called Stella and recalls her weirdly shaped clitoris every time he orders a pint. Perhaps he should change to Fosters because Elaine Foster's clitoris was a delectable sea shell. "Has the, excuse my French, fucking bitch thrown you out?"

"You shouldn't listen to idle gossip."

"I just adore idle gossip." Noisier sucking through the straw and he has to admit she does make it sound tantalisingly obscene. He stares at the mass of curly orange hair and swallows the comment he was about to make, taking another mouthful of Stella instead. They would have to turn the lights off. The dark – that's it – something to do with the dark.

"Another?" He indicates the thankfully empty glass as she most suggestively licks the length of straw.

"A large one."

He hates to admit that this show of orange legs and the suggestive straw licking are turning him on. Carrie Brattle, pregnant or not, dumped in the overflowing dustbin of history. He snatches the straw and, I am the man around here style, marches to the bar.

"A Stella and a large vodka please. No straw." The peroxide blonde barmaid, thirtyish at a pinch, decent body, more than decent sized tits and not the least hint of orange anywhere visible, executes a decent pout.

"You're that Spencer Perceval bloke." Quite a pronounced local accent. She would have to keep her mouth shut or at least not speak. "You're doing that Question Time from the Town Hall."

"Indeed I am, sweetheart. Indeed I am." She is taking her time at the lager tap.

"She your girlfriend then?" A dismissive nod in the direction of the curly very much visibly orange Helen Huntingdon, who is watching the exchange with undisguised amusement.

"My Research assistant." Equally dismissive… wouldn't touch it with a barge pole.

"You married then?"

He shakes his head. Any port in a storm has always been the Perceval motto. He leans confidently on the bar. "My room number is 363." Of course she has checked that out already and doesn't reply, busying herself with scooping ice cubes into the tall glass. As she pours the vodka, he can only too easily visualise those hands at a less mundane task. Stella once again comes to mind, although Elaine Foster was no slouch with the hands taking ownership stuff.

"Shall I put these on your bill, Sir?" She pouts poutier than the word.

He nods and thinks she can probably read his mind and, as he reaches for the drinks, she leans closer still. "I don't finish until eleven o'clock." A most confidential whisper that reverberates all the way down his body.

He leans closer so that their foreheads are almost touching. "Come up then, sweetheart. Come up then." His prize winning schoolboy smile that used to be infallible. It was the smile that got through Jane wifey's defences that first time all those years ago, or so he fondly believes.

Helen Huntingdon is grinning in a weirdly fixed way. He is sure she must have a screw loose somewhere. There seems to be even more of the orange legs on display.

"So that's you sorted then, lover boy."

"You lip read?"

"I don't need to, lover boy." She picks up the fresh glass. "Where's the straw?"

"Oops. I forgot." He takes a generous slurp of Stella.

There is a somewhat, he fondly hopes, sort of meaningful silence. He studies the roundish orange haloed face properly for the first time. A well-ordered everything in its place face and a surprisingly cute turned up nose. Starey eyes… brown he thinks… a bit scary actually. Yes brown. One noticeably muddier than the other, the left one as you look at the freckly face. Definitely a bit scary. He has no real take on freckles and perhaps he could fit her in before the barmaid. Another slurp of Stella.

"What's she called?"

"Who?"

"The tarty barmaid."

"I never asked."

The come on giggles appear to be genuine and he is taken aback. His antennae really are fucked up big time and he blames Carrie Brattle. Not to mention the fat shrew cow who has probably changed the fucking locks again. She really is a pain… he is beginning to wonder if it is worth the lack of effort.

"I might be jealous." Out of nowhere Ginger nut executes the poutiest game set and match pout of the night so far.

"What!"

"Only joking." The giggles are threatening to get out of control. The peroxide blonde barmaid looks daggers and Spencer Perceval has one of those moments when he wishes he was gay.

Tuesday 17th October 8.58pm

Jane Perceval really is an excellent cook when she puts her mind to it – the Coq au vin to die for literally melting in the mouth. He didn't realise he was so hungry; he is missing too many meals. Sir Godwyn glances round the vastness of the romantically candlelit dining kitchen and luxuriates in the divine comedy of domestic bliss; admittedly soothing to the soul after such a trying day. He has even read a bedtime story to the youngest girl, with the other two pretending not to be listening with their bedroom doors open. The oldest girl, his daughter he supposes, is turning into a real beauty. All this could have been his for the asking – what a frightening thought. If he was not so well fed he might well shudder, but instead drinks more of the excellent red wine. Jane herself has taken a lot of trouble with her appearance, has always scrubbed up rather well, and is only too well aware of his predilection for little black numbers. She needs to lose some weight but now is not the time to be picky… an Arizona ravine of cleavage showing off the extra pounds rather fetchingly. She can still just about get away with an exceedingly short black dress with hints of suspenders and stocking tops. The self-same slender legs of the younger Jane, who had been introduced by her father as the fatted sacrificial calf all those years ago.

If she holds her head in a certain quizzical position she can almost disguise the double chins that she pointedly refuses to acknowledge in the mirror, preferring to push together and admire the bigger breasts. The nipples are surprisingly much more sensitive; they do not tell one that in the diet manuals.

He taste swallows some more of the rather decent Vouvray. It is always a bonus to drink the silly boy's rather decent wine prior, that is, to enjoying the silly boy's more than rather decent wife. Mind you he did enjoy the silly boy's stunning wife several times on her wedding night, after the silly boy passed out, nearly choking on his own vomit. It might have been a blessing. "You look gorgeous my… darling."

"Good enough to eat?" She can still just about get away with arch-suggestive coy. "Most certainly my… darling." This is all rather pleasant and he taste swallows more wine, whilst she swallow swallows more wine. Ruby red lipstick kisses a blatant promise on the glass.

"Shall I open another bottle?"

"Most certainly my… darling." Although three bottles might be a tad excessive. Still – eat, drink and be merry for tomorrow is another ticked off day.

She weaves ever so invitingly across the kitchen in stockinged feet to the built-in wine rack. The most generous bottom also benefiting from the weight gain regime of chocolate cake and cream buns. All of it wasted on the silly boy but then it always was wasted on the silly boy…silly boys will always be silly boys…useful tools though.

As if on cue the mobile phone squared off close to his left hand resonates to Parsifal and for a few seconds he hums along to the tune and then checks the caller. Jane is pouring more red wine with intense concentration. Once upon a time her beauty took one's breath away just like on her wedding night, when all she was wearing was a garter. The eldest daughter is most definitely taking up the baton.

"Yes, Helen." It is not advisable to say 'my dear' and most certainly not 'darling' because Jane can be so touchy. There are long-standing jealousy issues. Helen will understand because she is an exceedingly intelligent, if somewhat off the wall, young madam. Infectious in the right way if one is in the right mood. The mental health issues are, in his opinion, somewhat exaggerated, and Nanny surprisingly agrees, but then Nanny has her own agenda.

He listens even more intently, watched just as intently by the scrumptious oozing layered cream cake of a woman, who is swallow swallowing more wine... perhaps the word should be guzzling. She has that determined look sheening her shining face that George Meredith knows only too well. The thin black strap on her right shoulder has slipped off to reveal as much cleavage as it is possible to reveal, before nipples come into play. Any minute now she will come and sit portentously on his lap and that will most definitely be that.

"Very well, Helen. By the way Rosalie Murray will not be able to make Question Time on Thursday." He listens. "Yes most unfortunate. She is unfortunately indisposed." He listens some more and checks his fingernails. Jane Perceval is baring her teeth maliciously at the thought of Rosalie Murray being unfortunately indisposed. She guzzle guzzles more wine in celebration.

"Inform the silly boy in the morning. Bye for now." He ends the call. "Your sad excuse for a husband has sloped up to his room at the hotel in a fit of pique." A dry lip twitch. "There to await what I am reliably informed is a tarty peroxide blonde barmaid."

Sir Godwyn is pleased that dear Helen is following his instructions to the letter. She is such an accommodating girl in her own cooky way. One just needs to take on board the mental health issues, which of course he does take on board.

"I hope the little shit catches something incurable." She guzzle guzzles more wine. No more impromptu Sunday afternoon fucks for that little shit. She guzzle guzzles more wine.

"I am changing the fucking locks tomorrow." She only swears when she is well on the way to being well pissed.

Displaying concentration at its acutest she breathlessly sets down the empty lipstick smeared wine glass as if it might shatter at the slightest breath. Then she levers herself purposefully to her stockinged feet, and holding onto the edge of the table for dear life, shuffle shuffles round to his side of the table and plumps down in his lap. He doesn't wince. Venus descending by the school of Rubens, with definite touches of the master on the substantial bottom. Perhaps a touch also on the thighs, not to mention the bosoms, where nipples are now very much in play.

"Time for dessert." She just about manages to articulate as she nibble nibbles an ear and then suck sucks an ear and then swallow swallows an ear. The furry mole of his right hand has burrowed up her skirt. There is a time and a place and without question this is the time and this is the place.

With this woman there are always echoes of that memorable first time.

"I just love dessert." Are the last words he is allowed to speak. There have not been a lot of words in their relationship.

Tuesday 17th October 9.22pm

A very much Johnny John Eames, earlier known as harder, leaves the Westminster apartment arm in arm with a cat got all the cream in the dairy Cecilia Hunt. They are walking to her favourite Cantonese restaurant. Not surprisingly they are both hungry, having burned off God alone knows how many calories.

First of all they need a drink. There is a convenient public house –The Lord Melbourne – at the corner of the street. The only other customers at this time on a Tuesday evening are two suited and booted middle-aged men. They make no bones about intently watching the older man and the younger woman take their drinks to a wobbly table for two. Must be a Vicars and tarts party.

"That's a bit tasty." Murmurs the one sipping gin and tonic who had ordered vodka and tonic. "A bit of all right." Agrees the one sipping vodka and tonic who had ordered gin and tonic. The spotty teenage barman nods in agreement, not being certain which one they are talking about.

Tuesday 17th October 9.26pm

Marion Fay is resisting taking off the gorgeous eye wateringly expensive lingerie. No strategic holes on display, although holes will be incorporated in the Amelia Sedley new season's designs. Holey knickers set to become the next must have in lingerie fashion.

"Come here, Mmeeeee..."A most definitely not wearing any kind of underwear Amelia Sedley wheedles from the bedroom. That lady certainly knows how to project a wheedle.

Marion Fay hopes no one is listening at the door. She doesn't trust that sly girl with the staring eyes that never seem to blink. Marion is admiring the undies effect reflected in the floor-to-ceiling bathroom mirror, having never dreamt she would ever possess such lovely intimate coverings. Until she escaped by marrying the wrong man it was her mother who chose her undergarments.

That was what her mother called them, and eminently sensible undergarments at that. Always too warm in winter and always clammy in summer. After she was married to the perv, but her perv, he wanted her wearing crotchless panties so that he could take her at any time of his choosing. Most certainly not warm in winter and she suffered some dreadful colds – pleasantly breezy in Summer though.

"Come on, Mmeeee..."

Marion is revelling in making the, she has discovered, incredibly brittle Amelia Sedley beg for it. There is a whole menu of takeaway naughtiness to be explored that puts even those memorable stolen afternoons with the Vicar's wife in the shade. John Eames never had the remotest idea but then he wouldn't, would he?

"Going to start without you, Mmeeeeee..."

Marion Fay edges closer to the mirror which clouds with her breath and stares at the oddly colourless eyes staring back that reflect startlingly with the henna make-up. Screwing up her mouth in a gesture reminiscent of her brother, she bares her teeth. There is a chip broken from a lower molar from when her late husband the perv got more carried away than usual. In fact the day he got carried away for good. He should never have said what he said after what he had done. They will never find the body.

Marion is never afraid of them because most of them are morons. Proved by her brother being found not guilty... I mean!

She licks her lips, savouring the taste of the ludicrously expensive lipstick, and squeezes her breasts together inside the pink lacy bra and releases them to spring apart... very impressive. She slips off the bra... even more impressive. She has always been more than happy with these breasts which developed early and led to much spotty schoolboy gropings.

From the bedroom are projected the unmistakable sounds demonstrating that the International superstar airhead has indeed started without her Mmeeeee. She really is a voracious whatever the word; Marion Fay cannot think of the right word and so sticks out her tongue at the thought of her brother, who can always think of the right word.

She stares appraisingly in the mirror at the chocolate button nipples. Suckling randy schoolboys is the nearest thing she has ever come to suckling a child. The nasty little scroggs used to beg to be tossed off by the top-heavy schoolgirl, and sometimes she had agreed for their week's pocket money. Sometimes she had agreed to go all the way, but she demanded several weeks' pocket money and use of a condom for that...cash and condom up front.

She slips off the matching pink panties and stares critically at her lower body. Legs a trifle too thick but only a trifle. Thighs ditto. Belly ever so slightly wobbly.

Amidst much giggling they had shaved each other this morning and so her fanny is lovely and smooth to the touch, the clitoris prominent as always. The perv said it was a miniature cock but then he was a perv after all. She half turns and studies her backside. So shapely rounded that she almost fancies herself, intrusive birthmark and all.

"Mmeeeee...Mmeeeee"

"Coming, sweet cakes."

The very much naked Marion Fay strides magnificently purposefully into the bedroom and is ready to spring a few more surprises. Anyone listening at the door will hear rather a lot of noise and some half-hearted protests.

Lucy Snowe primly purses her lips and thinks that Amelia Sedley is demeaning herself. Although the noises give her an idea and, unlike most of her ideas, this one is only verging on insanity.

Tuesday 17th October 11.23pm

Helen Huntingdon is propped up against several pillows reading Jane Eyre to calm her nerves. She always reads Jane Eyre to calm her nerves. It isn't really nerves, she just likes to pretend she might have nerves as a cover for other things.

This hotel room would have remained empty if Spencer Perceval and Carrie Brattle had still been an item. The room is hot and stuffy and so Helen has taken off her shorty pyjamas, the ones with the cute bunny rabbits, not to be confused with the ones with the cute teddy bears. She pauses in her half hearted reading and takes off the pink framed reading glasses that she only ever wears when she is alone. It is not the reading glasses that would shock but the fact that the curly orange wig is on its stand on the dressing table. Helen Huntingdon is totally bald and has no body hair whatsoever; the faint eyebrows being etched on. After several painful misunderstandings in the past, only Goddy is currently in on the secret.

She is acutely aware of the muffled and, occasionally not so muffled, noises emanating from the next bedroom, but will not give them the satisfaction of knocking on the wall. She hopes they do not break the bed that is all, because the accounts department will be even more unhappy. There is an adjoining door which Helen has ensured is locked. There had been some hopeful rattling of the handle earlier – to quote Spencer Perceval: no way, José – a girl likes to be remembered. The locked door is a chastity belt. As a pubescent teenager she had discovered strange sensations in her bits and pieces when she read about Crusader ladies and their chastity belts.

Back to Jane Eyre. Whenever Helen tries to picture Mr Rochester he has Sir Godwyn Lydate's features. She giggles at the thought and touches her bits and pieces. He had been so protective when she had that trouble with the Police over one of the misunderstandings. They had said she was a nutcase, which was not very nice. Sir Godwyn had arranged bail and she was never charged. She had been enormously grateful and felt obliged – still feels obliged.

The noise next door has stopped and someone is using the bathroom. Helen turns down the corner of the page of the battered sixpenny Penguin paperback, arranges it squarely on the bedside table and turns off the bedside lamp. Now she can let her imagination run as wild as the Brontë sisters on the bleak Yorkshire moors beyond Haworth Parsonage. She throws off the covers and imagines it is Mr Rochester Lydate touching between her legs… fondly touching and delicately exploring and then more urgent touching. It never takes long and she grunts once in the back of her throat. That is all. All very neat and tidy. She likes things to be neat and tidy. Going with yourself is so much neater and tidier than going with a man.

Currently Sir Godwyn is her one concession to messy consensuality. She giggles. He is such a mogadisish man. She and she alone knows what she means.

Noisily sucking her fish fingers she then composes herself to sleep neatly and tidily. Settling down and foetally sucking a thumb. She believes she was probably at her happiest in the womb. It was being born when things started to go wrong.

A few minutes later the muffled and not so muffled noises restart in the adjoining bedroom but Helen Huntingdon is soundly asleep and hardly moves throughout the night.

Tuesday 17th October 11.36pm

A barefooted Nina Balatka stifles a yawn and answers the intercom of the Chelsea Harbour apartment. She was in bed but not properly asleep. There is so much on her mind.

"It's me." Call me Jack believes he has earned the right to be recognised in these two words.

She presses the buzzer and clutches the Chinesey dragon tailed kimono tight around her bed warmed body. A gift from Julius Verinder after a trade mission to China. No gifts of jewellery – just a beltless dragon tailed kimono. The first throes of passion didn't last very long in every sense.

"You look tired, Jack." She blink blinks her eyes. "I didn't think you would come tonight."

He is bone weary. That is what confession does to such a man.

"Aren't you pleased?"

She doesn't look very pleased.

"Of course." To prove the point she leads him by the hand into the western prairie of the bedroom, all the way to the ridiculously outsized bed. She slips off the beltless kimono, slides under the covers and, as an afterthought, holds open the covers to reveal a sight for sore eyes. He undresses as if the clothes are ten ton weights and she studies his body in the shadows of the worst possible taste, Onyx bedside lamp. The black and white photograph angled to be seen when she wakes.

They hold fiercely in a kind of rehearsed desperation and out of nowhere he is sobbing into her neck. She strokes and coos his name and makes rash promises, which she has no intention of keeping. Very soon she will not need to make any promises to anyone.

They do not make love and soon he is deeply asleep in her arms, flattening her breasts as much as they can be flattened. They will probably make love in the morning as she thinks that would probably be a sensible move. Nina Balatka eventually falls into a troubled sleep and will thankfully, on waking, remember the rude dream.

Tuesday 17th October 11.54pm

A most pensive Shirley Keeldar is blondly blue-eyed staring out of the window of the Grande suite at the Savoy Hotel. Revived by the hot shower she is nursing a tumbler of neat vodka and is wearing a bathrobe that cannot disguise her shapely figure. Old Father Thames is glinting balefully in the hazy moonlight, and there are dim seeking lights marring the bulk of the Festival Hall.

For once her gaze is not seeking far off Galaxies but is focused on the moonlit waters. She is even aware of the blobs of bird lime on the window frame. Somewhere there are chimes of midnight a few minutes too early.

She is not one to indulge in overmuch introspection… after all, she is one of the chosen few… a mover and a shaker… a doer and a getter…a gilded creature of the sunlight…a daughter of the morning.

Goddy saw to that, and Goddy sees to that, despite her many frailties. They have been on and off lovers most of their lives. Although lovers is probably the wrong word. There probably is no right word. They have a shared history that has been oftimes a blessing and occasionally a curse, but never ever self-indulgent. Although she has to smile indulgently at this contentious thought.

Over a rather good dinner she and Jack had discussed the next moves. They had been awkward with each other, which was not really surprising, as they had picked and prodded at her favourite dishes and absent-mindedly sipped a rather decent Claret. He had of course been recognised. The glancing over diners no doubt speculating why he was very much tête-à-tête with a person of the opposite sex other than the worldwide Amelia Sedley. A beautiful woman it has to be said. Perhaps not hiding her years as well as Amelia Sedley it might perhaps be thought.

Shirley had been wearing a little black dress, Godwyn's favourite of all her little black dresses, and had briefly wondered if there was too much cleavage for her age, before dismissing the thought out of hand; one is as young as one's cleavage.

The female diners were slyly looking at Jack, but the male diners were most definitely slyly looking at Shirley Keeldar's cleavage.

After the meal they had decided it was a good idea to go their separate ways... for tonight anyway.

They were both in difficult moods and theirs is a relationship of uncoordinated parts, like a lesser known Dickens serialised novel.

The vodka glass is somehow empty, a regular occurrence these days, and she crosses to the drinks cabinet and pours another generous portion. She needs to think. She thinks better on neat vodka – her great grandmother was a Russian Countess after all, and for a brief time a lover of Count Tolstoy no less.

The mobile phone buzzes and it is a message from Tom Sawyer. They must meet up whatever the danger. Ring me. NOW.

Wednesday 18th October 8.33am

S hirley Keeldar has slumbered a fairytale sleeping beauty slumber and it is the insistence of the old-fashioned bakelite ring tones, rather than a Prince's kiss, that drags her up reluctantly from the mermaid depths. The mobile phone is under the pillow. A habit that she resolves to break. She grunts and retrieves the bloody thing; rolling onto her back she squints at the screen hoping it might be Tom; they had talked for over an hour last night and have agreed on a meeting. Phone sex being so perfunctory.

"Yeah."

"You and your little black dress are all over Twitter sphere. The Prime Minister no less is a like and he should know better. There are a lot of nastily jealous women out there."

"Good morning, puss."

"I must admit you look fucking amazing." One of those Becky pauses. "For your age." As this doesn't elicit a response she ploughs on regardless, Becky fashion. "You are now a mystery blonde. Quote. Unquote." Still no response. "Are you alone?"

"Of course."

Becky sniggers a smutty schoolgirls in the dorm snigger and Shirley just cannot be bothered. Unlike Becky she was never the smuttiest schoolgirl in the dorm by a country mile. The acute embarrassments of Shirley's own schooldays still linger in the early waking moments after certain recurring dreams.

Shirley luxuriantly stretches and extravagantly yawns. "Where are you, puss?"

"In the office." Another of those Becky pauses. "Someone has to do some work."

"Fuck off." Shirley yawns.

"That reminds me." The beginnings of a snigger. "Uncle Goddy phoned earlier and said you were not answering your mobile. Told him you were probably engaged in activities of an uncontactable and probably deviant sexual nature. He seemed a bit put out."

"Are you trying to annoy me?"

"Yeah."

They both laugh. Any manufactured tension between the two of them usually ratchets up to unperturbed laughter. Shirley wishes that Becky liked Jack more – wishes that Becky liked Jack at all – most certainly wishes that Becky approved of Tom Sawyer.

"Where is Goosey gold?"

"Not here."

"A lovers' tiff?"

"We are highly unlikely ever to reach the stage of lovers' tiffs."

Thank God for that and Lady Rebecca realises that this is all the information she is going to get. "Listen up, mystery blonde. Amelia Sedley's People have been in touch and they are even less happy bunnies than usual. The new movie, whose name escapes me, premieres next Monday at the Odeon Leicester Square. They need superstar megabitch and Goosey gold to at least appear to be an item. Mystery blondes are not in the script. Comprende?"

Shirley can hear the gap toothed grin.

"Particularly mystery blondes who wear little black dresses scarcely covering their considerable frontal assets."

"I will take that as a compliment." Shirley settles comfortably against the pillows and admires the considerable frontal assets from above. Not bad at all, age or no age. "What do you suggest, puss?"

"Tell the truth." She pauses for this revolutionary advice to fully sink in. "My finger is poised even as we speak, to respond to the millions out there who lead such sad fucking lives that they follow every piss and every fart of Project Jack. God help us all."

"What exactly is the truth?"

"For fuck's sake do not go all philosophical on me, Shirl." Shirley hates being called Shirl and only Becky ever has the brass nerve to get away with it. "The truth is that you are his fucking agent and you were finalising his conquest of the American Colonies not the conquest of your considerable frontal assets. End of story."

"Yeah. Okay."

"Whoosh. The truth the whole truth and nothing like the truth has vroomed into the ether." There is a brief silence. "Now contact Jacko boy gold and tell him to get his sorry ass very publicly over to the Ritz."

"Isn't he there already?"

"No. He isn't fucking there already."

"Okay. Okay. I will track him down. Bye, puss puss."

"Meow." The phone goes dead.

Shirley heaves a sigh of relief. Becky can be exceedingly trying at times. It is probably the centuries of aristocratic inbreeding diluted by the occasional serving wench or stable groom. Although Shirley should talk.

First things first, she must ring Goddy.

"Hi. It's me."

He does indeed sound more than a bit put out. He is going to Leeds to be on hand for Question Time in Leeds Town Hall and has suggested a surprise replacement for the unfortunately indisposed Rosalie Murray. He has spoken to that creep Spencer Perceval who agrees… now there's a surprise. Goddy thought Shirley ought to know as Jack Bellingham is also appearing.

"Do you think Camilla French is a wise choice after the fiasco on the Politics show?" She queries and stretches and inspects the left foot and the blood red toenails and then the right foot and the blood red toenails. She has taken Becky's advice on the colour. "I suppose you could put it like that." She replies to his annoyed response. Godwyn sounds even more put out; Shirley has never queried the wisdom of his moving and shaking. Perhaps she isn't thinking straight or perish the thought – his sure touch is not quite so sure as the anniversary birthday approaches.

Wednesday 18th October 9.02am

Sir Godwyn Lydate could perhaps occasionally perhaps be accused of perhaps occasionally being a fool to himself perhaps. So he fully realises that, if he has a weakness, if one can call it a weakness, it is that he just cannot resist this particular Biblical temptation. He was never ever a child in the strict sense of the word and never had childish things to put away. It is not an excuse merely a comment because he never excuses his behaviour. That is for others to do if they dare. Even in the current politically correct climate he intends to get away with murder, or worse.

Elf-like Camilla French looks up startled from the computer screen as well she might. The desk is cluttered. She is always meaning to tidy up but there is never enough time. She is just not good with time.

It is no exaggeration to say that she cannot believe her eyes. "What on earth…?" Which he thinks is a great improvement on… 'what the fuck?'…

The very last person in the world she would have expected to walk through her Commons office door has just walked through her Commons office door, and closes it firmly and decisively – she never closes her office door. Someone should have stopped him…as if.

With a dry lip twitch he removes a pile of papers from the only visible visitor's chair, sits down and composes himself, shooting his cuffs and adjusting the knot of the old Etonian tie that never needs adjusting. Then and only then, he crosses the immaculately trousered legs.

Apparently quite settled he stares, it could well be approvingly, at the clinging on by her fingertips Shadow Minister. There is talk in the lobbies that she will be unceremoniously sacked in the pending Shadow Cabinet reshuffle. Not even a sideways move… just sacked. According to certain impeccable sources, storming out of the Politics Show was the last straw. No one is taking bets any more.

There is even salacious gossip about this bred in the bone spitfire telling the Leader of the Opposition, in no uncertain terms, to keep his wandering hands to himself. Although this is not universally believed because he tends to go for tall, willowy and much too young. Camilla French is none of these things.

"Good morning, my dear Camilla."

She is an immoderately clever woman – always top of any class by a country mile. A double first at Cambridge at not her first choice of College but that only spurred her onwards and upwards. There are those who say she is too clever for her own good but they are usually less clever men. She despises second-rate brains and shows it and, despite the ever open office door, does not inspire loyalty.

"What on earth do you want?"

He is blatantly looking her over and she rarely, if ever, gets blatantly looked over; she rarely, if ever, gets looked over at all. She is only too well aware that she possesses the scribbled features of a Beatrix Potter scrapped creation. Not exactly ugly… shall we say no given lines of beauty. Character in spades definitely and a fierce courage shining through the adamantine eyes most definitely. Beauty no…definitely not. And, of course, she is small of stature.

She appears disconcertingly frumpy in the shapeless grey sweater and baggy black trousers. There is no point in taking any trouble over her clothes; she is no Rosalie Murray… Camilla French definitely believes that legs are for walking on.

"What I want, my dear Camilla." No dry lip twitch. "Is to save your Political career from going down the toilet."

She thinks talk of toilets is in bad taste. "Why?"

"Ah! That is the sixty four thousand dollar question, my dear."

She has only ever been not exactly afraid, she will not admit to that, but certainly apprehensive of two people in her life.

The first person being her one and only boyfriend in her second year at Cambridge. He had felt she should feel grateful for his attentions and made her do things of a sexual nature that she would have preferred not to know about, never mind partake of. Enough said. The second person is sitting not twelve feet away and giving the appearance of being very much at home. More at home than she has ever felt in this place.

She was forgetting. There was Daddy of course and so that makes two and a half.

She is probably more overwrought than usual but she thinks number two is looking her over not unlike her one and only boyfriend at Cambridge, when he picked her up in the College library on a rainy Tuesday afternoon. The awful thing was that she was grateful at first.

"So answer it."

She is determined to put her courage to the sticking place since reading rather a lot of Shakespeare recently... all our yesterdays have lighted fools the way to dusty death.

He tut-tuts and waves an admonishing index finger – a superbly manicured finger that has been prodded in countless pies and other places. Camilla has recently acquired the habit of biting her fingernails; she desires to bite them now but womanfully resists the temptation. She will not show any weakness.

"You are such a clever girl, Camilla and yet you drape yourself in the moth-eaten mantle of crass stupidity to the Manor born." No dry lip twitch. "Although of course it was I who was to the Manor born – you, my dear, were born to the less than salubrious suburbs of...?" He leans forward. "Where was it again?" He knows damn well.

"Oldham."

"Ah! Of course. Oldham." He makes it sound like an outer circle of hell – some sulphurous place where Dante, with eyes averted, would have ushered Virgil through as quickly as decently possible. Of course he has read Dante in the original Italian and so has Camilla French.

She purses her lips in a way that Beatrix Potter would, without hesitation, rub out and draw again. She crosses her arms and too late realises that the gesture, whilst defiant, highlights quite decent sized breasts. The one and only boyfriend had sneered that they were almost worth putting up with the rest of her body. She uncrosses the arms and scratches a wrist instead. Is she clever enough? Attack might not be the best form of defence but attack is the only gambit she is comfortable with. Attacking has got her where she is today. She cannot hold back a wry smile... perhaps a defensive attack.

"I thought the ever so fragrant Rosalie Murray was your protégée of the moment." She makes protégée sound like something the cat brought in – two can play at that game. She hates cats almost as much as she hates Rosalie Murray.

She senses instinctively that he has effortlessly forced a wrong move and it is unwise to sacrifice even a pawn to such a Grand Master. Of course she could always tell him to fuck off out of her office and sweep all the pieces off the board. The thought calms her down.

"Do you think I see you as a protégée, my dear Camilla?"

"I am not your dear Camilla." There goes a Bishop.

He pauses for thought; no one but no one pauses for thought quite like Sir Godwyn Lydate. "You entered this shitty bear pit with your eyes wide open because you craved power." He holds up a silencing hand. "Yes. Yes. I realise that you thought you hoped to change the world for the better and all that nonsense. Taken as read. Really and truly it is all about power. You have put up with the arrant imbeciles and the arse licking place men because you craved power. Because you crave power." He leans closer still. "It is all slipping away even as we speak, my dear. The arrant imbeciles and the arse licking place men are laughing behind your back." She knows they are... she bloody well knows they are. "The Leader who isn't fit to lace your boots is about to enjoy throwing you naked to the wolves."

He is... he bloody well is. She is not sure about the naked bit though.

Despite everything, Camilla French is watching fascinated, almost an out of body experience. This man will no doubt teach Machiavelli a thing or two when they meet up in the afterlife. Let's hope Dante is there to record it.

"So what do you want?"

He likes that. A very clever question in the circumstances and he would have expected nothing less. Abruptly he stands up and stalks to the window overlooking Parliament Square and Westminster Abbey.

Camilla loves to wander, of course unrecognised, in the Abbey. The calming sense of all those centuries of English history shaped, unfortunately, by men like Godwyn Lydate. She watches him looking down with all the ingrained authority of a thousand years of power and privilege. It was his ancestors who built the Abbey and even with her wall to wall cleverness she will never be part of it. Her mother had been so proud when Camilla became an MP...imagine our little Camilla... who would have thought it, the poor woman had said to anyone who would listen. She had died on the operating table the week before Camilla took her seat in the Commons.

There are tears in her eyes. She will not bloody cry. If she does cry it will, as usual, be alone.

He crosses the room and perches on the corner of the cluttered desk claiming the space as his own as a Scion of the ancient house of Lydate. This close she is aware of the no doubt expensive cologne. A most pleasing scent she has to admit. They even smell different these people.

He is very much looking her over. She is a regular Church goer and takes great comfort from the pomp and ceremony of the High Church of England. She has flirted with Rome but she has to take account of her mother's ghost. Just like her mother, she possesses an excellent hymn singing voice. The God to whom she prays on her knees every night she believes is a Just God. The God of Dinah and of Ruth as well as the God of Abraham and of Isaac. She would not go as far as to say that God is a woman...most certainly transgender.

"The choice is yours, my dear Camilla. The choice is yours." The centuries honed voice that is melodious and enticing. Not sweet doves those eyes, he thinks, but they see so much in their endeavouring and miss so much. "Academia of course beckons with a Fellowship at your old Cambridge College, yours for the asking." How on earth does he know that? "A safe harbour for the rest of your days." He glances towards the window. "Perhaps a trifle premature at your age." A dry lip twitch. "Happy birthday by the way." There are no cards on display but he probably also knows that she was a premature baby, that her mother nearly died giving birth and was unwell for the rest of her life. "So much promise not realised and so many might have beens to endure in the dank and dusky Fens."

The silence between them is not at all threatening. It has been said that he can charm the birds off the trees when he puts his mind to it. Charm his way into any woman's knickers. He would get a shock if he could see Camilla's knickers…she resists a knowing smirk because he would probably know what she was smirking about.

"At least they want me."

He appears to ignore the response, his free leg swinging like the pendulum of a grandfather clock tick tocking in the marbled halls of some ancient family Seat. She had once been invited to Lydate Hall with a group of new MPs but her mother had been taken seriously ill. She never made it.

"Or there could be all the power and the glory you have ever dreamed on." He knows a touch of Shakespeare rarely comes amiss with the likes of Camilla French.

That's it. He has said it and now it has some substance. Without thinking she crosses her arms and stares beady-eyed at the perfect knot in the old Etonian tie. She has to reluctantly admit that the colours suit his complexion. Showing that she is not without courage, she meets the stare of the compelling powder blue eyes. He appreciates that.

"Why me?"

"For my purpose." He emphasises the my. "You are in the right place at the right time. So much of power and glory is about place and time, don't you think? Infinitely better to be a Cromwell than a Charles Stuart. One just needs to be aware of the pendulum swinging."

Then as an afterthought. "My dear Camilla." A challenge to which she does not feel it politic to respond. The silence now tantalisingly stretches like one of those elastic bands littering the littered desk. Another of her recently acquired bad habits – fiddling with an elastic band when she has a decision to make and sometimes they snap.

"What is your purpose?" She emphasises the your.

He does not answer at once but stares admiringly at his own swinging highly polished burgundy brogue. Dear Lydia is so energetic with shoe polish as with so much else. He looks up. Camilla has an excellent bone structure and some decent make-up would make all the difference. She needs to accentuate the more than acceptable breasts. He has never seen her legs but takes them as read. He notices the askew sheet of paper with many crossings out and doodles. She sees where he is looking. "Your resignation statement." It is not a question.

"I have no intention of being pushed."

Sagely he nods as if in agreement. The pride of the French's being a small insignificant thing when set against the pride of the Lydates.

"Tell me, my dear, do you have legs?"

"Of course I have legs." Indignation actually suits her off key features and she folds her arms even more indignantly, as he rather thought she would.

"I will take your word for it for now."

"Are you making fun of me?" She hates to be ridiculed. In the Primary school Christmas concerts she was always the smallest fairy stuck at the end of a row out of the way; the one with a broken wand. Daddy always laughed his socks off and started calling her Tinkerbell, causing other people to laugh their socks off. Not her mother though… she never laughed her socks off.

"Yes."

"Then please don't." Daddy even laughed his socks off when he was on his deathbed and Camilla dropped his false teeth on the awful stained carpet of the Nursing Home. She loathed touching false teeth, but of course he knew that. Her mother had touched her arm in sympathy and had picked up the false teeth and glared at Daddy; Daddy's second wife had glared at Mother; Daddy had choked his socks off.

Sir Godwyn Lydate glances to the window and she glances too. The heights of the Abbey just visible from where she sits, as drawn in on herself as far as it is possible to be without damaging vital organs.

"You know, my dear, there is an early Sixteenth Century Lydate buried in the Henry the Seventh Chapel in the Abbey." She knows that. "He was a turncoat at Bosworth Field and won the battle for that upstart nobody Henry Tudor."

"I know." She knows the wording on the tomb by heart.

"You know such a lot, Camilla French."

There is a timbre to his voice that tells her she has lost the chance to tell him to fuck off out of her office. She knows she was never going to say that anyway. She knows that he is appraising her two best bits and not caring that she knows; a thousand years of debauching serving wenches and other men's wives breeds that survived arrogance. He has not answered the question and she will not ask a second time nor will she uncross her arms. At least he isn't laughing his socks off.

"Your Leader is a dead man walking." He holds up a finger. "Firstly, I will ensure that you are not sacked next week." She had not realised it would be so soon. "Or any other week." He holds up two fingers. "Secondly, I have secured an appointment for you this morning at an exclusive beauty parlour that is usually booked months ahead." He holds up three fingers. "Thirdly, this afternoon you are booked, all at my expense, at the most exclusive haute couture establishment in London." He holds up a silencing hand. "Even in these supposedly enlightened times a woman needs to look her best to gain maximum advantage."

He holds up four fingers. "Fourthly, tomorrow night you will appear on Question Time in place of the unfortunately indisposed Rosalie Murray." He holds up five fingers. "Fifthly, I am taking you out to dinner this evening to discuss what you will and will not say on national television. Early tomorrow morning we will travel to Leeds." She is a bit too far away for him to discover whether or not she has knees. "Any questions?"

She opens and shuts her mouth several times and oddly enough she doesn't remind him at all of a guppy of any kind. The rubber bands are out of reach and so she nibbles at the skin around a bitten fingernail. He leans over and slaps the hand away. "Nasty habit." She thinks about a rubber band and then thinks better of it.

"What are you saying?"

"I would have thought that was perfectly clear to a person of your high octane intelligence." He almost smiles and it is a bit scary. "The only person to obtain a higher Mensa score than you, my dear, was my good self."

She resists the temptation to ask by how much.

"The Leadership?"

"Of course."

"You can do that?"

"We, my dear. We can do that."

"Jesus." She never ever takes the Lord's name in vain.

It is her turn to lean closer. She has never leaned closer to anyone. That is if you except the small frightened fairy leaning close to the stocky fairy next in line, who had leaned back with knobs on. Daddy thought it hilarious when Camilla tumbled off the stage and was led away sobbing by her Mother.

"Why me?" She has to admit that the cloistered academic life did not appeal as much she was beginning to pretend. There was a creeping sense of dread that she did not want to define.

He holds out a hand. "Come, Cinders, your carriage awaits and you shall go to the Ball." The driest of dry lip twitches. "Or rather my limousine is parked outside on double yellow lines. My chauffeur knows your itinerary, my dear, and will accompany you." He is not to know that this could well be a mistake.

She takes hold of the cool hand and he pulls Camilla to her size three feet. She so rarely smiles. "What would you have done if I had told you to fuck off out of my office?"

"I would have fucked off out of your office."

She smiles now.

Wednesday 18th October 10.32am

The By Royal Appointment Clerical outfitters on Pall Mall exudes the appropriate hushed and reverent atmosphere. The Reverend John Eames is being assiduously measured to the quarter inch for his Bishop's raiment by the elderly man, who could be taken for a Bishop himself, albeit a defrocked Bishop.

From time to time the rubbery mouthed Measurer glances to where the extremely attractive young lady is seated. Rather nice legs, although this Establishment is not at all used to hosting quite so much female thigh. The rather severe spectacles only adding to the somewhat intrusive allure.

She must be a daughter, surely, or a favourite niece perhaps. Although the manner in which she is appraising the soon-to-be, God help us, Bishop of Staines is a touch leery – a word he seeks any excuse to use since last Friday's Times crossword. Most definitely five letters across or down and most definitely leery.

"Are you certain I need these?" The soon-to-be's voice a trifle too loud – for goodness sake this is not the back of the Church. Hard to believe the sorts of people being made Bishops these days. He blames the Government.

"They must be worn in the House of Lords." Thank goodness he does not yet have to call him my Lord.

"That colour really suits you, Johnny." She purrs in the manner of the Measurer's widowed sister's unspoiled half tamed Siamese cat. Not a daughter then and probably not a favourite niece either. These people… my God… these people… they are not in the same league as Archbishop Hugh. Now there is a proper man of God.

The Reverend John Eames admires himself in the old-fashioned mirror sloping on its rickety stand, then momentarily focuses on the Garden of Eden background of Cecilia Hunt who bestows a dinky little wave. The Measurer looks to the Heavens as the soon-to-be bestows a dinkyish little wave in return. The Measurer is not aware that the little madam sticks out her tongue and gives a slender finger to the broad back of the dirty old Measuring man.

Unaware of this sacrilege, the dirty old Measuring man coughs into the hollow of his hand and for some reason, the future Bishop John of Staines takes this as a mark of approval.

Wednesday 18th October 10.59am

Jack Bellingham, only following orders, ignores the shouted questions of the media frenzy as he ducks out of the taxi at the Ritz Hotel. He has slept well and feels much more balanced. Sleeping well is vital to his well-being and he has always been able to fall asleep within minutes, even in the stale sweat infested cell he shared with Sikesy. The bed he woke up in this morning was a world away from that much creaking lower bunk. Waking up entangled with the muscle toned limbs of Nina Balatka was not the least bit like waking up underneath his cell mate's threatening body bulge. Syksey inevitably announcing his waking with a cacophony of rumbling farts, echoing belches and feverish scratchings.

The same Porter recognises Jack and touches the neb of his uniform cap. Thoughts of the Bulgarian chambermaid's latest demands are put to one side. He is not as young as he used to be and a nice cup of tea on waking is becoming more and more of a tempting option.

The Hotel manager, who was forewarned, is ready and waiting to escort Hero Jack to the lift. The Porter follows at a respectful distance, holding his uniform cap at present arms. There is no way he wants to upset the bastard of a Hotel manager for a second time this morning. He hates to think what would happen if the bastard found out about the Bulgarian chambermaid who has learned several new words.

Jack thinks he recognises the only one of her People who is there to meet him when the lift arrives on the second floor.

An extortionately pretty girl in a theatrically vacant sort of way, where vacancy adds an almost psychedelic quality to the extortion. Very shapely to follow down the corridor, but then they are all very shapely to follow down the corridor.

And there are the gruesome twosome esconced together, like Tweedledum and Tweedledumette, in the Ancien Regime sitting room of the Ritz Hotel suite that stinks of competing heady perfumes.

"Jack...ee!" Squeals the mega one, who is prevented from running into his arms as she had intended. There will be a bruise. "Where have you been?" As though he has been out of the room only a few minutes and she just cannot live without his presence. He remembers the movie well – not one of her best.

Appraisingly he meets his bloody sister's appraising eyes. She is not to know what he has divulged to Shirley Keeldar; the brother and sister having sworn in actual blood never to tell a living soul. He ought to feel guilty, except that it gives him a slim advantage in the wordless struggle of wills that has been their lives together since before they were born – forever and forever teetering on the edge of something unimaginably worse.

He will never know if she turned up every day to the trial hoping he would be found guilty. Some days she reminded him of one of those crones avidly knitting at the foot of the guillotine, dropping stitches every time a severed head tumbled into the bloody basket.

"Well hello, brother mine." They could always out stare each other turn and turn about. The crafted insults more daggers than broadswords.

"Fancy seeing you here of all places, sister yours."

"A nice surprise?"

"Not at all." She is not sure if he means the nice or the surprise. He always was a cunning bastard with the stiletto. In response she crosses well-manicured smooth legs for him to admire, and then crosses two well-manicured smooth hands on top of an equally smooth knee, the spearmint green fingernails setting off the flesh tones. The dress she is wearing must have cost several arms and several legs and he cannot fail to appreciate that it accentuates the delta of their mother's curves. His bloody sister turned quite a few heads every day in Court, including that wall eyed detective bloke.

Amelia Sedley is fucking annoyed that she is becoming marginalised here and stares narrow eyed at Jack as if it is all his fault. On second thoughts she thinks that becoming marginalised in a room with these two might not be a bad thing after all.

"You are just in time, brother mine." Deftly he raises a quizzical eyebrow, which reminds Amelia Sedley of that remarkably randy leading man in the last but one movie that sort of flopped; he never sort of flopped. She needs to take several deep breaths here. "Just in time for a threesome, brother mine." Several more deep breaths.

"Hey just hang on one cotton picking minute." The two pairs of oddly colourless eyes swivel in unison and stare at Amelia Sedley as if she has just crawled out from under a stone. Nobody has ever looked like that at Amelia Sedley… never. She doesn't say anything else. When she looks down at the hands clasped in her lap the brother and sister renew that relentless hundred years war of eye contact.

"You so so enjoyed the threesome with the Vicar's wife, the ever so fragrant Dora Eames." Marion Fay extravagantly licks her lips. "Although not quite so fragrant by the time we had finished." She nudges Amelia. There will be a bruise.

Amelia needs to fucking reassert herself here, she really fucking does, she is losing the plot big time. "What the fuck is going on here?" The voice is not quite right – too quavery – she needs direction here.

"Shut the fuck up." There has been such a lot of doing as she is told in her gilded life that she shuts the fuck up. No doubt there will be some sort of cue – there usually is some sort of cue.

Marion Fay is admiring her own toenails, the same spearmint green colour as her fingernails, and mews up her mouth in that exact same gesture. Amelia Sedley closes her eyes for all she is worth.

"Come and sit next to sweet cakes, brother mine." The big sister bestows an uncatalogued smile on her twin brother. "We have been trying out different perfumes for sweet cake's new range of fragrances."

"So that's why it stinks like a brothel?"

"No, brother mine, that is something else entirely." The follow up laughter is Western frontier Saloon gal raucous that makes Amelia flinch. She is not sure that this is the safest place in the world to be right now.

A sitting next to sweet cakes Jack, sniff sniffs at the nape of Amelia's classical swan's neck and she shudders. "I like that one. What's it called?" He is thinking of a gift for Shirley Keeldar. He is not yet equipped to know that he is reading Shirley Keeldar wrong.

"Seduction," Amelia Sedley croaks.

Marion Fay stretches an arm across Amelia's world-famous chest, that Movie Reel magazine called the eighth wonder of the world. "Smell that, brother mine."

"Not bad."

"Articulate." Marion takes a sniff of her own arm. "Not my choice. Smells a bit like an open grave in the rain." She grins conspiratorially with the exact same shape of mouth. Amelia Sedley is still not getting any cue and so eyes tight closed is the best option. She might wake up.

"Shall I tell you about the threesome with the Vicar's wife, sweet cakes?" Amelia cannot trust her voice, which for an actress is not good. She is beginning to think there is something not quite right about these two. A suspicion that has been growing about Marion in particular throughout the morning. Something definitely not quite as it should be, cogs unhinged and swivelling in the opposite direction. Reflected in those eyes are things that should not have been seen. Seductive though – absurdly seductive. Best not to look until prompted.

"It was the day after John, sorry Jack, was found not guilty. I'd been having a thing with Dora Eames for several weeks. It helped me through a difficult time."

"And you were having a thing with her husband the Vicar," Jack interjects.

"We never had a threesome." So that's all right then. "On that particular day John, sorry Jack, went to the Solicitors…"

"Useless sods."

"Let me finish please. Went to the Solicitors to discuss compensation for wrongful arrest but lost his temper and walked out." She whispers in Amelia's ear. "And not in a nice way." She leans forward from the waist and grins wickedly at her twin brother. "You just never know with… Jack."

Amelia Sedley stays as quiet as the quietest mouse in a children's nursery rhyme. If she could find her voice she would ask them to leave but knows that might not be a good idea. She wonders if any of her useless fucking People are within earshot.

"So he came back unexpectedly and walked in on two naked ladies being very naughty indeed." She strokes Amelia's bare arm and Amelia shivers. "In fact we had just reached a delicate point in proceedings." That raucous laugh again only more raucous…it is throwing out time at the Western frontier Saloon. She nudges Amelia hard in the ribs and there goes another bruise. "You know what I mean, sweetcakes? Of course you do." Amelia has opened her eyes and is staring off into the distance, possibly as far as the limitless plains of Wyoming. She wishes she was there right now on the Dude Ranch she owns and rarely visits, and wonders if letting out a scream would be too too melodramatic.

She perfected a wondrous scream in the one and only movie where she was nominated for best supporting actress. No fucking Oscar there either.

"The dirty bugger sneaked up the stairs." Another dig in the ribs. Jesus fuck... another bruise. "Avoiding the one that creaked and there we were approaching the point of no return on the mountain road and no brakes." Marion Fay is only too well aware that Jack is absentmindedly stroking Amelia's bare thigh. She always knows when his thoughts are in a dark place, which is most of the time. Amelia's eyes are tight closed.

"To be fair, sweetcakes, the dirty bugger waited until we had well and truly finished before joining us in bed." Only the threat of a raucous laugh this time. "You just will not believe it, sweetcakes, it was the prim and proper, butter wouldn't melt in her mouth, Vicar's garden party wife, and she pregnant by another man not her husband, who begged the first fuck. You know what they say, sweet cakes... first fuck is the deepest."

"I didn't know she was pregnant."

"You don't know everything, brother cakes." Not even the threat of a raucous laugh. "I thought the two of them would never stop banging away." Marion throatily giggles, which is a marginal improvement on the raucous laugh. "She even watched the second fuck which was over in no time at all. They often say that about second fucks, sweetcakes." Amelia flinches but she is not dug in the ribs this time. "Then she begged thirds, the greedy cow. After a brief rest, because he is partly human after all, brother mine duly obliged."

Amelia groans and knows the medication is a waste of time. It is an incurable illness... it really is an incurable illness.

"To be honest, sweetcakes, I left them to it in the end."

Marion Fay eases down the strap of Amelia Sedley's pink flowery top and exposes half of the eighth wonder of the world.

Amelia Sedley dare not open her eyes. No fucking medication known to man is going to save her now. She might as well give herself up to whatever these twisted siblings conjure up with smoke and mirrors.

There is a knocking at the door. "Fuck off." One of them shouts.

Lucy Snowe does not like that at all... not one little bit does she like that. She is storing everything up... boy is she storing everything up. It is all going into her mental little black book.

Wednesday 18th October 11.40am

A most reverently thoughtful Archbishop chews an arm of the tortoiseshell reading glasses and gazes serenely out of his study window. A team of gardeners is clearing up dead leaves in the Palace grounds. There is a regiment of trees that are quite lovely in summer, or so he has been told. He has an aversion to trees, and dead leaves in particular, going back to a horrid shrouded October Wednesday morning during his first weeks at Eton. He had been rolled in dead leaves as a punishment for sneaking on one of his classmates. The little shits had stuffed dead leaves in his mouth until he believed he was choking his young life away.

He has not the self-awareness to think that, on balance, that might have been a good thing.

That frightful morning wanting to cry out for Nanny Beatrice, but choking all the more. Then Godwyn Lydate magically appeared on the scene and ordered the little shits to cease and desist; they had slunk away rubbing leaf mould off their shitty little hands. Even at that age one did not cross Godwyn Lydate. He had helped snivelling little Hugh Clavering to his feet and taken a firm grip of his arm, whilst the shivering and shaking little boy spat out mouldy earthy leaves; a bitter taste of the Underworld.

Nothing he can ever do will adequately repay that marvellous man for that and numerous other favours, but he tries his best. And to be fair he thinks his best is very good indeed.

He chews some more on the tortoiseshell reading glasses and ponders on the keynote speech he will make in the House of Lords next week. It will be an important contribution to the debate – Sir Godwyn has seen to that.

There is a knock at the door.

"Come."

"Coffee, your Grace." A deep voice for a woman. The lovely big black eyed olive skinned creature carries the hallmarked silver tray. A rattling cup and saucer, not to mention the hallmarked silver coffee pot and the hallmarked silver milk jug and the hallmarked silver sugar bowl with solid silver sugar tongs.

She is flaunting the Lyons Corner House waitress uniform, which is precariously stretched across the expansive bust; several buttons have already pinged. She sets the tray down on the neat and tidy desk, then looks boldly to where the naughty spanker of earlier this morning has turned from his contemplation of, no doubt, things Spiritual. She knows all about Priests and their, no doubt, things Spiritual. After all flagellation is in several books of the Bible, or so claimed one of the village Priests, before beating Anna's backside black and blue.

"Will that be all, your Grace?"

"No that will not be all." Imperious is as Imperious does. He needs to recover some dignity after the proceedings of earlier this morning which got somewhat out of hand. He wonders if he might have met his match on things not at all Spiritual.

"You have an appointment at twelve o'clock, your Grace." The unfathomable darkness behind the eyes is as bewitching as a starless sky on a moonless night seen through an uncurtained window of a castle tower. It is a long time since he has written any bad poetry and now he feels the urge. Yes… well.

"It can wait."

"Yes, your Grace."

"This cannot wait." He indicates, with the tortoiseshell reading glasses, the tell-tale bulge in his trousers.

She buries the thought that there is more often than not a tell-tale bulge in men's trousers where Anna is concerned. After all, this is a great improvement on being pawed by the slobbering brother-in-law, who seems to have disappeared without trace off the face of the earth. The beanpole Chef is already bare bones of the Bronze Age.

"Come here, woman." In the manner of Adam commanding an Eve created of his rib before it all went so badly wrong. Obediently she crosses the thick pile carpet with a suggestive crinkle crinkling of the old-fashioned uniform which, with those several buttons having pinged, is more than ever precariously stretched across the expansive bust. She stands close so that he is only too well aware of her body heat, the garlic on her breath and the underlying scents of scrubbed sweat. She wears no other perfume and, anyway, traditional perfumes make him sneeze. It started with that stupid doused in cheap perfume waitress at Oxford, who was just asking for it and then screamed blue murder when she got it. He soon shut her up. Of course, thanks for the later shutting up must go to Sir Godwyn.

The Archbishop gingerly sets aside the tortoiseshell reading glasses because, after that extempore overexuberant incident of yesterday, they are his only unbroken pair. This woman's black eyes reflect thousands of years of peasant cunning and naked peasant flesh, adorned by guttering candlelight and conjoined shadows flickering on flaking plaster walls. He really must write down some bad poetry. It has been far too long.

"Take off all your clothes and serve my coffee naked." A quivering smile. "You naked not the coffee." There is not a trace of stray laughter in the air.

"No stockings?" The deep voice, that if one closes one's eyes could almost be a man's voice. Eton has a lot to answer for.

"No stockings." Clearing his throat as if he is about to commence one of his signature Royal Wedding addresses in Westminster Abbey or St Paul's.

He limps over to the cleared desk and, with some difficulty, takes his seat in the leather captain's chair which used to be his holier than thou father's favourite chair, from which to admonish his least favourite, but only legitimate son. He stares at his nervous hands on the desktop. He is never nervous before an Easter sermon or a Royal address. Nervously he nudges the printout of Sir Godwyn's email of suggestions for the House of Lords speech. It just needs to be clothed in Hugh Clavering's banal words and the finishing touches of pompous morality that he intones better than anyone.

He absolutely does not look at the just asking for it waitress shedding her clothes. He is only too well aware that she is deliberately taking her time unhooking and then tantalisingly peeling down the 1940s stockings... everything must be authentic. He pretends to be unaware of her crossing to the desk on those pummelling bare feet. He has his dignity.

"Shall I pour the coffee, your Grace?" It is a rare Himalayan coffee, a gift from that delightful girl at the Chinese embassy. She had also served him naked after shedding a waitress uniform; the bust, it has to be said, a trifle disappointing.

"Yes." More a squeal than anything else. "Yes." A bit better. "Pour." Much better.

She lifts up the hallmarked silver coffee pot as if it weighs nothing at all and deftly pours into the china cup. She has never served naked and quite likes it. It is surprising that her greasy brother-in-law didn't think of it for his own after hours delectation. Delectation the word used several times by the Archbishop yesterday. She intends to learn a lot from this particular man of the cloth just, as a young girl, she had learned such a lot from several village Priests. She will certainly teach him a thing or two in return, as she taught several village Priests a thing or two in return. She has generous instincts.

"Milk, your Grace?"

"Yes." She leans closer as she pours the full fat milk, the lovely big bosoms momentarily in his face so that it is hard to breathe.

"Sugar, your Grace?"

"Two lumps." His voice muffled. There is an insolently polite knock at the study door which is ignored, as she expertly wields the solid silver sugar tongs and withdraws the bosoms.

"'Stir it." She stirs with a solid silver spoon. "Take a sip. It might be poisoned." There is the pre-taste of dry leaves in his mouth.

She, of course, realises that he is more than a touch mad – the distillation of a thousand years of privileged inbreeding. But then she is a result of thousands of years of village peasant inbreeding. It is just that the madness takes a different form. It is always interesting when two forms of madness propagate...they are not to know yet that she conceived last night, or it might have been this morning. So that this silence is indeed pregnant.

She takes a generous sip and smacks her lips and sets the china cup back on the China saucer with no hint of a rattle. The coffee is not poisoned. She has resisted the temptation to grab at her throat and make choking noises. This is no laughing matter.

Now, and only now, this Prince of the Church drinks in, with avid eyes, the lovely big naked creature, with the primeval blackness caved between gloriously meaty thighs.

"Not poisoned?"

"No, your Grace."

Rather shakily he takes up the fine china cup of coffee smeared with the red lipstick that he painted on her mouth this morning and then painted on her nipples. He adores the taste of this particular brand of lipstick. She stands passively knowing her place… or so he thinks he ought to believe.

"Will that be all, your Grace?" As if she will walk naked out of the room. Shakily he places the china cup back on the rattling saucer.

"I have spilled some coffee on my trousers." He just about has enough breath to finish the sentence.

"Shall I take care of that, your Grace?" He cavalierly nods his head and fixes bloodshot eyes on the depressingly dull oil painting of a former Archbishop of the late Eighteenth Century. No one remembers his name now of course… he was a Clavering and they used to call him the madcap Archbishop. They do not call him anything now. The naked woman kneels at his feet and unzips his trousers. The sounds that escape from his throat are scarcely human, but then neither is her toothsome grin and the protruding tongue.

Wednesday 18th October 12.07pm

Spencer Perceval noisily slurps strong black coffee and with bleary teddy bear eyes checks his mobile phone. The screen is blurred. Fuck. He chews a thumbnail.

"You look like shit." Helen Huntingdon is immaculately immaculate in a pale grey handmade business suit, with a tight skirt very much on the short side. Pale grey blouse with a dinky bow and lots and lots of pale yellow tights that might not be a colour to everyone's taste, and of course topped off by the curly orange hair.

"Fuck off." But his heart is just not in it. She could almost feel sorry for the useless twat.

"No message from the little woman?"

"Fuck off and she certainly isn't little." He tosses the mobile phone on the spare chair at their table in the bar area of the Queens Hotel. "Arse like a rhinoceros." An intriguing image that Helen Huntingdon plays around with for a few time wasting seconds.

"Not at all like my arse then?" She crosses pale yellow legs and adjusts the short skirt accordingly. He wishes she would sit fucking still.

"Don't fucking start that cock teasing shit again." Noisily he slurps more coffee and must admit he does feel like shit. The two bottles of champagne at three o'clock in the morning, not to mention the coke snorting, might have been several steps too far. There have been too many of those steps recently. He thinks it might well be the first time he has had sexual congress with an actual real life nymphomaniac; a well pissed and drugged up nymphomaniac at that.

It is just his bad luck it is her fucking day off and that she has taken ownership of his bed like a praying mantis on heat. He did well to escape whilst she was gushing a pee with the bathroom door wide open. His wife locks the bathroom door when she goes for a pee. Carrie Brattle…well…Carrie Brattle had her own take on exhibitionist peeing.

"You missed breakfast." Give that girl a shiny medal for stating the bleeding obvious he doesn't say. There is something creepily almost frightening about this weirdo he definitely doesn't say. "The full English was absolutely yummy scrummy." He doesn't like to point out that he partook of an alternative full English. "Lovely juicy sausages." They even smoked after sex and no one who is anyone smokes after sex anymore. He rubs his eyes and throatily coughs. They had smoked rather too much… everything was rather too much. Another tick in the worst pick-ups he has made box. He cannot even remember her fucking name. His memory is more and more a black hole, as Helen Huntingdon can testify.

"Have I missed anything apart from an absolutely yummy scrummy full English?" He fails dismally in the mimic. Her resulting giggles are certainly beyond his powers to even attempt to mimic.

"All is in hand." She girly girly flutter flutters surely fake eyelashes in a way that anyone watching might think suggestive. "Had a meet at the BBC studios and told them you were indisposed. Didn't tell them that the noise through the wall of your indisposition woke me up this morning and interrupted my beauty sleep." She certainly does not tell him that she quite satisfactorily took care of her own resultant urges with a minimum of fuss. There is nothing wrong with her memory.

He is fucking not going to apologise. Never in a million zillion years.

"Don't worry, lover." She leans closer and pat pats his knee. One can take the girl out of Sir Godwyn Lydate but one cannot take Sir Godwyn Lydate out of the girl. "Your Auntie Helen has taken care of everything. Showed lots of leg and assured the all-male ensemble that you will be present and correct at this afternoon's run through."

"Fuck."

"By the looks of you, lover boy, and the noise of your indisposition, rather too much fuckee fuckee." She makes slits of her two eyes and then giggles into a cupped hand and leans back to publicly reveal rather a lot of the pale yellow tights. They are definitely tights and not stockings. A most tempting display. What the fuck is wrong with him?

"I agreed four o'clock at the Town Hall for the run through and blow jobs all round." More manic giggles without the cupped hands. Jesus Christ he can see her fucking tonsils. "Don't get jealous, lover. I was only joking."

Blearily he stares into the drained coffee cup as if there are unlucky fortunes to be divined and keeps staring until the giggling has run out of steam. This is one weird chick.

"Do you want something to eat, lover?"

"Just more coffee." He flicks the blonde fall of hair away from his face. If she studies him closely, which she does, she can see that the fine edge of his boyish good looks is being inexorably eaten away by dissipation. Plus he really is a nasty spiteful two timing forgetful little shit, although not totally lacking the boyish charm that has been his stock in trade for so long. Getting less boyish and less charming by the day. He has got away with it for so long that the loss of getting away with it is going to come hard – she suppresses a giggle.

Helen is no snob but already he has sunk to the level of tarty peroxide blonde barmaids. Carrie Brattle was an aberration of a lifeboat that he should have clung to for dear life.

Just as blearily he watches the weird chick march to the bar to order more coffee. Certainly not an arse like a rhinoceros he has to give her that. In fact rather an encingly neat and shapely arse from the School of Carrie Brattle. Not the original but a very good copy. He emits a gurgled moan at unbidden thoughts of the lost world of Carrie Brattle. The flower bedecked barge pushed off from Avalon and she was not on board to accompany the body of the fallen king.

Namby-pamby bitch. For fuck's sake anyone who is anyone has abortions these days – just a different form of the morning after pill. He checks the time on the gold Rolex and it is a total fucking blur.

Perhaps he should have tried harder last night with the undoubtedly up for it Helen screw loose, who is returning with the coffees. No Helen of Troy but eminently beddable, firmish tits from what he can make out and Business class legs. Just a pity about the Wizard of Oz orange hair. On the plus side, he could not imagine screw loose extemporising eye watering moves with an empty champagne bottle at five o'clock in the morning. He couldn't help worrying that he turned out to be a bit of an anti-climax following on from the champagne bottle.

"I've ordered myself a club sandwich with chips on the side."

"Where do you put it all?"

"Wouldn't you like to find out?"

There she goes again. He cannot make up his mind whether or not she is playing hard to get or just playing hard. Or knowing his luck probably just playing get. He thinks he knows what he means.

"I would like to put something else in your mouth."

He is a trier she will give him that. "The sausage theme again, lover?"

Not too much of a giggle, thank Christ, and when she crosses her legs he is sure he gets a flash of something not pale yellow.

"Who knows?" She carefully arranges the short skirt, the crotchless tights being a bit of a challenge. That's better. She takes up the cup of coffee – she does so enjoy a caffeine rush. She has crossed her heart and hope to die promised Goddy to stay off the hard drugs; it was part of their bargain to take the prescribed medication without fail…one out of two ain't bad.

"Who knows what?"

"Precisely." She is gazing suggestively over the rim of the cup. It just has to be suggestive… there is no other word for it.

"Look, Helen."

"Yes, lover." She is even sipping the coffee suggestively.

"We have oodles of time before the run through so why don't we go to your room and get naked." A crude chat up line that nevertheless worked on Carrie Brattle, but then he was not to know. A bit of soreness downstairs so he might have to take it easy at first… he blames what's er name mantis, the champagne bottle girl.

Helen pertly sets down the cup and purses orange lips, as if she is giving his quite reasonable suggestion due consideration… on the one hand and then on the other hand.

"Why not your room, lover?"

Will the nymphomaniac coked up barmaid have gushed off? Probably not but then quick thinking has saved the Perceval bacon more than once. "It's a bit of a mess." Not to mention well… not to mention. And then he serves up a Formula One it never fails winning smile. "So your room then, babe?"

"Your coffee is going cold."

"Fuck the coffee."

"I thought you wanted to fuck little old moi."

"I do, babe. I so do, babe."

She sips more coffee… on the one hand and then on the other hand.

Two ladies of a certain age at the next table are glancing over not quite surreptitiously enough. It takes practice.

"Oh! I forgot to tell you, Spencer." She deftly lifts a piece of fluff off a pale yellow knee as if it is a particularly nasty insect, smooths the knee and admires the resultant smoothness. Most definitely a screw loose. "Rosalie Murray has pulled out of the Show."

"Fuck."

She ostentatiously treats it is a question. "I am still weighing up your tempting offer. Camilla French is taking her place."

"No fucking way José."

"Sir Godwyn Lydate has arranged it directly with the DG."

Spencer Perceval has no option but to stare off into the distance, big-game hunter fashion, as far as the bottles of spirits lined up behind the bar. He could do with a stiff drink. Who fucking cares anyway which Political tart comes on the Show. The only difference being that he hasn't banged Camilla French. As far as he knows, no one has banged Camilla French – probably not even Camilla French.

Unintentionally he catches the roving eye of one of the ladies of a certain age at the next table who caught out coyly smiles. A quite presentable brunette and nicely turned out but must be fifty if she's a day. A not as picky as he used to be Spencer returns the smile, and she goes into a whispering huddle with the other lady of a certain age who, from what he can make out, is not quite as presentable. His eyesight is not what it was and he worries that he might need glasses. Fuck. The other one would be a decent third in a threesome. It really would have to be a threesome…sizeable tits though… a bit of a toss up.

"How do you do it, Spencer?"

"What?" He forgot for the moment where he was. He really must cut down on the booze and the substances. The blackouts can be quite disturbing. Sometimes he cannot remember the doings of the night before.

"Another conquest." Moving on from tarty barmaids to overdressed grannies she doesn't say.

"Are you taking the piss?"

"You have this stunning, if I do say so myself, young lady deciding whether to get naked with you and, there you are, making sheep's eyes at other women."

"She was making sheep's eyes at me." He has never made sheep's eyes at a woman in his life… the very idea. "She was making sheep's eyes at me."

"Spencer, love. The answer is yes."

He takes a moment out of his manufactured indignation to absorb the breathlessly whispered words and to make sure he has heard correctly. He stares so abjectly bleary eyed that she struggles not to giggle, which would ruin the moment.

Whilst screw loose is not stunning she is not at all bad. Most certainly acceptable legs with the usual stuff at the top of the legs… they all have that. To prove it she crosses and uncrosses the legs in question. A most definite hint of something not yellow.

"What did you say?"

"I said the answer is yes, lover."

In his more than somewhat fevered imagination he can already feel the pressure of those legs pincered round his lower back. It might be the fag end of the cocktail of substances but he is almost good to go . He should be wearing a Superman top. Pity about the curly orange hair but he can always close his eyes – the trouble is he might fall asleep. Anyway the, shall we say, mature threesome can go on hold and, to be honest, it might have been expecting a bit too much.

He pushes back the chair, stands up too hurriedly and almost falls over. Not a good image, as coffee spills into the saucer as he grabs the back of the chair. Recovering, he transmits the second best lets go and get naked without further ado grin, which is a tad wavery. But there you go – still pretty damned potent. It has never failed yet.

"Where are you going, Spencer?" In her turn she is transmitting a puzzled somewhat nonplussed expression, that lends her features more than a passing resemblance to a Sixteenth Century New England village idiot. She has uncrossed those legs and is primly tugging down the shortish skirt. The pale yellow knees are welded together in the manner of an Agatha Christie village spinster about to unmask a murderer. It looks as though it would take an acetylene torch to unweld the knees.

"Upstairs to get naked, babe. You said yes. You said yes." He holds on tight to the chair which is a bit wobbly but is there… most definitely is there in the here and now.

"I said yes to taking the piss." She only just manages to spit out the words before collapsing into the giggliest fit of giggles so far.

Spencer Perceval looks on in sheer disbelief. "Cunt." He hisses and, composing himself with the utmost dignity he is able to muster in his current state, he sidles purposefully to the other table, where the two fifty something women have been fascinatedly watching the Spencer Perceval and yellow legs show. Thankfully he drops into an uninvited chair. The two ladies are now part of the show. How exciting!

"Ladies, can I buy you a drink?"

The quite presentable brunette who had coyly smiled coyly, smiles coyly. "We really shouldn't, Mr Perceval."

The less presentable one with shortish grey hair offputtingly resembling a Second World War, abandoned on the battle field, German helmet does not coyly smile. "It's a bit early, Mr Perceval."

"Please. Call me Spencer." He formally shakes hands with them both. The less presentable one has soft melting hands and tits fighting their way out of the size too small dress with a couple of sly buttons undone. Possibly more a first reserve than a makeweight in a threesome – he is nothing if not fair.

"You see, Spencer." The quite presentable brunette takes the lead – there is always a pushy one. "We are having a coffee and then going to do some shopping at Harvey Nicks." There is a hint of a Geordie accent or somewhere up there near Hadrian's Wall. The Romans were not stupid.

"We had a big breakfast." Murmurs the less presentable one. It is hard not be distracted by the rising and falling of the fighting chest. So that was where she put the big breakfast.

"Please, ladies. I hate to drink alone."

"What about the young lady?" Asks the quite presentable brunette without looking at the young lady in question, who is intently checking her mobile phone. Spencer has his back to the devious fucking psycho. "I wouldn't drink with her if she was the last woman on earth."

The quite presentable brunette holds a shocked hand to her mouth and glances at the less presentable one. This is all very dramatic and so unreal to be chatting to the actual real life Spencer Perceval. They are both fans of the Show and avid readers of the gossip magazines on their fortnightly hairdresser visits. If the stories are to be believed there have been some very racy goings on, making the half-hearted wife swapping at West Shields golf club very tame by comparison. Not that Maria Branwell has ever taken part.

"Are you staying at the hotel?" He asks most politely.

The quite presentable brunette, in an out of place homely gesture, brushes down her pleated pale blue skirt. There are black tighted knees on display but not much else. To be honest it makes a pleasant change and is quite restful after the seated gymnastics of the nut job who thankfully he cannot see from here. "Just last night, tonight and tomorrow." She leans closer as if about to divulge some juicy gossip to the person under the next hairdryer, wafting lots of a not unpleasant perfume. "We managed to get tickets for Question Time tomorrow evening."

"Then we must drink to that." He clicks his fingers to summon the bartender. The less presentable lady appears about to say something and then thinks better of it when she catches the quite presentable brunette's eye. Maria Branwell has had long practice of knowing when to keep her mouth shut. She cannot help feeling guilty after last week's aberration when she most definitely did not keep her mouth shut.

He had spotted the bottle earlier. "A triple Black Label and one lump of ice. Just one lump mind. Ladies?" He doesn't bother looking at the male bartender, which is his way with male functionaries. After last night's experience it might well be his way with female functionaries in future.

"Vodka and slimline tonic please, Spencer." The quite presentable brunette stares at his lips for some reason. Just wait until she tells the girls back at West Shields golf club. They call themselves girls, but the youngest admits to a doubtful forty eight.

"Same here." The less presentable one also stares at his mouth – possibly a Pictish custom when accepting drinks from a sort of famous stranger.

"Exceedingly large ones as the Bishop said to the waitress." With a wave of his hand he dismisses the bartender, who cannot help but glance admiringly at the determinedly texting leggy girl in the pale yellow tights and the outrageous curly orange hair.

"Spencer really, we shouldn't."

Equally dismissing the half-hearted comment he takes hold of the quite presentable brunette's clammy hand – a paper thin wedding ring. "I don't know your name." The hand is not softly melting but hey it's a hand.

"Harriet O'Connor and this is Maria Branwell."

"Delighted to meet you both." Theatrically he kisses the captured hand and then lets it go. Doesn't want to overdo it and is only too well aware of the partly suppressed giggling from behind his back, where the chair is pushed back. Psycho is leaving without waiting for the club sandwich with chips on the side. He is now feeling a tad peckish.

Both ladies of a certain age watch the orange haired leggy girl leave the bar with over much swaying of slim hips for their liking. The bartender would not agree. Maria Branwell experiences a sudden inexplicable feeling of foreboding and the taste of last week's aberration lingers.

"She is very attractive." Murmurs Harriet O'Connor.

"Not as attractive as you, Harriet," Spencer interjects before Maria thingy can put in her six penneth.

"Oh! Spencer for goodness sake." Harriet lightly slaps his arm and is still blushing from the kissed hand. "I am fifty one years old." She is actually fifty four years old and cannot help being delighted at the outrageous compliment. She avoids catching boring goody-goody Maria's eye; if Harriet only knew.

"I do not believe it, Harriet."

"Stop it." Another less gentle slap. She really likes him saying her name; it brings her out in goose bumps. There is now a quite becoming blush to her cheeks. Luckily no one can see the blush flowering on her chest.

He grasps his slapped arm, pretending to be injured, and Harriet sort of tinkly laughs. Maria does not sort of tinkly laugh, although she gives it a failed attempt, because she doesn't like to be left out. She is often left out of things, particularly since she flatly refused to take part in the disgusting golf club wife swapping. Before last week's aberration she had always seen sex as an invasion of her body to be repulsed if at all feasible. She has no children.

The drinks arrive and Spencer raises his tumbler, not noticing there are two lumps of ice. He needs this. Boy does he need this. "To us."

It is patently obvious that neither lady is quite sure how to respond, particularly Maria what's er name, who gazes inquiringly at the triple vodka she is holding as if it has appeared by magic. Most odd.

Harriet O'Connor rallies and gamely raises the frosted glass. "To us." She glances at Maria who is gazing vacantly at her own frosted glass. She hopes Maria is not going to have one of her turns. That would be too much.

Harriet is beginning to think it was a mistake to take pity on the silly moo with her so-called dicky heart. "To us," Harriet firmly reiterates and is rewarded with a most suggestive boyish grin. She blushes on the blush – most becoming. Naturally he is not aware of the blush on the blush flowering her chest. The girls will never believe this, whatever it is. Harriet doesn't quite believe it herself. He is not quite as handsome as he appears on television, a tad jowly, but then who is she to talk.

Maria Branwell takes a gulping swallow of the magic brew. Then another. Then belches. "Pardon me." No matter how much she drinks she will never forgive herself for what happened last week. There were extenuating circumstances, but even so, and she gulps another swallow.

Harriet O'Connor raises her well defined eyebrows to the heavens and Spencer Perceval signals for more drinks.

Wednesday 18th October 12.59pm

Jack Bellingham is beginning to think that Spencer Perceval should take on a lesser role in this state of the nation novel. After all he is a shallow and inconsequential person and not at all in the mould of Sir Godwyn Lydate.

Speak of the devil, Sir Godwyn carries the package, which has been hand delivered by a courier from the Chinese embassy, to the kitchen table. Smoked salmon and a box of eggs taking up space, not to mention two bottles of his favourite lunchtime Burgundy... the perfect lunchtime drink for sharing anticipations of the flesh.

With a narrow eyed pensive expression that bodes ill for some unfortunate personage, he methodically cuts the string and carefully opens the brown paper parcel. The paper and string can be reused – one of Nanny Linda's thrifty habits...waste not want not.

Equally narrow eyed pensively he reads the handwritten note displaying exorbitantly neat, backward sloping handwriting. Li Soo Ying cannot make lunch today... sincerest apologies. Something has come up. She will contact him to rearrange when convenient. To add insult to injury there are several spidery kisses and what appears to be a lipsticked kiss.

Sir Godwyn tap taps the scented note against an even more pensive mouth. He believed he had outgrown such childish games.

The package contains the ravishing silk dress she had been wearing at the Downing Street Reception. He holds out the dress to its full length and presses the silky material to his grim Reaper's face, inhaling the tantalising perfume. Tossing the dress to one side he uncorks a bottle of Burgundy, pours half a glass and swirls the reflecting ruby liquid and sniffs appreciatively, before swallowing a mouthful. Breaths in deeply. "Excellent." He holds the glass to the light. "Quite excellent." This glorious vintage will outlive the Chinese strumpet. The mobile phone on the kitchen table pings, he checks the number and opens the message. The Mount Rushmore expression intensifies as he studies the selfie taken by Li Soo Ying.

A naked Li Soo Ying is standing legs apart with her back to an ornate mirror so that everything she thinks worth seeing is on show. She is deluding herself, because there is nothing on display that every woman does not possess in equal if not more abundance.

With a shock of surprise he recognises the mirror and what it shows of the room and, looking more closely, he most definitely recognises the room – this is a miscalculation of epic proportions. As if she is so much trailer trash he forwards the image to Gilbert Markham without comment. She will not get away with this. The Chinese hate to lose face – by the time he has finished no one will want to look at Li Soo Ying's face.

She is for the moment dismissed from his thoughts as he checks information on his mobile phone. He thought so – a meeting of the National Gallery Patrons Trust this morning to which his apologies were sent. He glances at the antique kitchen clock that dear Lydia checks daily with Greenwich Mean Time, and finger marks into his mobile phone the number that, of course, he memorised, touches the screen and waits. It is answered on the third ring.

A background noise of London traffic. "Is that you, my dear?" He listens. "It is indeed." Listens some more. "I did promise you that I would ring, my dear." Another taste of wine and he listens some more. "There is now some urgency on the Chair's role I mentioned on the Art in schools Quango." Sip. Sip. "Are you free for a working lunch at such short notice?" Sip. Sip. "Excellent." The anticipations of the flesh are back on track. More substantial flesh than the scrawny Chinese strumpet. There is ample time for one necessary and one not so necessary telephone conversation. He is on the phone to the droning Leader of the Opposition when the doorbell chimes. It is pleasing that she has arrived sooner than he anticipated. Other people's lateness is something he finds incredibly trying.

"Indeed. Indeed." He intones as he unhurriedly crosses the polished oak flooring of the hallway. Dear Lydia daily polishes the floor on her hands and knees, occasionally the polishing is interrupted and occasionally abandoned… she really is a treasure.

He opens the door and mouths 'come in' to Marian Fairburne who mouths back 'can she use the little girls' room?' He nods and points to the sign less toilet door. She makes an embarrassed mew with much lipsticked lips and tiptoes on high heels to the door indicated.

"So we are agreed." He walks back to the kitchen. She will find her way, as doubtless she was a girl guide in her teens. The Arbroath smoked salmon is plated and the eggs from the Norfolk farm are in the jug ready to be whipped… such a delicious word.

"Yes. Yes. Of course. Your secret is safe with me, Tom." He pours more wine with a sensuous glug glug glugging into the two inscribed glasses whose inscriptions always impress. "No need, my dear fellow. No need."

He is aware of the toilet flushing and, as preludes go, it is pretty hard to beat, as are the nervously hesitant click clicking high-heeled footsteps on the polished oak floor. An enquiring head peers round the door and he beckons with the free hand and she tiptoes into the kitchen and deprecatingly smiles and waits. The Chinese strumpet could learn a lot from this Home Counties abundance of housewife. It is far too late for that.

It is hard for Marian to believe that she is actually inside Sir Godwyn Lydate's actual home… his lair so to speak. Although she doesn't feel a bit like a fly… hang on that's a web surely. She really can be giddy when she is so nervous. Stop it, Marian, and she mentally slaps a wrist. She cannot help but pretend not to notice that he is wearing a rather naughty apron with two hands at the front grasping large bosoms with vivid pink nipples peeping through sausage fingers. She glances away – the last thing she needs is a fit of the giggles. She is just glad she decided to wear this slinky pale green dress, which shows off her own ample bosoms to near perfection. No vivid pink nipples though. Stop it, Marian. Stop it. Another mental slap of a wrist. She had fervently hoped he would be at the Patron's Trust meeting and the disappointment at his apologies nearly made her cry. The last time she had cried was when Timmy their cat had been run over – she is not a crier.

"That's fine by me, Tom. Must go now, duty calls. Indeed. Indeed." He ends the call and comically raises trimmed eyebrows. "The Leader of the Opposition really should stop listening to rumours." She knows the name of course – Thomas Love Peacock – she was recently in the same crowded reception room. A rather aloof man was her impression. She did not take to him at all.

She pretends not to notice the strips of silky dress material cut up and scattered on the floor as Sir Godwyn captures her two, plumpish in a nice way hands. She gasps and he appreciates that. "You look divine, my dear." He kisses both, plumpish in a nice way hands and then both plumpish in a nice way cheeks. He doesn't let go of the hands and she doesn't make any move to take them back. It is hard to believe that yesterday these captured hands were kneading dough in her perennially untidy kitchen that drives her husband to distraction.

For some reason, which she dare not even begin to fathom, she had decided not to wear her wedding and engagement rings this morning. Her husband wouldn't notice anyway and nor would he have noticed the rather racy Amelia Sedley branded underwear she is wearing. He is immune these days to her dressing and undressing. The days are long gone when putting on or taking off knickers could lead to impromptu lovemaking and on two occasions – both by mistake – impromptu baby making.

"You look good enough to eat, my dear." He really is a most charming man. Still holding the plumpish in a nice way hands, he takes her by surprise by kissing her full on the recently, touched up in the taxi, lipsticked mouth.

She is not at all used to this sort of thing and has rarely contemplated being unfaithful to her rather dull and, these days, also rather grumpy husband. He sneers at her rather a lot, which she doesn't like, and tries to make her feel stupid. She is most definitely not stupid.

Just the once she had strayed and that really was an aberration bitterly regretted the next morning. She couldn't get dressed fast enough and escape the seedy hotel room. She was on tenterhooks until her next period eventually arrived a few days late. The unwelcome discharge had, thank goodness, responded to antibiotics.

In the here and now, without any thought process, she is most definitely kissing back and they are somehow in a possessive clinch. Her bosoms are most definitely heaving just like in the romance novels that she avidly reads. The nipples as blindingly tender as they used to be when she was first married. She had forgotten that lovely enticing feeling, but then she has forgotten so many lovely enticing feelings. It is by no means certain that it is Sir Godwyn who instigates tongues. There were lots of tongues that one and only time best forgotten.

It is Sir Godwyn who breaks the clinch and holds her at arm's length. He does so love these Christmas morning gift wrapped boxes of surprises, which he never had as a child. Never ceasing to be amazed by the twists and turns of chance, the Chinese strumpet dismissed from his thoughts for the moment, even as Gilbert Markham is enjoying the nude selfie of Li Soo Ying. There is no written text attached but he perfectly understands the subtext.

"You really are a glorious woman." Marian is staring wide-eyed and open mouthed, the tip of that exploring tongue tantalisingly visible. A woman who has blossomed in her forties, the somewhat bland prettiness of the eager young wife having filled out in all the right places. A woman of natural substance. So rare in his wide experience.

"Are you hungry, Marian?"

She shakes her head, causing the Wedding Anniversary gift pearl earrings to dance clockwise around the maypole. She is too breathless to speak.

"Shall we eat later?"

She nods her head and sets the pearl earrings dancing anti-clockwise round the maypole. He releases the plumpish hands and takes off the naughty apron, a gift from a well known Royal personage, and drapes it neatly over the back of a chair.

Then he enfolds the glorious woman, who has stepped out of the high heeled shoes, in an even more possessive clinch. This time the necking is fierce and tooth jarring and she is only too well aware of the hardness demanding against her groin. She cannot stop herself demanding back, only more so. Someone moans in the stygian depths of the kiss that even a Rodin would struggle to replicate.

It would ruin the mood to divulge that she is not on the pill and, in fact, has never been on the pill. There is no way she is going to mess about with the practically unused coil that, on a whim, she had stuffed in her handbag this morning.

The mobile phone on the table pings and is ignored as they leave the kitchen leaning together hand in hand.

Jack Bellingham sucks the bloody pen that seems to have a life of its own and is lost in thought. None of this is what he imagined on those Prison mornings when he woke up from weirdly dreamless sleeps, beneath the ever intrusive bulge of Sikesy, snoring fit to wake the dead; the thoughts of the projected state of the nation novel keeping him as sane as he will ever be. This is not that novel.

Wednesday 18th October 2.05pm

The lunchtime rush, such as it was, has petered out and the Queens Hotel male bartender is keeping a weather eye on that little shit's table. He might be somebody quite famous, so Emily on Reception reckons, but he has the worst manners John Everson has ever experienced in his all too truncated career. Clicking his shitty little shit fingers, summoning more and more drinks and ordering John to be quick about it. John angrily rub rubs a half pint glass the cleanest it has ever been rubbed. If looks could annihilate, but of course John Everson's looks never can.

It is Charlotte the barmaid's day off and they are sort of seeing each other… the main reason being she is very much available. She is not the only one he is sort of seeing, although Charlotte isn't married; unlike Emily who is also very much available whilst her much older husband is working abroad. But then John just cannot get enough so that's all right. A previous sort of girlfriend had suggested he should get help, but then in his opinion she had frigidity issues. Neither Charlotte nor Emily has frigidity issues.

John Everson is disgusted at the behaviour of the two well-dressed middle-aged women. Decent respectable Church going types should not be getting rat arsed at this time of day in such a vile man's company. It is obvious at twenty paces that the man is bad news. When the two ladies first arrived at the bar to order coffees the decent looking brunette, who reminds John of his once upon a time sexy Auntie Mary, had been on the phone and had boredly said 'love you' to someone, probably a husband. She doesn't look of the age to boredly say 'love you' to someone other than a husband. Mind you, his sexy Auntie Mary was full of surprises of that nature, and at the time he had thought her quite ancient.

Now the decent looking brunette is allowing the shitty little shit to stroke her leg, a silly grin on her face, the make up going south, half-heartedly not quite knocking the stroking hand away. Not as silly as the grin smeared on the face of the grey-haired lady who hasn't spoken for some time. John checks the BBC tab – seven large drinks each so far. There goes another attempt at shitty little shit finger clicking. John has a good mind to accidentally trip on purpose and pour the drinks all over the arrogant little shit, but John cannot afford to lose this job; something tells him that the shitty little shit would make damn sure he lost his job.

Removing the empty glasses he replaces them with fresh ones... the bowl of peanuts is untouched. The plate with a half-eaten club sandwich and several congealed chips he refuses to take away... his very own fuck you gesture that goes unnoticed amidst the drunken cavalcade. "Will that be all, sir?" You wanker.

He is waved away as if he is a piece of dirt, and now the waver awayer has his right arm round the decent looking brunette's shoulders. It is disgusting; she must be fifty if she's a day. Well preserved though... John wouldn't kick her out but, to be perfectly frank, John wouldn't kick any woman out. He wonders if the poor biddy is aware of how much leg she is showing...sexy Auntie Mary used to show a lot of leg when she was well pissed.

Now they are rubber lipped necking. This is getting ridiculous and he wonders if he should do something. Perhaps take a picture on his mobile and share it on Twitter. That would put the cat among the pigeons.

The grey-haired lady is intently watching the rubber lipped necking, as only the totally rat arsed can intently watch, and is striving to say something.

If the Nazi hotel manager sees this John could be in big trouble. The grey haired lady sort of signals to John to come back to the table. It appears that her lips are even more rubbery and John leans closer. The fixed rictus grin is really a bit off putting. Like she is going to have a fit or something. Very nice tits though.

"Yes, madam?"

With surprising strength she grabs hold of his nearest arm and John leans as close as he thinks appropriate in the circumstances. Very nice tits indeed. There is a desperate mute appeal in the washed out blue eyes that are finding it impossible to focus. He could be anybody. She is lizard licking the uncoordinated pieces of rubber. "Need..." She takes several shuddering breaths and John just prays she isn't going to puke.

"Yes, madam?"

"Pee...pee..."

JESUS. He frantically looks around. The shitty little shit and the decent looking middle aged brunette who reminds him of sexy Auntie Mary, who is probably best forgotten after what happened at his cousin's wedding, are weaving their way to the lift.

"Sir! Madam!" He shouts but not too loudly. The lift doors open and close and they are gone. Just like that. He turns back to the abandoned grey haired lady who is staring at John with those pleading washed out blue eyes. She is not rictus grinning anymore and that is something. Now she just looks as though she has had a minor stroke. It might be his overheated imagination but he thinks she might be flexing stomach muscles.

"No. Sweetheart, no." He takes hold of both the hands and the thick wedding band is cold to the touch. "Hold on, sweetheart. Hold on, there's a good girl." A phrase normally used in far different circumstances. Thank Christ there are no other customers as he Monty Python strides across the deserted foyer to the Reception desk. No sign of the Nazi hotel manager, thank Christ. She will blame John. She always has to blame somebody. He cannot afford to be sacked from a third job in as many months.

Thank Christ it is Emily on duty who offers a lovely remembering smile.

"Emily love." She is conspicuously all lovely delicate ears. "There is a lady in the bar who is about to piss herself."

The coquettish smile slips somewhat to be replaced by a puzzled smiley expression – not one he has ever seen and which quite suits the angular dark features. He really must get a grip. "She's so rat arsed that she cannot get up out of the chair." He grabs hold of one of Emily's slim smooth hands and is aware, as always, of the bulbous wedding ring that she always takes off before they go at it. Yesterday there was a minor panic when she forgot to put it back on afterwards, and they eventually found the bloody thing under the bed. "Please hurry, love."

"I wouldn't do this for just anybody." She squeezes hands and smiles a promise… a smile he most certainly does recognise. "You owe me one, lovie."

"I will give you more than one."

"Promises. Promises." She gives him a peck on the cheek knowing he always gives her more than one. "Watch the desk, lovie."

Thank Christ there is still no sign of Attila the Hunness. John is still in his probationary period, and was eternally grateful that Nazi lady was too vain to wear reading glasses when she glanced at the forged references.

Nor could the Bride of Attila hide the fact that she appreciated that the handsome, if he does say so himself, young… well youngish man made no secret of admiring the eye watering cleavage; a ploy that usually works with women of a certain age. She must be forty if she's a day… no doubt gagging for it. It being his only trump card. She wouldn't have to smile though, her toothy crocodile smile being even more disturbing than the grey haired lady's rictus grin.

He knows he is a fool to himself. Losing his job at the Metropole Hotel over a misunderstanding with a lady guest who was similarly rat arsed. Afterwards the cow tried to pretend she wasn't gagging for it. At the age of twenty nine he really must start to learn from his mistakes. The only difficulty is knowing where to begin.

Here comes the lovely Emily sashaying across the foyer and executing a twirl for his eyes only. "You owe me big time, lovie." She leans suggestively on the counter. "Only just got the old biddy to the toilet in time."

"Where is she now?"

"Slumped in a chair in the bar minus these." She takes balled up tights and sensible white pants out of her pocket. "We need to get her up to her room." She stuffs the tights and sensible white pants back in her pocket.

"If she is sharing with the other biddy who disappeared upstairs with that television bloke then that could be a no-no." John gives the impression of a cross dressing Bo Peep who will never ever find the sheep.

Emily consistently worries about John. She doesn't worry at all about her much older husband who is working in Saudi for six months on a lucrative contract. One of the things she finds endearingly attractive about John is his constant air of potential helplessness in the face of impending disaster. Like a character from an unfinished P.G Wodehouse novel; she once started to read a P.G Wodehouse novel believing "Full moon" was about something else entirely. Of course John is handsome in a what's it sort of way. Vacuous is the word.

He can be forgiven just about everything for his Olympian performances in bed.

"We cannot take the risk. We must dump her in one of the water damaged rooms." They are both taken aback at his initiative.

"Not the one we use, lovie." He suspects Emily is a bit of a romantic at heart. They have only been at it for just over a week but it seems longer. They had progressed from a bit of fooling about goosing in the back office to frantic all-night sex, without the flowers and chocolates in between stages.

Emily rummages through an untidy desk drawer and then hands John a battered room card. "This is the room next door to ours. You get her up there, lovie and I will keep a watch on the bar. It's quiet anyway at this time."

He is frowning in that adorable naughty little boy lost way and she could kiss him all over. She has kissed him all over on several occasions. "Go on, lovie, hurry before Gestapo lady shows up." She leans closer, grabs his ears and kisses the screwed up mouth briefly but passionately. "There will be more where that came from later."

John just cannot believe the old biddy is such a dead weight. After a struggle he manages to get a decent wrestler's hold and half carries the silly biddy towards the lifts.

Emily is fondly smiling; talk about Monty Python morphing into the Keystone cops. At the sight of John manfully struggling with the comatose old baggage Emily's heart lurches. The mixture of the sublime and the ridiculous is a potent combination. Throughout the last glorious however many days she has been in the state of constant randiness. Just being near him makes her tingle in places, where a recently married lady should not tingle, except in the company of her lawful wedded husband. There really is no future for her and John. She tells herself it is just the needs of a twenty three year old red-blooded girl married to a much older man, who is not there most of the time to do the necessary. Even when he is there there is not overmuch necessary carried out. The truncated honeymoon was just that.

Now John is propping the comatose old baggage against the wall and she begins to slide down as he reaches for the lift button. He cannot make up his mind whether to stop the slide or go for the button; it would be hilarious if it wasn't so potentially disastrous. Emily will be sort of devastated if John gets the sack, and so she rushes over to the rescue and presses the button.

"Thanks, love." He is out of breath and Emily just wants to take him to bed and love him to pieces.

Thankfully the lift doors close cutting off the Boxing Day Pantomime scene. Emily has to admit that John is not the brightest button in the box, but then bright buttons need such an awful lot of polishing. With an inwardly pensive look on her dark angular face, a look that always annoys her much older husband because he is never sure what, if anything, she is thinking, a thoughtful Emily Prescott walks slowly back to the Reception desk.

It is a good job that her much older husband doesn't know what she is thinking at this moment. She shivers at the thought because he can be insanely jealous for no reason…well there were several reasons…but even so…he should be so lucky.

John props the silly biddy in the far corner of the lift and takes a well-earned breather but she begins to slide down and he has to react quickly. "You really are a stupid biddy, sweetheart."

He never thought to ask Emily to look up the biddy's name. Anyway it would be the choice of two and knowing his luck he would probably pick the wrong one.

Propping the biddy up, he is conscious of the intrusion of those very nice tits and gives the nearest one a bit of a squeeze; lovely and squashy and reminiscent of sexy Auntie Mary. This Auntie works at the rubbery lips but not even a grunt, the eyes tight closed and the eyelids flickering. The lift bell pings and he makes an executive decision to carry her, bride over the threshold fashion, to the door of the water damaged bedroom. Thankfully it is only a few steps from the lift – she is no lightweight. Thank Christ there is no one around on this floor.

He does the propping up thing again.

Thank Christ the battered key card works at the second attempt. The stupid biddy has slipped down to the floor and is very much showing everything she's got, reminiscent of a pissed as a newt sexy Auntie Mary at his cousin's wedding.

The washed out pale blue eyes are open and staring at the floor at John's feet. Now that the bladder has been well and truly emptied there resides a pagan contentment of Viking proportions. Somewhere, floating on the ocean waves lapping at her subconscious, is the stray flotsam thought of something vital just out of reach. She has a morbid fear of drowning but that is not it. Then the wave surges over everything as she is hauled to her feet and the screen goes blank in a whirlpool of weird contentment. She cannot even wonder why she is so far out at sea... she hates the sea.

"Come on, sweetheart." He has taken a firm grip under her armpits and realises she is only wearing one shoe. Shit. The other one must be in the lift. Shit. Shit.

Instead of bride over the threshold fashion he unceremoniously drags the stupid biddy backwards, and the other shoe comes off. He drags the dead weight body as far as the stripped down bed in the mouldy smelling bedroom, and with a match winning effort hoists the deadweight aboard the much stained mattress. The dress has concertinaed above the waist exposing a concave belly button as well as everything else. The sight of the belly button is somehow more disconcerting than the sight of the everything else, including a recent Brazilian very much on display. More recent even than Emily's Brazilian by the look of it.

He straightens out a leg bent under at an awkward angle. Boys really should not play with dolls that have such realistic limbs. A moan escapes from the cavernous depths and a choke threatens which is, thank Christ, swallowed down.

He should have stopped serving that table but then the shitty little shit would have caused no end of trouble. None of this is John's fault... not one bit of it. He is beginning to believe he is just one of life's innocent victims.

The room telephone ringing reverberates and he picks up the receiver with both shaking hands and doesn't speak.

"John, lovie?"

"Yeah." He manages to croak.

"You all right?"

"Never better." The ragged breathing from the bed is getting on his nerves.

"Gestapo lady is on the warpath."

"Shit!"

"Appropriate. Told her you have a stomach upset. She is not a happy Hun." The receiver is covered and he is aware of muffled voices. Then she whispers. "Got to go. Stay there, lovie."

Unable to control his facial muscles, he perches on the edge of the manky mattress and grins manically at nothing in particular. He studies the senseless biddy and the everything else. It will be some time before she starts coming round and she will not remember anything beyond the fifth treble gin. The ragged breathing has settled into a ragged breathing holding pattern, with the occasional gasp, as if she is trying to articulate something that is lost in translation. He is tempted... sorely tempted... the deadliest sin of all if he did but admit it. After all, he is only human, and it is such a pity that the poor cow is missing out. Why should the other slapper have all the fun? Life can be so unfair. He really will be doing her a favour... he really will...I mean she has had the Brazilian and everything and so she must be expecting some fun and games... stands to reason.

A couple of minutes later the telephone rings. The reverberating ringing finds him standing by the bed looking down to where he has lowered the straps of the slapper doll's dress, the white bra straps likewise. The naked breasts with brown saucered nipples rising and falling on the ragged breathing pattern are quite magnificent. Calling them nice didn't do them justice. It was a crime to keep them covered up. He is doing the world a favour if the world did but know it. Reluctantly he answers the phone.

"John, lovie?"

"Yeah."

"What are you doing?" Nothing. Honest to God absolutely nothing.

"Sitting on the toilet."

"This is no time for one of your silly jokes. Gestapo lady is at the perimeter fence. Told her it must've been something you've eaten at the hotel. That has shut her up for the time being. Stay where you are, lovie." The telephone goes dead.

He stands at the side of the bed and hesitantly touches a breast and less hesitantly squeezes a nipple. For a few seconds the stupid biddy opens wide the washed out blue eyes and stares wide eyed at the ceiling and there is some attempted movement of rubbery lips.

"You gagging for it sweetheart?" Course she is.

Always happy to oblige a lady, he makes sure the door is locked and takes off his trousers and underpants. If she were properly conscious she would most certainly be begging for it now, just as sexy Auntie Mary begged for it on several occasions, and boy did she get it as the fourteen year old John duly obliged… talk about the University of life. Here goes. He just prays the telephone doesn't ring to put him off his stride.

It is such a clear blue sky, so close that Maria could almost touch the blueness if only she could move her arms. Poor Maria cannot understand why the precarious life raft is rocking so much on the calm nameless sea. Nor understand why her self-effacing husband is invading her body so aggressively. Because on the rare occasion she allows invasion he is always so gentle and apologetic, because of her dicky heart. She begs him to stop but her voice is wafted away on the tropic breezes. It is hurting and he is making such a lot of noise; he never ever makes a lot of noise but, of course, there was a lot of noise during last week's aberration. He surely cannot be biting her boobies – he never ever bites her boobies because she will not allow it. Surely he is not sucking her nipples so greedily. Then the invaded body spectacularly lets her down and she tumbles overboard on a wave of such gloriously intense pleasure that it quite takes her breath away. As she sinks down down down to the sea bed she tries hard not to breathe. There is an unaccustomed looseness to her limbs that carries her down and down and then she breathes. Only there are no breaths to be had on the sea bed. A last thought is that her husband must have found out. She was stupid – really really stupid.

Wednesday 18th October 2.45pm

Helen Huntingdon is zip mouthed staring at the do not disturb notice hanging upside down on the handle of Spencer Perceval's bedroom door. Surely to God he has not taken one of those respectable middle-aged ladies to bed. Not even Spencer Perceval would do that... of course he would.

She knocks on the door. No reply. Knocks louder and there is a scurried movement inside. "Open up." She knocks and knocks. "If you do not open up I will get the management to bring a key."

She stands back hands on hips and glares at the offending door which glares back.

After a few seconds the door is clumsily unlocked and opened just far enough for a peroxide blonde head to peep, half tamed mink eyed, around the door jamb; just a head like one of those spooky make-up heads that are cast aside by young girls on Boxing day. This head looks as though it has passed through several grubby pairs of childish hands on the way to the dustbin.

"Well... well... well."

"What do you want?" A mean throaty grasping voice tinged with elemental contempt. Helen Huntingdon is good on voices and is even better at elemental contempt.

"Is he in there?"

The peroxide blonde dishevelled head rapidly withdraws but not rapidly enough for a fired up Helen Huntingdon.

The door is barged open before it can be locked and the naked body attached to the head endeavours to cover its rudely exposed nakedness as best as it can. After wasting a withering glance Helen's gimlet eyes roam the room. She kicks an empty champagne bottle just for the hell of it. She peeps under the bed and wishes she hadn't. Checks in the bathroom and wishes she hadn't. There is lumpy puke all round the toilet basin, not to mention shit smeared on the toilet seat.

Back in the bedroom she stands hands on slim hips, Boadicea watching Roman Colchester burning fashion, and out stares the naked bimbo who has decided to give up the unequal task of covering her modesty. She knows she has nothing to be modest about – quite the reverse in fact.

"You have been stood up, doll." A contemptuous smile that would surprise and delight Sir Godwyn Lydate. "Even as we exchange pleasantries lover boy is no doubt fucking someone else." She takes a step towards the naked woman who, to her credit, stands her ground. "You look like shit, doll."

"You can't talk to me like that, you stuck up cow and don't call me doll." It is hard to fake credibly indignant, with battered make-up daubing a clown's face painted by a three year old child in a tantrum.

"Get dressed and get out."

"I need a shower." She has a local accent that grates and Helen so dislikes local accents that grate. She once spent a waste of a week in Rotherham, of all places, for reasons she would rather forget.

"You deaf as well doll?" This time the naked bimbo does take a step backwards. "You have got two minutes and then I call the Manager. Imagine my shock horror at unearthing a naked tarty barmaid in the one and only Spencer Perceval's bedroom."

Helen licks an index finger and dabs the white powder remnants on the bedside table and theatrically tastes. "A cokehead naked tarty barmaid at that." Now the arms are triumphantly crossed. Rome trembles – Caesar is long dead – the Barbarians are at the gate.

Charlotte wisely gives up on the losing battle of trying to preserve overrated dignity and pads naked round the room in search of scattered clothes. She is not ashamed of her body so put that up your stringy arse and smoke it, you stuck up cow, she doesn't say.

The curly orange haired stringy arsed stuck up cow is watching with actual curled lips. It takes all of Charlotte's self-control not to launch herself and grab a handful of ridiculous orange curly hair. It would not be the first time she had engaged in a catfight and she has sharp claws. Only this time she would get the shock of her life.

"I can't find my knickers."

"One minute left and counting." That lippy smirk just begs to be slapped into the middle of next week. "I am sure it is not the first time you will have gone without knickers."

Charlotte dresses hurriedly under the withering steely gaze. She is rarely intimidated by women and she is not intimidated now... no she fucking isn't. She knows only too well when retreat is the best option to live to fight another day. Unlike Napoleon and Hitler, she is nothing if not a survivor.

"Thirty seconds."

"All right. All right." She is fastening the shocking pink bra with fingers and thumbs difficulty. At last. Then she adjusts the rather short uniform skirt that is the same Burgundy shade as John Everson's uniform waistcoat and trousers.

Pretending to be on her own with all the time in the world, she calmly fastens the buttons of the cream uniform blouse with the Keeldar Group emblem flowered on her left breast. It is a match for the blouse worn by that other superior stuck up stringy arsed bitch, Emily thingy. An A-level in domestic science and she thinks she's it. The emblem is not as rounded, though, on Emily thingy's blouse and Charlotte smirks in her turn; a minor triumph is a triumph of sorts.

"Time is up." Helen Huntingdon opens the door and stands to one side.

"Can I have a quick look for my knickers?"

"Out."

Charlotte scuttles out of the lousy bedroom, just praying that no one is lurking in the corridor. She knows she is not looking at her best and so it would just be her luck. The door slams and she gives the finger to the slammed door.

Then, checking to right and left, she bolts for the back staircase. This is the last time she gets picked up by a hotel guest, although she did say the same thing the last time and the time before that. There is always randy John boy who is always up for it. Although he can be a bit rough, not that she minds, she can be equally rough back. She smirks some more as she disappears down the back staircase. She has indeed gone without knickers on many occasions…so stick that up your stringy arse you stuck up bitch.

Helen sniffs and wrinkles up her nose, in the manner of Stout Cortes surveying the carnage of the battlefield, when victory has been assured over the Aztecs by the use of muskets. Then she rings reception. A nicely spoken girl with a not unpleasant wafty voice… local accent but not unduly so. There is a brief polite exchange of pleasantries. Helen requires the room to be serviced without delay.

"Yes madam."

"The older ladies who were drinking in the bar earlier – what is their room number?"

"Sorry, madam, I cannot give out that information.'

A pause and then, voice not raised– "Just give me the fucking room number or get me the fucking manager because there are things going on in this fucking hotel that that need to be investigated." It usually works – there are always Peyton Place secrets and lies to be unearthed in hotels. After a face-saving pause and replying in a shaky wafty voice, the nicely spoken girl gives the room number.

"Thank you. You have been most helpful."

The room shared by the two ladies in question is on the next floor up and Helen takes the stairs because she doesn't get enough exercise. There is no do not disturb sign upside down or the right way up. She raps on the door. Then louder. And louder. "Open the door, Spencer."

"Who is it?" He still sounds well pissed.

"Open the fucking door, you prat."

"It's not convenient." Although the prat in question struggles to articulate convenient. This could all go spectacularly tits up; if Goddy finds out he will look for someone to blame, and he no doubt will find out. That thought spurs her on.

"Open the fucking door, you moron." She knows he is programmed to obey orders and would have made a half decent Nazi stormtrooper shot down in the first wave of attacks at Stalingrad. After a few tantalising seconds the door is opened just far enough for Spencer's dishevelled head to poke out – no child would want to play with this head on Christmas morning. She pushes her way into the room; a sense of déjà vu is wasted on Helen Huntingdon, as she sniffs up the unmistakable nose tingling scents of much recent sexual goings on. The stupid middle aged woman, who should be ashamed of herself, is not visible in the tangled bedding of the two single beds haphazardly pushed together. Spencer Perceval is idiotically clutching a hand towel at his waist and swaying in the breeze.

"What's up, doc?" He fails miserably with one of those killer grins; more a Cromwellian death mask.

"The run-through is at four o'clock."

He dismissively shrugs his somewhat rounded shoulders and the soiled hand towel drops to the floor. "Oops."

If he believes this is any kind of clincher he is sadly mistaken – that boat has well and truly sailed. There is a sound of stomach curdling retching echoing through the closed bathroom door.

Helen determinedly goes to investigate and is met with the vision of the naked middle-aged woman, who should be ashamed of herself, embracing the toilet bowl and seeking to retch politely and dismally failing. At least she closed the door. A spreading, but still shapely backside, size fourteen bikini pale against a suntanned body. A pale backside give away bruised and reddened.

The bent over body spasms and she retches some more… wretch very much the word here. Tight lipped Helen Huntingdon bestows a much younger sisterly squeeze of a meaty shoulder and with dire purpose walks back into the bedroom.

"Have you been spanking that poor woman?" The stupid woman has now morphed into a poor woman. Helen abhors violence to women… well…to most women anyway.

"The horny bitch fucking begged for it. Fucking begged for it." He is nakedly swaying and it is not a pretty sight despite a decent sized cock – Helen Huntingdon is nothing if not fair.

"Liar." She is not to know or care that he is telling the truth.

"We got a bit carried away." The vile secretion is actually smirking.

"You are a vile secretion." If she could bear to get any closer she would slap his stupid face. On second thoughts she would punch his stupid nose. "You are the vilest man I have ever met." Not quite true but near enough for these purposes.

The insult sobers him somewhat, as he is not used to this kind of talk from a mere underling. A female mere underling to boot. Women and underlings occupy the same lower Saturn ring of Spencer Perceval's perverse Universe.

"Who the fuck do you think you're talking to…?" Wisely deciding not to say bitch, he takes a half step forward and raises a fist. Helen stands her ground and defiantly stares with hands on hips. She knows exactly where she will kick out if he takes one more step. It is a tempting target and it will be a great pleasure.

"Don't you dare come any nearer."

He gladly stops in his tracks and tries the hands on hips thing in his turn, but looking so ludicrous he is risking a fit of giggles. This is not turning out well.

Psycho is not buckling at the knees or anywhere else. He looks down…yep… still dangling invitingly.

"The horny bitch begged for. Begged for it." He sneers to add to the lack of attractiveness of the sight. "Fucking begged for it."

"Did you use a condom?" Stupid question time.

He shakes his head and sniggers. "You know how it is, we got a bit carried away. Know what I mean? Anyway she said she's in the change."

"You are beyond vile."

"She fucking loved it. Fucking loved it." Even though he is telling the truth he wisely decides to leave it there. There might be more than one screw loose on the other side of no man's land. She has really scary eyes and no man's land is not a good place to be naked.

More wall-to-wall retching from the bathroom and Helen checks her watch, a gift of which she is inordinately proud. "Your own room is being cleared up even as we speak and the tarty barmaid has been evicted. I will order a pot of coffee. Get dressed. Go to your room. Have a shower and a shave. Drink the coffee. You are doing the run through. End of." A veritable verbal machine gun repulsing the first wave of attacks. It would take a brave man to crawl out of the shell hole and fight on. He is not a brave man.

"I am not finished with the very willing Mrs thingummy." He doesn't even sound convincing to his own ears.

"You are doing the run through." She holds up the shocking pink mobile phone. "Sir Godwyn?"

He thinks about calling her a cunt and thinks better of it, because he has not totally lost his survival instinct.

"Get dressed. Go back to your room. Do exactly as I have said. Or else." She shakes the shocking pink mobile phone. She doesn't give him the satisfaction of watching him getting dressed and, instead, goes back into the bathroom and, with some difficulty, because there is not a lot of room, kneels next to the poor woman who takes up rather a lot of space. Helen drapes a comforting arm across the broad shoulders and tries not to breathe in. Unlike with the tarty barmaid, every last gobbet of vomit has gurged into the toilet bowl – gurged is a word she has just invented, but does seem to cover things rather well.

This poor woman has gurged very neatly. Just a pity about everything else of a gurging nature that has occurred.

"There. There." She doesn't even know the stupid poor woman's name. At least she appears to have stopped retching and is merely spitting out bile, which is stringy dribbling down her chins, and snaking between the substantial breasts. In a different situation Helen might well be jealous. "That better?" Not quite the end of stupid question time. Helen notices livid bite marks on one of the substantial breasts and the poor woman starts to blubber. The door of the bedroom slams shut... the eternal toss pot is still able to enact fits of pique with a certain aplomb.

Helen awkwardly gathers the poor blubbering package of mottled flesh in a very much younger sisterly, possibly even eldest daughterly embrace...a daughter born to a youthful first marriage. The substantial breasts rather getting in the way as substantial breasts are prone to do. "What is your name, sweetheart?"

"Harriet." She chokes out through the snot drooling sobs and Helen strokes the messed up hair and offers shushing noises. There are merest hints of grey roots... this is probably not the time or the place to mention the fact.

"You are safe now, sweetheart." She sincerely hopes so anyway, although there is no accounting for human quiddity. Being a practical girl at heart Helen tears off some tasteful pink roses toilet paper and wipes the poor woman's nose and chins. "Blow." Like an obedient child the poor woman blows. "There. That's better."

This reminds Helen of the role that Amelia Sedley played in that Second World War movie about the fall of Paris in 1940. Helen watched it three times and still didn't get the ending; the middle was a bit of a challenge as well. The ending was good though.

"I didn't... I didn't..."

"Shush now, Harriet." You certainly did thinks Helen... you most certainly did, breasty lady. Helen etches the tear stained face with nimble thumbs; it is not as much of a riotously painted clown's face as the tarty barmaid; an older child perhaps has coloured it in. The nimble thumbs brush away lots and lots of streaky mascara. Perhaps not a good idea...a bit of an at bay zebra effect with the pursuing lion in a mid air leap.

"He's not worth it, sweetheart." She much younger sisterly, or perhaps eldest daughterly, kisses the furrowed brow in a weirdly comforting gesture; weirdly comforting for Helen, that is. Furrowed brows are not good at Harriet's age. "Let's get you to the bed, Harriet and then you can have a nice lie down." Harriet knows there is nothing quite like a nice lie down when ... well... when you feel like a nice lie down.

The poor naked woman, she means poor naked Harriet, leans heavily against very much fully clothed Helen Huntingdon, as they weave their unsteady passage towards the nice lie down. Helen hopes she doesn't get any substances on her clothes; she knows who will be footing the dry cleaning bill.

There are times when Harriet O'Connor really appreciates a nice lie down in the afternoons. She needs to think about all the stuff that happened, which was not a bit like the genteel wife swapping, with almost apologetic please and thank you couplings, of the West Shields golf club set. She wishes she could have a nice lie down on her own king-sized bed with tasteful matching accessories and wake up to a nice cup of Ringtons tea. But then...

Theatrically Harriet collapses on this haphazardly pushed together bed, which creaks ominously. The kind, attentive girl in the somewhat lurid tights, and with weird orange hair, sorts out the tangled bedding. God bless her. There are some tell-tale stains best ignored in polite company. Helen touches, but not in a suggestive way, the livid bite marks on Harriet's left breast.

"Does that hurt, sweetheart?" It is a long time since anyone called Harriet O'Connor sweetheart.

Harriet nods and is having difficulty focusing. She has only ever taken cocaine once before. She should have learned from that experience which did not end well.

"Any other bites?" Harriet doesn't like to admit to any and to be honest she finds the questioning and touching just a tad intrusive. She feels she ought to say something to elicit sympathy.

"He was very rough." The kind, attentive girl purses her lips and narrows her eyes in due remembrance. She is not the sort of person to get on the wrong side of... but then neither is Harriet O'Connor. The kind, attentive girl sighs and covers up the substantial breasts and delves in a shoulder bag.

"Here, take two paracetamol." Helen realises it is like putting a sticking plaster on a gaping machete wound and, with difficulty, manages to keep the giggles at bay...it was a good job she didn't have a machete to hand earlier.

"I can't swallow without water."

Jesus Christ – keeping a tight hold of her wafer thin patience, Helen fills a cracked glass in the bathroom and then, matron fashion, watches over as Harriet drains the glass. Not quite Amelia Sedley's Florence Nightingale in that movie whose name Helen always forgets, but a decent understudy for the long shots, with the inevitable sounds of gunfire in the distance.

"Thank you."

"You're welcome. Now get some rest, Harriet."

"You are being very kind." There is a catch in her voice that is smeared with a hint of Geordie that Helen actually doesn't dislike. She hopes the stupid woman isn't going to burst into tears though because, in truth, Helen is all sobbed out.

Cameras rolling...The kind, attentive girl with the posh voice kisses the furrowed brow in a very very much younger sisterly whatever way. "Try to get some sleep. Knit up the ravelled sleeve of care and all that."

"Would you close the curtains please?"

For fuck's sake!

The room seems so empty after the kind, attentive girl with the slightly scary eyes has flounced out and Harriet thankfully closes her own eyes. She needs to properly think things through – but not now. There are too many conflicting emotions. She had been determined to hold back at first with Spencer, but failed miserably. She had done things and said things that any decent meat and two veg suburban housewife would find reprehensible. Even the girls at the golf club would be shocked. She must stop thinking now because she needs to gather all her strength to be exhausted. She is just glad she wore the lacy black knickers, even though they are now in tatters. Spencer was very forceful and Harriet has always been a sucker for forceful men – it is just a pity she didn't marry one, the useless sod. She is falling asleep with a smile on her swollen lips that would so annoy Helen Huntingdon, who so dislikes that kind of smug self-satisfied smile on other women. A falling asleep final thought is she was glad she had indulged in the bikini wax. There is no thought to spare for Maria Branwell, who had the bikini wax under protest, the daft cow. Very soon the sound of rhythmic gurgling snoring fills the room where the curtains are partially closed.

Wednesday 18th October 3.25pm

Sir Godwyn Lydate, comfortably propped up against lace fringed pillows, is checking his mobile phone, and very much aware of a naked Marian Fairburne, legs entwined as if by artistic design. It could be an early study by Manet for an unfinished and now lost painting – 'stolen lust in the afternoon' an appropriate title. It has been a week of lovely surprises to outweigh the unpleasant surprise of the duplicity of the Murray woman, known as Robyn to her disappointed parents. He purses his lips. The Jury is still out on the punishment that will be meted out. There must always be cause and effect; an eye for an eye and a tooth for a tooth and that includes the Chinese strumpet – so make that punishments.

He taps in the number that has tried to reach him three times in the last hour. No message because the paranoid moron believes messages might get in the wrong hands. He wouldn't recognise a wrong hand if it grabbed him round swollen testicles.

"Yes, Prime Minister."

A rosy cheeked Marian Fairburne glances up startled from where her face is resting in the crook of his protective arm. Godwyn intimates a smile and she three-quarter smiles back, her body tantalisingly languid and more paganly satisfied at its core than it has ever been in all the wasted years... that could be the working title of an early draft of a T.S. Eliot poem. A bit overdramatic perhaps, as she sighs and snuggles closer. At first he had been so gentle and understanding, less gentle but very understanding as things developed. Not at all gentle in the end; she sighs contentedly.

"Indeed, Prime Minister."

Goodbye to the boring housewife she contentedly thinks. Goodbye to the mother of no use anymore to grown-up career-pursuing daughters. Goodbye to the boring Marian who reads, some might say, trashy romance novels for a bit of excitement in her life. Now some might say she is actually living in a trashy romance novel. Daringly she kisses an exposed nipple in its circlet of dark hairs and is pleased when he shivers. She doesn't think he was at all disappointed when things got less gentle. In fact she is quite sure he wasn't the least bit disappointed. She never knew she had such hidden carnal depths and, for once in her life, she is not the least bit worried about consequences. It is quite certain that Godwyn has a way with consequences.

"It will not come to that, Prime Minister."

The emerging butterfly will not and cannot be forced back into the chrysalis. There was an out of season midsummer madness to it all – intimations of T.S. Eliot again. Her eldest daughter's Master's dissertation had been on T.S. Eliot's fourth Quartet. Marian had started to read it and given up. She has been told often enough that she is not the brainy one in the family.

"Leave it to me, Prime Minister."

He ends the call and tosses the mobile phone into the tangled bedding and, with a glance at the painting of Aphrodite awakening and stretching, hanging on the opposite wall, strokes the generous curves of an ordainly fleshy thigh of which Aphrodite would have been proud.

Dear Marian insinuates such a lovely, soft, caressing plumpish in a nice way hand to which, being only flesh and blood, he cannot fail to respond. "You really are a naughty girl."

No one has ever called her a naughty girl, even when she was a naughty girl. "You are a naughty boy." It is a long time since he was called a naughty boy. She is now being a very naughty girl indeed.

Wednesday 18th October 4.05pm

Jack Bellingham is only too well aware that he is losing control of his own state of the nation novel. Just for instance he would like to write his bloody sister out of the story, but he is not at all sure she will allow herself to be written out. As for Sir Godwyn Lydate, the black biro seems to have a life of its own and Jack appears to be merely the honorary watcher-on and holder of the pen. At least it is obvious that Spencer Perceval will soon write himself out of the story without any help from Jack…although of course there is the unknown quantity of Harriet O'Connor, who will need a great deal of watching.

In any case Jack is not sure he is fitted to be the hero of his own life. He had believed that spilling the beans to Shirley Keeldar would act as some sort of closure and might even allow him a stab at being heroic to his own eyes, but now he is not so sure. In her turn Shirley had spilled some beans, although he is not certain that she was telling the whole truth. If only partly true, there was some information that he might be able to use against Sir Godwyn should it prove necessary. The strike would have to be swift and deadly otherwise the consequences do not bear thinking about. Collateral damage will take on a whole new meaning.

Anyway back to his bloody sister who has been left victorious in the field in bed with a strangely subdued, almost cowed, Amelia Sedley. The International movie star seemingly having met her match in the manic sexual obsessive department.

In truth Jack had been glad to make his escape. Not that either of them tried to stop him. In fact Amelia Sedley's mind appeared to be very much elsewhere and quite separate from the victorious field of her naked body.

It is pleasant to be strolling through Green Park in the pale October sunshine seeking the safety valve of being alone. It is hard to break the habit of surreptitiously eyeing up the girls, only now they are eyeing him back not at all surreptitiously. There are giggles and whispers and nudges and backward glances. There will be no more loneliness in a crowd which used to be the loneliest place of all…the place where he belonged for so long.

He pauses at the Bomber Command Memorial and, ignoring a group of Japanese tourists posing for photographs, wonders if, unlike the Japanese tourists, he can borrow a sense of perspective. After all, he is not falling to earth trapped in a blazing Lancaster bomber knowing his lovely young pregnant wife is waiting at home, fervently praying for his safe return. One day she will marry someone else and the unborn child will grow up calling someone else Daddy; that someone else will enjoy that lithe, only too willing body of the young widow. A searing pain. Then nothing.

Jack inhales several deep breaths and strolls up Piccadilly avoiding catching anyone's eye. It has been agreed between her People and his persons that he will escort Amelia Sedley to the Premiere of 'Sacrifice' at the Odeon Leicester Square next Monday evening. His sister was not discussed and there was no item called the elephant herd in the bedroom. This sister it was who struck the blow that killed her husband after they had made love and he was naked and vulnerable. It had been done Cluedo style, with a metal golf statuette that her husband had won for a hole in one.

In mitigation Mlud, three weeks earlier the bloody sister had surprised the naked murderee in the marital bed with the naked five months pregnant next door neighbour, whose husband was abroad on business. There been lots of tears and never agains and Jack's sister had pretended to forgive. She had patiently awaited her chance and it had been her idea to dispose of the body where it would never be found. The following week the pregnant next door neighbour had somehow fallen down the stairs and lost the baby. She would never speak about it. The next door neighbours sold their house and moved to Cornwall.

Pointedly ignoring the turning heads and sly glances, he strolls past the Ritz Hotel, avoiding the media presence, and is now looking into the sun slanting windows of Waterstones bookshop on Piccadilly. Staring in book shop windows inevitably reminds Jack of that long weekend spent with his mother in the bookshop town of Hay-on-Wye. She was a voracious reader, as in so many other things, and had been recovering from what Jack always suspected was a miscarriage, although she would never talk about it. She liked to pretend that such matters were aberrations of her closeted subconscious. Things that happened to other people that she just happened to get caught up in through no fault of her own. Her fervent prayers of course gave the game away because not only God was listening.

Anyway... enough of that. He has not read a book from beginning to end since his arrest; what was happening in his own life made the contents of novels, even Russian novels, tame by comparison. He borrowed books from the prison library but could never concentrate for more than a few minutes at a time. Sikesy had sneered that reading books was for puffs and sissies. Anyway, shagging Prison Officer Dora Spenlow on the bottom bunk with Sikesy watching would not appear in any borrowed novel.

Taking a deep breath, Jack glances over his shoulder to make sure the ghost of his mother is nowhere to be seen, before guiltily sidling inside Waterstones.

It is becoming a day for deep breaths; the lady Prison Psychiatrist would be moderately pleased. She was never more than moderately pleased and forever on the alert; but not alert enough as it turned out. Right legs in the wrong place and there was never a right time.

There is an unmistakable dustic aura about bookshops that never ceases to make Jack feel comfortable in his own skin. The massed ranks of books standing mute guard over his hopes and fears, a comfort even his mother could not spoil. Although she tried – boy how she tried.

As usual he gravitates to the fiction section, and there is something vaguely familiar about the leggy girl in skin tight blue jeans with strategic designer tears, natural sunlit auburn hair tied in a ponytail. She is standing to the right and skimming a book she has taken from the Classics section. There is no one else close by as he edges nearer and, becoming aware of his presence, she turns her head, flicking the sunlit ponytail.

"Hi." She smiles shyly.

"I didn't expect to find you here." Or anywhere else for that matter.

"Me neither." She turns everything else. "I mean..."

"I know what you mean, Celia." He tries a pleased not expecting to see you smile, and it seems to work. It appears that his smiles have stopped appearing vaguely sinister. Practice makes perfect – one of his mother's many maxims and she should know.

"You remembered my name." A winsome smile. None of her smiles will ever have been sinister. Expressive brown eyes. Celia. Celia. Celia Brook, that's it.

"Of course I remember your name, Celia Brook."

Talk about truth being stranger than fiction. It would be hard to believe this coincidental meeting if written in a novel. She is blushing, which suits her one spot complexion of the pretty girl next door of any street anywhere any time. She would have fitted well into the burgeoning Nineteenth Century, most probably as a put upon Governess pursued by the father of the family; living forever on the edge of shameful seduction.

"What are you reading, Celia?"

She holds up a thick paperback edition of the collected novels of Mark Twain.

"Let me see."

She meekly hands over the weighty paperback. This close he is very much aware of her distinctive perfume, not expensive but overtly woodlandish and redolent of misty summer mornings in a Bavarian forest – not that he has been within a hundred miles of a Bavarian forest. He cannot help but reflect that the overall effect is more potent than the ridiculous cost per ounce stuff dolloped on by Amelia Sedley and her bubonic partner in smells. Peeking above the neck of Celia's pale blue blouse are intriguing tattoos of butterflies in flight and he cannot help but wonder.

The book is open at 'A Connecticut Yankee at King Arthur's Court'. Jack offers a quizzical twitch of an eyebrow and she colours up some more. The girl next door found out in some misdemeanour that she had agonised over, just knowing she would get found out, like that time behind the bike sheds.

"It's a long time since I have read any Mark Twain." He flicks through the pages.

"I haven't read him at all." The cute turned up nose turns up cutely and there is a hint of peppermint on her breath. The too generous but somehow it works mouth very much in the right place at the right time. A hint of cigarette smoke on the clothes. Spying on girls smoking outside offices and pubs used to be always a bonus. They never gave the previous John or Johnny a second glance.

"Let me buy you this book." £12.95. The original Penguin would have been sixpence in old money. At Hay-on-Wye a battered copy was fifty pence.

"No... really." She looks down at her scuffed shoes and wishes she was wearing her going out heels and best frock. Celia hasn't worn her best frock since finishing with her long-term boyfriend for sleeping with her best friend, who had borrowed the best frock.

"I insist and please let me buy you a coffee as well."

"You don't have to waste time on me." It is not a pose because she is not that kind of girl.

She had never in her wildest dreams thought they would ever meet again. I mean... the most famous man on the Planet. She has dreamt about him of course and just hopes he cannot read the dreams in her face. She is hopeless at hiding her thoughts, which is why she will probably lose her lousy job. She has been all at sixes and sevens since splitting with her cheating long-term boyfriend.

"I would love to waste time on you, Celia Brook." Instead of sounding corny he sounds sort of sincere. She traces semicircles with the toe of a scuffed shoe.

"If you're sure?" Seated at a table for two, Celia Brook scoops the froth off the medium cappuccino – asking for large would have seemed unladylike – and she licks the spoon clean. "I love the froth." The expressive brown eyes are watchful and she is only too well aware that people are looking over at their table and whispering. She cannot help but feel a bit of a fraud, whilst guiltily revelling in the experience that she will pick over later.

"What are you thinking, Celia?" She thinks he has the naturally caressing voice of a man you can trust. After all he didn't pinch her bum on Friday evening like most other male guests; that sleazy so called celebrity chef actually grabbed a handful of butterfly tattooed bum cheek…if looks could kill.

"I was just." Lick. Lick. "You know, thinking." She puts down the licked clean spoon. "After all you could be sitting here with Amelia Sedley."

"God forbid." He theatrically shivers and, truthfully, could not think of anything worse.

"I thought you two were an item." They certainly seemed an item from where Celia was standing on Friday evening.

"All fabricated." He slurps coffee. "A publicity stunt put together by our People."

"Really?" She is impressed that he has People but is not at all sure about the fabrication thing. She is aware she now has serious trust issues.

"Yeah." He slurps more coffee and wipes froth off his lips with the back of his hand. A habit that used to annoy his mother, so a habit that his bloody sister assiduously perfected.

"She was all over you on Friday."

"Marginally better than a rash I suppose." Celia giggles and screws up her eyes. Not in the least bit a silly manufactured girly giggle… everything about this girl is natural. He tries not to think about the butterflies in flight. Out of left field. "You got a boyfriend, Celia?"

Her face clouds over, her eyes fill with tears and to stop herself losing balance she flattens her hands on the scratched Formica table top. The hurt and the pain painfully obvious even to Hero Jack.

"Sorry." He leans across the table and covers her flattened hands that are surprisingly cool to the touch. "That was impertinent of me."

"No. It's all right." The covering of his warm hands steadies her resolve not to break down in public. She would never forgive herself. After the breakup she had cried for two days solid… the lousy cheat didn't deserve that much regret. "We had been together nearly four years." There is something sturdy in her character that goes unrecognised; a sturdiness that you would pass in the street without noticing; a sturdiness she does not realise that she possesses.

"You don't have to talk about it, Celia. You really don't." The cool hands are warming up and she is jolly well not going to break down…so there.

"My mum was taken ill and I had gone home for a few days." She is staring at his covering hands and their, she wishfully thinks, delicate pianist's fingers. "I came back to our rooms earlier than expected." She cutely sniffs up the cute turned up nose. "My boyfriend was in bed with my best friend." She doesn't mention the best frock tossed on the floor… and to add insult to injury, a pair of matching knickers and a discarded bra that her best friend had also borrowed without asking. Not that it seemed all that important in the scheme of things.

"Shit." He hopes that doesn't count as a swear word.

"It turned out she was two months pregnant with his baby."

"Shit."

It seems appropriate to squeeze both hands. She tries for a deep breath. An expert on deep breaths, he takes several to show empathy.

"I'm okay now."

"You sure?"

A bit of a wan smile. "Well, fairly okay." The expressive brown eyes more expressive than eyes have any right to be. "I am back living with my parents." An even waner smile. "Fairly sad at twenty nine." He had thought she was younger.

"Where do they live?"

"St Albans."

"Not too far then?"

"Forty minutes or so from King's Cross. Depending." She bravely smiles, her too generous but it works mouth painting such a generous brave smile. "I haven't told anyone else." She would normally have told her best friend but of course that was out of the question.

"Your parents?"

"Just that we split up." A pregnant pause. She will never ever speak her boyfriend's or her best friend's names ever again and that is her wall of resolve. "My parents didn't like him anyway."

He squeezes hands and she shyly nudges back.

"I'm really glad you told me, Celia." A unique heartrending unpublished short story, but profoundly normal like all the most compelling short stories. He knows what he means. If only he could write as well as this, natural as nature intended, girl speaks from the heart.

Celia stares at their by now intermingled fingers. She wears no rings. She had dragged off the diamond engagement ring there and then and had thrown it at the naked couple, who were very much still conjoined together on the bed, and staring at Celia as if she was the intruder. The ring is probably now adorning the third finger of her best friend's left hand. She really must stop thinking of Cynthia – Oh heck – as her best friend, because she is done with best friends.

"I will have to get back to work."

"You like your work?" It is the ordinariness that takes him by surprise as she corkscrews her mouth and the cute nose turns up even more cutely.

"It's all right."

"Only all right?"

"Most of the guests treat me like a lump of meat…" A wry self-deprecating smile… "And a cheap cut at that." She eases her fingers out of his loosening grip. "I really must go."

"Can I have your phone number, Celia?" He is at a bit of a loss what to do with the released fingers.

"Why?" She appears genuinely taken aback. This girl needs no direction on the banalities of day to day life.

"I would like to take you out to dinner."

"You don't need to do that because you feel sorry for me." She has had enough of that with her parents, although they mean well and she loves them dearly. She has tried ever so hard to stop feeling sorry for herself and they don't help…God love them.

"I would just like to see you again, Celia."

She visibly thinks this over and then even, more visibly, comes to a decision. "I would like that… but…" The eyes have it again. A pity eye men are so thin on the ground. She realises that whatever words she chooses they will sound trite.

"…I am not, you know… that sort of girl."

"I am really glad you are not that sort of girl, Celia Brook."

They exchange phone numbers, but she believes in her heart of hearts that they will never meet again. He is just being kind and she will never dare to ring. There are always daydreams though, and night dreams that she has no wish to control.

Wednesday 18th October 7.05pm

Standing too close to the cracked bathroom mirror, because she is more short-sighted than she will ever admit, even to herself, Camilla French gazes intently into its three-quarter length. So rarely does she appraise her own body that it is almost like sneaking a voyeuristic peek at the body of a stranger. It is a long time since anyone else has admired the pert breasts and the orangey nipples gazing back with equal short-sighted intensity. She strokes the palm of her left hand across the pleasingly flat belly – no abortions – no children and no vestiges of childbearing to leave their marks.

Then shyly she touches the smoothness between her legs, a result of this afternoon's intrusive Brazilian wax. The vee of curly nut brown hair has disappeared as if by magic. She smooths out the delicateness of her porcelain white thighs and appraises her thinner than she would like legs, that have also been waxed, although deforested might be a better description. The body of a stranger indeed.

The small feet with their toenails painted pillar box red to match the pillar box red acrylic false fingernails. She never realised there are so many shades of red.

She gazes surprisingly enraptured at the stranger's naked body. If you ignore the forty something face, which she does, you might think it the body of someone in their late twenties or early thirties. Well… possibly no older than mid-thirties.

She swivels sideways to admire the ever so neat bottom. Her mother always called it a bottom – look after your bottom, Camilla and your bottom will look after you. It was her bottom that had been the preference of her one and only boyfriend at Cambridge – her one and only boyfriend full stop.

Now the unavoidable face… late thirties at a pinch. She touches flecked with blonde highlighted hair, expensively styled, eyebrows plucked and shaped and face massaged. It could certainly be the elfin features of someone late thirties. Yes… she will settle for that. Not too far out of sync with the body.

She swivels once more to admire the ever so neat bottom and idly wonders if Sir Godwyn is a bottom man. Not that he will get anywhere near this bottom tonight. She certainly does not see herself as a collectable item – the very thought.

She really must shake herself out of this verging on sensuous trancelike state. She is not at all used to being well and truly pampered to within an inch of her life. At the mention of Sir Godwyn's name nothing was too much trouble. The ruggedly handsome Chauffeur, Gilbert Markham, had been really really sweet… nothing was too much trouble as he sat and waited. She knows that he caught more than a sneaky glimpse in the mirrors of Camilla in her new exceedingly brief undies, and she had felt oddly excited. It is a long long time since she has felt oddly excited in that way. The intrusive Brazilian wax only notched up the excitement.

She edges closer to the cracked bathroom mirror and the tangible smoothness between her legs is quite breathtaking. She hates to admit it but she likes it. No doubt Gilbert would like to be touching the smoothness as she is touching it now. Stop it, Camilla!

She remembers the horror in her early teens when hair sprouted between her legs and she thought she was a freak. The smooth touch takes her back to the happiest days of childhood after her Father had run away with Auntie Flo and there was just Camilla and her Mother.

With a heartfelt sigh she stretches and yawns luxuriously. She really must get a move on, she is being picked up at 7-45 and has yet to work out the intricacies of the suspender belt. She waves a shy goodbye to the naked stranger in the mirror who waves back just as shyly. She wishes she was going out to dinner with the ruggedly handsome Gilbert Markham.

Stop it, Camilla!

Wednesday 18th October 8.03pm

Harriet O'Connor wakes with a snorting grunt. It was not a good dream because it involved her useless husband, but happily it fades quickly, as all her dreams fade quickly these days. Sometimes she doesn't think she has dreamed at all.

She is disorientated. This is not her bed because the mattress is too hard and she is naked and not wearing a nightie – she always wears a nightie – sometimes silky if she is in the mood. More and more these days she is not in the mood for her sad excuse of a husband, except when needs must and, come hell or high water, she has always catered to her musting needs.

Tentatively she reaches out her left hand. She is alone. Just for a minute she thought…

She has a crushing headache and her mouth tastes foul. The flickering eyes slowly adjust to the less than darkness in the stuffy room, most definitely not her own bedroom, which explains the bed. Hastily closed curtains at the window do not quite meet in the middle. That clinches it.

A car horn toot toots angrily; car horns never toot toot angrily, or otherwise, in their quiet, exclusive cul-de-sac of six bedroom executive homes, with distant sea views on a clear day if you stand on tiptoes in the smallest bedroom. She needs to get a grip here. The useless sod usually brings her a nice cup of Ringtons tea when she wakes up after a nice lie down. For goodness sake, she is not at home for goodness sake. She rolls onto her back, winces, and out of a waking habit, rub rubs her slightly wobbly belly. She really must get to grips with the latest diet whose name she has forgotten. There have been so many latest diets to forget. Tattered Crusader banner remnants of pleasure are reawakened by the rub rubbing hand – then she remembers some of it. "Oh! My God" She splutters out loud and guiltily turns on the bedside lamp at the second attempt. She is definitely alone and unbidden thoughts are colliding thick and fast, but first things first…she desperately needs a pee. She scurries bare footed to the bathroom, being careful of the troublesome corns. She is not at all sure that the ridiculously young Podiatrist knows what he is doing. Neither is she sure that the gentle toe massaging, though pleasant, is strictly necessary.

Perching, not so squarely, on the wobbly toilet seat she vaguely remembers being sick earlier and a sort of helpful girl with scary eyes. It is uncomfortable to pee, she remembers some more and holds her splitting head in her hands, but it doesn't help.

Whatever possessed her to do what she did? She knows only too well but, thank the Lord, she is in the change and so no worries about late periods anymore.

Even so, the naughty boy was irresponsible not to use a condom...or rather condoms. It is the rule of West Shields golf club wife swapping... no condom: no can do, is the one and only rule. She splashes her face with lukewarm water from the cold tap, thirstily drinking from cupped hands, then snatches up the hand towel from the floor and dries her face – vigorously depositing smears of smeary make-up on the towel...not her problem.

Then she looks in the mirror and wishes she hadn't. She always looks terrible with hangovers; she groans abstractly as she becomes aware of the livid bite marks on one of her substantial breasts. She has to admit to herself that they both got a bit carried away. She had said things... rude things... done things... really rude things.

"Oh! My God." She speaks aloud and feels a little bit better for hearing the sound of her own voice.

Bereftly she touches the spreaded brown nipples that feel, she is not sure of the right word. Well sucked. The two words will have to suffice as the shades of his greedy mouth and teasing teeth are poised in the ether. "Get a grip, Harriet," She admonishes the blurry image in the mirror. She talks to herself more and more these days, and has become her own best friend and worst enemy. "He shouldn't have done that," She whispers. "I have never ever done that before." She will never ever be able to tell the girls at the golf club, which has always been half the pleasure.

She totters back to the bedroom clutching a glass of lukewarm water held in both hands, which she sets down most carefully on the bedside table. Then she rifles through her, she tells everybody, genuine designer handbag – and it is – and roots out some paracetamol. Swallowing four tablets she snuggles back under the duvet, pulling it up to her chin, and drifts back to sleep idiotically smiling to herself. He really was a very naughty boy, although no one can blame him for getting a bit carried away. She quite liked being called babe. Turn over, babe has a certain ring to it. Very soon sounds of rhythmic gurgling snoring fills the partly curtained room.

Wednesday 18th October 10.55pm

Camilla French kicks off the absurdly pinching high heel shoes and is not sure whether or not to be disappointed. She collapses into the least uncomfortable of the two uncomfortable second-hand armchairs, which fight for space in the pint sized lounge area of her dingy apartment – that is all she needs, or so she frequently tells herself... somewhere to lay her head. Camilla has never had an interest in possessions. Not that she has ever had many possessions to take an interest in. She has always been a soft touch for the various charities she supports.

She rubs her sore eyes – she was too vain to wear the rather unflattering spectacles she needs when her eyes are tired. The menu was a blur and so she graciously allowed a blurry Sir Godwyn to order the food and wine. She has never had an interest in food and wine but both were rather good.

There is so much to ponder about their secret discussions. It reminded Camilla of a painting that hangs in her Cambridge College dining hall; Elizabethan Courtiers plotting by candlelight... all men, of course. Tonight there was candlelight and there was most certainly plotting. Academia no longer beckons; she could not resist being enticed into his confidence, or as far into his confidence as he deemed necessary and he knows that she knows that.

She is surprisingly bone weary and cannot be bothered to pour herself the usual small brandy. Small brandies at bedtime being her secret vice. How sad is that? It will be impossible to sleep with the ideas teeming and lading in her overactive brain.

With Gilbert watching in the rear mirror Sir Godwyn had chastely kissed her on the cheek as the limousine pulled up outside her door. He had not asked to come inside and she was disappointed that she was not allowed to refuse. Not allowed to let Gilbert Markham hear the refusal.

She must get undressed because the absurdly expensive designer dress is getting creased. The snooty haute couture woman, who nevertheless paled at the mention of Sir Godwyn's name, had not offered an encouraging word, whereas a watching on Gilbert had said this dress looked stunning.

She is not used to wearing stockings and the suspenders are digging into the lilywhite thighs. Sir Godwyn had told her she looked radiant. Well he would say that, wouldn't he? She believed that she was looking her best, which is probably as good as it gets.

She sighs contentedly and doesn't think she will read from Wuthering Heights tonight. Her own turned upside down real life needs to be arranged in well-written sentences, necessary paragraphs, not to mention accompanying illustrations.

There is so much to ponder that there should be a stronger word. She will just close her eyes for a few moments. Gilbert was so sweet, not the least bit fidgety whilst she was trying on so many dresses. She is glad she chose his favourite.

Wednesday 18th October 11.18pm

Leaning back on an invitingly comfortable settee, Jack Bellingham is shuffling through scribbled notes of the state of the nation novel, at his elbow a tumbler of Double Black whisky. The Grande suite at the Savoy Hotel faintly redolent of the scents of Shirley Keeldar that never quite go away.

He is thankfully alone, mobile phone turned off, and for some reason that he dare not fathom, he cannot stop thinking about Celia Brook, who is not that kind of girl. He wonders what role that fey innocent seeming girl, and her tantalising flight of butterfly tattoos, will play in the never ending story. A walk on part or something more defining; for her sake he hopes just a walk on part. Time will tell… time always tells… just ask Marcel Proust. Jack has always meant to read Marcel Proust's 'In Search Of Lost Time' and has made several abortive starts.

He imbibes a rich smoky mouthful of whisky. Earlier this evening he shared a picnic meal with Nina Balatka and Emily Rowley at the Jermyn Street Gallery. The Window man canvases are, in Nina's own words, good to go. The words of a Nina Balatka who confirmed that all the launch machinery is in place and also good to go; that lady can smell money. There will be all the usual paraphernalia including mugs, tea towels and not forgetting a catalogue and prints and fridge magnets and, of course, at Jack's insistence, there will be Exhibition pens and bookmarks.

Shirley Keeldar has become involved and the Exhibition will be opened by Window man himself with Window lady, aka cupper of the balls, at his side. There will be a post-launch party for the great and the good. Shirley will ensure the attendance of minor Royalty and senior Politicians, and of course Sir Godwyn Lydate and guest.

No prices will be fixed to the first five Window man paintings until the very last minute. The Artist insists there will be more Window man canvases; glancing over the existing five canvases a visiting Shirley Keeldar had reserved Window man three, whatever the price. That particular Window man reminding her more of Tom Sawyer than Jack. A fact that she keeps very much to herself.

Emily Rowley had stared and stared at Jack politely munching picnic food and, even more politely, sipping Argentinian red wine from an Egon Schiele Exhibition mug. Her flat green eyes more like fake emeralds than fake emeralds; perhaps the next series of paintings will be Picnic man. Hard to know what the weird girl is cooking up. He was not to know that she was actually thinking the next series could well be Window man ravishing the artist – several positions. Like Turner, she always paints from life.

Although her own thoughts were moored elsewhere, Nina Balatka had been aware of Emily Rowley staring drink eyed at Jack. To be honest she was keeping an eye on Emily Rowley rather than Jack.

After the Exhibition Nina will be a wealthy woman, no blackmail required. Her mother would have been so proud she would have cried tears of joy that, in her lifetime, she never had cause to cry. Unlike her mother, from now on Nina Balatka will only go to bed with men of her choice. That might include Jack or it might not…the Jury is out on Sir Godwyn Lydate. Although she realises that decision could well be out of her hands. They will certainly be rich.

Jack all alone imbibes more whisky and is reading scribbled notes appertaining to Sir Godwyn Lydate. He had not intended the old Etonian sexual predator should dominate the foreground, or the background for that matter, as he is threatening to do. The rapacious sexual appetite is making Jack nervous; rapaciousness is contagious after all. The sense of entitlement is awesome and frightening. It is hard to believe Shirley Keeldar's revelations but they must surely be true. She has no reason to lie. What is true is that Sir Godwyn Lydate is a most dangerous man and that is not a good thing for the state of any nation.

They say that the battle of Waterloo was won on the playing fields of Eton – Jack believes that the battle was won in the back streets of Manchester and Liverpool and Leeds.

He sucks the Egon Schiele Exhibition pen. Perhaps he should kill off Sir Godwyn without further ado and do the world a favour and save the Prime Minister's bacon. The killing off being something acceptably dramatic… a terrorist car bomb in Whitehall…or the arch fornicator shot by a jealous husband. A suitably Nineteenth Century comeuppance. After all a Nineteenth Century Lydate had been wounded in a duel with a wronged husband. Unfortunately the wronged husband had been shot through the heart in the same duel and the adulterous pregnant wife abandoned. It is food for thought.

The door of the Grande suite is thrown open and typhoon Shirley bursts into the room taking it for granted that she will be welcomed with open arms.

"Sorry I'm so late, darling." He had no idea she was late. She sweeps up the empty whisky tumbler and carries it to the drinks cabinet. She pours more whisky for Jack and pours herself an extremely large vodka on the rocks. She plumps herself close to Jack on the invitingly comfortable settee. He doesn't mind at all.

"I am making notes for the novel I've been meaning to write for as long as I…" He pauses. "…have been meaning to write a novel."

"I hope I have a starring role." She kisses a prominent ear and slurps vodka. "Under an assumed name of course."

He does not reply and she pats his knee. "Not detailing all our bed stuff I hope, darling. By the by I have some good news on the book front."

He looks bemused as she kisses the sticky out ear.

"Your book on the Brontës."

"Charlotte Brontë's married year?" Now he sounds bemused.

"The very one." She gulps more vodka. "The University Publishers have been in touch and they want to republish urgently. They have been inundated with enquiries since the delectable Lady Rebecca plugged the book on Twitter." She gulps more vodka. "They have sold all the remaindered copies at full price and taken thousands of orders for a second printing. They want an up-to-date photograph and so the delectable one is obliging." Shirley would be lost without that girl.

"There wasn't a photograph in the original."

"That was then and this is now." Nothing further needs to be said.

They are companionably silent for several minutes with no pregnancies, phantom or otherwise, involved. Shirley is apparently lost in her own thoughts whilst Jack scribbles away. He has definitely decided Sir Godwyn will be blown to pieces in a terrorist attack. After all he was behind the mishandled drone attacks killing and maiming hundreds of innocent women and children in Palestine.

In the natural order of things it is, of course, Shirley who breaks the silence. "You remember Sir Godwyn Lydate whom you met at the BBC?" Arrested in midsentence he glances sideways at the heart stopping Pre-Raphaelite profile. Surely she cannot read his mind.

"Yeeees...?" She has his full attention.

"You remember that I told you the Head waiter at Sir Godwyn's restaurant had disappeared, the restaurant where you lunched with Amelia super what's it?"

"Yeeees...?"

"Well the body of the head waiter has been dragged out of the Thames below Tower Bridge."

"Christ!"

"Foul play is not suspected."

This time the silence is charged and there is no other word.

"Do you suspect foul play?" He asks.

"Of course."

Jack pensively sucks the Exhibition pen. It appears Sir Godwyn Lydate will not allow himself to be written out of the story. A terrorist attack would probably leave him unscathed but killing and maiming many innocent bystanders.

Wednesday 18th October 11.28pm

Sir Godwyn Lydate is blissfully unaware how close he came to being the victim of a terrorist outrage. Alone in his study in his Albany apartment he is sipping his favourite single malt whisky of the moment. He has telephoned the 'widow' as he for the moment categorises Sarah Newton. The funeral is arranged and Sir Godwyn will attend. She sounded surprised and gratified, as well she might. No discretion needed. A mere pawn it might be thought, however ornately carved… ornately carved or not, pawns are an integral component of the game and of course one never knows… that is the beauty of the game.

Through an immense magnifying glass he is studying his latest philatelic acquisition. He has bid much more than he intended at auction for a two penny blue cover from Doncaster to Leeds, clearly date stamped 2 May 1840 – four days before the official first day of the introduction of postage stamps. Four large margins and the stamp only just touched by the distinctive Maltese cross. The Certificate of authenticity from the Royal Philatelic Society of which he is a Vice President.

"You beauty." He whispers which leads to idle thoughts of Marian Fairburne. He tears his gaze away from the miniature profile of Queen Victoria to the oil painting on the wall, above the bookcase containing the Dickens and Trollope first editions. A bashfully naked woman staring out from all of four centuries ago. There are those who believe the Rubens is a copy. They can believe what they want.

He arranged Marian in the same pose and had taken several photographs. The one with a sex sated smoky grin being his favourite; even Rubens at his best would have struggled to capture that coy bemusement – would have captured the flauntingly generous body most certainly but not that coy, bemused, lopsided promissory shape of lips. They are to meet again very soon.

Then there is Camilla French. He knew that she would take great delight in turning him down so he didn't ask; that is a game promising many twists and turns. The makeover had been spectacular and heads had turned in the restaurant. Heads never turn for Camilla French. Such a fiercely intelligent creature, she is now very much onside and he is absolutely certain that there will be no Rosalie Murray moment. There is so much in play he sighs contentedly and that reminds him. The text from the Foreign Secretary's permanently disgruntled wife. She has laid hands, her words, on the incriminating documents. They must meet secretly and they will meet secretly.

He stretches and yawns luxuriantly. The afternoon and early evening lovemaking with a surprisingly inventive Marian is catching up with him. He hates to admit that he is not as young as he used to be. An early start in the morning and so sensible to get some sleep. He will probably dream of the luscious Marian Fairburne or, perhaps, Camilla French who was quite intriguingly attractive in the treacherous candlelight and not in the least bit a pawn.

The mobile phone vibrates to Parsifal and he checks the caller. "Can't you sleep, my sweet Helen?" He listens.

Wednesday 18th October 11.28pm

The bar area of the Queens Hotel is busier than earlier and they are lucky to get a table but then lucky used to be his middle name.

"You really are a piece of work, Spencer."

Spencer Perceval realises this is not a compliment. Helen Huntingdon remains immaculate, but scarier, although she has only merestly touched up her make-up and the pale yellow tights have stayed pale yellow. The weirdo is staring at him in an oddly speculative way. There is something he is definitely missing here.

The run through went as well as could be expected. Afterwards they dined with the Production team and Spencer had been all over the Producer's wife. In the end Helen reluctantly intervened to stop him being punched on the nose. Surely she can relax now… surely nothing can go wrong. Spencer has not yet become a total parody of himself. She fervently hopes that will be someone else's problem.

With manufactured distaste she watches him down a large whisky in one swallow, rub his eyes, throatily cough and brush a wayward lank of blonde hair away from his flushed face. She idly wonders how deep the predictability goes as he orbits a cavernous yawn. Probably goes as deep as the name on Blackpool rock. Not that she has ever been to Blackpool or sucked any kind of rock. She stifles a giggle. Perhaps not the most appropriate of similes when in the presence of the forgetful Spencer Percival.

"That poor woman."

"She was totally fucking up for it. Totally fucking up for it."

"So you say." There you go. No one will believe him even when he is telling the truth. He thinks he might be losing credibility in certain quarters. Harriet what's er name said she was a bad girl and needed spanking and naturally one thing led to another – it always does –everyone knows that. Not to mention that Producer tosser's wife who had allowed Spencer's hand up her skirt under the table. She had licked her lips and trapped his hand between her lovely squashy bare thighs, for Christ's sake…totally fucking up for it…just a pity her husband was sitting across the table.

"I thought the run through went well." He signals the bartender for another large one. Watching demure screw loose demurely sipping vodka is making him thirsty. She is not bothering to lick the rim of the glass in a suggestive way; he gets the impression that if he was the last man on earth and she was the last woman there would be no future for the human race.

The treble whisky arrives. He doesn't take any notice of the bartender. If he did he would see that he looks green at the gills and that his hand is shaking. Helen Huntingdon notices.

"Had a text from Sir Godwyn." She drops the name into the void and so he gulps whisky. Just the mention of that name can bring him out in a cold sweat and a rash, even when he has done nothing wrong. Well nothing wrong-ish anyway.

"He is coming up in the morning with Camilla French."

Spencer emotes moody pensive as well he might. A look which she hates to admit rather suits his fading good looks – such a pity. Of course, it doesn't matter in the dark.

"Is he giving her one?"

"You are so crude, Spencer."

He recalls that Housemaster's rather tasty wife at Eton. The rumour being that Godwyn Lydate was the only boarder who didn't need to fantasise about that fading Swedish beauty. Lucky sod. There were even rumours about the Headmaster's somewhat feisty Scottish wife and the parentage of the unexpected baby. Not to mention Hugh Clavering's mother with the basketball tits…rumour had it they were spotted very much at it behind the cricket pavilion during the annual Parents versus first eleven match; her husband was an Umpire.

He drains the whisky. "I've had enough." She knows he doesn't mean the whisky, as he pushes back the chair and heads for the lift, staggering only slightly.

She studies his departure with a marked lack of interest. There will no doubt be a bottle of Scotch secreted in his room. The slippery slope gets slipperier by the day or, in his case, by the hour. She gives herself up to her own thoughts. It is highly unlikely that Goddy is giving one to Camilla French, or old iron knickers as she has been christened by Helen Huntingdon.

Sipping the vodka, and for nothing better to do, she studies the vacuously handsome bartender. He looks as though he could collapse at any moment and has twice taken a slug of whisky when no one was looking; no one, that is, except Helen Huntingdon. This youngish man looks to be the guardian of all the guilty secrets that reside with Goddy. He would not make a good spy. The prettyish Receptionist is also keeping an eye on him. There is more to this than meets the eye – secrets and lies indeed…move over Peyton Place.

She is pondering whether she deserves a second vodka, when the lift doors open and Spencer Perceval reappears like a third rate genie from a rusty lamp heading inexorably towards his Nemesis. He practically falls into the vacant chair and has great difficulty in getting his breath. He looks as though he has been pursued by a lost Legion of ghosts and she hopes he is not having a heart attack. That would be really inconvenient. Helen Huntingdon notices that the bartender is staring open mouthed and so is the prettyish Receptionist. Much much more to this than meets the eye.

"What on earth is wrong?" Helen has a bad feeling about this and it is as well not to ignore her bad feelings.

His mouth is making shapes but the sound is turned off. He looks as though he has run into a brick wall that had no right to be there.

"What? What?" She hopes she might have to slap his stupid face. "What on earth is wrong?"

"There is a dead woman in my room."

Thursday 19th October 12.03am

Fully dressed, Camilla French has fallen deeply asleep in the least uncomfortable of the two uncomfortable second-hand armchairs. She never falls asleep, fully dressed or otherwise, in a chair of any description. It is only the insistent ringing of the off key doorbell that forces her to surface from a sensuous dream that goes against every inclination of her mind but apparently not of her body. For a few seconds she is perilously disorientated. The vivid dream so vivid that it takes a few disappointed moments to realise it is only a dream after all. She has not enjoyed such a vivid erotic dream for some time and it is perhaps a good thing she is fully clothed. In the past she has never been able to prevent dreamily masturbating herself awake.

The off key doorbell is not going to go away. Reluctantly she struggles to her stockinged feet and instinctively smooths the creased, obscenely costly, silk dress courtesy of Sir Godwyn. She is acutely aware of crab pinching suspenders in all her waking movements, as she tugs open the squealing door, which is just a common or garden door. There are no common or garden squealing doors in erotic dreams and it is not the man from the erotic dream anyway.

"A change of plan, my dear." Sir Godwyn Lydate asserts his way into the cramped apartment. She wonders if he was expecting to discover her blowzily naked under a hastily dragged on revealing dressing gown. Probably not and, anyway, she doesn't possess a revealing dressing gown. The blowzily naked is probably pushing it a bit as well. "We are driving up to Leeds now."

"Why?" She extravagantly yawns and luxuriantly stretches and is slow to realise that it is most definitely a sight for sore eyes.

"I will explain on the way."

She realises he is in one of his signature aggressive no-nonsense 'do as I say' moods. So reminiscent of Daddy, before he thankfully ran away with the recently widowed and even more recently pregnant Auntie Flo. Just like Daddy, Sir Godwyn is such a larger than life personality and it is such a small apartment.

"Is your case packed?"

She nods and yawns. "I need to go to the toilet." The bathroom door doesn't lock. In fact the door doesn't close properly. It has never mattered.

"Do hurry up, my dear."

She knows he is outside the door but can do nothing about breaking wind and then the gushing wee.

As she emerges she cannot meet his eyes, and without a word he carries the overnight case to the waiting limousine. A tense looking Gilbert Markham stows the case in the boot. He had realised when he stowed Sir Godwyn's larger case that he had forgotten all about Rosanna Spearman's shoe. He must not forget his promise because she will be grateful and a second bite of the cherry will be most acceptable…not to mention plan B.

As the limousine speeds away Camilla settles herself in the farthest corner, wishing there had been time to dispense with the stockings and the all-pervasive suspender belt. She is not used to her legs being so visible. To make up for the discomfiture she listens most intently as Sir Godwyn succinctly explains the reason for the sudden change of plans. She makes no comment and knows he appreciates it. She intercepts Gilbert's glance in the rear view mirror. He is not to know he was very much naked and aroused in her dream – but then so was she.

Sir Godwyn is on the mobile phone to Henry Wititterly, the recently appointed Home Secretary, who knows better than to complain about being disturbed at such a late hour. He holds a hand that, a few seconds ago, was caressing between her wide apart smooth legs, over the naked young female Researcher's mouth. One cannot be too careful.

There will be a Police motorcycle escort waiting at the first motorway junction.

With nothing to say, Camilla closes her eyes and is soon dozing, dimly aware that she has been covered with a travelling rug. She absently smiles her thanks but doesn't open her eyes and soon is sound asleep. Sir Godwyn listens to the gentle adenoidal snoring, finding it appealingly restful. He will not sleep and instead watches the motorway flash by as the speed limit is of course exceeded. There are Police outriders at front and rear with blue lights flashing. Just one minor manifestation of his power and glory. It is thinking time. There is never enough time to think. There is now.

Gilbert Markham finds the gentle adenoidal snoring not in the least bit restful as he intently watches the road ahead and the flashing blue lights. Imprinted on his mind's eye are those surprising glimpses of Camilla French in skimpy lacy underwear, spied through a gap in the changing room curtain.

Thursday 19th October 2.33am

Helen Huntingdon is the Night Watch… a watching likeness that even Rembrandt would struggle to capture in all its manic watchfulness. She has spoken to Sir Godwyn, as she must think of Goddy in this situation, on the shocking pink mobile phone clutched now in her hot, medium sized hand. She is caressing the phone unthinkingly with finger and thumb.

He sounded calm and collected. She would expect nothing less.

He even appears calm and collected as he strides across the hotel lobby accompanied by the hunk of a chauffeur carrying two overnight cases as if they weigh nothing, and also accompanied by old iron knickers herself. Only a highly polished, much improved version of old iron knickers; the Crusaders have unexpectedly returned from the Holy Land. Their ladies have hurriedly bathed in rose petals and cinnamon, and anointed their bodies with precious oils from the mysterious Orient. The Chastity belts will be ceremoniously unlocked, then stand well back.

Helen Huntingdon uncrosses lots and lots of pale yellow legs, secreting the shocking pink mobile phone in the pocket of her smart jacket and goes to meet the group halfway. She knows only too well that if one meets potential trouble on one's feet it stops being so troublesome and she is taller than any of them.

Standing to his full height Sir Godwyn takes hold of both the hot medium-sized hands which is a good sign. She knows that once they are touching she has the advantage. The hot medium-sized hands have it just about every time.

"Where is he?"

"Safely tucked up in bed with a certain Harriet O'Connor."

"The peroxide blonde tarty barmaid?"

"No." He is such a good listener. "A middle-aged housewife he picked up in the hotel bar at lunchtime today." He is caressing her lifelines, which is a very good sign. "It is her friend who is the dead body in his room." He decides it will be inopportune to say it makes a change from the library.

Sir Godwyn sighs theatrically. "Who was it said that the gods themselves are powerless against stupidity?"

"Schiller." Camilla French answers without any hesitation.

Helen ignores the clever clogs interjection. "I thought it best to get him out of the way." She smiles at Goddy and his excuse for a heart inches towards a lurch. "The lady did not protest overmuch." Not at all actually.

Sir Godwyn squeezes the captured hands and Helen is only too well aware that Camilla French is staring intently at Helen's curly orange hair. She probably guesses. Clever old iron knickers.

Sir Godwyn searches into Helen's eyes, one darker brown than the other, and appears satisfied. She goes noticeably cross eyed when she is not taking the prescribed medication. "Good girl." She knows what he means. Reluctantly he lets go the smooth enticing medium-sized hot hands. One has to keep up appearances.

At the sound of subdued voices, the temporary Hotel manager emerges crab scuttling from her cubby hole of an office. She has kept well away from the really scary girl after they crossed swords earlier, when the really scary girl had insisted they must wait for someone called Sir Godwyn Lydate. She would brook no argument and had made some awful threats. Caroline Helstone has no doubt that the scary girl would have carried them out. Even the ex-pugilist night porter, with a several times broken nose and only two cauliflower ears, has made himself scarce.

"My name is Caroline Helstone, the Hotel manager." She was just about to go off duty when all this nonsense blew up and, as yet, she has not found anyone to blame.

"Sir Godwyn Lydate," He announces and bows slightly from the waist in the manner of a high ranking German Baron of the 1890s. No doubt an advisor to the Kaiser after the dismissal of Bismarck. This man effortlessly exudes power as he looks her over and, fancifully, she thinks she might as well be naked. She has checked: he is someone mysteriously important at the very heart of Government. In no uncertain terms she has been ordered to fully cooperate. Standing next to the handsome chauffeur is a smallish woman in an inappropriately sensuous, much creased silk dress. The elfin face is vaguely familiar; a most intense and disconcerting stare.

"This is all most unfortunate." Caroline needs to assert her somewhat battered temporary authority. Sir Godwyn is making no bones about eyeing up the spectacular cleavage but she would expect nothing less. "Most unfortunate." She needlessly adds, not meeting any eyes.

"Indeed."

"Your…" She hesitates as well she might. "…young lady arranged for a medical man." Under protest she doesn't say… very much under protest. She will have to make sure that human punch bag of a night porter doesn't blab. She will not have her temporary authority undermined any further… no indeed. She might have to buy his silence in kind. It would not be the first time she has bought silence in kind…no indeed.

Sir Godwyn almost smiles benignly at Helen Huntingdon, the young lady in question, who really is a one-off. "His verdict?" He asks.

"Heart attack." Helen makes him aware that there are things unspoken for his ears only.

He realises that Caroline Helstone is the sort of person so often, mistakenly, overlooked in the scheme of things; who then impose themselves indiscriminately. This stocky, busty, muscular woman could be formidable in the right or wrong circumstances. There needs to be more cleavage control – the nuclear option should always be a last resort.

"The Police must be informed, Sir Godwyn."

There she goes. "I do not think there will be any need for that, my dear."

Caroline Helstone is acutely aware that there is a dire threat in the ensuing silence. She is only too well aware of the sweat under her arms. "The Police must be informed. It is Company policy." So that's that, threat or no threat. Put that in your pipe and smoke it Mister Southern big shot.

"Caroline. May I call you Caroline?" The cleavage contents actually heave, but Sir Godwyn will not be distracted with Helen looking on.

"I suppose so." He takes possession of a cushioned elbow and steers the heaving cleavage towards her cubby hole of an office. Caroline Helstone is not sure she likes this one little bit... not one little bit. The touch of his hand is quite disturbing. He closes the office door and she is not at all sure that she likes that. It is like being shut up in a broom cupboard. She is just not sure at all. The previous time she had been shut up in a broom cupboard against her will was in the Children's home, when that awful man had done unspeakable things to the naked twelve year old Caroline.

"Caroline, my dear, we have a situation here that can go one of two ways." He articulates the ultra-posh commanding voice that brooks no interruption; she does not interrupt. "Either this situation can go spectacularly tits up." She is startled but he is looking her in the eye and no sign of anything resembling a smirk. "And I will then be forced to inform the Chairman of your Hotel Group, Sir Bernard Keeldar, who is a close personal friend." A few moments of absorbing silence. "That you have been most unhelpful." She licks exceedingly full lips. "Most unhelpful. In fact that your attitude has caused untold damage to the Keeldar Group's reputation. The share price, as you are no doubt well aware, is already vulnerable."

She was not at all aware of that and is finding it hard to breathe.

"On the other hand I can inform my good friend Sir Bernard Keeldar that you have been, shall we say, most accommodating. That in fact you are deserving of a significant promotion." He is standing so close that the scent of his aftershave is addling her senses and she blink blink blinks. "In fact it would not be going too far as to say that the flagship Hotel beckons."

"The Savoy?" She cannot stop herself whispering in awe.

"Indeed." He leans even closer, as if they are about to kiss... most disconcerting. She just stops herself puckering the rarely kissed lips. "The position of Deputy General Manager has become vacant." As of this moment in fact. He takes it as a good sign that the cleavage is once more heaving. By no means a secret weapon; the bikini atoll well named.

"Of course, Sir Godwyn, I quite agree." She is not sure to what she is agreeing but the words sound appropriate and, importantly, most accommodating.

"I thought you would, my dear. I thought you would."

"Is there anything I can do?"

"I am sure there will be, my dear." He presses an index finger to the rarely kissed lips. "It would be best if you stay in here until my return." He makes it sound like General MacArthur quitting the Philippines.

Helen Huntingdon hadn't realised that she was scarcely breathing as Sir Godwyn reappears not accompanied by the bruiser bitch. It had taken all of Helen Huntingdon's considerable talents of threat to put the chunky bitch in her place. She had thought it might come to blows. The boxer looking night porter had looked on aghast at the thought of having to break up a no holds barred cat fight.

"Come with me, Helen, my dear." He of course notices that Camilla French is unthinkingly sharing most of her personal space with Gilbert Markham. Human cupidity never ceases to amaze and delight. "It will be best if you stay out of this, Camilla, my dear. Wait here with Gilbert." Something tells him this will not be a hardship.

As soon as the lift doors close, Sir Godwyn sweeps Helen Huntingdon into his arms and they delight in a most deep seated kiss.

In the lobby Gilbert Markham steers a willing Camilla French to the bar area where someone has forgotten to lock the bar grille. "I need a drink."

"Me too." She perches nervously ladylike on a two seater settee, only too well aware that the much creased silk dress is shorter than she would wish, given all the circumstances.

"What's your poison?" He never ever says what's your poison.

"A small brandy please."

Two large brandies in hand he arranges himself next to Camilla on the two seater settee, not too close and not quite touching.

"Cheers."

"Cheers."

Neither of them is quite sure of the next line although Gilbert Markham knows what he would like to say. Feeling the warmth of the brandy whirling in the pit of her stomach it is Camilla French who puts her courage to the sticking place.

"I didn't properly thank you for being so kind to me yesterday, Gilbert." She had impulsively kissed him on the cheek when he dropped her back at her apartment in the late afternoon. Some might have thought that was thanks enough.

"Gil. Please."

"You were so patient and understanding that it made the whole thing so much less of an ordeal." She smiles wanly. "It must have been so boring for you... Gil."

"It was certainly not boring." Just like Camilla's, his voice bears traces of his North West upbringing. "You are a beautiful woman and it was a privilege to see you being transformed."

She sips more brandy. "The ugly duckling turning into a swan."

"You were always a swan."

"Oh! Gil. You're so sweet." She kisses him on the same cheek and offers a vagrant grin that makes something definitely lurch.

"I caught a glimpse of your undies when you were trying on dresses." He knows she knows because their eyes had met in the reflecting mirrors, her mother's advice concerning bottoms proving opportune.

"That weird curly orange haired girl has christened me old iron knickers." The warmth of the brandy is deliciously spreading.

Gilbert Markham gulps more brandy. "From what I could see I would have christened you sexy knickers."

A very much rosy cheeked Camilla French studies the lees of the brandy swirling in the balloon glass. It is quite wonderfully disconcerting to be sharing brandies with such an inordinately attractive man at this time and in this place. A man who is treating her as a woman and nothing else. No apparent subtext... no apparent hidden agenda... he just wants to get in her sexy knickers.

She knows she has to say something in case he thinks he has gone too far. She finishes the brandy, sets aside her balloon glass, takes the other balloon glass from his hand and finishes that brandy as well, before setting his glass aside.

Then she takes deliberate possession of both of his strong fierce hands and edges closer. "I think, Gil, that that is probably the nicest thing anyone has ever said to me." She smiles somewhat crookedly and, taking them both by surprise, kisses Gil full on the lips.

Sir Godwyn Lydate and Helen Huntingdon are standing hand in hand like naughty children, staring down at the wretchedly naked body of the very much late Maria Branwell.

"This is how she was found?"

Helen nods. "The dress and bra bundled on the floor. No knickers or tights in the room."

"Strange." He leans closer to the dead body. "Very strange." There are what appears, from his wide experience, to be dried semen stains slugging the inner thighs. A well-built woman but everything in the right proportion. A recent Brazilian wax... such a waste.

"As you can see there has been recent sexual activity." She sounds disapproving.

"So I do indeed see." He dry lip twitches. This girl really is a delight of pretence as in everything else. "But not Perceval minor?"

"He was in bed with the woman's friend all afternoon, then the run through and then at dinner afterwards, where he made a prat of himself with the Producer's prat of a wife. So no, not him." She sounds disappointed.

They both study the fading bite marks visibly flowering the substantial breasts like fading autumn blooms. Helen cannot help but be envious of the substantial children's birthday party blancmangey breasts... except of course the poor woman is dead. "It looks like they got a bit carried away." She squeezes his hand. They both know all about getting carried away. They cannot be in the same room without needing to touch. In the bedroom the need is everything but it is never quite enough... that is the unspoken dilemma.

"Indeed." He squeezes back.

"Her friend said she had, in her words, a dicky heart."

"How has the friend taken the news?"

"She was more concerned with comforting the blubbering moron." They ponder the existence of the blubbering moron, and of what use his existence serves in the grand scheme of things, before coming to the same conclusion.

"I must arrange things with the manager woman." It will do no harm to pretend he has forgotten Caroline Helstone's name. "This will become the two women's room and their room will become Perceval's room. The friend will return to this room in the morning after a night of illicit passion and shock horror discover the body." The fingers are now tightly entwined. "The poor woman passed away peacefully in her sleep. Such a pity. No one to blame."

"What about the recent sexual activity?"

"Clean her up, my dear. No one needs to know, least of all the grieving husband."

"And cover her up." The substantial blancmangey breasts are beginning to get on Helen's nerves. She was never invited to any children's birthday parties after that first time. The word got round and so blancmange was a no no for Helen.

Meanwhile Caroline Helstone is staring wide eyed at her square, some might cruelly say, manly hands resting lumpily on the small desk, which takes up most of the space in the claustrophobic room. A vodka bottle secreted in the bottom drawer the nearest thing she has ever got to a trousseau. The office is definitely more of a cubby hole, a place of transit like her life so far. She is waiting patiently for that man to return. Patience has had to become one of her virtues; she is not sure she has any other virtues. They were buried along with her memories of the sex abuse at the Children's home. She was always thankful she was not one of the pretty ones because they rarely, if ever, moved on from the abuse.

Now she is beyond tired and knows she will not sleep; the sleeping pills are useless and she has been so damned tired recently, knowing that her temporary job is forever under threat. The Regional Manager hates her guts, even though she let him slap her around during sex, and even that didn't work. He hasn't spoken to her since slamming out of her bedroom on the top floor as if she was the deviant. There is something inherently disturbing about Sir Godwyn, whose rich aftershave scent lingers in the claustrophobic atmosphere. She pretends she has made the choice to leave everything in his hands, as it makes her feel marginally less of a failure, which is probably as good as it gets. Failure is the word she is fighting a losing battle to keep out of her thoughts, forever on the periphery. Caroline knows she is incredibly needy and dares not show it and thus comes across as a bit of a harridan. She knows she shows far too much cleavage that is not a big enough asset to keep a man – the one-night stands rarely morphing into two-night stands. The hour of misaligned sex with the pervy Regional Manager not even morphing into a two hour stand.

She is certainly no looker, with squat somewhat rounded figure, but she is incredibly willing. Staring at her squat hands she is only too acutely aware that she has always been a tall beautiful woman trapped in the wrong body… although that tall beautiful woman would certainly not have survived the Children's home. The pretty ones were foully abused, often by several men at a time, and usually had their first abortions at twelve or thirteen and invariably ended up as druggies on the Game. For as long as she can remember she has been a crypto feminist. Her childhood heroine was the suffragette who died under the King's horse at the Derby…Emily something or other. She always daydreamed of doing something as brave and noble and historic. She likes to pretend that she doesn't need men… not that men show much of an interest anyway. Even in the Children's home she was only abused if no one else was available. In recent times she has had to make it blatantly obvious that she is available, and even has a schoolgirl crush on that pathetic barman with the forged references.

Something has gone badly wrong somewhere – something has come unstuck. She opens the bottom drawer and glugs Asda own brand vodka. It helps. Secreting the bottle she places the square hands firmly in her capacious lap as she gazes at the closed door. Perhaps Sir Godwyn Lydate will prove to be a real life Merlin the Magician; after all, he has made a life changing promise. Since when do men keep life changing promises to women like Caroline Helstone? Never, that's when. She scratches the finger where she once wore a cheap engagement ring that didn't fool anyone – incredibly willing doesn't take a girl very far at all.

She is thinking about another glug of vodka, and why not, when the door opens and there is Merlin very much in the flesh as he squeezes round the desk, perches on the corner, almost touching with the free swinging leg. From up there he will have a spectacular view of the off piste alpine slopes.

In that ultra-posh commanding, yet caressing, voice he comprehensively explains what needs to happen and she, of course, agrees. She can even manage one of those toothsome smiles that are disturbingly reminiscent of some long forgotten memory.

"I will contact my good friend Sir Bernard Keeldar in the morning, my dear." He checks the impressive antique Rolex. "Or should I say later this morning."

She possesses a surprisingly summery, if somewhat toothy, smile. He does so relish a work in progress. Almost Rodin with a block of marble – almost – one should not get carried away.

"Did you really mean what you said?" She asks and, much to her surprise, he retrieves one of the square hands out of the capacious lap.

"You have been most helpful, my dear and I am resolved to take care of you." It is so unexpected. No one has taken care of Caroline since her parents were killed when she was nine years old; there are tears in her eyes. It has all been too much. She blink blinks.

If it is not her imagination, a little finger is caressing the lined palm of the square hand; the ring hand once upon a brief time. She has always dreamed of owning delicate hands like that pretty Receptionist who is always making sheep's eyes at the pathetic barman... Emily something or other.

"I don't know how to thank you." The cleavage is most susceptibly heaving.

"I will most assuredly think of something, my dear Caroline." She knows she is now in his power and she doesn't care. There can be no power as absolute as that experienced by those vulnerable children at the Children's home.

"You will need to finalise things here, my dear."

"That won't take long."

All she owns in the world doesn't take up much space in the spartan two rooms on the top floor, which comes with the job. All she possesses in the world will fill a medium-sized suitcase.

"You have a really ennervating smile, Caroline, my dear." She blushes – she never ever blushes. "I will arrange your accommodation in London." For several more audible heartbeats he keeps hold of the square hand. "I have been thinking, Caroline." He knows he would have made an excellent Louis XIV plucking, say, a washerwoman from obscurity just for the hell of it. "I might have a much more important job for you than mere hotel work." Except that the real Louis XIV only went on looks. Such a short-sighted policy.

She doesn't believe you can dismiss Deputy General Manager of the actual Savoy Hotel as mere hotel work but says nothing, only too well aware that she is prone to say the wrong thing, make the wrong move, snatching at absurdities as if they are life belts. Sometimes a bit of a bull in a china shop and sometimes a lot of a bull in a china shop. Discretion rarely if ever getting the better part of valour.

"Is there a man in the picture, my dear?" He is admiring the cleavage as if it is a work of art on which he might bid if the price is right. Instead of saying mind your own business you nosy sod and stop staring at my tits, she emphatically shakes her head. "A woman?" She even more emphatically shakes her head and toothily smiles. She has smiled more in the last few minutes than in the previous six months, and each succeeding smile is less and less disturbingly reminiscent. "So nothing to keep you here. I have great plans for you, my dear."

She gives off an enticing perfume that is hard to categorise.

"What plans?" She has unearthed a voice of sorts and not a question that can upset anyone…surely?

He is loosely holding the hand which she could reclaim at any time. "Now that would be telling, my dear." He has compelling almost hypnotic azure blue eyes that you might believe could see into your soul. She hopes not… it is a very private place although perhaps there are no private places any more. There were most definitely no private places at the Children's home and a distinct absence of soul.

"I will send for you in a few days and then we shall see what we shall see." He old-fashionedly kisses the loosely held hand and then he is gone, leaving in his wake the heady scents of the aftershave as his mark. Caroline Helstone pinches herself and it bloody hurts. She is definitely not dreaming.

She holds the kissed hand to her burning cheek. She will take the remains of the vodka and retire to her meagre two rooms to indulge in a lovely sensuous bubble bath, her other illicit pleasure. That is what she will do… a lovely sensuous bubble bath… just the thing for tingly nipples and tingly other things as well. She even smiles to herself at the thought that the ex-bruiser night porter, George Edmonds, will probably need to be paid in kind. He will be a vast improvement on the creepy Regional Manager who can now go and fuck himself. She smiles even toothier – it wasn't her fault the creep couldn't keep it up. A little bird tells her that George will definitely be able to keep it up.

Sir Godwyn strides across the silent hotel lobby and passes two overnight cases side by side like the unclaimed baggage of an airport luggage carousel. The night porter dodges out of sight knowing when to make himself scarce. At the edge of the bar area Sir Godwyn pauses and takes in the unexpected tableau a deux. Not something he expected to have to take in at this stage of proceedings – the best laid plans of mice and men and all that. Camilla French is perched on Gilbert Markham's lap and some very intense necking is taking place, with Gilbert's free hand caressing a bare lilywhite thigh above the visible stocking top – a most tantalising and thought-provoking situation.

Sir Godwyn coughs into his hand. Nothing. He coughs louder – then louder still. They adjust the clinch and stare at him with dazed expressions on faces swollen in the shadows. Stare, would you believe, as if he is intruding. The caressing hand remains trapped in the cleft of lilywhite thighs. There is no use crying over spilled milk – he never does cry over spilled milk. He goes as close as seems polite in the circumstances and drops a room key card on the table. "It might be advisable, my dears, to take yourselves to this bedroom tout de suite." A dry lip twitch and he strides away and cannot resist glancing back to see that they are necking even more frantically; something tells him they are not going to make it to the bedroom in time. Picking up his own overnight case he crosses hurriedly to the lift, wondering if the time is right to make his own plunge into the unknown, in the manner of Camilla French. Nanny Linda has been nagging recently that he must get married and have children to carry on the dynasty – she calls it a dynasty. She says he is not getting any younger and Lydate Hall needs the pitter patter of tiny feet. Despite past experiences she has always been a bit of a romantic. Perhaps he should give in to the inevitable. He is indeed not as young as he used to be. He would not wish to give up his ladies – that would be too much to ask. He might have to be even more circumspect than usual. Albany would be off bounds to Lady Lydate. The bedroom door is slightly ajar and Helen is expectantly naked on the bed, grinning that off kilter promissory grin that makes his excuse for a heart almost flip.

The curly ginger wig is on its stand and she is ostentatiously sucking a finger. "I started without you." Making her intentions absolutely clear, there are three condoms neatly arranged on the bedside table.

Locking the door he rapidly undresses and then takes her in his arms on top of the covers. Always, like that first time that took them both by surprise, they must look at each other and touch each other. There is not a hair on her body. He kisses the smooth scalp and she always coos at their secret shared. Then he, newborn baby fashion, suckles each of the blush pink nipples.

She road tests the rock hard erection through practised fingers; that first time he had very messily prematurely ejaculated at this point and she learned from that mistake. She is not to know that it was a tremendous compliment, that the only previous time it had happened was the first time with the Headmaster's much younger Scottish wife at Eton. Although he had more than made up for it later that balmy afternoon, and on many other afternoons and on one memorable weekend in Dunoon…it was not as easy to meet up after the baby was born.

For some reason, tonight he is even more eager than usual, far too eager for overmuch foreplay and as he reaches to the bedside table for a condom his fingers are uncoordinated.

"You're in a hurry tonight, Goddy." She suppresses a giggle. "Let me do that." She expertly rolls on the condom. She doesn't like mess although she has sometimes made an exception for Goddy. With the stronger medication she has been advised the pill doesn't always work. She is an old-fashioned girl…that sort of Russian roulette is for the marriage bed.

"I want you, sweet girl."

"I want you, Goddy." In the bedroom he is Goddy.

They are both telling the truth for once. Well, at least the truth of the moment, the most beguiling truth of all. Montaigne said there is no other truth.

In the adjoining bedroom behind locked connecting doors, the stiffening covered up to the chin corpse of Maria Branwell is oblivious to the unmistakable noises of passionate lovemaking. Noises that go on for longer than she would deem strictly necessary if she was able to hear. Then, when after a brief pause the noises start-up again and the bed head bang bangs against the wall, she would be truly shocked… the invasion of Sicily followed immediately by the invasion of Normandy. But then oblivion is just that – the word brooks no argument.

Four floors above, John Everson is sitting up in bed in their water damaged hotel bedroom. He is hugging his knees and wishing he had the courage to make a run for it…it would not be the first time he had lacked the courage to make a run for it.

Sheets and pillows have been borrowed from an unlocked store room and the lovely, to her own eyes in the mirror Emily, is stroking up and down his knobbly backbone. They have not made love and she wants to make love.

"John, lovie, it was not your fault. You were not to blame."

He wishes she would just shut up and go to sleep and stop repeating the same stupid thing over and over again. As far as she is concerned he came to Reception to beg the pass key to Spencer Perceval's room… the stupid old biddy had had a stupid heart attack. Emily agreed the body should be dumped in the little shit's room – a brilliant getting them off the hook plan. The last thing she wanted was to see the dead body. No. No. Thank you very much.

The only fly in the ointment, more a bluebottle really, is that Emily doesn't know and must never never never know about the tell-tale bodily secretions. John really is a fool to himself. He should have used a condom. What if they test every man in the hotel? It doesn't bear thinking about. He shivers and gives off a salty moan. He is so wound up he half expects the Police to arrive mob handed at any moment and burst the door down. The building is so quiet this time in the morning. Too damn quiet if the truth be known – the truth must never be known.

"John, lovie." She is beginning to get exasperated. "You are not to blame. It wasn't your fault the old biddy got pissed out of her skull." Which is true. "If anyone it was that Spencer Perceval's fault." Which is also true. "Let him sort it out. Come here, silly boy."

He allows himself to be gathered in her lovely smooth arms and lovely smooth legs and lovely smooth everything else. She would not want to gather him in her lovely smooth arms and lovely smooth legs and lovely smooth everything else if she knew about the bodily secretions. She must never know. Never. Never. Ever.

She presses him protectively against the lovely squashy breasts and is not to know that he has often fantasised about the no doubt even squashier breasts of Grupenfuerer Caroline Helstone. These squashy breasts are more than adequate as squashy breasts go.

He just hopes that making love to Emily will not be an anti-climax.

"That's more like it, lovie." A relieved Emily whispers a wet kipper kiss. "I want you." She murmurs. He is not the sort of man to realise that the poor deluded girl might actually want something else entirely.

Three floors below, Spencer Perceval is scared out of his wits. He has never seen a dead person and never touched a dead person. The awful thing is that at first when he entered the bedroom he thought the naked woman wanted a piece of the action. She couldn't be blamed for that. "Hi, babe." He had burbled, trying to remember where he had hidden the bottle of whisky. "Great tits, babe."

It was only when he gave a welcoming squeeze to one of the great tits that he realised something was not quite right. The flesh was chilled and when he properly focused he realised the mouth was slack and the lifeless eyes were staring unblinking at the ceiling.

The scream had been silent but no more heartfelt for that. Screw loose will never fucking believe him was his first thought; they will never fucking believe him was his second thought. This is it, he had thought. This is fucking it.

Now he cuddles from behind the cushiony warm backside of Harriet O'Connor, who is gurgling snoring. His arms just about encircle the considerable breasts. Screw loose had said she would sort it out and with Screw loose he has to believe that these things stay sorted.

He must stop thinking about it and get some sleep. He cannot function on too little sleep, as the events of today have proved. As soon as Screw loose had gone he had made love to Harriet and vice versa. It had been soon over, but very nice, and they had clung to each other for a long time afterwards. He had whispered he was sorry and she had whispered she was sorry. Although what she was sorry about he was not at all sure.

She had stroked his face and he had kissed her nose. He called her Harry and she had liked that. Some gentle kissing and then she had turned over and gone to sleep. Soon his rattling snores mingle with Harriet's gurgling snores, as in sleep that knits up the ravelled sleeve of care, he cuddles closer. In her sleep she smiles and presses back.

Thursday 19th October 5.47am

In bed in the Grande suite of the Savoy Hotel, notes of the state of the nation novel propped against his knees, a wakeful Jack sucks the Exhibition pen. This is not at all what he intended. The death of that poor woman has led to a wall-to-wall lovefest. He had intended that the Police should be involved – after all, it is a suspicious death. The contemptible John Everson had taken advantage of the drunken woman – not to beat about the bush, it had been statutory rape and the heart attack a direct result – manslaughter at the very least. Jack would have liked to see the perpetrator grilled by that bastard Chief Inspector Stephen Guest, who had not been able to keep his ill assorted eyes off Jack's bloody sister in Court.

The abandoned behaviour of supposedly prim and proper Camilla French has also rather taken his breath away. At least at this moment she is in an actual bed safely ensconced in the muscled, tattooed arms of Gilbert Markham and is free at last of the intrusive suspender belt and everything else. At least their second and third delirious comings together were not spied on by the broken nosed, cauliflower eared night porter. Jack sighs… something tells him we have no doubt not heard the last of the night porter…the archetypal walk on part one might think. One could, of course, be wrong.

Jack is only too well aware that the precipitate actions of Sir Godwyn Lydate will deny justice to that poor silly woman. Her presence is already fading from these pages, unlike the presence of the tenaciously half-baked Helen Huntingdon who had been meant to fade from these pages.

She could well be a uniquely restraining influence making Sir Godwyn even more formidable – not a pretty thought. Samson- willed Harriet O'Connor was also meant to fade from these pages. Unfortunately she has the potential to be the saving of Spencer Perceval from himself… not that he knows it yet.

Jack is going to be extremely careful about walk on parts from now on but of course the damage is done. Shirley Keeldar mumbles in her sleep and, in the here and now, Jack puts the pen and notepad to one side and enacts his own spoony shaping to the generous curves of this particular most shapely warm backside. She mumbles some more and his last thoughts before dozing off are to wonder if he can somehow conjure Chief Inspector Stephen Guest into action. Although there is no way he wants to get on the wrong side of Sir Godwyn Lydate… not to mention the formidable Harriet O'Connor. This book writing stuff is fraught with all kinds of difficulties.

Thursday 19th October 7.17am

The lovely mirrored Emily has kissed John Everson awake. He has slept surprisingly well considering.

"I need to be getting up, lovie."

Nevertheless she holds him tight as he yawns and coughs and the squashy breasts have it, as he subdues a wayward thought of the Reich Fuhrer's cleavage. He is relieved that he has woken with his usual mountainous hard on. Thank God for that. Things are back to normal.

"There is no time, lovie." She doesn't sound all that convincing – not being a spiritual sort of girl.

"There is always time." He is feeling much more his old self, like yesterday was only a bad dream. It's the last time he does a favour like that, he decides, as Emily takes possession of the hard on.

"We will have to be quick, lovie." They are never usually quick – they will be this morning.

Thursday 19th October 7.23am

Spencer Perceval wishes he could stay here forever and ever amen, safe in the arms of the not at all ghostly Harriet O'Connor. She has kissed him awake and part of him wishes that she hadn't; he is no sleeping beauty. She is gently caressing his floppy hair which is all very pleasant. He doesn't know what to say… he doesn't know what to do… he doesn't know what to think.

"I'm really really scared, Harry." Is what he does manage to spit out and she kisses the tip of his nose.

"Don't be silly, pet. I'm here." And she is most definitely here, solid and fleshy and incredibly desirable in a solid and fleshy way. The considerable breasts, quivering every time she breathes, giving a whole new meaning. She is more here than he has any right to expect or deserve and, to give him his due, he does dimly realise this fact.

"I don't know how she got in my room."

Harriet O'Connor is now cradling his head in her expressive hands. "Don't cry, you silly boy."

She kisses and kisses his ready tears, tasting the salt and licking her lips. "I believe you." These are words he never expected to hear from anyone ever again. Her fond gaze momentarily hardens. "She always was a jealous cow. She was after you to spite me." She doesn't care to think such behaviour was totally out of character. Spencer is not at all sure he would like to get on the wrong side of Harriet O'Connor. She is one of the few women he has ever met who could take on his wife in a fair fight and most probably slog out a draw.

"I wouldn't have done anything."

"I know that." She kisses and kisses his blubbery salty lips. "She got what she deserved." To tell the truth he is not really sure about that. "I will take care of you, Spencer."

"Will you really?" He really really wants to be sure about that, wants all the nasty stuff just to go away just like it did when he was a spoiled child.

"We have something special, Spencer, pet."

"We do. We do." Neither of them has awareness of the ridiculous, which is just as well.

"Nothing and no one will come between us, pet." It doesn't seem appropriate to point out that they are both married to other people. He is not really a details person. He is not to know that Harriet O'Connor always gets what she wants and gets rid of what she doesn't want, as her philandering third husband will soon find out.

"Nothing. Nothing."

This time the kisses are more lingering and she instigates tongues. He is not sure he is really in the mood and winces as she bites his neck.

"You think we have time, Harry?" The lost schoolboy voice that tugs at the linings of her stomach. He really needs to get some backbone, although she has enough backbone for a first eleven of Spencer Percevals.

"There is always time, Spencer, pet."

"I want you, Harry."

"You've got me, pet." As she goes on to prove it he totally forgets about not being really in the mood. Carrie Brattle might never have existed.

Thursday 19th October 7.38am

Goddy is adeptly soaping up a giggling, but not too much, Helen Huntingdon immersed in the tepid bath that they are most definitely sharing.

"I'm going to have the cleanest tits in the world." She giggles, but not too much, and snuggling back against his body inside the safe harbour of his clenching thighs, she turns her head and they kiss.

"Did you mean what you said earlier?" She whispers somewhat huskily, as he is now soaping between her legs.

"I said so many things earlier, my sweet." They spear with tongues.

She breaks off. "I don't mean all that rude stuff." She giggles but not too much. "Although that was goodly goodest."

"I meant it." He presses his chin into a shoulder cleft. "You haven't said yes." He licks a soapy earlobe and then licks the bald skull.

"I am giving your proposition due consideration."

"Cheeky madam." He weighs the wet and glistening breasts with his wet hands and is not sure... not at all sure. Unfortunately a pregnant Jayne Peel is not a possibility, and somehow this deliciously naked creature, despite all her perverse mental absurdities, has also sneaked under his radar.

"Well?" There is so much he doesn't know and so much she has never revealed. He does know that if it can possibly be avoided, he does not want to risk losing this gloriously insane girl from his busy schedule. "Well?" There could of course be another way.

"Are you really sure, Goddy?"

Of course not. "Absolutely."

"But why me?"

"I wish I knew, my sweet girl. I wish I knew." Because neither Nanny's first choice nor pregnant Jayne Peel are available, he does not say.

She presses her trim bottom backwards and elicits the correct response. "I do love being your sweet girl." She turns her head and their close eyes meet. "It would not be easy, Goddy." She has few illusions. She is not sure either... not at all sure.

"Nothing worth having is ever easy, my sweet girl."

"That's just words, Goddy and you know it."

She is weighing it up, knowing all about his weakness for women and their weakness for him because, after all, she is one of those weaknesses. She knows he will not change and she would not want him to change. Two weekends ago at Lydate Hall, Nanny Linda confided so much during their unexpected exchanges on the circular bench at the base of the famous kissing tree. It had been a disconcerting weekend. Nanny Linda is still a handsome woman and Helen had not needed to ask if they were still occasional lovers; she knows Nanny Linda appreciates discretion. Nanny had said it was time he was married. Time for an undisputed heir and spare for the Lydate dynasty.

Nanny Linda had said he needs a wife who can take what is available and not grieve over what is not available. She had taken hold of Helen's hand and had whispered, although there was no one to overhear – he needs a wife who is able come to terms with all that he cannot give. Then she had squeezed the hand and said something rather unexpected – the wife must be out of a unique mould and must be unbreakable.

"The answer is yes, Goddy." She hears herself say from a long way away.

"My sweet girl." He actually sounds relieved that the decision has been taken out of his hands. She knows full well it is not a love match in the traditional sense and, if it was, she would be scared out of her remaining wits. It is very all sorts of nice things, though. There is the touching which is nicest of all...only there is not enough of that. Perhaps there is not enough of anything. Perhaps she should have asked for more time because there is oodles of that.

Then of course there is Lydate Hall which will pass down to her son. She has no doubt she will have a son. She even knows his name and his pet name, which she alone will use.

They dry each other on the big fluffy hotel towels and go back to bed. This time there is rather a lot of mess – the old-fashioned girl not so old fashioned after all.

Thursday 19th October 8.06am

The former call me Jack is standing at the picture window of the Grande suite at the Savoy Hotel rubbing his chin and pondering ponderingly. He has ordered omelette à la Arnold Bennett for two and is waiting on room service. Unfortunately, a running late Shirley Keeldar has rushed off to a breakfast meeting at the American Embassy – a meeting she had pretended to have forgotten. There are concerns about security for Jack's forthcoming trip to the United States. The First Lady wishes to meet Jack.

Shirley had explained that the Ambassador is a close personal friend of Shirley and, of course, is acquainted with Sir Bernard.

There is no matchstick girl, or matchstick boy for that matter, to draw Jack's attention from the pondering. There are lots of matchstick people going about their daily goings about. He has never felt so remote from other people's ideas of reality, not even when he was enmeshed in his most far-fetched Heath Robinson daydreams. He greets the feeling of remoteness as an old and trusted friend.

There is a knock at the door not as tentative as might be expected. "Come in."

He is aware of the clattering of the trolley but does not look round. According to Amelia Sedley it is what famous people do – ignore the help unless it is being fired. Sometimes Jack thinks that might be a fatal mistake.

"Will there be anything else, Mr Bellingham?" He recognises the voice and turns on his heel to see the busty waitress who so annoyed Lady Rebecca Sharp.

He is puzzled. Now that he looks closely she is an organically lovely girl endeavouring to be merely every day pretty. Auburn hair tied in a severe ponytail, no visible make up and everything most shapely under the deliberately ill-fitting waitress uniform. In her turn she is watching with eyes far too observant.

All this he computes in the quick glance of the voyeuristic secret daydreamer. As if embarrassed she looks down, it might be thought shyly at her clumpy shoes. He walks across the deep pile carpet until they are only a few feet apart. No scents of perfume.

"What is your name?"

"Jane Fennell, sir." She is apparently fascinated by the awful clumpy shoes. "No Y in Jane."

He decides to test out his new found Superhero status just for the hell of it. There must surely be prescribed limits even for Masters of the Universe.

"What else would you suggest, Jane no Y Fennell?"

Now she does make eye contact and he cannot make up his mind whether she is amused or not, her eyes a nameless shade of dark blue give nothing away. Not that it matters.

"What did you have in mind, sir?"

He is not at all sure. She does not appear to be the least bit discomfited and he takes back the shy. "My friends call me Jack." The ultimate in deluded chat up lines one might think.

"Do they?" She is not at any kind of disadvantage and he has every right to be as intrigued as she intends.

"Why don't you join me for breakfast?" He looks pointedly at the trolley. There are two settings.

"I would lose my job." No sir he notices… that didn't last long. She is coyly circling a toe of an awful clumpy shoe and it is patently obvious that she is not at all used to awful clumpy shoes.

"Sit down, Jane no Y fennel. We both know you are not a genuine waitress." That is much better…much more masterly.

"Can we drop the no bloody Y thing?" A posh unwaitressy voice.

"Please sit down." She shrugs – whatever – and sits down and glances at the chunky watch on a slim wrist…it has stopped…some props are just bloody useless.

"Who are you?"

"Can't you guess?" She has a deep dark blue eyed stare that could, on a good day, out stare a green eyed yellow Idol on the road to Kathmandu.

"I know you are spying on me."

"Why on earth would I spy on you?" A very posh voice indeed.

"You tell me." He moves to the trolley and sweeps the covers off the plates. The plate that was intended for a supposedly forgetful Shirley Keeldar, he puts on the table in front of Jane Fennel, and pours some coffee. Then he sits down at the far end of the settee and begins to eat. Within a few seconds she follows suit. She is actually quite hungry and the aromas of the omelettes had been tummy rumblingly enticing. She butters a slice of toast, sips black coffee and feels it is only polite to comment. "This omelette a la Arnold Bennett is delicious." It is all she can do to stop herself laughing out loud and that would never do. Inappropriate laughter at mealtimes was a leg slapping offence at boarding school.

"A signature dish of the Savoy." He cannot stop himself bragging.

"I know." She would know of course, and is eating hungrily but elegantly. Not eating elegantly was also a leg slapping offence at boarding school. "Anna of the Five Towns is one of my favourite novels." More wholemeal toast nibbling putting him in his place.

"Where is the Honourable Lady Rebecca Sharp this morning?" She executes a demi-Royal wave of the fork. "Not lurking in your bed I hope." Jane would not be at all surprised. Lady Rebecca is not a girl to lose any opportunity to open her legs. She was legendary at school even after she had been expelled – an expulsion that led to the resignation of three teachers and the suicide of another.

"No. My bed is empty." He does that sideways smile. On someone other than a People's hero it would appear even creepier.

"Who was the breakfast intended for?" She knows that Lady Keeldar left in a scent scattering hurry. Jane had wondered if there had been a threesome. Not that she has anything against threesomes, although she is not really a threesome morning person.

"Wouldn't you like to know?"

"No, not really." She resumes elegantly eating without a care in the world. She is going to have to formulate some response to this unexpected turn of events and it had better be good. It will be. Unexpected is her middle name she likes to think.

"Is Jane Fennell your real name?"

She deigns a withering look and it most definitely works. "Of course." She nibbles wholemeal toast. "The Honourable Lady Jane Fennell actually." Another demi-Royal wave of the fork. "Lady Rebecca didn't recognise me without make-up." A demi-Royal pause. "And of course wearing this awful outfit."

"Did you go to the same school?"

"Two years below actually." She pat pats the corners of her mouth with the voluminous napkin and smiles condescendingly. "And I wasn't expelled either." More pat patting at the corners of her mouth. "I could tell you a thing or three about that unladylike lady."

"She doesn't like me."

A thinking about getting pregnant pause follows, as Jane is actually thrown and gazes at him with renewed interest. She does so like to be surprised by men and, somehow, it is the most unexpected men who surprise the most. She does not yet realise that call me Jack is probably the most surprising man she is ever likely to meet, or that sometimes surprises can be very nasty indeed.

"Really. You are actually sort of cute in a far out kind of way. Great ears." She sips black coffee and nibbles wholemeal toast. "You have certainly got Sir Godwyn Lydate on the back foot." She puts down the china cup on the china saucer without any hint of a rattle – breeding will out. "Oops. Me and my naughty mouth." She suggestively licks her noticeably enhanced lips. "By the way if I were you I would steer well clear of the yid bitch." No names. No pack drill.

She sits back very much at her ease crossing her legs more like a fashion model than a waitress. There is a deliberate snagged ladder in the black tights – the devil is in the detail. "She is bad news."

"She came on to me."

"I know, I was there."

He on purpose slurps the lukewarm coffee and considers consideringly.

"So tell me, my friend Jack, how are things so far?"

"Confusing." He on purpose slurps more lukewarm coffee. "Very confusing."

"You need to be choosy about the company you keep."

"Anyone else I should steer clear of?"

She stares appraisingly; the sticky out ears are definitely sort of cute. "The real question is who you should not stay clear of." She smooths down the awful uniform which crinkles noisily over her slender thighs. "The utterly gorgeous Lady Shirley Keeldar is well known for picking up, using, and then discarding unsuitable men."

"Do you see me as unsuitable?"

The deep dark blue eyed appraisal is surprisingly thorough, almost as if she is studying a portrait on an art gallery wall, at a private viewing of course, and deciding whether the colours are too garish now that the painting has been cleaned. Whether the brushstrokes etch the true meaning or more likely not. "As for Amelia Sedley, well, nuff said."

She purses her lips and studies unpainted fingernails – the devil is very much in the detail and she is sick of hearing that phrase from Sir Godwyn. Yawn. Yawn. "My friend Jack." A covert smile; her grandmother had been a Special Agent during the war behind enemy lines and all that. "This is a Jungle and you need to be a Tiger."

"Perhaps I am a Tiger."

"Perhaps you are." She works on the beginnings of an actual yawn.

"Would you like me to prove it?" He thinks about edging closer but there is something inherently intimidating about this girl. In one of his unrealistic daydreams she would be naked by now and begging for mercy. He is not to know of course that she recently crawled naked on Sir Godwyn's bed pretending to be a lioness.

"My name is not Julia Verinder."

At least he was right not to edge closer and that is something. This Masters of the Universe thing is not as easy to pull off as it might appear.

"Neither am I Lady Rebecca Sharp."

"I get the drift."

"Good." She smooths the noisy crinkly material over slender thighs. "And anyway you have a train to catch." No point in asking how she knows that. "I am most certainly not a dispenser of quick fucks." An expensive education really shows.

She purses the noticeably enhanced lips and studies her fingernails, which will be painted later on today now that her cover, such as it, is blown. At least she will not be put up against a wall and shot like Granny. She allows a clumpy shoe to drop from the foot of the tantalisingly crossed leg and flexes the foot. It is several weeks since she had congress with a foot man. Jack waits patiently for her to break the silence she has engineered and she takes her time, flexing her toes and thinking possibly rose pink or perhaps vermilion. She likes the sound of that. Vermilion – from the Latin Vermiculus…that expensive education again.

"However." The deep dark blue eyes are now appraising him without any trace of humour. "I am by no means a nun."

"Nor are you a waitress." So there.

"No indeed." She offhandedly sighs in mock regret. "I will tell you what, my good friend Jack, I will give you my phone number. How's that?"

"Thank you."

"Don't mention it." She recites the number, puts on the awful clumpy shoe and rises elegantly to her feet, taking him by surprise by squeezing her breasts together under the noisy crinkly uniform top. "Some of this is padding by the way." A wicked grin or at least what he takes to be a wicked grin – he is not an expert. "Must go. Duty calls. Time and Tide and all that." When she has gone, leaving the trolley behind, he pours out the dregs of the lukewarm coffee.

Thursday 19th October 9.08am

At the dinky kitchen bar Reverend John Eames is contentedly munching white toast and staring thoughtfully at Cecilia Hunt, who is also munching white toast just as contentedly and no less thoughtfully. The rather severe rounded spectacles lend a blithe academic glaze to her pretty face. She is wearing one of Rosalie Murray's collection of clingy dressing gowns – the one with butterfly motifs.

"You eat so sexily."He mumbles with his mouth full.

She playfully smacks his hand and waits until she has swallowed all the toast. "You are a silly bugger, Johnny." It is said without rancour. One might almost say it is said with affection. "I assume you mean eating toast?" She adds and then before he can rudely reply. "What do you want to do today, Bish?" He grins and is about to rudely reply. "Apart from that."

She sips coffee and grins over the rim of the filched House of Commons mug found at the back of a cupboard. "I am going to ration you from now on." She has to laugh at his crestfallen expression. He would be a lousy poker player. "No more than six times a day."

They both laugh. They do so like laughing together and can laugh together at the smallest thing. Sometimes they laugh together at things that are not funny at all. "That means you only have four left today."

"The second time this morning doesn't count, surely?"

"It most certainly does count, you cheeky bugger." She presses a telling finger to his lips. "I am surprised the neighbours didn't bang on the wall." The neighbours had banged on the wall in the small hours.

Retrieving her finger she tap taps the nearly empty House of Commons coffee mug against baby teeth; weirdly she has never lost her baby teeth. She is not sure how to arrange the necessary words, which is a rare occurrence. She is never usually short of the right words in any given situation.

"Johnny?" That will do for starters.

"Mmm…"

"I really like being with you, Johnny. More than with anyone." She stares into the dregs of coffee. "The sex is really brill. You've obviously had plenty of experience."

"Not really." He is not sure where this is going…Mary Thorne said exactly the same thing, only she said brilliant.

"I don't mind because I've been around the block a few times myself." She picks up the mug and swirls the coffee dregs. There is no help there.

"It's just. You know." The borrowed dressing gown is gaping open to reveal a tempting pale brown nipple. He tries to concentrate on what she is saying. She notices where he is looking and draws the dressing gown tighter. "Pay attention, you dirty bugger."

"I am. I am." He has such an infectious grin that she has to smile, and then deliberately be seen to compose herself.

"It's just. You know. This is my job." That pulls him up short. He finds it impossible to read what is going on behind the severe round spectacles. She can shut up shop whenever she chooses. He wishes he could do that. "What do you mean?"

"I am one of Sir Godwyn Lydate's people and I have been entrusted not to let you out of my sight." She winces at the hurt in his shocked face. "You knew that." It is not a question.

"Yes I suppose so." A short trousered grazed kneed schoolboy who has lost with his second best conker.

"Having said that, Johnny, I like you a lot."

"I like you a lot, Cecilia."

She reaches a cool slim hand across the table and they clasp fingers. "Actually I'm beginning to like you more than a lot." A wan smile. "And it's not just the brill sex." More stray thoughts of Mary Thorne.

"Same here."

"But we mustn't, Johnny. There is no future for us and you are going to marry Rosalie Murray. That is why you are here and that is why I am here."

"I don't want to marry Rosalie Murray."

"Johnny. Johnny. The Danegeld. Never forget the Danegeld." They are now clasping both hands as if their lives depended on it. She is not sure which one of them is treading water more than the other. The dressing gown is gaping open but he is staring at the clasped hands.

"Did Sir Godwyn Lydate tell you to sleep with me?" It has been nagging at him. He is only too fallibly human. She is also staring at their clasped hands, her eyes rapidly blinking behind the round spectacles. She knows her life has been a lie for such a long time, so whatever the consequences, she will not lie now. "Yes." A still small voice.

"I see."

"Surely you knew that." A stiller smaller hollowed out voice. "Surely?"

"I suppose so." Bang goes the prize twentyer conker.

For once he will have to take the lead role. She knows that and he knows that. There is largely untested tensile strength hewn in his character that people do not realise is there, until on all too rare occasions they unexpectedly come up against it. "You know, Cecilia, when I said I like you a lot." She stares at the white knuckles of the clasped hands. "I think I am falling in love with you." It doesn't sound the least bit stupid and that is the trouble – it doesn't sound the least bit far-fetched and that is also the trouble. She wishes that she wished it did sound far-fetched.

"I am not frightened of Sir Godwyn Lydate."

"Well you should be, Johnny."

"I want to be with you."

"I want to be with you." Is not what she intended to say. She has never felt such nameless dread and yet felt so safe in her life. Her always understanding mother would understand only too well and Cecilia is only too well aware of what her sound advice would be.

"I am not scared of a man who beats up defenceless women." She cannot shape an answer to that. "Have you slept with him?"

With only a slight hesitation she nods her head. She is staring at his face as if to remember every last detail before he goes off to the war. Carriage doors are slamming, engine steam is swirling and the whistle blowing. She wants him so badly it hurts and he is going away, perhaps forever. She wishes she understood any of this because it was never supposed to happen. She has been foolhardy and it is out of character. Out of the character she has so painstakingly fashioned. But it is not the first time.

"I don't want you to sleep with him ever again."

He doesn't know what he is asking but she nods her head. In the highly charged here and now she could almost believe anything possible. Stupid stupid tears are rolling down her cheeks and she doesn't do stupid stupid tears. Her mother had repeated the mantra that she must always stay strong. Her mother had always stayed strong, despite what happened at the Harry Hotspur club, and never indulged in stupid stupid tears.

"Cecilia, we are going to visit Staines. We are going to visit my Cathedral."

She is beginning to sob for real and how stupid is that? She snatches off the stupid round spectacles and rubs her eyes.

The Reverend John Eames, God love him, takes her in his arms and fondly kisses the tears away. "Stop it, you silly girl." He whispers and kisses more tears away. She is trying to say something as she gulps and gulps and gulps. He ever so fondly kisses away more tears and does not want to remember fondly kissing away Mary Thorne's tears, but he does remember.

"Who or what is there to be frightened of?" He holds her at arm's length. "If you say Sir Godwyn Lydate I will take you over my knee and smack your bottom."

She rubs and rubs her eyes, attempts a laugh on a sob and takes several deep breaths. "Sir Godwyn Lydate." She gasps.

Thursday 19th October 9.28am

Camilla French and Gilbert Markham are devouring full English breakfasts in the crowded hotel restaurant. There are three racks of toast on the table. "I have never been so hungry." She mutters between greedy mouthfuls.

"This sausage is delicious." He mumbles in turn.

She pauses and smiles courageously. "Not as delicious as your sausage." She is delighted and relieved that he blushes to the roots of his chestnut hair.

"Camilla!" He swallows some sausage, some eggs and some beans as he glances guiltily around the restaurant.

Now all at once unsure of her ground. She leans closer and whispers, "Was I good?"

Without any hesitation: "You were amazing."

Now it is Camilla French's turn to blush to the roots of her chestnut hair. She has never shared a shower with anyone before and most certainly never had sex in a shower. She tries not to think about the wasted years of showering on her own merely to get clean.

They eat in silence for a couple of minutes. She digests more than the food.

"Have you been with many women, Gil?" She also loves the taste of his name in her mouth.

He cuts up more sausage and bacon and doesn't meet her gaze. "Quite a few."

"I'm not surprised." She is putting a brave face on the sudden stab of ridiculous jealousy. She has no right to be jealous and she will not be jealous. She is not a silly schoolgirl with a crush. She needs to grow up; her schoolgirl crushes never went anywhere anyway. "I don't suppose Sir Godwyn is going to be too happy." She butters toast. "About us."

"He's very adaptable."

"What does that mean?" She pauses in the toast buttering.

"He will have adjusted his thinking." He stares at Camilla through eyes that have seen her vulnerable and naked in the breathless moments after lovemaking has run its course. It is a very exclusive club…only two men can say that…and one of those is dead. "He is prepared to retreat and attack from a different place; he is never beaten."

"You admire him?"

"He's been good to me." He doesn't say that he would take a bullet for Sir Godwyn, but he would.

"Will he accept us?"

Gilbert Markham doesn't like to say that there is no us or that he doesn't do relationships. She was a great shag…that's it. Hopefully there will be some more great shags where they came from. Sufficient unto the day is one of Sir Godwyn's sayings that Gilbert has taken to heart.

Talk of the Devil. "Good morning, my dears, may we join you." It is not a question.

He is arm in arm with Helen Huntingdon, who is attempting an impression of the purring cat that got all the cream in the dairy, and almost succeeding. She is dressed in a smart dark blue business suit and polka dot tights.

"Of course." Camilla waves a welcoming fork and feels acutely embarrassed and does not want to feel acutely embarrassed.

Sir Godwyn pulls out a chair for Helen and takes his seat next to her with Camilla on his other side. In the doorway the temporary manager is looking on anxiously and a waitress rushes over to take their order.

"Two full English breakfasts, my dear, with all the trimmings."

"Coffee or tea, sir?"

The waitress is a slim, exceedingly pretty girl with everything very much in the right place and Sir Godwyn holds her gaze. She has been told in no uncertain terms that he is someone very important and she must watch her p's and q's. She appears exorbitantly pretty in the waitress uniform – the Archbishop would be in seventh Heaven, or perhaps has already reached eighth Heaven. Surely hers is just a walk on part…surely? "Coffee for myself and tea for the young lady, my dear."

The slim, exceedingly, not to say, exorbitantly pretty waitress is only too well aware that she is being appraised from behind by the great man as she crosses the room. That is probably why Hitler lady is giving her a hard stare. It is by no means the first time.

Helen Huntingdon rests a possessive hand on the great man's thigh and he dry lip twitches at the insouciance of the gesture. "You look radiant this morning, my dear Camilla." She is wearing a pale blue dress that suits her colouring; those fashion ladies know their stuff.

"If I was a medical man do you know what I would prescribe for just about any illness?" Asks Sir Godwyn to the table at large but no one replies. "A cock in a hole. It works every time." Helen Huntingdon giggles, but not too much.

Camilla French, who has never felt so exposed in her life, looks at Gilbert Markham for support, but he is looking for answers in the remains of his congealing breakfast and has apparently lost what remained of his appetite.

"Gilbert?"

"Yes, Sir Godwyn." A meaningful pause.

"Have you had enough?"

"Yes, Sir Godwyn."

"Good. I've got a little job for you."

"Yes, Sir Godwyn."

"Run along now and I will text you later."

Camilla French watches her sometime demon lover depart without even a backward glance. He passes the slim, exceedingly pretty waitress with the fetching boyish haircut, as she crosses the restaurant with a tray of food. They exchange brief glances. Camilla pushes back her chair as the slim exceedingly pretty waitress hip swayingly approaches with the tray.

"Where are you going, Camilla, my dear?"

"I have finished."

"No. No. My dear. You have only just started." A dry lip twitch. "We need to talk." The slim, way beyond merely pretty waitress is putting down the tray and avoiding all and every eye contact for all she is worth…eye contacts have got her into much trouble in the past.

"Thank you, my dear, this all looks rather scrumptious." The smile doesn't reach his luminously pale blue eyes as she pours coffee and then the tea, and knowing she is under observation by the Gestapo, ignores the leggy girl's hand stroking the important man's thigh; although she does find it oddly disturbing. "I suspect nearly as scrumptious as you, my dear." He speaks ever so softly and she does a double take, meeting his gaze and discerning in his luminous pale blue hypnotic eyes that she hadn't misheard at all.

"What is your name, my dear?"

"Laura." She is unexpectedly short of breath. "Laura Standish."

"Such a lovely name." She is for the moment dismissed and crosses the restaurant with the empty tray not knowing what to think. She doesn't know if he was coming onto her or was just being an important person who always can – she has known a few of those. Not for the first time she wonders if the uniform skirt is a bit on the tight side, a bit too come and get me if you're important enough big boy.

"What did he say?" Hisses the death's head manager.

"Nothing." And Laura escapes into the kitchen. She has been propositioned many times. It is a hazard of the job. But never quite like this, that is if it was a proposition, and has never felt resultant guilty excitement quite so much. There was something behind those luminously pale blue eyes that was utterly compelling. She sidles up to the head waiter who always pretends to be hard of hearing.

"I need the toilet."

"Be quick about it, sweetheart." As usual the bald coot squeezes a handful of her bum; the girls all call him the perv and so do the boys for that matter. Locking the cubicle door she sits on the toilet to puzzle out her thoughts. She has not had a serious boyfriend for some time; although occasional one night stands… well quite a few one night stands. A girl has her requirements and men, even useless tossers, have their uses.

She checks the Mickey Mouse watch, a Christmas gift from a useless tosser, and decides she might as well have a pee seeing as she is here, and eases down black tights and 'little miss naughty' motifed panties.

As she idly wonders what turns that man on she checks between her legs… not shaved for a couple of weeks and she wonders if he likes it smooth. She needs to pull herself together but then she has needed to do that for some time.

She leans back spreading her thighs and her right index finger, almost of its own volition, strums the shell like clitoris. There has been overmuch strumming recently. Surprisingly she is nearly there…she doesn't hear the ladies' toilet door open and close. She is in her own little world imagining that man watching; those luminous pale blue eyes watching…that man unzipping his trousers and releasing the hard… she jerkily comes with several ratcheted moans and doesn't hear the ladies' toilet door open and close.

She washes her hands at the sink, thinks about washing between her legs and decides not. Studying her face in the mirror, her flushed cheeks giving a daub of colouring to her native paleness. She decides to undo one more button on the uniform blouse hinting at a cleavage. Not in the Fuhrer manager's class, but not bad. She has always been quite happy with her tits. She takes a deep breath and heads for the door. There is a spring in her step and she intends to stand close to that man. She knows that standing close to a man is something she does rather well, and cannot help wondering if he might guess.

Meanwhile, the man in question, has finished his full English breakfast and is admiring Helen Huntingdon's appetite, as she pinches a sausage from his plate and the remains of a fried egg. He sips black coffee. "You really have an appetite, my dear." It is not appropriate to call her sweet girl in company and she will certainly not call him Goddy.

"So have you." She giggles suggestively, which is as far as she dare go, and wipes her lips with the serviette and studies the resultant stains. Disapproving, Camilla French thinks it is a bit like blowing your nose and studying the resultant contents of the handkerchief – one of her Cambridge boyfriend's more annoying habits. She is not at all sure what is going on here. She does realise, of course, that these two have spent the night together…but somehow they are seeking to convince each other that it is more than that. She is not sure she wants to know. Whatever it is, will be in the interests of Sir Godwyn Lydate – that is for sure.

"Helen, my dear, off you go now and sort out that poor woman's body."

Obediently dear Helen pushes back from the table and crosses the restaurant to several appraising glances. The polka dot tights certainly make a statement.

"She really is a delightful creature." With that she is dismissed. "So, Camilla dear heart, you never cease to surprise me." He is texting whilst waiting her response.

There are several answers to this but she is not sure which one to choose, so the ball remains in his court which is what he intended. He is about to speak when she surprisingly replies against serve.

"I will never apologise for my feelings." A pause that Jack would recognise only too well. "Godwyn." She thinks he might be appraising her with new respect. She likes to think so anyway although she might be wrong. He is certainly looking at her rising and falling chest with something or other that she knows is deliberate. This is unchartered territory and stupidly, she wishes that Gil was here to hold her hand knowing that somewhere there be dragons. "Don't you have feelings?" She is beginning to sound like one of those drippy women on daytime television that she so despises. A night of unlooked for passion and she is going to pieces…she has to be better than that.

"All the time, my dear." She opens and shuts her mouth and he dry lip twitches. "As we speak, Gilbert is on his way back to London to do a little job for me." The luminously pale blue eyes are as luminously pale blue as the recent cloudless late summer afternoon she spent alone at Dedham Vale, imagining she was back in Constable's time. "Later today Helen will be accompanying the poor woman's body back to the north east and doing another little job for me." He looks off into the distance at the stunningly pretty waitress purposefully approaching with lots and lots of meaningful eye contact. Suddenly Caroline Helstone appears from stage left, grabs poor Laura's arm and steers her forcefully out of the restaurant and possibly out of this book. Sir Godwyn winces…another formidable lady with so much anger to be channelled to his advantage.

"Now where was I? Ah! Yes." There are Wagnerian ring tones. He picks up the phone and reads the text from Jane Fennell. Camilla is about to speak but he holds up a restraining hand and replies to the text. Then and only then he brings the focus back to the surprisingly attractive, in its own way, elfin face and the, not at all, elfin rising and falling chest in the pale blue dress. "You really need to grow up, Camilla." She opens and closes her mouth. "Gilbert is not the love of your life. Gilbert is not the love of anybody's life. End of." He leans forward. "You have bigger fish to fry and you know that. I will overlook last night's unfortunate episode. You got carried away. It happens to the best of us. It will do you good. End of."

She opens and closes her mouth. There is nothing to say.

"We are playing the biggest game of all, you and I. Do you want to play the biggest game of all? Do you? Do you?" He hisses. "Because if not say so now and you can take the next train back to London. Gilbert will of course be otherwise engaged." The voice is pitiless and the voice is cruel.

She swallows hard and stares short-sightedly at the uncollected plates, then at the salt and pepper cruet and at the coffee pot and at the teapot and at the cups and saucers. Then and only then does she stare at the unrelenting features of Sir Godwyn Lydate, who takes hold of her nearest hand in a complicit gesture that almost brings tears to her eyes. "Camilla, dear heart, we must not lose sight of our goal." She does not want the touch of his hand to be comforting and disturbing. "Do you want it?"

She chews her bottom lip. "I want it." There is nothing else to say.

"Good." He squeezes the hand. "Good. We have work to do, you and I."

"I am sorry."

"Never ever be sorry." He lets go of the hand and pushes back the chair. "The first port of call is Spencer Perceval's bedroom. I looked in earlier with Helen. He is holed up with the redoubtable Harriet O'Connor, who is a most formidable lady I am glad to say."

"Will he be alright for tonight?"

"The formidable lady will make sure of that."

Rigid mouthed Caroline Helstone watches the two of them leave the restaurant heading for the lift and neither of them glances her way. Laura Standish is nowhere to be seen.

Thursday 19th October 10.17am

The door is opened by fully dressed and meticulously made up Harriet O'Connor, who does not stand aside. "Can't you leave him alone?"

She is also an attractive woman in her own way, although handsome is probably the word Sir Godwyn would pluck out of the ether. A similar build to his very own Scottish Pearly Queen, the priceless Lydia Robinson. Definitely more hard edged... an intriguing woman in a limited way. The intriguing woman in a limited way stares challengingly at Camilla French.

"Who are you?"

Sir Godwyn answers, "This is the Right Honourable Camilla French MP a Shadow Minister of State. You will hear much more of her doings from now on. Please stand aside."

"He is resting."

"If you do not stand aside I will make sure you regret your insolence." A voice from the Underworld. She needs to learn the limitations of her remit and she will.

"Let them in, Harry. It's all right." A voice from somewhere else entirely.

Pretending reluctance she stands aside; they both know that she would have stood aside anyway.

Sir Godwyn pauses in the doorway to allow Camilla to enter the bedroom first – always the perfect gentleman.

"A most distinctive perfume, Harriet, my dear."

"Yours also, Sir Godwyn."

They are momentarily eyeball to eyeball. She is brave, he will give her that. Limited intelligence behind the greenish slightly bloodshot eyes. She will not require a great deal of intelligence for her designated role. An element of confident stupidity will indeed be useful. She is of course the first to look away.

"I do hope we understand each other, Harriet, my dear."

"So do I." See what he means?

Spencer Perceval is half dressed wearing garish striped boxer shorts and an open necked pink shirt. The pillows are propped up on the bed and he is sitting with his bare knees up to his chest; at Harriet's insistence he has bathed and shaved. The expression on his pasty face would make his darling wife howl with glee.

Harriet O'Connor is now sitting on the bed fondly stroking that pale face and Spencer fondly kisses the stroking hand. Then the stroker glares challengingly at Camilla French, who feels she is somehow intruding on a private tragedy that will not end well.

"He is not an animal in a zoo," Harriet snaps, the north east accent more noticeable in her supportive anger.

It is Sir Godwyn who replies. "No unfortunately he is not." He walks to the window overlooking a busy, bustling City Square and the equestrian statue of the Black Prince, a platform for scores of squawking pigeons. Then he turns his back to the pale sunlight.

"I have every confidence in you, my dear Harriet. You will ensure that he is there tonight." It is not a question.

The liquorish allsorts of a couple are holding hands like lovesick teenagers. Spencer Perceval has closed his eyes as if pained by just about everything except the holding of hands.

"Of course."

"Then there is nothing further to be said." He walks towards the door and a much relieved Camilla French follows in his wake.

"What about poor Maria?" Harriet has been made to ask.

He turns on his heel to see that Harriet is dry eyed and in control. It could well be that Spencer Perceval's luck has changed. Although Sir Godwyn does not think it will end well either.

"One of my assistants is dealing with everything. She is accompanying the poor woman's body home and will comfort the bereaved husband." It is not the first time that Helen Huntingdon will have comforted a bereaved husband.

"That scary girl?"

He does not deign to reply and, instead, intones in a voice that brooks no argument. "Such a tragedy. Heart attack in her sleep. No one to blame. You have other things to think about."

"I know." Her gaze sees and ups his gaze. She knows he could call her bluff if he was so inclined.

With a hand in the small of her back he guides Camilla French out of the bedroom. Two is most definitely company and any more than two most definitely a crowd.

"It's going to be alright, pet." They overhear as the door closes. Their eyes meet; they are both thinking the same thing.

Thursday 19th October 10.27am

Jack Bellingham has purchased a Spectator magazine at King's Cross station and is skimming through the pages, when he becomes aware of an unfamiliar scent close by. It is not the scent he was expecting. The other three seats of his first-class table are also reserved in the name of Jack Smith and are unoccupied.

"We really are going to have to stop meeting like this, my friend Jack." It is Jane Fennell looking down on him. Not the waitress Jane Fennell of earlier this morning – but Jane Fennell playing Jane Fennell, wearing a black and white figure hugging designer dress with a matching designer shoulder bag slung elegantly over one shoulder. He cannot see her legs. Tasteful understated make-up, except the red lips winningly smiling and showing lots and lots of white teeth. Jane Fennell the waitress did not show a lot of teeth. This Jane Fennell sits across from Jack and shuffles along next to the window to be opposite. A little bird tells her that he was expecting someone else.

"Be a sweetie pie and lift my case onto the rack." A Gucci overnight case that he lifts with ease.

"Isn't this nice?" Then with a mischievous grin she pushes her just this side of sizeable breasts together. "Told you not as eye watering as earlier but all mine." She settles herself and deposits her designer shoulder bag on the adjoining empty seat.

"Isn't this where I ask what on earth you are doing here, Jane no Y Fennell?" He glances out of the window; he is definitely expecting someone else. She knows that if he is expecting Shirley Keeldar he is going to be sadly disappointed. Jane really does despise that woman.

Jane offers such a red lipped toothy enchanting smile, one might be led to believe. "I am to be your shadow and not in the political sense."

"My shadow?"

"Sir Godwyn Lydate's orders, sort of cute one." With a shuddering shudder the train starts up gliding smoothly out of King's Cross station. "Only just made it." Unlike someone else and she grins even more mischievously. "I am not to let you out of my sight, oh friendly one."

"I might have something to say about that." Shirley Keeldar had promised faithfully and he was going to show her his mother's grave and everything.

"Just think how it works both ways, sort of cute one. You will have me in sight at all times of the day and night. Now isn't that an enticing prospect?" An exceedingly posh voice that has intonations of Rebecca Sharp; they are probably distant cousins or something. "Don't upset me by saying you do not find that an enticing prospect, sort of cute one?"

"Do you always do what Sir Godwyn Lydate commands?"

"Always." She puts on a serious face, that doesn't quite work, and growls like a lioness and bursts out laughing. "You look so hangdog, sort of cute one."

"I do not take orders from Sir Godwyn Lydate or anyone else."

She pouts exceedingly red lips; he is not to know the shade is vermilion. "In the limited time available I have made a real effort to look my absolute bestest." A little girly voice.

"You look absolutely gorgeous."

"Thank you, kind sir." A demure smile this time.

The clattering catering trolley is approaching. "Do you think it's too early, my cute friend Jack, for a drinky poo?"

"What would you like?"

"Gin and tonic." A pensive smile. "Make that a large one. It has been a stressful morning and I do like large ones."

They laugh almost in unison. She mistakenly believes the ice has been well and truly broken. She will soon find out that her optimism could well have been misplaced. Skating with call me Jack is always on thin ice.

Thursday 19th October 10.42am

Shirley Keeldar has wrapped smooth bare man trap legs around the frantically thrusting naked torso of the American ambassador and she noisily and genuinely orgasms; the bastard can do it every time. She is followed just as noisily and genuinely several seconds later by the frantically thrusting American ambassador.

For several minutes they are unspeaking, getting their breaths back in each other's arms. These are stolen minutes – the best minutes. He is not as young as he used to be, although he refuses to admit it most of the time, and this is by no means the first time a working breakfast has finished up in bed. Not to mention the occasional working lunch…only this time the working breakfast started in bed.

When he has more or less rearranged his scattered senses into some sort of working order he whisper kisses to make her shiver. "We really must do this more often, honey." It is what he had whisper kissed that first time at a weekend shoot at Lydate Hall. That first time, when they had both been taken very much by surprise at their overwhelming desire for each other.

"That's what you always say." She had not intended that it should happen today because she had faithfully promised to go to Leeds with project Jack, who is far too trusting – a murdering innocent abroad one might think.

She instigates some gentle post coital tonguey kissing and, as always, his catcher's hands explore all over as much as he can lazily reach of her luscious peach of a body. With difficulty she breaks the instigated kiss and inserts an index finger into his mouth, which he nibbles with the perfect teeth of a Mid-West rodent at large.

"One of these days, Tom, my darling, we are going to get found out." Secrecy is part of it but only a small part. She is one of the few people Thomas Sawyer allows to call him Tom; the others being his elderly mother who forgets his name anyway, and his much younger fourth wife. His first wife only ever refers to him as that fornicating bastard; the second wife doesn't refer to him at all. The third wife is dead of natural causes relating to drugs and alcohol.

"Mary is back in the States as her mother is ill again." She was back in the States when they met at Lydate Hall. His attempt at sounding disappointed fails miserably. She strokes the sides of his head knowing he finds it irresistible and he closes his eyes and moans.

"You have the touch of an angel, Shirley."

"A fallen angel." He is not to know she is telling the truth.

"The best kind." He would not say that if he knew. This time he instigates some less gentle tonguey necking, but they have not breakfasted and somebody's stomach is rumbling.

Earlier, as soon as the door had closed, they were in each other's arms, all the hopeful New Year Resolutions blown away at the first chimes of midnight. She was only too well aware of the urgency of their joint and several needs. More than once they have said they must break things off… let things cool. Instead it gets hotter every time. It is something neither of them sought and something he thinks neither of them wants to control. It is something he knows must be ended in his own good time, or so he fondly believes.

"I'm hungry." She kisses the tip of his nose. "Let's eat, my darling."

"I've already eaten." He grins that trademark Huckleberry grin. "It was delicious."

"You are incorrigible, Tom Sawyer." She playfully slaps an arm and snake slides out of his reach and python slithers out of bed. He avidly watches as she steps into the hastily discarded cream lace panties, then the flesh-coloured tights as she divinely wriggles a fine ass. She arms up the cream lace bra, then the crumpled designer dress designed to accentuate all the divine curves of her body; a luscious almost overripe peach of a body that he thinks he knows in every intimate detail. Thinks he probably knows better than the bodies of any of his wives. She always leaves him wanting more and he is not used to that with women – surely the ending cannot be postponed much longer, because there are other considerations. There are always other considerations for this consummate surviving Politician. She stands with hands quite magnificently on curved hips.

"Mr Ambassador, I want my breakfast." She stamps her foot but the edgy smile gives her away, or perhaps not. There are mysteries yet to be solved and he is not sure he appreciates that. He likes to know his women inside out…or even outside in.

"Come back to bed, honey." He pleads. Last week she had hurriedly dressed and then at his pleadings, undressed again in a sexy striptease routine. "Please, honey."

She sits on the bed but not within reach. "I am hungry and we need to talk about Project Jack's impending trip to the States." She thinks better of reaching out to touch his outstretched supplicant's hand. "Then if you are a very good boy …?" She licks her lips as suggestively as lips have ever been suggestively licked outside of an Arizona brothel.

"Are you going with Project Jack to the States?" He leans back against the pillows, his hands behind his sleek head. She knows he is in great shape and does not look anything like his age, which he admits to fifty four.

"Not sure yet."

"Stay here, honey. We can meet more often with Mary away." He gives the narrow eyed stare he has perfected to advance his career. "I want you all to myself, honey."

"Tom, my darling, we are both married to other people."

"We both married money." There is no answer to that and she picks at the coverlet, momentarily mazed in thought.

"Penny for them." He has become more Anglicised than he cares to admit.

"We do not meet often enough to only see each other." He doesn't like it but he knows exactly what she means. It might be for the best to end it all soonest and suck up the temporary pain. Best for all concerned, particularly his career.

"That can be changed." Is actually what he says.

"Tom, my darling, we both know we have to be careful. The scandal would finish your career."

He knows that is true and cannot afford for that to happen. His political ambitions are sacrosanct and one day – one day the Oval Office.

She is about to say something and changes her mind. There is a dangerous volatility to Tom Sawyer that is best avoided.

"I want you, Shirley." They both know that that is not enough. It is good to say it though.

"I want you, Tom." She takes hold of the proffered hand knowing the surge of urgency has temporarily passed. "Let's eat."

In the adjoining room, he sends for fresh coffee and they devour delicious flaky croissants. He has hurriedly dressed, but has left off his tie. They hope that as far as anyone guesses it is just an extended breakfast on a complicated issue and, luckily, it is Sally's day off. They are crossing a tightrope without a safety net and that cannot go on.

"You know the First Lady has the hots for your Project." Shirley sticks out her tongue. He knows exactly what she will have been prepared to do to ensure that the Project signed on the dotted line. Unfortunately he doesn't think he will ever tire of this woman of his own volition and that should be a warning.

"How is that going to pan out?"

"The First Lady always gets what she wants." As he knows only too well.

Shirley mews up her mouth. "If it ever gets out…"

"It never gets out." A grim smile. "What happens in her pants stays in her pants."

That seems to be that for now and Shirley knows that these are shark infested waters. She delicately pat pats the corners of her mouth with the Eagle crested napkin and Tom watches fascinated. He will never tell Shirley that some nights he wakes up in a cold sweat because she is not there. If Mary is in the bed on those nights, then he takes his wife hard and brutally. She always begs for more and gets it. The terrible irony being that meeting Shirley has revived the physical side of his loveless marriage. Sally is just a bit on the side.

There are the notes of the Star-spangled banner and he answers his cell phone and listens. There is a wound-up edgy strength to this man that shows in all his bodily movements, even answering a cell phone.

"Very well." He ends the call and smiles at the cell phone. "The Chinese ambassador has cancelled lunch. There is some crisis." He pushes back his chair. "We are going back to bed where we belong." Not something an ambitious politician should say out loud because walls have ears…careless talk costs lives.

He stands tall to his six foot two and a quarter inches, holding out a hand like a Roman Emperor of the late Fourth Century demanding of his Empress's much younger half sister.

She pushes back her chair. "Have you been a really good boy?"

This time the smile is everywhere. As they make their way out of the room back to the tumbled bed, he is feeling up her fine ass and they are both smiling avidly in the lost before moments. From out of nowhere he is reminded of the High School Prom when he and his teenage date went in search of a quiet place. His first experience of going all the way, as they used to call it back then. The first time he became aware of the potency of avid lost before moments. It was just a pity the way it ended; but then there is a pity in all endings. He must end it with Shirley but has not the courage to tell her that Mary is pregnant. The morning after a particularly brutal night of lovemaking, because Shirley was not there, Mary claimed she was sure she was pregnant. She was right.

Thursday 19th October 11.13am

A dapper Sir Godwyn Lydate stands at the top of the entrance steps of the Queens Hotel breathing deeply of the misty morning air. It is so good to be alive, so good to be one of the gilded ones of the Earth and Master of all he surveys. He glances at the statue of the Black Prince in City Square, not one of his favourite historical characters, a loser in the end after such promising beginnings. Dying too early of a nasty debilitating disease and missing out on the Crown. No surprises really that his son should lose the throne... sons of losers are losers twice over. There are, of course, exceptions that prove the rule.

The mobile phone vibrates in his pocket. "Yes, Jane, my dear." He is contemplating statues of naked nymphs also adorning City Square. "Excellent." Not unlike the marbled naked figure of Helen Huntingdon when she poses scarily nude for his eyes only. "You know what to do, my dear." He ends the call. Such an obedient girl, the would-be lioness, although a bit too scrambled for her own good. A wee bit fey, although she is the sort of girl to forgive and be forgiven for most things.

Another invigorating breath. Camilla French has gone for a lie down, claiming she is bone weary this morning and he dry lip twitches. Camilla French is not used to being bone weary. Aimlessly his eyes flicker over the insignificant people going about their significantly insignificant lives, one or two attractive women as always catch the eye. There are always attractive women to catch the eye, one of God's little jokes. He yawns and stretches and then his roving eye is floating log snagged by a girl sitting alone on the bench in a nearby bus shelter. She is blubbering and being pointedly ignored by the insignificant people in the bus queue. He is at a loose end and damsels in distress are such a lovely distraction. If they did not exist they would have to be invented. Of its own volition the queue Red Sea parts to let the great man through. Perching on the narrow uncomfortable bus shelter bench next to the blubbering girl, he takes possession of her hot little hand. It is the right thing to do to a damsel in distress. The Black Prince, who caused a few of his own, would undoubtedly approve. Sir Peregrine Lydate had stood by the Black Prince's side in the French wars; there were rumours about the parentage of the Black Prince's surviving son. The insignificant people in the queue are ignoring even more so. He takes no account of them one way or the other...he has never taken part in a queue.

"What on earth is wrong, my dear girl?" It takes a few moments for the dear girl to be able to articulate coherently. She makes no attempt to reclaim the hot little hand.

"I've been sacked." Sir Godwyn cannot prevent an image of Fourteenth Century French towns overrun by English soldiery.

"Tell me all about it, my dear Laura." She has not walked out of the book at all.

"The cow said I… said I…" A fresh burst of choking tears and he lets go of the hot little hand to retrieve an initialled handkerchief from his pocket. In his experience an initialled handkerchief rarely goes amiss where there is a damsel in distress.

"Here, my dear, do stop crying. Wipe your eyes and blow your nose. That's a good girl."

He waits patiently, taking even less account of the insignificant people, whilst Laura takes her time doing as she is told. Such an awful brown windsor soup coloured short overcoat not adequately covering the cheap cut waitress uniform, that nevertheless shapes in all the right places. It will all have to go. She lustily blows her nose and angles her head to acknowledge the unlooked for kindness. She makes to hand back the initialled handkerchief.

"Keep it, my dear."

She screws it up in hot little hands, staring red eyed at the resultant Rubik's cube. "She…she said I was making up to the guests…and…and… I'd taken an unauthorised toilet break." The crude cow had said a lot more but there is no way Laura can repeat it in present company. She had not been aware of the ladies' toilet door opening and closing.

As the hot little hands are otherwise engaged he slips his arm through hers making suitable clucking noises. He does so thrive on this sort of potential situation. Has always believes that forging one's own luck creates the best luck of all and has always realised that women are wired differently. Knowing only too well that one can receive a nasty shock if one is not on one's mettle.

The shades of green double-decker bus arrives and the queue begins to shuffle along. The damsel makes a half-hearted attempt to scramble to her feet, but scarcely resists when he keeps firm hold of the trapped arm. Neither of them notices that the bus is advertising Amelia Sedley's latest movie.

"I need the money." She dry sobs. "I am behind with the rent." Another dry sob. "And other stuff."

"Dear. Dear." The double-decker bus has swallowed the wartime ration queue whole, leaving the two of them alone… alone is probably not the correct word. The thought crosses his mind that she might have been waiting for him to leave the Hotel; not that it matters – he has nothing against giving fate a nudge. "Have you a boyfriend, Laura?"

After a momentary pause she shakes her head. She had thought about lying to save face but there is no point. She is in deep shit. The cow. The awful shitty cow. She will be thrown out on the street. Shit…shit…shit.

"There there, my dear." She is beginning to shake and shiver. "There is a coffee shop over there. I will buy you a coffee and we can talk properly."

He is so very kind. She knows he is an important man because even the shitty cow is scared shitless. At a window table she stirs and stirs the milky coffee, at a loss because she had not thought any of this through and knows she looks like shit. She will have to stop thinking the word shit, otherwise she will need to go to the toilet for a shit and that will ruin everything.

"What will you do now, my dear?"

"I don't know." The vibrant greeny blue possibly bluey green eyes fill with tears. Because it is getting on his nerves he stops her stirring the coffee and masterfully takes possession of both hot little hands. This damsel in distress thing is really quite straightforward.

"Would you like to get your job back, my dear?"

"The cow would make my life hell."

He doesn't think it appropriate to reveal that the cow will soon be leaving for pastures new. "We must put our thinking caps on, my dear Laura." He has such lovely luminous pale blue eyes that seem to see into her soul. Not much to see there. "You are no relation to the Hertfordshire Standishs, are you, my dear?"

She shakes her head. She is not sure where Hertfordshire is. He squeezes the hot little hands.

"It is probably a good thing, my dear. Awful prigs. For a mercifully short time Gerald Standish was my fag at Eton. Horrid little sprog. Had to beat him senseless more than once. Something in the city now, I understand, which explains an awful lot."

She has no idea what he is talking about, but the posh voice is so soothing that she could just lay her weary head on his shoulder, go to sleep and wake up in a different time and place. She is not sleeping well these days, what with money worries and everything. The stupid cow of a GP refuses to give her stronger sleeping tablets. She has had to revert to plan B and take matters into her own hands so to speak.

"You are a very, very pretty girl Laura. All this is such a shame."

"I look a mess." She thinks is probably a better shitless way of putting it.

"A very pretty mess though."

She cannot stop herself almost smiling through the tears. The pressure of his strong hands is really comforting and she stares at their entwined fingers. She used to be very good at working out puzzles.

"That's much better. Would you like me to help you, Laura?"

The luminous pale blue eyes are making her feel warm all over, which is a really, really nice feeling. She realises he will want something, probably sex, because that is what they all want, but shit – she means hell – nobody else is getting it at the moment. It used to be a big deal but not anymore. She has lost count of the losers and tossers she has allowed in her pants. "Yes please." One of those still small voices that he finds so enervating.

He doesn't beat about the bush. "How old are you, Laura?"

"Twenty three." Well, twenty four next week, but she is the only one counting. Another smile that is just this side of a grin. She is one of those women whose graded smiles are apparently genuine, lending her features the looks of a medieval Madonna on one of the less accessible walls of the Uffizi. A beguiling look and as timeless as time itself – he is getting a bit carried away. He must stop reading Spinoza in the wee small hours.

"How old are you?" She asks to prove that two can play at this verbal footsy game. She prefers actual footsy games.

The dry lip twitch is verging on a smile; he has never ever grinned. "Much more than twenty three, my dear Laura."

There is a reflective pause. "I don't know what to do."

"We will think of something, Laura, my dear."

She stares into his eyes and he stares back.

"I don't know your name." She knows she is not very good at this sort of thing whatever it is. She usually gets picked up in pubs or nightclubs when she is well pissed. Internet dating has been a dead loss.

"Godwyn."

"That's a really nice name." She doesn't add that she has never been with a Godwyn. Plenty of Bens and Robs and Pauls, not forgetting the odd Peter and not to mention a couple of Zaks. Her last proper boyfriend, if you will, was called Simon. A lot of bloody use he turned out to be when he was needed. She had to face it on her own. She could provide a football team of useless tossers to play a team of self-absorbed wankers.

"Where do you live, Laura?"

"A pokey flat on Meanwood Road." His thumbs are caressing the receptive palms of her hot little hands. It is really, really nice. "Until I get thrown out." She thinks he knows how to treat a lady…well… posh people know all sorts of things like that.

"We must stop that happening, Laura, my dear."

This is all rather pleasant and thought provoking and, if he is honest, the thought provoking is a bit of a surprise. Now that he really studies her face he realises that she could be much more than exceedingly pretty. Make-up too garish and too much face powder. The reality is that, given her current situation, another five years and the prettiness will fade rapidly. Another ten years and she will be a dowdy seen it all waitress no man will take the time of day to chat up at the table; there will be no second glances on the street and no sly thigh pressings on the top deck of a double-decker bus.

And, most importantly, no powerful man intrigued by a certain something that is impossible to define. Something bred in the bone, something that he feeds on. Unless he intervenes there will be a succession of declining losers and what is bred in the bone will be irretrievably lost without trace.

Sir Godwyn releases even hotter little hands and extracts his cheque-book from his inside jacket pocket. He knows it is old-fashioned but it works well as gestures go. He opens the cheque-book and retrieves the Mont Blanc pen from the same pocket. All done with several muted Cavalier flourishes.

She reads the bank name upside down. "I've never heard of Martins Bank." She is now at a loss what to do with the released hot little hands.

"The posh people's Bank my dear. A similar set of crooks to the other banks only they charge more." That reminds him. Mental note. Those German Bankers must be taught a severe lesson. They will be. "How much do you need, my dear?"

"Why are you doing this?"

"Why do you think, my dear?"

She is not at all sure how posh people would phrase it. "To get in my knickers." Knickers are definitely posher than pants.

"Most assuredly, my dear, but that is the least of it."

She looks puzzled, as well she might, but doesn't mind being out of her depth – she is a quick learner.

"You will belong to me body and, more importantly, soul."

"I don't think you'll be getting much of a bargain." She has not the remotest idea what a soul might be worth.

"That is for me to decide, my dear Laura." The driest of lip twitches. "How much do you need?"

She is rubbing one hand nervously on top of the other. She must resist the temptation to scratch because she doesn't think that posh people scratch. "I owe three months' rent and two thousand on credit cards." She might as well be hung for a sheep as a lamb. "And a thousand pounds overdraft." She chokes back an unintended sob. "The Bank is getting really nasty." If it is the same Bank it has the ring of truth.

Meticulously he writes out the cheque, not quite mouthing the words. "Any middle names, my dear Laura?" She shakes her head. "Shall we say…" He meets her stunned gaze; it has not yet sunk in that this could well be for real. She really could be stunningly beautiful and it would have been such a waste. She is a lucky girl, a great loss to a generation of provincial wasters. As a work in progress there is much to be achieved, in many ways the more work in progress the better for the end product. Upper class girls are prone to bouts of self-assertion which can be rather trying. "Let me see…" He taps the pen against his ever so slightly prominent front teeth. He does so manifestly enjoy teasing out proceedings. "Shall we say ten thousand pounds?" He doesn't think she will understand Guineas.

Her finely shaped jaw literally drops and, staring into his pale blue eyes, she expects him to say 'fooled you' then put the fake cheque-book and exploding pen away.

"Of course that is just for now until I can arrange your Platinum card. Make sure you pay off all your debts otherwise I will be cross. Buy some new clothes. You are now in my employ."

It takes several moments to find any semblance of a voice. "Are you serious?" She is not sure what she anticipated but whatever it was it wasn't this.

With a flourish, her knight in shining armour tears off the cheque and pushes it across the scratched Formica table top. She has not drunk any of her coffee. "I will arrange for the cheque to be cleared within the hour." She is getting used to the dry lip twitches. "After all, I am a Director of the Bank."

She stares at the copperplate handwritten cheque made out for ten thousand pounds, as if it might disappear in a puff of smoke if she touches it. He has guessed correctly that ten thousand pounds is beyond her wildest dreams. As far as she is concerned he can possess every square inch of her body and her soul, no questions asked.

"Do pick it up, my dear. It won't bite you." He puts away the cheque book and the pen that doesn't explode.

"I can't take this." A voice…yes it is definitely her voice speaking of its own volition and she feels like punching the stupid voice on the nose.

"Do pick it up, my dear."

She picks it up and the deed is as good as done. He glances at the antique Rolex watch. "Do you have a little black dress, my dear Laura?" She nods her head wondering if it might be too little but it is definitely black. "Wear it tonight and I will meet you at eight o'clock in the bar of the Hotel." He takes out his wallet and peels off six £50 notes. "Get your hair done. Is there somewhere you can get advice on make-up?"

She knows she uses too much make-up. "Boots."

"Excellent." He hands over the money. "Bin this coat."

"There is one I have seen in Top Shop. It is really nice."

"Then buy it." He reaches across the scratched Formica table and cradles her modelled chin. She doesn't mind in the least. After all he has bought the chin and it fits perfectly in his palm. "I think you will scrub up rather well, my dear Laura." Little does he know.

"Shall I buy some sexy undies?" There are some incredibly sexy undies in Victoria's Secret that she has coveted and never been able to afford. He gazes, it might well be, fondly into the greeny blue or is it bluey green eyes. She will definitely scrub up very well indeed. Perhaps not an early May date, but a May date nonetheless, and at such an affordable price.

"Have there been many men in your life, Laura?" So posh. She can learn posh. Just look at Posh Spice. He is very direct with his questions. She is not used to that. Perhaps it is a posh thing.

"A few." She would hate to actually count them up.

He is caressing her chin with a gentle thumb and it is really nice.

"A few, a few, too few for drums and yells may creep back silent up half known roads." His pale blue eyes really are hypnotic and the voice washes over her body like scented oils… not that she has ever bathed in scented oils. She has such a definitively puzzled smile. The contours of her face really are just, and only just, this side of perfection. An accident of birth is just that. A bargain indeed.

"Is that poetry?"

"Indeed it is poetry, Laura Standish. Indeed it is." Some more thumb caressing. "You are a living poem, my dear Laura, definitely more Keats than Wilfred Owen. I shall look forward to learning you by heart."

"That's really nice." She wishes now that she had paid more attention at school and not messed about with the Chavs, deliberately getting excluded as many times as possible.

He leans closer and, without thinking, she meets him halfway for a chaste kiss on the lips. His breath smells so posh and he, in turn, tastes the salty residue of her tears.

"Sexy undies would be an excellent idea, my dear." What a pleasant waste of an hour.

Thursday 19th October 1.58pm

Torn sandwich wrappers, empty coffee cups and several empty gin and whisky miniatures litter the first-class table. Jane Fennell stares out of the train window as though at a foreign country. It has just been announced that they are approaching Wakefield Westgate station.

"I have never been this far North." She is probably anticipating cobbled streets and shawled women wearing clogs; not to mention the whippet racing and Knurr and Spell.

He has been trying to decide which undomesticated wild animal she reminds him of. Possibly some rare species of North American wildcat sighted occasionally from a safe distance. There is definitely a wildness in this stunning girl that matches a wildness in his own character and should give any man pause.

"Do you have a boyfriend?" It is a question that has taken him some time to screw up his courage to ask. He is still intimidated by the Lady Rebecca tribe.

"That is a very personal question, my friend Jack." She is not in the least put out. The colour of her eyes more a shadowed mountain stream colour that is darker than blue. Not a colour you would even see mixed on Emily Rowley's palette. "Since you ask the answer is no one special."

The train squeals to a halt at Wakefield Westgate Station and Jane looks out of the window at drab people milling about on the drab platform. An attractive, fortyish, flame haired woman stares in the window as she walks slowly past. The same woman had walked up and down the carriage several times, as if screwing up courage to speak to the People's hero.

Throughout the stop-start journey Jane Fennell has minutely studied Hero Jack, and is only too well aware that he is the worst embodiment of the word enigma. A word that has been used to describe herself on more than one occasion, usually involving kinky sex or, on one best forgotten occasion, the lack of it. She needs to keep a sense of balance, which comes naturally enough anyway. She has been called a cold fish by more than a few men friends and, with one notable exception, none has ever progressed beyond temporary fuck buddy. Sir Godwyn is just Sir Godwyn.

"Sir Godwyn does not encourage us to have boyfriends."

"Sir Godwyn says." He mimics in such a spoiled posh voice that she is forced to laugh out loud. She hates to laugh out loud in public. It does not suit the lay of her face.

"Indeed he does, my dear." She mimics in her turn and is probably the loser by a short head.

The train shudders forward and, along with all the other passengers, they both automatically glance out of the windows. The attractive fortyish flame haired woman is standing with a small case at her feet determinedly catching Jack's gaze. He smiles and she smiles back and then she isn't there. Jane Fennell has seen the brief encounter of sorts and for some unfathomable reason thinks of a captured Boadicea at the end – go figure.

She studies Jack with renewed interest and knows that, despite contrived appearances to the contrary, he is no innocent abroad. Christ! He is a cold blooded murderer. A pronounced not guilty murderer but a murderer nonetheless. She feels sorry for him on a certain Dantean level and, on another level, would not kick him out of bed; no Beatrice she. A good thing given the circumstances. Sir Godwyn does indeed say.

"You know, Jack, you have to be watchful." Yes… that is the word. "You are fair game and it is the hunting season." She knows all about hunting seasons – not to mention fair game.

He mews up his mouth and meets her gaze head on. There are so many contradictions it is impossible to know where to start.

"I know."

"People like Shirley Keeldar take whatever they want and, literally, hang the consequences. They do not give. They take. They even take when they are giving. She is probably the most dangerous person you have met so far." He is not at all sure about that, but then what does he know.

"That is until I met you, Jane no Y Fennell."

"Jack, my sort of cute one, I am not in the same league as that woman. No man has topped himself because of me."

He appreciates she is giving genuine advice, and that it does not appear to be a put up job and, as far as he knows, she has no axe to grind. Although he doesn't feel able to follow through on this revelation at this time.

"How close are you ordered to stay to me?"

"Not to let you out of my sight." She smiles at the thought of the flame haired woman's utterly pagan smile, fashioned to entice an unsuspecting Roman Guard. "Think of me as a second skin."

"I need the toilet."

"Then so do I."

He is not sure if she is joking, and remembers where he has seen that attractive fortyish flame haired woman before. His only excuse being that so much has happened in the interim.

Thursday 19th October 2.46pm

Gilbert Markham is peering through the overgrown privet hedge, camera at the ready. A pity it is not a rifle. Whilst reasonably well hidden he still has a perfect view of the Percevals' front door. Arriving by Tube he had walked past the Foreign Secretary's car parked two streets away. Pathetic really, the sad git would not have lasted two minutes in the killing fields. Gilbert, dressed in his camouflage gear, is reminded, as always, of his days in the Regiment. Staying still and silent on watch, senses alert and mind on hold for hours on end. There are so many things to miss from those days of rare companionship.

He is well aware that Rosanna Spearman cannot resist glancing furtively out of her window. She has promised him a meal later – a takeaway no doubt. She wants to talk about her estranged husband, making it crystal clear that she wants Gilbert to spend the night in her bed – to do it properly this time – as she put it. He has no objection. She is lovely meaty and several veg and there is nowhere else to be tonight. Sir Godwyn will not be around to interrupt proceedings.

There goes the door of the Perceval house. Click. Click. Click. They are kissing on the doorstep. Click. Click. Click. Unbelievable. She is wearing a short dressing gown shop windowing lots of bare legs. Now the idiot is feeling up her bare arse in full view of the apparently deserted street. Unbelievable. Click. Click.

He could take them both down with two bullets... the first bullet in the small of the sad git's back and, as he falls, the second bullet in her soft belly. She would take several minutes to noisily die and the screaming would remind him of that mountain village in Afghanistan.

This bellied woman waves as George Meredith hurries down the drive, peering guiltily from side to side. Click. Click. Walking quickly as if that will make any difference. She is watching him all the way down the street...another lovely meaty piece. Out of bounds to Gilbert for so many reasons but, knowing Sir Godwyn, that could always change.

Gilbert will have to tread carefully after getting carried away last night. To be fair Jesus Christ himself would have got carried away. Camilla French was so hot for it he was surprised he didn't receive third degree burns. He thought there were no surprises left where women are concerned.

He waits for ten minutes before creeping stealthily round to the back door of Rosanna's mansionette. He knocks three times, smiling at the memory of his foster mother's favourite song. The door is unlocked and he slips inside and the door is hastily locked and bolted. She is really getting into the part.

"Did you get what you need, Gil love?" She is breathless with the excitement of it all. Just like being in a movie. She is wearing tight jeans that shape her ample arse and a scarlet top that clings to the more than ample bosoms.

In answer he holds up the camera and then takes her in his arms. It is Rosanna who eventually pulls away. She is no pushover. "We need to talk, Gil, love"

"That sounds ominous, Roz."

"Don't be silly." She moves reluctantly away to take a seat at the huge marble kitchen dining table that was not her choice. The twelve white leather chairs were not to her taste either. She indicates the chair next to hers and he sits down.

"I'm really scared, Gil, love." The chins quiver. "Felix is being a real bastard over the divorce." Her expressive gunmetal grey eyes beseeching his complicity. "I feel so alone."

"You are not alone, Roz." He, strong man, takes possession of the hands clasped in her capacious lap. All at once he is exhausted and bone weary and would love to lay his head in this pillowed lap and sleep.

There was not a lot of sleep last night with Camilla French or the night before – the Lady Rebecca Sharp as inventive as ever. He has ignored her recent texts.

"You look tired, Gil, love." She frees one of her hands to stroke the side of his face; he needs a shave. He is one of those men who, unlike her husband, needs to shave twice a day. "All that driving and everything."

"I'll be fine. I need a stiff drink, that's all."

"Help yourself, love." She indicates the vast array of bottles of spirits. "Pour me a large vodka and small tonic, there's a love." He pours himself a generous Platinum label Scotch on the rocks and a large vodka with a splash of tonic. He knows how she likes it.

They both swallow generous slurps and set their glasses side by side on the marble table, holding hands again as if it is the most natural thing in the world. He feels naturally at ease with this generous woman and tells himself he is not just here for what he can get. He thinks she probably knows that; women of a certain age seem to have unerring instincts where that sort of thing is concerned. They often go against instincts, but that is another story.

"He has threatened me." She takes a deep shuddering breath. "He says he knows some dangerous people who will hurt me unless I move out."

"You have changed the locks?"

She nods. "This morning he hammered on the door shouting terrible things and I had to let him in. He has given me forty eight hours to get out." Another shuddering breath. "He said some really, really terrible things." Tears sparkle in her gunmetal grey eyes. "He said I was a fat whore and I would get nothing."

Gilbert holds the hands tight. "Where is he living?"

"There is an apartment a couple of streets away that he doesn't know I know about where he takes women. I know he is seeing some young woman at the moment because he let it slip accidently on purpose. She only sounds to be a slip of a girl."

"I will take care of it." There is a steely Barbarian mercenary look in his eyes that did for Varus's lost Legion. She can well believe he has killed men in the line of duty. Being a kind and decent woman she does not consider that there might have been women.

"He said dangerous people would take turns raping me before cutting me up." She is fighting back the tears. She rarely cries. "I am so sorry to put all this on you, Gil, love. We've not even been to bed properly yet."

"We had some time yesterday before I was summoned."

"It was a lovely couple of hours."

"There will be lot more of those, Roz." He hopes it doesn't sound too lovey dovey.

"I really like you, Gil."

"I really like you, Roz." On a tour of duty you took any available woman when you had the chance. No ifs or buts. You never knew if it might be the last time. Some of the lads liked it best when the chosen woman struggled or fought back. The Lads had their own code – no morals involved – morals were for civilians.

"Are you hungry, Gil?"

"Famished."

"Indian or Chinese?"

Thursday 19th October 3.03pm

The man and woman are sitting hand in hand, more or less hidden on the back row of the shadowiest pews in the vaulted interior of the Medieval glory that is Staines Cathedral. There has been worship on this site since early Saxon times and there is a definite chill in the musty air of all those wasteful centuries.

The Reverend John Eames is staring wide-eyed and attentive towards the distant altar, where many candles are burning to lighten the gloom. There is a palpable sense of incense all around. Cecilia Hunt is staring at John Eames through the severe round spectacles.

"I feel I belong here." He is speaking in appropriately hushed tones; nonetheless his voice carries. His gaze shifts to the intricately carved pulpit from where he will deliver his Sermons; the words of the Gospels and the words of the Prophets. "I feel it is right, Cecilia. Don't you?" Always that sliver of anxiety making Cecelia want to take him in her arms and make better whatever it threatens to be. She really hopes this is not another false dawn; her Mother has been nagging it is time to settle down with a nice man. Something her Mother was never able to do. One cannot blame her after what happened.

"Yes, Johnny, I do." And she really, really does.

"I feel I belong here." Is his solemn reply and for a few blessed minutes the man and the woman remain in companionable earthly silence. He is overcome by the sheer Majesty of this most Holy Place, where generations of men and women have bowed their heads, if not their souls, and sought the Lord their God. Sought something mysteriously mystical outside themselves and their daily grind.

Cecilia Hunt is overcome with intricate feelings for John Eames. She did not see this coming and wishes she could pray for guidance. As the next best thing she needs to speak to her Mother.

"I have always believed in God, Cecilia." The tone is even more hushed, as she squeezes his hand and thinks that if one is to believe in God then this is the place to do it.

"I don't mean the old man with a beard. I mean a great power beyond our knowing. Nothing else makes sense. The theory of evolution is for self-deluded fools. If our ancestors evolved from sea creatures where are all the inbetween skeletons?" Another hands squeeze.

"There are dinosaur skeletons and then human skeletons but no inbetweenies. We were created and we evolved to our circumstances; evolved within our creation."

"What about Piltdown man? The missing link?"

"Proved to be a forgery." She didn't know that.

A few more minutes of blessed silence. In the distance a stooped man in untidy Clerical garb kneels briefly in front of the altar and then hastens briskly away. There is no one else in sight.

"When you think how complicated human beings are we just must be created by an amazing power. Women in particular." He smiles at a Cecilia, who is shadowed magically mystical in the candle flaring gloom, severe round spectacles and all. "Nurturing babies inside your bodies and then giving birth to a helpless child. How could a helpless child survive on its own?" He thinks he is getting the beginnings of a Sermon.

Cecilia, who quite likes the idea of a baby, kisses his ear and tears spring to his eyes.

"I love you, Cecilia." He really must forget about saying the same thing to Mary Thorne, who has texted that they need to speak. It never rains but it pours.

"I love you, Johnny."

There – it is said in this most Holy Place and not in a darkened bedroom. Not even Sir Godwyn Lydate is as powerful as the Lord God of hosts, or whatever is out there. Or at least that is what Cecilia Hunt fervently hopes, as she stares at the distant altar and clings to Johnny bending his head in prayer. She is not to know that some of his prayers have been answered.

Thursday 19th October 2.40pm

At the Queens Hotel in Leeds it has been arranged that Jack Bellingham and Jane Fennell are allocated adjoining rooms. The pretty Receptionist doesn't bat an eyelid under Jane Fennell's challenging stare. Jane Fennell is very good at challenging stares. Emily Prescott doesn't think it appropriate to ask Jack for an autograph – she thinks of him as Jack and is following him on Twitter. She does indulge in a gaze into the oddly colourless eyes. She watched the Phineas Finn Show but he is much more handsome in real life. There is a definite aura.

He glances at the name badge adorning her left breast and she has no doubt he is imagining her naked breasts and the colour of her nipples. She is used to that. She has no false modesty and self-awareness has never held her back from a catalogue of misapprehensions.

"Thank you." Another lingering glance at the angled badge. "You have been most helpful, Emily."

An answering gleaming smile… a not unattractive girl and decent tits.

"Please let me know if there is anything else, Mr Bellingham." She is surprised that the Fennell woman has a proprietorial hold of his arm and that her stare is very challenging indeed. Whatever happened to Amelia Sedley?

The somewhat battered porter carrying their overnight cases leads them to the lift and presses the button with an elbow. Emily Prescott is prettily thoughtful as they disappear from view. There was a definite attraction in the exchange of gazes; she has never been unsure of her sexual powers if, sometimes, a tad delusional. If the truth be known she is getting a bit cheesed off with John Everson, who can be really stupid sometimes, and she wonders if he is not quite all there.

Emily is, of course married, but that has never held her back from the passions of the moment.

She wonders if there is more to that old biddy's death than meets the eye. John appears really more upset than he should be. This morning in bed he lost the hard on almost immediately, knocked her hand away and not even a ten second wonder. Reluctantly she had to look after herself and he didn't even watch. Now he has gone off sick and so that tarty bitch is behind the bar, no doubt giving the eye to everybody in trousers. At least Emily is choosy… well… most of the time anyway. Anybody is allowed the odd mistake. She avoids the eye of the somewhat battered porter crossing from the lift and pointedly ignores his knowing wink. That particular night was probably a mistake although they are all similar in the dark.

Thursday 19th October 7.09pm

At Agnes Grey's London apartment, Rosalie Murray tops up the bathwater with practised toes from the hot tap and then settles back at her full length. These old-fashioned baths are really accommodating and scented bubbles are making desert island wavelets around the archipelagos of her breasts. At least she can look at her breasts without shuddering. She hasn't dared look in the mirror but Agnes Grey says her face is beginning to heal. Lots of discoloured bruising but that is, apparently, a good thing according to Agnes Grey. Rosalie can now partially see out of the black eye – another good thing.

One could almost believe that this is not the first time Agnes Grey has tritely doled out this sort of asinine comfort. Rosalie Murray has done a lot of thinking because there has not been much else to do. Watching television gives her a headache and the radio is even worse. One thing is certain – she does not intend to wait on Sir Godwyn high and mighty Lydate's pleasure. She made an almost fatal strategic error; she can see that now and will not make the same mistake again. Nor will she meekly accept the ordained punishment like the penitent she is pretending to be. She has cried a lot with Agnes around, but intends to pay that man back in kind or perish in the attempt.

It does not sound so melodramatic when she thinks the words. Rosalie is not sure she will ever forgive Saint Agnes Grey for seeing her at her most vulnerable and for cleaning her up most intimately when she had, for God's sake, pissed herself. Even as a child she had never ever pissed herself, for God's sake. The humiliation of the whole thing burns in her throat and tears at her heart. The bastard should have finished her off when he had the chance.

Earlier Rosalie said that she didn't feel well and would have a bath and go to bed, and so an on edge Agnes Grey had gone out for a couple of hours. Rosalie had done her own bit of espionage and knows that Agnes is secretly meeting that tosser John Caldigate. They are trysting, if that is the word, at a nondescript hotel near King's Cross. Saint Agnes really should not leave her mobile phone lying around when Rosalie has one goodish eye.

Rosalie does not think that Sir Godwyn high and mighty Lydate would be at all happy at not so saintly Agnes after all. Rosalie would take great pleasure in most intimately cleaning up Agnes Grey at her most vulnerable.

The stored selfies were most revealing. There is certainly a whole lot more to Agnes Grey than meets the eye. Lucky old John Caldigate... or not, as the case may be.

First things first and second things second. Rosalie grimaces a smile at the banal thought. It doesn't hurt as much to smile, laughing would be a different matter entirely. One day she will laugh at the bastard's open grave.

She has no reason now to marry that dullard John Eames, who is, as far as she is concerned, a mere support system for a cock. She had enjoyed the threesome but thinks that candid pleasure made her careless. She will not be that careless ever again and so no self-indulgent threesomes for the foreseeable future. From now on her body is a weapon of choice to be deployed sparingly.

The scented water lapping at her bruised chin is restful and soothing. Somehow in the past few days she has forgotten how clever she can be when she puts her mind to it. Convincing herself that she was outwitted by Sir Godwyn because she was careless.

That was stupid but the inherent cleverness remains, and the despicable way he behaved has forced her to redefine something of herself. She knows how Boadicea felt, and she must avoid Boadicea's fate. Seeing nothing ridiculous in comparing herself to the doomed Queen of the Icenii.

"Bastard." She says out loud. "Bastard." Louder. "Bastard." She shouts.

She knows exactly what she is going to do. Time to get out of the bath and make a phone call. Be very afraid, Sir Godwyn high and mighty Lydate...be very afraid.

Thursday 19th October 8.02pm

A blissfully, as yet, unaware Sir Godwyn Lydate, Lord of the Earth fashion, crosses the lobby of the Queens Hotel heading towards the noisier than he would like bar area. As far as he is concerned the problem that is Rosalie Murray is well on the way to being solved once and for all. As far as a potential problem of Agnes Grey – well we shall see what we shall see.

The rather pretty drab girl on Reception returns his bequeathing smile. She is not to know that Laura Standish is in pole position... so much of life's winnings is about luck. Not to mention chance and circumstance – a not unattractive pretty drab girl nonetheless.

He Grand Masterly pauses at the entrance to the noisier than he would like bar area and glances round. No sign of Laura Standish; he does so hate being kept waiting. There is never any excuse for not being punctual. He walks to the bar and catches the eye of the peroxide blonde barmaid, who looks anxiously over his shoulder to see if the scary girl is anywhere about.

"A large Glengoyne, my dear. No ice. No water." He is aware in his peripheral vision of some rather spectacular crossed legs on a bar stool. Shiny black tights, certainly not stockings with such a short black dress, which is more a pelmet really, and low-cut, enhancing a more than acceptable cleavage. The exceedingly pretty, not the least bit drab, face is vaguely familiar and the exceedingly pretty, not the least bit drab, brunette holds up a tall glass in greeting.

"I started without you, Godwyn." A cheeky red lipped smile revealing fetching dimples that he had not noticed earlier.

"Laura?" This is ridiculous. It feels like an unrehearsed scene from a second-rate movie, as she knocks back the remains of the drink. A gesture deliciously out of kilter with her svelte looks.

"Same again, my dear?"

"Vodka and gin. Lots of ice."

"What an interesting combination." He thinks this girl might turn out to be even more endearingly surprising than he anticipated. One just never can tell.

The clever girl has taken his advice…the eye make-up just right, the boyish hair effectively styled… this really is remarkable.

"I feel like Julia Roberts in Pretty Woman." Even her voice is more assured with much less of a local accent. He has never heard of this Julia Roberts person, rather he is reminded more of Pygmalion… George Bernard Shaw being the favourite playwright of his early Oxford days.

"You look absolutely stunning, my dear Laura."

Lots more red lipsticked smile with teeth all present and correct.

The drinks have arrived promptly. The barmaid is aware that he is somebody very important and the manager has told her that any drinks are on the house.

"These are on the house."

He appraises the peroxide blonde barmaid properly and thinks that dear Helen might have been a tad judgemental; the girl appears not all that tarty. "Thank you, my dear."

Reluctantly she has to waste her time serving someone else, disappointed he didn't make a point of looking at her name badge. There is something familiar about that striking red lipsticked girl who is stroking his arm.

"Cheers."

"Cheers." Laura knocks back half the drink. It is hard to equate this girl of such shining potential with the promisingly indistinct waitress of this morning. It is such an enticing game. The Archbishop has never entirely grasped it, never progressing beyond the indistinct waitress bit.

"My. My. You will be getting pie eyed, my dear Laura."

"I always like to get a bit pissed early on."

"Indeed." He sips neat single malt whisky. "Don't get too pissed, my dear Laura, because I have plans for later."

She eyes him boldly over the rim of the ice frosted glass which she licks with the tip of a pinky tongue, which of course is bought and paid for like everything else.

Impossible to equate these shiny legs and the no doubt usual attachments with the pathetic sobbing girl at the awful bus stop. It is amazing what a true artist can achieve in such a short time.

"Don't worry, Godwyn, I never get that pissed." Not very often anyway. Only on rare occasions has she ended up in a strange bed with some random tosser, not knowing how she got there. The next morning sometimes allowing hangover sex, but occasionally not if her eyes have focused properly. She even more boldly meets his gaze and is not sure what the carnal power is, but she knows she possesses it in spades when she puts her mind to it. Purchased pinky tongue licks purchased red lips.

There is a polite cough and reluctantly they break eye contact and Laura stops stroking his arm.

"Camilla, my dear."

Camilla French had studied the scene from a safe distance, fascinated by the preying mantis display, which she more fully appreciates after Gilbert Markham and all that.

Watching Sir Godwyn most definitely enjoying being pawed by the, just asking for it, beautiful young woman has brought a Biblical scene to mind. Camilla has always read the Bible, more so recently than for many years. The book of Genesis comes to mind and he is Jacob with the maidservant Bilhah who bore him a son. She was also most beautiful and most desirable and low born.

Camilla catches the eye of an out of focus bearded man standing at the bar, who raises a glass and smiles. He could well be Abraham the Patriarch. For the first time in her life Camilla knows she is alluring, and that she has Sir Godwyn to thank. All his faults are powerful faults and the fault lines deep and dangerous. She crosses the room avoiding the out of focus bearded man's inviting eye; Abraham had many wives.

She coughs politely.

"Camilla, my dear." He turns, she hopes not too reluctantly, away from the provincial vamp ....no... that is unfair...and takes hold of Camilla's hand. His touch does stir sensations in intimate parts of a woman's body. A gift and a curse, no doubt shared by both Jacob the seducer of the maidservant Bilhah, and by Abraham the Patriarch with many wives. "You look ravishing, my dear." Laura Standish narrows expertly mascaraed eyes, taking in all that is visible of the smallish woman, who is dressed in an expensive dark blue trouser suit with a pale blue silky blouse buttoned to the neck. All set off by a stylish pearl necklace. Laura is trying to decide if ravishing trumps stunning. She thinks not. "Allow me to introduce Laura Standish." The dry lip twitch." Not one of the Hertfordshire Standishes but a Standish nonetheless."

"Pleased to meet you, Laura." Camilla French realises this close up that she was being really unfair and she hates to be unfair. There is an insouciance of beauty about this girl that is just this side of adorable. She instantly likes the girl. There is an open hearted honesty behind the kittenish eyes that is most beguiling.

"Likewise, I'm sure." Laura knows this attractive small woman will be somebody else important, and bats back what appears to be a genuine smile. Laura feels more at ease than she usually does with challenging women; usually expecting to be put in her place.

"Camilla is on Question Time tonight."

"You must be somebody important?"

"Not really." A genuine self-deprecating smile and Laura likes that.

"She most certainly is important, my dear Laura. A Shadow Minister no less."

"That does sound important." The two unalike women exchange verging on complicit smiles, intriguing Sir Godwyn who is so rarely intrigued these days. He had been prepared for a Paddington Bear staring contest and it is Laura Standish, who is the shadow of nothing whatsoever, surprising him the most.

"That murderer bloke is on as well." Laura's voice has not quite found the settled tone. "Jack thingy. I am following him on Twitter." She does not realise that she is actually following the Honourable Lady Rebecca Sharp on Twitter.

"Now now, my dear Laura, he was found not guilty." Sir Godwyn touches her bare arm and she smiles an at ease smile.

"He did it though." This surprising girl has an innate ability to command the high ground. Camilla French thinks Sir Godwyn Lydate might not realise what he is stoking into life. These Biblical maidservants are made of stern stuff.

"Talk of the devil."

There is a murmured hush in the bar area as the People's hero enters arm in arm with a striking girl in a full on above the knee crimson frock. It could not be a more dramatic entrance had there been a fanfare of Shakespearean trumpets stage left, and it demands a Prologue. The striking girl in the full on above the knee crimson frock steers her captive towards the threesome at the bar.

"My dear Jane." Sir Godwyn kisses the striking girl on both cheeks, surprised by the flush on her cheeks, because she is normally such a pale girl. "How good to see you." As if this meeting is a rather pleasant unexpected surprise in a series of pleasant unexpected surprises. The two men nod to each other, man to man fashion, and Sir Godwyn makes the introductions. Both Camilla French and Laura Standish take stock of the current most famous human being on Planet Earth. Camilla French with pale red lips pressed together, because she does not approve of murder however apparently justified. And she does mean apparently.

Laura Standish gazes with redder lips slightly open; an enticing look which she carries off to native perfection. Sir Godwyn has edged closer and is pressing against her shiny black legs. She feels like the first prize in a fairground coconut shy, and is not sure she likes it – but what the hell. Not quite sober she aspires to be more than a prize – even a first prize. She knows what she means and the cheque has cleared – so what the hell.

"How are things, my dear Jane?" There is something going on here and Laura, where is bloody Hertfordshire anyway, Standish intends to find out. Camilla French knows only too well what is going on.

"Couldn't be better, Sir Godwyn." An incredibly poshly polished voice. This Jane person pouting a naturally pouty mouth, glances, it might be thought, dismissively at Laura. A glance that could be likened to the sweep of a lighthouse beam at midnight on a Cornish headland. Then glances at Camilla French and raises a quizzical plucked eyebrow. Camilla French pretends not to notice. She is not in the mood for quizzical plucked eyebrows raised by posh little madams, never having been a posh little madam.

"Excellent." Sir Godwyn is revelling in the unspoken interplay as he presses a thigh against Laura's shiny black legs. Laura's make believe billydoo in the ladies toilet seems a lifetime ago and things have moved on apace. If this was a novel it would be hardly believable and truth is indeed stranger than fiction.

"We really need to be going, Sir Godwyn." The pushy posh Jane glancer is holding tight to the People's hero as though, given half a chance, he might bolt for the hills.

"Indeed we should, my dear Jane. Indeed we should." Sir Godwyn finishes the whisky with a flourish. Laura Standish had been hoping for another drink. That smarmy looking bearded bloke, who looks vaguely familiar, is getting an eyeful of her legs. But then so is Hero Jack, who does not appear the least bit smarmy.

She is not to know that Jack is thinking what a tantalisingly beautiful girl with such amazing legs. She reminds him of one of his more attractive students, who had more than once pointedly ignored him in the street; he has forgotten the ignoree's name. The days of being pointedly ignored in the street have apparently gone the way of the Dodo.

Their eyes meet and Laura smiles. There is something tantalisingly just out of reach masked behind her innate beauty. He is acutely aware of Jane Fennell's body heat, a woman who has indeed not let him out of her sight. She follows orders to the letter, a girl born out of time, designed more for 1930s' Germany and could be a Mitford sister reborn. She certainly sounds like one and would, no doubt, have caught the wandering eye of an oversexed Adolf Hitler.

"Where is Spencer Perceval?" Camilla French feels someone should pose the elephantine question.

"The redoubtable Harriet O'Connor, that hammer of the Picts, has escorted the dear boy to the Town Hall." The dry lip twitch. "She didn't think that meeting in a bar before the Show was a good idea." The silence contains more than an element of stunned surprise on the part of those intimately acquainted with Spencer Perceval.

This delightfully saucy girl is most definitely pressing back. He is also aware that she is indulging in a stare exchange with Jack Bellingham, the Jury's favourite.

"Spencer agreed?" Jane Fennell sounds incredulous – she knows Spencer Perceval's predilections only too well. The only man she knows who can perform satisfactorily when dead drunk, although somewhat spoiled by the fact that he can never remember anything afterwards…after she has given of her best a girl likes to be remembered afterwards.

"Shall we say he went along with the suggestion."

Jane Fennell is aware that Jack is feeling up her arse. Not that she minds, in fact quite the reverse. Their impromptu screwing this afternoon had been most assuredly satisfying in all areas. There is no way he will not remember anything afterwards. She feels that she is literally glowing, a rarity these days. She is not at all happy about Jack eyeballing Sir Godwyn's latest leggy appendage of doubtful pedigree. She hopes Jack is not imagining feeling up the appendage's arse, and Jane assertively wiggles her own arse until he breaks eye contact with the appendage and smiles down at Jane.

She has plenty of ideas for more impromptu screwing later and has even packed the ill-fitting waitress uniform. In her varied experience of men some dressing up role-play rarely comes amiss and one gets so bored with the nurse thing. There are only so many places one can stick a thermometer. And schoolgirls… well really!

"Come then, my friends, once more into the breach," Sir Godwyn intones and someone sniggers.

Arm in arm with Laura Standish, Sir Godwyn leads the way and Camilla French brings up the rear. The bearded bloke, who would be mortified to be thought smarmy, watches them all the way out. That naughty little waitress Laura something or other doesn't recognise Philip Whiteoak with his recent Ayatollah beard. Mind you she was well pissed that night and it was three months ago. She was still pissed the following morning when he memorably took her from behind…well…memorably for him anyway.

Being pragmatic he turns his attention to the busty barmaid who is definitely hovering with intent.

"Same again, love and whatever you want."

"That would be telling."

That's tonight fixed up then. Better touch base with the wifey before he goes into full seduction mode. The barmaid is actually quite fit.

"Cheers, love."

"Bottoms up."

Thursday October 19th 10.46pm

Risking a blinding headache, Rosalie Murray is staring with one goodish eye and one blurred eye at the old-fashioned colour flickering television set. Everything about Agnes Grey's late mother's apartment is disturbingly old-fashioned, like being trapped in a 1960s' William Hartnell playing Doctor Who time warp. Unlike the saving grace bath, the television is well past its sell by date.

If Rosalie Murray has anything to do with it, Agnes Grey is approaching her very own sell by date. Not only has Agnes seen Rosalie at her most vulnerable, but she must have been the one who betrayed her to Sir Lucifer Lydate and, at that thought, she tugs the borrowed dressing gown tighter around her naked body… the weapon of choice to be used sparingly.

She is nurturing this visceral hatred for both of them – nurturing more successfully than she nurtured the recently aborted child. A cowardly decision made in the heat of the moment and regretted that same day and at some time every single day since.

She strives not to think about having, weirdly, only found true forgetfulness in the act of procreation. She has to grimace at the irony knowing that, since the abortion, she has fucked around more than somewhat indiscriminately. It is not her fault.

Her mind wandering, she is aware of the voices of the Question Time panellists. She has to admit that John Eames was a great comfort in the immediate aftermath. An inherently good man despite all his frailties, and their coming together on the altar steps the nearest thing she has ever approached to a glimpse of Paradise. John Eames is the opposite of Sir Godwyn Lydate, that inherently evil man despite all his strengths. One day she will spit on his grave. More than that…one owl hooting midnight hour she will piss on his grave and that might go some way to evening things up.

Now she pays attention. Camilla French, or rather a buffed up version of Camilla French, is answering a leading question with sincere confidence and aplomb. She is bloody good and the audience applauds enthusiastically, and a confident seeming Spencer Perceval delivering a witty throwaway comment, occasions more shared laughter. There will be no walking off set tonight; how the mighty and all that.

Now Jack Bellingham is mouthing words amidst interrupting cheers. Rosalie cannot prevent the tears running down her bruised and battered cheeks, clouding vision that is already clouded. She should have been there. She will have revenge; she must have revenge.

She has made a phone call to set it all in motion. He was surprised but could not disguise that he was intrigued…an overused word but appropriate on this occasion. Tomorrow the fightback begins. She looks round the old fashioned, colour flickering, high ceilinged room with distaste, tugging the borrowed dressing gown even tighter. Tomorrow her body will be used purely as a primed weapon and, for once, being a woman in the political bear pit will work in her favour.

The first step is to leave this place and seek sanctuary, but not in any Church where there is an altar. She must come to terms with her loss and move on. Tomorrow is another day. The paucity of the banal thought is not lost on Rosalie Murray, as the pounding headache threatens.

Thursday 19th October 11.52pm

They are gathered round a table in the bar area of the Queens Hotel like characters at the denouement of an Agatha Christie novel, where the plot is unravelled on the last page by Hercule Poirot and his little grey cells. The peroxide blonde barmaid, avoiding Spencer Perceval's eye, is pouring champagne for the assembled company. Not Sir Godwyn's choice of champagne but champagne nonetheless. At his insistence there are proper goblets and he raises one in a toast of his own devising.

"I thought that all went rather well."

Jack Bellingham raises his own goblet and imbibing a generous mouthful, also thinks it went rather well. Jane Fennell follows suit. Sir Godwyn thinks she is looking particularly apple scrubbed luscious this evening. Not letting the not guilty one out of her sight seems to agree with the feisty little madam, but she needs to be careful. She has not the native resilience of Shirley Keeldar. He glances at Camilla French who is taking a few exploratory sips. She in turn glances at delightful Laura Standish, a girl of appetites who has finished her glass of champagne in two gulps.

Without being asked, the peroxide blonde barmaid refills Laura's goblet and returns to the bar, where bearded Patriarch Philip Whiteoak is somewhat precariously perched on a bar stool. He stops trying to catch naughty Laura, the once upon a time willing waitress's eye.

"I am off at midnight." The peroxide blonde whispers. "Go to your room and I will join you in a few minutes."

He whispers back. "I've got a terrible horn, love."

"So have I." The silly sod has no idea what's in store. She is just in the mood to shag his excuse for brains out.

She watches him weave his way towards the lift, his somewhat staggering exit ignored by the round table of toffee nosed gits. Not Laura Standish, of course; she is just a common or garden tart…no toffee at all involved. She wants to be careful, that's all, because that toffee nosed lot don't take prisoners. There are no flies on Charlotte.

The pugilistic battered porter is limping towards the bar counter looking Charlotte over with avaricious eyes of a born loser, who still dreams of winning that last fight. He was never a loser and he did win his last fight. She knows that one night stand was probably a mistake… still, any port in a storm is an acceptable motto in Charlotte's world. He might turn out a useful stopgap if there is another storm. He possesses all the right equipment in more than adequate proportions, and he certainly has stamina. They most certainly went the full ten rounds and then some.

"You alright, George?"

"Yes, Charlotte love. And you?" He has a disturbing habit of talking to her tits…not that he can be blamed.

"Not so bad, love." She is preparing to leave. She doesn't want beardy boy to go off the boil… not the mood she's in. "See you tomorrow, George love." She turns away before he can say anything else. He watches her leave clutching the bottle of champagne, and there is a look of longing in his eyes – that was a hell of a night – the things that girl got up to. Then he glances at the champagne swilling table of rich buggers and wonders if they will order any more drinks. He recognises the small tasty little piece who was getting banged last night. He got some smart pics on his mobile. The tasty small piece catches his eye and looks away. He is not to know he is only a blur in the background. She is hardly touching her champagne.

"Drink up, Camilla, my dear." Sir Godwyn is finding it hard to keep his hands away from the tempting nearness of Laura Standish, who has kicked off a high heeled shoe and is rubbing a crinkled sole against his tensed calf muscles.

"I think I will go to bed." Is Camilla's yawning reply. "I am really whacked." She cannot help wondering if Gil has become as yesterday as Helen Huntingdon appears to have become.

"I am not surprised, my dear." He raises the tumbler. "See you in the morning." As she passes his chair he takes hold of her arm. "You were superb, my dear." She knows he means Question Time, but there are always several sub agendas with this most disingenuous man.

"Thank you, Godwyn."

He would have made a first class Old Testament King of Judah.

"Sleep well, my dear."

She glances at the Night porter; his face is blurry, but there is something vaguely familiar about him.

Camilla is well aware that he is watching her departure, and resists the temptation to wiggle her ever so neat bottom. That would not do at all. Being appraised merely as the shape of a woman is such a double-edged experience.

Alert on the watchtower, Harriet O'Connor prevents Spencer Perceval reaching for the champagne bottle and Sir Godwyn watches on in genuine admiration. The sole of the crinkled foot rubbing against his clenching calf muscles is most promissory.

"I think we will retire as well, Sir Godwyn." There is now more posh in Harriet's voice than really works, and the smile does not reach her eyes. He is glad that he has arranged for dear Helen to check things out on the banks of the Tyne – very much out of sight out of mind.

"Very well, my dear and good night to you both." Spencer Perceval avoids eye contact with anyone as he is led to the lift by Harriet O'Connor's firm hand in the small of his back. She resents Sir Godwyn's right to benediction.

"How are the mighty fallen." Simpers Jane Fennell, who will never forgive Spencer Perceval, although it was partly her own fault for allowing herself to be handcuffed to the bed. She was not to know that he would pass out clutching the key. She somehow doesn't think that formidable old biddy will allow that to happen. She will probably handcuff Perceval to the bed and throw away the key. Jane sniggers at the thought.

Sir Godwyn does not reply as she expects, being too taken up with the visibly active sole.

Jack is studying the hefty night porter sneaking a glass of whisky – he knows it is just a walk-on part, but then so was Harriet O'Connor's role. Now it seems she might be going to play a more substantial part. That was not at all envisaged.

Jack just does not seem to be able to handle walk-on parts – Jane Fennell, for instance, who has taken ownership of his free hand, started life as a nondescript waitress serving breakfast in the Grande suite of the Savoy Hotel. He was not to know she was one of Sir Godwyn's people. The same Sir Godwyn who is now heading for the lift, an arm round Laura Standish's exceedingly trim waist. No need for three guesses... a very lucky man, thinks Jack, even with Jane Fennell holding onto anything within reach.

"Let's go to bed, Jack." She whispers just to prove the point. As Jack and Jane... at least she isn't called Jill... remorselessly head for the lift, arms round each other's waists. He wonders if the pugilistic night porter will develop into a meaningful role. He hopes not because you, he means one, would not want to meet him down a dark alley. It is hard to think coherently with Jane Fennell whispering urgent rude somethings into a sticky out ear.

George Edmonds, Noah like, watches them depart two by two; and one of those all in the right place birds reminds him of that waitress who is always eyeing up the blokes. George tried it on but she told him to 'fuck off, you sad git' – which wasn't very nice. George sees the murderer bloke necking with that skinny posh bit of stuff as the lift doors close. Some blokes get all the luck. George likes to think he is a realist and knows his limitations. These birds tonight were Premier League and he is strictly bottom half of League Two. His current girlfriend, in the loosest sense of the word, is a part-time prostitute. George met Una Campbell in the Armley massage parlour where she works to boost her wages as a care worker. She prefers caring for old people so she can nick money to further boost her wages, plus some of the old fellas are only too happy to pay good money for a hand job or a blow job.

He likes to think the two of them have a sort of understanding. They actually sort of like each other and make each other laugh. She always insists on a condom which is fair enough. There is one old fella she lets go all the way without a condom every Tuesday morning, but then he pays through the nose, so fair dos. Finishing the whisky he washes up the glass and closes the shutters on the bar. It will be quiet from now on with just the occasional guest staggering back from the fleshpots. The occasional brought back woman sneaking out... but that will be much later. He recently caught Una Campbell sneaking out but neither of them mentioned it afterwards.

Settling himself in his cosy cubby hole he plays back what he recorded last night of that tasty little piece going like the clappers. When he goes off duty at six o'clock in the morning he will go to Una's pad and, if she is in the mood, give her a bit of a seeing to before she goes off to work. If he shows her this footage she should be well and truly up for it. More often than not she asks for money before allowing any seeing to, and that's fair enough. They are not exactly love's young dream. She did reluctantly agree to a freebie there and then, after he caught her sneaking out of the Hotel. He is playing back the video for the third or possibly fourth time, when a voice behind his hunched shoulders nearly gives him a heart attack. "What the hell is that, George?"

"Jesus fucking Christ. You nearly gave me a heart attack, woman."

This temporary manager woman is always sneaking around. He is sure she expects to catch him with a woman...luckily she didn't catch him with Una, although it only took five minutes. He has dropped the mobile and Caroline Helstone picks it up. For some unaccountable reason this plug ugly ex-boxer is the only member of staff with whom she feels the least bit comfortable. She is not sure she wants to know why that should be.

"Christ, George, when did you record this?" She is playing it back for the second time and knows he is getting an eyeful of her cleavage... there is a valiantly grim simplicity to George she finds oddly comforting and, with George, she doesn't feel out of her depth. There is telling it like it is and then there is battered about George Edmonds, who is a man's man in the best possible way. The sort to make the right kind of woman feel valued.

"Last night in the bar." He switches on the kettle. "Dirty buggers."

"You can say that again."

"Dirty buggers." She throatily chuckles even though she saw the joke coming from outer space.

"Cuppa?"

"Yes, thank you, George."

"I know how you like it."

Here comes another one and she doesn't mind playing along. "Do you really?"

"From behind." She would allow no one else to get away with this sort of comment. It is as though the Hotel at this time of night is an enchanted kingdom. Not a bad guess either.

"You are a naughty boy, George."

With his best attempt at a wicked grin he hands over the Leeds Rhinos mug of milky tea with two sugars. She takes a tentative sip. "You know who this woman is, don't you, George?"

He shakes his head. Unless she plays Rugby League he would have no idea.

"She is Camilla, I think it's French, a Shadow Minister and is tipped to be a future Prime Minister." Caroline is playing the recording back for the third time. "She was on Question Time tonight with that Jack Bellingham." She intercepts the blank look. "That murderer who got off."

"Oh! Him." As if murderers who get off are ten a penny. George slurps his strong brown tea with three sugars from a matching Leeds Rhinos treble winning mug – the one with the chip – he is nothing if not a gentleman after his own lights.

"You realise this could be pure dynamite, George?"

"What do you mean, woman?"

"The media will pay a small fortune for this footage. That little lady was incredibly indiscreet." Caroline reflects the avaricious gleam in the big man's red setter reflective brown eyes and, not for the first time, wishes she had seen George in the boxing ring. Rumour has it he was magnificent... a gladiator in full armour who usually won by a knockout. It is only outside the ring that he is, apparently, a loser. "On the other hand Sir Godwyn Lydate might be eternally grateful." That could be worth more than money.

"That snooty bloke whose arse they all lick?" Including you, woman, he doesn't say. He has eyes and ears and battered common sense.

"That's him."

George is breathing close over her shoulder as they look over the incriminating footage together. "You can even see their faces. She is a horny little madam." Caroline Helstone has to admit it is making her feel somewhat horny. They are certainly going at it. It is some considerable time since she has had one of her trademark one night stands. Not one of the most memorable either, more of a half night stand.

"A tight arse." George is breathing even more closely over her shoulder and she can smell the whisky on his breath. She would discipline anyone else on the spot.

"Stop that, George." He has the brass nerve to feel up Caroline's arse that could never in a million years be described as tight. An arse though; most definitely and lots of it. She playfully knocks his hand away. "Stop it, George." Another dismissible offence let go.

She thoughtfully hands back the mobile phone and they sip their respective teas. She pointedly ignores the heavyweight contender bulge in his trousers. She is not that desperate. Who is she kidding?

"What shall we do about the footage, woman?"

"We?"

"I can't do it on my own, woman." He knows only too well that he has taken a few punches too many over the years. He watches her contemplatively sipping the hot sweet milky tea and blowing the cloudy steam. Unlike Una Campbell, who is a bit stringy apart from up top, this lady is lots of fleshy woman everywhere. Just the way he likes it…chance would be a fine thing.

"I will need to think about the best thing to do." She sets down her mug. "Now I'm off to beddy byes." She cannot resist glancing speculatively at the heavyweight bulge. Who is she kidding indeed?

"I'm off duty at six, woman."

She doesn't reply as she slips out of the cubby hole. He is a trier, she will give him that, and she is really cheesed off with having to take care of things on her own. She has never felt comfortable about taking care of things on her own since that particular creepy bloke at the Children's home, who insisted on watching and then coming all over her budding tits.

Smiling to himself, George relishes the hot sweet tea. Occasionally when he was boxing he didn't go for the easy knockout but kept things going to win on points. It was sometimes more satisfying that way. The trouble was…yes well… the trouble was.

Friday 20th October 2.08am

Flint eyed, Gilbert Markham adjusts the Regimental balaclava to a military setting and glides expertly from shadow to shadow at the rear of the target property. There are no lights showing – the enemy is not expecting an attack at this hour – Gilbert has no sense of an ambush. He has sneaked away from Rosanna Spearman asleep and gently snoring. A woman of much more body than Camilla French and a surprisingly gentle soul. She is a woman to tug at the heart strings, needing protecting from her frailties and the world at large, particularly in the person of her husband. This is where it starts… this is where it ends.

Invisible in the shadowest shadows he listens – nothing out of the ordinary, just the usual made up sounds of a London suburban two o'clock in the morning. Soundlessly he breaks the window pane and reaches inside and opens the rear door… the third floor apartment is his target. This ground floor room is some sort of disused scullery and the door at the far end is unlocked. Like taking candy from a baby…not at all like that mission in Kandahar that served as a warning to them all…at least to the few who survived.

Meticulously he climbs the worn carpeted stairs on the balls of his feet, pausing only once at a creaking stair which he will avoid on the way down. Then he continues and listens at the first floor apartment door of the married couple with a baby… he has done his research… no sounds. Then the second floor apartment of a recently divorced woman… probably in bed with her much younger boyfriend with whom she cheated on her husband… no sounds… all passion spent. Good solid doors in these Victorian houses well-built for the upper middle classes of the 1870s. It will take a bomb to wake anyone up… no need for that… unlike Kandahar. Learn from your mistakes the unspoken Regimental motto. Bury your dead then get right royally pissed and have a woman.

The target apartment is on the third floor. It takes all of twenty seconds to pick the lock. Then he is inside and silently closing the door, his eyes already accustomed to the darkness. With the pencil torch he checks behind the first door to reveal an untidy living room. The second door a bathroom and a toilet ditto untidy with a smell of cheap disinfectant. The third door opens onto an untidy junk room. By process of elimination this fourth door must be where his unsuspecting quarry lies. The door is slightly ajar and Gilbert slips inside like a night time bogeyman from a gothic tale brought to life – he listens – rhythmic breathing – male. No one else in the room, so no complications; it is hard to predict how females will react. Collateral damage of a female nature to be avoided if at all possible – unlike Kandahar. This particular sortie brings it all back. They were good men who never made it back and could not learn from their mistakes, get right royally pissed and have a woman.

Not bothering to be soundless any more he walks across the bedroom floor and pulls back the duvet. The man sleeps naked. That makes it easier. Gilbert sniffs. There has certainly been a woman here… a sleep disorientated voice. "Frances?" Straight out of some vivid dream into a waking nightmare. Only seconds…it might as well be a lifetime. "Katie?"

"Fraid not, lover boy."

"What the…" Felix Spearman is dragged unceremoniously out of the bed and held tight in a basic training hold. It feels good. It always feels good. The target cannot speak with a strong arm round its neck that could be broken with one practised movement.

"Now you listen, Felix, you piece of steaming horse shit and you listen good." The arm round the throat is tightened. The target begins to choke; his brain will be struggling to piece together what is happening. Just as it should be. Unlike Kandahar the victim understands English.

"I am the appointed representative of Rosanna Spearman of this Parish." He will not say wife. She is above that. Another squeeze. Some more choking. Which is as it should be; a choking target cannot shout a warning. He must never forget Kandahar.

"You will not threaten the lady in any way. Do you understand?" Another squeeze and some more choking. "Do you understand?" He slightly loosens the classic hold. The nodding dog in rear car window nod nods.

"Ca …ca…can't breathe."

Gilbert is not under orders on this mission so the buck stops here. He tightens the hold and the only answer is a squealing sob that is strangled into a choke. He knows in his heart of hearts the ideal solution, sorted once and for all. No comebacks and he was never here.

Nothing to go tits up in the future. Furthermore they are still married and so Rosanna will inherit everything…she will be a rich widow. Gilbert has seen the will that the stupid shit threatened to change tomorrow. Sometimes tomorrow never comes.

With an accomplished twist he snaps Felix Spearman's scrawny neck and lets the instantly lifeless body tumble to the floor like so much useless rubbish. The shit is voiding his bowels; they always void their bowels. It was something in their training they were told to expect. The headless chicken syndrome the Instructor had said. They had all laughed like drains.

Gilbert clicks on the low wattage bedside lamp and, with scarcely a glance at the huddled corpse, he checks the bedside table – a used condom in the ashtray – he thought so. Let's hope his last act of sexual congress on this earth was memorable. Nothing much else of any use in the bedroom, except the mobile phone which Gilbert pockets. No booby traps here.

Best not to linger when the mission is accomplished. The shitty smell is not very pleasant either… he had forgotten the shitty smell. He turns off the low wattage lamp and reverts to night-time bogeyman mode. No one saw him arrive and no one will see him leave.

Back at HQ, Rosanna's kitchen, he peels off the plastic surgeon's gloves and secretes them at the bottom of the rubbish bin. He sniffs… it needs emptying. He will do it in the morning. This lady needs a man about the house.

Pouring himself a well-deserved large whisky, he sits at the kitchen table scrolling the dead man's state of the art mobile phone. Nothing much of interest except full frontal selfies of two extremely pretty barely teenage girls, one of whom he recognises. So this one is Frances. Silly silly girl…tasty though…a younger version of her mother.

Tapping the mobile thoughtfully against his teeth, which were reconstructed after Kandahar, he wonders if Frances is the one who shared the condemned man's last condom – or Katie perhaps. He might need to find out. These are the sort of things that Sir Godwyn needs to know.

"Gil, love." He has not been aware of the yawning and stretching Rosanna Spearman entering the kitchen lighted only by the cooker light, and clutching a seen better days woollen dressing gown to her generous body. That is what happens when your attention wanders. She sees that he is fully dressed. "Where have you been at this time of night, love?" She is blink blinking sleep from her eyes and appears adorably confused. He pulls her onto his lap and she doesn't resist. "I woke up to go for a wee and you were gone."

"I'm back now." A tonguey kiss and a distracting hand stroking the Delphic curve of a lovely meaty thigh. Instinctively she traps the hand between the lovely meaty thighs.

"I woke up from a naughty dream." She hoarsely whispers.

Enough said. He stands up with the woman in his arms and carries her upstairs like a bride over the threshold, as if she weighs nothing. She loves that. She was never carried over the threshold by Felix and has not giggled girlishly for such a long time.

They tumble together on the once upon a time marital bed. It is always the same after a kill this brutally urgent need for a woman… any woman. Even so he is glad it is the widow Spearman and not some squealing Arab tart.

Friday 20th October 3.32am

Wide awake as wide-awake is, Jack Bellingham is staring at the hotel bedroom ceiling, which is artistically dappled by the rustling curtain reflected streetlights of a rainy City night that could be anywhere. Unlike Emily Rowley he is no artist but he knows what he likes – one of his Mother's many facile sayings as they traipsed round numberless art galleries, where she always made sure her opinions were overheard by all and sundry. Whatever his mother admired his sister disliked with equal intensity, and the inevitable slap followed unless his sister managed to dodge out of reach. Their Mother wisely pretending to ignore the stuck out tongue. To this day his bloody sister will not enter an art gallery if her life depended on it.

The naked girl stirs in his arms and Jack wonders where it all went right. The reality has made all those carefully constructed Meccano daydreams appear pretty tame – banal is the word that comes to mind – a word he used often in his lectures on Nineteenth Century literature.

Jane Fennell mumbles in her sleep and unconsciously rearranges her slim leggy thigh draped across his torso. It is a sensuous movement and no Meccano involved. They have done things that he could not have envisaged in his wildest imaginings. At least, unlike Amelia Sedley, Jane Fennell got his name right in the throes of passion. Surely Jack is not a hard name to remember.

One thing he does know is that the People's hero does not need to understand women; the formerly closed book simply opens of its own accord with no blank pages to fill in. Jane Fennell is such a sensuously demanding creature that he dare not move his arms in case she wakes up. He does not want to understand why he wishes it was Celia Brook stirring in his arms and draping a leggy thigh across his torso. Jane Fennell possesses some interesting hidden tattoos, particularly on her lower belly, but this yearning is about much more than hidden tattoos. Something about being with Celia Brook makes him appear as normal to himself as he will ever be. She is the girl next door and he is the boy next door… Jesus Christ… if only.

Friday 20th October 5.42am

Rosanna Spearman wakes Gilbert Markham with gently insistent butterfly kisses. October falls but Midsummer is in the air to celebrate a time of the dying of butterflies. It is a most pleasant way to be woken from a not very pleasant dream that he refuses to think of as a nightmare. It is always the same after a kill, the only remorse is in dreams. "Another naughty dream, Roz?" He mumbles, knowing there is no lurking danger in coming luxuriantly awake in these scented moments next to this woman.

"Very naughty." A seamless move from timely butterfly kisses to tonguey necking and this time the inevitable lovemaking is gentle and, it has to be said, verging on loving – not a word with which Gilbert Markham is usually on speaking terms.

It only takes a few minutes and they are both inordinately satisfied. The insistence of the gentle rhythm fitting their bodies together seamlessly into a two piece jigsaw of intense pleasure.

"That was so lovely, Gil." She whispers, tight in his arms. She cannot believe how much pleasure her body can give and receive. Felix never took her in his arms afterwards, and the men she took to pay him back merely slam bang thank you ma'ams. Not lovers in any sense of the word.

"The same here, Roz." He kisses a glittering diamond studded earlobe and she shivers. In these few moments, she is so much at peace with his sticky slackness squashy against her soft belly. She wishes they had met twenty years ago when she was a stunning beauty with a taught belly and not an ounce of fat.

If they had met then she would not have fallen for Felix with his seductive distortions and exaggerations. Controlling her every thought and deed. Then, of course, Rosanna stopped being so very young and it all started to go horribly wrong. She wants to get back to the better person she could have been if she had never gifted Felix her virginity.

Rosanna finds it hard to hate anyone but she must learn to hate Felix. Sleepily she breathes into Gil's throat that smells so manly; Felix never smelt manly.

"Roz?"

"Mm… love."

He is stroking gently along her backbone and she wishes she could stay like this forever, and has not wished that for a very long time.

"Last night I went to see your husband." He will not speak his name. The enemy does not have a name.

She is all at once wide awake and eases backwards to study his face that is still flushed with the all-consuming lovemaking.

"Gil, you shouldn't have." Her gunmetal grey eyes are indelibly grey, as they search his face that she is gently stroking. "You really shouldn't have, love."

"I wanted him to leave you alone."

"Oh, Gil love, he will never do that." She knows it has always been Felix's mission to make her life as miserable as possible and she has grown accustomed to it.

"I want to look after you, Roz."

She cannot prevent instant tears streaming down her own flushed cheeks. Felix had once said the same thing, although she had been very young and innocently trusting at the time. She hadn't known then that he was a congenital liar.

"That is really sweet, Gil, but Felix is a cruel man."

"Not any more he isn't."

She eases further back searching in his eyes that give nothing away. If there is a mirror to Gilbert Markham's soul it is not in the eyes. She is not at all sure she understands the way this is going.

"What do you mean?"

He has worked out what he is going to say. He would have told her last night but needs musted. She could be easily frightened off like an uncaged canary. She looks so satisfyingly attractive in her confused uncertainty and the gently insistent lovemaking has taken years off her age. He resists the urge to kiss the questioning lips which would only delay things further.

"He took a swing at me when I told him to leave you alone." She could well believe that... Felix has never been good with being told what to do. "We struggled and he fell awkwardly against a table." Now he is stroking her teary cheeks with braille fingertips. She is so glad Gil wasn't hurt. Felix can be unpredictable and violent. He once cut her with a kitchen knife. She hasn't told Gil that Felix slapped her face yesterday making her lips bleed. She was so ashamed to be treated like that. She didn't deserve that.

"Was he hurt?"

"I think he broke his neck."

It takes several alarm clock ticking seconds for Rosanna Spearman to compute the words. All the time the braille fingertips are gently stroking her face and brushing away the tears with gentle thumbs.

"You mean...?" She stares not quite horrified into his face. "...he is dead?"

"It was an accident, Roz."

He knows this is the moment of truth and holds her seeded body tight so she cannot see his face. He knows that if she is the least bit perceptive his face might give him away. She relaxes as he strokes up and down the finely ridged backbone.

"What are we to do, Gil, love?"

So far so good. They are in this together. "Nothing."

"Nothing?"

He holds so tight that she cannot ease away and she doesn't struggle.

"He cannot hurt you any more, Roz."

She knows this must be true although it is hard to believe. The hard slaps really hurt yesterday and a tooth has been loosened. He shouldn't have done that. She didn't deserve that.

"You are safe now, Roz."

"Safe?" Such an alien concept. She has lived on the crumbling and dangerous cliff edge of threat and malice for so long.

"I will look after you, Roz." At this moment he wants to believe that he can be the better man she deserves, which she does believe without question.

The sound that escapes from deep in her throat is halfway between a croon and sob; an ancient woman to ancient man sound first heard in the flame shadowed Neolithic caves of northern Europe. She presses her body fiercely to his body and he holds her body just as fiercely and in these moments they are a one piece jigsaw.

She is glad that Felix is dead. Glad. Glad. Glad. So glad that Gil is alive. The sticky softness is hardening against her soft belly and she avidly seeks his mouth.

Friday 20th October 6.24am

George Edmonds mutters the short, half remembered prayer he used to recite before his later fights, when he was starting to lose his nerve. He inhales a deep shuddering breath as he knocks on the door of Caroline Helstone's rooms. This would by no means be the first time he has badly misread a woman. He has not felt this nervous since before his last ever bout in the ring, which he won by a knockout that broke his hand. His opponent was in a coma for several weeks and neither of them fought professionally again. For a couple of years they had exchanged Christmas cards; his opponent's cards written by his wife.

The door opens and Caroline Helstone gives him the once over, and thinks if you look beyond the battered face, the broken nose, and the cauliflower ears he is a fine looking man. She is wearing a sensible maroon woollen dressing gown that has seen worse days. There is no disguising the sculpted shape of her substantial breasts.

"What kept you?"

Before he can painstakingly assemble a suitable reply, she has turned on bare heels and walked across the sitting room, towards what turns out to be the cramped by the three-quarter bed bedroom. By the time he has politely closed the door, rubbed his shoes on the worn smooth welcome mat and followed the bare heels into the bedroom, she has shed the faded maroon dressing gown.

The bedroom is illuminated by a low wattage bedside lamp. If he had been aware of the painting of Venus rising out of the waves, he would think this was a version that any red blooded man would be glad to see come to life.

"You like what you see, George?" He has hurriedly undressed and she can see that he does indeed like what he sees… she is a magnificent looking woman in her own way. The breasts are even breastier than Una Campbell's breasts, which are out of proportion to her scrawny body…these breasts are not at all out of proportion. He nods and there is no need to assemble a reply.

"Right." She sits on the three-quarter bed which noticeably sags; it is going to be a bit crowded in there. "We do it in the dark and you never ever tell a living soul… ever." He nods and she smiles, or at least George takes it for a smile because she is showing an awful lot of teeth. "It is not polite to keep a lady waiting." She turns off the low wattage bedside lamp and swings her legs onto the bed which audibly sags even more.

Friday 20th October 7.48am

Helen Huntingdon breathes in several lungfuls of salty North Sea air and sighs, it might be thought, contentedly. No ifs or buts she loves the seaside, redolent of memories of the happy uncomplicated years of her childhood – the time before she was twelve and three quarters and her Mother remarried.

At this time on this October Friday morning the windswept sands of West Shields-on-Tyne are deserted, apart from a well preserved middle-aged man wearing a flat tweed cap set at a jaunty angle, who is walking a limping small dog. He is not trying to disguise the fact that he is eyeing up this striking looking girl with the curly orange hair and the silver glittery tights.

She is staring out to sea, where a dinky toy looking oil tanker is crossing the far horizon. It is a good place to think and she needs to think. She is usually an instinct sort of girl but realises she needs to think. Instinct is all well and good, but thinking is thinking after all, she thinks.

The dead woman's husband is a really decent, uncomplicated man who is only too happy to be comforted. If she didn't know better she might think he was relieved his wife is dead. Which is ridiculous because he cried … a bit.

She has never questioned Goddy's instructions in the past but she does so now. She is only too well aware that he lacks a moral compass; even so she is not at all sure it is appropriate to insult his blushing bride-to-be by sending her to comfort a bereaved husband, in whatever way she deems appropriate. He wants the loose ends tied up 'whatever it takes', being his exact words.

Finding out all about Harriet O'Connor has been easy. It is the whatever it takes comforting bit that does not sit well with, what she thinks of, as her possibly new status. After all Goddy had no reason to offer marriage to get in her knickers because he was in them already. She cannot help wondering if it is all a bad taste cosmic joke.

Ted Branwell has insisted she call him Ted; his late wife always called him Edward. So far he has been comforted with a few tit squashy cuddles, not the worst she has ever dispensed.

He smells really nice and has a kissable mole on his neck, a sore temptation to an instinct kind of girl. He confirmed that poor Maria enjoyed a dicky heart. Helen gathered there was not a lot of sex, sounding like the occasional birthday and every other Christmas sort of treat. Although, in the last few days before she died, Maria had behaved rather strangely – Ted didn't go into details – no doubt he will spill the beans all in good time.

Maria Branwell's funeral will take place next week and Helen has agreed to stay and give moral support to poor Ted. There are no children, not that Helen sees herself as a child substitute, otherwise those tit squashy cuddles would not be at all appropriate. It has to be said that Ted wears his age well. He could be a much older brother. Helen has always wanted a much older brother.

Helen shields her eyes against the glare of the low sun reflecting off the North Sea. The dinky toy tanker has almost crossed the horizon and a dinky toy fishing boat is chugging out of the harbour. The well preserved middle aged man with the limping small dog in tow is leaving the beach. She has made his day with her loose skirt blowing against her body in the blustering wind. More than once exposing just about all of the glittery tights. He is not to know she has farted several times into the blustering wind, blaming the chicken curry Ted made last night. He fancies himself as a bit of a cook; Maria was never able to stand too long in the kitchen. To be honest Maria sounds to have been a bit of a wet lettuce.

Ted has insisted Helen stay at the house – more a mansion really, with stunning cliff top sea views and seven bedrooms all ensuite. She made him laugh by saying she must have a pee in every toilet. He has a really infectious laugh. He said don't forget the three toilets downstairs. Then made her giggle by saying the toilet at the back of the triple garage doesn't have a door. She had called him a cheeky man and slapped his arm…he had certainly seemed to be comforted.

Ted has made his money in scrap metal – where there's muck there's brass – he has intoned several times to make her smile her besterest smile. He confessed that he and Maria had married late, both in their mid 40s. Maria had had several unhappy love affairs and, reading between the lines, appears to have had issues about sex. Ted had always been too busy for love affairs and Helen thinks he probably paid for sex, which is really sensible when you are building up a business. Probably tax-deductible as well.

Before they were married Maria had been his part-time secretary, occasionally letting him get in her knickers – Ted's phrase – in between and sometimes during her ill-starred love affairs. Reading between the lines Helen thinks Maria probably let him get in her knickers for strategic reasons. She gathers that the infrequent knicker getting in was not all that memorable. Even so, the strategy paid off.

Ted said Maria seemed always to go for unsuitable men and Helen had smiled and said join the club. Ted had laughed saying any bloke who got in Helen's knickers was a very lucky man indeed. Then he had at once genuinely and shamefacedly apologised for saying something so inappropriate. She had really liked that and attempted her least scary smile and told him not be silly. There is an inherent niceness about Ted that is alien in the planetary constellation of Sir Godwyn – sometime Goddy – Lydate and all his works.

The trouble with this thinking is that her thoughts always chase off down the thoughtful equivalent of rabbit holes.

Ted told her, that following a particularly messy breakup with some grade A1 tosser with issues, they had somehow drifted into sharing his house. It just seemed more convenient in every way. He had rattled around in the big house on his own and, after the break up, she couldn't afford the rent of the riverside apartment. It seemed an ideal solution to their mutual loneliness. They had somehow ended up married – sneaky bitch, Helen had thought but not said. Ted had always wanted children, but soon after they were married, Maria was diagnosed with congenital heart trouble. There was even less knicker getting in after that.

Helen strolls towards the edge of the sea where sliced cream cake waves, whipped up by the north east wind, are crashing over the pebbly sand. She wishes her feet were bare like when she was that happy go lucky child before her Mother remarried. What are the waves saying? That was in some book or other. It might have been Dickens she thinks. Such a lot of things seem to have been Dickens.

The waves have always been such a soothing gobbledygook sound to her troubled grown up self. She wonders if being Goddy's blushing bride will be all it's cracked up to be. Not that it is really being cracked up to be anything at all. He will be the epitome of an absent husband. She is not at all sure that she desires her function in life to be a dropper out of an heir and a spare for the Lydate dynasty.

She cannot imagine her lack of ease at Lydate Hall will change once she is the nominal Chatelaine of that brooding Elizabethan pile, with the formidable Nanny Linda listening at doors and peeping round corners and poking in drawers. What she doesn't find out her crafty husband does find out. Helen finds the crafty husband disturbing and, unfortunately, not a little exciting. She calls it the Lady Chatterley effect. Some people think Helen is a bit simple, but they could not be more wrong. Scary yes – simple no.

She has heard rumours about Sir Godwyn's – she means Goddy's – Mother and the gardener, who still works on the Estate. She has no wish to follow suit. The gardener must be in his late 60s but hung like a donkey and randy as a goat according to Nanny Linda. According to village rumour she should know.

If she were to become Lady Helen Lydate, a virtual prisoner at Lydate Hall, she might not be able to resist age old forbidden temptations. She knows only too well she has big resistance issues. There is a definite north east chill in the air. Helen has left the borrowed fur coat in the car that Ted insisted she should also borrow. A reconstructed MGB GT in racing green that drives like a dream. Ted bought it for Maria as a birthday surprise. She moaned it was impractical and never drove it and Helen surmises there was no birthday knicker getting in of any kind. The more Helen learns about Maria, the more she dislikes the frigid cow. Although of course the frigid cow is dead and not yet buried. Helen walks back across the pebbly sands towards the tatty flag bereft excuse for a promenade, where the borrowed car is parked. The tweed flat capped middle-age man is leaning on the rusty promenade railings, and making no secret of ogling the attractive girl, with a loose skirt wrapping round shapely thighs; even the small panting dog appears mesmerised.

"Morning." Harriet O'Connor's husband touches the neb of the jauntily angled tweed flat cap. They are always on the lookout for newcomers to join the golf club wife swapping circle – there would be a fight over this delicious leggy piece. She distractedly smiles a greeting and fumbles in her shoulder bag for the car keys. Bob O'Connor knows that she has travelled from Leeds with poor Maria's body, which is now resting at the Funeral Parlour on Fowler Street, opposite the original Harriet's fashion boutique.

He also knows the vintage sports car belongs to that boring old fart Ted Branwell, rich as Croesus and thick as two short planks. The butt of most of the boys together jokes at the golf club; decent player though. The sports car roars throatily away and Bob O'Connor turns to stare at the incoming tide. The dog yawns and coughs and avidly licks its private parts. Bob knows he shouldn't be glad that Maria is dead; even he knows that is going a bit too far. He has to admit it has resolved possible worrying complications. He has been worried and he is not the worrying kind. He had called at Branwell Towers, which is what they all call the massive cliff top mansion, to leave Ted a new style eight iron that Bob had promised and kept forgetting. It was a few days before the girls were going on their trip to Leeds and a sobbing Maria had answered the door. There had been a letter from the hospital and it was not good news. Ted as per usual was away on business. Bob O'Connor screws up his mouth and, as pensive as Nelson at Trafalgar, stares out to sea. How the hell he and Maria Branwell ended up half clothed and frantically fucking on the hall carpet he still cannot, for the life of him, fathom and then, would you believe, fucking naked in several positions in the marital bed. At one point in proceedings, when he was taking her from behind, she had made so much noise he thought the selfish mare was having a deliberate heart attack there and then – going out on a high so to speak. Great tits though, really great tits but, to be honest, he was glad to get away. He made a promise of sorts that they would meet up when the girls got back from their trip. Bob is not one look a gift horse in the mouth, even a gift horse with a dicky heart.

Well now there is one less problem to be arsed about. Harriet texted that she is going to London for a few days on a buying trip. He rubs his hands together… while the cat's away the mouse will most certainly play. There is that tasty new manageress at the newly opened twentieth Harriet's fashion boutique; Cramlington is far enough away for the mouse to most definitely get away with it. The bonny lass is recently divorced…he rubs his hands together even more so…in his experience of divorced lasses she will be gagging for it.

Friday 20th October 9.44am

Sir Godwyn Lydate is not at all sure and he does not like being not at all sure. When he is not in the physical presence of Helen Huntingdon he cannot define why he cannot keep his hands to himself or his brain in neutral. He is not at all sure that this is a proper basis for a marriage. Marriage itself has been an alien concept since childhood, and nothing that he has witnessed since has changed his mind.

He sips strong black instant coffee out of a much faded Everton mug and stares out of the grimy window of Laura Standish's pokey apartment. Cosy though, most certainly cosy. She possesses the knack of cosiness along with other surprising attributes and there are such pleasant Laura scents everywhere. Apparently this is Meanwood Road and he had not intended to be here. It was not in his plans. He thinks he might be thrown by all this dynastic nonsense instigated by Nanny. He is not at all sure.

"Penny for them?" Laura has materialised, sipping strong black instant coffee from a Manchester United mug.

"They are not worth it, my dear Laura." He dry lip twitches and holds up the faded mug. "Which team do you support?"

"Neither." Sip.Sip. "The refuse of previous boyfriends."

"Have there been many previous boyfriends, Laura?"

"Now that would be telling." She nudges him coyly. It had been on the tip of her tongue to say the rest of the Premiership and half the Championship but, on second thoughts, realised that he might take it the wrong way. She is not going to spoil the effect she created by appearing surprised and delighted like a first time virgin on the far side of the pain barrier.

"It is a busy road."

"You get used to it." There is something inherently – he is not sure of the word – innocent – no most certainly not that. Guileless possibly as close as he can get to describing this girl. "We'll be talking about the weather next." She pokes him in the ribs and he pretends to wince. She really is a delightfully natural girl but more than that. There is a hurt in there somewhere that he would like to reach to make better. He so rarely feels that about other people's hurts, most of which he causes. The right words are proving so elusive this cloudy October morning, when he really should be somewhere else. He wonders if some nameless hound is catching up with the Master of Lydate Hall. He stupidly let his guard down with Rosalie Murray and knew he was doing it… doubly stupid …being stupid just to see what happens is way beyond Nemesis.

"A kiss for them."

In reply he sets down his mug and she sets down her mug as he takes her in his arms. They kiss tenderly and lingeringly. She is wearing the little black dress from last night but not the shiny black tights or the infinitesimal lacy black knickers; both mislaid somewhere in the intense lovemaking of last night and this morning. Lovemaking of a depth of purpose that he could not help comparing favourably to his verbally betrothed. Afterwards they had breakfasted in his bed at the Hotel, and a naked Laura had coyly hidden in the bathroom whilst the food was delivered. Laura leaves a man wanting more and after breakfast they had made love again. Helen Huntingdon leaves a man counting his balls.

"It was really nice… you know…everything." She burrows into his neck so he cannot see her face. "I didn't think I would like it so much." Her voice is muffled. "You know… everything." It is the truth the whole truth and nothing but the truth and she doesn't have to swear to God.

"Me neither." He kisses the top of her head… such sweet scented fine hair. If Judge Helen Graham was a Revelation then this girl is the Annunciation.

"Cheeky sod." He can feel her smiling. "You knew I was a bit of hot stuff."

"My darling Laura you are so much more than a bit of hot stuff." The resonant sensuousness in his voice makes her ease out of the clinch and stare into his serious face. It was at his insistence that he had accompanied her home in the taxi. She had said there was no need but he had insisted they walk out of the Hotel together arm in arm. There was no sign of Hitler's twin sister; Laura had worried that one of those myopic stares would have spoiled everything. After all, she was not wearing knickers and yesterday the cow had called her a dirty little wanker. Laura knows that something will spoil everything; something always does.

"What do you mean?"

That is a good question and one that he is not sure he is ready to answer at this juncture.

"I like being with you, Laura, very much indeed." He stares so intently into her eyes that she needs must stare back like a surprised Nymph at the water's edge…she thinks his eyes are like a cloudless sky and she gently strokes his unshaven face, which of itself is an omen. He captures and kisses the stroking hand.

"At least you're my cheeky sod." It is not what she had meant to say. In her experience men run a mile at any possessive word or gesture.

Sir Godwyn's pale blue eyes flare in surprise. This is not what was intended. If he was writing this page he would tear it up and start again. It is almost as if he is being written out of some story or other, which is patently ridiculous.

They kiss tenderly and lingeringly and it is Laura who breaks the clinch.

"I thought you had a train to catch?"

"There will be other trains." Is not something he thought he would ever say; Rhett Butler he is most assuredly not. She leads him by the hand to the pokey but cosy bedroom dominated by the second hand double bed. She is a neat and tidy girl, there are no clothes scattered about and if he was able to think straight he would like that. There is a row of well-worn teddy bears on the window sill and a large teddy bear propped up between the pillows on the bed. She shrugs off the dress almost shyly, which is strange as they have both explored each other's bodies most intimately.

He undresses and they stare at each other's bodies as if memorising every line and curve. He merestly touches her delicately honey coloured nippled breasts and she lays a flat hand on his quite hairy chest A few grey hairs – she likes that. They do not speak, the words are not yet invented or have been forgotten from the human race.

She turns back the threadbare duvet and picks up the well-loved teddy bear which she kisses and places on the floor next to the bed, with its face to the wall. He thinks the gesture charming, not knowing it is a well-worn ritual. The site of naked Laura Standish bending over is utterly compelling. There will indeed always be other trains.

Friday 20th October 10.06am

Naked as the day she was born, Caroline Helstone is making furry animal crooning noises in the depths of her throat. Bulkily naked, George Edmonds is caressing her substantial breasts and teasing gobstopper nipples with his teeth and tongue. She has been ravished, there is no other word. She been ravished several times and is confused by the welter of accrued sensations. He is such a forthright and insistently generous lover, surprising for such a big man in every way. She had not seen any of this coming but then she wouldn't, would she? She has noisily orgasmed more than once and she never orgasms without the intrusion of her own practised fingers after the event.

She cannot stop herself helplessly moaning as his fingers delve between her legs and his tongue and teeth savour her breasts and nipples.

She ought to want to stop this madness. She has to be on duty by eleven o'clock and is expecting to hear from Sir Godwyn, and badly needs a bath. Instead she moans helplessly and reaches for the renewed bigness to guide it back inside where they both fear it belongs.

"George, love." She whispers and that is all.

She is a gorgeous woman, such a revelation after the brisk and efficient and time constrained couplings with Una Campbell. Unlike Una Campbell this brazenly meaty woman cannot get enough.

He needs to play his cards right, and he so rarely does play his cards right. To be fair…it is often not a full pack. He gnaws a love bite into her exposed neck and she bucks and arches her back as he plunges even deeper inside Fingal's flooded cave. She is making a lot of noise but so is George, and it is a good job there is no one listening at the door. If anyone was filming it would be very blurry indeed.

Friday 20th October 10.24am

Gilbert Markham and Rosanna Spearman are seated at the state of the art kitchen table littered with various legal documents. Gilbert is reading through the embossed, sealed will and sipping real black coffee, whilst Rosanna is sipping real black coffee and watching Gil reading the embossed, sealed will. He looks so ruggedly handsome it quite takes her breath away. He makes her feel ashamed of playing around to get back at a Felix, who didn't care anyway; the late Felix that is, and she smiles.

She is not proud of giving herself to rotters like Spencer Perceval, and worse. She wants to forget all that. She knows it is early days but she feels so unthreatened and relaxed with Gil. She feels like a proper woman. Even Roz realises that sounds crass, but there we are.

"You definitely inherit everything." He has such a bewitchingly wicked grin that overturns her heart. "Every last penny."

"Are you sure, Gil, love?"

He holds aloft the embossed will document in a Roman triumph. "It's all here, duly signed and duly witnessed."

"He was going to change his will. He said so yesterday."

"He sure as hell is not going to change it now." The wicked grin even more wicked. "You are a wealthy woman, Rosanna Spearman." He shuffles the other documents. "There are deeds here for several properties, including this house, and the apartment house where he met with his unfortunate accident. There are other properties including an office block, and lots of Share certificates. At least a half a million in various cash bank deposits. There will probably be more when everything is gone through properly."

"Oh, Gil, love!" She covers her mouth with her left hand in a habitual gesture she uses when taken aback; she used it often in this kitchen until she gave up her half-hearted attempts at cooking. Another occasion was when the late Felix called her a useless cow after she burned some sausages and he slapped her face. She is glad he is dead. The sausages were edible. "Are you sure you're alright, Gil, love? Felix's accident must have been a terrible shock?"

He leans across the table and kisses Roz full on the lips. "I'll get over it." He collects all the documents together. "We will put these back in the safe." It had been child's play to open. "And wait on events as they say."

She follows him through to Felix's study and watches as he returns the documents to the wall safe, then spins the combination tumbler and replaces the painting of the Hay Wain. It is strange to think that Felix will never again sit in the brown leather captain's chair and tell her to fuck off.

"I wonder when his body will be found?" She hugs herself in the cream lace dressing gown.

"Soon, I should think, and my money is on the girlfriend." He was about to say girlfriends but doesn't want to hurt Roz any more than necessary. Although on second thoughts it will probably make no difference.

"It will be a shock for the poor girl." Roz feels sorry for any woman who fell under Felix's malign and destructive influence.

"Let me show you something."

She follows him back to the kitchen, a room to which they both gravitate as shared territory… the bedroom and the kitchen.

"More coffee, Gil, love?"

"Please."

Setting down two flowered china mugs she takes a seat next to him; being close to this man is as natural as breathing. She knows she mustn't rush things; the last thing she wants to do is to frighten him off. They kiss and he fondles a naked breast. Then he hands over a mobile phone which she recognises.

"Felix's phone." So as not to be distracted he covers the fondled breast with the cream lace dressing gown. He has showered and dressed ready for any message from Sir Godwyn. He is surprised he has not heard anything, but then Sir Godwyn has been a bit unpredictable recently. It will be sensible to have that plan B in place. Rich widows do not grow on trees.

"Do you recognise the girl?"

Rosanna stares wide eyed at the naked selfie and covers her mouth in that habitual gesture.

"It is Frances, one of the Perceval girls next door."

He thought so. Sir Godwyn will need to know.

Rosanna, keeping her mouth covered by her hand, is remembering that this was how she looked at that tender age, when she was first seduced by Felix. A much younger Felix in his defence. She uncovers her mouth. "She is only just fifteen." To be fair Rosanna had been nearly sixteen.

Gilbert recalls the used condom leaking in the ashtray on the bedside table. "Scroll down. There is another girl."

She scrolls down to a naked selfie of a dark-haired girl about the same age. The look on this face is most definitely come and get me. "She is vaguely familiar."

"I think he might have been seeing them both."

She hands back the mobile phone and takes several deeply shuddering breaths. "They are only children." She herself was only a child.

"He was a piece of work."

Rosanna is staring at her hands on the table top, so so glad that Felix is now very much in the past tense. She has already discarded her wedding ring. It is hard to see Gil as an Angel but he has certainly answered her prayers. She will never openly admit that every night she prayed for Felix to be out of her life. She never actually prayed for his death but, of course, it might have been implied.

Gilbert doesn't feel he can intrude on thoughts visibly squeezing the natural generosity out of her lips. He wonders if he ought to text Sir Godwyn, although the great man does not like to be harried. He has told Gilbert on more than one occasion to wait patiently and, whenever the call comes, to respond immediately no matter what he is doing. Sometimes a call comes at the most inconvenient moments.

"He was a bastard." The voice is as gunmetal grey as her eyes staring at Gilbert. "A total bastard." She hates to swear and the word tastes odd in her succulent mouth.

"You can say that again, Roz."

She takes hold of his nearest hand. "When his body is found the Police will come here."

"There is nothing to link you with the accident, Roz."

"They must not find you here, Gil, love."

She is no doubt right because she will be nervous and it might raise suspicions. She is not skilled at hiding her feelings.

"I will let you know when they have been and gone." They both acknowledge the subtext.

"As soon as his death is confirmed you must contact the lawyers."

"I will." She smiles a relieved smile. She does not reveal that it might be slightly awkward since she has slept with all three of the partners...but not at the same time.

Friday 20th October 11.06am

Camilla French is not sure whether to be relieved or insulted as she stares across the table at the empty first-class seat, Sir Godwyn Lydate being conspicuous by his absence as the train pulls out of Leeds station. On the other side of the aisle Spencer Perceval and Harriet O'Connor are sitting opposite each other holding hands in full view on the table top like prosaic Mills and Boon lovers. It should be totally ridiculous but somehow it is ridiculously touching. Feeling as though she is intruding, Camilla French checks her mobile phone; no message from Gil but several messages from the Leader of the Opposition. It is hard to believe that Sir Godwyn is staying behind with that rather common girl with the incredibly short black dress – that is unfair – she is an exceptionally pretty and likeable girl; not the least bit common in so many senses of the word.

Camilla must be missing something. Her antennae have never been tuned to this sort of thing. She glances across the aisle where the attractive, well-dressed, middle-aged woman has taken charge of more than the hands of alley cat morals Spencer Perceval. Camilla wishes her all the luck in the world. She recalls a Foreign Office Reception when the alley cat had squeezed a handful of her bum and whispered an obscene suggestion and she had slapped his face. He had merely grinned ruefully and moved away to try it on with someone else; a few minutes later she saw him disappearing to the toilets with Rosalie Murray in tow.

Now he whispers something, quite probably obscene, and the attractive, well dressed, middle aged woman attempts a giggle and playfully slaps his wrist. Camilla French cannot believe her eyes as they head off down the aisle hand in hand, she hopes towards the restaurant car but she cannot be at all certain. She is most definitely missing something. Colouring up she remembers herself and Gil losing it big time in the bar area of the Queens Hotel. It was a good job there was nobody around. She sits back in the seat and closes her eyes. She needs to get a grip and needs to focus. There is much work to do now that she is not going to be sacked and now that Sir Godwyn has outlined some of his plans. The Leader of the Party wants a meeting and it must be arranged – 'soonest' – the tosser's favourite word of the moment.

Uninhibited sex with Gilbert Markham has opened a can of worms of long suppressed desires and must be handled. A proper time and place must be found in her busy life for sex, hopefully with Gilbert but, if not, there are plenty of other fish in the sea. No doubt Sir Godwyn will demand his pound of flesh…there she goes mixing metaphors again. It appears that he is more than competent at satisfying women, so fair enough.

Having made the decision that she needs to be satisfied on a regular basis from now on, Camilla French opens her eyes. She opens the tablet on the table top and replies to the Leader of the Opposition. She will start as she means to go on.

Friday 20th October 11.28am

Jack Bellingham is standing arm in arm with a pinch faced Jane Fennell, staring down at his mother's scarce tended grave, where the plastic flowers look pathetic. Despite the clear blue sky there are occasional gusts of a chill October wind in the north eastern corner of Adel churchyard. In these parts October winds have been dangerous down the ages. Jane Fennell shivers and wishes she was somewhere else. Sir Godwyn is unobtainable and so she is staying as close as close to the People's hero. Not that he seems to mind one way or the other. She is not used to that.

There is much to be said for closeness but there is also much to be said against closeness. She enjoys a bloody good shag or three as much as the next up for just about everything posh girl, but there is a frightening quality to his brain numbing couplings that makes her uneasy – and if Jane Fennell is uneasy there is something to be uneasy about. In the extremes of passion he had demanded things that made her shiver, without a chill north east wind seeking out her vulnerable bits and pieces.

"Can we go now, Jack?"

He ignores the question and stares across to the unmarked grave of Lily Dale. There are no pathetic plastic flowers there. It was her own fault but even so… even so…he is grateful that he so rarely dreams.

They are unaware of an unmarked Police car in the car park opposite the Memorial lychgate. Chief Inspector Stephen Guest is intently watching through second hand binoculars; intently watching John, now known as Jack, Bellingham, and the unknown very pretty woman hunching her shoulders against the biting wind. More than once his superiors have told the Chief Inspector to drop the case. There is no case. Orders have come all the way from the Home Office. He cannot do it… it is not his way.

"I will get you, sonny." He whispers.

The mobile phone on the passenger seat pings. It is a message from his much younger, work colleague third wife, who has got annoyingly clingy since discovering she is unexpectedly pregnant. He thinks he might be too old to be an unexpected father, but the deed is done and he is not one to cry over spilled milk. He is one to cry over spilled murderers getting away with it. Jack and Jane are also unaware that they are being spied on from the Vicarage kitchen window. The Reverend John Eames's long-suffering ex-wife is standing arm in arm with Alice Vavasor's husband. Gordon Vavasor is wearing John Eames's tatty old dressing gown much more stylishly than John Eames ever managed. She is wearing a pink dressing gown that clings to her naked body, the pregnancy not yet showing.

They have spent the night together and only just come down for a belated breakfast. She has told him that she is pregnant and he has assumed he is the father, which is almost certainly the case. Their affair started three months ago and has been pretty intense. She will, of course, never ever in a million years mention those three, perhaps four times with her Mother's doctor. They had both got carried away in the moment… well alright… several moments. Most certainly she will never ever mention the threesome involving the man now standing at his mother's grave arm in arm with a very pretty girl, who looks frozen stiff. The frantic coming together of their rampant bodies that afternoon at Jack's mother's house was memorable indeed. Her flesh forever tingles in the memory. She knows if Jack wanted her again she would not be able resist. Marion Fay was a timely interlude but Jack was something else entirely.

"He's an odd bloke." The unknowing Gordon Vavasor has a deep manly voice which had first persuaded her to bed, on the afternoon of July the thirteenth to be precise. He had only come to repair the boiler, but she had not taken much persuading. There was no question of taking the part of a blow up doll. It was like waking up from a Sleeping Beauty sleep; not that she has ever thought of herself as beautiful. She needs to put that memorable threesome afternoon out of mind. "The bird looks a bit of hot stuff."

"Unlike me."

"You are the hottest bit of stuff on the planet." The deep manly voice as always caresses intimately and scooping the woman in his strong arms they passionately kiss, just like they had passionately kissed on the afternoon of July the thirteenth. She had only asked if he wanted a cup of tea. "Let's go to bed." He whispers, just as he had on the afternoon of July the thirteenth, into an ear that he kisses as he had kissed it then, the boiler in pieces on the kitchen floor… he never did get his cup of tea.

"We've only just got out of bed." She whispers back and wonders if they ought to be careful with her being pregnant, because Gordy can be quite vigorous, but she doesn't say anything to spoil the mood. She intends that he will leave Alice Vavasor and that they will be living together, perhaps even married, before the child, that is almost certainly Gordy's child, is born.

The generous unexpected divorce settlement means that she has no money worries and, of course, as an only child there will very soon be her Mother's modest Estate. The large detached house in Colchester is empty now that her Mother has protestingly moved into the Hospice. The decrepit, smelly mongrel dog has been put down.

Gordy is feeling up her bare backside, not knowing that is where the trouble started with her Mother's doctor. It had been a night time emergency call and Dora was wearing the same dressing gown and nothing else.

"You are a naughty boy." She huskily whispers.

"You are a naughty lady."

There is no way she will ever ration Gordy's access to her body as she did with John Eames, carrying out the minimum of wifely duties minimally. It was always good thinking time but a new life beckons and it has to be better. They do indeed go back to bed. She must put Jack out of mind and not wish it was him feeling up her bare backside with intent, as they climb the stairs and out of this story; going on past experience, that is by no means certain.

"Please can we go now, Jack?"

In answer he does something that takes Jane's breath away, frightening her out of all proportion and making her wish for other things in faraway places. He spits on his mother's grave.

Chief Inspector Stephen Guest is not sure he believes what he has just witnessed through the second hand binoculars. The mobile phone on the passenger seat pings and is ignored. Jack Bellingham and the extremely pretty girl in tight jeans with holes in strategic places, are now walking towards the Memorial lychgate. Stephen Guest slides down in the driver's seat.

Friday 20th October 12.29pm

Gilbert Markham is as invisible as it is possible for a human being to be, in the strategic bushes on the opposite side of the street, and has turned off his mobile phone. He was trained to remain immobile, except for his nose and ears, for hours on end. It only takes half an hour before he is watching a frowzily pretty, dark-haired young girl in the maroon school uniform and black tights, skirt hitched short, use a key to let herself in through the communal front door. She glances nervously over her shoulder but is not aware of Gilbert. There is no one else to be seen. She is the come and get me girl on the late husband's mobile phone.

A couple of minutes later there is a piercing scream and Gilbert allows himself the thought of a bleak smile.

A few minutes after the piercing scream, two police cars race screeching down the avenue and block the road outside the three-storey house. Four minutes later an ambulance duly arrives. He feels like shouting that there is no need to rush.

Gilbert scarce breathes as the sobbing maroon uniformed schoolgirl is led out of the front door, leaning on the arm of a most attractive uniformed Police woman – Gilbert remarks to himself – on these reconnaissance missions it is only possible to remark to yourself.

"There there, Katie you will soon be home." The most attractive Police woman has a Scottish accent. They slide into the back seat of the police car and the red eyed schoolgirl looks out of the window directly at Gilbert's hiding place. It is a good job he is scarce breathing. She looks away as an overweight male Police officer comes out of the front door and glares challengingly up and down the deserted avenue. Gilbert lines up a headshot – lowers his aim – a throat shot causes maximum pain and a more agonising death and, of course, there is no scream.

The Police officer levers himself with difficulty into the driver's side and smiles reassuringly at Katie, at the same time slyly copping a look at her displayed legs. The marked police car screeches away. Gilbert has seen all he wants to see. They will inform Rosanna Spearman and the new widow will attempt distraught. Perhaps some of her grief will be genuine, since she believes it was an accident.

Is Roz really that stupid?

For the silly showing off her legs schoolgirl called Katie, the horrors are only just beginning. It is odds-on that she and not Frances was the sharer of the condemned man's last condom. Discovering the stinking corpse could well put her off sex for the foreseeable future, although she returned the fat copper's reassuring smile, knowing he was not so slyly copping a look at her legs, so perhaps not.

Friday 20th October 1.07pm

"This is all very mysterious, Rosalie." Robert Peel sounds a smidgen put out as he follows her shapely rear down the gloomy hallway into a high ceilinged living room. Agnes Grey is absent and they are alone in the apartment that belonged to her late Mother. Rosalie really is quite magnificent from behind in a tight skirt; it is almost worth missing lunch with the delightful Li Soo Ying. Lunch has been rearranged to a late supper this evening, so all's well that ends well.

The message had been urgent…a matter of life and death… he must come in alone …no advisers… not a bit Rosalie's style.

The owner of the magnificent rear walks to the high window lighting the high ceilinged room with reflective sunlight, and spots the watchful Security people in the street below. Robert Peel loves all the trappings and fripperies of high office, and believes that he was always destined to be Prime Minister. Some delusions are more dangerous than others.

"What is this all about, Rosalie?" There is weariness in his voice that is out of character.

Waiting a few heartbeats to heighten the dramatic effect, she turns to face the Prime Minister.

"Jesus Christ."

Then just as dramatically she crosses the old-fashionedly furnished room to stand a few feet away. The open-mouthed Prime Minister and First Lord of the Treasury for once is lost for words. "We need to talk, Robert." There is a lisp shaped on the swollen lips and he wonders if she has lost some teeth, recalling Agnes Grey's Mother taking out her false teeth in this very room, and the intense pleasures that followed.

Somewhat distractedly he opens and closes his mouth. The right words are usually within reach in the ether, but not this time. He must make an effort. He has his position to think about.

"Who did this?" He doesn't recognise his own voice that has been said to charm the birds from the trees; or more realistically charming his way into certain women's knickers. He has always believed that every great person must have a weakness to prove his or her humanity. He knows that he is not suited to portentousness but he cannot help himself.

"Sir Godwyn Lydate." She answers in a Lady Macbeth Act three, scene two, gloom laden voice that is portentous to perfection.

He opens and closes his mouth. The grandiloquent phrases into which he tends to lapse more and more these days are redundant.

"Sit down, Robert, and I will get you a drink." It is with relief that he sinks down onto a not very comfortable 1960s style sofa, which he remembers from his clandestine visits to Agnes Grey's Mother. They do not know it is the sofa on which Agnes Grey's Mother so recently choked to death, in the manner of

Mrs Gaskell, after rather too adventurous impromptu lovemaking not involving Robert Peel. For once his personal comfort is taking second place and the spring prodding his backside is of no relevance, except as a prod to memories.

The battered woman sits on the same sofa but not too close, as if being battered is contagious. She hands him a generous tumbler of neat whisky and, just in time, he resists lifting the tumbler in a toast and slurps gratefully. From the borrowed jewelled necklace down, the woman facing him is the eminently desirable Rosalie Murray of fable, as usual displaying lots of very nice legs and quite stunning cleavage – well known to the public gallery of the House of Commons. The face, though, is hideously bruised, one eye practically closed like a boxer at the end of twelve rounds who is about to lose on points.

"In God's name, why?"

The voice that replies, if one ignores the lisp, is the voice of Rosalie Murray, but with a hardness of unforgiving edge that he doesn't recognise. "He thought he would use me to destroy you."

Robert Peel drains the tumbler and resists the temptation to smash it to smithereens in the old-fashioned fireplace; it is not the time for futile Edwardian gestures; he never ever thought he would think that. "Why?"

"This is Sir Godwyn Lydate we are talking about." It is hard to believe she so recently shared that bastard's bed and was so exquisitely pleasured by his all too knowing wiles, believing that all her dreams had come true. Almost believed in Father Christmas, not to mention the tooth fairy. As a precocious child she had never ever believed in Father Christmas, and most certainly never believed in the tooth fairy.

"Get me another drink, Rosalie. Please." When she turns her back she is still an eminently desirable woman. Regretfully it had never been the right time to try it on with Rosalie Murray. Agnes Grey's Mother was a different kind of regret.

He slurps even more gratefully. "Jayne has done one of her disappearing acts and I think Godwyn is behind it."

"Very likely." She has of course heard the malicious rumours; everyone except poor Robert appears to have heard the malicious rumours.

"She has not been the same since that last miscarriage." And of course finding her husband naked in bed with a naked Florence Dugdale. He had certainly proved his humanity and no mistake.

"He will use the poor woman against you."

"You certainly tell it like it is, Rosalie." He is not at all sure about the poor woman thing. Some of the things she said. Dear dear. Some of the things she said. Thoughtfully he swirls whisky, acutely aware of the closeness of the very nice legs. He knows he really should not be thinking very nice legs. "Are you no longer his creature, Rosalie?"

She is about to reply indignantly that she was never his creature, thank you very much, but knows only too well that would be untrue. They must be as honest with each other as it is sensible to be. For their purposes there has to be an authorised version of the truth. After all it works for the Bible.

"Look at my face, Robert." Somewhat guiltily he tears his gaze away from the very nice legs to the battered face. "There is your answer."

Instinctively he reaches out his free hand which is grasped in her moist hands. A gesture of sympathy they both simulate and appreciate in their different ways.

"What are we to do?" He asks with a show of genuine humility. This woman is strong in a crisis, he is weak in a crisis, so he must take from her strength, as he always takes from the strength of others. He has cunning in spades and she knows that. He will need physical and moral courage, but she is not at all sure he has that.

"Bring him down."

The appalling words swirl in the atrophied atmosphere like the smoke of a thousand beacons signalling the approach of the Spanish Armada.

"Can we do that? Can we?"

"We have no choice."

Robert Peel takes comfort from the tenor and tone of her unforgiving voice. She could be a most effective understudy for one of the avenging Furies of ancient fable. He was a Classics scholar at Cambridge where he met Jayne. It had been love at first sight and they had been so happy once upon a time, when she was in ignorance of his discrete indiscretions. Rosalie Murray is unaccountably touched by the tears running down his cheeks, which are beginning to show the ravages of the good life. Rosalie's looks will heal and his will not. She knows better than most that he has never ever quite got his head round the important stuff – the life and death stuff.

"We can do this, Robert. We can do this." He nods sagely and she prises the empty tumbler out of his hand and takes firm hold of both fleshy hands. "We need to strike quickly."

"Strike?"

"He is not expecting to be attacked."

"Attacked?"

"I have gone through Agnes Grey's computer files." Agnes Grey could not be blamed for assuming that Rosalie had abjectly surrendered like the others. He shakes his head in disbelief. What on earth led him to insinuate his way into Agnes Grey's knickers at her Mother's funeral? "I have found something we can use for starters." He shakes his head again. To be fair the Grey daughter had been unbelievably enthusiastic, reminiscent of her Mother, which seemed as fitting a tribute as any.

"Starters?"

"For fuck's sake, Robert, stop repeating everything I say." He is getting used to the lisp, which is actually rather sexy.

"Sorry."

"Stop fucking apologising." She wonders if she ought to slap his face, so she releases his hands and slaps his face.

"Jesus." He holds a hand to his shocked face. Jayne had hit him much harder in the aftermath of the naked girl in the bed discovery – how was he to know she would come back a day early?

"We have to focus because if he finds out what we are doing he will try to destroy us."

He resists the temptation to say 'destroy?'. The good eye in the battered face is fiercely burning with a hatred that he finds frightening and yes – and yes – not a little exciting.

"You cannot stay here, Rosalie." That is more like it. "We must find a safe place."

She too finds it all not a little exciting, as if they are taking part in a real-life thriller novel.

"Where do you suggest?" It never does any harm to pander to his innate vanity.

"Ten Downing Street." There has always been a vacuous quality to Robert Peel that is not as apparent when he is called on to save his own skin. "Jayne's rooms are vacant." A grim, having been caught out smile that somehow works. "He will never think to look for you there." Rosalie wonders if he ought to do more grim, having been caught out, smiling for the cameras. "Something tells me she will not be coming back anytime soon."

Surely he must have heard the malicious rumours, but if not, this is not the time to rock the good ship Revenge. She needs him focused and onside. He doesn't focus very often but when he does he can be formidable... but only in short bursts. "As few people as possible must be in the know." In a gesture that almost takes her breath away he gently strokes her bruised cheek and she struggles not to flinch. "We will sneak you in the back door."

"We?" Now it is her turn.

"I will involve Florence Dugdale." He forestalls the inevitable question. "She was appointed by me personally and not by Sir Godwyn. In fact she was appointed against his advice."

"You are certain she is not one of his people?"

"I would trust her with my life." As a standing joke Florrie calls herself his peeler. In truth surprising them naked in bed was the last straw for Jayne Peel, who sought solace in the arms of Sir Godwyn, who happened to be there. The rest is likely to be history.

Rosalie knows they will have to trust someone. "Very well. The first thing she can do is collect some clothes and necessities from my apartment. The sooner I am secreted away the better." Fetching and carrying should put pushy Florence Dugdale in her place.

"Let's go." He pulls her to her feet. "Please call me Bobby."

Friday 20th October 1.49pm

Seated on a knife slashed memorial bench in Meanwood Park, five minutes' walk from Laura's pokey yet cosy apartment, Sir Godwyn Lydate is ensconced arm in arm with the stilled Laura Standish. They have agreed it is unseasonably warm for the time of year and, as a result, she has coyly poked him in the ribs and he has edged close to a smile. She is holding tight to his arm, fearing that these good feelings will not last and that something will happen to spoil things. Something always does happen to spoil things; it is Laura's law.

He has said that he must return to London later today but wishes he could stay longer. She would like to believe him because…well because a girl like Laura Standish likes to believe that fairy tales come true. A part of her never wanted to grow up after what happened.

For once, the great man is content to be an onlooker of his surroundings and do absolutely nothing about them at all. As content as he will ever be with the loved up girl cleaving to his side and the contours of her body filling his mind. These particular surroundings are composed of facile young women with screeching children in pushchairs; older women walking dogs and the occasional elderly couple, walking slowly, wrapped up in their own worn down two selves… he can almost appreciate the cosmic joke.

There is no need to exchange banalities, something else he appreciates in this most surprising girl. The waitress already consigned to history – the Archbishop would be appalled. She is content to share the silence. Such a rare quality these days. He is sorely tempted to stay tonight but tomorrow's meeting at Lydate Hall is vital. He must go and there will be other nights as there are other trains. He will make sure of that.

Smith Jones Robinson, the multinational Pharmaceutical Company, are sending their top man from Geneva to seal the deal, and tens of millions of pounds are at stake for the Lydate coffers. If it follows the pattern of the previous meeting there will be the outrageously gorgeous Swiss, honey blonde, Mia Fischer to warm his bed. They think they know his Achilles heel and it does no harm to let them think so. He sighs deeply, appreciating the fact that Laura doesn't offer another penny for his thoughts and is smiling at her own thoughts, with such a delicately engraved smile of that Uffizi Madonna on the hidden wall. The painting might have to be restored and moved to a more prominent place. He does not think that Mary and Joseph would have indulged as wantonly as he and Laura had earlier – of course one never knows. One wouldn't be able to guess by looking at this enchanting profile.

One might think the past few hours had been an aberration of sorts. There really is no time for sitting here doing absolutely nothing in the pale autumn sunshine, in this sheltered corner of the park, and luxuriating in just being with this most beguiling creature. He closes eyes and turns up his face to the Sun God in the manner of the heretic Pharaoh Akhenaton…the Pharaoh he would most like to have been. A Pharaoh whose mind was no doubt filled by the contours of Queen Nefertiti's body.

There is a sense of phoney war… not quite foreboding…not quite that. Perhaps he is catching some of Laura's doubting thoughts. The mobile phone in his pocket rings to Parsifal and he checks the caller. "Yes, my dear." He listens and Laura turns her head to watch him listening and wonders if he will enjoy her soul as much as he has enjoyed her body. Wonders if she will enjoy him enjoying her soul as much as she has enjoyed him enjoying her body. Surely a girl can wonder?

"Where is she?" His face is all at once closed and threatening and she is aware of his body stiffening. "You have done the right thing, my dear Caroline and I am on my way." He ends the call.

"We need to go, my dear."

"A problem?"

"Shall we say a situation."

Holding hands like common or garden lovers, they walk unhurriedly out of the park and the flame haired woman walking a frisky, tongue lolling, cross breed dog thinks they make an odd couple. She also thinks she might have seen the man somewhere before, although she cannot think where. The girl is very beautiful, with such a lovely figure and a naturally graceful walk. The flame haired woman watches enviously as they disappear from view and then, feeling the need to go, hurries away in search of the Park toilets.

Friday 20th October 2.16pm

Caroline Helstone is at a loss what else to do and that big daft lovely bugger George Edmonds is intently watching Caroline Helstone being at a loss what else to do.

"Sir Godwyn is on his way." Caroline attempts to take hold of the distressed girl's hand in a comforting gesture, but the distressed girl pulls away into a corner of the battered sofa, holding herself tight in her own arms and staring at nothing whatsoever.

George Edmonds shifts his gaze from Caroline Helstone. He recognises the exorbitantly pretty girl who went off with that murderer bloke last night.

He had glimpsed them necking in the lift. Something has gone badly wrong since that passionate moment, because George has not seen someone so abjectly distressed since he insisted on facing the pregnant wife of the opponent of his last fight. This one is not weeping and beating him with clenched fists which make it worse somehow.

George is not good at woman stuff, but he is good at clenched fist stuff. This lass has taken some punishment, evidenced by finger mark bruises on her swan's neck, and a flowered bruise on a downy cheek. Although not weeping she is, not quite silently, keening in the back of her bruised throat and rocking gently to and fro, like a winding down clockwork doll whose mechanism is worn faulty with overuse, and is about to break down and be unrepairable.

Caroline Helstone takes hold of George's huge hand and squeezes and George squeezes back, but not too hard, being only too well aware of his own strength since that final fight. They both feel better for the companionable contact almost as much as from the no holds barred sex – but not quite. Caroline is pleasantly aware of the places he has been and strives not to smile, otherwise it will be difficult to wipe the inappropriate smile off her face.

"It looks like he tried to strangle the poor lass." George thinks he whispers.

"Shush, love." Caroline does whisper and squeezes hands. "Sir Godwyn will soon be here, love." Caroline feels that she ought to plough on, although she has felt out of her depth since the Receptionist, Emily thingy, brought the girl to Caroline's rooms. All the distressed girl kept repeating was Sir Godwyn... Sir Godwyn... Sir Godwyn.

Luckily Caroline and George had already climbed out of the shared bath and were drying each other on Hotel towels. At the insistent knocking they had dressed hurriedly, after a fashion, and Emily thingy had given George a knowing look. She should give knowing looks, the little hussy.

Caroline doesn't feel able to ask the poor girl's name and doesn't think she would get an answer anyway. It does feel good to have the bulk and strength of George at her side, even though he is no bloody use. He is here and that is the thing, and for once in her life she is not on her own.

"Would you like a cuppa, love?" George asks the distressed girl in his best attempt at addressing a distressed girl voice.

Much to Caroline's surprise the girl focuses her gaze on George and, much to Caroline's discomfort, studies the lovely big man for several hangdog seconds. Caroline had dressed herself hurriedly after the knock at the door, having previously ignored the telephone, and thinks she might well have put her knickers on back to front. This is not the time or the place to confide the fact in George, who would say something rude and make her giggle. He had said quite a few rude things in the bath and she had giggled rather a lot. Then he had done some rude things and she had stopped giggling. They would have gone back to bed after the towel caressing drying, if it had not been for the intrusive knocking at the door.

The poor nameless girl shakes her head, winces and goes back to staring at nothing in particular. At least she has stopped rocking backwards and forwards and the keening is now inaudible to the human ear.

Caroline is just thinking that she would love one of George's cuppas when there is rapping at the door and, all in a thankful rush, Caroline opens the door to find Sir Godwyn Lydate with a buffed up version of that sneaky wanking waitress at his side. Caroline is all glared out and lets it go, hers not to reason why. She stands aside as the great man dominates into the room and, after a slight hesitation, the sneaky wanking waitress follows and their eyes meet briefly. Time has moved on and Caroline offers the briefest of nods.

Sir Godwyn crosses to the battered sofa and takes a seat next to the poor girl and takes hold of both her hands. She half-heartedly resists and manufactures the oddest of shapes with her mouth.

"Jane, my dear. Tell me."

Such a gentle caressing voice and Caroline glances with new respect at the intently watching Laura Standish. She will have to stop thinking of her as the sneaky wanking waitress. They are more partners in crime so to speak.

The poor girl Jane takes a deep shuddering breath, frowning as if she is trying to recall something from a long time ago that she would rather forget and Caroline sympathises.

"What happened, my dear?" The caressing voice and the caressing touch of accomplished hands appear to be drawing the poor girl reluctantly back into the land of the touching. She licks and licks her swollen lips and winces. Caroline becomes aware that her own lips are somewhat swollen. She must not bloody smile.

"You are safe now, Jane, my dear."

In trying not to cough George struggles with a strangled gurgling in his throat. The poor girl looks at George and appears to see something there that calms her down, causing Caroline an unwanted stab of jealousy.

"He tried to kill me." A gritty, unharnessed, unrecognisable voice that is not her own; posh though, thinks Laura Standish, who is gazing intently at the finger mark bruises on the poor girl's elegant neck... most assuredly posh. Laura will forgive the slighted comments of last night...she is that kind of girl.

Sir Godwyn attempts to take Jane in his comforting arms but she resists and, reacting without thinking to save any embarrassment, Laura Standish walks across to the battered sofa.

"Let me, Godwyn." No Sir after all that they have so intimately shared. Not Goddy... not yet anyway. Caroline Helstone notices and purses her lips, but only momentarily, because time and tide wait for no man or woman.

Without demur the great man moves to one side and Laura eases down, taking the poor unresisting girl into her arms as the floodgates open.

"There. There." Jane Fennell sobs her heart out on the nice kind girl's shoulder. "Let it out, sweetheart. Let it all out." Laura's strokes the untidy bed swept hair, shushing and cooing and kissing a diamond studded ear. Jane is so sorry... so very very sorry.

Sir Godwyn looks on with undisguised admiration. There is so much more to the enrapturing Laura Standish than even he ever thought possible; he was wrong... she is an incredibly early May date at a bargain price. He knows that such thoughts are grossly unfair and possibly sexist, although meant as a compliment. He takes no account of social trends.

"There. There. You are safe now. Shush. Shush."

Caroline Helstone is gobsmacked as she presses close to George Edmonds on the other more battered sofa. They are quite naturally holding hands without giving it a second thought, both instinctively aware of each other, but they must concentrate on matters in hand.

At last the tears are drying up and the gut wrenching sobbing becoming less and less intrusive, as Jane Fennell holds tight in Laura Standish's comforting arms.

Sir Godwyn glances at Caroline Helstone and the muscle bound bruiser who is holding tight to her hands for all he is worth. Or is it the other way round?

"You did absolutely the right thing, Caroline, my dear." He cannot help but notice the livid love bites on her neck.

"All she would keep repeating was your name."

The dry lip twitch. "How did she get here?"

"The Receptionist said something about a plain clothes Policeman leading the poor love into the lobby."

"That explains it." He had recognised the detective from the trial sitting in the foyer.

"He wanted to come up here but she wouldn't let him."

"A clever girl."

Caroline Helstone purses her lips for real and does not reply because there is a limit. Sir Godwyn is now paying due attention to the broken nosed, cauliflower eared, what Jane Fennell once upon a time would have called an appendage. Sir Godwyn of course recognises the hotel porter who was not always a hotel porter. These two are quite obviously recently stapled together lovers. He can only think the dastardly deed has been done since his little talk with Caroline in her cubby hole. He is certain she does not possess the guile to have dared to lie.

"I saw you fight."

George Edmonds looks startled, as well he might. He is not at all used to being admiringly appraised by such an important person. Important people do not waste their no doubt valuable time admiringly appraising the likes of George Edmonds.

"It was at the Albert Hall when you fought to be the heavyweight contender."

George nods his head and bites his lips at the unexpectedness. It feels so good that Caroline tightens her hold with her hands being so fleshy in his big fists. She is all woman and no mistake, but he mustn't think about that for the moment.

"It was the only bout I ever lost." A craggy excavated voice that rumbles like distant thunder.

"In my opinion you were unfairly disqualified."

"It was a fix, guv."

Now it is Sir Godwyn's turn to nod, although he does not bite his lips, as he takes in this particular tableaux a deux and all its implications. He is not one to miss such an opportunity. The shock of what has happened to poor dear Jane has refocused him with a vengeance which, all things considered, is just as well.

"How long have you been lovers?" No beating about the bush.

Caroline Helstone opens and closes her mouth but George Edmonds replies without hesitation. "Since six thirty this morning, guv." A broken toothed smile that makes Sir Godwyn think about a dry lip twitch.

"Is it more than a one night stand?"

"I hope so, guv."

"Caroline?"

"So do I." She gazes fondly at George who gazes fondly back with several knobs on. They appear to be as ridiculously smitten as taken by surprise new minted lovers are ever likely to be smitten.

"I have spoken to Sir Bernard Keeldar, my dear Caroline, and informed him that you are coming to work for me in London. I have a special role lined up for you and I also have a special role in mind for... George, isn't it?"

"George Edmonds, guv."

"Of course. There is a convenient apartment which you can move into together if that would suit?"

George Edmonds doesn't hesitate. "It would suit real fine, guv." Caroline Helstone merely opens and closes her mouth. It had crossed her mind, drawing on past experience, that George might have had his fill so to speak.

"Excellent." For several more seconds he looks at them both in turn. "This little Edwardian melodrama that you have witnessed never happened."

"What Edwardian melodrama, guv?"

"You and I will get on very well, George." And he turns his full attention to the other tableaux a deux, where the very much defeisted ex-lioness Jane Fennell is preternaturally stilled, pretending for all she is worth to feel safe in Laura Standish's arms. She is not sure she will ever feel safe again in the same room as a man...she is no doubt wrong.

Laura has watched the conversation with fascinated interest. Who would have thought it? Nazi lady tamed by that big lump George Edmonds. Perhaps Laura was a bit hasty turning him down when he tried it on. The real reason being that she wasn't pissed enough and the time of the month was all wrong. That used to be the story of her life.

"Was it Jack Bellingham, my dear Jane? Did he really try to strangle you?" Sir Godwyn asks and Laura feels the clasped head nod, and she nods at Sir Godwyn in turn. Then she listens to the gasping whisper.

"She says he called her awful names." There is some more gasping whispering that Laura does not repeat and no one asks.

Caroline Helstone purses her lips, although it is not really her place to do so. In truth she is not used to being sidelined and sees that Sir Godwyn is pursing his lips much more pursingly than she could ever manage. She is really really glad she didn't try to sell that footage to the media. She might have had to blame George and that would not have been fair as things have turned out.

Sir Godwyn strokes Laura's arm. "I think it would best if you take poor Jane back to your apartment, my dear Laura."

"Are you sure, Godwyn?"

"Just for the time being. Apparently she trusts you and it will be for the best." He leans forward and kisses Laura full on the lips. "I will send for you both." Another kiss full on the lips.

It is a promise…she thinks posh people probably keep promises sealed with a kiss… she hopes so anyway. Being bought and paid for she cannot argue anyway, not that she wants to argue, because all of this beats waiting at crappy tables and having your arse pinched by all and sundry. Even the loved up Nazi lady is looking at Laura with new respect… wonders will never cease. Jane Fennell holds as tight as tight to Laura, as they leave the temporary manager's quarters, giving the comic impression that they are coming next to last in a Primary School Sports day parents' three legged race. No one smiles or dry lip twitches. George Edmonds watches them leave and as usual chews on his own thoughts.

When they have gone Caroline Helstone seizes the moment. "George has something to show you, Sir Godwyn."

Three times Sir Godwyn plays back the footage of Camilla French and Gilbert Markham very much at it. He is watched intently by the new minted smitten lovers, who are clutching hands for all they are worth. Sir Godwyn tap taps the mobile phone against the ever so slightly prominent front teeth.

"You took this, George?"

"Yes, guv."

"Were you going to sell it to the media?"

"Yes guv." He cannot tell a lie. Well he can…but he is a lousy liar.

Then Sir Godwyn points the mobile phone at Caroline Helstone. "You, my dear, are an extraordinarily clever girl." Then he points the mobile phone at George Edmonds. "And you, my truthful friend, should hold onto this lovely lady for dear life."

"Yes, guv."

That having been said, the great man lapses briefly into hidden depths of thought, before secreting the mobile phone in his pocket. "I will keep this, George." There will be no leading into temptation.

"Yes, guv."

Sir Godwyn is about to say something else, when rudely insistent knocking shakes the door on its hinges and, guilty as charged, Caroline Helstone jumps to her size seven bare feet. She glances at Sir Godwyn who, not at all surprised at the intrusion, curtly nods as the rude knocking is renewed even louder.

She has scarcely opened the door when Chief Inspector Stephen Guest forces his way limping into proceedings, closely followed by a becomingly flustered Emily Prescott. "I tried to stop him…" She is equally becomingly out of breath after running up the stairs to beat the lift – it was a dead heat. She needs the exercise but that was ridiculous. "He wouldn't take no for an answer…"

"None of this is your fault, my dear." Sir Godwyn gets in first as he stands to his full height to out face the comically irate slouchy detective. "Some people have no breeding whatsoever." Not to mention posture.

The Chief Inspector is finding it difficult to articulate his bitterly angry frustration. He had the prize within his grasp – he had the bastard – he bloody well had the murdering bastard. "Where has that poor girl been taken?"

Seizing her chance, a slightly less breathless Emily Prescott decides to interject her six penneth. Prettily flustered really works, thinks George Edmonds; it is not certain what Sir Godwyn Lydate is thinking. "He tried to stop them leaving the hotel and Laura told him to fuck off and kicked him in the shins and he fell over." Emily decides to leave it there before she bursts into a fit of giggles. It was very funny.

Except it is not at all funny that the Chief Inspector turns on her and spits out his pent up bile. "You will be charged as an accessory."

"Leave the poor girl alone."

Now the Chief Inspector turns on Sir Godwyn Lydate under the appalled gaze of Caroline Helstone, who is aware that it is not a wise move to turn on Sir Godwyn Lydate. Someone should tell the bloke… they really should.

"As for you…" Some prehistoric instinct of self-preservation decides the Chief Inspector to withhold the insulting names. "I demand to know where the poor girl has been taken. If you do not tell me I will arrest you here and now and you will accompany me to the Station."

"Do policemen actually parrot those words outside second rate Agatha Christie novels?" Asks Sir Godwyn in a bored tone to no one in particular.

Opening and closing his fists the Chief Inspector takes an ill-advised step forward. The misaligned eye even more misaligned.

"That's far enough, buddy." The voice of George Edmonds resonates in the room.

"Thank you, George." Is Sir Godwyn's polite response. "I can handle this."

"Answer the question," Stephen Guest practically shrieks.

An enthralled Emily Prescott is just glad no one has told her to leave the room because this is better than Emmerdale any day. She has clocked the Fuhrer lady holding hands with George Edmonds and thinks wonders will never cease – so much for not telling a living soul.

Emily has to admit, at least to herself, that George's body servicing was by no means the worst she has ever experienced. Unthinkingly she catches his eye and he winks as if he can read her mind; she colours up and now her attention is taken up by the posh bloke who she is aware is mysteriously powerful, who has taken out his mobile phone and tapped a number. She can hardly wait.

"Home Secretary?... I'm fine and you, Henry...?" A lip flexing listening pause. "No really don't mention it, Henry, it was the least I could do." More listening and lip flexing. "It is very kind of you to say so but the reason I am ringing, dear boy, is a little local difficulty..."

The audience, each in their different ways, watch fascinated as this preternaturally great man explains the situation in as few words as humanly possible, all the time examining his manicured fingernails. They are all acutely aware of the Chief Inspector's stentorian breathing as Sir Godwyn listens to the response and, without a word, and with a look of utter distaste, hands the mobile phone to Chief Inspector Stephen Guest, giving the impression it will be carefully wiped afterwards.

"The Home Secretary, Henry Wititterly, would like a word."

Now all riveted eyes turn to the mottle faced Upholder of the law. George Edmonds hates coppers with good reason. Caroline Helstone is wary of the Police since a blobby sleazebag Superintendent used to come to the Children's home and take his pick. She only went with him the once, when she was the only girl available. That was more than enough. Not for the first time, she was eternally grateful she was not one of the pretty ones.

Emily Prescott has no thoughts either way, as she catches Sir Godwyn's eye and smiles one of her out of this year's autumn catalogue of enticing smiles that almost work, which is graciously accepted. An all too obviously rattled Chief Inspector Stephen Guest, who has not spoken a word, hands the mobile phone back with a shaking hand. Sir Godwyn does not let the phone touch his ear.

"Thank you, Henry and I am sure that the Chief Inspector now fully appreciates the situation... by the way I am arranging a little get together at Lydate Hall next weekend...just a select few... I would be delighted if you and

Harriet could join us…excellent…I will look forward to it…give Harriet my love." Nothing more needs to be said.

Emily Prescott is beyond impressed. For several weeks she has been a participant in Harriet Wititterly's pricey, but hopefully effective, bust enlargement programme. Endorsed by no less a personage than the actual Amelia Sedley of fabled bust. Sir Godwyn ends the call with a flourish and, momentarily forgetting where it has been, tap taps the mobile phone thoughtfully against his ever so slightly prominent front teeth. Buxom Harriet Wititterly is such an enthusiastic Labrador of a lover, and incredibly discreet. There is the baby to think about and of course Henry's meteoric career, which Sir Godwyn has aided and abetted…quid pro quo.

Sir Godwyn recalls to mind the assembled company, who are waiting on his words with varying degrees of bated breath. "I will reiterate the Home Secretary's comments that the Bellingham case is closed. There is no Bellingham case. Now go."

"That poor girl ran from his house and said she had been attacked. She was in a hell of a state. I only brought her here because she insisted. She was beside herself." Stephen Guest thinks about taking a step towards the sanctimonious posh bastard but, very much aware of the lurking bulk of George Edmonds, thinks better of it. "He half killed the girl."

"A misunderstanding. I take it you were parked outside the mother's house." He doesn't wait for a reply. "If you continue with your unauthorised harassment I will personally ensure that your career is over or my name is not Sir Godwyn Lydate. Now go."

Stephen Guest bug eyed glares at each of them in turn, as if imprinting their faces on his memory for future reference. Only Emily Prescott is slightly discomforted, as she has never been in trouble with the Police. The miscast eyes are most intimidating. At a loss for words and not able to punch anyone, because there are witnesses, the detective slams out of the door and, within a few seconds, they hear an animalistic bellow of impotent rage. They are not aware of the clenched fist beating against the walls of the descending lift.

"That went rather well." A dry lip twitch and that is all. "Caroline, my dear, take the weekend to clear things up here and I will expect you in London on Monday. I have things for you to do… George…?"

"Yes, guv."

"Can you sort out things your end over the weekend?"

"Yes, guv." It will not take long to gather his few possessions from Una Campbell's apartment. She will probably be glad to see the back of him if the truth be known. She has been a bit sharp recently and dropped certain hints that he has pretended to miss. Una thinks he is punch drunk.

"Excellent. You can travel down together. There will be things for you to do as well, George." He turns to the pretty drab girl, although he is not at all sure that drab is the right word. There are not the depths of Laura Standish but no doubt everything will be in the right place.

"I don't know your name, my dear?"

"Emily. Emily Prescott."

"Well, Emily, my dear, I have something I would like you to do for me as well."

"Yes, Sir Godwyn." She is a quick learner. If this man knows Harriet Wititterly then he is very important indeed. Emily would love to meet Harriet Wititterly and her world famous bust. Not in a sexual way of course. Emily Prescott is very certain of her sexual orientation thank you very much.

"Come, Emily, my dear, I think we might be intruding."

"Yes, Sir Godwyn."

He quite likes the sound of his name ballooning out of her orange lipsticked mouth as he guides her to the door; the pressure of his hand in the small of her back is not the least bit intrusive.

When they have gone, Caroline and George, as they must now think of themselves as a couple, remain in hand holding silence for a few blessed moments and then a few more.

"All that carry on has made me a bit horny, woman."

"Me too, George, love."

They disappear hand in hand into the bedroom and close the door. The rest of it can wait because this cannot wait, is the shared thought, as they rapidly shed their clothes; her knickers are indeed on back to front.

Friday 20th October 3.34pm

Blissfully unaware of his narrow escape from arrest, Jack Bellingham has made the phone call he always knew in his heart of hearts that he would make, sooner rather than later. She did not sound the least bit surprised. Spread eagled naked on his bed, staring at the ceiling of so many bedraggled boyhood memories, as the afternoon shadows begin to close in, which is the time of day he always feared the most. The pale sunshine of earlier has given way to dark clouds threatening a storm. He knows he got carried away with no Y Jane but it was not all his fault. He had every right to think she was up for all of it – every right and she started some of it anyway. He does see the strangling thing might have been a step too far. Knows that he descends into a darker place when aroused like that. Not a good place. A very dangerous place in view of what has happened in the all too recent past.

He needs to stop thinking about it. She was beginning to get on his nerves anyway with her grating posh voice…Stop it, Jack…stop it…please…please. She should be so lucky. Most women would give their right arm to be up for all of it with the one and only People's hero. Perhaps not Celia Brook, but then she is not that kind of girl. He doesn't want to think about Celia Brook at this time and so will not think about Celia Brook at this time. Nor will he think about the lady prison psychiatrist. She was another one just asking for all of it. There is a rap rap knocking at the house door and he takes several deep sea breaths and remains spread eagled. The house door opens and closes, is locked and bolted and footsteps mount the stairs, including the giveaway step that creaks. It would take a lot more than a bit of bodily fooling about to scare this woman. No no Y Jane she.

Prison Officer Dora Spenlow, for it is she, pauses in the doorway for effect. Taking her time, she studies the naked man on the bed, spread eagled as if staked out by a Sioux raiding party. The spectacular erection briefly holds her New England gaze.

"I see you are expecting me, Johnny boy." She is wearing a tight fitting dress accentuating every last painterly curve and fissure and tell tale bulge of underwear. Her only surprise is that it has taken the stupid sod so long to ring. She shakes her frizzy blonde curls and fashions that rare transforming demi-smile. "You in trouble, Johnny boy?" Without being asked, she is beginning to undress under his intently watchful gaze, revealing pink knickers and a yellow bra. There is no question of a striptease routine. He attempts a smile of sorts. Not easy after all he has been through.

"Probably."

"I did warn you, you stupid sod."

"I know." Spectacularly naked in her turn, she crosses tit wobblingly to the side of the bed and stands with legs apart. Jack reaches out a tentative hand and deftly strokes a fleshly Rubenesque thigh, lingering over the healing bruises and lingering, even more so, over the soft insides of both thighs.

"Did you hurt the woman, Johnny?" She demi whispers, ever so slightly out of breath.

"I suppose so."

"You need looking after, Johnny boy."

"I know." She kneels down in a weirdly shadowy remembrance of his praying mother, and strokes the spectacular hard on... more demi-whispering and more than slightly out of breath. "This beats the underground holding cell or the bottom bunk with Sikesy watching." She teasingly takes a portion of his hard on in her mouth and Jack groan moans. All at once she releases the salivered portion and grins. "You push me around, Johnny boy and I will break your fucking neck."

"I know."

Then without further ado the Rubenesque woman out of time climbs on top. "This had better be good, Johnny boy, cos I don't wanna waste my day off." And she groans, or it might be moans, as she mounts the spectacular erection. It is weird that, for once, that wanker Sikesy is not watching and…well… wanking. Soon the only sounds to be heard in Jack's mother's dust moted house of dark secrets, are the frantic wheezy bouncing of the bedsprings and the moans mingled with the groans several times removed.

Friday 20th October 3.48pm

A surprised Laura Standish opens the squeaking door of her pokey but cosy apartment to find Emily Prescott on the threshold. They have never been great friends; more acquaintances aware of each other's presence in a shared survival space.

"Sir Godwyn asked me to bring the poor love's overnight case." They both look down at the Gucci overnight case for confirmation.

"You had better come in, Emily." Emily only lives five minutes away, but she has no wish for this real life Soap Opera to come to a premature close, and so follows Laura into the somewhat tiny sparsely furnished lounge.

"Very bijou."

"Fucking small you mean." They both genuinely laugh and know they could become bosomish pals, given a fair wind.

"Where is the poor love?"

"Safely tucked up in my bed. The doctor gave her a strong sedative." Laura also thinks about saying the poor love, but thinks that might be going a bit too far. "She's spark out."

"You actually got a doctor to visit?" If it is the same Practice Emily uses then she has problems getting a Surgery appointment at three weeks' notice.

Laura grins an infectious grin. "It's amazing what a blow job can get you."

"Laura, you didn't!" Truly shocked, Emily Prescott holds a hand to her mouth; Emmerdale is just not in the picture.

"It didn't take long. It never does. Tea?"

Emily follows the luscious shape of Laura, which she has always secretly envied, into the pokey kitchen area redolent of stale food. "Are you serious?"

"He's not all that bad looking but married with kids. You should try it. I hate waiting in that lousy sweaty waiting room to see one of those female doctor bitches." She fills the kettle. "Only of course I don't wait in that lousy sweaty waiting room anymore."

"Laura!" There doesn't seem anything else to add and it has to be food for thought. If it is the doctor Emily thinks Laura must mean, he's not all that bad looking and that smelly waiting room is awful. For a few moments they stand facing each other in the confined space, their arms crossed, knowing they are weighing up alternatives and that these are crucial moments.

"You slept with that Sir Godwyn?" Emily is not good with meaningful silences and knows she talks too much. Her much older husband has said it often enough, although she thinks it is just an excuse to stick his cock in her mouth at every opportunity.

"I most certainly did."

"You will think me cheeky for asking…"

"He was brilliant."

For once Emily opens her mouth and nothing comes out or goes in. She is not at all used to that and takes a deep breath. "He knows Harriet Wititterly."

"The tits woman?"

"The bust expansion programme is really effective." Emily tries not to be offended as they both look appraisingly at her bust shaped in the monogrammed uniform blouse. "I have gone up two bra sizes." Well one and a bit anyway depending on the make…a slight exaggeration never hurts a girl.

There is another weighing up the alternatives silence and this time it is Laura Standish who breaks the silence. "I'm quite happy with my tits, thank you very much. Milk? Sugar?"

Friday 20th October 4.21pm

Lucy Snowe, the scary eyed listener at doors, does not possess a great sense of smell, but is nevertheless nauseated at the rank odours clinging in the fetid bedroom; it is hard to believe it has come to this. Takeaway food cartons and takeaway food scattered about the close curtained room, empty champagne and empty vodka bottles and used drugs wrappings of every hue and colour. Lucy Snowe is truly appalled at the size of the dildo gripped in the apparently lifeless hand of Jack's…she thinks of him as Jack because they will soon be together for all eternity…the apparently lifeless hand of Jack's sister who is brazenly naked, legs wide apart, on the football pitch bed. Some people have no shame.

There are what appears to be several pairs of balled up panties stuffed in his sister's mouth and Lucy Snowe hopes they are clean panties. She is very particular about that sort of thing. The sister is staring at the ceiling with those oddly colourless, unblinking eyes.

Lucy Snowe pinches a sisterly cheek. Nothing. She does not really want to pinch anything else. That would be really intrusive and far too personal. Jack would not approve. If she had a make-up mirror she would hold it to the slack mouth. She does not breathe through her nose because the lifeless woman has voided her bowels, which is not very nice. Even with Lucy's almost non-existent sense of smell the stink is not at all nice. Being a practical girl, Lucy Snowe draws open the curtains, opens a window and heaves a deep breath. That's better. If she had a proper sense of smell it would be unbearable.

At the other side of the bed she bends close to the slackened face of an equally brazenly naked, legs wide apart, Amelia Sedley. Her eyes are closed and it does not really look like the actual Amelia Sedley. With difficulty, Lucy prises out the balled up panties from this mouth.

She thinks there might have been a distant moan and this one has certainly not voided her bowels… Lucy is not at all sure that mega superstars should ever void their bowels.

Now that Lucy looks closer, she notices that the right hand is, of its own volition, rhythmically opening and closing and there is a tourniquet tight on the upper arm.

She tut tuts, shaking her head and squeezes a perfectly crafted nipple. There is another distant moan. Just to show there are possibly no hard feelings at being sacked earlier she squeezes the other perfectly crafted nipple… no distant groan. She sort of caresses a perfect breast and the nipple hardens… no distant groan but the eyes are now open and unfocused. Still sort of caressing a perfect breast Lucy Snowe leans close and can almost smell the rancid breath.

"You shouldn't have said those nasty things. It was very hurtful to be called that. You know, Amelia, you can sometimes be a really nasty person and it demeans you." She squeezes a perfect breast. She has decided there most definitely are hard feelings. "I will not forgive you."

She crosses to the wardrobe, opens wide the mirrored doors and takes in the literally hundreds of dresses. Again she tut tuts and shakes her head…although shaking her head makes her feel really really dizzy. "No one needs all these dresses, Amelia, with all the starving children in the world. They really really don't."

Lucy Snowe retrieves the ebony, pearl encrusted, dress she has lusted after ever since spying on Amelia Sedley trying it on and casting it aside. Shrugging off her own cheap High Street copy of another Amelia Sedley creation, she wriggles into the pearl encrusted original. It fits perfectly and she smooths the svelt outlines of slim thighs and shapely bottom, and admires the effect in the full-length mirrored door.

"Just wait till my Jack sees me in this, Amelia." She cat walks to side of the bed. "You will be history, sweetheart." Her very own take on Bette Davis. She snorts a series of manically choking giggles.

Then she notices the absolute smoothness between the billion dollar legs and realises she will need to wax even closer before her Jack has his way with her, as he most certainly will. She knows that, with him being shy, he is waiting for his Lucy to make the first move.

There is knocking at the door.

"Fuck off." She shouts in a decent imitation of Amelia Sedley and manically choky giggles some more – the word giggling does not cover it. She narrow eyed studies the naked body of the legendary Amelia Sedley and touches and pinches and strokes to elicit another far away groan. "I am just as desirable as you, Amelia, if not more so." She purposefully compresses her lips together and slaps the slack face hard. "You really should not have sacked me just because you caught me listening at the door. The things you called me were unforgivable."

Another hard slap… and another. The finger marked head lolls backwards and forwards, like an out of favour ragdoll retrieved from the dustbin for just this purpose. The useless tongue attempts to lick cracked lips and there is a long lost effort at speaking. "It is no good saying you're sorry now, Amelia. It is far too late for that. You see no one else knows you sacked me because that…" And she points. "…smelly dead woman dragged you back to bed. Yes she's dead and very smelly and you are in big trouble, smoothy."

Then Lucy Snowe presses the tip of a finger to her own dimpled chin and appears theatrically lost in thought. "Unless… unless…" She watches as the depthless eyes of a thousand posters attempt to focus and fail miserably. The useless tongue cannot find its way back into the slack mouth and she looks really really stupid. "Unless I help you out, Amelia. Would you like that? Would you? I am not sure you deserve it." Another hard slap…and another.

Lucy Snowe leans closer and whispers into a diamond studded ear. She has always lusted after diamond earrings. "I will take care of everything, Amelia." The lovely head of a million desires half turns, and Amelia Sedley dimly recognises that sneaky idiot of a girl with the staring eyes who listens at doors. What is she doing here? Why is she grinning like a village idiot? And then the pillow covers the face that launched several thousand ships and everything is blackness.

Friday 20th October 8.03pm

The chauffeur driven limousine meets Sir Godwyn Lydate at King's Cross and Gilbert Markham stows the overnight case in the capacious boot, and realises he has not arranged the promised repairs to the widow Spearman's shoe. Probably no need now that she is a rich widow and cannot get enough of it, poor cow. Five minutes after he set off for the Station she had phoned to say that the Police had paid a visit. They were very sympathetic and she had managed to cry a little. She wants Gilbert to come round and he has promised.

After a silent journey the limousine is waved through the ornate gates of Lydate Hall by uniformed Security. Gilbert is hoping he will not be needed further tonight. As if he can read minds Sir Godwyn, who has been texting and reading texts throughout the journey, breaks the silence. "Do you have plans for this evening, Gilbert?"

"Yes, Sir Godwyn."

"Do they include Camilla French?"

"No, Sir Godwyn."

"Then you will not be needed."

"Thank you, Sir Godwyn."

"But stay in touch. One never knows."

"Of course, Sir Godwyn."

Gilbert realises that Sir Godwyn is in one of those moods that bodes ill for some poor bugger, or more likely buggers, and he will be glad to make himself scarce. He can now give his thoughts to the well done meaty and several veg exceedingly rich and grateful widow – otherwise known as plan B.

As always, Sir Godwyn is greeted at the palatial front doors of Lydate Hall by Nanny Linda. They embrace and, as always, share a lingering kiss. Gilbert hovers with the overnight case.

"You look well, Goddy."

"You too, Nanny." As if they have not met for several months.

Then Nanny turns to Gilbert and allows a kiss on the softened cheek.

"Gilbert has plans for this evening." Sir Godwyn watches on proprietorially.

"Then give me the case, young man and off you go." Nanny squeezes his arm fondly and gives the hunky chauffeur one of those penetrating stares, reserved for men she has allowed in her bed on several memorable occasions. "Who is the lucky lady?" Another squeeze of the arm to indicate that Nanny Linda does not do jealousy, but has a prior call should she be so minded.

"No one you know, Nanny."

"Off you go then, you naughty boy." They both know that Nanny knows just how naughty he can be when encouraged; not that he needs much encouragement, as she has found out to her delight. Something tells him he might be getting the priority call pretty soon, as she allows another kiss on the softened cheek. Sir Godwyn glances at his watch.

The door closes on a suitably flush faced Gilbert and Nanny Linda smacks Goddy's arm. "You are such an impatient boy but then you always have been."

"I am hungry, Nanny." He knows he should contact Shirley to update her on the Project that could be going spectacularly tits up. He is not proud of himself that something petty is holding him back.

"Dinner is in twenty five minutes, so you have time for a quick shower. Your young lady has been shopping in town today."

"A little black number?" He has cheered up already.

"Very much so. She really has a lovely figure... "

They are walking arm in arm towards the showpiece marble staircase. "But...?"

"No buts." She responds. He had learned so much at Nanny's knee and oftimes on Nanny's knee. "You and I know more than most about needs of the blood and the bone."

At the foot of the stairs he takes Nanny in his arms, pressing her chest tight against his chest. It is no contest. "It is always you, Nanny." There is a catch in his voice. "Always." Neither of them says it was never going to be enough and nor would they want it to be…perish the thought.

She kisses an ear. "I know, sweet boy. Now go and get ready or I will get cross." When he was a boy he used to smack his bottom when she was cross and, more often than not, kiss it better. With a tempting sway of child bearing hips, Nanny heads for the kitchen to superintend the girls from the village, who help out when the Master is in residence. Silly flighty things that always need watching and Nanny purses her lips. She does so worry about her sweet boy. There needs to be a legitimate heir to all of this and she knows Carrie Brattle's cannot be the chosen womb; Carrie Brattle is a bed warmer, and there have been more than enough of those. Another one is arriving tomorrow. Nanny also fears that the outrageously fey Helen Huntingdon will slip through the net… a pity… good breeding stock, the Huntingdons. She is going to have to put her thinking cap on. As she approaches the kitchen she hears the deep voice of her husband and some silly girly responses. No doubt later he will walk a particular silly flighty thing back to the village. Nanny is thankful for small mercies.

Friday 20th October 8.13pm

Laura Standish and Emily Prescott are halfway down the second bottle of perfectly acceptable Co-op Chenin Blanc. They both feel glad of exclusively female company tonight and for not dissimilar reasons. The remains of the Chinese takeaway litter the floor and Laura is sitting, cross legged, in her fashionably torn jeans, at Emily's feet. Emily, in her work uniform, is slouching in the only chair. They have chatted about so many inconsequential things, it has been really relaxed and girly.

"I really like you, Laura."

Emily drains the glass and Laura pours some more wine.

"I really like you, Emily."

"Should you check on your guest?"

"The doc said she will be out for several hours."

Emily giggles and Laura joins in only more so. "I can't believe you gave the doc a blow job."

"He's quite well hung."

They both burst out laughing and Emily spills some wine on her blouse. "Oops…"

"I think we're getting a bit pissed."

"I must say I hate that doctors' waiting room if you can get an appointment at all. The Receptionists are real cows."

"Well you know what to do."

They sip warm white wine in companionable silence, thinking their own thoughts for a few moments. Laura Standish is wishing that Godwyn had stayed the night; she was not exaggerating when she said it was brilliant and she is getting moist just thinking about it. She knows that she is bought and paid for…but even so, Laura Standish is not the kind of girl to hide her light under a bushel.

"What are you thinking, Laura?"

"Nothing much."

"Me neither." Laura tops up both glasses and is glad they bought three bottles when they ventured out for the Chinese takeaway. "Are you still seeing that John Everson?"

"He's done a bunk."

Laura doesn't think it will be a good idea to say she thought he was a total tosser. "Plenty more where he came from." Unfortunately she thinks.

"I know."

After a thoughtful pause Laura decides the truth should out. "He tried it on with me, you know."

"I'm not surprised." Emily could write a thickish book about her bad choices in men. They companionably sip more warm white wine. It does not seem the right time to bring up the fact that Emily is, in fact, married.

"That Sir Godwyn bloke is very attractive in a mature kind of way."

"I know."

"Is he well hung?"

"Very." That topic of conversation apparently exhausted, they stare at the false flames of the electric fire. Laura can now afford to keep on all the bars all day and all night if she wishes. Last winter was a bugger, using just one bar. She was forever catching colds. "You know that tits thing, Emily?"

"The bust enhancement programme."

"Harriet thingy."

"Harriet Wititterly."

"What do you have to do?"

"I thought you were happy with your tits?" Damn… she meant to say bust.

"I am but an extra inch or so wouldn't come amiss." She wondered if Godwyn found her tits a bit disappointing, although to be fair he did fondle them rather a lot. He was certainly eyeballing the Nazi lady's spectacular cleavage… but then so was everyone else, including Laura. It is hard to believe her and punch drunk George morphing into an item.

"There are some nasty tasting pills to boost your growth hormones and there is some special cream you have to massage in a certain way three times a day."

"Show me." Emily hesitates and Laura laughs that infectious laugh. "Don't worry, I'm not a Lezzie." She slurps some warm white wine. "I've got some dosh spare and I might give it a go." Laura hates not to be doing things and if there is nothing to do she will find something and, given past experience, probably the wrong thing.

Emily roots in her somewhat scuffed, seen better days, shoulder bag to retrieve a dog eared leaflet which she hands to Laura. "That tells you everything."

Laura has trouble focusing. "Shit." Then she holds the leaflet further away. "That's better." There are several diagrams showing how to massage and a topless photograph of a very attractive middle-aged woman. "Is that Harriet thingybob?" Emily nods and slurps more warm white wine. "It certainly worked for her." They both giggle and Laura turns over the leaflet. "Christ it's expensive."

"My husband bought me it as one of my birthday presents. The six-month programme."

"I had forgotten about him."

"So had I." More giggling. They are both really enjoying giggling in unison. It is so girly and…well…so girly.

"Still I've got plenty of dosh now."

"From Sir Godwyn?"

"Yeah. He's bought me body and soul." She makes a face that Emily is not equipped to read, giving them both pause for thought as Laura tops up their glasses. He had stroked Emily's bum in the lift and she hadn't complained because it made her quite tingly and receptive but she will keep that to herself. "We need to open another bottle."

"I should be going."

"Stay the night. There's a spare sleeping bag." When it got really cold last winter Laura used to sit around in the sleeping bag.

Emily doesn't take any persuading. It is a long time since she felt so relaxed and…and well …so relaxed. Sitting in the only chair she crosses and admires her own legs, knowing she has a lot to be thankful for, if only her much older husband and his intrusive cock would stay abroad permanently.

Laura puts the open leaflet on the threadbare carpet and massages her own breasts outside the woollen pink Primark top.

"Not like that." Emily drains the glass of warm white wine and reaches into the seen better days shoulder bag for a tube of cream.

"I take this to work because you have to massage three spaced out times a day without fail." She unbuttons and shrugs off the wine dampened monogrammed blouse and unhooks the white lacy bra which drops to her waist. She has nothing to be ashamed of. "Like this."

She squeezes the shocking pink cream onto both hands and begins to massage both wobbling breasts in an anticlockwise direction, then clockwise, then up and down and finally down and up. She repeats the pattern. "You have to do this for five minutes three times a day."

Laura is watching mesmerised." You have great tits, Emily."

"Thanks." She hopes she isn't blushing.

"Doesn't doing that make you feel a bit horny?" The nut brown nipples are visibly hardening.

"A bit." Emily glances at the old fashioned clock on the mantelpiece. "It is nice though. Really relaxing."

In her turn, game for anything Laura pulls the woollen Primark top over her head and unhooks the brand new pale blue lacy bra which drops to the floor. She reaches for the tube and squeezes some of the shocking pink cream onto both hands.

"You don't need much." Instructs Emily as she continues the rhythmic massaging. "That's it. Six times with each action then move onto the next one." Emily considers her new best friend's action critically. "A bit gentler."

"That's what I told him last night."

They both giggle. "Stop it or I will forget where I'm up to." Emily glances at the clock.

"You're right, Emily, it really is relaxing."

"I know. You've got a really nice bust as well, Laura. Lovely pale nipples." Which are also visibly hardening.

Laura looks down. "Yeah they're not bad. Never had any complaints." Well... just the once and that miserable tosser should talk.

"What would anyone think if they could see the two of us doing this?" They both try not to giggle and fail miserably.

"All we need is a man."

"Any man."

"Exactly."

As a statement of intent Emily thinks it is as good as it gets. She is not to know the depths of Laura Standish that Sir Godwyn Lydate has quite clearly divined. That is the thing about new best friends: it is hard to know where to start.

Friday 20th October 10.06pm

Nanny Linda Bertram, Tressel as was and could well be again, watches Sir Godwyn ascending the magnificent Adam staircase with his arm possesively round Carrie Brattle's trim waist in the little black dress. A slightly unsteady Carrie Brattle... that girl can certainly put away the booze...not to mention the rich food....she should weigh fifteen stones. She has such lovely long legs in the seamed black stockings, Nanny knows they are black stockings because she helped out when Carrie had trouble with the suspender belt. Nanny has never been tempted by a woman, otherwise she would have been sorely tempted.

Goddy is in one of those viscous moods that mean the receiving strumpet will probably get more than even she has bargained for. Nanny knows those viscous moods only too well. Unfortunately she is getting a bit long in the tooth to match them these days, except in short bursts. Smiling she switches to unbidden thoughts of Gilbert Markham.

Quietly Nanny approaches the kitchen and pauses at the slightly ajar door. Two of the three giddy village girls have already left for the walk home, arm in arm, confiding God knows what gory secrets. The other girl has, of course, stayed behind to help clear up the kitchen. Nanny knows the village only too well. Despite the modern day commuter element it is still an English village, in the true black hearted sense of the word… a nasty spiteful lustful place – Nanny's place.

The high ceilinged, dimly lit kitchen is conspicuously empty, the ancient dishwasher chug chugging to a rhythm all its own. Nanny coughs loudly and there is a scuffle in the adjacent utility room. The village girl who stayed behind, unsurprisingly, is Alice Gamwell. Not really a girl to be exact, more a young widow, and a serial cheating young widow at that; the young husband of two months' duration having been run over, six weeks ago, by his own tractor…he always was a stupid boy. Far too stupid to realise that his shapely young wife was servicing most of the Lydate Arms darts team, not to mention the village cricket eleven, the scorer and the two groundsmen. After a suitable interval Alice appears extremely flustered, fastening the top button of her blouse – busty like all the village girls through the generations, including Nanny of course. She doesn't meet Nanny's gimlet eyed stare. Everyone but everyone goes in fear of Nanny Bertram, Tressel as was and could well be again. "The surfaces need wiping down and then you can go."

"Yes, madam."

"I have no doubt my husband will see you safely home."

"Yes, madam." Alice Gamwell stares hard at her own shoes – yes – definitely shoes. She knows the randy sod is having trouble zipping up his trousers.

She told him to wait until they got to her cottage but the randy sod has no patience. Last night they ended up shagging in the undergrowth near the Hall gates. She got stung on her bare arse and then Security shone a bloody torch to cop an eyeful, the dirty sods.

"You have missed fastening one of the buttons on your blouse."

"Yes, madam." Alice Gamwell checks before carefully unfastening and even more carefully refastening the buttons. Taking her time with her substantial bust almost bursting out of the borrowed bra. She has brass nerve, this young woman. There is even a village rumour that she was spotted at her wedding reception in a cloakroom with the best man, his trousers round his ankles, and enjoying frantic activity that should have been reserved for the marriage bed. Of course the best man is the captain of the Lydate Arms darts team and opening batsman of the village cricket team. There are other rumours, of course, because there always are rumours. Alice's late husband's funeral has entered village folklore, involving the Undertaker and, if the rumour is to be believed, the stand-in Curate whose wife was six months pregnant.

Nanny's sad excuse for a husband now puts in a belated appearance, showing off one of his trademark, self-deprecating, what me grins. He has served his purpose over the years and theirs was never a love match and he has had to put up with a lot. When they were teenagers they thought they were in love and it was only after the baby died that they knew better. Still, they decided marriage was the least worst option. She had suckled Goddy and he has been more to her than any child or any husband.

"So there you are." Nanny pretends to sound surprised. No one is meant to be fooled. He thinks about making an excuse and thinks better of it. He knows his place and wants to keep it, against all the odds.

"Alice is going to clean down the surfaces and then you can make sure she gets home safely." What happens in the home is another matter and it would not be the first time a Village girl has had to be paid off.

"Yes, alright." He is finding it difficult to stand properly. That little vixen has been at work with her soft little hands; he has never known hands so well designed for the purpose. Apart from her mother of course. Nanny gives him a hard stare, knowing it is a waste of time – in sickness and in health, for richer or poorer means just that – it does not say anything about being caught with trousers unzipped.

"When you get back you can sleep in the dressing room."

"Yes, alright." Nothing new there then.

"Breakfast will be served at eight o'clock. The Swiss delegation will arrive by ten o'clock."

"Yes, alright."

When the bossy cow has gone, he makes a grab at Alice, who slips out of his clutches. "No, George, wait until we get to my place. We can do it properly in bed." These days she much prefers to do it properly in bed because at twenty three she is beginning to feel her age.

She begins to hurriedly wipe down surfaces, at the same time keeping a watchful eye on his movements. Alice really likes George and, for an older bloke, he knows how to satisfy a girl. He has taught her a thing or two, which is quite surprising. She knows she takes a hell of a lot of satisfying, but that's just the way she was created. Her mother's the same. She thinks that George might well have satisfied her mother at one time but is not certain. Still, keeping it in the family is a village tradition. "Right. I'll get my coat."

They sneak out by the kitchen door which latches on the lock as it closes behind them. Unseen by the intemperate lovers, Nanny watches out of a first floor corridor window, as the shadowy couple walk arm in arm down the moonlit driveway, in a parody of the Atkinson Grimshaw 'Lovers by moonlight' in the Lydate Hall picture gallery. They pause for some brief distinctive necking, before moving on at a quicker pace, even more arm in arm. Alice Gamwell's is the first cottage they will reach at the edge of the village and they will be there in ten minutes. It is a tied cottage and Goddy has let the widow remain after the tragic accident. Nanny has no doubt he will collect the rent in kind as and when; years ago she had heard, but not seen, Goddy more than satisfying fifteen year old Alice Gamwell at the edge of the woods. Nanny has never felt the same jealousy towards George, even when they were youngsters and believed they were in love. Since the baby died there has never been room in her heart for anyone but Goddy. The shadowy couple have disappeared from view and will soon be at it. Nanny smiles grimly and thinks she knows the devious little game that Alice Gamwell imagines she is playing. She would get the shock of her life if allowed to win.

She listens at the door of Goddy's bedroom. They are certainly very much at it and Carrie Brattle is making a lot of noise, which is only to be expected in the circumstances. Nanny had her pencilled in as a noisy comer. Nanny remembers that time Goddy was in one of these viscous moods and they had broken the bed. Nanny had been much younger then and they had continued rutting on the floor. She could not help making rather a lot of noise.

She smiles fondly at the memory and, taking a deep breath, walks down the thickly carpeted corridor to her own bedroom. It is early, but she might as well get some sleep whilst she can. When Goddy is at home she always sleeps naked and never used to get much actual sleep when Goddy was at home. It is sometimes difficult to know where all the years have gone.

Saturday 21st October 12.08am

"**S**omething is just not right. I just fucking know it in my water."

Shirley Keeldar has covered her nakedness with a Savoy Hotel bathrobe and is pacing the bedroom floor. Ambassador Thomas Sawyer, who is sitting up in bed with his hands behind his head, doesn't need any encouragement.

"Come back to bed, honey." They have picked at a room service dinner and hardly consumed any of the vintage wine. Although she has been somewhat preoccupied, they made love and he is considering risking staying the night, and, in preparation, has turned off his cell phone. There is a situation developing in China that he will need to check on later.

Shirley has tried ringing Jack at intervals throughout the afternoon and evening and he is not answering. Neither is Goddy and neither is Jane Fennell who, Shirley knows, Goddy had arranged to shadow Jack, with all that that implies.

She tries Jack again and it goes to voicemail, where she has already left a handful of messages "Jack, for fuck's sake ring me."

"Honey." He admonishes, not liking to hear her swear, because a woman swearing taints his shifting sands idea of proper womanhood. His wife Mary never swears in his hearing...his first wife swore a lot when the marriage was breaking down and she was drinking to excess.

Ignoring the interruption, she taps in a number that she has resisted calling. She hates Becky to think that she panics unnecessarily.

"Hi, puss, sorry to ring at this time." There is loud music in the background. "Really sorry. Can you speak up... that's better. Jack is not answering his phone. Something is not right. I just know it." She listens. "He is not at the Hotel in Leeds. I checked only a few minutes ago. He must be at his Mother's house. Something has happened. Goddy knows something and is ignoring my calls. We just cannot afford for this to go pear-shaped." She speaks all in a rush and gulps on an intake of breath. She will not be reliant on her fucking sad excuse for a husband. She fucking will not. No one can appreciate the pain she suffers – actual physical pain – when he bales her out bestowing one of those pitying looks, the self-serving bastard. Demanding his own unique take on a pound of flesh. Tom Sawyer yawns and closes his eyes in a Buffalo Bill show of exasperation. He has been informed this afternoon that Mary is coming back earlier than intended next week. Her mother has rallied… she would…it is as if the bitch is telepathic. He wonders if that is why he is taking this risk staying overnight with Shirley. He wants this woman but what can he do? He repeats to himself. What can he do?

"We need to fucking sort this, puss." A catch of desperation laces her voice. She has been an absolute fool. She should have gone up to Leeds with Jack. She promised she would accompany him to visit his Mother's grave. There would have been no problems. He was eating out of her hand and this affair with Tom is heading towards the inevitable at a rate of knots. "I am going up to Leeds now." There would have been no Jane fucking Fennell who is involved in all of this somewhere.

"No, honey," Tom commands but she is not in the mood to be commanded and covers the phone with her hand. "Shut up, Tom." Then she listens some more. "Yes he is…" She looks at Tom who raises his eyes to the heavens. He is not at all sure he likes the way this is panning out. "You are a star, puss. I will have a quick shower and meet you downstairs."

"Why are you doing this, Shirley?" He asks of the shapely robed figure that is, for God's sake, retreating to the bathroom – not honey anymore. "Come back to bed."

At the bathroom door she turns and does that hands on hips thing he finds kinda sexy. Mary does it too but not as sexily as either Shirley, or Sally at the Embassy.

"It is not all about you, Tom, and I need to sort this."

"Leave it until the morning and catch an early train." His most reasonable and really there can be no argument because I am right voice; a voice that all his wives and lovers would recognise only too well. Shirley struggles to disguise her own frustration at her stupidity and his lack of empathy.

"I need this to be sorted."

"More than you need me?" She thinks about answering. Thinks better of it and retreats into the bathroom. This is not the time and certainly not the place for truth or dare.

He hears the shower running and is furious that she has not put him first in the time slot that he has allocated in his busy schedule. He is accustomed to being put first… Mary would have put him first, so would Sally at the Embassy. He reaches for the cell phone on the bedside table and switches it on. There are a plethora of messages blinking away and he checks the most recent one from Sally at the Embassy. "Shit… Christ…"

He sniffs at himself and he definitely needs a shower before heading back to the Embassy. The last thing he needs is for any suspicions that he has been AWOL with a woman. Sally is getting a bit possessive – a transfer might be on the cards. He hears the shower turned off and jogs naked into the bathroom, disturbing a frowning Shirley vigorously drying herself.

"I need a shower. Got to get back. There has been a coup in China. The President is under arrest and his wife has taken over. This is a serious as it gets." With that he slams the shower door shut. Shirley Keeldar continues drying herself and wonders if Goddy knows.

The way she feels about Goddy at this moment she hopes not. At this moment she does not give a flying fuck about China one way or the other and, instead, gives up a silent prayer. She so rarely gives up silent prayers that she imagines God looking down in amazement as she makes a rash promise that she probably will not be able to keep. God probably knows that.

By the time Thomas Sawyer comes out of the shower she has gone. He has got more to think about than the cupidity of women. He needs to get a handle on things. He will get a handle on things or his name is not Thomas Sawyer, future President of the United States of America.

Saturday 21st October 12.42am

"Fuck off." Shrieks Lucy Snowe, in a passable imitation of an irate Amelia Sedley, to answer the knocking at the door. Her impersonation has got better and better as the evening has progressed. She is sitting naked and cross legged in a chair close to the open window, holding herself tight in her own arms. She is shivering and covered in goosebumps but the stink is not as bad here. She is glad she has such a poor sense of smell. She is wearing the genuine diamond earrings extracted from body two's ears. Lucy snorty giggles; body two, as she now thinks of Amelia Sedley, will not be needing them and body two didn't feel any pain when one of the ears was torn as the ear ring was ripped off…serves body two right for saying those nasty things…body two will not be saying nasty things anymore.

Scattered over the floor are several dresses that Lucy has tried on… she just cannot make up her mind. It feels wrong somehow to be wearing clothes when the other two are naked and not entering into the spirit of things. As a child she was always accused of not entering into the spirit of things… at any gathering the obdurate child would usually bite the nearest available hand and be sent hungry to bed.

Anyway, bodies one and two are not doing anything exciting and are just lying there staring at the ceiling. Boring really. She has thought about closing their eyes but she doesn't want to touch the nasty smelly things, now that body two has also voided its bowels. She might catch something. She once caught herpes and she vowed never again to touch persons anywhere where it wasn't necessary…of course Jack will be an exception and he will be here soon. Her Jack would never give his beloved a dose of herpes. She thinks she will choose the orange dress with the tassels, which sets off her figure to absolute perfection. She must look her best for her Jack. She knows her best is very good indeed.

There is some really sexy underwear in the drawer and the girl must start as the girl means to go on. There must be some mystery; not wearing knickers in the past has led to some awkward situations. She has never been quite sure how to handle awkward situations.

The door handle rattles. Her teeth are chattering and she cannot be bothered to shout fuck off. After all it might be her Jack. It probably is her Jack. Taking a deep breath of freshish air she scoots to the open underwear drawer and chooses really sexy peach coloured knickers, because she loves peaches. Her titties are so firm that she never needs a bra.

Then she shrugs on the orange dress with tassels, knowing it will look better on her than it ever looked on body two. She checks in the mirror…perfect… and her bare feet give it a gypsy element that she really likes, her toenails are a vivid red that really works…she loves vivid red and she bets that her Jack loves vivid red.

The door handle rattles.

"Coming, my Jack." She skips across the room, trying not to breathe in, and unlocks the door throwing wide her bare arms.

Saturday 21st October 1.06am

Nanny Linda knocks gently on Goddy's bedroom door, knowing only too well that he hates to be disturbed in such circumstances. Even Nanny has had to gird her courage to the sticking place, or some such, as she opens the door and slips inside the darkened room, crossing with actual bated breath to his side of the bed. She breathes in the unmistakable aromas of recent energetic lovemaking and cannot help but be pleased that they are not quite as distinctive as her own age ripened aromas.

The girl is snoring almost a manly snore. Goddy never snores. Her useless excuse for a husband snores like a pig when he is allowed in her bed. He is only to be used in emergencies, which are few and far between these days. Gently she shakes Goddy's bare shoulder and he wakes instantly.

"What is it?" Instantly alert, he switches on the bedside lamp and rubs his eyes. He has only been asleep for a few minutes and it promised to be the kind of sleep that follows Fauvist lovemaking; the sleep he craves and so rarely gets.

He got it with Laura Standish and believes he will probably always get it with Laura Standish – definitely more food for thought.

"What is it Nanny?"

Carrie Brattle does not wake, only the snoring misses a few beats.

"Agnes Grey is downstairs and must speak to you urgently." Knowing Carrie Brattle's place in the order of things, Nanny doesn't bother to whisper.

He stares into Nanny's muddy brown eyes seeing anxiety and distress. The look she cannot hide when she is worried for her darling Goddy. It is at these moments that he knows how much he cares for Nanny, as unselfishly as cares for anyone – up until now.

"Pass me the dressing gown, Nanny."

A silk dressing gown with dragon motifs is abandoned over the back of a chair; he agilely swings his bare legs out of bed and stretches. His disturbance of the bedclothes exposes the shapely bare and bruised buttocks of Carrie Brattle, who moans in her sleep but doesn't wake. The lay of her body gives the impression that she might never wake again, a false impression of course. The little black dress is tossed on the carpet, together with the stockings and the suspender belt that was a lot easier to take off than put on. There is no sign of any panties.

"Thank you, Nanny."

He is fully awake and slips into the dressing gown as Nanny covers up the naked sleeping girl, mentally tut-tutting at the tasteful devil tattoo adorning one masterly sculpted buttock. In Nanny's opinion tattoos are for muscle bound stevedores and burly drunken sailors.

"Was she worth it?"

"They are so rarely worth it beyond the moment, Nanny." They both know exactly what they mean – the loss of self in the moments of exquisite climax; the drug that cannot be bottled. "You are always worth it, Nanny."

"Yes... well." More than enough said, she leads the way out of the bedroom and he follows. She is wearing the sensible woollen dressing gown he bought several Christmases ago. She will no doubt wear it until it is threadbare.

"What is all this about, Nanny?"

"She wouldn't tell me."

Pursing his lips and wishing he had time for a shower, Sir Godwyn follows Nanny down the magnificent staircase, recalling that it was Plautus the Roman who said a woman's best smell is the smell of nothing... the smell of Laura Standish who is more in his thoughts than he would wish.

An anxious Agnes Grey is waiting at the bottom of the magnificent staircase looking whey faced and ill at ease. She has never intruded herself before now and so this must be serious.

"Would you bring some strong black coffee to the library, Nanny."

"Of course." She heads for the kitchen.

"This way Agnes, my dear." Not Miss Grey to mark the seriousness of things that they might have to face together. Now it is his turn to lead the way. The library is his inner sanctum. Agnes Grey has never passed the threshold that very few people have passed. Those very few do include Daiyu Chen, the Chinese President's wife.

"Sit down, Agnes." He indicates a leather armchair, and is very much in control...she would expect nothing less.

She is acutely aware that the visible vein is throbbing at her right temple but she can do nothing about it. Her close-cropped mousey hair, greying at the temples, could do with a good comb. That is the least of her concerns.

She resembles a not unattractive Queen Victoria in early middle age, about to impart some unpleasant information to a recently appointed Minister; the slightly bulbous eyes slightly more bulbous than usual in their uncertainties.

As he pours a neat whisky, she glances round the floor-to-ceiling bookshelves that dominate the high ceilinged room. Ladders reach the higher shelves and there must be tens of thousands of books.

"A drink, Agnes, my dear?"

She is intimidated that he is calling her Agnes. How silly is that? She shakes her head.

He seats himself in the opposite leather armchair taking a generous gulp of whisky and sighing contentedly. He really is an incredible man. She coughs and takes a deep breath and believes his enemies have already left it too late. They have also underestimated Agnes Grey... but that is only to be expected.

"I am really sorry to disturb you like this, Sir Godwyn." She can smell a woman on him and wishes it was her smell – stop that, Agnes – she needs to collect her thoughts.

"It must be serious, Agnes, my dear."

"There are two things that I thought you ought to know without delay, Sir Godwyn."

"In the circumstances, Agnes, I think we can drop the Sir."

For a few moments she is at a loss and is even more intimidated, as he crosses bare legs and adjusts the fall of the silk dressing gown. The dragon motif is suitably fierce.

"There has been a coup in China. The President is under arrest and some reports say that his wife has been declared the new President."

He taps the cut glass tumbler against his ever so slightly protruding front teeth. "I see." The calculations are in full swing. This has happened much sooner than he expected. It was always a possibility.

"Daiyu Chen has tried to contact you." They are interrupted by Nanny bringing in the tray of coffee cups and saucers and the coffee pot. She pours coffee and knows that neither of them takes milk or sugar.

"Thank you," Agnes mutters as she is handed a cup and saucer and strives to control the resultant rattle. "Have a drink of coffee, dear and you will feel much better." Agnes knows that Nanny tolerates her existence, which is probably as good as it gets with Nanny. Gingerly she sips coffee. It is just the right temperature and she less gingerly sips some more.

Nanny places Sir Godwyn's cup and saucer on the antique side table next to his chair.

"Thank you, Nanny."

"I will be in the kitchen if you need me." She touches his shoulder in a gesture that would bring tears to his eyes if he was a different person.

When the door has closed Sir Godwyn sets down the whisky glass.

"If I am not mistaken you have further news, Agnes, my dear."

Gratefully she most carefully sets down the cup and saucer on the polished parquet floor. Clutching her hands in her lap she stares at the dragon motif as if for inspiration. She is not able to stare into his luminously pale blue eyes glinting in the lamplight, and instantly resolves not to see John Caldigate again. It has gone too far and must stop; it is becoming too self-indulgent. There is just too much at stake, and she has not come this far to risk everything for sexual gratification like her mother did once too often…she will not do that…it was not a pretty sight. "Rosalie Murray has gone into hiding."

"How on earth did that happen, Miss Grey?" He sounds very calm and collected. She thinks it is probably not a good sign.

"She seemed so cowed and defeated so I thought she would be safe to leave on her own." A deep breath. "I was only gone for an hour to pick up some papers from the office. I am really sorry."…..no she cannot say it… "Sir Godwyn." Agnes Grey rarely gets away with things and has more than a nodding acquaintance with consequences.

He purses his lips and studies the pleasant looking woman clutching her hands anxiously in her pleasant lap. She looks as though she wouldn't say boo to a goose, would, in fact, be mortified to be seen anywhere near a goose; there are deceptive looks and then there is Agnes Grey. In the present circumstances he will forgive her just about anything because he knows she will never be disloyal. Loyalty is the lingua franca of the day and so he has decreed that she is worth her weight in gold. "There is no use crying over spilled milk, Miss Grey."

"No, Sir Godwyn." She is glad they are back on a proper named footing and stifles the tears that might not be needed.

"First things first. I take it you have spoken to Daiyu Chen."

"Over an hour ago. I tried to ring you. She sounded really frightened."

"Then it is my turn to apologise." Thank goodness and the trade mark dry lip twitch to boot.

"She said that Robert Peel is refusing to take her calls."

Sir Godwyn uncrosses bare legs and sits forward in the chair. "How dare he make that decision without speaking to me?"

She might as well plough on. "I think it is something to do with Rosalie Murray. One of my neighbours took great pleasure in telling me there were Security people swarming all over the street. I think Robert Peel has secreted her away." The great lover Robert Peel, she doesn't think – a big disappointment, unlike John Caldigate – stop it, Agnes.

Sir Godwyn leans back in the creaking leather armchair, fishing in the pocket of his silk dressing gown to retrieve his mobile phone. Turning on the phone he taps in a number and it rings several times before cutting out to voicemail. Sir Godwyn glares at Agnes Grey who presses back into the chair as far as she can without actually becoming part of the leather upholstery.

"He knows it is me and is refusing to answer."

She knows not to say anything as he snatches up and drains the cut glass tumbler of whisky, then tap taps the empty tumbler against the ever so slightly protruding front teeth.

"We need to move quickly, Miss Grey. This is a Shechemites moment."

"Yes, Sir Godwyn." Not understanding what he means but something Biblical no doubt. She will have to look it up because the Bible is not really her province.

"I have rather taken you for granted recently, my dear Miss Grey."

"Not at all, Sir Godwyn."

The driest of dry lip twitches. "Are you still seeing John Caldigate?"

A momentary pause. "I was until today, Sir Godwyn." She stares at the hands clasped in her lap and just knew this was coming.

"You really are a treasure, Miss Grey."

She looks up startled because this was not the response she was expecting and he is looking at her... there is no other word for it... fondly. Of course she is not to know of his unfolding plans where loyalty is deemed beyond price.

"I will not see him again, Sir Godwyn." A promise is a promise is a promise.

"Nonsense, Miss Grey. In fact I will need you to contact him later this morning." A pause for effect. "Although not in the Biblical sense. All that naked flesh can sometimes get in the way." As he knows better than most.

"He will be with his family for the weekend." Is all she can think to say.

"He must be contacted. Affairs of State, Miss Grey. Affairs of State."

She doesn't reply, thinking that parroting 'yes, Sir Godwyn' is not really appropriate. It only takes a few seconds to work most of it out. People rarely realise that Agnes Grey is extremely bright, assuming that a person's appearance denotes everything, whereas with certain people, appearance is merely the tip of the iceberg – shipping beware.

"I see that the penny has dropped, Miss Grey."

"Yes, Sir Godwyn." Now it is appropriate.

"It is time you came out from the shadows, Miss Grey."

"Yes, Sir Godwyn." In truth she quite likes the shadows.

"Have I ever told you that you bear a striking resemblance to Queen Victoria in her prime?"

"No, Sir Godwyn." She understands this is a compliment, and takes it as such.

He taps another number into the mobile phone and waits several rings. "Sorry to disturb you, Henry. You sound a bit out of breath, my dear fellow." He raises eyebrows at Agnes Grey. "Those nubile Research assistants can be very demanding." He listens and studies his manicured fingernails. "Of course your secret is safe with me, Henry. Harriet will not need to feel scorned and react accordingly." A suitable pause. "Has the PM tried to contact you?" He gazes at Agnes Grey. She really is a pleasantly attractive woman if you peer behind the mask of deliberate blandness. Her loyalty must be suitably rewarded. "I realise you were otherwise engaged. Check your mobile phone." A most pleasantly attractive woman and not a woman of trifles. "You have missed several calls and texts?" Now he stares beyond Agnes Grey to the bookshelves; a stare as bleak as a Saharan midnight under a full moon. "Tell me." He listens with disappeared lips that should make his enemies very afraid indeed. Agnes Grey is very glad she is not his enemy and can almost feel sorry for the duplicitous Murray woman. "Of course you must go to the meeting, my dear Henry, and afterwards you must come to Lydate Hall. Bring the delightful Polly Taylor as you will need a nubile Researcher to hand." He listens. "Never mind how I know. The important thing is that Harriet will never know. Keep in touch." He ends the call. It is always fraught with difficulties when the wife is the money.

"They are coordinating things from Downing Street and will have secreted the Murray woman in the First Lady's vacant rooms. Predictable is his middle name."

Agnes Grey smiles knowingly at her suspicions being confirmed.

"The game is afoot, my dear Miss Grey and I fear the consequences will be grave indeed." At this point, only he is aware how grave. "It appears that the gruesome twosome are moving against me even as we speak."

"We should have taken the Murray woman out of the equation." There is so much left unsaid in this statement that they both appreciate. There will be no prisoners taken in these trenches.

"Indeed we should have done so, Miss Grey. It is a mistake that will not be repeated."

The mobile phone rings to Parsifal and he checks the caller. "My dear Florence, I hope you are not taking undue risks."

He listens to the whispering voice and repeats for Agnes Grey's benefit. "She is ringing from the ladies toilet at number ten." He listens. "It is Agnes Grey whom I would trust with my life."

Agnes Grey cannot help mentally preening herself. She had been so worried about continuing the affair with John Caldigate but it was so very hard to stop. They had tried on several occasions and always ended up in bed. Really really stupid. She has done with dangerous affairs – or so she fondly hopes.

Sir Godwyn is listening so intently that Agnes thinks he has, for the moment, forgotten her existence. She scratches an itch on her left breast through the woollen cardigan. It is the spot where John sucked a love bite and she, of course, sucked one back.

"You must stay in place, my dear Florence, because I need to know their plans and movements. Things have gone too far for any kind of accommodation. You must take due precautions and you must dissuade the moron from making any public statements on China." He listens. "Don't worry about the Foreign Secretary and don't worry about the raid, Florence. They will find nothing incriminating there." Gentle soothing voice. "Stop crying, my dear, they will pay for this, believe me. They will pay for this." He listens. "Don't be silly, pillow talk is always useful and it will not be long before your assignment will be over. That's a good girl. Blow your nose and once more into the breach." He is gazing at Agnes Grey's crossed legs. "That's better. It will soon be over. Keep texting. Bye bye, sweet girl."

Now he is looking at Agnes Grey's face after glancing at the scratched breast... he cannot possibly know. Surely?

"Would you believe they are going to raid my office at dawn?" She holds a shocked hand to her mouth at this sacrilege. "There is no going back now, so I have some urgent calls to make, my dear. Go and get some sleep because you will need to be on full alert later. Go to Nanny in the kitchen and she will organise a bedroom."

He taps a long number into the mobile phone. As Agnes Grey is closing the door she hears him speaking Cantonese in that purple shade of voice he reserves for beautiful women. Daiyu Chen has been called one of the most beautiful women in the world.

Saturday 21st October 4.23am

"There is a light in the kitchen." For some reason Shirley Keeldar is hoarsely whispering. The car driven by Dickie Evans, Becky's latest potential conquest of the week, is at Shirley's insistence, parked a few houses down the road. He has been told to wait. He is waiting.

"You are sure he was all right to drive?" Shirley cannot stop herself asking. She really is almost at her wits end. Stupid. Stupid. Stupid.

"A bit too late to worry about that now. He is taking some strong antibiotics and not drinking which makes him even more boring than usual."

"He just seemed a bit erratic."

"He's just a fucking lousy driver and of course, from time to time, I was stroking his thigh." They both snigger only Becky more so. "He is desperate to get in my pants." Becky is wearing a little black dress; she went straight from Glencoras to pick up Shirley from the Savoy. Dickie Evans was the only sober person within reach.

"It is very good of him to drive all this way."

"It is what men do to get in my pants. He will get his reward now that he is well and truly primed, although it depends on why he is taking strong antibiotics." Another snigger and they have crept to the side door next to the lighted window where the plastic curtains are closed. There is a full moon and their eyes have rapidly become accustomed to the Pepsyian moonshine.

"Should I knock?" It is the silence after the journey that Shirley finds oppressive although, just at this moment, she would find noise oppressive.

"We have not come all this fucking way to skulk here for the rest of the night." With which declaration of intent Lady Rebecca Sharp aristocratically hammers on the door. It sounds obscenely loud in the quiet suburban night and reverberates more like 'bring out your dead'.

An owl hoots and Shirley jumps; she really has been a total fucking idiot and is grateful that Becky has not said as much. Becky is about to knock again even more aristocratically, when the door is snatched open by a dumpy woman with, what could best be called, an unforgiving face. A big woman in every sense of the word apart from height. It is the frizzy blonde curls that catch and hold Becky's stare and Becky spits out, "Who the fuck are you?"

"Likewise I'm sure."

The slithering accent grates and her bulk is blocking out most of the dim light from the kitchen. Shirley feels she had better step in here, because Becky can be so in your face confrontational when she is that way out. It rarely ends well.

"I am Shirley Keeldar and this is Becky Sharp, Jack's agents. We became worried when he didn't return our calls." Most reasonable… most apologetic… so sorry to disturb you in the middle of the night whoever you are. Quite unforgivable is the unspoken subtext.

Dora Spenlow weighs up the speakings and the non speakings of the very posh voices for several handfuls of heartbeats. "You must be fucking worried to have come all the way up from posh town at this time of night." Then she grins it has to be said somewhat unforgivingly. "You'd better come in, Lady Muck or the posh tart will be catching her death of cold in that ridiculous excuse for a frock."

The posh tart is about to backhand a cutting reply when she catches Shirley's eye. There is just too much at stake. Metaphorically biting her tongue is almost a physical pain for Becky Sharp. Actually biting her tongue would be less painful. In the insect dusted light of the single shade-less bulb, they both become aware, that the unknown woman in the rather common garish dress has a generously sculpted figure and an eye watering bust. Lady Rebecca Sharp is speechless with envy, which is probably a good thing. The busty one is giving them the twice over and Shirley cannot help wondering if the unknown woman is not quite all there. There is a sense of vacancy in her face that Shirley cannot quite put her finger on. Becky is not looking at the face.

"Is Jack here?" Most reasonable... most apologetic... so so sorry to be a bother.

"Oh yes! He's here the poor lamb."

"The poor lamb!?"

"Only joking." She grins even more unforgivingly. "Anyone less like a poor lamb it would be hard to dig up." Letting the slithering words sink in she turns towards Becky. "Haven't you seen a pair of tits before?"

"They are pretty spectacular."

Dora Spenlow weighs up this comment for several charged moments and decides it is a compliment. "Tits to die for, say the prisoners." She boasts proudly and Becky nods in full agreement...so that's all right then.

"Prisoners?" Shirley Keeldar is floundering here and all Becky can do is to discuss outsize mammaries with this weird intimidating woman, with wide apart eyes and a pug dog squashed nose, which reminds her of a much abused childhood pet.

"I'm a Prison guard at Armley jail and my Johnny, that is your Jack, phoned me in a bit of a state." She has the audience in the palm of her pensioner haddock portion size shaped hand. "He has been a bit of a vicious boy and slapped a lady around as vicious boys are prone to do." She is speaking thoughtfully and slowly. No one in their right mind would slap this lady around. There will be no interruptions. "He got a bit carried away and the lucky lady escaped his clutches and vamoosed into the blue yonder."

"Jane Fennell." Whispers Shirley to no one in particular and Dora Spenlow ignores the interruption. This woman could play the Glasgow Empire on a wet Tuesday afternoon and one would hear a pin drop, thinks Becky Sharp, who has only ever been to Scotland for the Grouse shooting.

"We have enjoyed a couple of half decent shags and then had a bit of a heart-to-heart. He needs watching, that boy, or one of these days he will be back inside for a very long time." That unmitigated grin makes Shirley's flesh creep. "Not that I would mind. I managed to keep him more or less on the straight and narrow inside if you know what I mean?" Shirley and Becky avoid looking at each other, thinking they might well know what she means and wishing they didn't. "Anyway it's lovely to meet you both and have a bit of a girly catch up, but I need to get home and get changed because I'm on the early shift." She sniff sniffs. "Oh! And have a shower."

"Where is he?" They are sensibly ignoring the fact that she is undoubtedly taking the piss and both have the feeling that with this formidable female the piss remains taken.

"Sleeping like a newborn babe. I dug out some sleeping tablets belonging to his late mother, God rest her soul. He needed to get some quality time away from himself if you know what I mean?"

"We need to take him back to London."

"Sorry, sweetie, he will be out to the world for a few more hours yet which is a good thing for the world." She moves to the door and Becky conjures with the vision of a baby elephant. "There is out of date coffee in the cupboard and not much else. I've written a note of the strong medication he was prescribed in prison. It's on the table with the last few tablets."

"Medication?"

"There was an unfortunate incident in prison. I told him he was a naughty boy twice over for stopping taking the tablets. He said he was sorry but I had to smack him anyway." They both stare mesmerised. "The medication balances out some haemoglobin, or some such shit, in his bloodstream. Without it he can become a bit, you know, unbalanced." That grin again in spades and she points to Becky. "The boys in prison would love you, sweetheart."

Then she is gone, leaving a huge vacuum behind in the dimly lighted, peeling at the edges kitchen.

"I would not like to get on the wrong side of that Amazonian throwback." Is Becky's considered opinion. "Or meet her down any kind of alley." A thoughtful pause. "Really great tits though."

"You think she meant it about smacking Jack?"

"Probably." Even more thoughtful pausing. "I must get a boob job. I really must."

Shirley ignores the sideswipe comment, which she has ignored many times in the past. "I had better go and check on him." Until Shirley has seen Jack with her own eyes she will not believe the worries of her own confection are over.

"I suppose I had better tell Dickie to come in from the cold."

Becky lifts the teenie weenie black dress above her waist and extracts an incredibly slim mobile phone from inside lacy black knickers.

"Becky!?"

"There is nowhere else to keep the fucking thing in this dress and it is not unpleasant when in transit."

"The boys in prison might get more than they bargained for with you."

"It is certainly an intriguing thought."

They both snigger and Becky shares Shirley's heartfelt relief, as she would do anything for this gorgeous woman, who is her own worst enemy. Becky makes no objection when Shirley takes her in her arms and squeezes for all she is worth.

"Thank you, puss." She whispers. "Thank you."

"Don't be a daft cow." Nevertheless Becky squeezes back and if they were oranges there would be no pips left.

Saturday 21st October 7.29am

Helen Huntingdon is relishing being out of things – as she thinks of it. Thanks to the sea air she has slept dreamlessly in this guest bedroom of Ted Branwell's house, and the bedroom is probably the size of her shared London apartment. Her flatmate is one of those flappy girls who seem to take up an awful lot of space for just one person. She is also untidy with successive boyfriends, who always try it on with Helen and, more often than not, succeed.

Ted Branwell had insisted on taking her out last night for a lovely meal at the local Italian Bistro. They drank rather a lot of red plonk, laughed even lotter and she was sure Ted was proud to be seen very much in her company. He really is a lovely man and he said that her giggle is infectious. Men rarely say that her giggle is infectious. Her last proper boyfriend – if you ignore Goddy, which is not easy – told her that her giggling got on his fucking nerves. Particularly, in his own words, when he was approaching the point of no return. It was the tickling beard what did it – she will never ever again have congress with a bearded man.

She stretches her arms and yawns luxuriantly. When they arrived back quite late last night she said she was whacked. She gave Ted a tit squeezy hug and a sort of sisterly kiss. He smells really nice and he patted her bum in a non-threatening, big brotherly, thanks for everything kind of way.

Over dinner she learned a lot about Harriet O'Connor to report back to base and is pleased that her first opinion of that pushy personage has proved spot on. Ted doesn't like Harriet and despises her husband who will shag anything that moves – Ted's words.

The lady – in the loosest sense of the word – would you believe, owns twenty fashion boutiques in the Tyneside area, and likes to la di da it over anyone who will allow it. She treated Maria as a bit of a lap dog. Helen is guiltily pleased that all she has seen of lap dog Maria Branwell is the dead body; just a pity that her magnushous tits couldn't be transplanted.

Helen has to giggle now at the thought of Spencer Perceval in the clutches of the Harridan of the North. If it was anyone else but Spencer she would feel sorry for the poor mutt. Ted said that boutique lady once came on to him, and wasn't best pleased when he removed her podgy hand from his thigh. Helen could scratch her eyes out.

There is a timid knocking at the bedroom door. "Just a minute." She jumps out of bed and crosses to the dressing table that is the size of a medium-sized dining table, and swiftly and expertly replaces the orange curly haired wig and then rushes back to the bed. "Come in."

Ted is sporting an in the worst possible taste, zigzag pattern dressing gown of many clashing colours and carrying two mugs of tea. Helen could well imagine the dressing gown being a Christmas gift from you know who...colour blind as well.

"Thought you might fancy a cuppa, pet. Hope I didn't wake you."

"I was just having a yawn and a stretch."

"Sorry I missed that." She giggles as he places a newish Newcastle United mug on the bedside table. "Strong and sweet, pet."

"Just the way I like my men." This time the giggle is a smidgen off key. She checks that her somewhat skimpy pyjama top is as in place as it is ever likely to be, and sits propped up against the pillows.

"Cheers, pet." He sits on the bed and raises his own lucky Newcastle United Fairs Cup winning mug, where the emblem is almost worn away. He has not yet plucked up courage to say he would love to take her to a match. Maria hated football but then Ted hates funerals.

"Bottoms up." She replies and takes a gulp. "Just what the doctor ordered." This is all so... she must make up a new word... delushous. No one has ever brought her tea in bed. The next morning most of her boyfriends couldn't wait to exit stage left. Not that Ted is a boyfriend... perish the thought. Although no one has ever looked at her with such adoration to set her nipples tingling. "That reminds me." She puts down the mug and reaches for two bottles of tablets on the bedside table. "Must be a good girl and take my medicine."

"Are you not well, pet?" He sounds genuinely concerned, which is not surprising after his experience with – spit spit – Maria and her tricky dicky heart. Helen doesn't answer whilst she concentrates on choosing, and then swallowing with a gulp of tea, the correct shapes and colours of tablets. Then she puts down the mug again and contemplates a reply. She knows that Ted is politely pretending not to be looking at her tits which, despite being on the small side, are adequately nippled and proving a challenge to the skimpy pyjama top.

Still, when all is said and done, Ted was used to Maria's fireworks on the Thames embankment spectacular display up top. Helen cannot help inappropriately wondering if he is disappointed and whether they are not worth taking a peek. Not that he has any place to be disappointed... no sirree... none at all. There is definitely more than a hint of tingle inducing adoration and he has most definitely taken a peek.

"You should know, Ted, that I have mental health issues."

"Poor pet." He quite naturally and sort of elder brotherly strokes a bare arm. He has a very nice touch in a sort of elder brotherly bare arm touching kind of way.

"Sir Godwyn Lydate got me out of a lot of trouble and I promised faithfully to take all the prescribed tablets without fail."

"Is he that important bloke you told me about?" He carefully puts down his lucky mug on the bedside table, next to the broken alarm clock that Maria had once thrown at Ted but missed.

"Yes, he has been very good to me." She frowns …in Ted's opinion adorably… and stares towards the picture window and the distant North Sea, as if she is drawn instinctively to the sounds of the inrushing waves, like that girl in the Dickens book he never understood at school.

"Poor pet." The hand gently squeezes. It is hard for Ted to believe that he is sitting here touching the bare arm of this beautiful vision. She reminds him of a Pre-Raphaelite painting he saw in an Exhibition his company sponsored at the Laing Art Gallery. Small delicate features and an other worldly aura only heightened by the curly orange hair and the mismatched brown eyes staring into another world. He liked the painting so much he bought it on the spot. Maria had hated it. He must retrieve it from one of the downstairs toilets.

"My stepfather raped me when I was thirteen." Which is partly true.

"Oh! Pet." He takes the lovely vision in his arms and she bursts into gushing tears. "Pet! Pet!" She is sobbing so much that he holds her so so tight, as if this will somehow stop the tears. He is not good with tears. Maria used to cry a lot when it suited. "Pet. Pet."

"So…so…sorry, Ted…" She is striving to bring the sobbing under control. She has never ever told anyone and she swore an oath never ever to tell anyone. It is that thing with Goddy. She knows it is that thing with Goddy that has got under her guard. There is no medication to take those memories away except that they were not at all bad…nor can it take away what she did.

"Let it come out, pet." Which is what he used to say to Maria although, whatever it was, never seemed to properly come out.

"Ne… never… told… any… anyone." Not that anyone would approve of how she turned the tables by threatening to tell her Mother and would not let her stepfather end the affair.

They hold each other tight for several minutes for all the world like doomed lovers on a Titanic film set, holding a pose. This is not a role that Ted Branwell, born to be a bit player, ever in his wildest dreams thought he might play. He cannot think of anything meaningful to say…which is just as well as he must surely follow the instincts of one of the few decent human beings in this story.

Saturday 21st October 7.43am

Talking of human beings, Sir Godwyn Lydate has showered and is impeccably casually dressed and checking the messages on his mobile phone. The Turnbull & Asser pink striped shirt open at the top button. Also seated at the kitchen table is Agnes Grey appearing somewhat crumpled in yesterday's blue pinstriped suit and pale blue blouse. She has just ended a phone conversation with John Caldigate.

Nanny has served them both toast and coffee and has been told everything. She has provided Agnes with clean underwear…there is no shortage of ladies' underwear of assorted sizes and styles at Lydate Hall.

"What about the Swiss delegation, Sir Godwyn?" Nanny always calls him Sir in front of other people because, above all else, he is the Master of Lydate Hall and no one must be allowed to forget that.

"That meeting must go ahead."

"Shall I prepare the Blue room? I take it they will be staying overnight." That foreign blonde strumpet she doesn't say in so many words, but he dry lip twitches nonetheless.

"Indeed, Nanny, and I will explain to them the circumstances. All they are concerned about is that the agreement is signed. This marmalade is excellent."

"Homemade, of course, Sir Godwyn."

He knows that nothing is ever wasted by Nanny Linda including her husband. "Where is George?"

She has a decision to make. It is something she will sort out in her own good time. "He is running an errand." She fights off a knowing smile.

The mobile phone resonates to Parsifal. "Thank you for ringing back so promptly, my dear. I take it your husband is not in residence." He listens." You think so? It sounds more serious than we thought. It would be best if I ring because you need to bring the evidence to Lydate Hall soonest. Things have taken an unexpected turn and you might need to prepare yourself for a most interesting turn of events, my dear Bunny." He ends the call and looks meaningfully at both women. At this precise moment they are the two most important women in his life; Daiyu Chen is in a special category all her own. There has been a long conversation on a secure line. She knows exactly what he is planning and has confirmed, after some initial confusion, that she has the full backing of the Military.

They have agreed the next moves and she confirmed, half an hour ago, that her husband has been executed and so any opposition is now very much on the back foot.

"Did you get hold of Gilbert wherever he has laid his head for the night, Miss Grey?"

"Yes, Sir Godwyn. He has arrived at Albany and has been met by Lydia Robinson and the extra security is in place."

"Excellent. And here?"

"A mouse will not enter the grounds without being detected." She pauses. "And dispatched."

"Excellent. Now to disturb that most unlikely of Lotharios, George Meredith."

Agnes Grey's mobile phone pings. "A message from the Home Secretary, Sir Godwyn. He is arriving at Number Ten."

"Acknowledge and tell him to come straight here after the meeting." A thoughtful pause. "Remind him about dear sweet Polly." They all know that Henry Wititterly is the kind of man to be constantly reminded of his indiscretions. Sir Godwyn taps in a number and it is answered on the seventh ring. "Good morning, my dear Jane, could you put George on the phone." He taps the fingers of his free hand impatiently on the kitchen table. "I know he is there and I haven't time for amateur dramatics. I am not at all cross. Just put him on the phone NOW."

Shocked and chastened, and very much naked, Jane Perceval wakes a naked and contentedly snoring George Meredith. They had made extensive love an hour ago and then drifted back to sleep. It is the first time they have spent a whole night together and would have made love again on waking…the girls are staying with her parents. "George, my dear fellow. Never mind how I know. Have you checked your mobile? Then check it now." He waits several impatient finger taps. "No you do not to go to Number Ten. You come to Lydate Hall without delay. Mary Ellen is on her way from Chevening. It is a matter of the gravest urgency." He listens. "You need to weigh in the balance a slightly overweight, naked and undoubtedly thrice fuckable Jane Perceval and unemployment, against a possible glittering future beyond your redoubtable wife's wildest dreams." He listens some more. "Excellent. Set off now."

He puts down the mobile phone, briefly closing his eyes and pinching the bridge of his nose. Both women watch with differing degrees of hero worship, knowing that they are privileged to be watching a force of nature in action. Only too well aware that this is history in the making…of how much history in the making they are not yet aware.

"Are you all right, Goddy?" Nanny momentarily forgets about Agnes Grey whom she must now learn to tolerate even more, because Nanny also values loyalty.

He opens his eyes. "Yes, Nanny, everything is now in place and this particular endgame is about to begin."

"The endgame?" Agnes Grey would never dare to call him Goddy – never in a million years.

"Yes, Miss Grey. The endest game of all." He knows she will soon work most of it out.

The kitchen door opens and there appears the apparition of a sleep numbed Carrie Brattle wearing Sir Godwyn's silk dragon dressing gown. She is greeted with various degrees of irritation and disgust. Agnes Grey would never in a million years dare to wear his silk dragon dressing gown so openly.

In her befuddled state Carrie had hoped to find Godwyn alone in the kitchen. She had woken up surprised she was on her own; she is not used to that after giving of her best in the dark watches of the night. Despite last night's pretty awesome, not to say, intrusive lovemaking, she had woken up extremely randy. She usually wakes up extremely randy. Weighing up the three blankly staring faces she decides it would not be appropriate to divulge this information at the present time.

"Carrie, my dear, I hope you slept well. Today is going to be rather a busy day with much coming and going. I suggest you shower and dress and Nanny will bring up your breakfast on a tray." Nanny purses her lips at the thought of that buttocky devil tattoo. "It would be advisable to keep to your rooms until advised otherwise."

The mobile phone intrudes Parsifal, he checks the caller and dismissed Carrie Brattle is already forgotten. She turns and leaves the kitchen with a defiant hip swaying swishing of the silk dragon dressing gown; the dragon shimmers seductively and now it is Agnes Grey's turn to purse lips. Of course she is not aware of the devil tattoo.

Saturday 21st October 8.08am

Shirley Keeldar slept naked and chaste in Jack's bed, not two words she would normally associate in the same sentence. He has snuffled and snaffled in his sleep, but not woken from the induced sleeping tablets slumber. Shirley, wondering how many tablets that gross woman administered, has slept only fitfully in the remnants of the night. It was hard to unwind from the events of the day. She had left her mobile phone at the Savoy in the rush to leave and feels bereft.

There was also a lot of noise from the next bedroom where Becky had obviously decided that Dickie's intake of strong antibiotics was no reason to prevent his knicker getting-in rewards, very much in the Plural with a capital P.

Shirley feels marginally better after a cold shower and discovers that the gross woman was not exaggerating about the contents of the kitchen cupboard. Still… a steaming mug of out of date instant coffee is just about better than nothing. She really is lost without her mobile phone. Perhaps one ought to consider Becky's method of mobile phone transportation.

She switches on Sky News and perches on the edge of an uncomfortable, probably never ever seen better days sofa. There are several tell-tale stains – best not go there. The giant television screen dominates the room and the coup in China is playing out. It appears that the President has been shot by dissident elements of the Army. A highly decorated glint eyed General is speaking to camera. In the corner of the screen is a picture of the President's wife, who Shirley recognises from that weekend at Lydate Hall, when Shirley and Tom Sawyer seduced each other. She had remembered thinking that Goddy was playing with fire with that slit eyed beauty, but then that is what he does. Shirley knew only too well that she was not playing with fire. According to the running translation caption at the bottom of the screen, the glint eyed General is confirming that the President's lady has now been declared President. She is no lady thinks Shirley, and has to smile at her own insouciance. The General appeals for calm and it comes across more as a threat, as he reiterates that the new President has the full backing of the Military. The General stares menacingly into the camera. Someone else one would not wish to meet down any kind of alley. Back to the studio…surprisingly no comment thus far from the British Government.

The next item. A photomontage of Amelia Sedley in the background. It takes several seconds for Shirley to compute what is being said by the platinum blonde studio bimbo. Shirley vaguely remembers the bimbo from some pissed up party or other, when the pissed up bimbo, whose husband had passed out, was led staggering to a bedroom by a pissed up Spencer Perceval. Then the words sink in. "Shit… fuck… shit." Is Shirley's response. Running upstairs she drags open the warped bedroom door and rushes into the darkened room. The fucking light switch doesn't work and anyway there is no fucking bulb. With no ceremony whatsoever she drags open the heavy damask curtains, pulling one half off the damaged curtain rail. She doesn't notice a car parked on the other side of the road from where she has been seen and duly noted as 'unknown at risk blonde'.

"What the fuck?" A naked Lady Rebecca Sharp is bouncing around on top of a bug eyed Dickie Evans, who is making a gallant effort at standing in for the inmates of Armley jail. Shirley does see what puss means – the tits are not very bouncy.

"It stinks like a brothel in here."

"Shirl, for fuck's sake." Becky has stopped bouncing but gallant Dickie has not focused his eyes or stopped weakly moaning. Hardly a moan worth the name.

"Amelia Sedley has been found dead in her hotel bedroom."

"Shit. Fuck."

"I need to use your mobile."

"On the floor over there." Dickie Evans is still weakly moaning and Shirley Keeldar has a modicum of sympathy. "Just let me finish up here, Shirl. It won't take long."

Shirley leaves the bedroom and Becky determinedly renews bouncing up and down with a vengeance. Poor Dickie is not moaning at all now. Shirley checks on Jack who is still dead to the world – an unfortunate thought in view of the demise of the International super corpse. On the giant, out of all proportion screen, in the gloomy tree branch scratching against the window room, they are showing extracts from Amelia Sedley's movies; this could take some time. Shirley taps in the number and presses the phone to her ear. She knows where it has been secreted and thinks it might have been used for other purposes in the wee small hours, when Dickie was taking a well earned pit stop, but what the hell… girls will be girls.

"Have you been trying to contact me?" It is hard to believe that the stunning beauty on the screen is gone with scarcely a projected whimper. "Yeah sorry, problems with my phone." She listens to one of the People and watches the screen at the same time. "Yes I see. Terrible. Really terrible." Shirley stifles an inappropriate yawn. "I am with Jack now in Leeds." On the acreage of screen they are now interviewing weeping fans gathering outside the Ritz Hotel. There is already a pile of flowers which a hotel porter is arranging in some sort of order and seeking to be conspicuous. He is being tit squashingly embraced by weeping young women, being as close as they will ever be to the fabled one. "Of course we will be back in London later today." She fucking hopes so anyway and ends the call. Thoughtfully she sucks the phone, then remembering where it has been, instead taps it pensively against a slender thigh.

"Was it drugs?" Lady Rebecca who is thankfully now wearing the little black dress appears in the doorway. Lots and lots of bare legs though, which Shirley thinks a bit racy this far North.

"There is to be a post-mortem. Evidently there were two bodies but they are keeping that quiet as it wouldn't play well according to her Person. The second body is Jack's sister. We need to get back as soon as."

Becky offers that gap toothed grin. "I think poor Dickie will need some recovery time… you know, Shirl, this could play out really well." She is intently watching the screen as more and more mourning fans are arriving. "Some people should really get out more or, in their case, stay in more. Let's think this through, Shirl. Jack arrives back after paying respects at his mother's grave and is led, possibly red eyed, into the hotel dumb with shock… I mean numb with shock." She is warming to her theme, forming her hands into a square to emphasise the points. "Jack still dumb and numb with shock arrives at the opening night. The Show must go on in Amelia Sedley's memory. Then. My God. Then the funeral. This could be mega, Shirl." It is obvious that his sister's demise does not enter her calculations, and why should it?

"That is all a bit cold."

"Just like this fucking house."

"The central heating doesn't seem to be working." Shirley makes to hand back the phone.

"Nowhere to put it, Shirl. Dickie made rather a mess of my knickers in his undue haste." That gap toothed grin again. "Not to mention the stockings. Quite a caveman to start with."

"What about the strong antibiotics?"

"He swore on his mother's life it was only a lingering chest infection. Which was good enough for me. Unless, of course, his mother is fucking dead."

Shirley shakes her head, it being her turn, for once, to take their excuse for shared moral high ground. "That latest attack of chlamydia has only just cleared up."

"What's life without a few risks?"

There is nothing more to be said so Shirley doesn't say anything.

"I'm fucking starving." Becky rubs her washboard stomach for emphasis. "Strenuous exercise always makes me ravenous."

"There was a McDonald's we passed last night on the main road."

"Right. I will snaffle the semi-conscious Dickie's car keys and bring back some lovely greasy grubbo."

"And coffees." Becky salutes and heads for the stairs lifting up her dress to reveal a neat bare bum, which she wriggles. She really is a one-off, which Shirley thinks is probably a good thing.

Saturday 21st October 9.22am

The Reverend John Eames, titular Bishop of Staines, and his very much female companion are ushered into the Archbishop's presence by a closed faced Chaplain Secretary. The closed faced Chaplain Secretary knows something is amiss, not to mention awry, and wants nothing to do with any of it. He has not remained in the service of four Archbishops by getting involved in things that are amiss or awry. The visitors are not announced and the Chaplain Secretary hurriedly withdraws with downcast eyes. It is best not to see certain things and certain things are best kept as certain things – the Chaplain Secretary will die in office if it kills him. The two unannounced ones pause as the door is firmly closed and are fighting off the inclination to hold hands like naughty children. Cecilia Hunt is wearing an ultra safe, below the knee, peppermint shades stripy dress that she has not had the occasion to wear until today.

She stares through round spectacles at the surprising Nativity scene without the baby Jesus. Cecilia is more alabaster pale than usual since they received the call from Sir Godwyn less than an hour ago. They are carrying out his instructions without question.

The Archbishop is majestically seated straight-backed on a Victorian style two seater settee, the dark eyed olive skinned woman cleaved at his side... there is no other word for it. No waitress she any more. No waitress she is dressed in an expensive looking maroon chiffon dress, very much above the knee. She is enthroned with those prominent bare knees primly together, one hand resting, it has to be suggested suggestively, on the Archbishop's gaitered knee.

Cecilia is fighting the inclination to burst out laughing... this is no laughing matter.

"Come." The Archbishop signals with a splendidly beringed hand. His deep-set brown eyes of a crossbred cocker spaniel appear oddly devoid of their usual myopic intelligence. The magnificent eyebrows have taken on a most disconcerting life of their own.

"You have not met my dear wife, Anna Clavering."

John and Cecilia cannot resist exchanging meaningful glances. Luckily the unexpected wife is staring into her declared husband's worshiping eyes. Cecilia is the quickest to react. She takes hold of John's elbow and guides him towards the oddest couple in every sense of the word.

"We are pleased to meet you, Mrs Clavering." There must obviously be no acknowledgement of the burlesque waitressing. Sir Godwyn was right to make a pre-emptive strike. The creepy Chaplain Secretary is no doubt an informant. The lady inclines her head and shanks a smile...the suggestion of a harelip is just that and nothing more.

"Your Grace, I believe that Sir Godwyn has been in touch."

"Indeed he has Miss...?"

"Hunt."

"Of course. Miss Hunt and the Reverend...?"

"John Eames."

"Of course. The Reverend John Eames, of course. I never forget a name." He covers the olive skinned hand that has possession of the gaitered knee. "My dear wife often remarks on my feats of memory."

Cecilia Hunt knows that she is much better equipped at dealing with congenital madness than poor Johnny, who is at a loss what to say. If she glances at him her heart will ache. This is no place for the aching of hearts. "When were you married, your Grace?"

She thinks Sir Godwyn must have been distracted. He sounded in one of those nameless moods, best avoided, when he rang. Perhaps the creepy Chaplain Secretary has been a tad dilatory.

"Yesterday by Special licence. It was love at first sight you know."

Even a determinedly composed Cecilia Hunt is finding words difficult to muster under the unforgiving black eyed stare of the waitress that never was. Cecilia realises that something has tipped Hugh Clavering over some metaphorical mental cliff edge. The black eyed woman seems to be hovering on the safer cliff edge of a triumphant smile. She alone knows the tipping point and Cecilia Hunt has no wish to go there.

"Sir Godwyn wishes you to convey the Bishopric of Staines on the Reverend John Eames now." So there can be no mistake. "Today."

"This is most irregular Miss...?"

"Hunt. It is within the Prime Minister's gift." And therefore Sir Godwyn's gift is the subtext.

"Most irregular, Miss… Hunt." He emphasises and the black eyed woman continues to be black eyed in a most black eyed way. "Most irregular."

Plough on. For Christ's sake plough on. "Nevertheless, your Grace, Sir Godwyn wishes it and the Church Commission does not need to be involved in this instance. Would you like me to phone Sir Godwyn, your Grace?"

"No. No. That will not be necessary Miss…?"

"Hunt."

"Miss Hunt. The piper pays the tune, Miss Hunt. The piper pays the tune." At this bold statement the Archbishop relapses into a most portentous silence. The black eyed woman raises and kisses his beringed hand and he deigns a mystical movement of lips, before relapsing into an even more portentous silence, and staring at some point over Cecilia Hunt's right shoulder. She strives not to look over her shoulder.

"Your Grace…"

Cecilia is interrupted by the deep-ish accented voice. Very like the voice of that waitress who never was. "Eez Grace eez communing wiz ze Almightee."

They dare not look at each other… they just dare not. The black-eyed apparent wife is pressing the beringed hand to substantial bosoms. The Almighty certainly resides in some unexpected places. John Eames coughs politely but Cecilia Hunt knows this is way beyond polite coughing.

After two or three minutes of communing. "Sir Godwyn…" Cecilia starts to say and the deep-set brown eyes are all at once focused on her own breasts. She had not been aware of the Almighty's sudden change of habitat.

"Yes. Yes. Yes…Miss…?"

"Hunt."

"Yes. Miss Hunt… Come forward. I won't bite." Cecilia Hunt is not at all sure of that, nevertheless they edge forwards to within touching distance, unthinkingly holding hands.

He addresses John Eames. "Kneel…?"

"John Eames."

"Kneel, John Eames." Now all at once the Archbishop is brisk efficiency. "Kiss the ring." John Eames kisses the ring. "I declare by the power vested in me that you are rightly and properly appointed Bishop John of Staines. You may kiss my ring." John kisses the ring for the second time and is unexpectedly anointed with the sign of the cross on his furrowed brow. "Go to God's work." They are waved away and it has taken all of thirty seconds.

Cecilia Hunt is made of sterner stuff. "Sir Godwyn suggested a few days away from your onerous duties, your Grace."

"He has spoken to my good lady wife and it has been settled that we will go away on our long delayed honeymoon. There is a Clavering property near Brighton… we are Clavering sauces you know – by Royal appointment." Then he intones in sing song tones. "Eat your heart out if it isn't Claverings the sauciest of sauces." And then in as normal as his voice gets. "The sea air will be most beneficial to my good lady wife. She enjoys delicate health."

They both glance at the black eyed woman, who looks as healthy as anyone is ever likely to look this side of Paradise. She could probably knock all three of them out with a single blow. Cecilia notices that the Archbishop's bushy eyebrows are executing intricate manoeuvres. "I think, my love, it is time for our afternoon lie down."

The dismissed supplicants resist looking at their watches to check where the day has gone. The black eyed woman is apparently unfazed and kisses the recaptured beringed hand. John Eames cannot help thinking that she would make a most formidable Bishop, causing the fires of Smithfield to burn anew.

Cecilia Hunt leads Bishop John by the hand towards the door, which he opens awkwardly and bangs his leg. They glance back to see the oddest of odd couples staring into each other's eyes as if the Almighty is in two places at once. The black eyed woman leans close and whispers into an Episcopal ear. The Archbishop emits a scarcely human sound.

The intruders thankfully close the door, both taking deep breaths and Bishop John rubs his bruised leg. Neither of them can think of anything to say that will not set off fits of giggles impossible to control. Thank heavens the creepy Chaplain Secretary is nowhere to be seen.

It is no good – she cannot resist. "You saucy thing." The dam of giggles well and truly bursts. The Chaplain Secretary tut tuts in his hiding place and cannot resist a self-satisfied smile.

Saturday 21st October 9.48am

Gilbert Markham, wearing civvies for this assignment, is sipping strong black coffee and sitting in Sir Godwyn's everything in its place Albany apartment kitchen opposite Lydia Robinson, who is also sipping strong black coffee. They have always been naturally at ease in each other's company, more than happy with their below stairs roles.

"A nice cup of coffee, Lyd."

She is never sure that she likes being called Lyd, but makes an exception for handsome hunky chauffeurs, who look even more handsome out of uniform.

"Thank you, Gil." He insisted some time ago that she call him Gil; it is only fair.

"This is a right carry on, Lyd."

"It certainly is, Gil."

"Dirty work afoot, Lyd."

"Yes, Gil." She leans closer dropping her voice... the slight Scottish burr still noticeable even after all these years. "You would think they would all have learned by now, Gil." She has never had less than total faith in Sir Godwyn and his powers to wreak destruction on his enemies. It goes without saying that his enemies are her enemies to the tenth generation.

"By the sound of his voice when he rang me, Lyd, there won't be any prisoners." It was most unfortunate that when Sir Godwyn rang, he and Roz had just started to make waking up love – both waking up very much in the mood, and had far too hurriedly finished off.

Lydia purses her lips and inclines her head as much as if to say it will serve them all right. Gilbert has never made a move on Lydia Robinson – he is well aware of her status as Sir Godwyn's occasional loyal knock off – sometimes more occasional than others. Gilbert once almost caught them in the bath together, but thankfully became aware of the splashing and groaning before it was too late. She is a handsome woman… there is no question about that.

"Sir Godwyn has insisted we must stay here on guard until he tells us otherwise." Lydia Robinson always feels it necessary to emphasise what is already known, as though it then sets the bleeding obvious neat and polished in her own mind. "All night if necessary."

"Your husband okay with that, Lyd?"

She looks at him oddly for several seconds over the rim of the mug. "There is a neighbour who looks in when I am otherwise detained." The words 'quite so' hover in the pine spray scented air.

To save further unexpected embarrassment there is a polite knocking at the kitchen door.

"Security, Mr Markham."

Gilbert sets down the matching mug and moves to the door. The muscle bound bald headed Security guard grins at Lydia Robinson who doesn't grin back. She's quite a decent piece he thinks – for her age. He wouldn't kick her out.

"They've been in touch from downstairs and your unwanted visitors are on the way up."

Gilbert Markham nods and glances at Lydia Robinson, who is still looking at him in rather an odd, almost calculating, way. There is a peremptory knocking at the front door. "How many of your people are on this floor?"

"Half a dozen, Mr Markham."

"Armed?"

"Oh! Yes."

Gilbert opens the door to face the potential intruders Sir Godwyn warned him about. He is surprised that there are only three and all of them suited and booted, with no signs of any weapon bulges. They must feel confident. Tossers.

Lydia Robinson looks on thoughtfully from the kitchen door. She is quick on the uptake where the opposite sex is concerned and she thinks she has been propositioned in a roundabout way, and crosses her arms beneath the considerable breasts. He is certainly a handsome fellow and no mistake, with a way of assessing a woman that causes tingles in all the right places; she believes that tingles in all the right places are there for a prosaic reason.

"What do you want?" The granite faced Security guard is standing behind Gilbert who is in full, legs apart, belligerent mode.

The man with the ridiculous pointy beard, who is standing slightly in front of the other two nondescript suits, Munich peace in our time waves a piece of paper. "We have a warrant to search these premises." So they found nothing in Sir Godwyn's office. Tossers. Someone will pay dearly for that intrusion.

"Let me see." Gilbert takes his time perusing the single sheet of paper. "This is not a warrant. This is an authorisation signed by the Prime Minister." In other words a worthless piece of paper he doesn't need to say.

"It is good enough."

"No it fucking isn't. To search the private property of a Privy Councillor you need a search warrant signed by either the Home Secretary or the Attorney General." Good luck with that thinks Gilbert Markham, because that ain't gonna happen anytime soon. "So fuck off and stop wasting my time." He throws the sheet of paper onto the floor. No one picks it up.

"You will regret this."

"Fuck off before I get Security to throw you out." Gilbert half turns to the granite faced Security guard who has taken a step forward. "Escort these intruders off the premises." The Security guard moves forward.

"You will…"

"Yes I know, regret it. Now fuck off."

The Security guard now comes to the fore. "This way, gentlemen."

"We will be back." Gilbert closes the door on the empty threat and turns to see Lydia Robinson studying his every move. She really is a one off sort of woman.

"Well done, Gil." She has a really lovely rare smile that lights up her face, lending a kind of brittle edged beauty. He shakes his head – he will be writing poetry next.

He follows the gloriously swaying hips back into the kitchen. "You know what, Lyd, this calls for a celebration."

"What do you mean, Gil?" She knows only too well what he means, as he brushes past her to the wine locker that Sir Godwyn never needs to keep locked.

"Champagne, Lyd."

"Gil, no." She holds a hand to her mouth glancing at the kitchen clock. "We mustn't. Not at this time, Gil."

"Those tossers won't be coming back." He disappears from view, leaving Lydia Robinson with a decision to make. She knows that she is anybody's after a couple of glasses of champagne, and Gilbert Markham is not just anybody.

In a natural, unthinking gesture she flattens her flowered dress against her thighs, wishing she wasn't so aware of tingling in all the right places. Sir

Godwyn has not been so demanding of late, but she has kept herself very neat and tidy down there, because you never know. The situation today almost feels like wartime. Her Granny used to talk about it and the tales she could tell. The Yanks were the worst. Her Granny lost count of the number of times she was taken up against a wall in the blackout. She suffered a permanently bruised bum until peace was declared.

Gilbert returns to the kitchen and holds up the bottle of champagne in a Roman triumph. "Seeing as we are stuck here we might as well enjoy ourselves, Lyd."

"I suppose so." She usually does her supermarket shopping on a Saturday morning, unless Sir Godwyn has arrangements, although he is usually away in the country at weekends.

Without being asked she takes two tumblers from the cupboard and brings them to the table, where a grinning Gilbert is popping open the champagne bottle and pours two generous measures.

"Confusion to Sir Godwyn's enemies." He toasts.

Of course she must drink to that. They both take generous gulps and Gilbert licks his lips. "This is the best stuff."

"Nothing but the best for Sir Godwyn."

"I can see that, Lyd."

She knows she is blushing and takes another generous gulp. This is not at all what she expected to be doing this morning. They will have nothing in at home, but the always eager widow next door neighbour will see Wilfred is alright – Lydia has her suspicions there.

Gilbert tops up the tumblers.

"It's a bit early to be getting pie eyed, Gil."

"It's never too early, Lyd."

She avoids meeting his direct gaze and takes another generous gulp... it is such a moreish drink. Her Wilfred says you can never get enough champagne... not that he gets much; not that he gets much of anything these days, what with his chest. Although there are those suspicions about the always eager widow next door neighbour. She looked a bit flustered, not to say hot and bothered, the other day when Lydia arrived home unexpectedly early.

Lydia sits at the kitchen table and takes another generous gulp. "I'm feeling a bit squiffy already, Gil." She certainly sounds a bit squiffy to her own ears.

In for a penny in for a pound, Gilbert sets down his tumbler and moving round behind Lydia, gently massages her neck and shoulders. The tension she wasn't aware of falls away like magic. "That'sh nish." She closes her eyes, giving in to the relaxing rhythm causing such pleasant ripples and wavelets through her whole body; there is a lot of body to be rippled and waveletted. "Really nish."

He kisses the back of her neck. "We mushn't, Gil." Then somehow he is kissing her lips and his tongue searching in her mouth. She is only too well aware that she is kissing and searching back, and that an exploring hand is somehow down the front of her flowery dress. The hardening nipples letting her down big time.

Saturday 21st October 10.23am

Helen Huntingdon and Ted Branwell have somehow found themselves naked in each other's arms in the guest room bed. His dressing gown and her pyjamas cast off on the bedroom floor. She feels so safe and protected and wants... needs to feel safe and protected more than anything else in the world. She doesn't want to agonise and weigh up alternatives...she hates agonising and weighing up alternatives... alternatives suck. She is breathing gently into his neck, nustling the kissable mole and listening to the seagulls screeching outside the window and the not so distant sounds of the waves breaking on the beach – Ted's private beach, would you believe?

His skin gives off such a lovely sea drift smell. They are both drifting in and out of sleep, not surprising considering that the lovemaking, which was not meant to happen, was at first gentle and apologetic on his part until Helen had urgently whispered, "I'm not made of glass, Ted." And it was Helen who had quickened the tempo so things became not at all gentle or apologetic. There is rather a lot of mess but Helen doesn't mind because it is Ted's mess and her mess of course. She never thought she would think that way about mess.

She kisses an ear and he is instantly awake. "That was lovely, Ted."

"You sure, pet?" He cannot quite believe what has happened... cannot quite believe that it is his hand possessively stroking the lovely bare somewhat sticky bottom.

She licks his ear. "You were amazing."

"Really, pet?" He cannot quite believe any of this. He has never, ever, even had inventive wet dreams as good as this.

"Ted, darling, would you call me your sweet girl?" Now she is gazing enraptured into his face and, being a simple soul, he doesn't think it the least bit scary. He has such lovely greenish concerned eyes that she wishes that she was called Hazel...her stepfather called her his sweet girl the first few times. Later he called her a conniving bitch.

"Yes, pet...yes, sweet girl." She doesn't feel a bit like giggling as she cuddles closer. He is turbulently aware of her blush pink nipples that he has avidly played with every which way, and are now pressed into his hairy chest. Maria had such pendulously inviting breasts, yet she would never let him avidly do much at all. She had said it was dirty. Maria had said a lot of things were dirty, including touching her bare bottom. He must stop thinking about Maria with this gift from God in his arms. It will almost certainly not last so he must make the most of it.

He will have such amazing memories to look back on in his old age. Perhaps he is being rewarded for his years of generous Charity giving. He wishes now that he had given more.

"Ted, darling…?"

"Yes, sweet girl."

"You are getting hard again."

"I know, sweet girl. I'm sorry." He often apologised to Maria for getting hard.

"Don't ever apologise for wanting me… Ted, darling?"

"Yes, sweet girl."

"Can I get on top?"

He swallows hard and nods his dizzy head. There is no way he can speak as this vision of unlooked for, naked, smooth loveliness slides out of his arms and determinedly climbs on top. Thoughts of the late Maria are scattered to the five senses. If he died at this moment from a heart attack, whist deep inside this wetly moaning and gyrating girl, it would all have been worthwhile. He is a simple soul and is not equipped to know that Helen Huntingdon homes in on simple souls. They are meat and drink to the Helen Huntingdons of this world.

Saturday 21st October 10.58am

The Swiss delegation from Smith Jones Robinson, the Multinational Pharmaceutical giants, are shown into the Blue room by Nanny Linda and Agnes Grey; just one of the many ways Nanny asserts her unique status. With only two people making up the delegation they are more a twosome than a delegation thinks Agnes Grey, who is a stickler for detail. A stern bald grey streaked bearded man and a, so stunningly beautiful it hurts, honey blonde Swiss cheese maiden, who conspicuously avoids catching Nanny's gimlet eyed gaze.

Mia Fischer had pretended that she didn't want to come today but, thankfully, Luca had insisted, or so she had told her husband, who misses her terribly when she is away from home. When the chairman of Smith Jones Robinson insists then it happens. He is a very straightforward man.

Sir Godwyn Lydate is not a straightforward man; Mia has to be honest for once and admit that Godwyn not being straightforward had been amazingly enjoyable during their two nights and one long afternoon spent together at Lydate Hall. She had been sore in many places for a week and had blamed a virus. She had to be very careful when making love with her besotted husband, who is also a very straightforward man and would be horrified at the new moves she had learned. He is very traditional, setting Mia on a pedestal, and ladies set on pedestals should not indulge in such things for fear of tumbling off.

Pedestals are tricky things, of course. Her husband knows her marketing role at the giant Multinational Pharmaceutical company is exorbitantly well paid – hence the luxurious lakeside villa. The poor love chooses not to be aware of the necessary input.

Mia takes a seat at the polished table and most carefully sets the brown paper parcel against a table leg and places a leather folder on the table. She adjusts the ever so tight cream skirt, which is very much on the short side, particularly as she is wearing stockings. Luca is looking at her legs. On the private jet from Geneva he was more than just looking at her legs and when she had closed her eyes – she always closes her eyes – she could well imagine he possessed several hands. At least he is very straightforward, not to say traditional, and it never takes long. It is a small price to pay.

"Sir Godwyn will be with you shortly." Thankfully the formidable woman Sir Godwyn calls Nanny withdraws. On that previous visit at the end of that memorable shared afternoon, the formidable woman had caught a semi naked Mia sneaking out of Sir Godwyn's bedroom clutching a torn dress... most embarrassing, particularly in view of...well...particularly in view of. That evening at dinner Mia had not dared look at Nanny. She was regretting wearing the black dress that lent a whole new meaning to the word skimpy, and was most definitely regretting not wearing knickers because there was a draught from an open window.

The pleasant looking, slightly dishevelled woman who has remained in the room, has taken a seat at the opposite side of the highly polished table. Agnes Grey is aware that the token human sacrifice is a stunningly beautiful girl with a Venus de Milo figure. She has also noted the statuesque legs in sheer flesh-coloured probably stockings... it is the company one keeps. Venus smiles at Agnes who smiles back; she seems a nice girl for all that.

"A crisis has blown up but Sir Godwyn did not want to postpone this meeting."

The glistening bald po faced man with the stern grey streaked beard looks startled; she knows he is the Chairman of Smith Jones Robinson. He has the sort of offset eyes that are never still, seeing everything yet seeing nothing of a woman. Agnes can only speculate as to why she finds his offset staring at her dishevelled breasts so pleasantly disturbing. She is her mother's daughter and no mistake.

"Nothing serious, I hope?" He speaks English almost too perfectly.

"Nothing that Sir Godwyn cannot handle," Agnes replies in lieu of her breasts, in a manner that brooks no argument. He looks at her face properly for the first time – a most pleasant looking woman; he finds the slightly dishevelled appearance most becoming. Hidden depths, he thinks and he thrives on hidden depths. She most pleasantly smiles and he visibly relaxes, holding out a hand for some papers that are efficiently handed over by the stunningly beautiful cheese maiden; not a lot of hidden depths one might think.

The stunningly beautiful cheese maiden, who is probably early thirties thinks Agnes Grey –there is a wedding ring – is gazing enraptured at a painting on the wall behind Agnes. A Botticelli nude; Botticelli would have drooled over this honey blonde Venus. The door bursts open and Sir Godwyn's arrival really should be greeted by a blast of trumpets and some hammed up declaiming of Shakespearean blank verse.

"So sorry to keep you waiting, my dear Luca." He deposits a buff manila folder on the table and the two men enthusiastically shake hands. "So lovely to see you again, Mia." He kisses both lightly powdered cheeks and only Mia is aware of the tip of his tongue. It is lucky that she has never blushed since losing her virginity on her thirteenth birthday. Liking losing it so much that she lost it the next day with a favourite uncle. Sir Godwyn takes his place at the table next to Agnes Grey. "You have met Miss Grey."

This factual statement is acknowledged by an inclination of Luca's head, whose quicksilver eyes momentarily linger on the most pleasant curve of dishevelled chest. With an effort he recalls himself to the moment. "Before we start, Sir Godwyn." Luca Grosch smiles, or at least does something complicated with his facial muscles. "Mia!"

The honey blonde beauty lifts the brown paper parcel off the floor and brings it round the table. Agnes Grey thinks Mia moves more like a supermodel and, as human sacrifices go, she would have the Aztecs drooling. Briefly their eyes meet and Agnes is sure the poor woman accepts such beauty as a curse as well as a blessing…Agnes hopes so anyway.

"Thank you, Sir Godwyn, for all that you have done…" Mia stares into his hypnotic pale blue eyes and remembers one particular thing he had done several times. She is not able to blush otherwise she would blush. "….to cement your relations with Smith Jones Robinson, we hope you will accept this gift as a measure of our regard." An ever so slight accent but otherwise too too perfect English in a caressing lilting voice.

"You are too kind, my dear Mia." She stands to one side whilst he unwraps the parcel – so many Christmases have come along since the barren Christmases of his boyhood. It is Agnes Grey who gasps when the contents are revealed.

"It is genuine," Mia breathlessly adds. "After the bath by Degas."

Momentarily stunned, Sir Godwyn takes in the colourful pastel shades of the naked woman with the towel clutched at squashed breasts. It is a painting he has desired for a long time, as he had told Mia when he had showed her round the Lydate Hall picture gallery on her previous visit. At his request she had undressed and posed naked beneath a painting by Modigliani. She had quite taken his breath away.

"I don't know how to thank you, Luca. It is quite splendid."

"Mia chose it," Luca Grosch replies without irony. "She has excellent taste."

Sir Godwyn tears his gaze from the painting and stares at the stunningly stunning beautiful woman standing beguilingly, almost to attention, waiting for orders. "Indeed she does. Indeed she does." He reverently passes the painting to Agnes Grey to admire and takes hold of both Mia's hands. They both know that later she will enact the self-same after the bath pose to the life. "I must think of some way of thanking you, Mia." She is most definitely staring back.

"Now to business." Luca Grosch breaks the spell and Agnes Grey carefully places the painting face up on the table. "Mia. The papers."

They all watch Mia sashay back to her place, sit down and unthinkingly adjust the tight skirt. She opens the leather case and hands more papers to her boss who passes copies to Sir Godwyn. With their heads close together he and Agnes Grey read their copies. Luca Grosch watches them with undisguised interest. The bland, pleasant looking woman has unexpectedly excited his interest. It is so rare for a mere woman to excite his interest these days. No beauty this pleasant looking woman, but then he finds that beauty only satisfies in the moment. He is no great lover, but this Miss Grey has touched something pagan in his soul. There is no knowing how deep might be the unplumbed depths. He swallows hard.

"All seems correct." Sir Godwyn glances across the table and then turns to Agnes Grey. "Miss Grey?"

"Yes, Sir Godwyn, all appears correct." She agrees, not daring to admit it was all a blur as her reading glasses remained in her handbag. The shiny, bald, grey streaked bearded man is staring at her in that certain way and she did not want to spoil things. The black framed spectacles are not the least bit flattering. Although on occasion John Caldigate did like her wearing the black framed spectacles and nothing else.

"You can do this?" Luca Grosch holds up his copies and it is his nature to dot the I's and cross the T's. Agnes Grey appreciates that.

"I can do this, Luca. The ban on aspirin will be based on the independent report of its newly discovered dangers and will commence on the agreed date." The driest of dry lip twitches. The damning independent Report has been written by the lovely Mia and her, almost as lovely, deputy. Now that would be a threesome made in heaven. "The National Health Service will order the agreed number of your manufactured replacement product Xprin from the agreed date."

Luca Grosh sits back eminently satisfied. Sir Godwyn has not missed the Swiss appraising Agnes Grey, and knows it can be used to his advantage. "Thirty million pounds sterling will be transferred to your Swiss bank account later today, Sir Godwyn. Further payments of the agreed percentage of sales will be paid at monthly intervals."

Two copies of the agreement are signed by the two men and witnessed by the two chalk and cheese women. Agnes Grey smiles pleasantly at Luca, who does that complicated thing with his facial muscles, imbibing the distinctive flowery scent which, on the off chance, Agnes has dabbed in several discreet places. There have quite often been off chances in the past.

"There is another matter, my dear Luca."

Luca coughs to clear his throat. "Indeed. Sir Godwyn?" Reluctantly he looks away from Agnes Grey…such a trim business like figure.

"The new Chinese President was sworn in an hour ago."

"The former President's wife?"

"Indeed, Luca."

"I understand that you two are very close, Sir Godwyn."

Sir Godwyn does not answer directly. Sometimes Luca Grosch steps very close to the line. "I have spoken to Daiyu Chen on several occasions over the past few hours and she takes my advice."

There is a charged silence in the Blue room, where a Lydate of the early Nineteenth Century had signed a secret agreement with several Bristol merchants to facilitate slave trade, despite the Royal Navy's supposed interventions. Naval captains were biddable in those days when bribes had been paid in bags of golden Guineas.

That early Nineteenth Century gathering had imbibed excessively of Canary wine to toast the secret agreement. That night a drunken Sir Percy Lydate had taken one of the Bristol merchants' drunken wives to his bed. The Bristol merchant in question was dead drunk and never found out about the cuckolding. So dead drunk that his exceedingly frisky, sobered up wife was able to stay in Sir Percy's bed until the following afternoon. Whenever afterwards the feisty lady rode to hounds, she fondly remembered that night and that day when she so joyously rode Sir Percy Lydate – the resultant child was, of course, the Bristol merchant's son and heir, who luckily bore a striking resemblance to his mother. There were no further children.

Mia is breathlessly shocked to realise that she is jealous and has no right to be jealous. Surely he did not do all those amazingly enjoyable things with the Chinese President's wife. She always appears so pristine and untouched by human hand. Now she is the Chinese President and it is ridiculous to be jealous. Mia has only ever caused jealousy and never partaken of it. "The Chinese market will be worth billions to the Pharmaceutical company that can strike an exclusive deal."

"You can do that?"

"I can do that."

"Come to Geneva as soon as you can. We will agree terms and arrange a generous down payment."

"I will look forward to that." He turns his head and stares into the wine dark eyes of the hauntingly beautiful Mia Fischer, and cannot wait for her to pose naked with the towel clutched at sumptuous breasts – he will have to be patient – the Home Secretary and the Attorney General arrived just before he came into the Blue room. They just had time to inform him that John Caldigate is apparently siding with the Prime Minister; the rumour being that he has been promised Deputy Prime Minister. Sir Godwyn made no comment. Now he goes to the door and opens it knowing Nanny will be hovering.

"Nanny, will you show Mia to her bedroom. The same room as last time. She will no doubt wish to freshen up."

"Yes, Sir Godwyn." He turns back to the room where all eyes are on the great man. "Agnes, my dear, why don't you show Luca round the grounds. We don't want Capability Brown's work to go unappreciated."

"Very well, Sir Godwyn." The two of them leave the Blue room together, not quite touching, but closer than might be thought socially polite on such short acquaintance.

Sir Godwyn knows all about Luca Grosch and his outdoor tastes and Agnes Grey, for the tasks ahead, will need her mind taken off John Caldigate. As Mia hesitantly brushes past he strokes her smooth downy arm. She shudders and they exchange x-ray glances. "Later, my dear." He murmurs and her answering smile promises everything that a man could desire and then some. There are just not enough days in the year.

Saturday 21st October 11.59am

Laura Standish and Jane Fennell are staring out of the kitchen window overlooking Meanwood Park, and are both munching toast; the bread is only three days out of date. There is awkwardness, but not as much as Jane Fennell might have expected, as she gratefully gulps milky coffee from a Stoke City mug.

"You feeling better, babe?"

"Yes. That stuff the doctor gave me really knocked me out, but I feel much better now." The flowering bruise on her cheek and the finger marks on her neck have certainly faded. Such a posh Home Counties voice. "Laura?" There is something intrinsically likeable about this local girl in the tight blue slashed jeans and the overlarge somewhat faded New York Yankees top, that is impossible to quantify or resist. "Before I became unconscious did I hear you giving the doctor a blow job?"

"Jane, really!?"

"There was an awful lot of manly moaning and, what sounded like, sucking noises."

"It got you treated in double quick time, babe."

"You are awful." They exchange sisterly nudges and any awkwardness evaporates. Sisterly nudges are a new experience for Jane Fennell, who is an adored only child.

"He was quite handsome," Jane admits. She is not at all sure that he needed to tap her bare tummy with his fingertips for quite so long, and so obviously ogle the diamond belly button stud and the suggestive tattoos that she now regrets.

"A decent sized cock as well." Laura Standish finishes the slice of toast and brushes the crumbs off her fingers. "Married with kids, so blow jobs are as far as it goes and then only in the interests of medical research."

Jane Fennell slurps more milky coffee and looks down at her bare feet. She only woke up a few minutes ago and has borrowed Laura's second best dressing gown. She was not aware of Laura coming to bed or getting up apart from the scents lingering on the bedclothes.

"Laura?"

"Still here, babe."

"Have you ever had really violent lovers?" She knows she needs to get yesterday compartmentalised if she is to move on. She will move on and it will never happen again.

"Several and some right nasty buggers." She touches Jane's arm. "Just put it down to experience, babe and if you ever get the chance kick the bastard in the bollocks." She speaks from past experience. They are both staring out of the grimy window at the Park, which is overrun with families at this time on a Saturday. There is a crowded children's playground in the distance. Jane finishes her coffee and sets down the mug. "I am sorry I was nasty to you in the bar on Thursday evening, Laura."

"Vodka off a duck's back, babe."

"Thank you for being so nice and thank you for giving the good-looking doctor a blow job to get me treated in double quick time." The exchange of sisterly smiles is as sisterly as it gets on so short an acquaintance. So sisterly in fact that Laura takes Jane in her arms and they hold each other for some time. It is Laura who breaks the clinch and steps back.

"You are a very pretty girl, Jane and you must not let this set you back. You don't deserve it and that bastard doesn't deserve to make you feel bad about yourself." She squeezes Jane's shoulders. "Now get showered and dressed. A colleague of mine from the Hotel stayed last night, and we are meeting her at the end of her shift to go out in town and get rat arsed."

"I'm not sure I'm up for it, Laura."

"Yes you bloody well are up for it. First of all we will have some retail therapy courtesy of Sir Godwyn. So do as you are told, young lady. New undies are a sure fire pick me up."

Laura is a bit taken aback when Jane steps forward and kisses her on the cheek.

Saturday 21st October 12.20pm

It is a long time since Gilbert Markham has shared a bath with anyone. He was seven years old and it was shared with his nine years old girl cousin, and he got the blame. This time of course it is very different. He is embracing a lovely big woman encased in his strong arms and muscled thighs. His mobile phone is balanced on the edge of the bath. If Sir Godwyn calls, Gilbert is ready.

In the meantime he roundly caresses her lovely big bosoms that are not the least bit floppy or flabby. She is a Pandora's box of a woman and he had not anticipated such a surprising turn of events.

She half turns her head and they wetly kiss.

"This will have to be our little secret, Gil."

They wetly kiss some more.

"We probably have tonight, Lyd." Something tells him Sir Godwyn will be otherwise engaged if today's events are anything to go by. But then you never know.

"That will be nice, Gil."

She is a woman of few words, most of those banal. The surprising lovemaking didn't need any words… a library book with a fascinating cover never opened to be read, and there could well be a hefty fine. She presses her resounding bottom into his groin expecting a response. She is not disappointed – there is nothing disappointing about Gil.

"Of course we do have now as well, Gil." She turns in his arms, offering that rare, so out of keeping, dimpled smile. There are promises and then there is Lydia Robinson's rare out of keeping dimpled smile. He knows he really ought to contact the widow Spearman, but that can wait. This cannot wait, as they even more wetly kiss and her workaday hands take full possession of the expected response.

Saturday 21st October 12.40pm

"This is not going well, Rosalie. This is not fucking going well. Where the fuck is George fucking Meredith?"

"We are trying to contact him, Prime Minister." Replies a living on her nerve ends Florence Dugdale, who is standing at the partly open door, mobile phone ostentatiously in hand. She knows that Rosalie Murray is watching her like a battle hardened hawk – a one eyed battle hardened hawk at that.

"We need to get a fucking handle on this fucking China fucking thing."

This priapic swearing is not a good sign; the more spoken fucks, the more the pressure is telling. Robert Peel is not as good with pressure as he thinks he is with fucks.

"Bobby, for Christ's sake, get a grip." Rosalie is itching to slap his slackened face, but not in front of that sly minx. She wouldn't trust her as far as she could throw her, which is not very far, because the minx is well stacked. Bobby goes for well stacked girls. Li Soo Ying being the exception that proves the rule.

"We need to get a fucking handle on this fucking China fucking thing." Repeating himself is another bad sign. He is pacing the living room in the absent First Lady's quarters, which at Rosalie's insistence has become the war room. Rosalie will not be seen outside this room.

"Sir Godwyn will be in touch with the new Chinese President." Florence cannot stop herself stating the obvious.

They all realise that that particular elephant has left the room and is roaming free in the deepest jungle.

"Fuck Sir fucking Godwyn fucking Lydate." Is the Prime Minister's spittle sprayed response.

Florence Dugdale makes no further comment except to glance at Rosalie Murray who hawk eyed devours the glance. Florence Dugdale thinks that Rosalie Murray has become very scary indeed. Rosalie Murray would like to make a comment but not in front of an ill at ease Florence Dugdale, who seems to have acquired a rather convenient stomach upset.

"Li Soo Ying assured you that the President – the former President – would come out on top."

Rosalie does not believe that the supper with Li Soo Ying was very much about the political situation in China; she knows a slitty eyed pushy tart when she sees one.

"Yes, Rosalie, and she was fucking wrong. Now the fucking Chinese fucking ambassador will not return my fucking calls." He cannot help wondering if the delectable Li Soo Ying is now thinking that she went to bed with the wrong horse. The wrong horse is starting to think she did. There is a knock at the partly open door and Robert Peel jumps…he jumps at every knock. The ever efficient Florence has a murmured conversation with the invisible messenger. Then quite deliberately closes the door and sucks in a deep breath. She would really like to be somewhere else, anywhere else would do. She has bad vibes about the way this is going. "Prime Minister?"

"What the fuck is it now?" He looks as though he might burst into tears at any moment.

"The former President of China has been executed and his widow has been sworn in as the new President and has the backing of the Military."

"Fuck. Fuck. Fuck. Fuck."

Rosalie Murray stares balefully out of her good eye at Florence Dugdale, as if the sly minx is making this up just to annoy Rosalie Murray. She wouldn't put it past the top-heavy minx.

It is now Rosalie Murray's turn to pace around the room. Florence Dugdale thinks the rabid woman gives off the essence of a mauled tiger stalking its revenge prey; any revenge prey will do...the preyier the better. "That Bastard is behind this." They both know which bastard she means.

"Even he cannot get the fucking President of fucking China fucking killed?" Pleads Robert Peel.

"The former President of China," Florence Dugdale unhelpfully points out.

Rosalie Murray's mobile phone beep beeps and she snatches it from the occasional table and listens and listens. If any other woman had such a battered face Florence Dugdale might well feel a modicum of sympathy.

"It is John Caldigate. The Albany building is in lockdown. There are armed Security people crawling all over the place. They will not let our people in the building. Short of a gun battle in the centre of London there appears to be nothing we can do."

"He has the second fucking search warrant fucking signed by the fucking Home Secretary." The Home Secretary and the Attorney General had refused to sign the search warrant and had stormed out of this morning's meeting. They are many things but they are decidedly not suicidal. The Home Secretary's signature was forged by Rosalie Murray.

John Caldigate it is still on the line and Rosalie Murray's spits out. "He was told it would make no difference if the search warrant was signed by Jesus Christ and all his Saints."

The Prime Minister slumps into an armchair like a puppet with all the strings maliciously cut. "We need evidence, Rosalie. We need proof. We need..."

Florence Dugdale can scarcely breathe because the atmosphere in the room is so feral.

"We need to get to your wife, Bobby. There is some reason she is hidden away and we need to find that reason." Rosalie Murray has a pretty damned good idea. "We need to move against the bastard without delay."

"There will be a private army surrounding Lydate Hall." Mutters the string-less fuck-less puppet. "She will not be there."

Rosalie Murray is thinking thinking thinking. Florence Dugdale opens the door wider as surreptitiously as humanely possible.

"Where are you going?" Rosalie Murray snaps.

"I need the toilet." When Florence has slipped out of the room, using as small a space as possible, Rosalie Murray gazes speculatively at the pathetic call me Bobby creature with its head in its hands. Even she is beginning to wonder if the game is worth the candle. She has no choice; this is the only candle in town. She cannot afford for it to be blown out.

Taking a deep sea breath she talks into the mobile phone. "Stay where you are, John and I will get back to you." She ends the call. "Bobby... Bobby!"

He dumb stares like a kicked puppy at Rosalie Murray who forges his name like an insult. "Don't you think it strange that bastard knows all our moves?"

"He knows everything."

"He is not clairvoyant… somebody is feeding him information." Without another wasted word she stalks out of the room she had not wanted to leave. Luckily there is no one in the adjoining room or in the corridor. The headless chicken syndrome betokens some advantages.

As feline as a mousing cat she opens the door of the ladies' toilets and tiptoes towards the three cubicles. The door of the far cubicle is closed and she hears the unmistakable, subdued, pleading voice of Florence Dugdale. The sly minx must think she has five minutes at least whilst they have more important things to worry about. There are no sounds of any stomach upset bowel movements and no smell. Rosalie Murray knew that those few unhappy weeks as a Girl Guide would come in useful one day…lots of smells there.

Rosalie tiptoes closer. "I must speak to Sir Godwyn as a matter of urgency. I don't care if he is in a meeting with the Home Secretary and the Attorney General. Tell him it is urgent. Yes I will wait. Please hurry, please." So much for the bastard opposing the sly minx's appointment and so much for Henry Wititterly and the Attorney tart. Rosalie Murray works through the odds. To be or not to be that is the question – whether tis better the bastard knows they have turned their attention to the Prime Minister's possibly, in Rosalie's surmise, pregnant wife as a get out of jail card, or not. She has heard rumours of a bolt hole in the Cotswolds. It is highly likely that Florence Dugdale has been ritually deflowered there. Rosalie Murray is in no mood for pussy footing about because time is of the essence – kill or be killed – metaphorically speaking. She decides it is rather to be than not to be and kicks open the flimsy cubicle door. A shocked Florence Dugdale almost experiences an involuntary bowel movement, despite sitting on the closed toilet seat with her clothing all present and correct. Now that would have been some payback thinks Rosalie Murray. Florence Dugdale drops her mobile phone on the floor as she is grabbed by the hair, dragged out of the cubicle and frog marched down the corridor, through the adjoining room and into the makeshift war room, where she is unceremoniously dumped on the floor.

She is so shocked she doesn't move. Rosalie Murray is furious that the duplicitous minx hasn't even pissed herself.

"Here is our nasty little spy, Prime Minister… our nasty little mole." She kicks Florence in the stomach, who curls up in the foetal position.

"Florrie! I cannot believe it." He cannot believe it…the intimate stuff they have done together and it was all a lie. The carrier bag to his peeler… all a lie.

An enraged Rosalie Murray kicks the prone body and the arms protecting the face.

"Rosalie, stop it. That's enough." He drags her away and she turns on him.

"She knows where your wife has been hidden away."

"Then she will tell me." They look down at the prone body, and he kneels and touches a hunched shoulder that is shaking with her sobbing. "Will you tell your peeler, Florrie? Will you, my little carrier bag?" Ignoring Rosalie Murray's sharp intake of breath Florence nods her head. He leans closer as she whispers an address in Chipping Camden. Still on his knees he turns to stare at Rosalie Murray and repeats the address. Without further comment she phones John Caldigate and gives him urgent instructions. She is not to know that he has been told to obey her instructions without question. She believes she is the puppet master and that John Caldigate will also do anything to revenge himself on Sir Godwyn Lydate – she has never been good at reading people. Robert Peel struggles up from his knees and slumps puppy kicked fashion in a chair, staring at the foetal girl sobbing into her covering arms. Such a lovely willowy girl and quite magnificent breasts…she ought to be forgiven for those breasts.

Not being without pity, Rosalie Murray hands him a neat whisky. He mumbles his thanks and drains the glass. "I would have trusted Florrie with my life."

"Luckily you didn't have to." It is time to move. The luxury of introspection can hopefully come later.

"Who can we trust, Rosalie?"

"We can trust each other and that has to be enough for now."

He is not sure about that, but takes a modicum of strength from this formidable avenging fury; his Greek is rusty but he thinks the Greek word most apposite.

"Caldigate must bring your wife here."

"Here?"

"Don't fucking start that again, Bobby." He just stops himself saying sorry. "We need to prepare ourselves. In the meantime…" She grabs Florence Dugdale by the hair, dragging her to her feet and frog marching her out of the war room. She will be locked away in that other minx bitch Lizzie Hasting's ensuite bedroom, to be dealt with later. Rosalie Murray would throw away the key, but then Rosalie Murray is making strange disjointed noises in the back of her throat. Rosalie Murray does not look at all well.

Saturday 21st October 12.59pm

Nanny Linda hands the mobile phone to an annoyed Sir Godwyn who has sent the Home Secretary and the Attorney General about their allotted tasks more hurriedly than he would have wished. Not wishing to be disturbed, he left his mobile phone with Nanny to monitor calls. It is not a role she relishes. "The Foreign Secretary and his wife are waiting in the Blue room."

"Thank you, Nanny. Yes Florence?"

He listens for a few moments, then holds the phone away from his ear and narrow eyed studies the screen. She has not rung off. "Florence, are you there?"

Nothing. He looks at Nanny. "What did she say?"

"That it was urgent."

"No hint what it was about?" A worried looking Nanny shakes her head. She cannot hide raw emotions where Goddy's welfare is concerned. The baby that suckled milk from her breast; the boy she believes she seduced and has never for one second regretted that belief.

"I think her cover might have been blown." He twitches lips at sounding like a third rate Secret agent in a fourth rate novel remaindered at the Book People. Then he taps the mobile phone against ever so slightly prominent front teeth. He senses a vengeful Rosalie Murray behind this and knows that Agnes Grey was only too right. They took their eyes off the hand grenade. He is not at all happy that one of his people has had to take a fall. George Edmonds never took a fall.

"There will be no prisoners taken." He mutters for Nanny's ears only. "We are the enraged Canadians at Vimy Ridge and we shout no quarter...no prisoners."

"Do be careful, Goddy." They hug and kiss on the lips. Both know that this is by no means the first time she has said this. They both know that he cannot always be careful.

George Meredith jumps to his feet as if he has been scalded as Sir Godwyn bursts into the Blue room; only Nanny knows why it is called the Blue room and does not think it at all amusing, because she remembers that day only too well. Grim faced Mary Ellen Meredith remains seated in the manner of a seasoned actress playing a more mature Queen Elizabeth the First receiving news of the approach of the Spanish Armada and concealing her fears.

"George, it is good of you to come." The two men awkwardly shake hands and Sir Godwyn kisses Mary Ellen on both apple juicy cheeks. Only she is aware of the tip of his tongue. Such lovely fresh and minty breath. "Bunny, you look radiant." No longer grim faced, she lopsidedly smiles...the Spanish Armada will be sunk without trace.

It is a unique smile that he always finds fascinating. A smile that can slide into a come on I'm up for it if you are whoever you are, given the right or wrong circumstances, smile. More like a more mature Queen Elizabeth the First receiving news that the Spanish Armada has indeed sunk without trace. "Let's get down to it." He moves a chair closer to Mary Ellen and sits down and looks across her weighty bosoms to a startled, rabbit caught in the headlights, George Meredith. There was no time to shower after receiving the urgent summons and he is aware of the several scents of Jane Perceval lingering on several parts of his body. He has enough survival instinct to know that he must keep quiet and let things pan out. He closes his eyes, conjuring up some memories of last night and this morning's many and varied delectations. He might as well so conjure as he is probably for the high jump anyway. He has been led astray and should not have listened.

"You have the evidence, Bunny?" She pushes the green folder closer to Sir Godwyn. "Excellent." He opens the folder and takes several minutes to peruse various purloined documents and email transcriptions. Whilst he is reading Mary Ellen kicks off a shoe to rub a warm stockinged foot against his calf. They exchange glances and the unique smile is most assuredly sliding. There is something about Mary Ellen Meredith that should only be uncorked at room temperature. He closes the file with a snap and George opens his eyes and cannot believe he ever thought he was ahead of the game.

"Well, well, my dear George, you have been taking bribes from the Israelis and the Saudis, as well as plotting against me."

George Meredith does not reply... there is no point. He looks at his wife of twenty three years as if seeing her properly for the first time. "Why?"

She, of course, does not reply; the look she returns is so contemptuous that she might be Queen Elizabeth the First sending her once upon a time favourite Essex to the scaffold. George is taken aback. He has always known that she blames him for their not having children, but he thought they had come to some sort of workable mutuality. He thought the trappings of High Office had become enough. He is not aware of any affairs, but then he wouldn't be aware. He knows that recently he has fucked around somewhat indiscriminately, but then his wife wasn't interested in sex... at least not sex with George. He is acutely conscious of her foot rubbing Sir Godwyn's calf, explaining a great deal that he prefers not to contemplate.

He knows she has been drinking a lot recently, but even so. He summons up the courage to face his masked executioner across his wife's somewhat dominating bosoms. From out of nowhere comes a desire to lay his weary head between those once upon a time bosoms. He knows it is far too late for that.

"You will want my resignation." He hopes against hope that might be enough.

Sir Godwyn Lydate studies George Meredith's hangdog face that appears to have aged over the past few minutes. Sir Godwyn can only wonder at this man's many and varied female conquests, particularly of Jane Perceval, who has always been choosy, in her own inimitable way, with her lexicon of lovers. He doesn't really think that George ticks any of the boxes – but what does he know? He can only think that this most unlikely Lothario has well hidden qualities. He must ask Jane the next time they are in bed together.

Sir Godwyn's Patrician gaze switches to Mary Ellen, Bunny to her intimates, the once upon a time apple cheeked country pursuits beauty. Still exceedingly attractive in a merry-go-round comfortable way. No tattoos on that substantial in a nice way bottom. An enthusiastic lover, in a ruddy cheeked rolling in the hay country girl kind of way. A pleasure to be taken occasionally and then savoured afterwards when she has thankfully gone. She had posed, for his delectation, as a Rubens nude and it was sensational. The smile is sliding all the time.

"Why on earth should I want your resignation, George?"

If one could hear a pin drop before, now one could hear an ant squeak. Sir Godwyn is savouring Bunny's shocked reaction. This is not what they had agreed, not why she has betrayed her husband. This is not why she let Goddy do unspeakable things to her nakedly receptive body beneath the Rubens nude... she cannot help but think of them as unspeakable things, even though she begged for more. In the cleaned up aftermath a fully clothed Society lady has her pride. When she is about to indignantly protest Sir Godwyn holds up a commanding hand.

"The Prime Minister will have to go." George Meredith looks on knowing that he is a mere pawn in whatever game is being played out in front of his bloodshot eyes. At least he is, apparently, still in the game. He must do his level best to ensure it includes Jane Perceval. "You shall have your revenge, Mary Ellen, but in a more subtly rewarding way. We need, and I mean we, we need George to remain undestroyed. He is classically in the right place at the right time and, as the most supportive wife of the replacement Prime Minister, the world will be your oyster."

"Prime Minister?" George Meredith is not to know that he is aping the current Prime Minister, or how fortuitous it is that Rosalie Murray is only in the room in spirit.

His interjection is naturally ignored. "We can run things together, Mary Ellen. You and I can be the puppet masters of the world. Think of it... just think of it."

Her own shining pale blue eyes stare into the hypnotic pale blue eyes of this man whose body she craves more than anything else in the world at this moment. She licks her lips and her smile has slid as far as it can go. Her foot is rubbing further up his leg and she needs him to want her as much in the here and now; as always that has to be good enough; their comings together over the years have always been in the here and now. A bemused George Meredith is watching the highly charged interplay between his wife and his betrayed saviour, who has galloped up to the gallows with a stay of execution.

"George, you will most certainly not be resigning, indeed you must prepare yourself for the highest Office of all." He is looking at George Meredith with a degree almost of pity – the word bemused was invented for this moment. "Now go and find Nanny and she will make you lunch. Mary Ellen and I have things to discuss." The caressing stockinged foot has reached as far as it can go.

There will be no pretend cavalier little boy to ride his make-believe steed to disturb this particular frantic coupling rocking the table. They could be a peasant and his long suffering wife from a painting by Bruegel, slaking their lust as and when. She has the figure for it and he most certainly has the lust for it.

Stoop shouldered, George Meredith is standing with his back to the Blue room door and can hear his wife of twenty three years pleading for it harder, and unbidden tears are running down his untended face. God in Heaven, he never wanted it to come to this. The false moves made, the wrong roads taken and an accumulation of cross words and a build-up of misplaced loyalties. For some unaccountable reason, at this time and in this place, he remembers their wedding night, as he hears his wife noisily endeavouring to hold back her climax. He had always fooled himself that they had been so much in love. On their wedding night she had pleaded for it harder as well. He had hoped against hope that there was to be an infinity of such nights stretching in front of them, as on that night she had also noisily endeavoured to hold back her climax. There would be children and they, or was it he alone, had decided on four children – two girls and two boys hopefully. Now all he can taste are the unbidden tears.

"George."

He opens his eyes and a concerned Nanny Linda is standing a few feet away.

"Come away, George." She has always liked George for his honesty of weakness and, brooking no argument, she takes him by the hand leading him unresisting to the kitchen that is her kingdom. She knows there are some things it is better for a husband never to hear if he is to retain a modicum of inate manhood…even a fool like George deserves that.

Saturday 21st October 4.08pm

The fragrant bell tinkle tinkles as the door of the Jermyn Street Gallery opens and closes. The most distinguished, moppily grey haired, as well preserved as money can buy sixty year-old man has studied the two paintings in the window. He has to admit they do nothing for him as he crosses to the several smaller paintings of female nudes on the wall. The most sturdy take it or leave it, square faced, striking woman with strategic white panties in different places on each painting, is much more his cup of tea. Most intriguing. Women, striking or otherwise, have more than once been his potential downfall. He has never been very good with women that say no and this doesn't look like a woman who would say yes without a fight.

"Can I help you?" Here is that sturdy, square faced, striking woman. Even more striking in the flesh. The painter has not done her justice – at least she is recognisable, not something that can be said of most modern art, including the offensive daubs in the window.

He bows slightly from the waist. "My wife has told me of the forthcoming Exhibition."

Nina Balatka, wearing skin tight, exclusively labelled black jeans and a cleavaged stripy black and white original blouse, inclines her head. She has agreed with herself that from now on there will be no expense spared on looking the part.

"Your wife?" It is the only polite rejoinder, as she brushes a strand of reddish blonde hair out of her pale, almost milky blue Slavic shaped eyes. The painter has definitely not done her justice and he cannot help wondering if the pubic bush is artistic licence…he hopes not.

"Shirley Keeldar."

"Then you must be…?"

"Sir Bernard Keeldar at your service." He had not intended to be wandering aimlessly down Jermyn Street on a decidedly nip in the air October Saturday afternoon.

He had other plans, but there are shady political shenanigans of the Godwyn Lydate variety afoot, so Helen Graham is not available. It is wise not to know the afooting and, as the titular Party Chairman, he will know soon enough. In any case, Helen's mind has been elsewhere most of the time since her sudden elevation. Sir Bernard does not appreciate his women having their minds elsewhere.

"Those paintings in the window?"

"They are sold." Thank God for that. "That is the artist who is having the Exhibition?"

"That is correct. The Window man series by Emily Rowley."

"Are they similar to the ones in the window?"

"Similar. Your wife has reserved one." Jesus. He supposes the monstrosity could be hung in one of the more remote toilets at their Scottish Castle. She would never know, she is rarely there. Abruptly he turns to the smaller paintings on the wall. "These are much more my cup of Darjeeling."

"They are for sale." She knows he is Chairman of the Keeldar Group, including Keeldar hotels. Their Group headquarters is a forty storey glass tower block in Canary Wharf. She once sold some Londonscapes round their offices, but was not allowed to venture to the Chairman's floor. They all whispered his name with awe, except for two very pretty young women, who made faces at each other and shivered theatrically.

"How much?"

"Five thousand pounds each."

"How much for all five?"

"Twenty five thousand pounds."

"Touché. I will take them all on one condition." She does not reply. He is minutely studying each painting in turn, his face a few inches from the canvases. She wonders if he is short sighted. She is not the least bit embarrassed. "That you deliver them personally."

He turns abruptly on the heels of the highly polished handmade shoes; he is dressed expensively as if for a casual day in the country. She knows he is one of the richest men in Europe, who could buy and sell Julius Verinder ten times over. He has interests in many countries including Poland – her mother worked at one of his factories until she was sacked, after being discovered in a compromising position with the Foreman. He was not sacked.

Sir Bernard's harder than nails slate grey eyes are stripping her naked… not that he will need much imagination since he has minutely studied the paintings.

"I am not for sale, Sir Bernard."

He frowns, rubbing his ultra smooth chin in a habitual gesture. He is not a handsome man but richly well preserved she thinks, as he comes to stand closer the scent of his Cologne is familiar. "I have no intention of buying you, young lady."

"That is good." She chances a smile that does not reach the eyes or display any teeth.

"Would you make an old man very happy… I don't know your name?"

"Nina. Nina Balatka."

"Would you make an old man very happy, Nina Balatka and have dinner with me this evening?"

There is something disarmingly bereft about this Captain of Commerce and Industry that she cannot quite put a finger on…something disarmingly intractable that elicits female complicity. She is now her own woman. She picks and chooses and is not picked and chosen. There is nothing to dislike about his untold riches and her stomach is rumbling. She has skipped lunch to spend time with Emily Rowley and it will be an opportunity to wear the little black dress that was wasted on slime ball Julius.

"Somewhere public?"

"One of my hotels – the Ritz – the Connaught – the Savoy – the choice is yours, Nina." He possesses a harassing voice which she is certain he reserves for women. He is not a man's man, nor, she thinks, much of a woman's man for that matter.

"Very well." She has no wish to be on her own this evening. "The Savoy."

"Thank you, Nina. I will send a car to pick you up. Shall we say eight o'clock?"

"Seven o'clock." Her stomach rumbles in anticipation.

"Very well. Seven o'clock it is."

She is taken by surprise when he takes possession of and kisses her right hand. No one has ever kissed her hand. Impecunious amateur artists hawking their Londonscapes round other people's offices, get frequently propositioned and their bums pinched on a regular basis. They do not get their hands kissed on any kind of basis.

"Until this evening, Nina." He opens the door and turns for a few seconds to study the living woman as if he will never see her again. "Please take those paintings off the wall. I do not want anyone else seeing you naked." Then he is gone and only the scent of familiar Cologne lingers. Nina Balatka holds a hand to her throat and gazes intently at the space where he has been. She is reminded of Sir Godwyn Lydate's touch on her shoulder at the TV studios, and is not sure she wants to be reminded of the touch of that ultimate chooser.

Saturday 21st October 6.06pm

The pent-up media scrum outside the Ritz Hotel Vesuvius erupts as the, all too recognisable, People's hero exits from a common or garden black cab. Appearing on the point of collapse, he is supported by a beautiful blonde and a beautiful younger virginal looking brunette. Dickie Evans had dropped them at the Duke's knockoff pad in Knightsbridge, so that Lady Rebecca could change out of her creased and crumpled little black dress. She is now wearing tight blue jeans with slashed holes and showing rather a lot of bare thigh for a virgin.

This madcap circus will go viral and Becky is not a girl to miss an opportunity to look her best. No one would guess that the sympathetic, schoolgirl looking, innocent arm holder spent most of the previous night on top of or underneath or occasionally sideways with the aptly named Dickie Evans. They might well guess if they could see Dickie Evans at this moment, who has crawled home to sleep possibly for a week, or possibly longer, and is deafeningly snoring.

Cameras are flashing and cameras are rolling as the composed women and the supported People's hero pause to admire the floral tributes and read a few of the heartfelt messages. Lady Rebecca thinks that some people really should get a life. There are shouted questions but they are too visibly upset to verbalise any response. This is all really too too much at this sad time. They are deferentially led into the Hotel foyer by the humble Porter, whom Shirley Keeldar recognises. He looks as though he has been up all night. Shirley does not know, nor of course would she care if she did know, that the Bulgarian chambermaid has learned two new words. Period and late.

Amelia Sedley's Security People are on guard in the foyer; exactly what they are guarding they are no longer sure. The same two black guys are at the lift but this time they hurriedly stand aside. In the current circumstances they have no wish to experience the rough edge of the feisty blonde's tongue. The People's hero has access to all areas.

The threesome is met on the second floor by the same two of her People, appearing suitably stunned by what has happened, but there are no tears. No one close to Amelia Sedley will shed tears, except for their jobs which were forever precarious.

"Thank you for coming and we are sorry for your loss." Intones the dry eyed attractive brunette who takes the initiative and addresses Jack. The equally, if not more so, dry eyed attractive redhead nods agreement and takes in all three with a sweeping glance. "The bodies have been taken away for post-mortems."

They lead the way down the corridor and are very conscious of being appraised from behind by the one and only Jack Bellingham, who is sticking to the dry eyed theme.

He is finding it hard to believe his sister has gone. Finding it even harder not to laugh out loud and punch the air. No doubt his Mother, wherever she is, would share the joke. It is to be hoped his sister is not heading for the same sulphurous place.

Shirley Keeldar had insisted that he take the prescribed medication, and so he is feeling oddly detached. He will stop taking the medication when he gets the chance. It was not all his fault with Jane no Y Fennel and he has the bruises to prove it.

They are shown into the fateful bedroom, although there is nothing to see beyond what any bedroom contains, namely a bed. The window is open and the curtains are rippling in the chill evening breeze. Brunette person shivers and stands close to Jack as redhead person glares at brunette person. "They were discovered by Lucy Snowe." Brunette person purses her lips and could give the expertly pursing Sir Godwyn a run for his money. "She has been sedated."

"It must have been a shock." Shirley Keeldar twitches her nose. There is a disquieting scent in the air. Jack is staring at the bed. It is hard to believe that sex on legs Amelia Sedley is a lump of flesh on a mortuary slab. He indulges in a deep sigh. There is something deeply philosophical here, if only he didn't feel too detached to articulate anything remotely coherent, never mind philosophical. He half expects his bloody sister to pop out from under the bed and say 'fooled you, brother mine'. He resists the temptation to check under the bed.

"Are you all right, Jack?" Shirley touches his arm in a gesture of commiseration that he thinks could well be genuine and nods his head. Both of Amelia Sedley's People wish they could touch his arm in fake commiseration.

"The lawyers are flying in from the States." Says the brunette who, being an expensively brought up girl, refuses to say attorneys.

There is always a pushy one, thinks Lady Rebecca Sharp, who is feeling freaked out in this arctic edged room. She is not good with dead bodies, even when the dead bodies are not here.

"There is a will?" Shirley goes for practical.

"I assume so." The brunette has sidled as close to Jack as she dare. She is wearing Amelia Sedley's favourite perfume.

That seems to be about it and the redhead feels it is time to assert herself – Loetitia can be such a pushy cow. "It is thought the opening night of the movie should go ahead on Monday as planned."

"Hell yes," Becky replies. What is it about brunettes and pushy, thinks the redhead.

"Do you agree, Jack?" Shirley feels there should be due deference to make them all feel worthy of the moment…there must surely be a movie…she must discuss with Becky.

He nods his head. Shirley has never had a sister but sympathises with Jack as much as she is able. After all, one of the dead women was his twin. Of course no one will ever know that the other dead woman was pregnant with his child.

For some unaccountable reason Shirley is feeling better about herself after ignoring several messages from Tom Sawyer. There really is no apparent reason why she should feel better about herself, although, of course, Jack the money is back and more or less in line. So the threat of her husband's unique take on a pound of flesh has retreated.

Becky Sharp is thinking she would throw a party if her older sister shuffled off this mortal coil – the nasty spiteful bitch.

There are shouts from the street below… 'we love you, Amelia.' They are humming in unison the tune from one of her more successful movies – no Oscar, though.

Shirley Keeldar takes one arm and Loetitia Parsons takes the other arm, as they lead Jack out of the bedroom. Pushy bitch, thinks redheaded Rachel Ray, who exchanges glances with Lady Rebecca, who raises her impeccably plucked eyebrows as they share sort of complicit grimaces.

Jack is being treated like an invalid. Only Lady Rebecca would not be horrified to know that inside he is dancing a jig. He indulges in yet another deep sigh and Loetitia Parsons sympathetically squeezes his arm.

"Bear up." She whispers. "Bear up."

Bravely he nods his head.

Saturday 21st October 6.29pm

Gilbert Markham is rudely woken by the mobile phone left within reach on the bedside table. He had not meant to fall asleep in the three-quarter bed in the small out of the way bedroom that Lydia Robinson uses when she stays over. They did not dare use Sir Godwyn's bedroom, as if it is haunted by his ghost whilst he still lives.

Gilbert had been taken by surprise by the engrossing lovemaking. Nothing much out of the ordinary, everything more or less straightforward and Bristol fashion… but lots of it. If looks can deceive then the absolutely nothing out of the ordinary, woman next door, looks of Lydia Robinson take the biscuit.

"Yes, Sir Godwyn."

A naked lots of Lydia is instantly fully awake. She hardly dares breathe, although a stray workaday hand rests somewhat possessively on Gilbert's hairy chest. Not that he minds. There are worse things than being possessed by Lydia Robinson's workaday hand.

"Of course, Sir Godwyn." Gilbert ends the call and strives to bring his breathing back under control. He cannot know. He cannot possibly know.

Lydia insinuates her nakedness into his arms and they lingeringly kiss, and everything about the kiss calms him down; she is such a calm and collected person. It is impossible to imagine Lyd being any younger than she is now.

"I have to go to Lydate Hall urgently." He kisses each saucered nipple of the heavily laden breasts and she smiles that rarely bestowed genuine cut diamond smile that lights up a room.

"It must be our secret, Gil." She does adore secrets and there have never been enough in her life. One more fierce, leaving for the front, tonguey kiss. With a fond farewell kiss of each saucered nipple he swings his bare legs out of the three quarter bed.

"He says for you to stay the night and to keep in touch, Lyd."

"You had better get a shower, Gil. He knows my smell."

"There is no time."

"There must be time."

Lydia Robinson listens to the thrumming of the shower and smiling a cat got the cream smile that would surprise her family and friends, and her invalid husband most of all. She strokes her expansive stomach and her smile widens. The shower has stopped.

"Our secret." She whispers, and knowing that Gil will come and seek out a goodbye kiss, she caresses her nipples and wonders if there is time after all. Lydia Robinson is a formidable woman who has never met Nanny Linda, but they would recognise much that is alike in each other. "Our secret." She whispers again, as Gilbert comes back into the bedroom and is stopped in his tracks by the sight of a come and get me Lydia Robinson caressing her own breasts. The smile is bewitching…she opens her legs. There is always time.

Saturday 21st October 8.04pm

Sir Godwyn Lydate is pacing round and round the table in the Blue room, watched by Nanny Linda. No one else is in the room and Nanny's nose twitches; Mary Ellen Meredith is such a ripe woman. Poor, honest, weak George – that particular nightmare is just beginning. Nanny has never thought it a good idea to marry for one sided love. Two sided love is tricky enough.

"For goodness sake, sit down, Goddy."

"They will pay for this." He is furious. Only Nanny dare face him when he is in this ferocious mood. Except, possibly, the formidable Lydia Robinson, superbly playing sympathetic dumb.

"I know, so sit down. You are giving me a headache."

He doesn't sit down but does stop pacing and leans with his knuckles on the polished table top. Icy blue eyes take in calm and collected Nanny Linda. There is no one else he would trust in this room when he briefs Gilbert Markham on the task ahead.

"Where is George Meredith and his good lady?" Nanny asks; they both relish, have always relished, the unsaid things. She knows that, for her own good, he is keeping something from her and she knows she will tease it out.

"They have gone back to Chevening. He will appear on the Spencer Perceval Show tomorrow to support the new Regime in China."

"The Prime Minister?"

"I think that cowardly little shit has rather got his hands full." The voice is cold, calculating and without pity. Just as she would expect and she thinks she might be able to guess what he is keeping from her in this misplaced show of Chivalry...she was never ever a damsel in distress. If she was aware of the existence of Laura Standish she might well be concerned, although of course, the Hertfordshire Standishs are first class breeders.

"Where are they taking Jayne Peel?"

"I will know for certain very soon."

"Lizzie Hastings is unhurt?"

"They locked the poor girl in an outhouse but she is unharmed." At this stage she must suspect nothing.

"You have not heard from Florence?"

"She will be somewhere in Number Ten." The pursing of lips is always a declaration of intent.

Nanny Linda can read him like a book, albeit a War and Peace size of book, with some pages annoyingly torn out. She has often thought of him as a Russian Prince of the early Nineteenth Century Romanovs – a bane to the retreating Napoleon.

"I am sure that Florence was trying to warn you that they are going to use Jayne Peel to attempt to destroy you." The lips cannot be pursed any more but he makes an attempt –occasionally there are not enough lips for purpose. "They presume Jayne is the weak link."

The reviled name of the apostate Rosalie Murray hangs in the static laden atmosphere of the Blue room; like a Seventeenth Century witch's curse. They both know what needs to be done – they used to burn witches, didn't they? "I am almost certain they will take Jayne to Number Ten because that is where they are both holed up." He will soon know the destination for certain and is counting on it being Number Ten.

"You have calculated the risks?" He knows Nanny has probably guessed.

"Of course." Of course...silly question.

"Where is the Chancellor?"

"In Washington arse licking the Yanks and I have told him to stay there for the time being. He is popular over there and that might prove useful."

For the foreseeable future John Browdie, Chancellor of the Exchequer, is dismissed from calculations. There are good reasons why he would not dare move against Sir Godwyn and he is a fence sitter – which is fine as there are plenty of fences to sit on in the United States.

"Lizzie will have recognised John Caldigate but not the others." Poor Lizzie does not possess Nanny Linda's deductive powers.

"Poor John Caldigate." She baits and he has no need to bite, as he knows that she has guessed.

There is a hesitant knock at the door and they exchange meaningful glances. Both acknowledging that what needs to be done will be done without compunction. There will be no recriminations and no regrets. He has not come this far to fail and she has not come this far to stand by and watch him fail. That will not happen.

"Come in." It is Nanny who commands.

A hesitant and watchful Gilbert Markham enters the Blue room and most carefully closes the door and stands almost to attention... old habits die hard. If Sir Godwyn's mind was not on other things he might think that, damp haired two showers Gilbert, appears somewhat guilty as charged.

The mobile phone on the highly polished table resonates to Parsifal and Sir Godwyn snatches at it and listens.

"Come and sit next to me, Gilbert." Nanny speaks softly and seductively, as only Nanny can. Something in her voice reminds him of Lydia Robinson. He knows that whatever is happening is something deadly serious, since only supremely trusted Nanny is in the room.

Sir Godwyn ends the call. "They are indeed taking her to Downing Street." They both think that the fools really should have displayed more imagination to play this most deadly of games. He looks searchingly into Gilbert Markham's pale and strained features, the pale blue eyes seeing only what they need to see. He and Gilbert have been through much together and they have forgiven and been forgiven on small matters. Perhaps it might not be too fanciful to believe that everything was leading to this moment.

"We need to move quickly. That man of straw will not be able to resist the theatrics of her arrival."

"I know," Nanny agrees.

Gilbert Markham looks nervously from one to the other, almost wishing he was back with the Regiment... almost.

Saturday 21st October 8.23pm

They are sipping quite excellent white Burgundy, the best vintage of the previous Century. Nothing but the best for the late Amelia Sedley. Remnants of room service meals are scattered around the room. The effects of the medication are beginning to wear off and Jack is trying to hide the fact. He is determined not to take any more. He had often succeeded in not taking medication in prison, aided and abetted by Sikesy, who was addicted to prescription drugs, as to so much else.

Feeling more himself, which he realises might not be a good thing for the rest of mankind, Jack is able to appreciate sharing this ostentatiously luxurious Ritz Hotel corner antique strewn lounge, overlooking Green Park and Piccadilly, with these four most desirable women. The brunette with the funny Christian name has insinuated herself next to him on a two seater chaise longue. Not that he is complaining. She is pressing thighs and he is most certainly not complaining about thigh pressing, now that the medication is definitely wearing off. She possesses that sort of opening night, any theatre anywhere, verging on beauty that is not uncommon in a great Metropolis. She also has the advantage that she is not the rapacious Amelia Sedley, although of course the rapacious one is now adorning a mortuary slab and will be rapacious no more. The redhead called Rachel is sulkily sharing a chaise longue with Shirley Keeldar, and appears somewhat put out. Jack smiles winningly at her several times until she smiles back – great teeth. He knows winningly smiling is a poor consolation for thigh pressing, but it is better than nothing.

Lady Rebecca Sharp is tapping into the tablet on her knees and, as usual, ignoring Jack, sitting half turned away from him. Then she addresses the room in general and Jack can be included if he is so inclined. "That's done. Twitter sphere has been informed that the People's hero is keeping vigil over the anointed and perfumed body of his tragic dead lover. Grief stricken, of course, he had to be restrained from flinging himself on the body that is so hauntingly beautiful in death. The legend will live on."

"Becky!"

"The body isn't here." The winningly smiled upon Rachel Ray finds she needs to point out the flaw in the statement. She is a very literal girl.

"The saddoes out there must never know that. Jesus. There must never ever be any talk of post-mortems." Becky makes a zipping motion across her mouth. She has taken charge and Shirley Keeldar is only too happy to take a back seat. She has a lot on her mind… there are several messages from Tom Sawyer that she cannot ignore for much longer. She knows she will enjoy ending things and wishes she did not.

"We are agreed then, people…?" Lady Rebecca looks searchingly at each of the three women in turn, but doesn't look at Jack searchingly or otherwise. "Jack will attend the opening night of 'Sacrifice' on Monday accompanied by the lovely Rachel and the lovely Loetitia wearing their choice of Amelia Sedley originals. They were like sisters to Amelia Sedley." Rachel Ray, who has imbibed rather a lot of the excellent white Burgundy, snorts into a cupped hand... anyone less like a sister than Amelia Sedley would be hard to imagine in your worst nightmares.

"Only those in this room will ever know the truth."

They are all staring at Lady Rebecca Sharp, except Jack, who is staring at Rachel Ray who is displaying rather a lot of unpressed thighs. She is only too well aware of where he is looking and feels like sticking out her tongue at pushy Parsons... another unlikely sister. She could tell a thing or two about that little madam...yes indeedy. She refills her glass.

"Are you alright with this, Jack?" Shirley Keeldar, as usual, feels the need to ask and wonders if they gave him too large a dose of the medication. The instructions were rather vague.

"Sure thing." He speaks out of the side of his mouth in an American drawl, causing Shirley and Loetitia Parsons to smile and Rachel Ray to snort laughter.

Lady Rebecca just glares and continues. "You two girls are going to be the subject of much media attention."

"I'll drink to that." Rachel tops up her glass.

"Don't you think you've had enough?" Loetitia snaps.

"Nope," Rachel replies and Jack laughs out loud, pressing thighs with funny Christian name, whilst admiring even more of Rachel's unpressed thighs; a spectacular thousand firework display to anyone who is a thigh man. Not to mention the now visible thigh tattoo of what he takes to be an Owl-like creature out of someone's worst nightmare.

"Do you think we should light some candles in the bedroom?" Loetitia Parsons shyly ventures, not wanting to upstage the formidable Lady Rebecca. "It will make it more authentic. There are hundreds of people outside staring up at the windows."

"Good thinking." Lady Rebecca orders candles on room service, which is a first. "Anything else?"

"Whersh Jack shtaying tonight?" Slurs Rachel Ray.

"What's it to you and you're showing your knickers." At least she is wearing knickers thinks Loetitia Parsons, who never had a sister and thinks it is probably a blessing. Rachel Ray sticks out her tongue and huffily pulls down the short skirt, but not to much effect, before slurping more wine.

"Good question though." Retorts Lady Rebecca. "After all, he is keeping a Vigil."

"Sure am." The side of the mouth drawl again and another snort of laughter from Rachel Ray who spills some wine. Shirley Keeldar is not at all sure about the prescribed medication. That prison woman was more than a soupcon intimidating. Shirley cannot help wondering if that Jane Fennell creature is just as culpable, if not more so. Perhaps a sex game went a bit too far and she cried wolf. Shirley has experienced a few of those in her time although she has rarely cried wolf. She knows for a fact that Becky is the wolf in her sex games.

"He should stay here," Shirley insists to assert some authority and looks at Becky tapping away on the tablet. "What now, puss?"

Loetitia and Rachel exchange glances, or rather a cross eyed Rachel fails in a gallant attempt to exchange glances. There is more to this than meets the eye thinks Loetitia Parsons. Rachel Ray thinks she needs the toilet rather urgently.

"Informing the sad gits that the People's hero is keeping an all-night Vigil. Of course by candlelight."

Jack watches the well pissed redhead weave her way out of the room, miraculously knocking over only one lamp in the process. This brunette with the funny Christian name presses thighs with a vengeance. He presses back because that is surely why thighs were created. He looks across at Shirley Keeldar, who is checking her mobile phone for the umpteenth time. "I'm really cream crackered. I need to lie down." He is faking his reaction to the mixing of white wine with medication rather well he thinks.

"The only vacant bedroom is the one where the bodies were found." Loetitia is resisting the temptation to stroke his thigh. She tells everyone that she dumped her long-term boyfriend several weeks ago. Whoever dumped who, the strain is beginning to tell.

"Are you all right with that, Jack?" Shirley is multi-tasking by curtly replying to a Tom Sawyer text…she will most definitely make him pay. Lady Rebecca is avoiding looking at Jack and that pathetic all over Jack brunette with very nice tits. But then all the late one's People have very nice tits as standard. Becky is definitely going to have that boob job. The Harriet Wititterly thing just hasn't worked. Despite religiously massaging three times a day, not even an eighth of an inch, and the tablets taste foul.

"Sure thing, pardner."

"We should be going, puss." Shirley Keeldar is concerned that Goddy is ignoring her messages. Something is going on. There is a reason why he didn't tell her about Jack and that pushy Jane Fennell.

"Sure thing, pardner." Becky apes Jack and no one laughs. Loetitia Parsons thinks the posh cow is being very disrespectful and Loetitia Parsons has no intention of being disrespectful in any way. This wine is rather good.

"You take care, Jack and we will see you in the morning." For very different reasons both women cannot wait to make their exits stage left. Luckily neither of them believes in premonitions.

"See you, pardners."

They walk side by side down the carpeted corridor. From the nearest toilet there are sounds of gagging retching. "Game set and match to brunette Person methinks." Murmurs Lady Rebecca Sharp.

"I wouldn't be too sure about that." Responds Shirley Keeldar, who, if not a believer in premonitions, does experience a prickle of unease.

Saturday 21st October 9.07pm

Florence Dugdale is stretched out on top of the bed covers in what used to be Lizzie Hastings' windowless suite at Ten Downing Street. She has used up all her useless tears and is staring swollen eyed at the shadowy ceiling. Her scalp is still sore and her ribs even sorer where she was viciously kicked. She is bitterly upset at having revealed the Chipping Camden hideaway. She had spent a glorious weekend there with Sir Godwyn, where they had secretly plotted getting her close to Robert Peel. She is even more bitterly upset at having betrayed Sir Godwyn. She will never forgive herself. She was both stupid and weak. More importantly perhaps Sir Godwyn will never forgive Florence – if she had any tears left she would weep.

The door has remained locked and no one has visited since she was unceremoniously frog marched here by that vile Murray woman. Florence Dugdale will pay her back if it is the last thing she does. She is incensed with herself that she surrendered so abjectly, and disgusted with herself for giving her body gift wrapped to creepy Robert Peel with no obvious end result. Not that it ever took him long to finish before, thank God, immediately losing interest. It never took more than a single tissue to clean things up; minimum foreplay and absolutely no after play. If she felt at all like smiling she would smile to herself at the pathos of it all. There has been lots of comings and goings and slamming doors. She has heard the vile Murray woman's raised voice several times. Florence is hungry and tries to take her mind off her rumbling stomach. She hates to miss meals of any kind because it throws her metabolism out something awful. Her twin sister is the same.

Thankfully there is an ensuite toilet so she has water on tap. There have been no toilet related indignities so she can be thankful for small mercies. That was one of her Mother's sayings. "Be thankful for small mercies and for God's sake stop crying, Florence." Not that her Mother was ever thankful for mercies, small or otherwise.

Oddly enough her Mother might have been proud that Florence, the less successful twin, was sleeping with the Prime Minister... sleeping being the operative word.

There are more raised voices outside the room and somebody is screaming and there are running footsteps. Florence swings her legs off the bed, smoothing down her skirt, and listening with her head on one side. Definitely screaming and she wonders what the hell is going on. Hammering on the locked door she shouts, "Let me out."

Saturday 21st October 9.28pm

"This claret is excellent, Sir Godwyn." Luca Grosch holds the cut glass goblet up to the light whilst, out of sight under the table, his left hand is stroking Agnes Grey's thigh underneath her little black dress. Agnes Grey is looking across the table at Sir Godwyn Lydate who inclines his head. Both men are wearing expensively tailored dinner jackets and both ladies are wearing little black dresses, which are famously de rigueur at Lydate Hall Saturday evening dinners.

"I am only sorry that we had to start dinner later than usual, my dear Luca." In his turn Sir Godwyn holds up his cut glass goblet in a wordless toast. The others would be shocked if they knew what he is wordlessly toasting. Mia Fischer is used to being desired… it is a blessing and a curse…she so rarely desires back…she does so now. She wonders why he is not stroking her thigh under the table and why his mind appears to be elsewhere.

The littler black dress has a plunging neckline and whilst Carrie Brattle filled a little black dress spectacularly, Mia's filling is on another plane entirely. He really must do something about Carrie Brattle, who is eating dinner off a tray in her rooms. He really must not think about Laura Standish at this time.

"I fully understand, Sir Godwyn. Affairs of State."

The two couples are seated either side of a small dining table in what is accurately referred to as the small dining room, used for more intimate dining. One could not get more intimate than this, thinks Sir Godwyn as he detects the giveaway movements of Luca's left arm.

He is aware that Agnes Grey has that anticipatory sheen to her eyes so reminiscent of her late Mother. He knows that she and Luca have most definitely experienced intimacy both indoors and outdoors. The long night is yet to come.

He knows from past experience that Luca has an outdoors preference. On his previous visit he had drunkenly revealed that having sex in a tent, in a blizzard on a Swiss mountain side is his ultimate fantasy. There is no accounting for perversion and dear Miss Grey will need to be on her mettle…he has every confidence.

"When are you flying back, my dear Luca?"

"Early tomorrow morning I'm afraid."

"Why doesn't Agnes fly back with you to prepare the way on the Chinese deal. There is no time to lose and she is fully in my confidence."

Sir Godwyn is not sure where Luca's left-hander has reached but Agnes Grey's eyes are rapidly losing focus in the manner of her Mother. This is all rather pleasant.

"You are sure of the Chinese deal?" Luca is a successful businessman first and a demented fornicator a close second.

"I spoke to Madam President whilst I was dressing for dinner. The Army is already rounding up possible dissidents and I am invited over soonest."

"Excellent. Agnes will be most welcome in Geneva." Agnes and Luca exchange most complicit facial movements. "She must stay at my lakeside villa as my guest." He has retained the luxurious villa as part of the divorce settlement from his third wife, the scheming bitch.

A pause for more lip smacking appreciation of the '61 Lafitte and Sir Godwyn watches them exchange even more complicit facial movements. A very English aristocratic dinner party thinks Mia Fischer – the Swiss can be so dull. She thinks about reaching for his hand but there is something in his demeanour that makes her hesitate.

"I think it might be a good idea, my dear Luca, if Mia stays over here for a day or two so that we can tie up loose ends on the aspirin ban."

"An excellent idea, Sir Godwyn."

Mia, who has not been consulted, is already pondering on a believable excuse to feed her worshipping husband. She had thought Godwyn would come to her earlier, but knows he is such an important man with so many responsibilities. And of course there is the China thing. She doesn't know anything about the China thing and has quite enough on her hands with the Swiss thing.

She idly wonders why Godwyn keeps glancing at the door, nor has he rung the bell to summon dessert. Mia has such a sweet tooth, but she would gladly skip dessert if he insisted. On her previous visit they had skipped dessert.

Outside the closed door there are the sounds of a commotion in the Great Hall. The door bursts open and the woman he calls Nanny enters without knocking. He will be furious. Mia settles an innocent glaze on her face, only this Nanny person is ignoring everyone else and staring at Godwyn for all she is worth. He does not appear the least bit angry. The Nanny woman is holding a hand to her substantial bosoms in a Victorian, melodramatic gesture.

"The Prime Minister has been shot."

"Is he dead?"

What an odd response, thinks Mia Fischer.

"It has just been on Sky News in the kitchen." Nanny had insisted on Sky News playing throughout the evening, despite grumbles from the idiot village girls. George Bertram knows better than to grumble, and didn't even raise eyebrows to match Alice Gamwell's raised eyebrows. "He had come out of the front door at Number Ten to greet his wife who has been away." Nanny still doesn't take any notice of the others. "He was helping her out of the car and he was shot in the head."

So definitely dead then, thinks Mia Fischer. Agnes Grey shoots Sir Godwyn an enquiring stare before they all rush from the table and follow Nanny, at an Olympic walk, to the kitchen.

The two unmarried village girls are clutching each other in frightened delight and staring open mouthed at the flat screen on the wall. Alice Gamwell is standing close enough to George Bertram to clutch him if she dare. Seeing that his wife's attention is on the screen, he strokes Alice's curvy arse. The next best thing to a hand clutch in the given circumstances. At the same time George sneakily eyes up the honey blonde Swiss beauty, who is standing close enough to clutch Sir Godwyn. Such a gorgeous figure – she really is a stunner, possibly only outshone by that hoity toity chinky piece.

That weirdo Grey woman is actually clutching the bald, bearded Swiss bloke. George is the only person in the kitchen not drinking in the dramatic coloured images on screen. His eyesight is not what it was and the screen is just a blur. He is far too vain to wear spectacles. Alice Gamwell presses close as he continues to stroke her curvy arse. Later he will imagine that Alice is the honey blonde Swiss beauty – not easy because Alice makes rather a lot of gratuitous demands in the throes of what might loosely be called passion.

There is a sense of unreality, as Sky News replays again and again, the truly awful scenes that resonate around the world.

Over and over again the Ministerial limousine pulls up to the shiny polished door of Ten Downing Street, which is opened by a designated flunkey. The Prime Minister insinuates into view, smiling his snake oil salesman smile, as he walks round to the rear door farthest from the building to be in full view of the tipped off media… for once he has outmanoeuvred that arrogant bastard. The satisfaction shows as he gives a brief 'hey I'm your kind of guy' wave to the crowds gathered outside the Security gates. A gentleman to his minor Public school bootstraps, he opens the rear door and stands back as his wife's elegant legs swing into view. Such lovely legs, thinks Alice Gamwell, as her own curvy arse continues to be stroked. Jayne Peel is half out of the car when the Prime Minister's grinning head explodes, like a target practice melon in the Jamaican Badlands, blood and brains splattering everywhere, including over the knee length grey day dress worn by the instant widow – not much brain matter, thinks Sir Godwyn. There are shouts and screams as armed and helmeted Police uselessly appear on screen, staring upwards, aiming their guns at the moon and the stars. Nanny Linda worries for Gilbert, as a blood and brains splattered Jayne Peel is hurried inside, closely followed by the unmistakable bulk of an attendant John Caldigate.

"Jesus Christ." It is Luca Grosch, non-conformist Church elder, who breaks the awestruck silence and is holding tight to Agnes Grey, who is holding tight back.

Nanny Linda feels she ought to say something. "Terrible. Terrible."

Mia Fischer tentatively seeks out Godwyn's left-hand. She would never admit to it, but seeing the British Prime Minister's head explode has touched a chord somewhere that was better left untouched. She licks her lips. There is a definite steely taste and she is acutely aware of the hot blood coursing through her veins. Agnes Grey catches Sir Godwyn's eye, knowing not to say anything until she has gathered her senses, which will not take long. The mobile phone in Sir Godwyn's dinner jacket pocket trills Parsifal.

"Yes, George, terrible. Go at once to Downing Street and take control. Put Mary Ellen on the line."

They are all fascinatedly watching the great man. The two unmarried village girls are hanging onto each other as if the next bullet could be for one of them. They will need to remember every detail to relate to the village. They all know Sir Godwyn is important but this is beyond mega. Alice Gamwell is wondering if she did the right thing after all and wishing she could turn back time.

"Mary Ellen." Calling her Bunny would not be appropriate in the circumstances. "Yes, terrible. Go straight to Downing Street and be seen arriving with George. They are going to get two and a half for the price of one. For God's sake don't let George wave or smile." Sir Godwyn does that dry lip twitch that George Bertram often tries to copy and fails dismally; it does amuse certain doe eyed village girls.

"Henry Wititterly and Helen Graham will join you. To ensure the smooth running of Government George will temporarily take over the responsibilities of Prime Minister." He listens for a few moments. "That is a good idea. Don't waste any more time. Go now."

He ends the call and the mobile phone immediately rings. "Yes, John." He listens. "Then let her do it. It will play well. Have you discovered Florence? Good. Tell her she is not in the least to blame." He listens. The village girls think he is superb at listening and they have never seen anyone listen quite so listeningly. "You have done well, John and, as promised, the role of Foreign Secretary will soon be vacant." He ends the call.

The great man looks at the television screen and holds up a silencing hand as Agnes Grey is about to speak. They all stare at the screen as a blood and brain splattered Jayne Peel appears on the steps of Number Ten. There are lightning flashes of cameras and a forest of microphones being thrust forward. Sir Godwyn thinks Jayne looks quite magnificent in the knee length high collared dress splattered in blood and brains; as fashion statements go it will never be bettered.

In the background stands a suitably grim faced and historically jowly John Caldigate and a red eyed Florence Dugdale with a handkerchief held to her face. Sir Godwyn thinks she is probably containing hysterical laughter.

Bravely the First Lady stares into the distance daring anyone to mistake her for a target practice melon in the Jamaican Badlands. The World listens spellbound to Jayne Peel who, in a not quite breaking voice, extolls her husband's courage and many virtues; his humanity and his dedication to the cause of furthering the human race; his like will not be seen again; and, on cue, she bursts into tears and is hustled back inside the safety of Number Ten by the bulk of John Caldigate, a willowy top heavy Florence Dugdale in attendance. It is Agnes Grey's turn to purse her lips with all due purpose.

The cameras remain focused on the closed door. The body has been hastily covered by a blanket, but a lifeless hand is visible.

Sir Godwyn exchanges glances with Nanny who is holding a pay as you go mobile phone in her right hand. He exchanges glances with Agnes Grey who has worked it all out and knows, in this one glance, that she is still trusted. There was good reason for her not knowing. It might have gone horribly wrong. Might still go horribly wrong.

The pay as you go mobile phone rings and Nanny holds it close to her ear. She listens and then ends the call and, almost imperceptibly, nods at Sir Godwyn. Nanny can stop worrying about Gilbert Markham. She should have realised he is professional to his fingertips.

"I wonder if you would excuse Nanny, Agnes and myself for a few minutes." Sir Godwyn calmly and collectedly addresses Luca Grosch and Mia Fischer. "Coffee and drinks will be served in the library and I will join you shortly." He glances at George Bertram who stands to attention, pretending he wouldn't know a female arse if it bit him on the bum. The two unmarried village girls are clinging together like determined to remain Siamese twins... the Master has such compellingly masterful pale blue eyes that see things so seeingly. "See to it, George."

"Yes, Sir Godwyn." George leads the way to the library, standing by the door as the honey blonde stunner and the bald, bearded geezer enter the book lined room. Without a by your leave the bald bearded geezer pours an exceedingly large whisky which he downs in one swallow and then pours another one... typical bloody foreigner. The honey blonde stunner collapses in a leather armchair and crosses quite magnificent legs; there is a most tantalising hint of stocking top and George swallows and, with a shock, realises that she is smiling at him. He thinks that tonight he will gag and tie up Alice Gamwell, like that other time, and then his imagination can roam free.

"Pour me a large vodka on the rocks, please, George."

"Yes, madam."

She sees his hand is ever so slightly shaking, which is only to be expected, as he pours vodka over ice cubes. He is quite handsome in a letting himself go sort of way. "Thank you, George." She thinks he is probably not at all straightforward either and, in a storm, would be an acceptable port.

"It is a pleasure, madam." They brush fingers and are both ignored by Luca Grosch who is swivel eyed staring at the gold embossed spines of some leather bound books. He sets a book straight and is making calculations just for the hell of it, his eyes roaming free.

Saturday 21st October 9.46pm

"I must speak to Godwyn." They both know that she will not be dissuaded, so John Caldigate looks imploringly at the puffy eyed Florence Dugdale, who avoids eye contact.

"I will keep trying, ma'am but his mobile is engaged all the time," Florence replies, knowing it is just not good enough. Jayne Peel paces in her sitting room where she and Goddy first came together on that very couch, where that floosy Florence Dugdale is sitting with her legs together for once. Jayne has suffered badly from morning sickness these past few days, there is a hollowness in her stomach but nowhere else. She needs a drink but dare not risk one because now, more than ever, their baby is everything. They are all conscious of the fists hammering on the locked door of the bedroom suite, where an infuriated beyond reason Rosalie Murray is now incarcerated in the place of Florence Dugdale.

It took bulky John Caldigate and two flunkeys to drag the screaming mad woman inside the room and the door key is burning a hole in his pocket as he tries, with limited success, not to take up too much space.

"Ma'am, you must change your dress." Florence thinks it macabre and distasteful to be still wearing that awful smelly thing.

Jayne Peel pauses in her pacing and looks down, as if just becoming aware of the blood and brains splattering the front of the knee length grey day dress. It would not have been her dress of choice had she known the starring role she would be called on to play. "Yes it has served its purpose." She stares dry eyed at the Florence Dugdale person whom she caught naked in bed with the Prime Minister…it was the last time Jayne saw him naked. "You know. Miss Dugdale, when I was a little girl I always daydreamed about being Jackie Kennedy on that sunny morning in Dallas, when President Kennedy was assassinated and she was splattered in his blood and brains. They were such compelling images, don't you think?" She pauses making balletic movements with delicate hands that has them both mesmerised. "Then the swearing in of President Johnson on Air Force One with Jackie at his side still wearing the ruined dress. Quite magical. Of course John Kennedy was a lying, cheating fornicator as well."

She stares meaningfully at Florence Dugdale who is not sure about any of this, and is just glad that they had finished when this woman discovered them naked in bed. Then had walked away without a word, followed by a nakedly scurrying Robert Peel. Florence had closed her ears to the raised voices, or rather the raised voice, and hurriedly dressed.

Jayne Peel is a compelling woman herself, thinks John Caldigate, although he is not at all sure about the magical… way out of his league, thank God. "Perhaps one should be careful what one wishes for." The new minted worldwide widow actually smiles at Florence Dugdale and it is such a lovely carefree smile that Florence does catch John Caldigate's eye. They are both in this together, whatever it is.

"Sir Godwyn? The First Lady wishes to speak to you." A much relieved Florence hands over the sweaty mobile phone and can reciprocate John Caldigate's heartfelt sigh of relief. Jayne Peel looks steadily at them both in turn, and if looks could turn to pillars of salt then this would be the one to do it. "I will tell you when you can come back in the room."

They are thus Royally dismissed and John Caldigate most carefully closes the door, and much to his singular amusement, Florence puts an ear to the door but can hear nothing.

John Caldigate blows out his cheeks and stares at Florence who, unlike the First Lady, is not out of his league. She is nice posh and he likes the cut of her jib. Pretty but not overmuch, with soft brown eyes that are his favourite colour of eyes; his wife's eyes are steely blue and not the least bit soft.

Florence's auburn hair is fetchingly a tad on the wild side. She has a lovely willowy yet busty figure. It is all too easy to imagine this lass in black stockings and nothing else...he swallows hard.

"What do you make of all this?" He swallows harder. "Florrie?"

"She is loving it." Here in the corridor the mad woman in the attic knocking from behind the locked door is much louder, then all at once stops and Florence rubs her bruised ribs. "She was superb out on the steps. Eat your heart out, Jackie Kennedy's ghost."

"She is a hauntingly beautiful woman but an iceberg at the core I think." John Caldigate appears puzzled at the acuteness of his own assessment, as well he might.

"The ultimate unattainable." Adds Florence, who knows that she is not the least bit unattainable. She hasn't the stomach for it. Neither of them dares to say out loud what they are thinking, because walls do indeed have ears and careless talk does indeed cost lives.

"Sir Godwyn has promised me the position of Foreign Secretary." He is bursting to tell someone. The telephone conversation with Agnes Grey this morning decided his allegiance, not that he was left with much choice.

"Congratulations." Florence has a sun sweeping smile when she puts her mind to it. Signs of her recent distress are inevitably fading and, reacting to her audience, she is making her voice less posh. She is good at the Chameleon thing if the circumstances warrant.

"I thought my political career was over. A week certainly is a long time in politics. Harold Wilson said that."

"I know," Florence replies and stares appraisingly at this big man standing with his feet apart and hands behind his back, dominating with his bulk. From personal choice she has always gone for big men, the late Prime Minister being the exception that proves the rule in every way. Sir Godwyn Lydate is just Sir Godwyn Lydate and well outside any classification.

"You will be out of a job now, Florrie?"

"Who said you could call me Florrie?"

He is taken aback, and she thinks his flare of confusion would suit a mid Nineteenth Century, out of his depth, mill owner facing rioting workers only one generation removed.

"Only joking, Caldy."

More relieved than he cares to admit he rocks on his heels and takes the plunge. He likes to think he is a taking the plunge, in the here and now, in the flesh kind of guy. "Come and work closely with me at the Foreign office, Florrie."

Only the slightest hesitation. "That would be nice, Caldy."

She will have to square it with Sir Godwyn but is sure he will welcome a spy in that particular off piste Everest base camp. She knows that John Caldigate is easily led, and if she knew about Agnes Grey she would not be at all surprised. She once came across Agnes Grey's mother in a compromising position, in a semi-public place, with another easily led Politician.

"So that's settled then." He looks as pleased as punch and smacks a big fist into a big palm and that, Florence thinks, is the trouble … the big man cannot hide his feelings of the moment. It is endearing, but dangerous in the snake pit in which they operate. She will have to work on that but, first, a little test of the clear blue shark infested waters.

"Your wife will be pleased, Caldy."

His face drops like a stone dropped by a gullible small child down a dried out wishing well and she restrains a smile. She has learned at the feet of the Master.

"She will be pleased at the status, that is for sure." So all is not well at Caldigate Towers.

"Chevening and all that?"

"And all that." He agrees and stares at Florence with a stray puppy dog longing that she finds touching and more than somewhat enticing. She will probably need more than a single tissue where John Caldigate is concerned. She must ensure that Mrs Caldy never discovers them naked in bed together, conjoined or otherwise. It does not bear thinking about.

There is a commotion as George Meredith and his wife, with a mottle faced Helen Graham in tow, arrive at the top of the stairs. George is visibly upset at having seen the body covered in a blanket, with the lifeless hand sticking out. There was no question of smiling and waving.

"Where is she?" Mary Ellen Meredith, of course, takes the lead – someone else who is loving it, thinks Florence Dugdale.

"On the phone with Sir Godwyn." Florence takes great delight in stopping the trio in their tracks. They stand around in awkward silence. Mary Ellen

Meredith is not at all happy to be kept waiting on that ridiculous Prima donna Jayne Peel's say so – who does she think she is?

"Awful to meet in these circumstances." Murmurs John Caldigate and three of them nod.

Florence likes him for saying it and their eyes meet. Mary Ellen Meredith takes in the willowy busty girl making sheep's eyes at that idiot John Caldigate. She has decent legs and an arresting figure but then they all have decent legs and arresting figures. There are going to be a lot of changes made round here and that's for sure.

Saturday 21st October 10.16pm

Shirley Keeldar and Becky Sharp have kicked off their toe pinching designer shoes, and are sipping warm champagne in the Grande suite of the Savoy Hotel. Staring mesmerised at the footage playing on Sky News.

"It would fucking happen today of all days." Mutters Becky as the Prime Minister's head explodes for the umpteenth time with the same results. "We need to manage the Amelia Sedley thing to best advantage."

"The poor bastard." Shirley Keeldar tops up their champagne. "He didn't deserve that."

"He was always a smarmy git." Is Becky's response as the coverage switches to the thousands gathering in Green Park, blocking Piccadilly and lighting candles to the departed Amelia Sedley – she will live forever declares one of the scrawled banners.

"No she fucking won't." Sips Becky Sharp. "You know, Shirl, we might be able to use the smarmy git getting his comeuppance to our advantage. I must think it through."

Shirley Keeldar sets down her champagne flute and disappears to the toilet for some considerable time. When she returns she sits closer to Becky Sharp and they hold hands. Becky hopes there is nothing amiss in the consequences after unprotected sex department.

"Becky?"

"Yep."

"Do you think Godwyn could have had anything to do with the assassination?"

"Yep."

"He wouldn't?"

"He fucking would." Becky sips warm champagne with more than half her mind thinking through the Amelia Sedley thing. She can already visualise a dumb, numb Project Jack, all in black at the opening night, supported by a tearful Tweedledum and a tearful Tweedledee… timing is everything. Live coverage is playing of a pasty faced George Meredith with his Grimms' fairytale wife at his side. He is hamming a speech on the steps of Ten Downing Street. In the background the Home Secretary and the Attorney General are trying to outdo each other in the we will never see his like again face thing. The body and its lifeless hand have been discreetly removed.

"George's wife is a handsome woman." They had once exchanged angry words at one of Goddy's weekends, but Shirley Keeldar feels like being magnanimous in the circumstances. George Meredith is saying that no stone will be left unturned in finding the killer or killers and this terrorist outrage... Sir Godwyn's dictated words... will not go unpunished. Robert Peel was a great man and his legacy will live on.

"I fucking hope not." Interjects Becky Sharp.

Shirley Keeldar knows that Becky can be a cold fish when she puts her mind to it, which is most of the time. It is no use naysaying.

"They are claiming it is a terrorist attack." Shirley Keeldar does not want to believe that Goddy is involved.

Becky Sharp has just thought of another ploy to turn to the advantage of the Amelia Sedley thing, and is only half listening but replies, "Who is the biggest fucking terrorist we know?"

Shirley Keeldar does not feel able to reply as footage is replayed of the First Lady's dramatic appearance on the steps of Number Ten covered in blood and brains, which gives Becky another brilliant idea.

Saturday 21st October 10.59pm

Nanny Linda has been listening for the expected knock at the unlocked kitchen door. The village girls and George Bertram have been despatched on their way. It would not at all surprise Nanny if that sad excuse for a husband tried to take on all three tonight. She has turned off the television and is sitting at the large square oak kitchen table nursing a mug of black coffee laced with rum. She knows that Luca Grosch and Agnes Grey have gone to one of their beds. No doubt what they have witnessed at second hand has given an edge to their mutual ingrowing appetites. She has to admire Agnes Grey's ability to move on with the minimum of fuss, just like her late Mother, who was a renowned unfussy mover-oner.

The Master and the Swiss cheese golden girl are in the library, murmuring sweet nothings in between his constant giving and receiving of messages. Then she hears their voices in the hall and only Goddy enters the high ceilinged, absurdly silent kitchen.

"You have sent her to bed?" There is something about the blonde bombshell that sticks in Nanny's craw.

"It was getting too much of a temptation." He is holding a three quarter filled crystal tumbler of neat double black whisky in one hand and the bottle in the other hand. He is not drunk but only partially sober.

"Go to her if you wish. I can look after Gilbert." He knows it is an admonishment of sorts.

"He should have been here by now." He sets down the bottle on the kitchen table and checks his antique Rolex wristwatch and then the large Victorian kitchen clock on the far wall, which Nanny sets every day to Greenwich Mean Time. Shades of Lydia Robinson, who at this moment, is alone in the three-quarter bed wondering if her suspicions are correct...she really hopes so. She yawns expansively and snuggles under the duvet and smiles that smile...she will sleep well tonight.

"He will have been cautious and not rushed things. He is a trained killer and equally trained not to be caught. He is the best and you know that is why he is your man." She knows about Kandahar.

"He rang to say he was clear of the Ministry building?"

"Yes."

For a few moments he studies this most formidable of women calmly sipping black coffee as if she hasn't a care in the world. There is a knock at the kitchen door and they both start as if the knocking is the most unexpected thing in the world. The intruder tries the handle and the door slowly creaks open.

"Gilbert?" It is Nanny who sets down her coffee mug and goes to meet the shadowy figure who slips inside and closes the door.

"Nanny."

"Oh! My sweet boy." She takes him in her arms as if he is a youthful Goddy who has committed some uniquely Goddyish schoolboy indiscretion and is being comforted for being himself. She sweeps sweated hair out of Gilbert's pale face and smooths the skin of his cold cheeks with india rubber thumbs. "We were worried, my boy." She can admit it now, as Goddy sinks the three quarter glass of whisky in two swallows. Even the Grand Master can wonder if a minor calculation has been overlooked leading to unintended consequences. He is only human after all.

"No need to worry, Nanny." Gilbert stares over Nanny's shoulder and Sir Godwyn holds up the empty glass in the mutest of toasts. Nanny leads Gilbert by the hand to the table, sitting him down in the chair close to her chair. She too sits down and keeps tight hold of the hand in her capacious lap.

"Whisky?" Sir Godwin holds up the half empty bottle.

"Please." They know they are now on a subtly different footing. Gilbert is a warrior who has returned, when there was every chance he might not return, and everything might have come tumbling down around their ears. Despite every calculation it was all down to him in the end. He was not found wanting.

Sir Godwyn pours more whisky in his cut glass tumbler and takes a common or garden glass beaker from an open shelf and pours a most generous measure, which he hands to Gilbert Markham. "Cheers."

"Bottoms up."

They imbibe generous mouthfuls of the deliciously smoky whisky and Nanny smiles a most possessive smile. It could not get better than this, one might think.

"There were no problems?" Sir Godwyn is surprised how composed Gilbert appears, as if assassinating a British Prime Minister is an everyday occurrence instead of only the second time in history.

"It went like a dream and you were right, Sir Godwyn. The view from that window was perfect and I couldn't miss. I was out of the building before they knew what was happening."

"I am forever in your debt, Gilbert."

"I am your man, Sir Godwyn, you know that."

Nanny squeezes the hand in her capacious lap. They are both her boys, her only living boys.

Sir Godwyn takes the lead. "We will carry on as normal for a few days then you must take a well deserved holiday, at my expense of course. Anywhere you like."

"I've always wanted to go to Bondi beach."

"Then to Bondi beach you shall go. For a few days we will carry on as normal and tomorrow morning you can drive me to Downing Street." Repeating himself is a sure sign of how much whisky he has drunk.

"Yes, Sir Godwyn."

With a cavalier flourish, Sir Godwyn finishes the whisky, and with a wave he leaves the kitchen; holding onto the gilded bannister he climbs the elegant staircase. He has drunk rather a lot of whisky but it has not blunted his carnal appetites. He has left the whisky bottle on the kitchen table as a token of complicity.

He politely knocks on Mia's bedroom door and after a few blatant seconds, she calls out, but not too loudly, "Enter." She is naked, sitting sideways on one of the gilded chairs clutching a towel to her breasts. Next to the chair is propped the Degas painting – after the bath – she is uncannily replicating the pose. She has even grossly lipsticked her mouth and rouged her cheeks; the devil is in the detail. One would have to believe that Degas would take many weeks to complete the painting, with this particular time travelling model posing before his rheumy eyes. Sir Godwyn closes the door and walks across the room with only the slightest of staggers, towards the painting come to life. The gloriously naked woman allows the towel to drop and watches the Master of Lydate Hall undressing. It is in moments such as these when she does not in the least regret the gift of her beauty, lending her power, however transient, over such a man.

The ultimate power in any age and at any time...the power of melded flesh...the power that destroyed Carthage...the power that destroyed Troy. Her eyes flare as she sees that she will once again not be disappointed. She is not to know, nor will she ever care to know.

Nanny Linda is stroking Gilbert's sackcloth and ashes face and he cannot prevent his eyelids drooping. "Finish the whisky, my boy. You will sleep in my bed tonight."

"I am dog tired, Nanny." The need for a woman after such an ordained kill will have to be delayed.

"I said sleep, dear boy. Can you think of a better place to sleep tonight than in my naked arms against my naked body?"

He shakes his head knowing she will be there at dawn when the need kicks in. They both anticipate that moment, remembering the previous survivor's fuck after a less auspicious kill.

"Good boy." Then she smiles her lustful village girl's smile better than any lustful village girl...even the three naked lustful village girls taking part in a foursome at this very moment in Alice Gramwell's bedroom – a rampant George Bertram taking all their breaths away. "I will be there when you wake." She supports Gilbert as they climb the magnificent staircase and he is practically asleep on his feet.

Saturday 21st October 11.32pm

Sir Bernard Keeldar cannot believe his luck. The stunning Polak woman has agreed to a nightcap in the Savoy Hotel suite that is reserved for the Group Chairman's use when in town. Since the latest unfortunate incident, which Sir Godwyn somehow managed to make go away, Sir Bernard has, of course, only been here with Helen Graham, who is now permanently otherwise engaged.

He has forgotten this one's name...Nina...that's it... Nina something or other foreign sounding. She is wearing a black dress moulded to her body and displaying a cleavage that literally makes his mouth water. He can hardly wait. It was good to be seen at dinner with such a curvy baggage hanging on his every word. It does wonders for one's reputation with the lower orders. Holding two generously half-filled brandy glasses he turns from the well-stocked drinks cabinet and takes in the crossing of splendid legs. Quite splendid. Why waste any more time? He replaces the two half-filled brandy glasses in the drinks cabinet...waste not, want not.

His mobile phone was turned off earlier because such interruptions only get in the way. He had prepared the ground over dinner... promised financial help in any way he can. Bragged about his connections and his financial support for the major Political Parties. The Prime Minister is in his pocket. Not forgetting his Royal connections of course. The Royal connections must have impressed this Nina something or other foreign.

She has told him something of her poverty stricken background and he only hopes she will not be too much of a pushover…he doesn't like them to be too much of a pushover.

Nina Balatka is wondering if it might have been a mistake to accept the offer of a nightcap this early in the game. This distinguished looking, somewhat elderly, boring, but tremendously rich, man has put down the brandy glasses and is staring avariciously at her crossed legs. She wonders if he has an old-fashioned Polish Nobleman's view of what a nightcap and only too visible crossed legs entails.

Despite his boring, but tremendously rich company, she has weirdly enjoyed the evening, having got some wear out of the little black dress bought by that grease ball Julius Verinder. She also enjoyed being lusted over by all the men in the restaurant, bar none, and several of the women. It does no harm to be lusted over. The waiters had taken it in turns to practically nose-dive down her cleavage. She covertly smiles.

"I think we can dispense with a nightcap, my dear." Encouraged by the covert smile, although that is not the word he would use, he holds out a liver spotted hand. "Time for beddy byes, my sweeting."

"I don't think so, Sir Bernard." He is not to know that she has sworn to her mother's ghost that from now on she will choose and not be chosen. He has not really listened because such men rarely do listen.

"Bernie, please."

"I don't think so, Sir Bernard."

"Don't play fast and loose with me, you little tart." This is going to be much more enjoyable than he had at first thought. For starters he grabs both her square hands and yanks the not so little tart to her feet. No one is going to believe this particular asking for it piece of white trash. Droit de Seigneur fashion he captures the not so little tart in his arms, pressing the bulge in his trousers into her groin and savaging her mouth with a sucking kiss. She is not kissing back. Good. Good. This is getting better and better. Soon she will be begging him to stop. No. No. No. He will take his Baronial dues here and now on the floor, then afterwards he will drag the half clothed, ravished body to bed and the real fun will begin…the pain out of nowhere is excruciating beyond measure and he didn't see it coming… the raised knee slams into the bulge in his trousers, and excruciating pain is suddenly all there is in this world or the next – only excruciating pain. He collapses to the floor and has no breath even to scream the foul obscenities that resonate in his brain.

The utterly composed woman standing over him, waits a few moments and then, bending close to his thrashing body spits into the frantically gurning face. "There were not enough of you this time." She thinks one spit is probably enough.

He is only dimly aware of the door slamming because he is sobbing with the excruciating pain and cannot stop.

Meanwhile Gilbert Markham is sleeping the sleep of many warrior returned centuries, returned safe in the strong arms of naked Nanny Linda. The excruciating pains exist only in his dreams and will be forgotten on waking on the spike of the all-consuming need. Nanny is breathing into the mask of his throat. Dawn cannot come soon enough as she moans in shallow sleep.

Sir Godwyn Lydate is thrusting his whisky fuelled penis into the river deep receptive body of stunningly beautiful Mia Fischer, whose smooth legs are draped over his shoulders like a Byzantine Emperor's cloak of victory. On the rising epic of her keening he suckles both bullet hard nipples turn and turnabout. Triumphantly revelling in damnation to his enemies, knowing all is for the best in the best of all possible worlds and nothing in his world will come tumbling down. As her keening rapidly approaches inevitable climax he knows that if one cannot fuck the world, then this is the next best thing. She is frantically thrusting back on her all-encompassing orgasm, raking his spine with sharp fingernails. He knows he must keep thrusting and thrusting. The winner takes it all and tomorrow is just another ticked off day. He is not writing this story, but he has no intention of leaving it when there is everything to play for. There will be no spilling his seed upon the ground as he enslaving thrusts and thrusts and she cries out his name, but is too far gone to be aware that it is the name of Laura that escapes his bitten lips. These are the briefest of moments when ecstasy approaches...ah!...ah!...these are the moments that cannot be written out. These are the moments on which humanity turns. These...these...ah!...ah!...

Jack Bellingham is standing at that bedroom window of the Ritz Hotel overlooking Green Park, avoiding the guttering candles, being careful not to be seen by twitching the curtains. Through the narrow gap he can discern the lights of thousands of mobile phones waving in unison to the chanting.

'Am—el—ia, we love you, Am—el—ia'... and the occasional discordant screech... 'we love you, Jack.' The brunette with the funny Christian name is gurgly snoring in the acreage of bed, and as usual dreaming of her ex-boyfriend's invasive cock. She will wake up randy.

Jack thinks he might well give up this writing lark. The bloody book never seems to turn out as intended – although of course tomorrow is another day and all that crap. The brunette with the funny Christian name snorts awake and huskily whispers words of promise that Jack could well have written.

"Come back to bed. Mmm still horny."

So he goes back to the bed to the welcoming body of the girl with the funny Christian name. He has never been very good with names. He is getting better at other stuff.

{to be continued in

THE SEVENTH COMMANDMENT – a hard one to keep]